(père) lived a life as .... his famous novels. He was born on July 24, 1802, at Villers-Cotterêts, France, the son of Napoleon's famous mulatto general, Dumas. His early education was scanty, but his beautiful handwriting secured him a position in Paris in 1822 with the duc d'Orléans, where he read voraciously and began to write. His first play, *Henri III et sa cour* (1829), scored a resounding success for its author and for the romantic movement. Numerous dramatic successes followed (including the melodrama *Kean*, later adapted by Jean-Paul Sartre), and so did numerous mistresses and adventures. He took part in the revolution of 1830, caught cholera during the epidemic of 1832, fathered two illegitimate children by two different mistresses, and then married still another mistress. (The first of these two children, Alexandre Dumas [fils], became a famous author also.) His lavish spending and flamboyant habits led to the construction of his fabulous Château de Monte-Cristo, and in 1851 he fled to Belgium to escape creditors. He died on December 5, 1870, bankrupt but still cheerful, saying of death, "I shall tell her a story, and she will be kind to me."

Dumas's overall literary output reached over 277 volumes, but his brilliant historical novels made him the most universally read of all French novelists. With collaborators, mainly Auguste Maquet, Dumas wrote such works as *The Three Musketeers* (1843–44); its sequels, *Twenty Years After* (1845) and the great mystery *The Man in the Iron Mask* (1848–50); and *The Count of Monte Cristo* (1844). *L'action* and *l'amour* were the two essential things in his life and in his fiction. He declared he "elevated history to the dignity of the novel" by means of love affairs, intrigues, imprisonments, hairbreadth escapes, and duels. His work ignored historical accuracy, psychology, and analysis, but its thrilling adventure and exuberant inventiveness continues to delight readers, and Dumas remains one of the prodigies of nineteenth-century French literature.

The Three Musketeers
by Alexandre Dumas

Translated by Lowell Bair

BANTAM BOOKS
TORONTO • NEW YORK • LONDON • SYDNEY • AUCKLAND

THE THREE MUSKETEERS
A Bantam Book

PRINTING HISTORY
The Three Musketeers *was first published in 1844*
Bantam Classic edition / July 1984

Cover painting, *Man with the Black Ribbons*, by Sebastien Bourdon.
Reproduction courtesy of Musée Fabre, Montpellier, France. Photography
courtesy of Claude O'Sughrue.

ISBN 0-553-21147-1

Published simultaneously in the United States and Canada

Bantam Books are published by Bantam Books, Inc. Its trademark,
consisting of the words "Bantam Books" and the portrayal of a
rooster, is Registered in U.S. Patent and Trademark Office and in
other countries. Marca Registrada. Bantam Books, Inc., 666 Fifth
Avenue, New York, New York 10103.

PRINTED IN THE UNITED STATES OF AMERICA

O   0 9 8 7 6 5 4 3

CONTENTS

PREFACE

In which it is established that, despite their names ending in os and is, there is nothing mythological about the heroes of the story I am going to have the honor of telling my readers.

About a year ago, when I was in the royal library doing research for my history of Louis XIV, I happened to come upon the *Memoirs of Monsieur d'Artagnan,* which, like most works of that time, when authors wanted to tell the truth without having to spend time in the Bastille, was printed in Amsterdam, by Pierre Rouge. The title attracted me; I took the book home, with the librarian's permission, of course, and devoured it.

It is not my intention here to analyze that curious work. I will simply recommend it to those of my readers who appreciate period pieces. It contains portraits sketched by a skilled hand, and although most of them are drawn on barracks doors and tavern walls, the reader will recognize pictures, resembling their originals as closely as those in Anquetil's history, of Louis XIII, Anne of Austria, Richelieu, Mazarin, and most of the courtiers of the time.

But, as is well known, what strikes the poet's capricious mind is not always what impresses the mass of readers. While I admired the details I have mentioned, as others will no doubt admire them also, what preoccupied me most was something to which I am sure no one else has ever paid attention.

D'Artagnan writes that when he first visited Monsieur de Tréville, captain of the King's Musketeers, he met in the ante-room three young men named Athos, Porthos, and Aramis, who belonged to the renowned corps into which he was soliciting the honor of being accepted.

I confess that I was struck by those three foreign names, and it immediately occurred to me that they were only pseudonyms, either invented by d'Artagnan to disguise names that were perhaps illustrious, or chosen by the three young men themselves when, because of dissatisfaction, a whim, or lack of money, they donned the simple garb of a musketeer.

From then on I could not rest until I had found some trace, in contemporary works, of those extraordinary names which had stirred my curiosity so strongly.

Merely listing the books I read for that purpose would fill many pages, which might be instructive but would surely not be very entertaining for my readers. I will therefore say only that when, disheartened by my fruitless search, I was about to give it up, I finally found, guided by the advice of my illustrious and scholarly friend Paulin Paris, a folio manuscript with the reference number of 4772 or 4773, I have forgotten which, entitled: *Memoirs of Count de La Fère, Concerning Some of the Events that Occurred in France toward the End of the Reign of King Louis XIII and the Beginning of the Reign of King Louis XIV.*

Imagine my joy when, looking through that manuscript, my last hope, I found the name of Athos on the twentieth page, the name of Porthos on the twenty-seventh, and the name of Aramis on the thirty-first.

The discovery of a completely unknown manuscript, at a time when historical science has been developed to such a high degree, seemed miraculous to me. I therefore quickly asked permission to have it printed, with the aim of some day presenting myself to the Academy of Inscriptions and Literature with the writings of someone else if, as is likely, I do not succeed in entering the French Academy with my own. That permission, I must say, was granted to me; I note this here in order publicly to give the lie to those malicious people who claim that we live under a government not very well disposed toward men of letters.

I am now offering the first part of that precious manuscript to my readers, restoring its proper title, and I promise that if it meets with the success it deserves, as I fully expect it to do, I will publish the second part without delay.

Meanwhile, since a godfather is a second father, I invite the reader to hold me, and not Count de La Fère, responsible for his pleasure or boredom.

All that having been said, let us go on to our story.

1

The Three Gifts of Monsieur d'Artagnan the Elder

On the first Monday of April, 1625, the market town of Meung, birthplace of the author of the *Roman de la Rose,* seemed to be in as great a turmoil as if the Huguenots had come to turn it into a second La Rochelle. A number of townsmen, seeing women running in the direction of the main street and hearing children shouting on doorsteps, hastened to put on their breastplates and, steadying their rather uncertain self-assurance with a musket or a halberd, made their way toward the inn, the Hôtellerie du Franc Meunier, in front of which a noisy, dense, and curious throng was growing larger by the minute.

Panics were frequent in those times, and few days went by when an event of this kind was not recorded in the archives of one town or another. Noblemen fought among themselves; the king was at war with the cardinal; the Spanish were at war with the king. And then, besides all this secret or open warfare, there were robbers, beggars, Huguenots, wolves, and lackeys, who were at war with everyone. The townsmen always took up arms against robbers, wolves, and lackeys, often against noblemen and Huguenots, sometimes against the king, but never against the cardinal or the Spanish. It was because of these habits that the townsmen, on that first Monday of April, 1625, hearing a commotion and seeing neither a red and yellow Spanish flag nor the livery of Cardinal Richelieu, hurried toward the Franc Meunier inn.

When they arrived there, they were able to see the cause of the tumult.

A young man . . . Let us sketch a rapid portrait of him. Imagine Don Quixote at eighteen, a Don Quixote without chain mail or thigh pieces, wearing a woolen doublet whose original blue had been transformed into an elusive shade between purple and azure. He had a long, dark face with prominent cheekbones, a mark of shrewdness; his jaw muscles were heavily developed, an infallible sign by which one can recognize a Gascon, even without a beret, and our young man wore a beret adorned with some sort of feather. His eyes were frank and intelligent; his

1

nose was hooked, but finely drawn; he was too big for an adolescent and too small for a full-grown man. An untrained eye might have taken him for a farmer's son on a journey if it had not been for the sword that hung from a shoulder belt, slapping against his calves when he walked, and against his shaggy horse when he rode.

For the young man had a mount, one that could not fail to attract attention: a small Béarn horse twelve to fourteen years old, with a yellowish coat, an almost hairless tail and sores on his legs. He walked with his head lower than his knees, which made a martingale unnecessary, but he could still do twenty miles a day. Unfortunately his good qualities were hidden by his strange color and his outlandish gait. He had come into Meung a quarter of an hour earlier through the Beaugency gate, and since in those days everyone was a practiced judge of horses, his appearance had caused a sensation that cast disfavor on his rider.

This was all the more painful to young d'Artagnan (such was the name of the Don Quixote astride that other Rosinante) because he was well aware of how ridiculous his horse made him seem, even though he was an excellent rider. That was why he had sighed when he had accepted the horse as a gift from his father. He knew that such an animal was worth at least twenty livres; the words that had accompanied the gift, however, were priceless.

"My son," the Gascon nobleman had said in the Béarn accent that Henry IV never succeeded in losing, "this horse was born on my estate nearly thirteen years ago and has never left it. That should be enough to make you love him. Never sell him, let him die peacefully and honorably of old age, and if you go to war with him, treat him with consideration, as you would treat an old servant. At court, if you have the honor to go there, an honor to which our ancient nobility entitles you, be worthy of your noble name, worthily borne by your ancestors for over five hundred years. For yourself, your relatives, and your friends, never tolerate the slightest affront from anyone except the cardinal or the king. Remember this: it's by courage, and courage alone, that a nobleman makes his way nowadays. Anyone who trembles for even one second may lose the chance that fortune offered him precisely at that second. You're young, and you must be brave for two reasons: first, you're a Gascon; and second, you're my son. Don't be afraid of opportunities, and seek out adventures. I've taught you to use a sword. You have iron legs and a steel wrist. Fight duels at the drop of a hat, especially since duels are forbidden: that means it takes twice as much courage to fight one.

"My son, all I have to give you is fifteen écus, my horse, and the advice you've just heard. Your mother will give you the recipe for an ointment that a Gypsy woman taught her how to make: it miraculously heals any wound that doesn't reach the heart. Make the most of all these gifts, and have a long, happy life.

"I have only one more thing to add: an example for you to follow. It's not my own, because I've never appeared at court and I've fought only in the wars of religion as a volunteer. I'm speaking of Monsieur de Tréville, who used to be my neighbor and had the honor of playing with our King Louis XIII—may God preserve him!—when they were both children. Sometimes their games turned into fights, and the king didn't always win them. The drubbings he got from Monsieur de Tréville made him feel great respect and friendship for him. Later, Monsieur de Tréville fought duels: five on his way to Paris, seven between the time when the late king died and the young one came of age—not to mention wars and sieges—and by now he may have fought a hundred! So in spite of edicts, orders, and decrees, he's now captain of the musketeers. The musketeers, my son, are a legion of heroes highly favored by the king and feared by the cardinal, who fears very little, as everyone knows. Furthermore, Monsieur de Tréville earns ten thousand écus a year, so he's a very great lord. He began like you; go to see him with this letter and take him as your model."

The elder d'Artagnan then buckled his own sword on his son, kissed him on both cheeks, and gave him his blessing.

When he left his father's room, the young man found his mother waiting for him with the famous recipe, which he could expect to use rather often if he followed the advice he had just been given. This time the farewells were longer and more tender—not that Monsieur d'Artagnan did not love his son, who was his only child; but he was a man, and he considered it unworthy of a man to let himself be carried away by emotion, whereas Madame d'Artagnan was not only a woman but also a mother. She wept abundantly, and, to her son's credit, his feelings won out despite his efforts to hold them in check as he thought a future musketeer should do. He shed many tears and was able to hide only half of them.

He left that same day, taking his father's three gifts: the fifteen écus, the horse, and the letter for Monsieur de Tréville, with the advice thrown into the bargain.

Traveling with that horse and that advice, he was an exact copy, morally and physically, of Cervantes's hero, with whom we so accurately compared him when our duty as a historian required us to describe him. Don Quixote took windmills for giants and sheep for armies; d'Artagnan took every smile as an insult and every look as a challenge. As a result, all the way from Tarbes to Meung his fist was constantly clenched and he put his hand to the pommel of his sword a dozen times. His fist never struck a jaw, however, and his sword never left its sheath. Not that the sight of his awkward yellow horse did not bring smiles to many faces, but since above the horse there was a sword of respectable size, and above the sword a pair of eyes that were fierce rather than proud, the passersby repressed their laughter, or, if amusement proved to be stronger than prudence, they at least tried to laugh only on one side, like ancient masks. D'Artagnan therefore remained majestic, and his sensitivity remained untouched, till he reached the town of Meung.

But there, as he was getting off his horse in front of the Franc Meunier inn—where no one, neither the innkeeper, the waiter, nor the stableman, came to hold his stirrup at the mounting block—he glanced at a half-open window on the ground floor and saw a tall, handsome, and rather grim-looking nobleman talking with two people who seemed to listen to him with deference. As usual, d'Artagnan assumed he was the subject of the conversation and listened to it. This time he was not completely mistaken: he was not being discussed, but his horse was. The nobleman seemed to be describing all the animal's qualities, and because his listeners showed great deference for him, as we have mentioned, they burst out laughing every few moments. Since a faint smile was enough to stir up d'Artagnan's irascibility, it is easy to imagine the effect produced on him by this loud laughter.

But first he wanted to have a closer look at the insolent stranger who was mocking him. He saw that he was a man in his early forties with dark, piercing eyes, a pale complexion, a prominent nose, and a neatly trimmed black mustache. He wore a purple doublet and breeches, and laces of the same color, with no other ornament than the usual slashes through which his shirt appeared. His doublet and breeches, though new, were wrinkled, as if they had just been taken out of a trunk. D'Artagnan noticed all this with the quickness of a careful observer, and no doubt also with an instinctive feeling that this man was going to have a great influence on his life.

While d'Artagnan was examining him, he made a particularly profound remark about the yellow horse, his two listeners laughed again, and, contrary to his habit, he let a faint smile appear on his face. This time there could be no doubt: d'Artagnan had really been insulted. Filled with this conviction, he pulled his beret down over his forehead, and trying to copy some of the court manners he had observed in lords traveling through Gascony, he walked forward with one hand on the guard of his sword and the other on his hip. Unfortunately, however, he was so carried away by anger that instead of the haughty, dignified speech in which he had intended to formulate his challenge, these blunt words were the only ones that came to his tongue, accompanied by a furious gesture:

"You there, hiding behind the shutter! Yes, you! Tell me what you're laughing at, so we can laugh together."

The stranger slowly moved his eyes from the horse to its rider, as though it took him a certain time to realize that this odd reproach was being addressed to him; then, when there could no longer be any uncertainty, he frowned slightly and, after a rather long pause, replied to d'Artagnan in a tone of irony and insolence impossible to describe.

"I'm not speaking to you, sir."

"But *I'm* speaking to *you*!" cried d'Artagnan, exasperated by that mixture of elegance and disdain.

The stranger looked at him with his faint smile for a few moments longer, then left the window, slowly walked out of the inn, passed within two paces of d'Artagnan, and stopped in front of his horse. His calm self-assurance and mocking expression had redoubled the amusement of his companions, who remained at the window.

Seeing him approach, d'Artagnan had drawn his sword a foot out of its sheath.

"This horse is, or rather was in its youth, the color of a buttercup," said the stranger, continuing his examination and addressing his two listeners at the window, seemingly unaware of d'Artagnan's exasperation even though the young man was standing in front of the window. "It's a color that's quite common in plants, but very rare in horses."

"You laugh at a horse because you're afraid to laugh at its master!" d'Artagnan said with a reckless fury worthy of his model, Monsieur de Tréville.

"I don't laugh often, sir, as you can see from my face, but I intend to keep the privilege of laughing when it suits me."

"And I don't want anyone to laugh when it doesn't suit *me*!"

"Really, sir?" said the stranger, calmer than ever. "Well, that seems fair enough."

He turned away and prepared to walk back into the inn through the front door, beside which d'Artagnan, when he arrived, had noticed a saddled horse.

But it was not in d'Artagnan's nature to abandon a man who had insolently made fun of him. He drew his sword completely and ran after him, shouting, "You've mocked me for the last time, sir! Turn and face me, so I won't have to run you through from behind!"

"Run me through?" said the stranger, turning around and looking at him with as much astonishment as contempt. "Come, come, my friend, you must be mad!" Then, in an undertone, as though talking to himself: "What a pity, when His Majesty is always looking for brave men to join his musketeers!"

No sooner had he said this than d'Artagnan lunged at him so fiercely that his mocking would indeed have been ended forever if he had not quickly stepped back. Seeing that it was no longer a laughing matter, he drew his sword, saluted his opponent and gravely stood on guard. But just then his two companions, accompanied by the innkeeper, attacked d'Artagnan with a stick, a shovel, and a pair of tongs. This was such a sudden and thorough diversion that while d'Artagnan turned to defend himself against the rain of blows, the stranger sheathed his sword and began watching the battle with his usual impassivity.

"A plague on these Gascons!" he said. "Put him back on his orange horse and send him away."

"Not till I've killed you, you coward!" cried d'Artagnan, holding firm against his three attackers and warding off their blows as best he could.

"More blustering! I swear, these Gascons are incorrigible! Keep him dancing, since he insists on it. He'll tell you when he's had enough."

But the stranger did not yet know what kind of man he was dealing with; d'Artagnan was too stubborn ever to ask for mercy. The fight continued a few more seconds, then d'Artagnan, exhausted, dropped his sword, which one of his assailants broke with a stick. Almost at the same moment, a blow on the forehead knocked him to the ground, bleeding and half unconscious.

That was when people came running to the scene from all

directions. Fearing a scandal, the innkeeper had his servants help him carry d'Artagnan to the kitchen, where his wounds were given perfunctory treatment.

As for the stranger, he went back inside and took up his place at the window. He watched the crowd impatiently, as though its continued presence caused him great annoyance.

Hearing the door open behind him, he looked around and saw the innkeeper.

"Well, how's that young hothead?"

"Are you safe and sound, Your Excellency?" asked the innkeeper.

"Yes, I'm perfectly safe and sound, but you haven't answered my question. What's become of our Gascon?"

"He's doing better," replied the innkeeper. "He's completely unconscious now."

"Really?"

"Yes, but before he fainted, he gathered enough strength to call for you and challenge you."

"He must be the devil in person!" exclaimed the stranger.

"Oh, no, Your Excellency, he's not the devil," the innkeeper said with a contemptuous grimace, "because we searched him after he fainted and found that he had only one shirt in his bag and only twelve écus in his purse. Even so, while he was still conscious, he said that if such a thing had happened in Paris, you'd have regretted it immediately, but that since it happened here, you won't regret it till later."

"In that case," the stranger remarked imperturbably, "he must be some prince of the blood in disguise."

"I'm telling you this, Your Excellency, so that you can be on your guard."

"Did he mention anyone's name, in his anger?"

"Yes. He patted his pocket and said, 'We'll see what Monsieur de Tréville thinks about this insult to a man who's under his protection.' "

"Monsieur de Tréville?" said the stranger, suddenly attentive. "He patted his pocket and mentioned Monsieur de Tréville's name? After he fainted, I'm sure you didn't neglect to look into that pocket. What did you find?"

"A letter addressed to Monsieur de Tréville, captain of the musketeers."

"Are you sure?"

"Quite sure, Your Excellency."

The innkeeper, who was not gifted with great perspicacity,

had not noticed the effect produced by his words. The stranger left the window, where he had remained with his elbow resting on the sill, and murmured with a worried frown, "Can it be that Tréville sent that Gascon after me? He's very young, but a sword thrust is a sword thrust, no matter who gives it, and a boy like that would be less likely to arouse my suspicion. Sometimes a small obstacle is enough to upset a great plan . . ."

He was lost in thought for several minutes. Finally he said to the innkeeper, "I'd like you to put that lunatic out of the way for me. My conscience wouldn't let me kill him. And yet," he added with a coldly menacing expression, "he's a hindrance to me. Where is he?"

"In my wife's room, on the second floor. His wounds are being dressed."

"Are his clothes and his bag with him? Is he still wearing his doublet?"

"No, all those things are downstairs in the kitchen. But since he's a bother to you . . ."

"Yes, he is, and he's causing a disturbance in your inn that decent people can't overlook. Go up to your room, make out my bill and tell my servant to get ready to leave."

"What! You're leaving us already, Your Excellency?"

"You know I am, since I ordered you to have my horse saddled. Hasn't it been done?"

"Yes, sir. As you can see for yourself, your horse is saddled and waiting at the door."

"Very well. Now do what I told you."

The innkeeper nodded and thought, "Can he be afraid of that boy?" But a stern look from the stranger put an end to his reflections. He bowed humbly and walked out.

"That young rascal mustn't see Milady,*" the stranger said to himself. "She'll be here soon; she's already late. I'd better ride out to meet her . . . If only I knew what's in that letter to Tréville!"

And, still muttering to himself, he headed for the kitchen.

Meanwhile the innkeeper, convinced that the stranger was leaving his inn because of the boy's presence, went to his wife's room and saw that d'Artagnan had finally regained consciousness. Telling him that the police would be sure to arrest him for having picked a quarrel with a great lord—for in his opinion the stranger

---

*A French word (from the English "my lady") used in referring to a titled English lady. (Translator's note.)

could only be a great lord—he persuaded him to get up and continue on his way despite his weakness. D'Artagnan, still half dazed, without his doublet, and with his head swathed in bandages, stood up and, pushed by the innkeeper, went downstairs. But when he reached the kitchen, the first thing he saw was the stranger standing beside a heavy carriage with two big Norman horses hitched to it, calmly talking to a woman inside.

The woman, whose face was framed by the carriage window, was between twenty and twenty-two years old. Being a quick observer, as we have already mentioned, d'Artagnan saw at a glance that she was young and beautiful. He was all the more struck by her beauty because it was foreign to the southern regions where he had always lived. She was pale and blond, with long, curly hair that hung down to her shoulders, big, languid blue eyes, pink lips, and hands as white as alabaster. She was talking animatedly with the stranger.

"So His Eminence has ordered me . . ."

"To go back to England without delay," said the stranger, "and notify him immediately if the duke leaves London."

"And what are my other instructions?" asked the beautiful traveler.

"They're in this box. You're not to open it till you've crossed the Channel."

"Very well; and what are you doing?"

"I'm going back to Paris."

"Without punishing that insolent boy?"

Just as the stranger opened his mouth to reply, d'Artagnan, who had heard everything, appeared in the doorway of the inn.

"This insolent boy will punish *you,*" he cried, "unless you escape from me again, as you did before."

"Escape from you?" said the stranger, frowning.

"I don't think you'll dare to run away in front of a lady."

"No!" exclaimed Milady, seeing the stranger put his hand to his sword. "Remember that the slightest delay can be disastrous."

"You're right," he conceded. "It's time for us to go our separate ways."

He took leave of her with a nod and leapt onto his horse while the driver of the carriage vigorously cracked his whip. He and Milady both left at a gallop, in opposite directions.

"What about your bill?" shouted the innkeeper, whose affection for his guest had turned to disdain when he saw that he was leaving without settling his account.

"Pay it!" the stranger called back to his servant, who tossed a few coins at the innkeeper's feet and rode after his master.

"Coward! Miserable coward! False nobleman!" cried d'Artagnan, rushing off in pursuit.

But he was still too weak for such an effort. He had taken no more than ten steps when there was a ringing in his ears, he felt dizzy, and a cloud of blood passed before his eyes. He fell in the middle of the street, still shouting, "Coward! Coward! Coward!"

The innkeeper went over to him. "He really is a coward," he said, trying to put himself on good terms with d'Artagnan, as the heron in La Fontaine's fable became reconciled to eating a snail at the end of the day.

"Yes, he's very cowardly," murmured d'Artagnan, "but she's very beautiful!"

"Who's very beautiful?" asked the innkeeper.

"Milady," d'Artagnan answered feebly, and fainted again.

"I've lost two guests," thought the innkeeper, "but I still have this one, and I'm sure I can keep him several days. At least I'll take in eleven écus."

Eleven écus was exactly the sum that remained in d'Artagnan's purse.

The innkeeper was counting on eleven days of convalescence at one écu a day; but he had reckoned without his guest. At five o'clock the next morning d'Artagnan got up, went to the kitchen, and, among several other ingredients that history has not revealed to us, asked for some wine, olive oil, and rosemary. Then, following his mother's recipe, he made an ointment, which he put on his many wounds. He changed the compresses himself and would not allow a doctor to be called in. Thanks to the efficacy of the Gypsy ointment and also, perhaps, to the absence of a doctor, by that evening he was back on his feet, and by the next day he had almost completely recovered.

But when he reached into his pocket to pay for the rosemary, olive oil, wine, and other ingredients—the only expense he had incurred for himself, since he had strictly fasted, although his yellow horse, at least according to the innkeeper, had eaten three times as much as could have been reasonably supposed for an animal of that size—d'Artagnan found only his threadbare little velvet purse and the eleven écus it contained: the letter to Monsieur de Tréville had disappeared.

He began by looking for it patiently, turning all his pockets inside out, rummaging in his bag, opening and closing his purse; but when he finally became convinced that the letter was really gone, he flew into another rage that nearly added more ointment ingredients to his bill, for, seeing him lose his temper and hearing him threaten to smash everything in the inn if his letter was not found, the innkeeper picked up a pike, his wife brandished a broomstick, and the servants armed themselves with sticks.

"My letter of recommendation!" thundered d'Artagnan. "Give it to me, or by God I'll run you all through like birds on a spit!"

Unfortunately one thing made it impossible for him to carry out his threat: his sword, as we have seen, had been broken in half during his first struggle. He had forgotten this, however, and was therefore taken aback when he tried to draw his sword and found himself armed only with a blunt stub eight or nine inches long, which the innkeeper had carefully put back into the sheath. The cook had furtively taken the rest of the blade, intending to use it as a larding pin.

But this disappointment would probably not have stopped our fiery young man if the innkeeper had not suddenly realized that his guest's complaint was perfectly justified.

"What could have happened to that letter?" he said, lowering his pike.

"Yes, where *is* it?" cried d'Artagnan. "First of all, let me warn you that it's addressed to Monsieur de Tréville and we have to find it. If we don't, *he'll* have it found, you can count on that!"

This threat intimidated the innkeeper. After the king and the cardinal, Monsieur de Tréville was perhaps the man whose name was most often spoken by soldiers, and even by civilians. There was Father Joseph, of course, but the terror aroused by the Gray Eminence, as the cardinal's close associate was called, was so great that his name was mentioned only in a whisper.

The innkeeper dropped his pike and ordered his wife and servants to do the same with their weapons; then he set the example by beginning to look for the lost letter.

"Is there something important in it?" he asked after several minutes of unsuccessful searching.

"There certainly is!" said d'Artagnan, who was counting on that letter to make his way at court. "It contains my fortune!"

"Bonds?" the innkeeper inquired anxiously.

"Bonds on His Majesty's personal treasury," answered d'Artagnan; since he expected to enter the king's service by means of that recommendation, he felt he could truthfully make this rather hazardous reply.

"Good heavens!" the innkeeper exclaimed in despair.

"But that doesn't matter," d'Artagnan continued with true Gascon self-assurance. "The money means nothing to me, and the letter means everything. I'd rather lose a thousand pistoles than lose that letter."

He could just as easily have said twenty thousand, but he was restrained by a certain youthful modesty.

All at once an idea flashed into the mind of the innkeeper, whose frenzied search had still yielded nothing.

"Your letter wasn't lost!" he exclaimed.

"What do you mean?" asked d'Artagnan.

"It was stolen."

"Stolen! Who . . ."

"The gentleman who was here yesterday. He went into the kitchen while your doublet was there, and he stayed there alone. I'm willing to bet he stole your letter."

"You think so?" said d'Artagnan, unconvinced. Knowing that the letter was important only to him personally, he saw no reason for anyone to take it. None of the servants or guests had anything to gain by it. "You really suspect that insolent gentleman?"

"I'm sure he's the one who did it. He seemed very upset when I told you were under Monsieur de Tréville's protection and even had a letter for him. He asked me where the letter was, and he immediately went down to the kitchen, knowing your doublet was there."

"Then he *is* the thief," said d'Artagnan. "I'll complain to Monsieur de Tréville and he'll complain to the king."

He majestically took two écus from his pocket and gave them to the innkeeper, who accompanied him to the door, hat in hand.

He mounted his yellow horse and rode without further incident to the Porte Saint-Antoine in Paris. There he sold the horse for three écus, which was a good price, considering that he had pressed him hard during the last stage of his journey. The dealer admitted he had paid that exorbitant sum only because the horse had such an unusual color.

D'Artagnan therefore entered Paris on foot, carrying his belongings under his arm, and walked till he found a room for rent that suited his meager means. It was an attic room on the Rue des Fossoyeurs, near the Luxembourg.

After paying the deposit, he took possession of his room and spent a good part of the day sewing trimmings on his doublet and breeches; his mother had taken the trimmings from a nearly new doublet belonging to his father and given them to him in secret. He then went to the Quai de la Ferraille to have a new blade put on his sword. Next he went to the Louvre, stopped the first musketeer he saw, asked him where Monsieur de Tréville's house was, and learned that it was on the Rue du Vieux-Colombier, which was near the room d'Artagnan had rented. He took this as a favorable omen.

Finally, satisfied with himself for the way he had behaved at Meung, without remorse for the past, confident in the present, and full of hope for the future, he went to bed and slept the sleep of the brave. In his case it was also the sleep of a provincial.

It lasted till nine o'clock, when he got up and prepared to visit the famous Monsieur de Tréville, who, in his father's opinion, was the third most powerful man in the kingdom.

2

Monsieur de Tréville's Anteroom

Monsieur de Troisvilles, as his family in Gascony was still called, or Monsieur de Tréville, as he had finally come to be known in Paris, really had begun like d'Artagnan, that is, lacking money but generously endowed with the daring, quick-wittedness and shrewd intelligence that often make the poorest Gascon country squire receive more from his paternal inheritance in expectation than the richest nobleman in Périgord or Berry receives in reality. In a time when violence was an everyday matter, his insolent courage, and still more insolent good luck, had enabled him to reach the top of the difficult ladder known as favor at court, climbing it four rungs at a time.

He was a friend of the king, who, as is well known, revered the memory of his father Henry IV. Monsieur de Tréville's father had served Henry IV faithfully in the wars against the Catholic League. Unable to reward him with money—which he lacked all his life, so that he always paid his debts with the only thing he never had to borrow: wit—the king authorized him, after the surrender of Paris, to take as his coat of arms a golden lion passant on gules, with the motto *Fidelis et fortis*. This enriched him in honor but left him scantily supplied with worldly goods, with the result that when he died his only bequest to his son was his sword and his motto. Because of this double gift and the unblemished name that went with it, Monsieur de Tréville was admitted into the young prince's household, where he served so well with his sword and was so faithful to his motto that Louis XIII, one of the best swordsmen in the kingdom, sometimes said that if he had a friend who was going to fight a duel, he would recommend himself as his second and then Tréville, or perhaps Tréville even before himself.

Louis XIII had genuine affection for Tréville—a royal, selfish affection, but still affection. In those troubled times, everyone in high position tried to surround himself with men of Tréville's quality. Many other noblemen could claim the epithet of "strong," which was the second part of his motto, but few could claim "faithful," its first part. Tréville was one of those few. He was also one of those rare people with the obedient intelligence of a mastiff, reckless valor, alert eyes, and hands always ready to act. He used his eyes to see if the king was displeased with someone and his hands to strike down that displeasing someone, who might have proved to be an assassin like Besme, Maurevers, Poltrot de Méré, or Vitry. For a time, all that prevented him from rising to great heights was lack of the right opportunity. He was constantly on the lookout for that opportunity and determined to seize it if it came within reach. Then Louis XIII placed him in command of the King's Musketeers, who, in fanatical devotion to their sovereign, equaled Henry III's Ordinaries and Louis XI's Scottish Guards.

The cardinal did not let himself be outdone by the king. When he saw the formidable elite corps with which Louis XIII had surrounded himself, this secondary, or rather this primary king of France decided that he too must have his guards. He therefore had his musketeers as Louis XIII had his. The two rival powers searched all the French provinces, and even foreign countries, for renowned swordsmen to place in their service. During their evening chess game, Cardinal Richelieu and Louis XIII often argued about the merits of their respective bodyguards. Each praised the bearing and courage of his own, and while they both openly opposed duels and brawls, each secretly urged his men to fight against the other's and felt deep sorrow or boundless joy at each defeat or victory. So we are told, at least, in the memoirs of a man who took part in a few of those defeats and many of those victories.

Tréville had appealed to his master's weak side, and it was to this shrewd approach that he owed the long and constant favor of a monarch who has not left a reputation for being very loyal in his friendships. He made his musketeers parade in front of Cardinal Richelieu with a mocking expression that made His Eminence's gray mustache bristle with rage. Tréville had an admirable understanding of war in that time, when, if soldiers were not living at the expense of the enemy, they lived at the expense of their compatriots. His own soldiers formed a legion of turbulent daredevils who recognized no authority but his.

Unruly, hard-drinking, and scarred, the King's Musketeers, or rather Tréville's Musketeers, invaded taverns, promenades, and public games, talking loudly, curling their mustaches, rattling their swords, and joyously clashing with the cardinal's guards when they encountered them. They would then make joking remarks as they drew their swords in the street. They were sometimes killed, but in that case they were sure to be mourned and avenged; they often killed, and then they were sure not to languish in prison, because Monsieur de Tréville would have them released. They worshiped him and constantly sang his praises, and, pugnacious ruffians though they were, they trembled before him like schoolboys before their master, obeyed him unquestioningly, and were always ready to die in order to wipe away the slightest reproach from him.

Tréville had used that powerful weapon first for the king and the king's friends, then for himself and his own friends. But in none of the many memoirs that have come down to us from that time is there any mention of his ever having been accused, even by his enemies (who were as numerous among men of letters as among men of the sword), of taking money for the services of his men. With a rare genius for intrigue that made him the equal of the greatest schemers, he still remained an honest man. And despite the roughness and fatigue of his military exercises, he was one of the most accomplished men of his day in the arts of gallantry, elegant flirtation, and seduction; he was as famous for his success with women as Bassompierre had been twenty years earlier, which is saying a great deal. He had thus reached the peak of the human condition: he was admired, feared, and loved.

Louis XIV's vast radiance dimmed all the lesser luminaries at his court. But his father, a sun unable to shine on many different worlds, did not prevent his favorites from having their own splendor, or his courtiers from proving their personal worth. Besides the levees of the king and the cardinal, there were then in Paris more than two hundred minor levees held in varying degrees of esteem. Tréville's was one of those most eagerly sought after.

Beginning at six o'clock in the morning in summer, and eight o'clock in winter, the courtyard of his house on the Rue du Vieux-Colombier was like a camp: fifty or sixty musketeers, who seemed to work in relays so that there would always be an impressive number of them, walked about fully armed and ready for anything. The staircase was large enough for our civilization to build an entire house in the space it occupied. Up and down it went Parisians seeking some favor or other, provincial noblemen eager to be enrolled, and servants in liveries of all colors bringing messages for Monsieur de Tréville from their masters. On long circular benches in the anteroom sat the elite, that is, those who had been summoned. Here, there was a hum of conversation from morning till evening while in his study next to the anteroom Monsieur de Tréville received visitors, listened to complaints, and gave orders; and like the king on his balcony at the Louvre, he had only to go to his window to inspect his armed men.

On the day when d'Artagnan presented himself, the assembly was impressive, especially to a provincial newly arrived in Paris, though it is true that this provincial was a Gascon and that, especially in those days, Gascons had the reputation of not being easily intimidated.

As soon as a visitor had passed the massive gate studded with long square-headed nails, he found himself in the midst of loud, playful, and sometimes quarrelsome swordsmen walking back and forth in the courtyard. Only an officer, a great lord, or a pretty woman could have made an easy passage through those turbulent waters.

D'Artagnan's heart was pounding when he stepped into the disorderly throng. His long rapier hung beside his slender leg and he kept one hand on the brim of his hat, with the half-smile of an embarrassed provincial who wants to put up a good front. He breathed more freely each time he had passed a group, but then he would realize that they were turning to look at him, and for the first time in his life, after having had a rather good opinion of himself till then, he felt ridiculous.

When he reached the staircase, it was even worse. At the foot of the stairs, four musketeers were playing a game while ten or twelve of their comrades waited their turn on the landing. The game was as follows: one of the four stood on a step above the three others, sword in hand, and tried to prevent them from coming up while they deftly fenced against him.

At first d'Artagnan thought they were using blunt-tipped fencing foils, but when he saw some of them receive slight wounds, he realized that their swords were fully sharpened. At each wound the fencers as well as the onlookers laughed wildly.

The man on the upper step was holding off his opponents with amazing skill. A circle had formed around them. The rule was that each time a man was touched he moved down one place on the waiting list for an interview with Monsieur de Tréville and the man who had touched him moved up one place. In five minutes all three attackers had been touched—one on the wrist, one on the chin, and one on the ear—by the defender above them, who remained unscathed and thus gained three places on the waiting list.

Though he tried hard not to show it, d'Artagnan was astonished at this pastime. He came from a province where hotheads were common, but he had never seen swordplay on such a trivial pretext, and the blustering bravado of those four men went beyond anything he had ever heard before, even in Gascony. He felt as if he had been transported into the land of giants where Gulliver was so frightened. And there was more to come: he still had to reach the landing and the anteroom.

On the landing, there was no swordplay. Instead, men were telling stories about women; and in the anteroom, stories about the court. On the landing, d'Artagnan blushed; in the anteroom, he shuddered. His lively, roving imagination, which in Gascony had made him dangerous to young chambermaids and sometimes to their young mistresses, had never, even in his wildest moments, conjured up half of those amorous wonders or a quarter of those gallant exploits, spiced with famous names and intimate details. And after his sense of morality had been shocked on the landing, his respect for the cardinal was scandalized in the anteroom. To his amazement, he heard open criticism of the policy that made Europe tremble and of the cardinal's private life, which so many powerful noblemen had been punished for trying to delve into. This great man, revered by d'Artagnan's father, served as a laughingstock for Monsieur de Tréville's musketeers. They mocked his crooked legs and stooped shoulders; some of them sang satiric songs about Madame d'Aiguillon, his mistress, and Madame de Combalet, his niece, while others made plans against his pages and guards. To d'Artagnan, all this seemed monstrous and incredible.

Now and then, however, when the king's name happened to be mentioned in the midst of the jeering at the cardinal, the mockers were silent for a moment, as if they had all been gagged. They cautiously looked in all directions and seemed afraid that their voices might have been heard through the wall of Monsieur de Tréville's study. But soon an allusion brought the conversation back to His Eminence; the jeering then resumed, and so did the outspoken comments on all his acts.

D'Artagnan was terrified. "These men are all going to be thrown into the Bastille and hanged," he thought, "and the same thing will probably happen to me, because listening to them makes me their accomplice. After always telling me how much I ought to respect the cardinal, what would my father think if he knew I was with these heathens?"

And so, as the reader will have guessed without being told, d'Artagnan did not dare to take part in the conversation. But he strained his eyes and ears to make sure he missed nothing, and despite his trust in his father's recommendations, his instincts and inclinations made him consider those men's outrageous behavior with more approval than blame.

Since he was a stranger in the crowd of Monsieur de Tréville's courtiers and had never been seen in the anteroom before, a servant came to ask him what he wanted. D'Artagnan humbly gave his name, stressed the fact that he was from Gascony, like Monsieur de Tréville, and asked the servant to request an audience for him with his master. The servant patronizingly promised to transmit his request in due time.

Now that he had recovered a little from his first surprise, d'Artagnan began examining the clothes and faces of the men around him.

At the center of the most animated group was a tall musketeer with a haughty face, dressed in a strange way that attracted everyone's attention. He was not wearing his uniform coat, which was not absolutely obligatory in those days of less freedom but more independence, but a slightly worn and faded sky-blue jerkin, and over this a magnificent gold-embroidered shoulder belt, glittering like water in sunlight. A crimson velvet cloak descended in graceful folds, revealing the luxurious shoulder belt, from which hung a gigantic rapier.

This musketeer had just come off guard duty. He complained of having caught a cold and coughed ostentatiously from time to time. It was because of his cold, he said, that he was wearing his cloak. While he talked loudly, conceitedly twirling his mustache, everyone, including d'Artagnan, enthusiastically admired his embroidered shoulder belt.

"It's foolish, I know," he said, "but it's the fashion now. And besides, I have to do something with my share of the money from my father's estate."

"Come, come, Porthos," said one of his listeners, "don't try to make us believe that shoulder belt came from your father's generosity: it must have been given to you by the veiled lady I saw you with last Sunday, near the Porte Saint-Honoré."

"No, on my honor as a gentleman, I bought it myself, with my own money," replied the musketeer who had been addressed as Porthos.

"Yes," said another musketeer, "just as I bought this new purse with what my mistress put in my old one."

"What I said is true," protested Porthos. "I paid twelve pistoles for this belt."

Admiration increased but doubt persisted.

"Isn't that right, Aramis?" said Porthos, turning to another musketeer.

This musketeer formed a sharp contrast with Porthos. He was only twenty-two or twenty-three, with an innocent, almost prim face, dark, gentle eyes, pink cheeks as downy as a peach in autumn, and a thin mustache that drew a perfectly straight line across his upper lip. He seemed reluctant to lower his hands, for fear their veins might swell, and he periodically pinched his earlobes to maintain their delicate rosy tint. He usually spoke little and slowly, bowed often, and laughed silently, showing his beautiful teeth, which gave evidence of the same meticulous care he devoted to the rest of his person.

He nodded in reply to his friend's question. This seemed to clear away all doubts about the shoulder belt. Everyone continued to admire it but no longer talked about it, and the conversation abruptly turned to another subject.

"What do you think of the story Chalais's equerry has told?" asked one of the musketeers, addressing his question to everyone in general.

"What has he been saying?" Porthos inquired condescendingly.

"He says that in Brussels he found Rochefort, the cardinal's right-hand man, disguised as a Capuchin, and that with that disguise he was able to take in Monsieur de Laigues, like the fool he is."

"Yes, he's a real fool," said Porthos. "But are you sure the story is true?"

"I heard it from Aramis," replied the musketeer.

"You did?"

"You know very well he did, Porthos," said Aramis. "I told you the story myself, only yesterday. It's not worth talking about."

"That's *your* opinion!" retorted Porthos. "Not worth talking about? You're quick to jump to a conclusion! The cardinal sets a spy on a gentleman and has his letters stolen by a traitor, a scoundrel, a bandit; then, with the help of the spy and the letters, he has Chalais beheaded on the stupid pretext that he wanted to kill the king and have the queen marry the king's brother! No one had the slightest inkling of all that; you told us about it yesterday, to our great satisfaction, and now, while we're still astounded at the news, you tell us it's not worth talking about!"

"Very well, then, let's talk about it, since that's what you want," Aramis said patiently.

"If I were Chalais's equerry, I'd make Rochefort wish he'd never been born!"

"And then the Red Duke would make you wish the same."

"The Red Duke!" exclaimed Porthos, clapping his hands. "Bravo, Aramis! That's a charming name for the cardinal! I'll make sure it becomes widely known, you can count on that. I've always said you were witty! It's a pity you couldn't follow your vocation, my friend—what a delightful priest you would have made!"

"It's only a delay," replied Aramis. "I'll be a priest some day. You know I'm still studying theology."

"He'll do as he says," Porthos assured the others. "Sooner or later, he'll be a priest."

"Sooner," said Aramis.

"He's waiting for only one thing before he finally decides to put on the cassock he hangs behind his uniform," said one of the musketeers.

"What is it he's waiting for?" asked another.

"He's waiting for the queen to give an heir to the French crown."

"Let's not joke about that, gentlemen," said Porthos. "Thank God, the queen is still young enough to do it."

"They say the duke of Buckingham is in France now," Aramis said with a sly laugh that gave a scandalous meaning to this apparently simple remark.

"Aramis, my friend, you shouldn't have said that," Porthos reprimanded him. "Your wit always makes you go too far. If

Monsieur de Tréville had heard you, he'd have made you regret it."

"Are you lecturing me, Porthos?" Aramis said heatedly, his eyes flashing.

"Be a musketeer or be a priest, but don't try to be both at the same time," replied Porthos. "As Athos told you the other day, you want the best of both worlds. But let's not lose our tempers; that would be useless, and you know what you, I, and Athos have agreed on. You're a frequent visitor at Madame d'Aiguillon's house, and you try to win her favors; you also visit Madame de Bois-Tracy, Madame de Chevreuse's cousin, and you're said to stand very high in her good graces. No, no, don't admit your good fortune, no one's asking for your secret, we all know your discretion. But since you have that virtue, use it with regard to Her Majesty. Anyone can say whatever he likes about the king and the cardinal, but the queen is sacred. If you talk about her, say only good things."

"Porthos, you're unbearably pompous. You know I hate being lectured, except by Athos. And someone with a shoulder belt like yours is in no position to be sanctimonious. I'll be a priest if it suits me, but in the meantime I'm a musketeer. As a musketeer I say whatever I choose, and I now choose to say that I'm about to lose patience with you."

"Aramis!"

"Porthos!"

"Gentlemen! Gentlemen!" cried the other musketeers.

"Monsieur de Tréville awaits Monsieur d'Artagnan," announced the servant, opening the door of the study.

At these words, everyone fell silent. The door remained open. D'Artagnan walked across the anteroom and into Monsieur de Tréville's study, thankful at having escaped the end of that strange quarrel.

3

The Audience

Monsieur de Tréville was in a bad humor. Nevertheless he greeted his young visitor politely and smiled when he heard him reply in a Gascon accent that reminded him of his own youth and his homeland, two memories that make a man smile at any age. He then stepped to the door opening into the anteroom, gesturing to d'Artagnan as though to ask permission to finish with the others before beginning with him, and called out three times, his voice becoming louder with each name and going from sternness to irritation:

"Athos! Porthos! Aramis!"

Porthos and Aramis, the two musketeers with whom we have already become acquainted, immediately left their group and walked toward the study. The door closed behind them as soon as they were inside. Their faces were not entirely serene, but d'Artagnan admired their look of ease, mingled with both dignity and deference. To him, these men were demigods and their leader was a Jupiter armed with thunderbolts.

When the door had closed, the hum of voices in the anteroom began again, perhaps stimulated by the summoning of the two musketeers. In the study Monsieur de Tréville, silent and frowning, paced the floor three or four times, passing in front of Porthos and Aramis, who stood stiffly at attention. Suddenly he stopped and looked them over from head to foot with an angry expression.

"Do you know what the king said to me last night? Do you know, gentlemen?"

"No, sir," they both answered after a moment of silence.

"But I hope you'll do us the honor of telling us," Aramis added courteously, with his most gracious bow.

"He told me that from now on he was going to recruit his musketeers from the cardinal's guards!"

"The cardinal's guards!" exclaimed Porthos. "Why?"

"Because he could see that his weak wine needed to be strengthened by mixing it with a more vigorous vintage."

The two musketeers blushed to the whites of their eyes. D'Artagnan was so embarrassed that he wished the floor would open and swallow him up.

"Yes, and His Majesty was right," Monsieur de Tréville continued with more animation, "because, on my honor, it's true that the musketeers cut a sorry figure at court. Last night, during the king's card game, the cardinal told a story with a sympathetic look on his face that exasperated me. He told how some of the fearless, ferocious musketeers—he looked at me and said those words with a sarcasm that exasperated me still more—had caused a disturbance in a tavern on the Rue Férou, and how a patrol of his guards—I thought he was going to laugh in my face—had been forced to arrest them. Do you hear that? They arrested musketeers! You two were there, don't deny it: you were recognized, and the cardinal mentioned your names! It's my fault—yes, my fault, because I choose my men. You, Aramis, why did you ask me for a uniform when a cassock would have suited you so well? And you, Porthos, why do you have that beautiful gold belt for a sword you're not willing to use? And Athos—I don't see Athos. Where is he?''

"Sir," Aramis answered sadly, "he's sick, very sick."

"Sick, very sick, you say? What kind of sickness does he have?''

"They're afraid it may be smallpox, sir," said Porthos, wanting to have his share of the conversation, "and that would be a great pity because it would ruin his face.''

"Smallpox? Do you expect me to believe that, Porthos? Smallpox at his age? No! He's probably been wounded, maybe killed . . . If only I knew! Let me tell you something, gentlemen: I won't have my musketeers going to low taverns, picking quarrels, and fighting in the street. I won't have them being laughed at by the cardinal's guards. His guards are calm, well-behaved, clever men who never cause a public disturbance—and wouldn't let themselves be arrested if they did! I'm sure they'd rather die than retreat one single step. *They* don't run away like rabbits: they leave that for the musketeers to do!''

Porthos and Aramis were quivering with rage. They would gladly have strangled Monsieur de Tréville if they had not sensed that it was his great love for them that made him speak as he did. They stamped their feet, bit their lips, and clutched their sword hilts with all their strength.

The musketeers in the anteroom had heard Monsieur de Tréville call Athos, Porthos, and Aramis, and from the tone of his voice they had known he was angry. Ten of them now had their ears pressed to the door. Their faces were pale with fury because they had heard everything said in the study, and they had been repeating the captain's insulting words to the other men in the anteroom. It had taken only a few moments for their fury to spread to all the musketeers in the house and the courtyard.

"So the King's Musketeers let themselves be arrested by the cardinal's guards," Monsieur de Tréville went on, inwardly as enraged as his soldiers, but keeping his voice under control and deliberately plunging his words into their hearts like so many daggers. "Six of His Eminence's guards arrested six of His Majesty's musketeers! Well, I've made up my mind. I'm going straight to the Louvre to resign as captain of the King's Musketeers and ask the cardinal to make me a lieutenant in his guards, and if he refuses, I'll become a priest.''

At these words, the murmur in the anteroom turned into an explosion. The air was filled with curses and blasphemies. D'Artagnan had a strong impulse to hide behind a tapestry or crawl under the table.

"It's true that there were six of us against six of them, sir," said Porthos, beside himself with rage, "but they took us off guard, and before we even had time to draw our swords, two of us had been killed and Athos was badly wounded. You know Athos, sir. He tried to stand up twice, and he fell both times. But we didn't surrender, no! They dragged us away by force. Then we escaped. As for Athos, they thought he was dead, so they left him lying where he'd fallen, without bothering to carry him away. There, that's the story. No one wins every battle, sir. The great Pompey lost the Battle of Pharsalus, and King Francis I, who was as good a man as any who ever lived, from what I've heard, lost the Battle of Pavia.''

"And I killed one of them with his own sword," said Aramis, "because mine broke with the first parry. If you like, sir, you can say I stabbed him.''

"I didn't know all that," Tréville replied in a somewhat softer tone. "The cardinal was exaggerating.''

Seeing that his captain was becoming calmer, Aramis dared to make a request: "Please don't tell anyone that Athos is wounded, sir. He'd be in despair if the king knew about it. And his wound is very serious, since the blade went through his shoulder and into his chest. I'm afraid he may . . .''

Just then the door curtain was pushed aside and a handsome but horribly pale face appeared.

"Athos!" cried the two musketeers.

"Athos!" repeated Monsieur de Tréville.

"I've been told you want to see me, sir," Athos said in a weak but steady voice, "and here I am. What are your orders?''

With these words he stepped into the room, impeccably dressed as usual. Deeply moved by this show of courage, Tréville rushed toward him.

"I was just telling these gentlemen," he said, "that I forbid my musketeers to risk their lives needlessly, because the king values brave men and he knows that the musketeers are the bravest men on earth. Give me your hand, Athos.''

Without waiting for Athos to reply to this affectionate welcome, he seized his right hand and gripped it vigorously, not noticing that Athos, despite all his self-control, winced with pain and turned even paler, which would have seemed impossible.

Athos's arrival had caused a sensation in the anteroom, for his wound was known to everyone despite all efforts to keep it a secret. The door had remained ajar, and Tréville's words were greeted by a joyous hubbub. Two or three musketeers, carried away by enthusiasm, drew back the door curtain and looked into the study. Tréville was about to rebuke them sharply when he felt Athos's hand tighten in his own and saw that he was about to faint. A moment later Athos, finally overcome by the pain against which he had been struggling with all the strength he had left, fell unconscious to the floor.

"Bring a doctor!" cried Tréville. "Mine, the king's, the best one you can find! Oh, my God! Athos is dying!"

Hearing this, men from the anteroom hurried into the study and anxiously crowded around Athos. Tréville had no thought of ordering them to leave. But their zeal would have been useless if his doctor had not already been in the house. Pushing his way through the throng, he succeeded in reaching Athos, who was still unconscious. Since he could not attend to his patient properly in all that noise and bustle, he asked to have him taken to a nearby bedroom. Tréville opened another door and showed the way to Porthos and Aramis while they carried their comrade. Behind them walked the doctor, and behind the doctor the door was closed.

Monsieur de Tréville's study, ordinarily held in great respect, now became an annex of the anteroom. The musketeers made loud, excited comments, ranted, fulminated, and vehemently cursed the cardinal and his guards.

A few moments later Porthos and Aramis returned; the doctor and Tréville had remained with Athos.

Finally Tréville also came back. Athos had regained consciousness and the doctor had said that there was nothing alarming about his condition: he had simply fainted from loss of blood.

Tréville made a gesture and everyone withdrew, except for d'Artagnan. He had not forgotten that he had been granted an audience, and, with his Gascon tenacity, he had remained standing in the same place.

When all the others had gone and the door had been closed, Tréville turned to face d'Artagnan. His mind was still in disorder from what had just happened. He asked his persistent visitor what he wanted. As soon as d'Artagnan gave his name, Tréville remembered everything.

"Excuse me, my young fellow Gascon," he said, smiling, "but I'd completely forgotten you. You must understand that an officer is like a father with greater responsibilities than an ordinary father. Soldiers are big children; but since I must see to it that the king's orders, and especially the cardinal's, are carried out . . ."

D'Artagnan could not hold back a smile, and from this smile Tréville judged that he was not dealing with a fool. He changed the subject and came straight to the point: "I still have very fond memories of your father. What can I do for his son? Tell me quickly, because my time isn't my own."

"When I left Tarbes to come here, sir," replied d'Artagnan, "I intended to ask you to take me into the musketeers, in memory of your friendship with my father. But from what I've seen in the last two hours, I realize what an enormous favor that would be, and I'm afraid I may not deserve it."

"Yes, it *is* a great favor, but it may not be as far above you as you think, or pretend to think. However, His Majesty has made a decision on the matter, and I regret to tell you that no one can become a musketeer until he has first proved himself by fighting in several campaigns, performing outstanding acts, or serving for two years in a regiment less favored than ours."

D'Artagnan bowed without speaking. He was more eager than ever to wear a musketeer's uniform now that he knew he would have to overcome great difficulties to obtain it.

"But," Monsieur de Tréville went on, giving him a piercing look, as if he wanted to see into the depths of his heart, "because I have such fond memories of my friendship with your father, as I told you, I want to do something for you. Young gentlemen in Béarn usually aren't rich, and I doubt that things have changed since I left the province, so the money you brought with you is probably just enough to keep you alive."

D'Artagnan drew himself erect with a proud expression that clearly said that he asked no one for charity.

"There, there, young man, I know that look very well. I came to Paris with four écus in my pocket, and I would have fought anyone who told me I couldn't buy the Louvre."

D'Artagnan stood up still straighter; thanks to the sale of his horse, he was starting his career with four écus more than Monsieur de Tréville had had at the beginning of his.

"As I was about to say," Tréville continued, "you must need to keep the money you have—no matter how large that sum may be. You must also need to improve yourself in the skills that become a gentleman. So I'll write a letter, today, to the director of the Royal Academy, and tomorrow you'll be admitted into it free of charge. Don't refuse that little favor. Some of our richest and noblest gentlemen ask for it without getting it. You'll learn riding, fencing, and dancing, and you'll make good acquaintances. Now and then you'll come back to report on your progress and tell me if there's anything more I can do for you.''

Even though he still knew nothing of court manners, d'Artagnan realized the coldness of this reception.

"Now I regret more than ever," he said, "that I don't have the letter of recommendation my father gave me for you."

"Yes, I was surprised that you'd made such a long journey without a letter of recommendation, since it's usually the only resource of a young man from Béarn."

"I had it, sir," said d'Artagnan, "and it was in proper form, but it was treacherously stolen from me."

He told what had happened at Meung and gave a detailed description of the unknown nobleman, with an ardor and sincerity that delighted Tréville.

"It's strange . . ." Tréville remarked thoughtfully. "Had you talked about me at the inn?"

"Yes, sir, I'm afraid I'm guilty of that indiscretion. I felt that a name like yours would protect me during my journey, so I used it often."

Flattery was common in those days and Tréville liked it as much as the king or the cardinal. He therefore could not help smiling with obvious satisfaction, but his smile quickly faded and he came back to the incident at Meung.

"Tell me, did that man have a faint scar on his temple?"

"Yes, as though it had been grazed by a bullet."

"Was he handsome?"

"Yes."

"And tall?"

"Yes."

"With a pale face and dark hair?"

"Yes, that's right. How is it that you know him, sir? Ah, if I ever find him again—and I will, I swear, even if I have to follow him into hell . . ."

"He was waiting for a woman?"

"Yes, but when she came, he talked with her for only a few minutes and then left."

"Do you know what they talked about?"

"He gave her a box and said her instructions were in it and she wasn't to open it till she was in London."

"Was she English?"

"He called her Milady."

"It couldn't have been anyone else!" murmured Tréville. "I thought he was still in Brussels!"

"If you know that man, sir," cried d'Artagnan, "tell me who he is and where I can find him, and I'll ask nothing more of you, not even to take me into the musketeers, because my revenge comes before everything else!"

"Give up all thought of it, young man! And if you ever see him coming toward you, cross to the other side of the street! Don't collide with such a rock: you'd be broken to pieces."

"Even so, if I ever find him . . ."

"Meanwhile," said Tréville, "if you take my advice, you won't look for him."

He stopped short, struck by a sudden suspicion. It seemed unlikely that d'Artagnan's letter had really been stolen by the man he so loudly claimed to hate. Was there some sort of treachery behind that show of hatred? Had d'Artagnan, or at least this young man who called himself d'Artagnan, been sent by the cardinal to gain his confidence and then betray him, as had been done in so many other cases? Tréville examined him even more closely and was scarcely reassured by the shrewd intelligence and false humility he saw in his face. "I know he's a Gascon," he thought, "but that doesn't mean he can't be in the cardinal's pay. I'll put him to a test."

"Young man," he said slowly, "since I know you're the son of my old friend even though your letter from him was stolen, I want to tell you some important secrets to make up for the coldness you must have noticed in me at first. The king and the cardinal are the best of friends; the apparent discord between them is meant only to deceive fools. I don't want a fellow Gascon, a handsome young man who has everything he needs to win advancement, to be taken in by that sham, as so many others have been. I want you to know that I'm devoted to both my powerful masters, that none of my serious acts will ever have any other goal than to serve them, and that the cardinal is one of the most brilliant men France has ever produced. Now that you know this, act accordingly. If, like some other nobleman, you feel enmity against the cardinal, whether it was aroused in you by your family, your friends, or your own instincts, tell me good-bye and we'll part company. I'll still help you in many ways, but without taking you into my household. In any case I hope my frankness will make you my friend, because I've never spoken to any other young man in this way."

And Tréville thought, "If the cardinal has sent this young fox to spy on me, he's sure to have told him that the best way to win my favor is to talk violently against him, because he knows how much I detest him. So in spite of what I've just said, this crafty agent of the cardinal is going to tell me that he despises him."

D'Artagnan's reply was quite different from what Tréville expected:

"Sir, I've come to Paris with intentions the same as yours. My father told me never to tolerate the slightest affront from anyone but the three foremost men in France: the king, the cardinal, and you." (Though his father had neglected to include Tréville with the two others, d'Artagnan felt that adding him could do no harm.) "I hold the cardinal and his acts in great esteem. If you were speaking frankly to me just now, as you said you were, I'm glad that I've also spoken frankly with you, because it means that you'll think highly of me for sharing your views. But if you mistrusted me when you spoke, which would be quite understandable, then I've cut myself off from you by telling you the truth. In that case, though, I'll still have your respect, and that's what matters most to me."

Tréville could not have been more surprised. D'Artagnan's shrewdness and frankness aroused his admiration, but did not entirely dispel his doubts. If d'Artagnan had been clever enough to deceive him, he would be an especially dangerous enemy.

"You're an honorable young man," said Tréville, shaking d'Artagnan's hand, "but for the moment I can't do anything more for you than I've already offered. My house will always be open to you. Since you can visit me at any time, you'll be able to seize any opportunity that may arise, so I think that eventually you'll get what you want."

"In other words, sir," replied d'Artagnan, "you're going to wait till I've made myself worthy of it. Well, don't worry," he nodded with Gascon familiarity, "you won't have to wait long."

And he bowed to leave, as though the rest were entirely his affair.

"Just a moment," said Tréville. "I promised you a letter for the director of the Academy. Are you too proud to accept it, my young gentleman?"

"No, sir, and you can be sure the same thing won't happen to this one as happened to the other one. I'll keep it till I've delivered it, and anyone who tries to take it away from me will pay for his insolence with his life!''

Tréville smiled at this cockiness, left his young compatriot in the window recess where they had been talking, went over to a table, and began writing the letter he had promised. Meanwhile d'Artagnan, who had nothing better to do, drummed his fingers on the windowpane and watched the musketeers leaving one after another, till they had all disappeared around the corner of the street.

After writing the letter, Tréville sealed it and came back to give it to d'Artagnan. But just as d'Artagnan was putting out his hand to take it, Tréville was astonished to see him start violently, flush with anger, and dash toward the door, shouting, ''He won't get away from me this time!''

''Who?'' asked Tréville.

''The miserable coward who robbed me!'' answered d'Artagnan. And he ran out.

''He's a madman!'' murmured Tréville. ''Unless that was only a clever trick to slip away from me when he realized he'd failed to carry out his mission . . .''

4

Athos's Shoulder, Porthos's Shoulder Belt, and Aramis's Handkerchief

D'Artagnan, furious, had crossed the anteroom in three strides and was heading for the staircase, intending to run down it, when he collided with a musketeer who had just come through another door. His forehead struck him on the shoulder, making him utter a cry, or rather a howl.

''Excuse me, but I'm in a hurry,'' d'Artagnan said without stopping.

He had taken only one step down the stairs when a hand seized his sash and brought him to a halt.

''You're in a hurry!'' said the musketeer, pale as a sheet. ''And because of that, you run into me, you say 'Excuse me,' and you think that's enough? Not quite, young man. Do you think that because you heard Monsieur de Tréville talk to us a little rudely today, you can treat us the same way? If so, you're mistaken. You're not Monsieur de Tréville.''

"I didn't do it intentionally," said d'Artagnan, recognizing Athos, who had been leaving after having his wound dressed by the doctor. "I said 'Excuse me,' and I think that's enough. Even so, I'll repeat that I'm in a hurry. Please let go of me so I can be on my way."

"You're not polite, sir," said Athos, letting go of him. "It's easy to see that you come from far away."

D'Artagnan had already run down three or four steps, but at Athos's remark he stopped short.

"Let me warn you, sir, that no matter how far away I may have come from, you're not going to give me a lesson in good manners!"

"That remains to be seen."

"Ah, if I weren't in such a hurry," cried d'Artagnan, "if I weren't running after someone . . .''

"You can find *me* without running after me. Do you understand?"

"Yes. Where?"

"Near the Carmes-Deschaux monastery."

"When?"

"Noon."

"I'll be there at noon."

"You'd better not keep me waiting, because if you're not there by a quarter past twelve, *I'll* run after *you* and cut off your ears."

"Don't worry, I'll be there at ten minutes to twelve," said d'Artagnan.

He started down the stairs again, as if the devil were at his heels. He had not lost hope of catching up with his enemy, who could not have gone very far if he was still walking at the same slow pace.

But at the front door Porthos was talking with a soldier. Between them was a space as wide as a man. D'Artagnan thought he would be able to dart through it, but he had reckoned without the wind. Just as he was about to pass between the two men, the wind blew Porthos's long velvet cloak in front of him and he ran into it. Porthos was evidently unwilling to part with it, because he stubbornly pulled it toward himself, with the result that d'Artagnan became entangled in it.

Hearing the musketeer swear, d'Artagnan struggled to free himself from the cloak that was blinding him. He was afraid he might have damaged the magnificent shoulder belt that we have seen. When he timidly opened his eyes, he found himself behind Porthos with his nose against the belt.

Alas, like most things in this world whose appearance is their main asset, the belt was golden only in front; in back, it was ordinary buff leather. The vainglorious Porthos, unable to have a whole golden belt, at least had half of one. It was now easy to understand why he had announced that he had a cold that made it necessary for him to wear his cloak.

"You must be mad to charge into people like that!" he shouted as he tried to rid himself of d'Artagnan, who was still struggling behind his back.

D'Artagnan finally emerged from the cloak, under the gigantic Porthos's shoulder.

"Excuse me, but I'm in a hurry; I'm running after someone, and . . ."

"Do you always forget to open your eyes when you run?" asked Porthos.

"No," replied d'Artagnan, nettled, "I keep them open, and sometimes I see things that others don't see."

Porthos may or may not have understood this remark; in any case, his temper flared.

"I warn you, sir, that you'll get yourself thrashed if you go on running into musketeers like that!"

"Thrashed? That's a harsh word, sir."

"A man who looks his enemies in the face isn't afraid to use harsh words."

"Oh, I'm sure *you* never turn your back on anyone!"

D'Artagnan was delighted with himself for having made this witty thrust. He hurried away, laughing loudly.

Porthos, fuming with rage, started after him.

"Later, later," d'Artagnan called back to him, "when you're not wearing your cloak."

"At one o'clock then, behind the Luxembourg."

"At one o'clock," d'Artagnan replied as he turned the corner.

He saw no one in the street he had just entered. The stranger had outdistanced him, even at his slow pace; or perhaps he had gone into a house.

D'Artagnan questioned everyone he met; he went as far as the ferry and came back by way of the Rue de Seine and the Croix-Rouge without finding any trace of his enemy. His frenzied search was helpful to him in one way, however: the more he sweated, the cooler his head became.

He began reflecting on the events that had just taken place. They were numerous and unpleasant. It was only eleven o'clock in the morning and he was certain that he had already turned Monsieur de Tréville against him by the rather abrupt way in which he had left him. Furthermore he had gotten himself into duels with two men who were each capable of killing three d'Artagnans. And they were musketeers, members of the corps he admired and respected with all his heart.

It was a sad predicament. Convinced that he would be killed by Athos, he worried very little about Porthos. But since hope is the last thing to die in the human heart, he finally came to believe that he might have a chance of surviving those two duels, though with terrible wounds, of course; and in case he actually should survive, he reprimanded himself for the future: "What a scatterbrained lout I am! That brave Athos was wounded in the shoulder, and that's exactly where I butted him! I'm surprised he didn't kill me on the spot; he had every right to, and the pain I caused him must have been terrible. As for Porthos . . . Ah, that's something a little funnier!"

In spite of himself he laughed, then looked around to see if his laughter might have offended some passerby. "Yes, with Porthos it's funnier," he thought, "but I was a scatterbrained lout with him too. I ran into him without warning, then looked under his cloak to see what wasn't there. Yet I'm sure he would have forgiven me if I hadn't made that remark about his shoulder belt—a veiled remark, it's true, but not veiled enough. Wretched Gascon that I am, I'd try to show off my wit even if I were being boiled alive! D'Artagnan, my friend, if you come out of this alive, which is unlikely, you must be so polite that everyone will admire you and take you as an example. Being thoughtful and polite doesn't mean being cowardly. Look at Aramis: he's gentleness and courtesy personified, but has anyone ever called him a coward? No, certainly not. From now on, I'll try to be like him in every way . . . Ah! There he is!"

As he had continued to walk during this inner monologue, d'Artagnan had approached the d'Aiguillon mansion, and in front of it he now saw Aramis talking lightheartedly with three gentlemen of the king's guards. Aramis also saw him, but since he had not forgotten that this was the young man in front of whom Monsieur de Tréville had spoken so angrily that morning, and since he was not pleased at the thought of encountering a witness to the scene in which the musketeers had been upbraided, he pretended not to see him. D'Artagnan, however, filled with his new resolve to be friendly and courteous, went up to the four men and gave them a deep bow accompanied by his most gracious smile. Aramis nodded curtly and did not return his smile. The four of them immediately stopped their conversation.

D'Artagnan was not so obtuse as to fail to see that he was unwelcome, but he lacked the social experience that would have enabled him to extricate himself gracefully from the awkward situation of someone who has approached a group of people he scarcely knows and interrupted a conversation that does not concern him. He was trying to think of a way to leave without making himself seem too foolish when he noticed that Aramis had dropped his handkerchief and inadvertently, no doubt, put his foot on it. D'Artagnan felt that he now had a chance to make amends for his boorishness. He bent down, picked up the handkerchief despite Aramis's refusal to move his foot, handed it to him, and said:

"Here's a handkerchief, sir, that I think you'd be sorry to lose."

It was richly embroidered and had a coronet and a coat of arms on one corner. Aramis's face turned crimson. He snatched the handkerchief from d'Artagnan's hand.

"Aha!" exclaimed one of the guards. "Now will you still try to tell us, discreet Aramis, that you're on bad terms with Madame de Bois-Tracy, when she's kind enough to lend you her handkerchiefs?"

Aramis gave d'Artagnan one of those looks that make a man realize he has just acquired a deadly enemy. Then he resumed his usual gentle expression.

"You're mistaken," he said. "This handkerchief isn't mine, and I don't know why this gentleman took it into his head to give it to me rather than to one of you three. And to prove what I say, here's mine, in my pocket."

He took out his own handkerchief. It was also quite elegant, made of fine batiste, which was expensive in those days, but it had no embroidery or coat of arms and bore only its owner's monogram.

D'Artagnan said nothing: he had realized his blunder. But Aramis's friends were not convinced by his denial.

"If the handkerchief really didn't belong to you, my dear Aramis, as you claim it doesn't," one of them said with mock seriousness, "I'd have to ask you to give it to me, because Bois-Tracy is my friend, as you know, and I wouldn't want anyone to make trophies of his wife's belongings."

"I recognize that what you say is justified," replied Aramis, "but I won't give you the handkerchief because you've asked for it in an offensive way."

"The fact is," d'Artagnan ventured timidly, "that I didn't see the handkerchief come out of Monsieur Aramis's pocket. He had his foot on it, and I thought that since he had his foot on it, it was his."

"And you were mistaken," Aramis said coldly, unmoved by this effort to make amends. He turned to the man who had said he was Monsieur de Bois-Tracy's friend: "Now that I think of it, I'm as much Bois-Tracy's friend as you are, so the handkerchief could just as easily have come from your pocket as from mine."

"It didn't, on my honor!" said the guard.

"If you swear on your honor and I swear on mine, one of us will obviously be lying. Let's do something better than that, Montaran: let's each take half."

"Of the handkerchief?"

"Yes."

"Good idea!" exclaimed one of the other guards. "Solomon's judgment! Aramis, you're a wise man."

They all laughed and, needless to say, the matter went no further. A short time later the conversation ended. They cordially shook hands and walked away, the three guards in one direction, Aramis in another.

D'Artagnan had stood a little off to one side during the last part of the conversation. "Here's my chance to be reconciled with that gallant man," he thought. And, with that good intention, he caught up with Aramis, who had left without paying any attention to him.

"I hope you'll excuse me, sir," he said. "I . . ."

"Allow me to point out to you, sir," Aramis interrupted, "that your conduct just now was ungallant."

"What!" cried d'Artagnan. "Do you think . . ."

"I think, sir, that you're not a fool, and that even though you've just come from Gascony, you know that people don't step on handkerchiefs without a reason. Paris isn't paved with batiste."

"You're wrong to try to humiliate me, sir," said d'Artagnan, whose quarrelsome nature was beginning to speak more loudly than his peaceful resolutions. "I'm from Gascony, it's true, and since you know that, there's no need for me to tell you that Gascons aren't very patient. When they've apologized once, even for a foolish mistake, they're convinced that they've already done much more than they had to.''

"What I said to you, sir, wasn't meant to pick a quarrel with you. I'm not a belligerent man, thank God. Since I'm a musketeer only temporarily, I fight only when I'm forced to, and always with great reluctance. But this time it's a serious matter: a lady's honor has been compromised because of you.''

"Because of *us,* you mean!''

"Why were you so tactless as to give me that handkerchief?''

"Why were you so clumsy as to drop it?''

"As I said before, sir, it didn't come from my pocket.''

"Then you've lied twice, sir, because I *saw* it fall from your pocket!''

"If you're going to take that attitude, my Gascon friend, I'll have to teach you some manners.''

"And I'll make you regret that you haven't yet become a priest, my pious friend! Draw your sword!''

"No, not here, at least. Can't you see that we're in front of the d'Aiguillon mansion, which is full of the cardinal's agents? How do I know he hasn't ordered you to bring him my head? Ridiculous as it may seem to you, I want to keep my head because I think it goes well with my shoulders. I'm willing to kill you, don't worry, but in a quiet, discreet place where your death won't bring you any glory.''

"That suits me, but I advise you to be a little less confident. Bring that handkerchief with you, whether it belongs to you or not; you may need to use it.''

"Is that a Gascon boast?''

"Are you postponing our duel out of caution?''

"It's true that caution isn't a very useful virtue for a musketeer, but it's necessary for a churchman, and since I'm a musketeer only temporarily, I must remain cautious. Do me the honor of meeting me at Monsieur de Tréville's house at two o'clock, and I'll take you to a good place for our purpose.''

The two young men bowed to each other, then Aramis walked off along the street that led to the Luxembourg. Seeing that it was close to noon, d'Artagnan headed for the Carmes-Deschaux monastery. "It has to be done,'' he told himself, "but if I'm killed, at least I'll be killed by a musketeer.''

5

The King's Musketeers and the Cardinal's Guards

Since d'Artagnan knew no one in Paris, he went to his rendezvous with Athos without taking any seconds, having decided to
accept those chosen by his adversary. He had also decided that
he would apologize to him as earnestly as possible, short of
showing weakness, because he was afraid that if the duel took
place, it would have the result that could always be expected
when a young and vigorous man fought an adversary weakened
by a wound: if he lost, he would double his adversary's triumph;
if he won, he would be accused of having taken an unfair
advantage.

Unless we have failed to depict our hero accurately, the reader
has by now noticed that d'Artagnan was no ordinary man.
Although he kept repeating to himself that his death was inevitable,
he did not resign himself to it as someone less courageous and
sensible might have done in his place. When he had reflected on
the different characters of the men he was about to fight, he
began to see his situation more clearly. He liked Athos's lordly
manner and austere expression, and he hoped that by apologizing
to him he could make him his friend. The shoulder-belt incident
gave him a hold over Porthos because they both knew that if he
was not killed he could make Porthos look thoroughly ridiculous
by telling the story everywhere, with all the proper dramatic
effects. As for the hypocritical Aramis, he was not greatly afraid
of him. If he got as far as his duel with him, he expected to kill
him, or at least spoil the good looks he was so proud of by
striking at his face, as Caesar had advised Pompey's soldiers to
do.

D'Artagnan's determination was fortified by what his father
had told him: that he must not tolerate the slightest affront from
anyone but the king and the cardinal. He therefore walked
swiftly toward the Carmes-Deschaux monastery, a windowless
building bordered by barren fields that, like the Pré-aux-Clercs,
often served as a dueling ground for men who had no time to
waste.

When d'Artagnan came within sight of the small field beside

the monastery, Athos had been waiting only five minutes and the clock was striking noon. He was exactly on time; not even the most rigorous judge of dueling conduct could find fault with him.

Athos, who was still in great pain from his wound even though it had just been dressed again by Monsieur de Tréville's doctor, was sitting on a stone and waiting for his adversary with the air of calm dignity that never left him. As soon as he saw d'Artagnan, he stood up and politely took a few steps toward him. D'Artagnan approached him with his hat in his hand, dragging its feather on the ground.

"Sir," said Athos, "I've asked two of my friends to act as my seconds, but they haven't come yet. I'm surprised that they're late: it's not like them."

"I have no seconds, sir," replied d'Artagnan, "because I arrived in Paris only yesterday and I don't yet know anyone here except Monsieur de Tréville. I was recommended to him by my father, who has the honor of being his friend."

Athos thought for a moment.

"So you don't know anyone but Monsieur de Tréville?" he asked.

"That's right."

"If you should die in this duel," said Athos, speaking half to himself and half to d'Artagnan, "I'll seem like a child-killer."

"I don't think so, sir," d'Artagnan said with a bow that did not lack dignity, "since you're doing me the honor of crossing swords with me when you have a wound that must seriously hinder you."

"Yes, it does, and I must say that you caused me great pain this morning. But I'll use my left hand, as I usually do in such circumstances. Don't think I'm giving you an advantage, though, because I can fence equally well with either hand. There's even a disadvantage for you: a left-handed opponent can be very bothersome if you're not prepared for it. I'm sorry I didn't tell you about it sooner."

"I'm grateful to you for your courtesy," said d'Artagnan, bowing again.

"You embarrass me . . . Let's change the subject . . . Oh! My shoulder! The pain has been much worse ever since you ran into me!"

"With your permission . . ." d'Artagnan began timidly.

"Yes?"

"I have a miraculous ointment for wounds. It was given to me by my mother, and I've used it on myself."

"Well?"

"I'm sure it will heal your wound in less than three days; and three days from now, when you've recovered, I'll still regard it as a great honor to give you satisfaction."

D'Artagnan said this in a straightforward way that made it clear he was motivated by consideration and not lack of courage.

"There's a suggestion that pleases me!" said Athos. "Not that I accept it, but it shows you have a noble heart. That's how knights in the time of Charlemagne spoke and acted, and we should all try to follow their example. Unfortunately, however, we're not living in the time of Charlemagne, we're living in the time of the cardinal: within three days our secret would become known, no matter how well we tried to keep it, and our duel would be stopped. . . . I wonder what can be keeping those seconds of mine!"

"If you're in a hurry," d'Artagnan said with the same directness he had shown a few moments earlier in offering to postpone the duel for three days, "and would like to dispose of me immediately, please feel free to do so."

"There's another suggestion that pleases me," said Athos, nodding graciously to d'Artagnan. "It shows that you have a sensible head as well as a noble heart. I like men of your kind, and I can tell that if one of us doesn't kill the other, I'll take real pleasure in your company after this matter is settled. We'll wait for my seconds, if you don't mind. I'm not in a hurry and it will be more correct that way. Ah, here's one of them now!"

The gigantic Porthos had just appeared at the end of the Rue de Vaugirard.

"What!" exclaimed d'Artagnan. "Monsieur Porthos is one of your seconds?"

"Yes. Do you object?"

"No, not at all."

"And here comes the other one."

D'Artagnan turned and recognized Aramis.

"What!" he exclaimed again, with even more surprise. "Monsieur Aramis is your other second?"

"You obviously don't know that Aramis, Porthos, and I are always seen together and that we're known to everyone, in the musketeers and the guards, at court and in the city, as the three inseparables. But after all, since you just came from Dax or Pau . . ."

"Tarbes."

". . . you can be excused for not knowing that," Athos concluded.

"If my adventure becomes known," remarked d'Artagnan, "people will see that you three gentlemen are even more inseparable than they thought."

Meanwhile Porthos had arrived. He greeted Athos with a gesture, then looked at d'Artagnan in astonishment. It is worth noting that he had put on a different shoulder belt and was no longer wearing his cloak.

"What . . . Why . . ." he stammered.

"This is the gentleman I have a duel with," said Athos, returning his greeting and pointing to d'Artagnan with the same motion of his hand.

"I have a duel with him too!"

"But not till one o'clock," said d'Artagnan.

"And *I* have a duel with him!" cried Aramis, who had just arrived.

"But not till two o'clock," d'Artagnan said with the same calm.

"Why are you fighting him, Athos?" asked Aramis.

"I'm not too sure; he hurt my shoulder. And you, Porthos?"

"I'm fighting him . . . because I'm fighting him," Porthos answered, his face turning red.

Athos, who missed nothing, saw a faint smile appear on d'Artagnan's lips.

"We had an argument over clothes," said d'Artagnan.

"And you, Aramis?" asked Porthos.

"I'm fighting him because of a theological matter," replied Aramis, giving his adversary a look that asked him not to reveal the cause of their duel.

Athos saw d'Artagnan smile again.

"Is that true?" he asked.

"Yes," d'Artagnan assured him. "We disagree on a passage in Saint Augustine."

Athos nodded and thought, "He's an intelligent man."

"And now that you're all together, gentlemen," said d'Artagnan, "allow me to apologize to you."

At the word "apologize," a cloud passed over Athos's face, Porthos smiled haughtily, and Aramis made a scornful gesture.

"You've misunderstood me, gentlemen," d'Artagnan went on, raising his head. The sunlight shone on his bold, finely chiseled features. "I'm apologizing in case I'm not able to pay my debt to all three of you. Monsieur Athos has the right to kill me first: that makes your claim worth much less, Monsieur Porthos, and yours, Monsieur Aramis, is worth almost nothing at all. I repeat, gentlemen, that I apologize, but only for that. And now, on guard!''

He confidently drew his sword. He was now in such a state of fiery excitement that he would have fought against every musketeer in the kingdom, as he was about to do against Athos, Porthos, and Aramis.

It was a quarter past noon. The sun was at its zenith and the place chosen for the duel was exposed to its full heat.

''It's very hot,'' said Athos, also drawing his sword, ''but I can't take off my doublet because my wound has begun bleeding again, and I'm afraid I might put you at a disadvantage by showing you blood that you haven't drawn yourself.''

''That's true, sir,'' replied d'Artagnan, ''and whether it's been drawn by me or someone else, I assure you that I'll always regret seeing the blood of such a gallant gentleman. I'll also fight in my doublet.''

''You've exchanged enough courtesies,'' said Porthos. ''Don't forget that we're waiting our turn to . . .''

''Speak for yourself when you have such coarse things to say, Porthos,'' Aramis interrupted. ''For my part, I think that what these gentlemen have said is thoroughly worthy of two noblemen.''

''Whenever you like, sir,'' said Athos, taking his guard.

''I was awaiting your orders,'' replied d'Artagnan, crossing swords with him.

But scarcely had the two rapiers touched when a group of the cardinal's guards, led by Monsieur de Jussac, appeared at a corner of the monastery.

''The cardinal's guards!'' cried Porthos. ''Sheathe your swords, gentlemen!''

But it was too late. The two adversaries had been seen in a pose that left no doubt about their intentions.

''Stop, you musketeers!'' shouted Jussac, walking toward them and motioning his men to follow him. ''So you're fighting a duel, are you? Haven't you heard of the edicts against it?''

''You're very generous,'' Athos said with rancor, for Jussac was one of the men who had attacked him two days earlier. ''If we saw you fighting, I promise you we'd do nothing to stop you. Let us finish our fight, it's a sight you'll enjoy.''

''Gentlemen,'' said Jussac, ''I regret to tell you that it's impossible. Our duty comes first. Please sheathe your swords and follow us.''

"Sir," said Aramis, parodying Jussac, "we'd be delighted to accept your gracious invitation if we could, but unfortunately it's impossible: Monsieur de Tréville has forbidden it. Continue on your way, that's the wisest thing you can do.''

This banter exasperated Jussac.

"We'll attack you if you don't obey!"

"There are five of them," Athos said in an undertone, "and only three of us. We'll be beaten again, and we'll have to die here, because I swear I'll never again face the captain after a defeat.''

Athos, Porthos, and Aramis stood shoulder to shoulder while Jussac drew up his soldiers in a line.

D'Artagnan made up his mind in an instant. This was one of those situations that decide the course of a man's life. He had to choose between the king and the cardinal, and once the choice had been made there could be no turning back. To fight would mean breaking the law, risking his life, and making an enemy of a minister more powerful than the king himself. D'Artagnan saw this clearly, but he did not hesitate. He turned to Athos and his friends.

"I think you're mistaken. You said there were only three of you, but it seems to me there are four of us.''

"But you're not one of us," said Porthos.

"It's true that I don't wear your uniform, but I feel that I have the heart of a musketeer, and I want to prove it.''

"Stand aside, young man," ordered Jussac, who had evidently guessed d'Artagnan's intention from his gestures and expression. "We'll allow you to leave. You can save your life if you hurry.''

D'Artagnan stayed where he was.

"You're a fine boy," Athos told him, shaking his hand.

"Well, what's your decision?" asked Jussac.

"We must do something," said Aramis.

"Our young friend is full of generosity," said Athos.

But the three musketeers thought uneasily of d'Artagnan's youth and lack of experience.

"We're only three men, one of whom is wounded," Athos went on, "plus a child, yet everyone will still say that we were four men.''

"But we can't back down!" Porthos protested.

"It's a hard choice," said Aramis.

D'Artagnan understood their hesitation.

"Put me to the test, gentlemen," he said. "I swear I won't leave here alive if we're beaten."

"What's your name?" asked Athos.

"D'Artagnan, sir."

"Then Athos, Porthos, Aramis, and d'Artagnan will fight together!"

"Haven't you decided yet, gentlemen?" Jussac called out again.

"Yes, we have," answered Athos.

"And what have you decided?"

"That we're going to have the honor of charging you," said Athos, raising his hat with one hand and drawing his sword with the other.

"So you're going to resist!"

"Does that surprise you?"

The nine men joined battle furiously but methodically.

Athos took a man named Cahusac, one of the cardinal's favorites; Porthos had Biscarat; and Aramis had to deal with two adversaries at once.

As for d'Artagnan, he was face to face with Jussac himself. His heart was pounding wildly in his chest, not from fear—he had no trace of it, thank God—but from a powerful desire to prove himself worthy of his companions. He fought like an enraged tiger, constantly circling his adversary, changing his stance and shifting his ground. Jussac loved fighting and had done a great deal of it, but he was hard-pressed to defend himself against this nimble adversary who kept departing from the established rules and seemed to attack from all directions at once, yet parried like a man who had the greatest respect for his own skin.

Jussac's patience finally abandoned him. Furious at being held in check by someone he had regarded as a child, he lost his head and began making mistakes. D'Artagnan, who lacked practice but was solidly grounded in theory, fought with even greater agility. Wanting to finish him off, Jussac made a full lunge at him, but d'Artagnan parried and, while Jussac was recovering his balance, slipped under his sword like a snake and ran him through. Jussac fell to the ground and lay still.

D'Artagnan anxiously glanced over the battlefield.

Aramis had already killed one of his adversaries. The other was pressing hard, but Aramis was in good condition and still able to defend himself.

Biscarat and Porthos had just wounded each other simultaneously: Porthos had received a thrust in the arm, Biscarat one in the thigh. But since neither wound was serious, they were now fighting all the more furiously.

Athos had been wounded again by Cahusac and was turning still paler but, fighting with his left hand, he had not retreated an inch.

The dueling code of the time permitted d'Artagnan to come to someone's aid. While he was trying to decide which of his companions needed him most, Athos's eyes briefly met his. His glance was eloquent. He would rather have died than call for help, but he could ask for it with his eyes. D'Artagnan understood and rushed at Cahusac from the side, shouting, "On guard, before I kill you!"

Cahusac turned to face him. The diversion came not a moment too soon for Athos, who had been sustained only by his vast courage. He fell to one knee.

"Don't kill him!" he called out to d'Artagnan. "I've got an old score to settle with him when my wounds have healed. Just disarm him . . . Good! Very good!"

Athos had seen Cahusac's sword fly twenty paces away. Cahusac and d'Artagnan raced toward it, one to pick it up, the other to prevent him. D'Artagnan was quicker; he reached it first and put his foot on it.

Cahusac ran over to the guard who had been killed by Aramis, snatched up his rapier and tried to return to d'Artagnan, but he was blocked by Athos, who had regained some of his strength during the pause d'Artagnan had given him and now wanted to resume fighting, for fear that d'Artagnan might kill his enemy.

D'Artagnan realized that he would offend Athos if he tried to interfere. A few seconds later Cahusac fell with his throat pierced by Athos's sword.

At the same moment, Aramis pressed the point of his sword to the chest of his fallen adversary and forced him to ask for mercy.

Porthos and Biscarat still remained. Porthos was jeering at Biscarat, sarcastically asking him what time it was and congratulating him on his brother's having been given command of a company in the Navarre regiment, but his mockery gained him nothing. Biscarat was one of those men of iron who fall only when they are dead.

Time was pressing. The watch might arrive at any moment and arrest all the combatants, wounded or not, Royalists or Cardinalists. Athos, Aramis, and d'Artagnan surrounded Biscarat and urged him to surrender. Although he was alone against all of them, and wounded in the thigh, he refused. Jussac, who had raised himself on one elbow, also told him to surrender. Biscarat was a Gascon, like d'Artagnan; he pretended not to have heard, laughed, and, between two parries, found time to point to the ground with his sword and say, parodying a verse of the Bible, "Here will die Biscarat, alone of all those who are with him."

"But there are four of them against you!" said Jussac. "I order you to surrender!"

"Ah, if you order me to, that's different," said Biscarat. "You're my commander and I must obey you."

He leapt back, broke his sword over his knee to avoid having to surrender it, threw the pieces over the monastery wall, and crossed his arms, whistling a Cardinalist song.

Bravery is always respected, even in an enemy. The musketeers saluted Biscarat with their swords and sheathed them. D'Artagnan followed suit.

Biscarat was the only one of the guards who was still on his feet. He helped d'Artagnan and the musketeers carry Jussac, Cahusac, and Aramis's wounded adversary to the porch of the monastery, leaving Aramis's dead adversary behind. D'Artagnan and the musketeers then rang the bell and, taking four of their opponents' five swords with them, began joyfully walking toward Monsieur de Tréville's house.

They walked arm in arm, taking up the whole width of the street and calling out to every musketeer they met, until finally they had formed a triumphal march. D'Artagnan was between Athos and Porthos. He felt drunk with happiness.

"I'm not a musketeer yet," he said to his new friends as they crossed the threshold of Monsieur de Tréville's house, "but at least I've been accepted as an apprentice, haven't I?"

6

His Majesty King Louis the Thirteenth

The incident caused a great stir. Monsieur de Tréville thundered against his musketeers in public and congratulated them in private. But since there was no time to lose in informing the king of what had happened, he hurried to the Louvre. It was already too late: the king was having a private conversation with the cardinal.

Tréville was told that His Majesty was working and could not receive him for the moment.

That evening he went to the king's card game. His Majesty was winning, and, since he was miserly, this had put him in an excellent humor. As soon as he saw Tréville he called out to him, "Come here, Captain, come here and let me scold you. Do you know that His Eminence came to complain to me about your musketeers and was so upset that he's ill this evening? What ruffians those musketeers are! They're all fit to be hanged!"

"No, Sire," replied Tréville, who realized the direction the conversation was about to take, "they're all gentle as lambs, and their only desire is never to draw their swords except in the service of their king. But His Eminence's guards are always picking quarrels with them, and for the honor of their corps the poor young men are forced to defend themselves."

"Listen to Monsieur de Tréville!" said the king. "Just listen to him! He sounds as if he were talking about a religious order! Captain, I'm tempted to take your command away from you and give it to Mademoiselle de Chemerault, since I've promised her a convent. But don't think I'll simply take your word for what happened. I'm called Louis the Just, Monsieur de Tréville, and we'll soon see . . ."

"Because I have faith in your justice, Sire, I'll wait patiently and confidently till it pleases you to hear me."

"Wait, then, but I won't keep you waiting very long."

The king's luck had just changed, and since he was on the verge of losing more than he had won, he was glad to have an excuse for stopping while he was still ahead. He stood up and pocketed the money in front of him, most of which he had won.

"Take my place, La Vieuville," he said. "I have an important matter to discuss with Monsieur de Tréville. I had eighty louis on the table: put the same amount in front of you, so that those who are losing will have no cause for complaint. Justice above all."

He then turned to Monsieur de Tréville and walked over to a window recess with him.

"So you maintain that His Eminence's guards picked a quarrel with your musketeers?"

"Yes, Sire, as always."

"Then tell me how it happened. As you know, a judge must listen to both sides."

"It happened quite simply. The musketeers involved were

three of my best men, whose names are known to you, Sire: Athos, Porthos, and Aramis. You've appreciated their devotion more than once, and I know that serving you means more to them than anything else in the world. They were going to have a picnic with a young Gascon I'd recommended to them this morning. The picnic was to take place at Saint-Germain, I believe, and they'd agreed to meet at the Carmes-Deschaux monastery. There they encountered Jussac, Cahusac, Biscarat, and two other guards, who certainly hadn't come there in such a large group without unlawful intentions."

"Aha! They must have come there to fight among themselves!"

"I'm not accusing them, Your Majesty, but I leave you to decide what five armed men could have been doing in such an isolated spot."

"You're right, Tréville, you're right."

"Then, when they saw my men, they forgot their own quarrels and thought only of their hatred for the musketeers. As you know, Sire, the musketeers who serve you are the natural enemies of the guards who serve the cardinal."

"Yes, Tréville," the king said mournfully, "and it's sad to see two factions in France, two heads of state. But it will end . . . You say the guards picked a quarrel with the musketeers?"

"It's likely, but I can't swear to it. You know how difficult it is to learn the truth, at least for those of us not gifted with the admirable instinct that has earned you the name of Louis the Just. . . ."

"Quite so, Tréville, quite so. But your musketeers weren't alone? There was a young man with them?"

"He's really only a boy, Sire, and one of my musketeers had recently been wounded. So two able-bodied musketeers, a wounded one, and a boy not only held their own against five of the cardinal's best guards, but left four of them lying on the ground."

"That's a victory!" cried the king, his face radiant. "A complete victory!"

"Yes, Sire, as complete as the victory at the Cé bridge."

"Two able-bodied men, a wounded one, and a boy?"

"I suppose he can be called a youth. And he fought so well that I'll take the liberty of commending him to your attention, Sire."

"What's his name?"

"D'Artagnan, Your Majesty. He's the son of one of my oldest

friends, a man who fought for your illustrious father in the religious wars.''

"And you say he fought well? Tell me about it, Tréville; you know I like stories of war and combat.''

King Louis XIII proudly twirled his mustache and put one hand on his hip.

"As I told you, Sire, Monsieur d'Artagnan is almost a child, and since he doesn't have the honor of being a musketeer, he was in civilian clothes. When the cardinal's guards saw how young he was, and that he didn't belong to the musketeers, they offered to let him leave before they attacked.''

"You see, Tréville!" the king interrupted. "They were the ones who attacked!''

"What you say is true, Sire. It's quite clear. When they offered to let him leave, he answered that since he was a musketeer in his heart, and completely devoted to his king, he would stay with the musketeers.''

"What a fine young man!" murmured the king.

"He did stay with them, as he said he would, and he's such a stalwart supporter of Your Majesty that it was he who gave Jussac the terrible wound that's made the cardinal so angry.''

"He's the one who wounded Jussac? He, a mere child? That's impossible, Tréville!"

"Yet it's true, Your Majesty.''

"But Jussac is one of the best swordsmen in the kingdom!"

"Yes, Sire, and he met a better one.''

"I want to see that young man, Tréville, and do something for him.''

"When will you deign to receive him, Your Majesty?''

"Tomorrow at noon.''

"Shall I bring him alone?''

"No, bring the four of them together. I want to thank all of them. Devoted men are rare, Tréville, and devotion must be rewarded.''

"We'll come to the Louvre at noon, Sire.''

"Come by way of the private staircase. There's no need for the cardinal to know . . .''

"Yes, Sire.''

"You understand, Tréville: an edict is an edict. Duels are still forbidden.''

"But this wasn't a duel, Sire, it was a common brawl, since

there were five of the cardinal's guards against my three musketeers and Monsieur d'Artagnan.''

"Yes, you're right," said the king. "Even so, come by way
of the private staircase.''

Tréville smiled. But since he had already accomplished a great
deal in making this child rebel against his master, he bowed
respectfully to the king and, with his permission, took leave of
him.

That same evening the three musketeers were notified of the
honor that had been granted them. Since they had known the
king a long time, they were not too elated. But d'Artagnan, with
his Gascon imagination, saw fortune within reach, and spent the
night dreaming golden dreams.

He went to see Athos at eight o'clock the next morning and
found him dressed and ready to go out. Since their meeting with
the king was not to take place until noon, Athos, Porthos, and
Aramis had decided to play tennis on a court near the Luxembourg stables. Athos invited d'Artagnan to join them. Although
he had never played tennis and knew nothing about it, d'Artagnan
accepted the invitation because he did not know what else to do
with his time till noon.

Porthos and Aramis had already arrived at the court. Athos,
who excelled in all sports, took d'Artagnan as his partner and
challenged the other two to a game. But with the first movement
he made, even though he was playing with his left hand, he
realized that his wound was still too fresh to allow him such
exertion. D'Artagnan was thus left without a partner, and since
he admitted he had no experience in the game, the others merely
practiced with him, without counting points. One ball, launched
by Porthos's herculean wrist, passed within a hairsbreadth of
d'Artagnan's face. It occurred to him that if the ball had hit him,
he might have been unable to present himself for his audience
with the king. In his Gascon imagination, his whole future hung
on that audience, so he politely bowed to Porthos and Aramis,
told them that he would play with them at some other time, when
he was better able to compete with them, and went to join the
spectators.

Unfortunately for him, among the spectators was one of
the cardinal's guards, who, inflamed by his companions' defeat
the day before, had sworn to avenge it at the first opportunity. Seeing d'Artagnan, he felt that this opportunity had
arrived.

"It's not surprising," he said to the man beside him, "that that young man was afraid of a ball: he's probably an apprentice musketeer."

D'Artagnan spun around as if he had been bitten by a snake and glared at the guard who had just made that insolent remark.

"You can look at me as much as you like," the guard told him, arrogantly twirling his mustache. "I still said what I said."

"And since what you said is too clear to need an explanation," d'Artagnan replied in an undertone, "I'll ask you to come with me."

"When?" the guard asked with the same mocking arrogance.

"Now."

"You know who I am, don't you?"

"No, and I don't care."

"You should, because you might be in less of a hurry if you knew my name."

"What is it?"

"Bernajoux, at your service."

"Very well, Monsieur Bernajoux," d'Artagnan said calmly, "I'll wait for you at the gate."

"Go ahead, I'll follow you."

"Don't follow me too closely; we mustn't let anyone think we're leaving together. We don't want spectators for what we have to do."

"No, we don't," said Bernajoux, surprised that his name had produced no effect on the young man.

D'Artagnan may have been the only man in Paris who had never heard of him, for he was one of those involved most often in the daily fights that all the edicts of the king and the cardinal had been unable to suppress.

Porthos and Aramis were so absorbed in their game, and Athos was watching them so attentively, that they did not see d'Artagnan leave. D'Artagnan stopped at the gate, as he had said he would do. A few moments later, Bernajoux also stepped outside. D'Artagnan had no time to lose, since his audience with the king was set for noon. He looked up and down the street and saw that it was deserted.

"It's lucky for you, even though your name is Bernajoux," he said to his adversary, "that you're only dealing with an apprentice musketeer. But don't worry, I'll do my best. On guard!"

"But this isn't a very good place," protested Bernajoux. "I

think we'd be less likely to be disturbed behind the Saint-Germain abbey, or in the Pré-aux-Clercs.''

"What you say is very sensible," replied d'Artagnan, "but unfortunately I don't have much time because I have an appointment at twelve o'clock. So, on guard, sir!''

Bernajoux was not a man who needed to have such an invitation repeated twice to him. His sword flashed in the sunlight and he attacked vigorously, hoping that his adversary's youth would let him be intimidated.

But d'Artagnan had served his apprenticeship the day before. Fresh from his victory and buoyed by his future favor, he was determined not to give an inch of ground. The two swords were engaged to the hilt, and since d'Artagnan stood firm, it was Bernajoux who stepped back. D'Artagnan took advantage of this movement: he disengaged his sword, lunged and pierced his adversary's shoulder. He then stepped back and raised his sword, but Bernajoux shouted that it was nothing, lunged blindly at him, and spitted himself on d'Artagnan's sword. D'Artagnan did not know how seriously his opponent had been wounded, for he did not fall or admit defeat, but merely stepped back in the direction of Monsieur de La Trémouille's residence, where one of his relatives was a member of the household. D'Artagnan pressed him relentlessly and would no doubt have finished him off with a third thrust if two other guards, hearing the sound of fighting and having seen d'Artagnan exchange a few words with Bernajoux and then leave, had not rushed out with drawn swords and attacked him. But Athos, Porthos, and Aramis appeared at almost the same moment and forced the two guards to turn away from d'Artagnan. Then Bernajoux fell. Since the two guards were now facing four enemies, they began calling for help from Monsieur de La Trémouille's house. When the men in the house came running out, the four companions shouted, "Musketeers! We need help!''

Such shouts were usually heeded, for the musketeers were known to be enemies of the cardinal and were liked because of their hatred of him. Guards from companies other than those belonging to the Red Duke, as Aramis had called him, nearly always sided with the musketeers in this kind of quarrel. Three guards from Monsieur des Essarts's company were passing by; two of them came to the aid of the four companions while the third ran off to Monsieur de Tréville's house, calling for help.

As usual, Monsieur de Tréville's house was full of musketeers.

They hurried to help their comrades. In the free-for-all that followed, the musketeers had the advantage of number. Their adversaries retreated to Monsieur de La Trémouille's house and succeeded in locking the doors in time. As for Bernajoux, he had already been carried into the house, seriously wounded.

The musketeers and their allies were still greatly agitated. They discussed setting fire to the house to punish Monsieur de La Trémouille's servants for their insolence in attacking the King's Musketeers. This idea had just been enthusiastically adopted when, luckily, a clock struck eleven. D'Artagnan and his friends remembered their audience, and since they would have regretted having such a fine exploit performed without them, they succeeded in persuading the others not to burn down the house. A few paving stones were thrown against the doors, but the doors held fast, and the attackers soon gave up, especially since those who had to be regarded as the instigators of the attack had already left and were on their way to Monsieur de Tréville's house.

By the time they arrived, Tréville had already learned of the clash.

"Hurry!" he said to them. "We must go straight to the Louvre and try to see the king before the cardinal has told him what's happened. We'll describe it to him as a result of yesterday's affair and he'll let them both pass together."

He went to the Louvre with the four young men but, to his great surprise, he was told that the king had gone to hunt deer in the Saint-Germain forest. Tréville had this news repeated to him twice, and each time his companions saw his face darken.

"Had His Majesty already planned that hunt yesterday?" he asked.

"No, Your Excellency," replied the servant. "The master of the hunt came this morning to announce that a stag had been isolated for him last night. At first His Majesty said he wouldn't go, but then he couldn't resist the thought of an enjoyable hunt and he left after breakfast."

"Has he seen the cardinal?"

"Probably. This morning I saw His Eminence's carriage with horses hitched to it, and when I asked where he was going, I was told, 'To Saint-Germain.' "

"Gentlemen," Tréville said to the four friends, "our meeting with His Majesty has been forestalled. I'll see him this evening, but I advise you to stay away from him."

This was such reasonable advice, especially coming from

someone who knew the king so well, that the young men accepted it without question. Tréville told them to go home and wait to hear from him.

When Tréville returned to his house, it occurred to him that he ought to take the advantage of being the first to register a complaint. He sent a servant to Monsieur de La Trémouille with a letter asking him to put Bernajoux out of his house and reprimand his servants for having had the audacity to attack a group of musketeers. But Monsieur de La Trémouille, already informed of what had happened by his equerry, who was related to Bernajoux, replied that it was he, and not Monsieur de Tréville or his musketeers, who had cause for complaint, since the musketeers had attacked his servants and tried to burn down his house. Tréville realized that an exchange of letters between them could go on indefinitely because each of them would naturally persist in his own opinion, so he decided to try to bring the debate to a close by going to see Monsieur de La Trémouille in person.

He went to his house and had himself announced.

The two men greeted each other politely, for while there was no friendship between them, there was at least respect. They were both honorable, greathearted men; and since Monsieur de La Trémouille, a Protestant who seldom saw the king, belonged to no faction, he ordinarily had no prejudices in his social relations. This time, however, his greeting, though still polite, was colder than usual.

"Sir," said Monsieur de Tréville, "each of us believes he has reason to complain of the other. I've come here so that we can clear up the matter together."

"I'll be glad to do that," replied Monsieur de La Trémouille, "but I must warn you that I'm well informed. Your musketeers are entirely in the wrong."

"You're so fair and reasonable, sir, that I know you'll agree to what I'm about to propose."

"I'm listening, sir."

"First, how is Monsieur Bernajoux, your equerry's relative?"

"He's in serious condition. He has a shoulder wound that's not dangerous, but he also has a pierced lung, and that's a very different matter. The doctor is pessimistic."

"Is he conscious?"

"Yes."

"Can he speak?"

"Yes, but with difficulty."

"Then, sir, let's go to him and ask him to swear in the name of God, before whom he may soon appear, to tell the truth. I'll accept him as the judge of his own case, and I'll believe what he says."

La Trémouille reflected for a moment, decided that the suggestion was quite reasonable, and agreed to it.

They went down to the room where the wounded man was lying. When he saw those two noble lords coming to visit him, Bernajoux tried to sit up in bed, but he was too weak. Exhausted by the effort, he fell back, almost unconscious.

He revived when La Trémouille held smelling salts under his nose. Not wanting to be accused of having influenced him, Tréville asked La Trémouille to question him.

Things happened as Tréville expected. Hovering between life and death, Bernajoux had no thought of concealing the truth: he described exactly what had happened.

That was all Tréville wanted. He wished Bernajoux a speedy recovery, took leave of La Trémouille, went back to his house, and sent word to the four friends that he was expecting them for dinner.

He also invited a group of distinguished people who were all anti-Cardinalists, so conversation during the meal was naturally on the subject of the two setbacks that His Eminence's guards had just suffered. And since d'Artagnan had been the hero of both victories, he was profusely congratulated. Athos, Porthos, and Aramis were content to let him be the center of attention, not only because they regarded him as their friend but also because they had received congratulations so often in the past that they were now quite willing for him to have his share.

At six o'clock Monsieur de Tréville announced that he had to go to the Louvre. But since the time for the audience granted by His Majesty had passed, he did not ask to enter by way of the private staircase; instead, he and the four young men sat down in the anteroom. The king had not yet returned from the hunt. They had been waiting no more than half an hour, in a crowd of courtiers, when all the doors opened and His Majesty was announced.

D'Artagnan quivered with anticipation, feeling that the whole course of his life was about to be decided. He stared anxiously at the doorway through which the king was to enter.

Louis XIII appeared at the head of a small procession. He was still in his dusty hunting clothes and high boots, and held a whip in his hand. At first glance, d'Artagnan judged that the king was in a bad temper.

His obviously stormy mood did not prevent the courtiers from eagerly stepping forward as he passed; in the royal antechambers, it was better to be seen with irritation than not to be seen at all. The three musketeers stepped forward with the others while d'Artagnan remained hidden behind them; but although the king knew Athos, Porthos, and Aramis personally, he walked past without speaking to them or even looking at them, as if he had never seen them before. However, he did look at Monsieur de Tréville, who returned his gaze so firmly that it was the king who turned his eyes away. His Majesty then went into his apartments, muttering to himself.

"Things are going badly," said Athos, smiling. "We're not going to be knighted this time."

"Wait here ten minutes," said Monsieur de Tréville, "and if you haven't seen me come out by then, go back to my house, because it would be useless for you to wait any longer."

The four young men waited ten minutes, a quarter of an hour, twenty minutes, and still Monsieur de Tréville did not return. Finally they left, worried about what was going to happen.

Tréville had gone boldly into His Majesty's study and found him still in a bad temper, sitting in an armchair and tapping his boots with the handle of his whip. Tréville calmly inquired about his health.

"It's bad," replied Louis XIII. "I'm bored."

Boredom was his worst disease. He often took one of his courtiers over to a window and said to him, "Monsieur So-and-So, let's be bored together."

"Bored, Sire?" said Tréville. "Didn't you have the pleasure of hunting today?"

"I hunted, but it was no pleasure. Everything's deteriorating these days, I swear! Either the animals have stopped leaving a trail or the hounds have lost their sense of smell. We started a ten-point stag and ran him for six hours. Then, just as he was about to turn and face the pack and Saint-Simon was already raising his horn to sound the kill, the dogs all charged off after a little stag no more than two years old. I've already given up falconry; now I'll have to give up stag hunting. Ah, I'm a very unhappy king, Monsieur de Tréville! I had only one gyrfalcon left, and he died day before yesterday."

"That was a great misfortune, Sire, and I understand your

despair; but I believe you still have quite a few falcons and sparrow hawks.''

"Yes, but I have no one to train them! Falconers are becoming scarce. I'm the only man left who knows the art of hunting. After me, it will all be over; hunting will be done only with traps, pitfalls, and snares. If only I had time to train pupils! But the cardinal never gives me a free minute, he's always talking to me about Spain, or Austria, or England! Speaking of the cardinal, Monsieur de Tréville, reminds me that I'm greatly displeased with you.''

Tréville had been expecting this; knowing the king as he did, he realized that all his complaints had been only preliminaries intended to stir up his courage, and that he had now come to what had been on his mind from the start.

"How have I had the misfortune to displease Your Majesty?'' asked Tréville, pretending great surprise.

"Is this how you perform your duties?'' the king continued, ignoring Tréville's question. "Have I placed you in command of my musketeers to have you idly stand by while they murder a man, instigate a riot, and try to burn down the city? But I mustn't be too hasty to accuse you; no doubt the guilty men are in prison and you've come to tell me that justice has been done.''

"On the contrary, Sire,'' Tréville replied placidly, "I've come to ask you for justice.''

"Against whom?''

"Against slanderers.''

"Ah, so you claim it's slander! Are you going to tell me that those three damned musketeers of yours, Athos, Porthos, and Aramis, and your young Gascon, didn't attack poor Bernajoux and wound him so badly that he's probably dying at this very moment? Are you going to tell me that they didn't lay siege to Monsieur de La Trémouille's house and try to set fire to it? That might not have been entirely blameworthy in time of war, since the house is a nest of Huguenots, but in time of peace it's a bad example. Tell me, are you going to deny all that?''

"Who told you that interesting story, Sire?'' asked Tréville, still unruffled.

"It was told to me by my wisest counselor, who watches while I sleep, works while I rest, and controls everything with a firm hand, in France and all over Europe.''

"You must be speaking of God, Sire, because I know of no one else so far above you.''

"No, I'm speaking of the man who carries the burden of the state on his shoulders, the only man who serves me, my only friend: the cardinal."

"His Eminence is not His Holiness, Sire."

"What do you mean by that?"

"I mean that only the pope is infallible; his infallibility doesn't extend to cardinals."

"What you really mean is that His Eminence deceives and betrays me. You're accusing him of treason. Admit it."

"No, Sire, I'm only saying that he's mistaken and misinformed. He's been unfair to your musketeers by accusing them hastily, without taking time to learn the facts."

"The accusation came from Monsieur de La Trémouille, the duke himself. What's your answer to that?"

"I might answer, Sire, that he's too closely concerned in the matter to be an impartial witness. But I won't say that, because I know him to be a man of integrity. I'm willing to accept his testimony, on one condition."

"What condition?"

"That you send for him and question him yourself, Sire, alone, and that afterward you see me before seeing anyone else."

"Granted. You won't dispute what the duke says?"

"No, Sire."

"You'll accept his verdict?"

"I will, Sire."

"And you'll agree to any compensation he may demand?"

"Certainly, Sire."

"La Chesnaye!" called the king. "La Chesnaye!"

Louis XIII's confidential servant, who was always standing outside the door, came in.

"La Chesnaye," said the king, "send for Monsieur de La Trémouille immediately. I want to see him this evening."

"Do I have your word, Sire," asked Tréville, "that you will see no one between the duke and me?"

"You have my word of honor."

"Till tomorrow, then, Your Majesty."

"Till tomorrow."

"What time, Sire?"

"Whenever you like."

"I don't want to come too early in the morning, Your Majesty, for fear of waking you."

"Waking me? Do you think I sleep? No, I've stopped sleeping; sometimes I dream, but that's all. Come as early as you like, at seven o'clock, let's say. But I warn you that you can expect the worst if your musketeers are guilty!"

"If any of my musketeers are guilty, Sire, they'll be placed in your hands and you'll dispose of them as you see fit. Is there anything else you wish to demand, Sire? Speak and I'll obey."

"No, there's nothing else. It's not without reason that I'm called Louis the Just. I'll see you tomorrow morning."

"God keep you till then, Your Majesty!"

However badly the king may have slept that night, Monsieur de Tréville slept still worse. Before going to bed, he had sent word to his three musketeers and their friend to come to his house at half-past six.

He took them to the Louvre the next morning without guaranteeing them anything; he made it clear to them that their favor with the king, and even his own, hung in the balance.

When they reached the foot of the private staircase, he told them to wait. If the king was still angry with them, they would leave without being seen; if the king consented to receive them, they would be called.

Tréville then went to His Majesty's private anteroom. There he found La Chesnaye, who told him that Monsieur de La Trémouille had been absent when a messenger went to his house the evening before, that he had come home too late to go to the Louvre, that he had arrived only a short time ago, and that he was now with the king.

Tréville was greatly pleased to hear this because it meant that no one would have a chance to influence the king between the duke's visit and his own.

No more than ten minutes had passed when the door of the study opened and the duke came out.

"Monsieur de Tréville," he said, "His Majesty just sent for me to ask how things happened at my house yesterday. I told him the truth: that my servants were entirely to blame and that I was willing to apologize to you. Since I've met you here, please accept my apology now, and please continue to regard me as your friend."

"Sir," replied Tréville, "I had such confidence in your integrity that I wanted you to be my only defender with His Majesty. I see I wasn't mistaken. I thank you for proving that there's still one man in France who can truthfully be described as I described you."

"Very good," said the king, who had been eavesdropping on the conversation from the other side of the doorway, "and since he says he's your friend, Tréville, tell him that I'd also like to be his friend, but that he's been neglecting me. For the last three years I've seen him only when I've sent for him. Tell him all that for me, because those are things that a king can't say himself."

"Thank you, Sire," said the duke, "but let me assure you that it's not the people you see constantly who are most devoted to you—with the exception of Monsieur de Tréville, of course."

The king stepped into the doorway.

"Ah, so you heard what I said. Well, so much the better. . . ." He turned to Tréville. "Where are your musketeers? I told you to bring them to me day before yesterday. Why haven't you done it?"

"They're downstairs, Sire, and with your permission La Chesnaye will tell them to come up."

"Yes, yes, have them come immediately. It's nearly eight o'clock and I'm expecting a visit at nine. Good-bye, Duke, and be sure to come back. Come in, Tréville."

The duke bowed and left. Just as he opened the door the three musketeers and d'Artagnan, preceded by La Chesnaye, appeared at the head of the stairs.

"Come here, my brave young men, and take your reprimand," the king said when he saw them.

The musketeers bowed and walked toward him; d'Artagnan followed them.

"The four of you have killed or wounded seven of His Eminence's guards in the last two days!" the king went on. "That's too many, gentlemen. At that rate, His Eminence will lose all his guards within three weeks and have to recruit new ones, and I'll have to have the edicts strictly enforced. I don't object to one or two from time to time, but I repeat that seven in two days is too many, much too many."

"Yes, it is, Your Majesty," said Tréville, "and that's why they've come to you, contrite and repentant, to ask forgiveness."

"Contrite and repentant!" said the king. "Hm . . . I don't trust those hypocritical faces. And I see that one of them is also a Gascon face. Come here."

Realizing that this compliment was addressed to him, d'Artagnan stepped forward with his most woeful expression.

"You told me he was a young man, Monsieur de Tréville, but he's only a child! Is he really the one who wounded Jussac so seriously?"

"Yes, and Bernajoux, too."

"Incredible!"

"Furthermore, Your Majesty," said Athos, "if he hadn't rescued me from Biscarat, I wouldn't be here now to pay you my humble respects."

"He's a real demon!" exclaimed the king. "I'm afraid he's going to leave a great many punctured doublets and broken swords in his wake. . . . Tell me, Tréville, Gascons are still poor, aren't they?"

"Sire, I must say that no one has yet found any gold mines in their mountains, though the Lord owes them such a miracle as a reward for the way in which they supported your father's claim."

"What you're saying, Tréville, is that since I'm my father's son, the Gascons put me on the throne. Well, I won't contradict you. La Chesnaye, go and search all my pockets for money, and if you can find forty pistoles, bring it to me. And now, young man, tell me honestly how it all happened."

D'Artagnan related his adventure of the day before in all its details: how he had been unable to sleep because of his joy at the prospect of seeing His Majesty, and had joined his friends three hours before the time of the audience; how they had gone together to the tennis court; how the fear he had shown at nearly being struck in the face by a tennis ball had led to his being mocked by Bernajoux, who nearly paid for his mockery with his life; and how Monsieur de La Trémouille, who had nothing to do with it, nearly paid for it with the loss of his house.

"Yes, that's exactly how the duke told me the story," murmured the king. "Poor cardinal! Seven men in two days, and seven of his best ones, too! But that's enough, gentlemen, enough! You've had your revenge for what happened on the Rue Férou—more revenge than you needed. Be satisfied with it."

"If you're satisfied, Sire," said Tréville, "we are too."

"I *am* satisfied," replied the king, taking a handful of gold coins from La Chesnaye and giving them to d'Artagnan, "and here's proof of it."

In those days, our modern ideas of pride had not yet come into fashion. A nobleman could receive money from the king's own hand and not feel at all humiliated. D'Artagnan therefore pocketed the forty pistoles that His Majesty had given him and thanked him profusely.

The king looked at the clock.

"It's half-past eight. Leave now, since I'm expecting a visitor at nine, as I said. Thank you for your devotion, gentlemen. I can count on it, can't I?"

"Oh, yes, Sire!" the four friends all cried out at once, and Porthos added, "We'd let ourselves be hacked to pieces for you!"

"Thank you, but try to stay in one piece; you'll be more useful to me that way," said the king. As the others were withdrawing, he turned to Tréville and lowered his voice: "There's no vacancy in the musketeers, and furthermore we've decided that no one can be admitted into them without first serving an apprenticeship. I therefore want you to place that young man in the company of guards commanded by your brother-in-law, Monsieur des Essarts. Ah, Tréville, I can't wait to see the look on the cardinal's face! He'll be furious, but I don't care. I'm within my rights."

He dismissed Tréville with a friendly gesture. Tréville rejoined his musketeers and found d'Artagnan dividing up his forty pistoles with them.

And, as His Majesty had predicted, the cardinal was furious, so furious that for a week he did not come to the king's card game. This did not prevent the king from greeting him graciously whenever they met, and saying in his most sympathetic tone, "Tell me about those two poor guards of yours, Bernajoux and Jussac. How are they doing?"

7

The Musketeers at Home

As soon as d'Artagnan was outside the Louvre, he consulted his friends about how he should spend his share of the forty pistoles. Athos told him to order a good meal at the Cabaret de la Pomme de Pin, Porthos advised him to hire a servant, Aramis urged him to take a suitable mistress.

The meal was prepared that same day, and the servant served

it. The meal had been ordered by Athos. The servant, a Picard, had been supplied by Porthos, who found him standing on the La Tournelle bridge, spitting into the water and watching the rings that formed on its surface. Porthos had decided that this occupation indicated a thoughtful, contemplative nature, and hired him without further recommendation.

Planchet—that was the Picard's name—was pleased by the lordly appearance and manner of the gentleman he assumed to be his new master. He was somewhat disappointed when Porthos told him that he already had a servant, named Mousqueton, that he had no need of another one even though he lived on a grand scale, and that he had hired him for his friend d'Artagnan. However, when he served the dinner given by d'Artagnan and saw him take out a handful of gold to pay for it, Planchet thought his fortune was made and thanked heaven for having placed him in the service of such a Croesus. He kept this opinion till after the meal, whose leftovers enabled him to make up for a long period of involuntary fasting. But when he made his master's bed that night, Planchet's illusions vanished. It was the only bed in the apartment, which consisted of an anteroom and a bedroom. Planchet slept in the anteroom on a blanket taken from d'Artagnan's bed. D'Artagnan did without it from then on.

Athos had a servant named Grimaud whom he had trained in his own special way. Athos was a very quiet man. In the five or six years during which he had lived on close terms with Porthos and Aramis, they had often seen him smile but never heard him laugh. His words were few but expressive; he always said exactly what he meant and nothing more, with no embellishments, frills, or embroidery. When he described events, he left out minor incidents.

Although he was handsome, intelligent, and barely thirty, he had no mistress, as far as anyone knew. He never talked about women. He did not object when others talked about them in his presence, but he made only bitter, misanthropic comments, and it was easy to see that this kind of conversation was unpleasant to him. His reserve, silence, and unsociability made him seem almost like an old man. To avoid changing his habits, he had trained Grimaud to obey him at a gesture or a movement of his lips. He spoke to him only in special circumstances.

Grimaud was devoted to him and had great respect for his intelligence, but he was also deathly afraid of him. Sometimes, thinking he had clearly understood a silent order, he would do the opposite of what his master wanted. Athos would then shrug and, without anger, give Grimaud a thrashing. On those days, he spoke a little.

Porthos, as we have seen, was totally different from Athos. He spoke not only a great deal, but loudly, and in fairness to him it must be said that he cared little whether anyone listened to him or not. He talked for the pleasure of hearing himself talk; he talked about everything but scholarly subjects, saying that he avoided them because of a deep hatred of scholars that he had acquired in childhood. He was less distinguished-looking than Athos. At the beginning of their friendship, his feeling of inferiority in this respect had often made him unjust to Athos, and he had tried to surpass him by the splendor of his clothes. But, wearing his ordinary musketeer's uniform, Athos would take his rightful place and relegate the ostentatious Porthos to a secondary rank merely by the way he threw back his head and put his foot forward. Porthos consoled himself by filling Monsieur de Tréville's anteroom and the guardrooms at the Louvre with tales of his amorous adventures, which was a topic that Athos never even mentioned. After a long series of love affairs with ladies from various segments of the French aristocracy, Porthos was now said to be on intimate terms with a foreign princess who cherished him greatly.

An old proverb says, "Like master, like servant." Let us now turn from Athos's servant to Porthos's, from Grimaud to Mousqueton.

Mousqueton was a Norman. His real name was Boniface, but Porthos had found this too peaceful and changed it to the more warlike name of Mousqueton. He had entered Porthos's service with the agreement that he would be given only lodging and clothes, but that both would be magnificent, and that he would have two hours a day in which he could work to satisfy his other needs. Porthos had accepted the bargain; it suited him perfectly. He had doublets made for Mousqueton from his old clothes and spare cloaks. Thanks to a clever tailor who knew how to make shabby garments look like new again, and whose wife was suspected of wanting to make Porthos depart from his aristocratic habits, Mousqueton was able to cut a very good figure beside his master.

As for Aramis, his character has already been described, and moreover we will see it developed more fully, along with the characters of his companions, as the story unfolds. His servant was named Bazin. Because Aramis hoped some day to take holy orders, Bazin was always dressed in black, as befits the servant of a churchman. He was a plump, gentle, placid man from Berry, in his late thirties. He spent his leisure time reading pious works, and when necessary he could prepare a simple but excellent dinner. He was as discreet as if he were deaf, dumb, and blind. His loyalty to Aramis was unshakable.

Now that we have at least a superficial acquaintance with the masters and their servants, let us turn to their homes.

Athos lived on the Rue Férou, near the Luxembourg. His apartment was composed of two small but attractively furnished rooms in a house owned by a woman who, though still young and beautiful, had been unsuccessful in her efforts to arouse his interest. A few relics of bygone splendor shone on the walls of his modest apartment. There was a richly damascened sword that apparently dated from the reign of Francis I. Its hilt alone, set with precious stones, would have been worth two hundred pistoles, but Athos had never been willing to sell or pawn it even at times of great financial distress.

Porthos had coveted that sword for a long time and would have given ten years of his life to own it. One day when he had a rendezvous with a duchess, he tried to borrow it from Athos. Athos took the money from his pockets, gathered his jewelry, ornamental braid, and gold chains, and offered it all to Porthos; but the sword, he said, would never leave its place until he moved out of his apartment.

Besides his sword, he had a portrait of a nobleman in the time of Henry III, elegantly dressed and decorated with the Order of the Holy Spirit. A certain family likeness between Athos and the man in the portrait seemed to indicate that this great lord was his ancestor.

Finally, a chest, adorned with magnificent examples of the goldsmith's art and bearing the same coat of arms as the sword and the portrait, stood on the mantelpiece and formed a sharp contrast with the rest of the furniture. Athos always kept the key to that chest on him, but one day he had opened it for Porthos, who saw that it contained only letters and papers, no doubt love letters and family papers.

Porthos lived in a large and apparently sumptuous apartment on the Rue du Vieux-Colombier. Each time he passed by his windows with a friend, Mousqueton would be standing at one of them in full livery, and Porthos would look up with a sweeping gesture and say, "That's where I live." But he was never found at home; he never invited anyone to come there; and no one knew what real riches might lie behind that sumptuous appearance.

Aramis lived in a little ground-floor apartment consisting of a dining room, a bedroom, and a small salon. The bedroom windows opened onto a dense garden that was impenetrable to the neighbors' eyes.

As for D'Artagnan, we have already seen his lodgings and become acquainted with his servant, Planchet.

D'Artagnan was very curious by nature, like everyone with a gift for intrigue. He did his best to learn the real identities of Athos, Porthos, and Aramis, for each of these pseudonyms hid an aristocratic name. This was especially obvious in the case of Athos, who was unmistakably a great nobleman. D'Artagnan questioned Porthos about Athos and Aramis, and Aramis about Porthos.

Unfortunately Porthos knew no more about Athos's life than what hearsay had told him. It was said that he had suffered great afflictions in his love affairs and that a monstrous betrayal had poisoned his life forever. What that betrayal had been, no one knew.

As for Porthos, except for his real name, which was known only to Monsieur de Tréville, along with those of his two comrades, there was little mystery about his life. Vain and indiscreet, he was as easy to see through as crystal. The only thing that might have misled an investigator would have been to believe all the good things he said about himself.

Aramis, on the other hand, while seeming to have no secrets, was actually steeped in mystery. He answered little when questioned about others, and eluded questions about himself. One day when he was talking with d'Artagnan and had mentioned Porthos's rumored affair with a princess, d'Artagnan tried to find out something about Aramis's own amorous adventures.

"And what about you?" he asked. "You're willing to discuss others' baronesses, countesses, and princesses, but . . ."

"Excuse me," Aramis interrupted. "I've mentioned Porthos's affairs to you only because he makes no secret of them and I've often heard him loudly proclaiming them. But believe me, if I'd learned about them from someone else, or if he'd confided them to me as a secret, I would never have breathed a word about them."

"I don't doubt it," said d'Artagnan. "But it seems to me that you're also familiar with coats of arms. I'm thinking of a certain embroidered handkerchief to which I owe the honor of your acquaintance."

This time Aramis did not become angry; he took on his modest air and answered affectionately, "My dear friend, don't forget that I want to be a churchman and that I avoid all social occasions. The handkerchief you saw hadn't been given to me: one of my friends had left it behind in my apartment. I took it so that he and the lady he loves wouldn't be compromised. As for myself, I have no mistress and I don't want one. I follow Athos's wise example; he has no mistress either."

"But you're not a priest, you're a musketeer!"

"Only in the interim, as the cardinal says. I'm a musketeer against my will and a churchman in my heart, believe me. Athos and Porthos brought me into the musketeers to give me something to do. Just before I was to be ordained, I had a little difficulty with . . . But that wouldn't interest you, and I'm wasting your time."

"Not at all!" cried d'Artagnan. "It interests me very much and I have nothing to do now."

"But *I* have things to do. First I must say my breviary, then I must write the poem that Madame d'Aiguillon asked me for, and then I must go to the Rue Saint-Honoré to buy rouge for Madame de Chevreuse. As you can see, my dear friend, I'm pressed for time, even if you're not."

Aramis shook hands with d'Artagnan and left him.

Despite all his efforts, d'Artagnan was unable to learn anything more about his new friends. He decided that for the present he would believe whatever was said about their past and hope for more extensive and reliable revelations in the future. Meanwhile he regarded Athos as an Achilles, Porthos as an Ajax, and Aramis as a Joseph.

The four young men spent their time quite pleasantly. Athos gambled and always lost, yet he never borrowed a sou from his friends, even though his purse was always at their disposal. Whenever he ran up a gambling debt, he woke his creditor at six o'clock the next morning to pay him.

Porthos was sometimes seized with a passion for gambling. If he won, he was insolent and ostentatious; if he lost, he disappeared for several days, then came back with a pale and melancholy face, but with money in his pockets.

Aramis never gambled at all. He was the most unsociable

musketeer anyone had ever seen. He always had to work. Sometimes in the middle of a dinner party, when the wine had gone to the other guests' heads and the conversation at table was so lively that it seemed sure to last another two or three hours, Aramis would look at his watch, stand up with a gracious smile, and ask to be excused because he had an appointment with a theologian. At other times he would return home to write a thesis, and ask his friends not to disturb him.

But Athos would smile that sad, charming smile that suited his noble face so well, and Porthos would go on drinking and swear that Aramis would never be anything but a village priest.

Planchet, d'Artagnan's servant, behaved admirably during the period of good fortune when he received thirty sous a day; for a month he was unfailingly cheerful and affable. But when the wind of adversity began to blow—that is, when the forty pistoles given by the king had been almost entirely spent—he began making complaints that seemed sickening to Athos, indecent to Porthos, and ridiculous to Aramis. Athos advised d'Artagnan to dismiss Planchet, Porthos agreed but wanted him to be beaten first, and Aramis said that a servant should never speak except to compliment his master.

"That's easy for you to say," replied d'Artagnan. "You, Athos, live in silence with Grimaud and won't let him say anything at all, so naturally you never hear any complaints from him. Porthos, you live in grand style and your servant Mousqueton looks on you as a god. As for you, Aramis, you're always absorbed in studying theology, and since your servant Bazin is a deeply religious man, he has great respect for you. But I have neither money nor social standing, I'm not a musketeer or even a guard—what can I do to arouse Planchet's fear, respect, or affection?"

"It's a serious problem," said Porthos. "Servants are like women: they must be quickly taught to behave as you want them to. Think it over and try to find a solution."

D'Artagnan thought it over and decided to give Planchet a thrashing as advance payment for future misconduct. When he had done this as conscientiously as he did everything else, he told him not to leave his service without his permission, because, he said, "I'm sure there are better days ahead for me, which means that your fortune is made if you stay with me, and I wouldn't be so unkind as to make you miss your fortune by letting you leave me too soon."

The musketeers admired d'Artagnan for the way he had dealt with Planchet. So did Planchet himself, and he said no more about leaving.

By now the four young men had begun sharing their lives. D'Artagnan, who had no habits of his own, since he had just come from his province and plunged into a world that was entirely new to him, soon adopted his friends' habits.

They got up at eight o'clock in winter, six o'clock in summer, and went to Monsieur de Tréville's house to get their orders for the day and learn what was happening. Although d'Artagnan was not a musketeer, he was always on guard because he always accompanied whichever of his three friends was on duty. All the musketeers knew him and regarded him as a good comrade. Monsieur de Tréville, who had appreciated him from the start and now had great affection for him, constantly recommended him to the king.

The three musketeers were very fond of their young companion. Because of the friendship that united the four men, and the need to see each other three or four times a day, for dueling, work, or pleasure, they had quickly become inseparable. They were often seen looking for each other between the Luxembourg and the Place Saint-Sulpice or the Rue du Vieux-Colombier.

Meanwhile, Monsieur de Tréville had not forgotten his promises. One day the king ordered Monsieur des Essarts to take d'Artagnan into his company of guards, as a cadet. D'Artagnan sighed when he put on his new uniform; he would have given ten years of his life to exchange it for a musketeer's cloak. Monsieur de Tréville promised him that he would become a musketeer after a two-year apprenticeship, which could be shortened if a chance arose for him to render the king a service or perform some outstanding act. D'Artagnan took careful note of that promise and began his service the next day.

Athos, Porthos, and Aramis now began accompanying d'Artagnan when he was on guard duty, as he had accompanied them, with the result that Monsieur des Essarts's company acquired four men instead of one when d'Artagnan joined it.

8

A Court Intrigue

Like all things in this world, the forty pistoles given by the king finally came to an end, and the four friends then fell on hard times. Athos briefly sustained the group with his own money. Then, thanks to one of the disappearances that were common with him, Porthos supplied their need for nearly two weeks. Next Aramis took his turn with good grace and contributed a few pistoles that he had obtained, he said, by selling his theology books.

Finally they resorted to Monsieur de Tréville, as usual, and he gave them an advance on their pay. But this was a short-lived solution for three musketeers who already had many unpaid bills, and a guard who was yet had none.

When they were about to run short of everything, they scraped together nine or ten pistoles and gave it to Porthos to gamble with. He lost it all in a streak of bad luck and ran up a debt of twenty-five pistoles besides.

Their straitened circumstances now became outright poverty. Followed by their servants, they roamed the streets and visited guardrooms, on the lookout for friends who would invite them to dinner, for they had followed Aramis's advice to be generous with meals in times of prosperity, so as to get them back in times of need.

Athos was invited four times and always brought his friends and their servants. Porthos had six invitations, and also let his friends benefit from them. Aramis had eight; he was a man who said little and did much.

Since d'Artagnan did not yet know anyone in Paris, he was able only to arrange for chocolate with a priest from his home province and dinner with an ensign of the guards. He led his little army to the priest, who lost a stock of food that was to have lasted him a month, and to the ensign, who made a heroic effort to satisfy their hunger; but, as Planchet said, no matter how big a meal might be, it could be eaten only once.

D'Artagnan felt humiliated at having been able to provide only a meal and a half—the priest's contribution could be counted

only as half a meal—in exchange for the feasts provided by
Athos, Porthos, and Aramis. He considered himself a burden on
them, forgetting that he had fed them for a month. His worry
prompted him to begin trying to think of a way to improve their
situation. He told himself that a coalition of four brave,
enterprising, and vigorous young men should have a better purpose than swaggering in public, taking fencing practice, and
joking in ways that did not always show great wit.

They were so closely united that they shared whatever they
had and each was always ready to help the others, even at the
risk of death. They made plans together and carried them out
either individually or as a group; they were like four arms that
sometimes joined in a single attack and sometimes separated to
ward off danger from any direction. Four men like that could
surely overcome all obstacles in their path, using either force or
guile, and reach any goal they chose, no matter how distant or
well defended it might be. D'Artagnan was surprised that his
companions had not thought of this before he did.

He racked his brain in search of a purpose to which that
fourfold force could be applied. He had no doubt that, like
Archimedes' lever, it could lift the world if it was properly
used.

Suddenly he heard a gentle knock on the door. He woke
Planchet and told him to see who it was.

From the fact that he woke Planchet, the reader should not
conclude that it was night. No, it was only a little past four
o'clock in the afternoon. Two hours earlier, Planchet had asked
for something to eat; d'Artagnan had replied with the proverb,
"Sleep is the poor man's dinner," and Planchet had taken his
advice.

He opened the door and showed in d'Artagnan's visitor,
an ordinary-looking man who seemed to be some sort of trades-
man. Planchet would have liked to hear the conversation, but
the man told d'Artagnan that what he had to say was important
and confidential, and that he wanted to speak with him alone.

D'Artagnan sent Planchet away and invited his visitor to sit
down.

There was a moment of silence during which the two men
scrutinized each other, then d'Artagnan nodded as a sign that he
was listening.

"I've heard you spoken of as a very brave young man," said
the visitor, "and because I believe you deserve that reputation
I've decided to confide a secret to you."

"I'm willing to hear what you have to say," replied d'Artagnan, instinctively sensing something that might be of advantage to him.

"My wife is the queen's linen maid," the stranger continued after another moment of silence. "She's a good woman, and quite pretty. Our marriage was arranged nearly three years ago, even though she had only a very small dowry, because Monsieur de La Porte, the queen's gentleman-in-waiting, is her godfather and has taken her under his protection . . ."

"Go on."

"Well, sir, my wife was abducted yesterday morning as she was leaving her workroom."

"Who abducted her?"

"I don't know for sure, sir, but I suspect someone."

"And whom do you suspect?"

"A man who'd been trying to force his attentions on her for a long time."

"Aha!"

"But let me tell you something, sir: I'm convinced that love has less to do with it than politics."

"Politics?" d'Artagnan said thoughtfully. "What makes you think so?"

"I don't know if I should tell you what I suspect . . ."

"Let me point out to you that I didn't ask you to come here. You came of your own accord and said you had a secret to tell me. If you've changed your mind, you can leave without saying anything more."

"No, sir, I'll stay. You seem to be an honest young man and I'll trust you. I think my wife was abducted not because of any love affair of hers, but because of a certain great lady's."

"Are you referring to Madame de Bois-Tracy?" asked d'Artagnan, wanting to give the impression that he was well acquainted with court affairs.

"Higher, sir, higher."

"Madame d'Aiguillon?"

"Still higher."

"Madame de Chevreuse?"

"Higher, much higher!"

"Do you mean the qu—" D'Artagnan stopped short.

"Yes, sir," the terrified man replied, so softly that d'Artagnan could scarcely hear him.

"And with whom is she having an affair?"

"Who else could it be but the duke of . . ."

"The duke of . . ."

"Yes, sir," the man said even more softly.

"How do you know that?"

"How do I know?"

"Yes. Either tell me everything or . . . You understand."

"My wife told me, sir, my wife herself."

"And who told her?"

"Monsieur de La Porte, her godfather, and the queen's confidential agent. He put my wife in Her Majesty's service so that the queen could have someone to rely on, since the king has abandoned her, the cardinal spies on her, and everyone betrays her."

"Ah, things are beginning to take shape," said d'Artagnan.

"Four days ago my wife came to me—one of the conditions of her service was that she could visit me twice a week, because, I'm proud to say, she loves me—she came to me and told me that the queen was very much afraid."

"Afraid?"

"Yes, sir. It seems that the cardinal is pursuing and persecuting her more than ever. He can't forgive her for the incident of the saraband. You know about that, don't you, sir?"

"Of course," said d'Artagnan, who had never heard of it before but wanted to seem well informed.

"And so now he's gone beyond hatred: he wants revenge."

"Really?"

"The queen thinks . . ."

"Well? What does she think?"

"That a letter has been sent to the duke of Buckingham in her name."

"In the queen's name?"

"Yes, to make the duke come back to Paris and fall into some sort of trap here."

"But how is your wife involved in all this?"

"She's known to be devoted to the queen. They want to separate her from her mistress, or intimidate her so that she'll tell the queen's secrets, or win her over so that she'll act as a spy."

"That seems likely," said d'Artagnan. "And you say you know the man who abducted her?"

"I said I thought I knew who he was."

"What's his name?"

"I don't know. All I know is that he's an agent of the cardinal."

"Have you seen him?"

"Yes, my wife pointed him out to me one day."

"Can you describe him in a way that would make it possible to recognize him?"

"Yes. He's a distinguished-looking gentleman with black hair, a swarthy face, piercing eyes, white teeth, and a scar on his temple."

"A scar on his temple!" cried d'Artagnan. "And with piercing eyes, white teeth, a swarthy face—he's my man at Meung!"

"He's . . . You say he's your man?"

"Never mind, it has nothing to do with what we're discussing . . . No, I'm mistaken: it simplifies things, because if your man is mine, then your revenge will also be mine, and I'll kill two birds with one stone. Where can I find him?"

"I have no idea."

"You have no information on where he lives?"

"None. One day when I took my wife to the Louvre, he was coming out just as she was going in, and she pointed him out to me, that's all."

"It's all very vague. . . . Who told you about your wife's abduction?"

"Monsieur de La Porte."

"Did he give you any details?"

"He didn't know any."

"Have you found out anything from other sources?"

"Yes, I received . . ."

"You received what?"

"I don't know if I should tell you."

"Again? This time it's too late to turn back."

"And I *won't* turn back, by God!" said the visitor, swearing to give himself courage. "As sure as my name is Bonacieux . . ."

D'Artagnan cut him short: "Your name is Bonacieux?"

"That's right."

"Excuse me for interrupting you, but your name seems familiar to me."

"It's possible, sir. I'm your landlord."

"Ah, you're my landlord?" said d'Artagnan, half rising to his feet and bowing to him.

"Yes, sir. And since I haven't bothered you one single time, even though you've forgotten to pay your rent for the last three months—I'm sure you were simply distracted by your important occupations—I thought you might take my consideration into account.''

"Of course, my dear Monsieur Bonacieux. I'm grateful to you for your tact. As I've told you, if there's any way I can help you . . ."

"I believe you, sir, and as I was about to say, as sure as my name is Bonacieux, I trust you!''

"Good. You said you'd received something. What is it?''

Monsieur Bonacieux took a sheet of paper from his pocket and handed it to d'Artagnan.

"A letter?''

"Yes. I received it this morning.''

D'Artagnan opened it, and since daylight was beginning to fade he went over to the window. Bonacieux followed him.

" 'Do not look for your wife,' '' d'Artagnan read aloud. " 'She will be returned to you when she is no longer needed. If you make the slightest effort to find her, you are lost.' Well, that's clear, as far as it goes,'' he remarked. "But after all, it's only a threat.''

"Yes, but it's a threat that frightens me. I'm not a swordsman, sir, not at all, and I'm afraid of the Bastille.''

"I don't like the thought of the Bastille any more than you do,'' said d'Artagnan. "If it were only a matter of fighting, I wouldn't mind.''

"But I was counting on you, sir.''

"Oh?''

"I've noticed that you constantly associate with a group of fine-looking musketeers, and since I know they're Monsieur de Tréville's musketeers and therefore enemies of the cardinal, I thought that you and your friends would be glad of a chance to help the poor queen and do something against the cardinal at the same time.''

"That was a reasonable assumption.''

"I also thought that since you owed me three months' rent and I'd never even mentioned it to you . . .''

"Yes, yes, you've already given me that reason, and it's an excellent one.''

"Furthermore, since I never intend to mention your rent for as long as you do me the honor of living in my house . . .''

"Very good.''

"And finally, since I'm willing to give you fifty pistoles if you should happen to be a little short of money for the moment, though I realize it's highly unlikely . . ."

"Excellent! You must be rich, my dear Monsieur Bonacieux."

"Let's say I'm well off, sir. I've accumulated enough capital to give me an income of two or three thousand écus a year. I made part of it in the drapery business and part of it by investing in the last voyage of the famous navigator Jean Mocquet, so that, you understand . . . Oh!"

"What's the matter?" asked d'Artagnan.

"Look, there!"

"Where?"

"In that doorway across the street: a man in a cloak."

"It's my man!" d'Artagnan and Bonacieux both exclaimed at the same time.

"This time he won't get away from me!" cried d'Artagnan, reaching for his sword. He drew it from its scabbard and rushed out of the apartment.

On the stairs he met Athos and Porthos coming to pay him a visit. They stepped aside, and he darted between them.

"Where are you going?" they both called out after him at once.

"The man from Meung!" he answered and disappeared.

He had more than once told his friends about his adventure with the stranger, and about the beautiful lady to whom the stranger had seemed to give an important message.

Athos believed that d'Artagnan had lost his letter in the fight, since he felt that a nobleman—and, from d'Artagnan's description, the stranger could only be a nobleman—would never stoop so low as to steal a letter.

Porthos saw nothing in the whole affair except an amorous rendezvous between a lady and a gentleman that had been disturbed by the presence of d'Artagnan and his yellow horse.

Aramis had said that since such things were mysterious, it was better not to delve into them.

And so Athos and Porthos knew what d'Artagnan had meant when he said, "The man from Meung!" in answer to their question. They continued up the stairs, assuming that d'Artagnan would return home after either catching up with his man or losing sight of him.

When they went into his room, it was empty. Fearing the consequences of the encounter that was probably going to take place between d'Artagnan and the stranger, Bonacieux, acting in accordance with the description of his character that he himself had given, had decided it would be best to make himself scarce.

9

D'Artagnan Proves Himself

As Athos and Porthos expected, d'Artagnan returned half an hour later. Once again he had lost his man. The stranger had vanished as though by magic. D'Artagnan had run through all the nearby streets, sword in hand, without seeing anyone who looked like the man he was trying to find. Finally he had done what he should perhaps have done at the start, which was to knock on the door against which the stranger had been leaning. But he had pounded with the knocker a dozen times in vain. No one had answered. The noise had brought some of the neighbors to their windows or doorways, and they had told him that no one had lived in the house, whose doors and windows were all closed, for the past six months.

While d'Artagnan was running through the streets and knocking on doors, Aramis had joined the two other musketeers, so that when d'Artagnan came back, the foursome was complete.

"Well?" the three musketeers asked together when they saw d'Artagnan come in with his face sweaty and contorted by anger.

"That man must be the devil himself!" he cried, throwing his sword on the bed. "He disappeared like a shadow, like a ghost!"

"Do you believe in ghosts?" Athos asked Porthos.

"I believe only what I see, and since I've never seen a ghost, I don't believe in them."

"The Bible tells us that we must believe in them," said Aramis. "Samuel's ghost appeared to Saul. It's an article of faith that I hope you won't place in doubt, Porthos."

"In any case," d'Artagnan went on, "whether he's the devil or not, whether he's alive or a ghost, an illusion or a reality, that man is bad luck for all of us, gentlemen, because his escape has robbed us of a chance to make a hundred pistoles, and maybe more."

"What!" Porthos and Aramis exclaimed together.

Athos remained silent as usual, and merely gave d'Artagnan a questioning look.

"Planchet," d'Artagnan said to his servant, who had just put his head near the partially open door in the hope of overhearing some of the conversation, "go downstairs to my landlord, Monsieur Bonacieux, and tell him to send us half a dozen bottles of Beaugency wine. It's my favorite."

"You have an open account with your landlord?" asked Porthos.

"Yes, beginning today," replied d'Artagnan. "And don't worry: if his wine is bad, we'll send him off to find some that's better."

"One must use but not abuse," Aramis said sententiously.

"I've always said that d'Artagnan had a better head on his shoulders than any of the rest of us," said Athos, and after stating this opinion, which d'Artagnan acknowledged with a bow, he lapsed into his customary silence.

"Don't keep us in suspense, d'Artagnan! Explain!" Porthos demanded.

"Yes, tell us what's happened, my friend," said Aramis, "unless a lady's honor is involved, in which case you'd better keep the story to yourself."

"Don't worry," said d'Artagnan, "no one's honor will be damaged by what I have to tell you."

He then told his friends exactly what had taken place between him and Monsieur Bonacieux, and how the man who had abducted Madame Bonacieux was the same man with whom he had clashed in Meung.

"You've made a good bargain," said Athos, after tasting the wine with the deliberation of a connoisseur and nodding to show that he found it good. "We can get fifty or sixty pistoles from your landlord. But first we must decide whether fifty or sixty pistoles are worth risking four heads."

"There's more to it than money!" cried d'Artagnan. "A woman has been abducted! She's probably being threatened, and maybe tortured, and all because she's faithful to her mistress the queen!"

"Be careful, d'Artagnan," said Aramis. "It seems to me that you're a little too concerned about what happens to Madame Bonacieux. Women were created for our downfall, and all our misery comes from them."

Hearing this pronouncement by Aramis, Athos frowned and bit his lip.

"It's not Madame Bonacieux I'm concerned about," said

d'Artagnan, "it's the queen. The king has abandoned her, the cardinal is persecuting her, and she's been seeing her friends' heads fall one by one."

"Why does she love what we hate most: the Spanish and the English?"

"Spain is her native country, so it's only natural for her to love the people of that country. As for your second complaint, I've heard that she loves not the English, but an Englishman."

"And I must admit that Englishman is worthy of being loved," said Athos. "I've never seen a more imposing man in my life."

"Not to mention the fact that he dresses better than anyone else," said Porthos. "I was in the Louvre the day when he scattered his pearls; I picked up two of them and sold them for ten pistoles apiece. And you, Aramis, do you know him?"

"As well as you do, gentlemen, because I was one of the men who arrested him in the garden at Amiens, where Monsieur de Putange, the queen's equerry, had taken me. I was still in the seminary at the time, and it seemed to me that it was a cruel affair for the king."

"Even so," said d'Artagnan, "if I knew where the duke of Buckingham was, I'd take him by the hand and lead him to the queen, if only to enrage the cardinal. Our only real enemy is the cardinal, gentlemen, and I must admit that if we could find some way to give him a really painful setback, I'd gladly risk my head to do it."

"And Bonacieux told you that the queen thought Buckingham had been lured back to Paris with a forged letter?" asked Athos.

"She's afraid so."

"Just a minute . . ." said Aramis.

"What is it?" asked Porthos.

"No, go on talking; I'm trying to remember something."

"I'm now convinced," said d'Artagnan, "that the abduction of that woman in the queen's service is connected with what we've been talking about, and maybe with Buckingham's presence in Paris."

"That Gascon is full of ideas," Porthos remarked admiringly.

"I enjoy hearing him talk," said Athos. "His Gascon accent amuses me."

"Now I remember," said Aramis. "Listen to this, gentlemen."

"Yes, let's listen to Aramis," said Porthos.

"Yesterday I visited a learned doctor of theology whom I sometimes consult for my studies . . ."

Athos smiled.

"He lives in an isolated, sparsely populated neighborhood," Aramis continued. "His tastes and his profession require it. As I was leaving his house . . ."

At this point Aramis stopped.

"Well?" asked d'Artagnan. "What happened as you were leaving his house?"

Aramis seemed to make a great mental effort, like a man who had begun telling a lie and then been brought up short by an unexpected obstacle; but his three friends' eyes were fixed on him, their ears were straining to hear what he would answer, and he could not turn back.

"The theologian has a niece who . . ."

"Ah, he has a niece!" Porthos broke in.

"Yes, and she's a very respectable lady," said Aramis.

The three others laughed.

"If you laugh or doubt what I say, I won't tell you anything!"

"We'll believe every word and be as silent as graves," Athos assured him.

"Then I'll go on. The theologian's niece sometimes comes to see him. She happened to be at his house yesterday when I was there, and I had to offer to accompany her to her carriage."

"So the theologian's niece has a carriage?" Porthos interrupted again; one of his faults was an inability to hold his tongue. "You've made a good acquaintance, my friend."

"Porthos, I've told you many times that you're very indiscreet, and that it turns women against you."

"Gentlemen, gentlemen," said d'Artagnan, who had begun to guess where the story was leading, "this is a serious matter, so let's try not to joke about it. Go on, Aramis."

"Suddenly a tall, dark man, obviously a nobleman . . . Now that I think of it, d'Artagnan, he was like the stranger you've described."

"He may have been the same man."

"It's possible. . . . He came up to me, with five or six men following ten paces behind him, and said to me politely, 'Duke, and you, Madame'—the 'Madame' was for the lady beside me—"

"The theologian's niece?"

"Quiet, Porthos!" said Athos. "You're unbearable!"

" 'Duke, and you, Madame,' he said, 'please get into this carriage without putting up the slightest resistance or making the slightest sound.' "

"He thought you were Buckingham!" said d'Artagnan.

"Yes, I think so."

"But what about the lady?" asked Porthos.

"He thought she was the queen!" said d'Artagnan.

"Exactly," said Aramis.

"This Gascon is devilishly clever!" exclaimed Athos. "Nothing escapes him!"

"The fact is," said Porthos, "that Aramis has about the same height and build as the Duke. But it seems to me that in a musketeer's uniform . . ."

"I was wearing an enormous cloak," said Aramis.

"In July? Is the theologian afraid you'll be recognized?"

"I can understand that the spy might have been misled by your height and build," said Athos, "but what about your face?"

"I was wearing a big hat," answered Aramis.

"All those precautions for a theology lesson!" said Porthos.

"Let's not waste time on idle talk, gentlemen," said d'Artagnan. "Let's leave now and try to find the draper's wife. She's the key to the mystery."

"Do you really think that a woman of such low condition can be so important?" Porthos asked disdainfully.

"She's the goddaughter of La Porte, the queen's confidential agent. Didn't I tell you that, gentlemen? And Her Majesty may have deliberately chosen someone of low condition to help her. People in high places are more easily seen, and the cardinal has sharp eyes."

"First," said Porthos, "let's agree on a price with the draper, and let's make it a good price!"

"There's no need for that," said d'Artagnan, "because I think that if he doesn't pay us, we'll be paid well enough by someone else."

Just then there was a sound of hurried footsteps on the stairs, the door was thrown open, and Bonacieux burst into the room.

"Save me, gentlemen!" he cried. "In the name of heaven, save me! Four men have come to arrest me! Save me! Save me!"

Porthos and Aramis stood up.

"Just a moment," said d'Artagnan, motioning them to put back their half-drawn swords. "Courage isn't what's needed here, it's prudence."

"But," Porthos protested, "we can't let . . ."

"Let d'Artagnan do what he thinks best," said Athos. "I

repeat that he has the best head of any of us, and for my part I'm ready to obey him. Tell us what to do, d'Artagnan.''

At that moment four guards appeared in the doorway of the anteroom. Seeing four musketeers standing with their swords at their sides, they hesitated to go any further.

"Come in, gentlemen, come in," said d'Artagnan. "You're my guests here, and we're all faithful servants of the king and the cardinal.''

"You won't try to stop us from carrying out our orders?" asked the man who seemed to be the leader of the group.

"Of course not. We'll even help you if necessary."

"Why is he talking like that?" muttered Porthos.

"Quiet, you fool!" Athos ordered him.

"But you promised me . . ." the poor draper said in an undertone.

"We can't save you unless we stay free," d'Artagnan whispered to him rapidly, "and if we try to defend you, we'll be arrested with you.''

"But it seems to me that . . ."

"Come, gentlemen," d'Artagnan said aloud to the guards, "I have no reason to defend this man. I saw him today for the first time in my life, and that was because he came to demand his rent, as he'll tell you himself. Isn't that right, Monsieur Bonacieux? Answer!''

"Yes, it's true," said the draper, "but he hasn't told you . . .''

"Not a word about me, my friends, or the queen," d'Artagnan whispered, "or you'll put us all in prison without saving yourself." He turned back to the guards. "Take him away, gentlemen." He pushed the dazed Bonacieux into their hands. "He had the insolence to demand money from me, a musketeer! Take him to prison and keep him there as long as possible. That will give me more time to pay.''

The guards thanked him profusely and took Bonacieux away.

As their leader was about to follow them down the stairs, d'Artagnan tapped him on the shoulder.

"Why don't we drink to each other's health?" he said, filling two glasses with the Beaugency wine that he owed to Monsieur Bonacieux's generosity.

"Thank you," replied the guard. "I'll be honored to drink with you.''

"To your health, then, Monsieur . . . What's your name?''

"Boisrenard.''

"To your health, Monsieur Boisrenard!''

"To yours, sir—and may I ask your name too?"

"D'Artagnan."

"To your health, Monsieur d'Artagnan!"

"And now let's drink to the king and the cardinal!" said d'Artagnan, seemingly carried away by enthusiasm.

Boisrenard might have doubted his sincerity if the wine had been bad, but it was good and he had no misgivings.

"What a vile thing to do!" Porthos said when Boisrenard had rejoined his men and the four friends were alone together. "The four of us stand by and watch a poor man being arrested while he begs for help, and then you, a gentleman, drink with a policeman!"

"Porthos," said Aramis, "Athos has already called you a fool, and I agree with him. D'Artagnan, you're a great man, and when you're in Monsieur de Tréville's place I'll ask you to use your influence for me in my career as a churchman."

"I don't understand you at all!" cried Porthos. "You approve of what d'Artagnan just did?"

"I certainly do," said Athos. "I not only approve of it, I congratulate him on it."

"And now, gentlemen," said d'Artagnan, without bothering to explain his conduct to Porthos, "all for one, one for all—shall we make that our motto?"

"But . . ." Porthos began.

"Put out your hand and swear!" Athos told him.

Yielding to the others' example, though still muttering to himself, Porthos held out his hand and the four friends repeated the motto proposed by d'Artagnan: "All for one, one for all."

"Good, now I want you all to go home," d'Artagnan said, as if he had been giving orders all his life, "and be careful, because from now on we're going to be at war with the cardinal."

10

A Seventeenth-Century Mousetrap

The mousetrap is not a modern invention; as soon as societies were formed and invented some sort of police, the police in turn invented the mousetrap.

Since my readers may not be familiar with the slang used at

police headquarters on the Rue de Jérusalem, and since, in the fifteen years I have been writing, I have never before employed the word with this meaning, I will explain what a mousetrap is.

When the police have gone to a certain house and arrested someone suspected of a crime, they keep the arrest secret and station four or five men in the first room of the house. These men open the door to all who knock, close it behind them, and arrest them. Within a few days, nearly everyone who regularly comes to the house has fallen into their hands. This is what is known as a mousetrap.

Monsieur Bonacieux's house was turned into a mousetrap, and everyone who came to it was arrested and questioned by the cardinal's men. It goes without saying that since d'Artagnan's room on the second floor had its own entrance, those who came to see him were not molested.

Moreover, the three musketeers were his only visitors. Each of them had been investigating on his own, without discovering anything. Athos had even gone so far as to question Monsieur de Tréville, which, considering the worthy musketeer's silence, had greatly surprised his captain. But Monsieur de Tréville knew nothing, except that, the last time he had seen the cardinal, the king, and the queen, the cardinal and the king had both seemed worried and the queen's eyes had been red, evidently from either weeping or lack of sleep. But the redness of the queen's eyes had not seemed noteworthy to him because she had wept a great deal and spent many sleepless nights ever since her wedding.

Monsieur de Tréville urged Athos to be vigilant in serving the king, and especially the queen, and asked him to repeat this to his friends.

As for d'Artagnan, he constantly stayed at home. He had converted his room into a listening post. From his windows he could see those who came to the house and were about to fall into the trap; then, since he had removed a section of the floor, so that only a single layer of wood separated him from the room below, where the interrogations took place, he was able to hear everything that was said.

After the person arrested had been thoroughly searched, the same questions were nearly always asked: "Has Madame Bonacieux given you something for her husband or someone else?" "Has Monsieur Bonacieux given you something for his wife or someone else?" "Has either of them confided anything to you in person?"

"If they knew anything," thought d'Artagnan, "they wouldn't be questioning everyone that way. Are they trying to find out whether the duke of Buckingham is in Paris and has already seen the queen, or intends to see her?"

He stopped at this idea. From everything he had heard, it seemed quite likely.

Meanwhile the mousetrap continued, and so did d'Artagnan's vigilance.

At nine o'clock on the evening of the day following poor Bonacieux's arrest, when Athos had just left d'Artagnan to go to see Monsieur de Tréville, and when Planchet, who had not yet made the bed, was beginning to do so, d'Artagnan heard a knock on the front door of the house. He then heard the door open and close; someone had been caught in the mousetrap.

He hurried to the hollowed-out spot in the floor, lay down and listened.

He soon heard cries, then muffled moans. This time there was no questioning.

"It sounds like a woman," d'Artagnan thought. "They're searching her, she's resisting, they're using violence on her—the foul brutes!"

It was all he could do to restrain himself from abandoning his caution and intervening in the scene taking place below him.

"But I tell you I'm the mistress of this house, gentlemen!" cried the poor woman. "I'm Madame Bonacieux! I'm in the queen's service!"

"Madame Bonacieux!" murmured d'Artagnan. "Am I lucky enough to have found the woman everyone is looking for?"

"You're precisely the person we've been waiting for," said one of the men below.

The woman's voice became still more muffled and a violent movement shook the walls. The victim was resisting as much as one woman could resist four men.

"Please, gentlemen, plea—" she said, and then she uttered only inarticulate sounds.

"They've gagged her and they're going to take her away!" cried d'Artagnan, leaping to his feet. "My sword! Ah, here it is! Planchet!"

"Yes, sir?"

"Go and look for Athos, Porthos, and Aramis. One of them is sure to be at home, and maybe all three. Tell them to come here as quickly as they can, armed. I just remembered: Athos is at Monsieur de Tréville's house.''

"But where are you going, sir?"

"I'm going through the window, to get there sooner. Put the floorboards back in place, sweep the floor, then hurry and do as I told you.''

"Oh, sir, you'll be killed!" cried Planchet.

"Quiet, you imbecile," said d'Artagnan.

He climbed through the window, hung from the sill for a moment and let himself drop. Luckily the second floor was not very high; his fall did him no harm.

He went to knock on the front door. "Now it's my turn to fall into the mousetrap," he thought, "but this is one mouse they'll wish they hadn't caught!''

As soon as he knocked, the tumult ceased. Footsteps came toward the door, it opened, and d'Artagnan rushed inside with his sword drawn. The door closed behind him, evidently moved by a spring.

The other occupants of the house, and the neighbors, heard shouts, stamping, the clatter of swords, and the sound of furniture being knocked over. Surprised by the noise, several people came to their windows to see what was causing it. They soon saw four men in black come flying through the door like a flock of terrified crows, leaving feathers—that is, scraps of their clothes—on the floor and the corners of tables.

D'Artagnan had won a decisive victory—without great difficulty, it must be admitted, because only one of the men had been armed, and he had defended himself only for the sake of form. The three others had attacked him with a chair, a stool, and a large pot, but a few light sword thrusts had frightened them off. In less than ten minutes, the battle was over and the enemy had fled.

The neighbors, who had opened their windows with the calm usually displayed by Parisians in that time of constant riots and brawls, closed them as soon as they saw the four men in black run away: their instinct told them that the fighting had ended, for the moment at least. Besides, it was late, and then, as now, people went to bed early in the Luxembourg quarter.

D'Artagnan was now alone with Madame Bonacieux. When he turned to her, he saw that she was sitting limply in an armchair, only half conscious. He quickly examined her.

She was a charming woman in her early twenties, with dark hair, blue eyes, a slightly turned-up nose, admirable teeth, and a fair complexion that was now partly pink. But those were the only things that might have caused her to be mistaken for a great lady. Her hands were white but not delicate; her feet were not those of a woman of quality. Luckily d'Artagnan had not yet begun to be concerned with such details.

When his examination of her had reached her feet, he saw a fine batiste handkerchief on the floor beside her. He picked it up, according to his habit, and recognized the same monogram he had seen on the handkerchief that had nearly made him fight a duel with Aramis. Ever since that day he had been wary of monogrammed handkerchiefs, so he slipped this one back into Madame Bonacieux's pocket without saying anything.

Just then she regained her senses. She opened her eyes, looked around the room in terror, then saw that she was alone with her rescuer. She held out her hands to him and smiled. Madame Bonacieux had the most charming smile in the world.

"Ah, it was you who saved me, sir!" she said. "Let me thank you."

"There's no need to thank me, madame," he replied, "because I did only what any other gentleman would have done in my place."

"You're too modest, sir. I'm deeply grateful to you, and I hope to prove it. But what did those men want with me? At first I thought they were robbers . . . And why isn't my husband here?"

"Those men were much more dangerous than robbers, because they're agents of the cardinal, and your husband isn't here because yesterday he was arrested and taken to the Bastille."

"The Bastille!" cried Madame Bonacieux. "Why? What has he done? He's the most innocent man who ever lived!"

And something like a smile mingled with the fear that showed in her face.

"What has he done? I think his only crime is being both fortunate and unfortunate enough to be your husband."

"Then you know . . ."

"I know that you were abducted, madame."

"Who did it? If you know, tell me!"

"It was a man in his early forties, with black hair, a swarthy face, and a scar on his left temple."

"Yes, that's the man, but I want to know his name!"

"I don't know."

"Did my husband know I'd been abducted?"

"He was informed of it by a letter from your abductor himself."

"And does he think he knows why it happened?" she asked with embarrassment.

"I believe he thought it was for a political reason."

"I doubted that at first, but now I agree with him. So the dear man never suspected me for a moment?"

"No, not for one moment, madame. He had complete confidence in your honor, and especially in your love for him."

Another smile, almost imperceptible, flickered across the beautiful young woman's pink lips.

"But how did you escape?" asked d'Artagnan.

"When they left me alone for a little while, I tied my sheets together and lowered myself from the window. I've known since this morning what was behind my abduction. As soon as I escaped, I came home because I thought my husband was here."

"You wanted him to protect you?"

"No, I knew the poor man couldn't do that. But since he might be useful to us, I wanted to tell him something."

"What is it?"

"I'm not free to tell you. It's a secret."

"In any case, this isn't a good place for us to talk. Even though I'm a soldier, I must advise caution. The men I drove away will come back with reinforcements, and if they find us here, we're lost. I sent my servant for three of my friends, but I don't know if he's been able to find them."

"You're right, we mustn't stay here!" she said in alarm. "Let's leave, hurry!"

She took hold of his arm and pulled him toward the door.

"But where shall we go?" he asked.

"First, let's get away from this house, then we'll see."

Without bothering to close the door behind them, they walked rapidly along the Rue des Fossoyeurs, turned into the Rue des Fossés-Monsieur-le-Prince, and did not stop till they came to the Place Saint-Sulpice.

"Now what are we going to do?" asked d'Artagnan. "Where do you want me to take you?"

"I must admit I don't know what to tell you," replied Madame Bonacieux. "I intended to send my husband to Monsieur de La Porte to find out exactly what's been happening in the Louvre the last three days, and if it was safe for me to go back there."

"I can go to Monsieur de La Porte," said d'Artagnan.

"It's not that simple: my husband would have been allowed

into the Louvre because he's known there, but you're not, so they'd refuse to let you in."

"But there must be some gatekeeper who's devoted to you, and if I gave him a password . . ."

She looked at him intently.

"And if I gave you that password, would you forget it as soon as you'd used it?"

"Yes, on my word of honor!" d'Artagnan said with unmistakable sincerity.

"I believe you. You seem to be an honorable young man; and besides, you may be richly rewarded for your devotion."

"I don't need any promise of a reward to make me serve the king and the queen. Consider me your friend and tell me what to do."

"But where can I stay while you're gone?"

"Isn't there a house where you can go and wait for Monsieur de La Porte to come to you?"

"No. I mustn't trust anyone."

"I have it!" said d'Artagnan. "We're not far from Athos's house, so . . ."

"Who's Athos?"

"One of my friends."

"But what if he's at home, and sees me?"

"He's not at home. I'll lock you in his apartment and take the key with me."

"What if he comes back?"

"He won't. And even if he did, he'd be told that I'd brought a woman who was still in his apartment."

"That would ruin my reputation!"

"No, because no one in the house knows you. Besides, we're in a situation where we can't worry about proprieties!"

"Yes, I suppose so. Where does your friend live?"

"On the Rue Férou, only a few steps away."

"Let's go."

They started off again.

As d'Artagnan expected, Athos was not at home. D'Artagnan obtained the key without difficulty, since he was known to be a close friend. He went up the stairs with Madame Bonacieux and showed her into the little apartment that we have already described.

"Make yourself at home," he said to her. "Lock the door from the inside and don't open it for anyone unless you hear three knocks like this.'' He knocked twice quickly and loudly, then once more gently, after a pause.

"Very well," said Madame Bonacieux. "Now it's my turn to give you instructions."

"I'm listening."

"Go to the gate of the Louvre on the Rue de l'Echelle and ask for Germain."

"Yes, and then?"

"He'll ask you what you want. Answer with these words: 'Tours and Brussels.' He'll then do whatever you say."

"And what shall I tell him to do?"

"Tell him to bring Monsieur de La Porte, the queen's gentleman-in-waiting."

"And when Monsieur de La Porte has come?"

"Send him to me."

"I will. But where and how will I see you again?"

"Do you really want to see me again?"

"Yes, very much."

"Then let me arrange it, and don't worry."

"Can I count on it?"

"I give you my word."

He bowed to her and gave her a heavily amorous look. As he was going down the stairs he heard her lock the door. He hurried to the Louvre and arrived at the gate on the Rue de l'Echelle as the clock struck ten. All the events we have just described took place within half an hour.

Everything happened as Madame Bonacieux had said. When he heard the password, Germain bowed; ten minutes later La Porte arrived. D'Artagnan quickly summed up the situation and told him where Madame Bonacieux was. After making d'Artagnan repeat the address, La Porte ran off. But after only a dozen steps he came back.

"Young man," he said to d'Artagnan, "let me give you some advice."

"Please do."

"You may find yourself in difficulty because of what's just happened."

"Do you think so?"

"Yes. Do you have a friend whose clock is slow?"

"Maybe I could find one, but . . ."

"Go to see him, so that he can testify that you were with him at half-past nine. In law, that's called an alibi."

D'Artagnan felt that this was sound advice. He ran to Monsieur de Tréville's house, but instead of going into the drawing room with everyone else, he asked to go to the study. Since he was well known in the house, no objection was made and a servant went to tell Monsieur de Tréville that Monsieur d'Artagnan had something important to tell him in private. Five minutes later, Monsieur de Tréville asked him what he could do for him, and why he was visiting him at such a late hour.

"Excuse me, sir," said d'Artagnan, who had set the hands of the clock back forty-five minutes during the time when he had been left alone, "but I thought that since it was only twenty-five past nine it wasn't too late to come to see you."

"Twenty-five past nine!" exclaimed Tréville. He looked at the clock. "That's impossible!"

"You can see for yourself, sir."

"Yes, it's true. I thought it was much later . . . Well, why have you come?"

D'Artagnan told him a long story about the queen; he described his fears for her and related what he had heard about the cardinal's plans with regard to the duke of Buckingham. He spoke with calm self-assurance and Tréville was all the more easily taken in because he himself, as we have already said, had noticed changes in the cardinal, the king, and the queen.

At ten o'clock d'Artagnan left Tréville, who thanked him for his information, urged him once again to be vigilant in serving the king and queen, and returned to the drawing room. But when d'Artagnan reached the foot of the stairs, he realized that he had forgotten his cane. He hurried back up the stairs, went into the study, and turned the hands of the clock to the correct time, so that no one could notice the next day that it had been tampered with. Then, sure that he would have a witness to prove his alibi, he went downstairs and left the house.

11

The Plot Thickens

Having paid his visit to Monsieur de Tréville, d'Artagnan took the longest way home, lost in thought.

What was he thinking about as he walked along, looking up at the stars, sometimes sighing and sometimes smiling?

He was thinking about Madame Bonacieux. For an apprentice musketeer, she was almost an amorous ideal: besides being young, pretty, and mysterious, she knew nearly all the secrets of the court, which gave her face a charming look of gravity, and she was suspected of not being insensitive to masculine attentions, which is an irresistible attraction for young men with little experience in love. Furthermore, d'Artagnan had rescued her from the demons who wanted to search her and mistreat her, and this had given her one of those feelings of gratitude that can easily develop into something more tender.

D'Artagnan's dreams moved so swiftly on the wings of his imagination that he already saw himself being accosted by a messenger from Madame Bonacieux, sent to give him a note asking him to meet her, along with a gold chain or a diamond. We have already mentioned that young men were not ashamed to take money from the king; we must also add that in those days of easy morals they were equally shameless with regard to their mistresses, who nearly always gave them valuable tokens of their love, as if they wanted to overcome the fragility of their feelings by the solidity of their gifts.

Men unabashedly used women as a means of advancement. Women who had nothing else to offer gave their beauty, and that is probably the origin of the proverb that says that the most beautiful girl in the world can give only what she has. Those who were rich also gave part of their money; many a hero in that gallant age would not have won his spurs, and later his battles, if it had not been for the well-filled purse that his mistress tied to his saddlebow.

D'Artagnan had nothing. His provincial scruples, which were feeble from the start, had been swept away by the unorthodox advice that the three musketeers had given him. Following the strange custom of the time, he saw Paris as if it were a battlefield in Flanders, the only difference being that in Paris it was women, rather than the Spanish, who were the enemy; in both cases the enemy had to be conquered and made to pay tribute.

But for the moment he was moved by nobler and more disinterested feelings. Monsieur Bonacieux had said that he was rich, and since he seemed to be a fool, it was likely that his wife held the purse strings. Self-interest, however, had nothing to do with d'Artagnan's initial attraction to Madame Bonacieux, and it played very little part in the love that had now begun to blossom in his heart. We say "very little" because the idea that a beautiful, charming, and intelligent young woman is also rich does nothing to weaken the beginning of love, and in fact strengthens it.

A rich woman can have all sorts of luxuries and aristocratic whims that serve to enhance beauty. Fine white stockings, a silk dress, a lace chemisette, dainty shoes, a fresh hair ribbon—these things do not make an ugly woman pretty, but they do make a pretty one beautiful. Money also has a beneficial effect on a woman's hands because they need to remain idle in order to remain beautiful.

Since we have not hidden the state of d'Artagnan's fortune, the reader knows very well that he was not a millionaire; he hoped to become one some day, but the time he had set for that happy change was still rather far off in the future. Meanwhile he was aware of how painful it would be for him to see the woman he loved longing for all the trinkets and finery from which women make their happiness and not be able to give them to her. When a woman is rich and her lover is not, she can at least give herself what he cannot give her; and although she usually pays for it with her husband's money, her husband is seldom the one who benefits from her gratitude.

D'Artagnan was prepared to become a tender lover, but in the meantime he was a loyal friend. In the midst of his plans for a love affair with the draper's wife, he did not forget Athos, Porthos, and Aramis. He thought of sharing her company with them during outings to the Plaine Saint-Denis or the Foire Saint-Germain. He would be proud to show off his conquest to them. And since walking makes one hungry, as d'Artagnan had already had occasion to notice, they would later have one of those charming dinners during which a man touches a friend's hand on one side and his mistress's foot on the other. And with a mistress like Madame Bonacieux, d'Artagnan would be able to help his friends in time of need.

But what about Monsieur Bonacieux, whom d'Artagnan had handed over to the police, loudly denouncing him after secretly promising to save him? We must confess to our readers that d'Artagnan gave him no thought, except to tell himself that he was glad to have him out of the way, wherever he might be. Love is the most selfish of all passions.

But we want to reassure our readers by telling them that although d'Artagnan had forgotten his landlord, or pretended to, on the pretext that he did not know where he had been taken, we have not forgotten him and we know where he was at that time. For the moment, however, we will follow our amorous Gascon's example by ignoring Monsieur Bonacieux; but we will come back to him later.

D'Artagnan had been walking along the Rue du Cherche-Midi, or Chasse-Midi, as it was called in those days, while he thought of his future love affair, talking to the night and smiling at the stars. It now occurred to him that since he was near Aramis's house he ought to visit him and explain why he had sent Planchet for him. If Aramis had been at home when Planchet arrived, he had undoubtedly hurried to Monsieur Bonacieux's house on the Rue des Fossoyeurs and found no one there, except perhaps for Athos and Porthos, and they must all be wondering what had happened. Their useless effort deserved an explanation, d'Artagnan told himself.

He was also aware that a visit to Aramis would give him a chance to talk about the pretty Madame Bonacieux, with whom his mind, if not his heart, was already filled. We must not expect discretion from a man who has just fallen in love for the first time; the joy inside him is so great that he must let it overflow, because otherwise it would choke him.

Paris had now been dark for two hours and the streets were beginning to be deserted. All the clocks in the Faubourg Saint-Germain had just struck eleven. It was a warm night. D'Artagnan was walking along the narrow little street that has now been replaced by the Rue d'Assas. A breeze from the Rue de Vaugirard brought him the fragrance of gardens freshened by the evening dew. In the distance he heard drinkers singing in taverns, their voices muffled by closed shutters. When he reached the end of the street, he turned left. The house in which Aramis lived was between the Rue Cassette and the Rue Servandoni.

D'Artagnan had just passed the Rue Cassette and recognized

the door of his friend's house, half hidden by a clump of sycamores and clematis, when he saw something like a shadow coming out of the Rue Servandoni. This something was wrapped in a cloak, and at first he thought it was a man; but then, from its small size and hesitant, uncertain gait, he saw it was a woman. As though not sure of the house she was seeking, she looked around, stopped, retraced her steps, then went off in her original direction again.

D'Artagnan was intrigued. "Maybe I should offer to help her," he thought. "From the way she walks, she must be young, and she may be pretty. Ah, yes . . . But a woman who's in the street at this time of night could hardly be doing anything but going to meet her lover. If I disturbed her rendezvous, it would be a bad way of striking up an acquaintance with her."

Meanwhile the woman was still walking, counting the houses and windows. This was not difficult, since there were only three houses on that part of the street, and only two windows overlooking it, one of them in the house next to Aramis's, the other in his own house.

"It would be odd," d'Artagnan thought, remembering the theologian's niece, "if that woman were looking for Aramis's house. But that seems to be just what she's doing! Ah, Aramis, this time you won't keep your secret!"

He furtively went to hide in the darkest spot on the street, a recess with a stone bench inside it.

As he watched the woman, the lightness of her step made him still more firmly convinced that she was young. He heard her cough. That cough, he thought, was a signal.

Then, either because her uncertainty had been ended by an answering signal, or because she had recognized her goal without help, she resolutely went to Aramis's shutter and tapped on it three times with her finger, at regular intervals.

"She *has* come to see Aramis!" d'Artagnan murmured. "So *that's* how he studies theology, the hypocrite!" He saw light suddenly shine through the shutter as the window behind it was opened. "He was obviously expecting her visit. Now he's going to open the shutter and she'll climb inside."

But, to d'Artagnan's great surprise, the shutter remained closed and the light disappeared. Thinking that something was sure to happen soon, he went on peering into the darkness and straining his ears.

He was right: a few seconds later he heard two sharp taps from the other side of the window.

The young woman in the street answered with a single tap and the shutter was partly opened.

It is easy to imagine how eagerly d'Artagnan watched and listened. Unfortunately the light had been taken into another room. But his eyes were accustomed to the darkness, and it is said that Gascons have the ability to see at night, like cats.

He saw the young woman take a white object from her pocket. She quickly unfolded it and he recognized it as a handkerchief. She pointed out one corner of it to the person in front of her.

This reminded d'Artagnan of the handkerchief he had found at Madame Bonacieux's feet, which in turn reminded him of the one he had found at Aramis's feet. Another handkerchief! What could it mean?

He had no doubt that Aramis was the person talking with the woman outside the window, but from where d'Artagnan was standing he could not see his face. His curiosity got the better of his caution. Taking advantage of the fact that Aramis and his visitor were absorbed in conversation, evidently about the handkerchief, he left his hiding place and quickly but silently went to one corner of the wall, from where he could see into the apartment.

He nearly cried out in surprise: the young woman was not talking with Aramis, but with another woman. He could see clearly enough to recognize the feminine shape of her clothes, but he could not make out her features.

The woman inside took out a second handkerchief and exchanged it for the one that had been shown to her. The two women said a few more words to each other and the shutter was closed again. The woman on the outside walked away, passing within four paces of d'Artagnan. She pulled down the hood of her cloak, but too late to prevent him from seeing that she was Madame Bonacieux.

He had already suspected it when he saw her take the handkerchief from her pocket, but he had decided that since Madame Bonacieux had sent him to ask Monsieur de La Porte to bring her back to the Louvre, it was highly unlikely that she would be walking the streets of Paris alone at half-past eleven, at the risk of being abducted a second time.

It was obvious, then, that she had gone out for a very important matter. And what is the most important matter for a woman of twenty-five? Love.

But had she exposed herself to danger on her own account, or at the request of someone else? That was what d'Artagnan wondered while jealousy gnawed at his heart as mercilessly as if he were already her lover.

There was a simple way to find out where she was going, and that was to follow her. He began doing it instinctively, without a moment's thought.

But when she saw him move away from the wall like a statue coming out of its niche and heard his footsteps behind her, she uttered a little cry and broke into a run.

D'Artagnan ran after her and caught up with her all the more easily because she was hampered by her cloak. She was exhausted, not from running, but from terror. When he put his hand on her shoulder, she fell to one knee and said in a choked voice, "You can kill me, but I won't tell you anything!"

He leaned down, put his arm around her waist and lifted her to her feet. Feeling from her weight that she was about to faint, he quickly tried to reassure her.

His words meant nothing to her, for they could have been spoken with the worst intentions in the world, but his voice meant everything because it was familiar to her. She opened her eyes, looked at the man who had given her such a terrible fright and, recognizing d'Artagnan, cried out joyfully, "Oh, it's you! It's you! Thank God!"

"Yes, God sent me to watch over you," he said.

"And is that why you were following me?" she asked with a coquettish smile. Now that she knew he was a friend and not an enemy, her fear had vanished and the playful side of her nature had reappeared.

"No," he answered, "I admit it was only chance that made my path cross yours. I saw a woman tap on my friend's window . . ."

"Your friend?" Madame Bonacieux interrupted.

"Yes. Aramis is one of my best friends."

"Aramis? Who's that?"

"Come, now, you're not going to tell me you don't know Aramis, are you?"

"This is the first time I've ever heard that name."

"And was it the first time you'd ever gone to that house?"

"Yes."

"You didn't know a young man lived there?"

"No."

"A musketeer?"

"No."

"So it wasn't Aramis you came to see?"

"Certainly not. And you saw for yourself that the person I talked to is a woman."

"That's true; but she's a friend of Aramis."

"I don't know whether she is or not."

"She must be, since she lives in his apartment."

"That's not my concern."

"But who is she?"

"I can't tell you. It's a secret."

"My dear Madame Bonacieux, you're charming, but you're also the most mysterious woman I've ever . . ."

"Does that turn you against me?"

"Not at all; in fact, I think you're adorable."

"Then give me your arm."

"Gladly. And now?"

"And now, escort me."

"To where?"

"To where I'm going."

"But where are you going?"

"You'll see, since you'll leave me at the door."

"Shall I wait for you?"

"That won't be necessary."

"Will you come back alone?"

"Maybe, maybe not."

"If someone goes with you, will it be a man or a woman?"

"I don't know yet."

"Well, *I'll* know!"

"What do you mean?"

"I'll wait till I see you come out."

"In that case, good-bye!"

"Good-bye?"

"Yes. I don't need you."

"But you asked me—"

"I asked to be helped by a gentleman, not watched by a spy."

"A spy! That's too harsh."

"What do you call someone who follows people against their will?"

"I call him indiscreet."

"That's too gentle."

"Very well, madame. I see I must do everything you want."

"I'd have given you more credit if you'd agreed to obey me at the start."

"Won't you give me any credit for repenting?"

"Have you really repented?"

"I don't know, to tell you the truth. But I do know that I'll do whatever you say, if you'll let me take you to where you're going."

"And you'll leave me afterward?"

"Yes."

"You won't spy on me when I come out?"

"No."

"On your word of honor?"

"On my word of honor."

"Then let's go."

D'Artagnan offered his arm to Madame Bonacieux. She took it with a smile that did not entirely conceal her anxiety. They walked to the end of the Rue de La Harpe. There she seemed to hesitate, as she had done on the Rue de Vaugirard, but then she recognized a door and stepped toward it.

"This is where I'm going," she said. "Thank you very much for your company; it saved me from all the dangers that would have threatened me if I'd been alone. But now that I've reached my destination, it's time for you to keep your promise."

"You won't be in any danger when you leave?"

"I may be stopped by robbers, but that's all."

"Aren't you afraid of them?"

"What could they take from me? I have no money on me."

"You're forgetting that beautiful monogrammed handkerchief."

"What handkerchief?"

"The one I found at your feet and put back into your pocket."

"Be quiet!" she said urgently. "If anyone should hear you, I'd be lost!"

"You see: you're still in danger," said d'Artagnan, "since a word frightens you and you admit that you'd be lost if anyone heard it." He took her hand and looked at her ardently. "Be generous, madame, confide in me. Haven't you seen in my eyes how much devotion and sympathy there is in my heart?"

"Yes, I have, and that's why I'll tell you my own secrets if you ask me to. But I have no right to tell other people's secrets."

"Then I'll discover them on my own. Since they may affect your life, I have to find out what they are."

"No, you mustn't do that," she said with a seriousness that impressed him. "Don't try to find out anything about what I'm doing, and don't try to help me. I ask it of you in the name of the devotion you say you have for me. Please believe me: I'll always be grateful to you for what you've done, but from now on you must act as if you'd never met me, as if I didn't exist.''

"And must Aramis do the same, madame?" asked d'Artagnan, nettled.

"I've already told you I don't know anyone by that name."

"You knocked on his window, and yet you don't know him? Come, come, madame, I'm not as gullible as you think!"

"You've invented that man in the hope of making me tell you what you want to know. Admit it."

"I'm not inventing anything, madame, I'm only telling the truth."

"And one of your friends lives in that house?"

"I'll say it again: yes, one of my friends lives in that house, and his name is Aramis."

"This will all be cleared up later," she murmured. "For now, there's no use discussing it any more."

"If you could look into my heart," said d'Artagnan, "you'd see so much curiosity that you'd take pity on me, and so much love that you'd satisfy my curiosity here and now. You have nothing to fear from someone who loves you."

"You're very quick to speak of love, sir!" said the young woman, shaking her head.

"That's because love has come to me quickly, for the first time, and I'm not yet twenty."

She looked at him out of the corner of her eye.

"I'm already on the trail of your secret," d'Artagnan went on. "Three months ago I nearly fought a duel with Aramis because of a handkerchief like the one you showed that woman in his apartment. It was marked in the same way, I'm sure of it."

"I'm tired of this whole subject, sir."

"Think of what would happen if you were arrested with that handkerchief on you. That would be dangerous, wouldn't it?"

"Why? The initials on it are mine: C.B., Constance Bonacieux."

"Or Camille de Bois-Tracy."

"Be quiet, sir! How many times must I tell you that? Since the risks I'm running aren't enough to stop you, think of the risks you may run too!"

"What risks?"

"Just by knowing me, you're risking being sent to prison, or even losing your life."

"In that case I'll stay with you every minute."

"Please leave me," she pleaded, clasping her hands. "In the name of heaven, in the name of a soldier's honor, in the name of a gentleman's courtesy, leave me! Listen—midnight is striking, that's the time when I'm expected."

"Madame," said d'Artagnan, bowing, "I can't refuse anything that's asked of me that way. Since you want me to leave you, I will."

"You won't follow me, you won't spy on me?"

"I'll go straight home."

"Ah, I knew you were a gallant young man!" exclaimed Madame Bonacieux, holding out one hand to him and putting the other on the knocker of a small door set deeply into the wall.

D'Artagnan took her hand and kissed it ardently.

"Oh, I wish I'd never met you!" he cried with that spontaneous bluntness that women often prefer to polite affectation because it reveals what is really in a man's heart and shows that his emotion has won out over his reason.

"I can't say the same," Madame Bonacieux replied almost lovingly, squeezing the hand that still held hers. "What's lost for now isn't lost for the future. Some day, when I'm free to speak, perhaps I'll satisfy your curiosity."

"And will you also satisfy my love?" asked d'Artagnan, overjoyed.

"I can't promise that. It will depend on the feelings you're able to arouse in me."

"Do you mean that so far . . ."

"So far I haven't gone beyond gratitude."

"You're too charming," d'Artagnan said sadly. "You're taking advantage of my love."

"No, I'm only accepting your kindness. But believe me, we'll meet again."

"You've made me the happiest man on earth! Don't forget this night, and don't forget your promise!"

"You can count on me. I'll remember everything, when the time comes. But now you must leave. Go! I was expected at midnight, I'm already late."

"Only five minutes late."

"Yes, but sometimes five minutes are like five centuries."

"That's how it is with someone who's in love."

"How do you know it's not someone in love who's waiting for me?"

"So it's a man!" exclaimed d'Artagnan. "A man!"

"Let's not begin arguing again," Madame Bonacieux said with a half-smile that showed a tinge of impatience.

"We won't, don't worry, because I'm leaving. I believe in you. I want full credit for my devotion, even if it's stupid. Good-bye, madame."

D'Artagnan abruptly let go of her hand and hurried off, as if he would not have been able to tear himself away from her without that sudden effort. She knocked on the door as she had tapped on the shutter: three times, at regular intervals. When he reached the corner of the street he looked back: the door had opened and closed, and she was gone.

He continued on his way. He had given his word not to spy on Madame Bonacieux, and even if his life had depended on learning where she would go next or who would be with her, he would have gone straight home, because that was what he had said he would do. Five minutes later he was on the Rue des Fossoyeurs.

"Poor Athos must be puzzled," he said to himself. "Either he fell asleep while he was waiting for me, or he finally went home and learned that a woman had been there. A woman in Athos's apartment! Well, after all, there was one in Aramis's apartment too. This is all very strange and I'm curious to know how it will end."

"It will end badly, sir, badly," replied a voice that he recognized as Planchet's; while he was talking to himself, as preoccupied people sometimes do, he had come into the alley at the end of which was the staircase that led up to his room.

"What do you mean by that, you imbecile?" asked d'Artagnan. "What's happened?"

"All sorts of bad things."

"What are they?"

"First, Monsieur Athos has been arrested."

"Arrested! Athos? Why?"

"They found him here and thought he was you."

"Who arrested him?"

"The guards brought by the men in black you chased away."

"Why didn't he tell them who he was? Why didn't he say he had nothing to do with the whole affair?"

"That was the last thing he wanted to say, sir. He managed to come close to me and whisper, 'Your master needs to be free now and I don't, since he knows everything and I know nothing. They'll think he's in prison; that will give him time. In three days I'll tell who I am, and they'll have to release me.' "

"Bravo, Athos!" murmured d'Artagnan. "That was worthy of your noble heart. . . . What did the guards do?" he asked Planchet.

"Four of them took him I don't know where, maybe to the Bastille or the For-l'Evêque prison. Two of them stayed with the men in black. They searched everywhere and took all the papers they could find. And while that was going on, two more of them stood guard at the door. Then, when they were finished, they all went away. They left the house empty and open."

"What about Porthos and Aramis?"

"I couldn't find them and they didn't come."

"But they may still come at any moment—you left word that I wanted to see them, didn't you?"

"Yes, sir."

"Stay here. If they come, tell them what's happened and ask them to wait for me at the Cabaret de la Pomme de Pin; it would be too dangerous here, because it's possible that the house is being watched. First I'm going to report on everything to Monsieur de Tréville, then I'll go to meet them."

"Very well, sir."

D'Artagnan stepped toward the door, then turned back to shore up his servant's courage.

"You won't be afraid to stay here, will you?"

"Don't worry, sir," said Planchet. "You don't know me yet: I'm brave when I put my mind to it; the main thing is putting my mind to it, and I've done that now. Besides, I'm a Picard."

"Good, I'm counting on you. I expect you to die rather than leave your post."

"Yes, sir. There's nothing I wouldn't do to prove my loyalty to you."

D'Artagnan was pleased to hear this. "It seems I've used the right method in dealing with him," he thought. "I'll use it again when the need arises."

His legs were a bit tired from all the running he had done that night, but they carried him to the Rue du Vieux-Colombier with admirable speed.

Monsieur de Tréville was not at home; his company was on guard duty at the Louvre and he had gone there too.

D'Artagnan felt it was urgent for him to tell Monsieur de Tréville what had happened. He decided to try to get into the Louvre. His uniform as a guard in Monsieur des Essarts's company would probably gain him admittance.

He walked down the Rue des Petits-Augustins and along the

river, intending to cross it at the Pont-Neuf. For a moment he had thought of taking the ferry, but on reaching the water's edge he had put his hand into his pocket and realized that he did not have enough money to pay his fare.

As he was approaching the Rue Guénégaud he saw two people come out of the Rue Dauphine and was struck by their appearance. One was a man, the other a woman. The woman's figure was like Madame Bonacieux's and the man closely resembled Aramis. Furthermore the woman wore a black cloak like Madame Bonacieux's and the man wore a musketeer's uniform.

The woman's face was hidden by the hood of her cloak, the man's by a handkerchief that he held over it. These precautions showed that they did not want to be recognized.

They began crossing the bridge. D'Artagnan also had to cross it, to reach the Louvre. He followed them.

He soon became absolutely certain that the man and the woman in front of him were Madame Bonacieux and Aramis. His heart seethed with jealousy and suspicion. He felt doubly betrayed: by his friend and by the woman he already loved as if she were his mistress. Madame Bonacieux had sworn she did not know Aramis, and now, a quarter of an hour later, she was with him.

D'Artagnan did not reflect that he himself had known her only three hours, that she owed him nothing more than gratitude for having saved her from the men in black, and that she had promised him nothing. He regarded himself as an outraged, betrayed, scorned lover; the blood of anger rose to his face and he resolved to clear everything up.

The man and the woman now knew they were being followed, and had quickened their pace. D'Artagnan ran past them, then came back toward them just as they were beside the Samaritaine, in the glow of a streetlamp that lighted that whole part of the bridge.

He stopped in front of them, blocking their path. The musketeer stepped back.

"What do you want, sir?" he asked in a foreign accent, which proved to d'Artagnan that he had been at least partly mistaken.

"You're not Aramis!"

"No, sir, I'm not Aramis. I'll excuse you because your surprise shows that you mistook me for someone else."

"You'll excuse me?"

"Yes. Let me pass, since I'm not the man you wanted to speak to."

"That's true, sir, but I do want to speak to this lady."

"But you don't know her!" said the foreigner.

"You're wrong, sir. I know her."

"You gave me your word as a soldier and a gentleman," Madame Bonacieux said reproachfully. "I hoped I could count on it!"

"And you, madame," said d'Artagnan, embarrassed, "you promised me . . ."

"Take my arm, madame," said the foreigner, "and let's continue on our way."

D'Artagnan, bewildered, remained standing in front of them with his arms folded. The musketeer walked toward him and pushed him aside. D'Artagnan leapt back and drew his sword. The foreigner drew his at almost the same moment, with lightning speed.

"In the name of heaven, Your Grace!" cried Madame Bonacieux, stepping between them and taking hold of their swords, one in each hand.

"Your Grace!" exclaimed d'Artagnan. An idea had just burst into his mind. "Excuse me, sir, but are you . . ."

"He's the duke of Buckingham," Madame Bonacieux whispered, "and now that you know it, our fate depends on you."

"Forgive me, madame, please forgive me," said d'Artagnan. He turned to the duke. "I love her, Your Grace, and I was jealous. You know what it is to be in love. Forgive me, and tell me how I can serve you, even at the risk of my life."

"You're a fine young man," said Buckingham, holding out his hand to d'Artagnan, who took it respectfully. "You've offered me your services and I accept them. Follow twenty paces behind us till we reach the Louvre, and if anyone spies on us, kill him!"

D'Artagnan put his drawn sword under his arm, waited till Madame Bonacieux and the duke had walked twenty paces, then began following them, ready to carry out the instructions of the noble and elegant minister of Charles I.

Fortunately he had no occasion to give the duke this proof of his devotion. The young woman and the handsome musketeer entered the Louvre through the gate on the Rue de l'Echelle without incident.

D'Artagnan then went to the Cabaret de la Pomme de Pin, where he found Porthos and Aramis waiting for him. Without explaining why he had sent for them, he told them that he had already finished with the matter for which he had thought he would need their help.

And now, carried along by our story, we will let the three friends go to their separate homes while we follow the duke of Buckingham and his guide through the winding passages of the Louvre.

12

George Villiers, Duke of Buckingham

Madame Bonacieux and the duke were admitted into the Louvre without difficulty: she was known to be in the service of the queen, and he wore the uniform of Monsieur de Tréville's musketeers, who, as we have said, were on guard duty that night. Moreover, Germain, the gatekeeper, had the interests of the queen at heart, and if anything happened, Madame Bonacieux would be accused of having brought her lover into the Louvre, that was all. She would accept the accusation; her reputation would be lost but, to those in high places, the reputation of a draper's wife had little or no value.

Once they were in the courtyard, she and the duke followed the wall for about twenty-five paces, then they came to a tradesmen's door that was unlocked during the day but usually locked at night. Tonight, however, it was unlocked and Madame Bonacieux opened it. They stepped inside and found themselves in darkness, but she knew all the twists and turns of this part of the Louvre, which was reserved for members of the household. She closed the door behind them, took the duke by the hand, groped her way to a staircase, and began climbing it. The duke counted two flights of steps. Then she turned right, walked along a hall, went back down another flight of stairs, took a few more steps, unlocked a door, and led the duke into a room lighted only by a nightlamp.

"Stay here, Your Grace," she said. "Someone will come."

She left and locked the door behind her, so that the duke was literally a prisoner.

It must be said, however, that even in his isolation the duke of Buckingham felt no fear. One of the outstanding traits of his character was love of the adventurous and the romantic. He was brave, bold, and enterprising, and this was not the first time he had risked his life in such a venture. He had learned that the supposed message from Anne of Austria, which had brought him to Paris, was a trap; but instead of going back to England, he had taken advantage of the situation in which he had been placed and sent word to the queen that he would not leave without having seen her. At first she had firmly refused, but then she had become afraid that her refusal might exasperate the duke and drive him to some rash act. She had already decided to see him and beg him to leave immediately when Madame Bonacieux, who had been given the mission of going to him and bringing him to the Louvre, was abducted. For two days no one knew what had become of her and everything remained in suspense. But as soon as she had escaped and made contact with La Porte, things resumed their course, and she had just completed the dangerous mission that, if she had not been abducted, she would have completed three days earlier.

When she had left Buckingham alone in the room, he stepped in front of a mirror. His musketeer's uniform suited him perfectly.

He was thirty-five, and rightly regarded as the handsomest and most elegant nobleman in France and England. The favorite of two kings, enormously wealthy, all-powerful in a kingdom that he stirred up or calmed to suit his fancy, George Villiers, duke of Buckingham, had undertaken one of those prodigious lives that remain through the centuries as a source of amazement for posterity.

Sure of himself, confident in his power, and certain that the laws governing other men could not touch him, he went straight toward his goal, even if that goal was so lofty that it would have been madness for anyone else even to consider it. Thus he had succeeded in seeing the proud and beautiful Anne of Austria several times and in dazzling her to the point of making her fall in love with him.

As he stood in front of the mirror, he restored the waves in his blond hair that his hat had flattened, curled his mustache, and, elated at approaching the moment he had desired so long, smiled at himself with pride and hope.

Just then a door hidden in a hanging opened and a woman

appeared. Buckingham saw her in the mirror and uttered an exclamation: it was the queen!

Anne of Austria* was then twenty-six or twenty-seven and in the full brilliance of her beauty. She carried herself like a queen or a goddess. Her emerald-green eyes were both soft and majestic. Her mouth was small and red, with the slightly protruding lower lip of the Austrian royal family; it was a mouth that could smile graciously or express deep contempt. Her skin was noted for its softness and smoothness, and poets of the time sang the praises of her incomparably beautiful hands and arms. Her hair, blond in early youth, was now light brown. She wore it curled and heavily powdered, and it admirably framed a face in which the sternest judge could have wished no other changes than a little less brightness in its coloring and a little more delicacy in its nose.

Buckingham stood spellbound for a moment. Even at balls, festivals, and military exercises, Anne of Austria had never seemed to him so beautiful as she did now, wearing a simple white satin dress. She was accompanied by Doña Estefania, the only Spanish woman in her service who had not been driven away by the king's jealousy and Richelieu's persecutions.

The queen took two steps forward. Buckingham knelt and, before she could stop him, kissed the hem of her dress.

"Duke, you know that message wasn't from me."

"Yes, I know it now, Your Majesty," replied Buckingham. "And I also know I was mad to think that the snow had melted, that the marble had lost its coldness. My only excuse is that someone in love is always ready to believe his love is shared. But my journey hasn't been a loss to me, since you've consented to see me."

"Yes, but you know why I'm seeing you, Duke: I'm seeing you out of pity; I'm seeing you because you've stubbornly insisted on remaining in a city where you're risking your life and making me risk my honor; I'm seeing you to tell you that everything separates us: the depths of the sea, the enmity of kingdoms, the sanctity of vows. It's sacrilegious to struggle against all those things. And finally, I'm seeing you to tell you that we must never see each other again."

"The sweetness of your voice covers the harshness of your

---

*Anne of Austria (1601–1666), queen of France, wife of Louis XIII, and mother of Louis XIV, was the daughter of Philip III of Spain (of the house of Austria; i.e., of the Habsburg dynasty) and Margaret of Austria. (Translator's note.)

words, Your Majesty. You speak of sacrilege, but sacrilege lies in separating hearts that God made for each other."

"You're forgetting that I've never told you I loved you."

"You've never told me that you didn't love me, either; and saying such a thing would show great ingratitude, because where could you find another love like mine, a love that neither time, nor absence, nor despair can extinguish, a love that contents itself with a stray ribbon, a fleeting glance, a word spoken in passing?

"Three years ago I saw you for the first time, Your Majesty, and I've loved you ever since that moment. Shall I tell you how you were dressed the first time I saw you? Shall I describe each ornament you wore? I can still see you: you were seated on cushions, in the Spanish fashion; you wore a green satin dress with gold and silver embroidery, and full sleeves over your lovely arms, and big diamonds; you had a ruff around your neck, and on your head a cap the color of your dress, with a heron feather in it.

"When I close my eyes, I see you as you were then; when I open them, I see you as you are now—even more beautiful, a hundred times more beautiful!"

"What madness to feed a hopeless passion with such memories!" murmured Anne of Austria, who did not have the strength to reproach the duke for having remembered her so precisely.

"How else do you expect me to live, since I have only memories? They're my happiness, my hope. Each time I see you, I add another diamond to the treasure in my heart. This is the fourth one you've allowed me to have, for in three years I've seen you only four times: I've just told you about the first one; the second one was in Madame de Chevreuse's house, and the third was in the garden at Amiens."

"Duke," said the queen, blushing, "don't talk about that evening."

"Oh, you must let me talk about it, Your Majesty! It was the happiest, most radiant evening of my life. Do you remember what a lovely night it was? How the air was soft and fragrant, how the sky was blue and sparkling with stars? That time, I was able to be alone with you for a few moments; that time, you were ready to confide in me, to tell me about the loneliness of your life, the sorrow in your heart. You held my arm; I felt your hair brush against my face whenever I leaned toward you, and each time I quivered from head to foot. Ah, my queen, you can't imagine the heavenly joy I felt! I'd give everything I have—my fortune, my glory, all the days I still have left to live—for another night like that, because that night you loved me, I'm sure of it!"

"It's possible that for a time I was under the influence of that place, that lovely night, the fascination of your look, all the things that sometimes combine to make a woman weaken. But as soon as you dared to make advances to me, my weakness ended."

"Yes, and another love than mine would have succumbed to your cruelty; but mine became more ardent and faithful than ever. You thought you would escape me by returning to Paris; you thought I wouldn't dare to leave the treasure my master had ordered me to guard. But what do I care about all the treasures and kings in the world? A week later I was back. That time, I gave you no cause for complaint: I'd risked my favor at court, and even my life, to see you for a few moments, and I didn't even touch your hand. You forgave me when you saw how obedient and repentant I was."

"But I was slandered because of what you did, as you well know. The king, urged on by the cardinal, took drastic action: Madame de Vernet was sent away from court, Putange was exiled, Madame de Chevreuse fell into disfavor, and when you wanted to return as the English ambassador, the king himself refused to accept you."

"And France must pay for her king's refusal with a war. If I can't see you, I want you to hear about me every day. What do you think is the goal of the expedition to Ré and the alliance with the Protestants of La Rochelle that I'm planning? The pleasure of seeing you! I know I can have no hope of leading an army into Paris; but when the war ends, the terms of peace will have to be negotiated, and I'll negotiate them. I can't be refused then. I'll come back to Paris, I'll see you again, and I'll be happy for a few moments. It's true that thousands of men will have paid for my happiness with their lives, but that doesn't matter to me as long as I see you again! All this may be madness, but tell me: what woman has a more ardent lover, what queen has a more devoted servant?"

"You're defending yourself with arguments that speak against you, Duke. The things you're presenting as proofs of love are almost crimes."

"You say that because you don't love me. If you loved me, you'd see those things differently. Ah, if you loved me, my happiness would be too great and I'd go mad! You've mentioned

Madame de Chevreuse—she was less cruel than you: the earl of Holland loved her, and she returned his love.''

''Madame de Chevreuse wasn't a queen,'' murmured Anne of Austria, deeply moved, in spite of herself, by the expression of such a powerful love.

''Then you'd love me if you weren't a queen? May I believe that only the dignity of your rank makes you cruel to me, that I'd have reason to hope if you were Madame de Chevreuse? Thank you for those sweet words, Your Majesty, thank you!''

''You've misunderstood me, you've misinterpreted . . . I didn't mean . . .''

''Silence!'' said the duke. ''If I'm happy because of an illusion, don't be cruel enough to take it away from me. You yourself have told me that I've been drawn into a trap, and it may cost me my life. It's strange: for some time now, I've been having forebodings of death.''

He looked at her with a sad but charming smile.

''Oh, my God!'' she cried out with a fear in her voice that showed that her feelings for him were stronger than she was willing to admit.

''I didn't tell you that to alarm you. I know such dreams are ridiculous, and I don't worry about them, believe me. But what you just said to me, the hope you almost gave me, will more than make up for anything that may happen to me, even losing my life.''

''I have dreams and forebodings too,'' said Anne of Austria. ''I dreamed I saw you lying on the ground, bleeding from a wound.''

''It was a knife wound in my left side, wasn't it?'' asked Buckingham.

''Yes! A knife wound in your left side! Who could have told you I had that dream? I've confided it only to God, in my prayers.''

''Now I know you love me. I want nothing more.''

''I love you?''

''Yes, you do. Would God send us both the same dream if you didn't love me? Would we have the same forebodings if our hearts weren't joined together? You love me, Your Majesty. And will you mourn for me?''

''Dear God, this is more than I can bear!'' cried the queen. ''You must leave now, Duke! In the name of heaven, leave! I don't know if I love you or not, but I do know I won't break my vows. Take pity on me and go. If you were to be killed in France and if I thought your love for me was the cause of your death, I'd never be consoled and my grief would drive me mad! Please leave, I beg you to leave!"

"How beautiful you are in your emotion! And how I love you!"

"Please leave and come back later, as an ambassador, as a minister, surrounded by guards to defend you and servants to watch over you—then I won't be afraid for your life and I'll be happy to see you again."

"Oh! Is what you're saying really true?"

"Yes . . ."

"Then give me a token of your esteem, something to remind me that this wasn't all a dream, something that you've worn and that I can also wear: a ring, a necklace, a chain."

"Will you leave if I give you what you ask?"

"Yes."

"Immediately?"

"Yes."

"You'll leave France and go back to England?"

"Yes, I swear!"

"Then wait here a moment."

Anne of Austria went to her apartments and quickly returned with a monogrammed, gold-inlaid jewel box made of rosewood.

"Take this, Duke," she said, "and keep it in memory of me."

He took the jewel box and again knelt before her.

"You promised to leave," she reminded him.

"And I'll keep my word. Give me your hand, Your Majesty, and I'll go."

Closing her eyes, she held out one hand to him and leaned on Estefania with the other, for she felt that her strength was about to abandon her.

Buckingham passionately pressed his lips to that lovely hand, then stood up.

"If I'm not dead," he said, "I'll see you again within six months, even if I have to turn the world upside down to do it."

And, faithful to his promise, he hurried out of the room.

Madame Bonacieux was waiting for him in the hall. She led him out of the Louvre as carefully as she had led him into it, and with the same good luck.

13

Monsieur Bonacieux

As the reader may have noticed, there was one man in all this who, despite his precarious situation, seemed to have been more or less forgotten by everyone: that man was Monsieur Bonacieux, a respectable victim of the amorous and political intrigue so common in a time that was both chivalrous and licentious.

Luckily, however, as the reader may or may not remember, we have promised not to lose sight of him.

The men who arrested him took him straight to the Bastille and then led him, trembling, past a group of soldiers loading their muskets.

He was then taken to a long, partly underground room, where he was subjected to coarse insults and brutal treatment. Seeing that they were not dealing with a gentleman, the guards treated him as if he were a complete nonentity.

After half an hour a clerk arrived with an order for him to be taken to the interrogation room, which ended his torture but not his anxiety. Prisoners were usually questioned in their cells, but Monsieur Bonacieux was not deemed worthy of that consideration.

Two guards seized him, led him across a courtyard and into a corridor where there were three sentinels, opened a door, and pushed him into a room furnished only with a table, a chair, and a magistrate. The magistrate was seated at the table, writing.

The guards brought the prisoner in front of the table and, at a signal from the magistrate, withdrew beyond hearing distance.

The magistrate, who till now had kept his head bent over his papers, raised it to see who was standing before him. He was a grim-looking man with a pointed nose, a sallow complexion, prominent cheekbones, and small, lively, inquisitive eyes; the sum of all these features gave his face the look of both a fox and a ferret. He had a long, flexible neck, and the way his head swayed above his black robe suggested a turtle putting its head out of its shell.

He began by asking the prisoner his name, age, occupation, and address.

The prisoner replied that he was Jacques-Michel Bonacieux, fifty-one years old, a retired draper, living at 11 Rue des Fossoyeurs.

Instead of continuing his interrogation, the magistrate gave him a long lecture on how dangerous it was for a man of humble condition to meddle in affairs of state. He then went on to praise the cardinal, that incomparable minister who overshadowed all ministers in the past and would serve as an example for all ministers in the future, a man so powerful that no one could oppose him with impunity.

After this second part of his speech, he glared at poor Bonacieux and told him to consider the seriousness of his situation.

Bonacieux had already considered it; he cursed the day when he had married Monsieur de La Porte's goddaughter, and especially the day when she became the queen's linen maid.

The basis of Bonacieux's character was a mixture of deep selfishness and sordid avarice, seasoned with extreme cowardice. His love for his young wife, being only a secondary sentiment, was no match for these primary elements.

He thought over what he had just heard.

"Believe me, sir," he said timidly, "I fully appreciate the power and wisdom of His Eminence the cardinal, the great man by whom we have the honor of being ruled."

"Really?" the magistrate asked skeptically. "If that were true, why would you be in the Bastille?"

"I wish I could tell you why I'm here, sir, but I can't because I don't know. I'm sure of one thing, though: it's not because I ever did anything displeasing to His Eminence, not knowingly, at least."

"But you must have committed a crime, since you're accused of high treason."

"High treason!" Bonacieux cried out in terror. "How can a poor draper who detests the Huguenots and the Spanish be accused of high treason? Think about it, sir: it's completely impossible."

"Do you have a wife, Monsieur Bonacieux?" asked the magistrate, looking at him with his little eyes as if he had the ability to see into the depths of his soul.

"Yes, sir," replied the draper, trembling. He sensed that this was where things were going to become complicated. "Or at least I had one."

"You *had* one? What have you done with her, if you no longer have her?"

"She was abducted, sir."

"Abducted? Ah."

Hearing this "Ah," Bonacieux felt that things were going to be even more complicated than he thought.

"And do you know who abducted her?" asked the magistrate.

"I think so."

"Who is it?"

"I can't say for sure, sir, I want to make that clear. I only have a suspicion."

"Whom do you suspect? Answer frankly."

Bonacieux was in a quandary. Should he deny everything or tell everything? If he denied everything, the magistrate might think he knew so much that he could not afford to admit anything; if he told everything, he would be showing his willingness to cooperate. He therefore decided to tell everything.

"I suspect," he said, "a tall, dark man who seems to be a great lord. I think he followed my wife and me several times when I took her home from the Louvre."

The magistrate seemed to feel a certain anxiety.

"What's his name?" he asked.

"I have no idea what his name is, but if I ever see him again, I'll recognize him instantly, I can guarantee you that, even if he's with a thousand other people."

The magistrate frowned.

"You say you'd recognize him among a thousand other people?"

"Well, I . . . I . . . ." Bonacieux stammered, realizing that he had blundered.

"You told me that you'd recognize him. Very well, that's enough for today. Before we go any further, I must notify someone that you know the man who abducted your wife."

"I didn't say I knew him!" Bonacieux protested, in despair. "I told you . . . ."

"Take the prisoner away," the magistrate ordered the two guards.

"Where do you want him taken?" asked the clerk.

"To a cell."

"Which one?"

"It doesn't matter. Any cell will do, as long as it has a good lock on the door," the magistrate replied with an indifference that horrified poor Bonacieux.

He groaned inwardly and thought, "I'm doomed! My wife

must have committed some terrible crime. They think I'm her accomplice and they're going to punish me too. She must have said she told me everything. Women are so weak! They're going to put me into a cell! 'Any cell will do,' because I'll only spend one night in it and tomorrow they'll take me to the gallows or the wheel! Oh, my God, my God, have mercy on me!"

He continued his lamentations aloud, but the guards paid no attention to them, being used to such expressions of despair. They led him away, each holding him by the arm. The magistrate quickly began writing a letter while his clerk waited.

Bonacieux did not sleep that night, not because his cell was too unpleasant, but because he was too apprehensive. He spent the whole night sitting on his stool, quivering at the slightest sound, and when the first rays of daylight slipped into his cell, it seemed to him that the dawn had taken on a funereal tint.

Suddenly he heard his door being unlocked and started violently. He thought they were coming to take him to the gallows. Instead, he was taken back to the interrogation room. He was so relieved that he nearly embraced the magistrate and his clerk.

"There have been some new developments in your case since last night, my good man," said the magistrate. "I advise you to tell the whole truth: that's your only chance to save yourself from the cardinal's anger."

"I'm willing to tell you anything, anything at all!" said Bonacieux. "Anything I know, that is. Just question me."

"First, where's your wife?"

"I've already told you she was abducted."

"Yes, but at five o'clock yesterday afternoon she escaped—thanks to you."

"She escaped? I should have known she couldn't be trusted! But I had nothing to do with it, sir, please believe me!"

"Then why did you go to see your neighbor Monsieur d'Artagnan, and have a long conversation with him?"

"Yes, sir, it's true: I went to see Monsieur d'Artagnan, I admit it. I shouldn't have done it."

"Why did you visit him?"

"I asked him to help me find my wife. I thought I had a right to bring her back home; now I see I was mistaken. Please forgive me."

"What did Monsieur d'Artagnan say?"

"He promised to help me. But I soon realized he'd betrayed me."

"Stop lying to me! Monsieur d'Artagnan made an agreement with you and carried it out: he drove away the policemen who came to arrest your wife, then he hid her somewhere."

"Are you telling me that he abducted her too?"

"Luckily Monsieur d'Artagnan is now in our hands," the magistrate went on. "You're going to be confronted with him."

"Good! I'll be glad to see a familiar face."

"Bring in Monsieur d'Artagnan," the magistrate told the two guards.

They brought in Athos.

"Monsieur d'Artagnan," the magistrate said to him, "describe what took place between you and Monsieur Bonacieux."

"But that's not Monsieur d'Artagnan!" exclaimed Bonacieux.

"What! This isn't Monsieur d'Artagnan?"

"No."

"Then who is he?"

"I can't tell you. I don't know him."

"You don't know him?"

"No."

"You've never seen him before?"

"I've seen him, but I don't know his name."

"What is your name?" asked the magistrate.

"Athos," replied the musketeer.

"That's not a man's name, it's the name of a mountain!" cried the magistrate, who was beginning to lose his head.

"It's my name," Athos said calmly.

"But you said your name was d'Artagnan!"

"No, I didn't."

"Yes, you did!"

"Here's what happened. The guards said to me, 'Monsieur d'Artagnan?' and I answered, 'You think so?' They told me they were sure of it, and I let them have it their way because I didn't want to irritate them. Besides, I couldn't be sure I wasn't mistaken."

"Sir, you're insulting the majesty of the law!"

"Not at all," Athos assured him imperturbably.

"You're Monsieur d'Artagnan."

"You think so too?"

"He's *not* Monsieur d'Artagnan," Bonacieux said to the magistrate. "I'm absolutely certain of it. Monsieur d'Artagnan is my tenant, even though he doesn't pay his rent, so you can be sure I know what he looks like. He's a young man, no more than nineteen or twenty, and this gentleman is at least thirty. Monsieur d'Artagnan is in Monsieur des Essarts's guards, and this gentleman is in Monsieur de Tréville's musketeers: look at his uniform, sir, look at his uniform!"

"My God, it's true!" murmured the magistrate.

Just then the door was thrown open and one of the gatekeepers of the Bastille brought in a messenger who gave the magistrate a letter.

"May the devil take that woman!" the magistrate exclaimed when he had read the letter.

"What woman?" asked Bonacieux. "I hope you're not talking about my wife."

"I *am* talking about your wife. Now your case is more serious than ever."

"I can't imagine why!" said Bonacieux, exasperated. "Would you mind telling me how my case can be made worse by what my wife does while I'm in prison?"

"She's following a devilish plan that she worked out with you."

"You're completely mistaken, sir, I swear! I know nothing about what my wife has done, I'm not involved in it in any way, and if she's misbehaved, I disown her and curse her!"

"If you don't need me any longer," Athos said to the magistrate, "send me somewhere else, because your Monsieur Bonacieux is an intolerable bore."

"Take the prisoners back to their cells," ordered the magistrate, pointing to Athos and Bonacieux in a single gesture, "and have them guarded more strictly than ever."

"If it's Monsieur d'Artagnan you need," Athos said with his usual calm, "I don't see how I can replace him."

"Do as I say!" the magistrate shouted to the guards. "And keep all this in absolute secrecy! You understand?"

When the guards took them away, Athos shrugged and Bonacieux let out a heartrending wail.

Bonacieux returned to the cell where he had spent the night, and he spent the rest of the day weeping, for he was a draper and not a man of the sword, as he himself had said.

At about nine o'clock that evening, just as he was deciding to go to bed, he heard footsteps in the hall, coming toward his cell. The door opened and guards appeared.

"Come with me," said an officer who had followed the guards into the cell.

"At this time of night?" cried Bonacieux. "Where are you taking me?"

"To where we've been ordered to take you."

"That's no answer!"

"It's all I can tell you."

"Oh, my God, I'm lost!" murmured Bonacieux.

He passively followed the guards, looking as if he did not know what he was doing.

He walked along the hall, crossed a courtyard, went through another part of the building, and finally, at the gate of the entrance courtyard, he saw a carriage surrounded by four guards on horseback. He was told to get into it. The officer got in beside him, and the door was closed and locked; he was now in a prison on wheels.

The carriage started off, as slowly as a hearse. Bonacieux looked through the barred window of the locked door, and being a true Parisian, he recognized each street from its stone posts, shop signs, and streetlamps. When they reached Saint-Paul, the place where Bastille prisoners were executed, he crossed himself twice and nearly fainted. He had thought the carriage was going to stop there, but it continued on its way.

Farther on, he was seized with even greater terror when they passed the Saint-Jean cemetery, where state criminals were buried. He was a little reassured when he remembered that they were usually beheaded before being buried, and that his head was still on his shoulders. But when the carriage moved toward La Grève, passed the pointed rooftops of the Hôtel de Ville, and entered the arcade, he thought his end had really come. He asked the officer to hear his last confession, and when this request was denied, he protested with such loud, piteous cries that the officer threatened to gag him if he went on deafening him like that.

This threat calmed him a little: there would be no point in gagging him if he was going to be executed at La Grève, because they were nearly there. The carriage crossed the sinister square without stopping. Now all he had to fear was the Croix-du-Trahoir. But that was precisely where the carriage seemed to be heading.

This time there could be no doubt: the Croix-du-Trahoir was where criminals of inferior rank were executed. Bonacieux had been deluded in thinking he was worthy of Saint-Paul or La Grève: it was at the Croix-de-Trahoir that he was going to end his journey and his life! He could not yet see the ominous cross, but he felt himself approaching it.

When they had come to within twenty paces of it, he heard the sounds of a crowd and the carriage stopped. This was more than he could bear, after all the other painful shocks he had suffered; he uttered a feeble moan, which might have been taken for the last sigh of a dying man, and fainted.

14

The Dark Stranger

The crowd had not gathered to wait for a man who was going to be hanged, but to look at one who had already been hanged.

After being stopped a few moments, the carriage moved through the crowd, went along the Rue Saint-Honoré, turned into the Rue des Bons-Enfants, and drew up in front of a low door.

The door opened and two guards came out. The officer pulled Bonacieux from the carriage, and the guards caught him, seeing that he was about to fall. Supporting him on either side, they led him through a passage, up a flight of stairs, and into an anteroom.

He had walked mechanically, as if he were in a dream, seeing things through a kind of fog, hearing sounds without understanding them; if during that time he had been told that he was about to be executed, he would have done nothing to defend himself and would not have opened his mouth to beg for mercy.

He remained on the bench where the guards had left him, with his back leaning against the wall and his arms hanging limply.

Then, since he saw nothing to show he was in danger, since the bench was comfortably padded, since the wall was covered with fine Cordova leather, and since big red damask curtains, held by gold cords, floated in front of the window, he slowly came to realize that his fear was exaggerated and began nodding his head and turning it from side to side.

Having made these movements without arousing opposition from anyone, he regained a little courage. He ventured to draw one foot toward the bench, then the other; finally, supporting himself on the bench with both hands, he stood up.

Just then an officer with a pleasing appearance opened a door curtain, went on talking with someone in the next room for a moment, and turned to the prisoner.

"Is your name Bonacieux?" he asked.

"Yes, sir, at your service," the draper answered weakly, feeling more dead than alive.

"Go in," said the officer.

He stepped aside for Bonacieux, who did as he was told and entered the room where he was evidently expected.

It was a large study whose walls were adorned with offensive and defensive weapons. The air was stuffy: there was a fire in the fireplace, even though September had not yet ended. In the middle of the room was a square table littered with books and papers over which a big map of the town of La Rochelle had been spread.

Standing in front of the fireplace was a man of average height, with a proud expression, piercing eyes, a broad forehead, and a long, thin face made still longer by a pointed beard surmounted by a mustache. Although he was only thirty-six or thirty-seven, his hair, mustache, and beard were turning gray. Even without a sword, he gave the impression of being a soldier, and the thin layer of dust on his buff boots showed that he had been on horseback during the day.

This man was Armand-Jean du Plessis, Cardinal Richelieu, not as he is usually depicted—bent like an old man, suffering like a martyr, with a broken body and a feeble voice, buried in a big armchair as though in an anticipated grave, living only through the strength of his genius, carrying on his struggle against Europe only by the unceasing effort of his mind—but as he really was at that time: a shrewd and gallant gentleman, already physically weak, but sustained by that mental power that made him one of the most extraordinary men who ever lived. After supporting the duke de Nevers in his Duchy of Mantua, and after taking Nîmes, Castres, and Uzès, he was now preparing to drive the English from the Ile de Ré and lay siege to La Rochelle.

At first sight there was nothing about him to indicate that he was a cardinal, so that those who did not know him had no way of guessing who he was when they saw him.

Bonacieux stood in the doorway while the cardinal examined him as if he were trying to penetrate the depths of his past.

"This is Bonacieux?" he asked after a moment of silence.

"Yes, Monseigneur," replied the officer.

"Very well, give me those papers and leave us."

The officer took the papers from the table, handed them to the cardinal, bowed low, and left.

Bonacieux recognized those papers as the records of his interrogations at the Bastille. Now and then the cardinal looked up from them and plunged his eyes into the poor draper like two daggers.

After ten minutes of reading and ten seconds of scrutinizing Bonacieux, the cardinal had made up his mind. "That's not the face of a conspirator," he thought.

"You're accused of high treason," he said slowly.

"That's what they told me, Monseigneur," said Bonacieux, giving his unknown interrogator the title he had heard the officer give him, "but I swear that I knew nothing about it!"

The cardinal held back a smile.

"You've conspired with your wife, Madame de Chevreuse, and the duke of Buckingham."

"I *have* heard my wife mention those names, Monseigneur."

"On what occasion?"

"She said Cardinal Richelieu had lured the duke of Buckingham to Paris to trap him and the queen with him."

"She said that?" exclaimed the cardinal.

"Yes, Monseigneur, but I told her she was wrong to say such things, because His Eminence was incapable of . . ."

"Quiet, you fool."

"That's what my wife told me, Monseigneur."

"Do you know who abducted her?"

"No, Monseigneur."

"But you have suspicions, haven't you?"

"I had some, Monseigneur, but they seemed to displease the magistrate at the Bastille, so I don't have them any more."

"Did you know your wife had escaped?"

"I found it out after I was in prison, Monseigneur. The magistrate was kind enough to tell me—he's a very gracious man."

Again the cardinal held back a smile.

"Then you don't know what's happened to your wife since her escape?"

"Absolutely not, Monseigneur; but she must have gone back to the Louvre."

"At one o'clock in the morning she still hadn't come back."

"My God! What's become of her?"

"We'll find out, don't worry. Nothing remains hidden from the cardinal. He knows everything."

"In that case, Monseigneur, do you think he'd be willing to tell me what's become of my wife?"

"Perhaps. But first you must tell me everything you know about her relations with Madame de Chevreuse."

"I don't know anything about them, Monseigneur. I've never seen Madame de Chevreuse."

"When you went to meet your wife at the Louvre, did she always go straight home with you?"

"Almost never. She usually had business with cloth merchants, and I took her to see them."

"How many cloth merchants were there?"

"Two, Monseigneur."

"Where do they live?"

"One on the Rue de Vaugirard, the other on the Rue de La Harpe."

"Did you go into their houses with her?"

"Never, Monseigneur. I waited for her at the door."

"What reason did she give you for going in alone?"

"None. She told me to wait, and I waited."

"You're an accommodating husband, my dear Monsieur Bonacieux!" said the cardinal.

And the draper thought, "He called me his dear Monsieur Bonacieux! Things are going well!"

"Would you recognize those doors?" asked the cardinal.

"Yes."

"Do you know thé numbers of the houses?"

"Yes."

"What are they?"

"Number twenty-five on the Rue de Vaugirard, number seventy-five on the Rue de La Harpe."

"Very good."

The cardinal rang a silver bell and the officer came in.

"Go and find Rochefort," he said so softly that Bonacieux could not hear him, "and if he's come back, bring him to me immediately."

"The count is here, Your Eminence," replied the officer. "He's asked to speak with you about an urgent matter."

This time Bonacieux had heard. " 'Your Eminence!' " he thought, knowing this was the title usually given to the cardinal.

"Then bring him in!" Richelieu said sharply.

The officer hurried out of the room, obeying the cardinal with the alacrity shown by all those who served him.

Bonacieux was still overwhelmed by what he had heard. " 'Your Eminence!' " he repeated to himself.

Five seconds after the officer left, the door opened and another man came in.

"That's him!" cried Bonacieux.

"What do you mean?" asked the cardinal.

"That's the man who abducted my wife!"

The cardinal rang his bell again. The officer reappeared.

"Take this man back to his guards and have him wait till I call for him again."

"No, Monseigneur!" Bonacieux pleaded. "It's not him! I was mistaken! It was another man. This gentleman doesn't look anything like him. He's an honorable gentleman, I'm sure he would never do anything so . . ."

"Take this idiot away!" said the cardinal.

The officer seized Bonacieux, pulled him into the anteroom, and turned him over to the guards.

After impatiently watching Bonacieux till the door had closed behind him, the newcomer stepped closer to the cardinal and said, "They've seen each other."

"Who?" asked His Eminence.

"She and he."

"The queen and the duke?"

"Yes."

"Where?"

"In the Louvre."

"Are you sure?"

"Absolutely sure."

"Who told you?"

"Madame de Lannoy. As you know, Your Eminence, she's completely devoted to you."

"Why didn't she report it sooner?"

"Either by chance or because she suspected something, the queen had Madame de Surgis sleep in her room, and kept her all day."

"Well, we've had a defeat; now let's try to make up for it."

"Count on me, Monseigneur. I'll do everything I can to help you."

"How did it happen?"

"At half-past midnight, the queen was with her ladies-in-waiting . . ."

"Where?"

"In her bedroom."

"Go on."

"Someone brought her a handkerchief from her linen maid."

"And then?"

"The queen showed great emotion, and her face turned pale in spite of her rouge."

"Go on, go on!"

"She stood up and her voice was unsteady when she spoke. 'Wait for me, ladies,' she said. 'I'll be back in ten minutes.' Then she opened the door of the alcove and left."

"Why didn't Madame de Lannoy come and tell you immediately?"

"Nothing was certain yet. Besides, the queen had said, 'Wait for me, ladies,' and Madame de Lannoy didn't dare to disobey."

"How long was the queen gone?"

"Three-quarters of an hour."

"Did any of her ladies-in-waiting go with her?"

"Only Doña Estefania."

"So the queen came back in three-quarters of an hour?"

"Yes, but only to get a little monogrammed rosewood box. Then she left again."

"And when she came back later, did she bring the box with her?"

"No."

"Did Madame de Lannoy know what was in the box?"

"Yes: the diamond tags that His Majesty gave the queen."

"And you say she came back without that box?"

"Yes."

"Does Madame de Lannoy believe she gave it to Buckingham?"

"She's sure of it."

"Why?"

"During the day, in her capacity as mistress of the robes, Madame de Lannoy looked for the box, showed concern at not finding it, and finally asked the queen about it."

"What did the queen say?"

"She blushed and said she had broken one of the tags the day before and had sent it to her jeweler to be repaired."

"You'll have to talk with the jeweler and find out if that's true or not."

"I've already gone to see him."

"What did he say?"

"No diamond tag has been sent to him."

"Good, Rochefort, we haven't lost yet . . . And perhaps this is all for the best!"

"I'm sure that with your intelligence, you'll . . ."

"I'll find a way to undo my agent's mistakes."

"That's just what I was going to say, Your Eminence, if you'd let me finish my sentence."

"Now, do you know where Madame de Chevreuse and the duke of Buckingham have been hiding?"

"No, Monseigneur. My men haven't been able to give me any definite information on that."

"I already have my own information."

"Really, Monseigneur?"

"Yes, or at least I think so. One of them must have been hiding at twenty-five Rue de Vaugirard, and the other at seventy-five Rue de La Harpe."

"Shall I have them arrested there?"

"Too late; they're probably gone by now."

"Even so, I could try."

"Take ten men from my guards and search both houses."

"I'll go now, Your Eminence."

And Rochefort left.

The cardinal thought for a few moments, then rang his bell again.

The same officer reappeared.

"Bring in the prisoner."

Bonacieux came back into the room. At a signal from the cardinal, the officer withdrew.

"You've lied to me," the cardinal said sternly.

"Oh, no!" cried Bonacieux. "I would never lie to you, Your Eminence!"

"When your wife went to the Rue de Vaugirard and the Rue de La Harpe, she wasn't going to see cloth merchants."

"What was she doing, then, for heaven's sake?"

"She was going to see Madame de Chevreuse and the duke of Buckingham."

"Yes, Your Eminence," said Bonacieux, summoning up his memories, "you're right. Several times I told my wife it was odd that cloth merchants lived in houses like that, with no signs outside, and she only laughed at me. Ah, Monseigneur," he went on, throwing himself at His Eminence's feet, "it's easy to see that you really are the cardinal, the great cardinal, the man of genius everyone reveres!"

Although his triumph over such a mediocre man as Bonacieux could scarcely be counted as a great victory, the cardinal savored it for a moment; then, as if a new thought had just occurred to him, he smiled, held out his hand to the draper, and said, "Stand up, my friend. You're a good man."

"The cardinal touched my hand!" Bonacieux said ecstatically. "I touched the great man's hand! He called me his friend!"

"Yes, my friend," the cardinal said in the benevolent tone he sometimes used, which deceived only those who did not know him, "and since you've been unjustly suspected, you're entitled to an indemnity. There are three hundred pistoles in this bag: take it and forgive me."

"Forgive you, Monseigneur?" said Bonacieux, hesitating to take the bag because he was afraid the supposed gift might be only a joke. "You were free to have me arrested, and you're now free to have me tortured or hanged, because your authority is unquestionable—and yet you ask me to forgive you? Surely you don't mean it, Monseigneur!"

"I see you're a magnanimous man, my dear Monsieur Bonacieux, and I appreciate it. Am I right in assuming that you'll take this bag and leave without being too dissatisfied?"

"Dissatisfied? I'm overjoyed, Monseigneur!"

"Then good-bye for now; I hope we'll see each other again."

"Whenever you like, Monseigneur. I'm at your orders."

"It will be often, because I've greatly enjoyed our conversation."

"Oh! Monseigneur!"

"Good-bye, Monsieur Bonacieux, good-bye."

The cardinal made a gesture. Bonacieux responded by bowing low and backing out of the room. The cardinal heard him shouting enthusiastically in the anteroom, "Long live Monseigneur! Long live His Eminence! Long live the great cardinal!"

Richelieu smiled at this exuberant expression of Bonacieux's sentiments, and when the shouts had died away, he thought, "There's a man who's now ready to die for me."

He began attentively examining the map of La Rochelle that, as we have said, was spread out on his desk. With a pencil he drew a line representing the dike that was to close off the harbor of the besieged town eighteen months later.

In the midst of his strategic meditations, the door opened and Rochefort came back into the room.

"Well?" asked the cardinal, standing up with a quickness that showed the importance he attached to the mission he had given the count.

"Your Eminence, two people stayed in those two houses: a woman twenty-six to twenty-eight years old, and a man of thirty-five to forty. She stayed four days, he stayed five. But she left last night and he left this morning."

"It was they!" said the cardinal. He glanced at the clock. "It's too late to pursue them now: Madame de Chevreuse is at Tours and the duke is at Boulogne. We'll have to reach them in London."

"What are your orders, Your Eminence?"

"Don't breathe a word about what's happened. I want the queen to feel perfectly safe, without even suspecting that we know her secret; let her think we're on the trail of some conspiracy or other. Send Chancellor Séguier to me."

"What have you done with that man, Your Eminence?"

"What man?"

"That Bonacieux."

"I've done the most that could be done with him: from now on, he'll spy on his wife."

Count de Rochefort acknowledged his master's superiority with a deep bow and withdrew.

The cardinal sat down again, wrote a letter, sealed it with his personal seal, and rang his bell. The officer came in for the fourth time.

"Send in Vitray," said the cardinal, "and tell him to get ready for a journey."

A short time later, the man he had asked for was standing before him, wearing boots and spurs.

"Vitray, I want you to go to London as fast as you can. Don't stop anywhere along the way. Deliver this letter to Milady. Here's a voucher for two hundred pistoles; take it to my treasurer and he'll give you the money. You'll receive another two hundred if you deliver the letter and come back within six days."

The messenger bowed in silence, took the letter and the voucher, and left.

Here is what was in the letter:

Milady,

Go to the next ball attended by the duke of Buckingham. He will be wearing twelve diamond tags on his doublet. Move close to him and cut off two of them. Notify me as soon as they are in your possession.

15

Magistrates and Soldiers

The next day, since Athos had not returned, d'Artagnan and Porthos told Monsieur de Tréville that he had been arrested.

As for Aramis, he had requested a five-day leave and gone to Rouen, for a family matter, he said.

Monsieur de Tréville was like a father to his soldiers. Each of them, no matter how obscure he might be, knew that as long as he wore a musketeer's uniform, he could rely on his captain for help and support as confidently as he would rely on his own brother.

Tréville therefore went to the office of the magistrate for criminal affairs as soon as he learned of Athos's arrest. The officer in command of the Croix-Rouge post was summoned, and inquiries revealed that Athos was being provisionally held in the For-l'Evêque prison.

Like Bonacieux, Athos had been interrogated in the Bastille. We have already seen his meeting with Bonacieux, during which he declared that his name was Athos and not d'Artagnan; till then he had said nothing for fear that d'Artagnan would be arrested before he had the time he needed.

He also declared that he knew neither Monsieur nor Madame Bonacieux, that he had never spoken to either of them, that before going to visit his friend Monsieur d'Artagnan at about ten o'clock he had spent the earlier part of the evening in Monsieur de Tréville's house, and that a score of witnesses could support what he said. He named several distinguished gentlemen, including Monsieur de La Trémouille.

The second magistrate was as taken aback as the first one by Athos's firm, simple declaration. He had hoped for the kind of revenge that magistrates liked to take against soldiers, but the names of Monsieur de Tréville and Monsieur de La Trémouille were more than enough to give him pause.

Athos was also sent to be questioned by the cardinal, but unfortunately His Eminence was absent; he had gone to the Louvre to see the king.

Monsieur de Tréville went to the Louvre at that same time, after having failed to find Athos at the For-l'Evêque prison. As captain of the King's Musketeers, he was entitled to see His Majesty at any time.

The king's animosity against the queen was deftly nurtured by the cardinal, who was much warier of women than of men in matters of intrigue. One of the main reasons for His Majesty's animosity was the queen's friendship with Madame de Chevreuse. Those two women worried him more than the wars with Spain, the conflicts with England, and the financial difficulties of the kingdom. He was convinced that Madame de Chevreuse served the queen not only in her political intrigues but—and this tormented him still more—in her love affairs as well.

Madame de Chevreuse had been exiled to Tours. When the cardinal told the king that she had returned to Paris and had eluded the police during the five days she had spent there, His Majesty flew into a violent rage. Capricious and unfaithful, he wanted to be called Louis the Just and Louis the Chaste. Posterity has found it hard to understand his character, since historians only report his acts, without giving the reasoning behind them.

The cardinal went on to say that while Madame de Chevreuse was in Paris, she had been in touch with the queen through a mysterious network of agents; that he, the cardinal, had learned the identity of the woman who served as the intermediary between the queen and Madame de Chevreuse, and that through her he had expected to get to the bottom of the intrigue; but that just as four policemen were about to arrest the woman so that the whole affair could be examined impartially and presented to the king, a musketeer had assaulted them and enabled her to escape.

As soon as he had heard all this, Louis XIII took a step in the direction of the queen's apartments, his face pale with that silent indignation that sometimes drove him to acts of cold cruelty. And yet the cardinal had not said a word about the duke of Buckingham.

This was when Monsieur de Tréville came in, impeccably dressed and showing no sign of emotion. Having guessed what was happening from the cardinal's presence and the king's expression, he felt as strong as Samson facing the Philistines.

Louis XIII already had his hand on the doorknob when he heard Monsieur de Tréville enter. He turned around.

"You've come at the right time!" said the king, who was unable to hide his feelings once they had been aroused beyond a certain point. "I've just heard some outrageous things about your musketeers!"

"And I, Your Majesty," Tréville replied calmly, "have some outrageous things to tell you about your magistrates and policemen."

"What's this you're saying?" the king asked haughtily.

"I have the honor to inform you, Sire," Tréville continued with the same calm, "that a group of policemen—worthy men, but evidently hostile to soldiers—entered a house, arrested one of my musketeers, or rather one of yours, led him through the streets, and imprisoned him at For-l'Evêque, acting on an order that they refused to show me. Furthermore, the musketeer they treated in this way is a man of irreproachable conduct with an almost illustrious reputation, a man known favorably to you, Sire: Monsieur Athos."

"Athos . . ." said the king. "Yes, I know that name."

"Let me remind you, Sire," said Tréville, "that Monsieur Athos is the musketeer who had the misfortune of severely wounding Monsieur Cahusac in that regrettable fight." He turned to the cardinal. "Monsieur de Cahusac has fully recovered, hasn't he, Monseigneur?"

"Yes, thank you," answered the cardinal, his lips tight with anger.

Tréville resumed his story: "Monsieur Athos had gone to visit one of his friends, a young man from Béarn who's a cadet in Monsieur des Essarts's company of guards. When he learned that his friend was absent, he sat down to read a book while he waited for him. A short time later, a horde of policemen laid siege to the house, broke open several doors . . ."

The cardinal made a sign to the king to indicate that this was part of the affair he had told him about.

"We know all that," the king interrupted, "because it was done in our service."

"In that case, Sire," said Tréville, "it was in your service that an innocent musketeer was arrested, placed between two guards like a criminal, and led through the streets while an insolent mob jeered at him; it was in your service that this was done to a gallant man who has shed his blood a dozen times for you, and is ready to shed it again."

"Is that really how things happened?" asked the king, shaken.

"Monsieur de Tréville has neglected to mention," the cardinal said placidly, "that an hour earlier his innocent, gallant musketeer had attacked and wounded four examining magistrates whom I had ordered to investigate, a matter of the highest importance.''

''I defy you to prove it, Your Eminence,'' Tréville retorted with his Gascon impetuosity and military bluntness, ''because Monsieur Athos—who, let me say confidentially, is a man of very high birth—did me the honor of having dinner with me that evening, and an hour before his arrest he was in my drawing room, talking with Monsieur de La Trémouille and Monsieur de Châlus, who were also my guests.''

The king looked at the cardinal.

''An official report is authoritative,'' said the cardinal, answering His Majesty's silent question, ''and the injured parties have drawn up this one, which I have the honor of presenting to you, Sire.''

''Is a police report worth as much as a soldier's word of honor?'' Tréville asked disdainfully.

''Come, come, Tréville,'' said the king, ''that will do.''

''If His Eminence suspects one of my musketeers of having done something unlawful,'' said Tréville, ''I'll request an inquiry myself, because I know I can rely on His Eminence's sense of justice.''

''Isn't it true,'' the cardinal asked imperturbably, ''that a young man from Béarn, a friend of the musketeer in question, lives in the house where the arrest took place?''

''Are you referring to Monsieur d'Artagnan, Your Eminence?''

''I'm referring to a young man to whom you've given your personal support, Monsieur de Tréville.''

''Yes, Your Eminence, that's Monsieur d'Artagnan.''

''Don't you suspect him of having given bad advice . . .''

''To Monsieur Athos, a man nearly twice his age? No, Monseigneur. And besides, Monsieur d'Artagnan was at my house that evening.''

''Oh? It seems that everyone was at your house that evening.''

''Do you doubt my word, Your Eminence?'' asked Tréville, his face flushing with anger.

''Certainly not!'' said the cardinal. ''I'd only like to know when he was there.''

''I can tell you that precisely, because when he came in I looked at the clock and saw that it was half-past nine, though I would have thought it was later.''

''And when did he leave your house?''

''At half-past ten, an hour after . . . the event.''

''But it's still true that Athos was arrested in that house on the

Rue des Fossoyeurs,'' said the cardinal, who did not question Tréville's honesty for one moment and felt his victory slipping away from him.

"Is it unlawful for friends to see each other, for a musketeer in my company to visit a guard in Monsieur des Essarts's company?"

"Yes, when the house in which he visits his friend is under suspicion."

"That house *is* under suspicion, Tréville," said the king. "Perhaps you didn't know that."

"No, I didn't know it, Sire. But although most of the house may be under suspicion, that can't be true of the part Monsieur d'Artagnan lives in, because I can assure you, Sire, from what he's said to me, that he's completely devoted to Your Majesty and has great admiration for His Eminence."

"Wasn't it d'Artagnan who wounded Jussac in that unfortunate encounter near the Carmes-Deschaux monastery?" asked the king, looking at the cardinal, who could not conceal his rancor.

"Yes, Your Majesty, and the next day he wounded Bernajoux. You have a good memory, Sire."

"We've discussed the matter long enough," said the king. "What conclusion shall we draw?"

"That concerns you more than me, Your Majesty," said the cardinal, "but for my part I'm convinced that the musketeer is guilty."

"And I'm convinced he's innocent," said Tréville. "But His Majesty has judges, and they'll decide."

"Yes, you're quite right," said the king. "We'll present the case to the judges and let them decide."

"But it's still sad," said Tréville, "that in these unfortunate times a blameless life and an unquestionably virtuous character don't spare a man the infamy of persecution. Believe me, Sire, the army will be indignant to learn that an honorable soldier has been subjected to harsh treatment because of a political matter."

This was a rash thing to say, but Tréville had said it with the intention of setting off an explosion that would ignite a fire, which would in turn produce light.

"A political matter!" exclaimed the king. "What do you know about political matters, Tréville? Don't meddle in things that aren't your concern, and don't complain to me about the way your musketeers are treated. You talk as if a musketeer couldn't be arrested without putting France in grave danger! All that agitation about one musketeer! Let me tell you something: I'll have ten of them arrested if I choose to, or a hundred, or the whole company! And if I do, I don't want to hear one word of complaint about it!''

"Since you regard the musketeers as suspect, Sire," said Tréville, "they're guilty. I'm ready to resign my command. His Eminence has made accusations against my soldiers, and I'm sure that sooner or later he'll also make accusations against me, so I may as well go to prison now, to share the fate of Monsieur Athos, who's already been arrested, and Monsieur d'Artagnan, who will probably be arrested before long.''

"Enough, enough!" said the king. "You Gascons never know when to stop!"

"Sire," Tréville said firmly, "either have my musketeer released from prison or order a trial for him.''

"He'll be tried," said the cardinal.

"Good. I'll ask His Majesty to let me plead his case.''

The king was afraid of an angry outburst between the two men.

"If His Eminence," he said, "didn't have personal reasons . . .''

The cardinal saw where the king was heading and went there before him.

"Excuse me, Sire," he interrupted, "but since you don't consider me an impartial judge, I withdraw from the case.''

"Will you swear to me, by the memory of my father," the king asked Tréville, "that Monsieur Athos was in your house at the time of the assault, and took no part in it?''

"Yes, I swear it by the memory of your glorious father, and by you, Sire, who are what I love and respect most in the world.''

"Please let me point out, Your Majesty," said the cardinal, "that if we release the prisoner now, we'll never know the truth.''

"Monsieur Athos will always be available to answer the magistrates whenever they choose to question him," said Tréville. "He won't desert, Your Eminence, I give you my personal assurance of it.''

"That's true, he won't desert," said the king. "He'll always be available to answer questions, as Monsieur de Tréville says. Besides," he added, lowering his voice and looking at the cardinal imploringly, "this is a chance to give them a false feeling of security. It will be a clever maneuver on our part.''

Louis XIII's cleverness made Richelieu smile.

"Then order the prisoner's release, Sire," he said. "You have the right of pardon."

"The right of pardon applies only to the guilty," said Tréville, who wanted to have the last word, "and my musketeer is innocent, so his release will be an act of justice, not of pardon."

"He's in the For-l'Evêque prison?" asked the king.

"Yes, Sire, and he's in solitary confinement in a cell, like a common criminal."

"I wish I knew what to do . . ." murmured the king.

"Order his release, Your Majesty, and that will be the end of it," said the cardinal. "Like you, I believe that Monsieur de Tréville's assurance is more than sufficient."

Tréville bowed respectfully. His joy was mingled with apprehension: he would have felt more confident if the cardinal had put up stubborn resistance, rather than suddenly giving in.

The king signed an order for Athos's release. Tréville took it, intending to deliver it without delay.

As he was leaving, the cardinal gave him a friendly smile and said to the king, "There are good relations between officers and men in your musketeers, Sire. It helps them to serve you better and it's a credit to them all."

Tréville continued on his way and thought, "He's got some underhanded scheme against me. No one can ever have the last word with a man like that. But I'd better hurry, because the king may change his mind, and putting a man back into prison after he's been released is harder than simply keeping him there."

He triumphantly entered the For-l'Evêque prison and freed Athos, who had still maintained his placid indifference.

Later, when he saw d'Artagnan again, he said to him, "You've had a narrow escape. Now you've paid for wounding Jussac. Maybe you won't have to pay for wounding Bernajoux, but I wouldn't count on it if I were you."

Tréville was right in mistrusting the cardinal and believing that there was more trouble still to come, for no sooner had he closed the door behind him than His Eminence said to the king, "Now that we're alone, Your Majesty, we can talk seriously. The duke of Buckingham came to Paris five days ago and left only this morning."

16

Chancellor Séguier Looks for the Bell that He Rang in His Youth

It would be impossible to describe the effect that these words had on Louis XIII. His face turned crimson, then deathly pale, and the cardinal saw that he had just regained all the ground he had lost.

"Buckingham in Paris!" he shouted. "And what was he doing here?"

"He must have been conspiring with our enemies, the Huguenots and the Spanish."

"No! He was conspiring against my honor with Madame de Chevreuse, Madame de Longueville, and the Condés!"

"Oh, Sire! What an idea! The queen is too virtuous for that, and she loves you too much."

"Women are weak. As for the queen's loving me, I have my own ideas on that subject."

"I still maintain, Your Majesty, that the duke of Buckingham came to Paris entirely for political reasons."

"And I'm sure he came for another reason. But if the queen is guilty, I'll make her regret it!"

"The mere idea of such a betrayal is repugnant to me, Your Majesty, but you've reminded me of something. I've questioned Madame de Lannoy several times, as you ordered me to do. Today she told me that last night the queen stayed up very late, that she wept this morning, and that she then spent several hours writing."

"She must have been writing to *him*! Cardinal, I want the queen's papers."

"But how can we get them, Sire? It seems to me that it wouldn't be proper for either of us to take them."

"Don't you remember how it was done with Marshal d'Ancre's wife?" the king said angrily. "Her house was searched, and then she herself was searched."

"Marshal d'Ancre's wife was nothing but a Florentine adventuress, Sire, whereas your exalted wife is Anne of Austria, queen of France."

"That only increases her guilt! The higher her position, the farther she's fallen! It's time I put an end to her love affairs and political scheming. She has a man named La Porte in her service . . ."

"Yes, Your Majesty, and I must confess that I think he's the key figure in all this."

"So you agree that the queen is deceiving me?" asked the king.

"I've said before, Sire, and I'll repeat it now, that the queen is conspiring against your power, but I've never said that she was conspiring against your honor."

"And I say that she's conspiring against both; I say she doesn't love me, that she loves another man, and that the man she loves is the infamous duke of Buckingham! Why didn't you have him arrested while he was in Paris?"

"The duke of Buckingham is King Charles the First's prime minister, Sire! Surely you couldn't have expected me to have him arrested! Think of the scandal it would have caused! And if your suspicions had proved to be justified—which I still doubt—the scandal would have been even worse."

"But since he came to Paris secretly and stayed in hiding, like a thief, you should have . . ."

Louis XIII stopped short, frightened at what he had been about to say. Richelieu leaned toward him expectantly.

"What should I have done?"

"Nothing, nothing . . ." said the king. "But you had him watched during the whole time he was in Paris, didn't you?"

"Yes, Sire."

"Where did he stay?"

"At seventy-five Rue de La Harpe."

"Where's that?"

"Near the Luxembourg."

"And you're sure that he and the queen didn't see each other?"

"I believe the queen's sense of duty is too strong to allow her to do such a thing, Sire."

"But they've corresponded: you told me she wrote for several hours today, and she could only have been writing to him. Cardinal, I must have that letter!"

"But—"

"I want it, at any cost!"

"Sire, allow me to point out that—"

"Why do you always oppose my wishes, Cardinal? Are you

betraying me too? Are you in league with the Spanish, the English, Madame de Chevreuse, and the queen?''

"Your Majesty," the cardinal replied with a sigh, "I never thought I'd hear you cast doubt on my loyalty.''

"I repeat, Cardinal: I want that letter.''

"There's only one way—''

"What is it?''

"To have Chancellor Séguier get the letter. That kind of thing is within the scope of his duties.''

"Send for him.''

"He must be at my house, Sire. I asked him to call on me, but I came here before he arrived, so I left word for him to wait.''

"Send for him immediately!''

"I will, Your Majesty, but—''

"But what?''

"The queen may refuse.''

"She may refuse to obey my orders?''

"Yes, if she's not sure they're from you.''

"Then I'll go and tell her myself, so that she won't have any doubt.''

"Your Majesty, I hope you'll remember that I've done everything I could to prevent a break between you and the queen.''

"Yes, Cardinal, I know you're very indulgent as far as the queen is concerned, perhaps too indulgent; we'll talk about that later.''

"Whenever it pleases you, Sire. But I'll always be happy and proud to sacrifice myself to bring about harmony between you and the queen of France.''

"Very well, Cardinal. Meanwhile, send for Chancellor Séguier. I'm going to see the queen.''

Louis XIII opened a door and began walking along the hall that led to the queen's apartments.

Her Majesty was with her ladies-in-waiting: Madame de Guitaut, Madame de Sablé, Madame de Montbazon, and Madame de Guéménée. In one corner of the room was Doña Estefania, her Spanish maid of honor, who had followed her from Madrid. Madame de Guéménée was reading aloud and everyone was listening to her attentively, except for the queen, who had asked her to read so that she could pursue her own thoughts while pretending to listen.

These thoughts, though gilded by an afterglow of love, were nevertheless sad. The queen was mistrusted by her husband, hated and persecuted by the cardinal, who could not forgive her for having rejected his amorous advances. She could not forget the example of the queen mother, who was tormented by his hatred all her life—although, if we are to believe contemporary memoirs, Marie de Médicis began by granting him the tender feelings that Anne of Austria had always refused him. The queen had lost most of her devoted supporters and close friends. It was as if she were under a curse that brought misfortune to everyone who came near her. Madame de Chevreuse and Madame de Vernet had been exiled, and La Porte had admitted to her that he expected to be arrested at any moment.

While she was absorbed in these somber reflections, the door opened and the king came in.

Madame de Guéménée instantly stopped reading. All the ladies stood up and silence fell over the room.

The king made no show of politeness; he went straight to the queen and said in a tense voice, "Madame, Chancellor Séguier will soon pay you a visit to tell you certain things. He'll be acting at my command."

The unhappy queen, who was constantly under threat of being divorced, exiled, or even brought to trial, turned pale beneath her rouge and could not help asking, "But why is the chancellor going to visit me, Sire? What will he tell me that you can't tell me yourself?"

The king turned away from her without answering, and almost at the same moment Monsieur de Guitaut, the captain of the guards, announced the arrival of the chancellor.

When the chancellor came in, the king had already left through another door.

A sickly smile was frozen on Chancellor Séguier's slightly flushed face. Since we will probably meet him again in the course of this story, the reader may as well become acquainted with him now.

This chancellor was an amusing man. It was Des Roches le Masle, canon of Notre-Dame and formerly the cardinal's servant, who recommended him to His Eminence as a man who could be trusted. The cardinal trusted him and was satisfied with his services.

Certain stories were told about him, including the following:

After a stormy youth he withdrew to a monastery to expiate, at least for a time, the sins of his adolescence. But when he entered that holy place, he did not close the door behind him quickly enough: the passions from which he was fleeing came in with him. He was constantly obsessed with them. He confided his torment to the superior, who advised him to ring the bell of the monastery each time he was tempted by the demon of the flesh, so that, hearing this sound, the monks would know that a brother was being assailed by temptation, and the whole community would begin to pray.

This advice seemed good to the future chancellor. He warded off the devil with the help of the monks' prayers. But the devil was not prepared to admit defeat and give up the foothold he had established; to the monks' efforts to exorcise him, he responded by redoubling his temptations, with the result that the bell rang loudly night and day, announcing the penitent's urgent desire for mortification of the flesh.

The monks no longer had a moment of rest. During the day, they were always going up and down the stairs leading to the chapel where they prayed; at night, between compline and matins, they had to get out of bed a score of times and prostrate themselves on the floor of their cells.

After three months, either because the devil gave up the struggle or the monks succumbed to exhaustion, no one knows which, the penitent returned to the outside world with the reputation of having suffered from the most terrible case of demonic possession that had ever been observed.

After leaving the monastery he entered the legal profession and eventually succeeded his uncle as presiding magistrate of the High Court. He became a supporter of the cardinal, which showed considerable sagacity; he was appointed chancellor, zealously served His Eminence in his hatred of the queen mother and his vengeance against Anne of Austria, prodded the judges in the Chalais affair, and encouraged the bloodthirsty efforts of Monsieur de Laffemas. And finally, enjoying the cardinal's full confidence, which he had earned so well, he was given the strange mission that had now brought him to the queen's apartments.

The queen was still standing when he came in, but as soon as she saw him she sat down again in her armchair and motioned her ladies to sit down on their cushions and stools.

"Why are you here?" she asked haughtily. "What do you want?"

"I've come in the name of the king, Your Majesty. With all the respect I have the honor of owing you, I'm under orders to search your papers."

"What! Search my papers? That's infamous!"

"Forgive me, Your Majesty, but I'm only an instrument of the king's will. Wasn't His Majesty just here to tell you to be prepared for my visit?''

''Make your search, then, since I'm apparently regarded as a criminal. Estafania, give him the keys to my tables and writing desks.''

The chancellor searched all the drawers for the sake of form, but he knew very well that he would have to look elsewhere for the important letter the queen had written that day.

When he had opened and closed a score of drawers, he had no choice but to overcome his reluctance and bring his mission to its conclusion by searching the queen herself.

He walked toward her and said hesitantly, with great embarrassment, ''Now I must complete my search.''

''What do you mean?'' she asked, not understanding, or rather refusing to understand.

''His Majesty is certain that you wrote a letter today and that it hasn't yet been sent. It's not in any of your drawers, but it has to be here somewhere . . .''

''Would you dare to touch your queen?'' she said, drawing herself up to her full height and looking at him with an almost threatening expression.

''I'm a faithful subject of the king, Your Majesty, and I obey his orders.''

''The cardinal's spies have served him well. It's true that I wrote a letter today and that it hasn't yet been sent. It's here.''

She put her lovely hand on her bodice.

''Then please give it to me, Your Majesty,'' said the chancellor.

''I'll give it to no one but the king.''

''If the king had wanted you to give it to him directly, Your Majesty, he would have asked you for it himself. He ordered me to ask you for it, and said that if you refused to give it to me . . .''

''Yes? What then?''

''In that case, my orders are to take it from you.''

''What are you saying?''

''I'm saying, Your Majesty, that the king has ordered me to take the letter from your person, if necessary.''

''This is horrible!'' cried the queen.

''I beg you to cooperate, Your Majesty.''

''Your conduct is intolerable!''

''The king commands and I obey, Your Majesty; forgive me.''

The queen's proud Spanish and Austrian blood rebelled at the insult.

"I won't permit it! No! I'd rather die!"

The chancellor bowed low, but it was obvious that he intended to let nothing prevent him from carrying out his orders. He stepped toward the queen, like a torturer approaching a prisoner in a dungeon. Tears of rage welled up in her eyes.

She was a very beautiful woman, as we have said, and the chancellor's mission was therefore a delicate one, but the king had become so jealous of Buckingham that he was no longer jealous of anyone else.

At that moment the chancellor must have looked around for the rope of the monastery bell; but, not finding it, he summoned up his courage and reached out his hand toward the place where the queen had admitted putting the letter.

She backed away from him, so pale that she seemed on the verge of death. She steadied herself against a table with one hand while with the other she took the letter from her bodice and gave it to the chancellor.

"Here's the letter," she said in a gasping voice. "Take it and relieve me of your odious presence."

The chancellor, who was understandably quivering with emotion, took the letter, bowed low once again, and left.

As soon as the door had closed behind him, the queen fell half-fainting into the arms of her ladies.

The chancellor brought the letter to the king without having read a single word of it. The king took it with a trembling hand, noticed that it bore no address, turned pale, slowly opened it, and then, seeing from the first words that it was written to the king of Spain, read it rapidly.

It was a whole plan of attack against the cardinal. The queen urged her brother and the emperor of Austria, who were being injured by Richelieu's persistent attempts to bring down the Austrian monarchy, to pretend that they were about to declare war on France, and to demand the cardinal's dismissal as the price of peace. But the letter did not contain one word about love.

The king, overjoyed, asked if the cardinal was still in the Louvre. He was told that His Eminence was awaiting His Majesty's orders in his study.

The king immediately went to him.

"You were right and I was wrong," he said. "The intrigue is

entirely political. This letter says nothing about love. It does, however, say a great deal about you."

The cardinal took the letter and read it with great attention; he then read it a second time.

"You can see how far my enemies are prepared to go, Sire," he said. "You're being threatened with two wars if you don't dismiss me. If I were in your place, I'd yield to that strong pressure. And the fact is that I'd be very happy to retire from public life."

"Surely you don't mean that, Cardinal!"

"Yes, I do, Your Majesty. My health is being destroyed by my constant work and the strain of all these fierce struggles. I doubt that I'll be able to bear the fatigue of the siege of La Rochelle; it will be better for you to replace me with Monsieur de Condé, Monsieur de Bassompierre, or some other capable soldier. I'm a churchman, yet I must constantly turn away from my vocation to concern myself with things for which I have no aptitude. Without me, Your Majesty, you'll have fewer difficulties in France, and you'll undoubtedly be more powerful in foreign affairs."

"I understand your feelings, Cardinal," said the king, "but rest assured that all the people mentioned in this letter will be punished as they deserve, along with the queen herself."

"Oh, no, Your Majesty! God forbid that the queen should ever suffer the slightest distress because of me! She's always regarded me as her enemy, although you can testify that I've always taken her side, even against you. If she'd betrayed your honor, I'd be the first to tell you to show her no mercy, but fortunately she hasn't done that; you've just had new proof of it."

"That's true, Cardinal. You were right, as always. But I still have good reason to be angry with the queen."

"And she has good reason to be angry with you, Sire. If she were to refuse to speak to you, I'd understand it. You've treated her so harshly . . ."

"That's how I'll always treat my enemies and yours, Cardinal, no matter how high their rank may be, or how dangerous it may be to treat them that way."

"The queen is my enemy, Sire, but not yours, far from it. She's a devoted, obedient, and irreproachable wife. Please be reconciled with her."

"Not unless she first comes to me and humbly asks me to forgive her!"

"No, Sire, you must set the example; you were the first to be in the wrong, since you suspected her unjustly."

"You expect me to make the first move? Never!"

"I beg you to do it, Your Majesty."

"How would I go about it, if I wanted to?"

"By doing something you know would please her."

"What do you have in mind?"

"Give a ball, Sire. You know how much the queen likes dancing. I promise you her rancor will vanish if you do that for her."

"Cardinal, you know I don't like social gatherings."

"The queen knows it too, so she'll be all the more grateful to you. Furthermore, it will give her a chance to wear the beautiful diamond tags you gave her for her name day. She hasn't yet worn them."

"We'll see, Cardinal, we'll see," said the king. In his joy at having found the queen guilty only of a crime that meant very little to him, and innocent of a sin that he feared greatly, he was quite willing to be reconciled with her. "But," he added, "I still maintain that you're too indulgent."

"Leave severity to your ministers, Sire," said the cardinal. "Indulgence is a royal virtue; use it this time, and you'll be pleased with the result."

Hearing the clock strike eleven, the cardinal bowed, asked the king's permission to withdraw, and again begged him to be reconciled with the queen.

After the seizure of her letter, the queen expected to be sternly reprimanded. She was therefore surprised the next day when the king came to her in a conciliatory mood. Her first impulse was to reject his overtures, for her womanly pride and queenly dignity had been so cruelly offended that she could not simply overlook what had happened. But finally, influenced by the advice of her ladies-in-waiting, she acted as if she were beginning to forget. When he saw that her attitude had softened, the king told her that he was going to give a ball.

A ball was such a rare thing for her that, as the cardinal had thought, when she heard the news the last trace of her resentment disappeared—if not from her heart, at least from her face. She asked when the ball would take place. The king answered that he would have to discuss it with the cardinal.

From then on, each day the king asked the cardinal when the

ball should be held, and each day the cardinal found some reason to postpone setting a date.

Ten days went by in this way.

A week after the scene we have described, the cardinal received a letter with a London postmark on it, containing only these few words:

> *I have them, but I do not have enough money to leave London. Send me five hundred pistoles, and I will be in Paris four or five days after I receive it.*

On the day when this letter arrived, the king asked the cardinal his usual question.

Counting on his fingers, Richelieu thought, "She says she'll be here four or five days after receiving the money. It will take four or five days for the money to reach her, and four or five days for her to come to Paris; let's say ten days. Allowing for contrary winds, unexpected delays, and a woman's weakness, let's say twelve days altogether."

"Well, Cardinal, have you decided?" asked the king.

"Yes, Sire," replied Richelieu. "Today is the twentieth of September; the municipal magistrates are giving a ball on the third of October. It's an excellent opportunity for you. You and the queen can go to that ball and it won't look as if you're making the first move toward a reconciliation with her. Incidentally, Sire," he added, "on the day before the ball, don't forget to tell Her Majesty that you want to see how the diamond tags look on her."

17

Monsieur and Madame Bonacieux at Home

This was the second time the cardinal had mentioned the diamond tags. The king was struck by his insistence and felt that some mystery lay behind it.

More than once the king had been humiliated to discover that the cardinal—who had an excellent network of secret agents, though it had not attained the efficiency of a modern police force—knew more about what was happening in the royal household than he himself did. He therefore decided to talk with the queen, learn some secret or other from her, and then report it to the cardinal; even if the cardinal already knew it, he would still have a higher opinion of the king.

The king went to the queen and, as usual, greeted her with new threats against the people who were close to her. She bowed her head without answering, hoping that the torrent of menacing words would soon stop. But that was not what he wanted; he wanted a heated discussion that would generate a flash of light, because he was convinced that the cardinal was engaged in some sort of machination and intended to give the king an unpleasant surprise, as he had done several times in the past.

Finally, by persisting in his accusations, he goaded the queen into speaking.

"You're not telling me everything that's on your mind, Sire," she said, irritated by his vague attacks. "What have I done? What crime have I committed? You can't be saying all those things because of a letter I wrote to my brother!"

Now it was the king who was under attack, and for a moment he did not know what to answer; then he decided to broach the subject of the diamond tags, even though the cardinal had told him not to mention it till the day before the ball.

"Madame," he said loftily, "there will soon be a ball at the city hall. To honor our good municipal magistrates, I want you to attend it in full ceremonial dress, wearing the diamond tags I gave you for your name day. Now you know what's on my mind."

This answer was a violent shock to the queen. She thought he knew everything, and that the wily cardinal had persuaded him to conceal his knowledge during the last seven or eight days. She turned very pale, supported herself on a console table with a hand that now seemed to be made of wax, and looked at the king with terror-stricken eyes, unable to say a word.

"Do you understand?" he asked, enjoying her agitation without knowing its cause.

"Yes, I . . . I understand," she stammered.

"You'll come to the ball?"

"Yes."

"With your diamond tags?"

"Yes."

Her pallor increased still more. He saw this and inwardly

gloated over it, with the cold cruelty that was one of the bad sides of his nature.

"Then it's agreed," he said. "That's all I had to tell you."

"When will the ball be held?"

Since she asked this question in an almost dying voice, he felt instinctively that he should not answer it.

"Soon," he said, "but I don't remember the exact date. I'll ask the cardinal."

"Then it was the cardinal who told you about the ball?"

"Yes," he replied, surprised. "But why do you ask?"

"And was it he who suggested that you tell me to wear my diamond tags?"

"Well, I suppose . . ."

"It was the cardinal!"

"Well, what of it? Does it make any difference whether the idea was his or mine? It's not a crime, is it?"

"No, Sire."

"And you'll come to the ball, won't you?"

"Yes, Sire."

"Good, I'll expect you to be there," he said, preparing to withdraw.

The queen curtsied, not because of etiquette but because her knees were about to give way beneath her.

The king left, delighted.

"I'm lost," the queen murmured to herself, "because the cardinal knows everything. He made the king come to me and tell me to wear the diamond tags. The king doesn't know anything yet, but soon he'll know everything. I'm lost! Oh, my God, my God!"

She knelt on a cushion and prayed, with her head between her quivering arms.

Her situation was desperate. Buckingham had gone back to London, Madame de Chevreuse was at Tours. More closely watched than ever, the queen sensed that one of her ladies was betraying her, though she did not know which one it was. La Porte could not leave the Louvre. There was no one she could count on to help her.

Overwhelmed by her isolation and the disaster that threatened her, she burst out sobbing.

"Is there anything I can do for you, Your Majesty?" asked a gentle, sympathetic voice.

The queen quickly turned around, for the expression of the voice clearly showed that it was a friend who had spoken to her.

Madame Bonacieux was standing in one of the doorways. She had been putting away dresses and linen in a small adjoining room when the king came in, and, unable to leave, she had heard everything.

The queen uttered a cry of surprise because, in her distress, she did not immediately recognize the young woman who had been placed in her service by La Porte.

"Don't be afraid, Your Majesty," said Madame Bonacieux, clasping her hands. Tears came into her eyes when she saw the queen's anguish. "I'm devoted to you body and soul, and I think I've found a solution for your . . . difficulties."

"Look me in the eyes," said the queen. "I'm betrayed on all sides; can I trust you?"

"Oh, Your Majesty!" cried Madame Bonacieux, falling to her knees. "I swear I'm ready to die for you!" These words came straight from her heart, and their sincerity was unmistakable. "Yes, there are traitors here, but I swear by the holy name of the Virgin that no one is more loyal to you than I am. Those diamond tags that the king asked you to wear—you gave them to the duke of Buckingham, didn't you? They were in a little rosewood box that he took with him when he left, weren't they? Am I mistaken? Isn't it true?"

"Yes, yes, it's true," murmured the queen, her teeth chattering with fear.

"We must get those tags back," said Madame Bonacieux.

"Yes, but how?"

"By sending someone to the duke."

"Who could be trusted with such a mission?"

"Rely on me, Your Majesty. Do me that honor and I'll find a messenger."

"But I'll have to write a letter!"

"Yes, Your Majesty, that's necessary. A few words in your handwriting, and your personal seal."

"That letter could mean ruin for me—divorce, exile!"

"If it was intercepted, yes; but I guarantee you that it won't be."

"Then I must place my honor and my life in your hands!"

"Yes, Your Majesty, and I'll save them!"

"But how? At least tell me how."

"My husband was released from prison two or three days ago; I haven't yet had time to see him. He's an honest, good-natured man who has neither love nor hatred for anyone. He'll do as I ask: he'll deliver your letter without knowing what it is, without even knowing it's from you."

The queen took the young woman's hands with deep emotion, looked at her intently, and, seeing nothing but sincerity in her beautiful eyes, kissed her tenderly on the cheek.

"If you do that for me," she said, "you really will have saved my honor and my life!"

"I'm happy to do what I can for you, Your Majesty, but you mustn't exaggerate the importance of my help. You've done nothing to put your honor in danger. You're only the victim of a treacherous plot."

"Yes, that's true. You're right."

"Please write that letter, Your Majesty. Time is pressing."

The queen went to a table on which there were pens, paper, and ink. She wrote a few lines, sealed her letter, and handed it to Madame Bonacieux.

"We're forgetting something essential," said the queen.

"What is it, Your Majesty?"

"Money."

Madame Bonacieux blushed.

"Yes, I must confess that my husband . . ."

"He has no money, is that it?"

"No, Your Majesty. He has money, but he's very stingy; that's his main fault. But don't worry, we'll find a way to . . ."

"I have no money either," said the queen. (Those who have read Madame de Motteville's memoirs will not be surprised by this reply.) "But wait . . ." She went to her jewel case. "I've been told that this ring is very valuable. It was given to me by my brother, the king of Spain, so I can do with it as I please. Sell it and give the money to your husband for his journey."

"He'll leave within an hour, Your Majesty."

"You see the address," said the queen, speaking almost inaudibly: "the duke of Buckingham, London."

"The letter will be delivered to him personally."

"I can't tell you how grateful I am to you!" cried Anne of Austria.

Madame Bonacieux kissed the queen's hands, hid the letter in her bodice, and hurried away with the lightness of a bird.

Ten minutes later she was at home. As she had told the queen, she had not seen her husband since his release; she therefore knew nothing of the change that had taken place in him with regard to the cardinal. This change, originally produced by the cardinal's flattery and money, had been strengthened by several

friendly visits from Count de Rochefort, who had convinced him
without much difficulty that there had been no shameful reason
for his wife's abduction, but that it had been only a political
precaution.

She found Monsieur Bonacieux alone, trying to restore some
semblance of order to the house. He had found most of the
furniture broken and the closets nearly empty, since the police
were not one of the three things that King Solomon mentioned
as leaving no trace of their passage. The maid had fled when her
master was arrested, so terrified that she had walked from Paris
to her native province of Burgundy.

When he came home, Monsieur Bonacieux had sent his wife a
message telling her that he was back. She had replied with a
message congratulating him on his safe return and saying that
she would visit him as soon as her duties allowed her some free
time.

That free time had taken five days to arrive. In other
circumstances, this would have seemed a little long to Monsieur
Bonacieux, but his visit to the cardinal, and the visits he later
received from Rochefort, had given him a great deal to think
about, and, as is well known, thinking makes time pass quickly.

Especially since Bonacieux's thoughts were all exquisitely
pleasant. Rochefort called him his friend, his dear Bonacieux, and
kept telling him that the cardinal held him in high esteem. The
draper saw himself already on the road to honors and fortune.

Madame Bonacieux had also been thinking, but about something quite different from ambition. In spite of herself, she kept
recalling that brave, handsome young man who seemed to be so
much in love with her. Having been married at eighteen to
Monsieur Bonacieux, and since then having always lived in the
midst of his friends, who were incapable of arousing tender
feelings in a young woman whose ideals were higher than her
station in life, she had remained insensitive to all attempts to
seduce her. But in those days the title of gentleman made a
strong impression on middle-class women, and d'Artagnan was a
gentleman. Furthermore he wore the uniform of the guards,
which, after the uniform of the musketeers, was the one most
appreciated by women; he was young, handsome, and adventurous;
he spoke ardently of his love for her and seemed to be yearning
for her to love him in return. All this was more than it took to
turn the head of a woman of twenty-three, and Madame Bonacieux
had just reached that happy age.

And so, even though she and her husband had not seen each

other for a week and many dramatic things had happened during that time, they were both rather preoccupied when they were finally reunited; he showed genuine joy, however, and stepped toward her with his arms open.

She leaned forward to let him kiss her on the forehead.

"We have to talk," she said.

"About what?" he asked, surprised.

"I have something very important to tell you."

"And I have some serious questions to ask you. Please tell me about your abduction."

"Not now. I . . ."

"Ah, I understand: you want to hear about my arrest and imprisonment."

"I heard about it the day it happened, but it didn't worry me because I knew you'd soon be released: you hadn't committed any crime, you weren't involved in any plot, and you didn't know anything that could be dangerous to you or anyone else."

"It's easy for you to talk like that!" he said, offended by her lack of interest. "Do you know I spent a day and a night in a cell at the Bastille?"

"Well, the day and the night are over now. Let's drop that subject and go on to my reason for coming here."

"Your reason for coming here?" he asked indignantly. "Do you mean to say that you didn't come here because you wanted to be with me, your husband, after being separated from me for a week?"

"That's my main reason, of course, but I also have another one."

"Then tell me about it."

"It's something that will interest you because our future fortune may depend on it."

"Our prospects for the future have changed greatly since the last time I saw you, and I won't be surprised if we're envied by many people within a few months."

"We will be, if you follow the instructions I'm going to give you."

"You're going to give me instructions?"

"Yes. You can perform a worthy act and make a great deal of money at the same time."

Madame Bonacieux knew that by speaking of money to her husband, she was attacking him at his weakest point.

But no man, not even a draper, was still the same after having talked with Cardinal Richelieu for ten minutes.

"A great deal of money?" asked Bonacieux, pursing his lips.

"Yes."

"About how much?"

"Maybe a thousand pistoles."

"Then what you want me to do must be something very serious."

"It is."

"Tell me about it."

"You'll leave immediately with a letter that I'll give you. You mustn't let anyone take it from you, or even see it, till you deliver it."

"And where will I deliver it?"

"In London."

"London! You must be joking—I have no business in London!"

"But others need you to go there."

"Who are those others? I warn you that I'm never going to do anything blindly again. I want to know what I'm getting involved in, and who I'm doing it for."

"An illustrious person is sending you, an illustrious person will receive you, and your reward will go beyond your wildest hopes. That's all I can tell you."

"More intrigue! No, thank you, I now know better than to get mixed up in things like that. The cardinal has opened my eyes."

"The cardinal!" exclaimed Madame Bonacieux. "You've seen the cardinal?"

"He sent for me," Bonacieux replied proudly.

"And you went to see him? Didn't you realize how risky that was?"

"I must admit I didn't have the choice of seeing him or not seeing him, because I was taken to him by two guards. I must also admit that since I didn't yet know him, I'd have been glad not to visit him if I could have avoided it."

"Did he mistreat you, threaten you?"

"He shook my hand and called me his friend. His friend! Do you hear that? I'm a friend of the great cardinal!"

"The *great* cardinal?"

"You're not denying that he deserves to be called great, are you?"

"I'm not denying anything. But I'll point out to you that a minister's favor can end at any moment. Only a fool will count on it. There are powers higher than a minister's, and they don't depend on one man's whim or the outcome of an event. We should be loyal to those powers and no others."

"I'm sorry, but I recognize no power but that of the great man I have the honor of serving."

"You're serving the cardinal?"

"Yes," said Bonacieux, "and as his servant I won't allow you to plot against the security of the state and work to further the intrigues of a woman who's not French and is Spanish in her heart. Luckily the great cardinal's vigilant eyes keep watch over everything and see into the depths of all hearts," he added, repeating a sentence he had heard from Rochefort.

His poor wife had counted on him and confidently told the queen that he would deliver the letter. She shuddered at the danger she had narrowly escaped, and for a moment she was crushed by a feeling of helplessness. But then, knowing her husband's weakness and greed, she regained some hope of making him do as she wanted.

"So you're a Cardinalist now!" she said. "You're working for the people who mistreat your wife and insult your queen!"

"Since individual interests are nothing in relation to the common interest, I support those who preserve the state," Bonacieux said grandiloquently.

This was another of Rochefort's remarks that he had carefully remembered, and he was glad that his wife had given him a chance to use it.

"What do you know about the state?" she said with a disdainful shrug. "You're an ordinary man with an ordinary mind. Be satisfied with what you are and support the side that will bring you the most advantages."

"Never mind preaching to me, just tell me what you think of this," said Bonacieux, patting a bag full of silver coins.

"Where did you get that money?"

"Can't you guess?"

"From the cardinal?"

"From him and my friend Count de Rochefort."

"Count de Rochefort! He's the man who abducted me!"

"That's quite possible."

"And you take money from him?"

"You told me yourself that your abduction was entirely political."

"Yes, but its purpose was to make me betray my mistress, to torture me till I told secrets that would damage her honor and maybe even put her life in danger."

"Your mistress is a treacherous Spanish woman, and whatever the cardinal does is right."

"I always knew you were a coward, a miser, and a fool, but I didn't know you were also a vile traitor!"

"You can't mean that!" cried Bonacieux, shaken by his wife's vehemence, for he had never seen her angry before.

She was encouraged by his reaction.

"I do mean it! You're contemptible! You're involved in politics now, you've become a Cardinalist—for money! You've sold yourself to the devil!"

"Not to the devil, to the cardinal."

"It's the same thing! Richelieu is another name for Satan."

"Quiet! Someone may hear you!"

"All right, I'll lower my voice, but only because I'd be ashamed for anyone to know what a wretched man my husband is."

"There's no need for you to insult me. Just tell me what you expect of me."

"I've already told you: I want you to leave immediately and deliver a letter. If you carry out that mission, I'll forget everything and forgive you. And," she added, holding out her hand to him, "I'll give you back my friendship."

Bonacieux was indeed a coward and a miser, but he loved his wife. He could not help being moved by what she had said. A man of fifty-one cannot hold rancor against a woman of twenty-three for very long.

She saw that he was hesitating.

"Well, have you made up your mind?" she asked.

"Think of what you're asking me to do, my dear. London is far away from Paris, very far, and the mission you want me to carry out may be dangerous."

"What does that matter, as long as you avoid the dangers?"

"I don't think . . . No, I won't do it! I'm more afraid of court intrigues than ever, now that I've seen the inside of the Bastille. It's a horrible place! Just thinking about it makes my flesh creep. They threatened to torture me! Do you know what that means? They put wooden wedges between your legs and drive them in till the bones crack! No, I won't go to London. Why don't you go there yourself? I think I've been mistaken about you: you must really be a man, a reckless, fanatical man!"

"And you're a miserable, stupid woman! So you're afraid of the Bastille, are you? Well, I'll have you arrested and sent there, by order of the queen, if you don't leave for London immediately."

Bonacieux was silent for a moment while he weighed the

queen's anger against the cardinal's. It seemed to him that the cardinal's was much heavier.

"If you have me arrested by order of the queen," he said, "I'll appeal to the cardinal."

Madame Bonacieux realized with alarm that she had gone too far. She looked at her husband's coarse face; it showed the unshakable stubbornness of a frightened fool.

"On second thought," she said, "you may be right. After all, a man knows more about politics than a woman does—and especially you, since you've talked with the cardinal. Even so, I thought I could count on your affection, and it saddens me to know that you don't care enough about me to indulge my whim."

"This is one whim that's too dangerous to indulge," he replied triumphantly.

"Then I'll give it up," she said with a sigh. "Let's not talk about it any more."

"I wish you'd at least tell me what I was supposed to do in London," said Bonacieux, remembering, a little late, that Rochefort had urged him to try to find out his wife's secrets.

Some instinct warned her that she should reveal nothing more to him.

"There's no need for me to tell you about it in detail," she said. "You were to buy one of those trinkets that mean so much to women, and you'd have been well paid for your trouble."

But he was not deceived by her evasive answer; it only made him think that the secret she refused to tell him was important. He decided to go straight to Rochefort and inform him that the queen was looking for a messenger to send to London.

"I'm afraid I must leave you now, my dear," he said. "Not knowing you were coming to see me, I made an appointment with one of my friends. But I'll only be gone a few minutes. If you'll wait for me, I'll come back as soon as I've finished with my friend, and then, since it's getting late, I'll go with you to the Louvre."

"No, thank you," she replied. "You're not brave enough to be of any use to me. I'll go back to the Louvre by myself."

"As you like. Will I see you again soon?"

"Probably. I hope to have some free time next week. If I do, I'll come back and put some order into our affairs. I'm sure they need it now."

"Good, I'll be expecting you. You're not angry with me?"

"Of course not."

He kissed her hand and hurried away.

As soon as he was gone she thought, "Now he's turned himself into a Cardinalist, the idiot! And I told the queen she could count on him! She'll think I'm one of those vile people brought into the palace to spy on her! Ah, Monsieur Bonacieux, I never liked you very much, but now it's worse: I hate you! And I swear I'll make you pay for this!"

Just when she said these words to herself, a tapping sound above her made her look up, and a voice called to her through the ceiling: "Madame Bonacieux! Open the little side door, I'm coming down to see you."

18

The Lover and the Husband

"Madame," d'Artagnan said as he came in through the door that the young woman had just opened for him, "allow me to tell you that you have a wretched husband."

"You heard what we said?" she asked, looking at him with anxiety.

"Every word."

"How?"

"By a certain method known only to me, the same one I used when I overheard your more animated conversation with the men the cardinal sent to arrest you."

"And what did you gather from my conversation with my husband?"

"Several things. First, that your husband is a fool, which is fortunate. Next, that you're in a difficult situation, which I'm glad to know because it gives me a chance to help you, and God knows I'll stop at nothing to do that. And finally, that the queen needs a brave, intelligent, and loyal man to go to London for her. I have at least two of those three qualities, and here I am."

Madame Bonacieux's heartbeat quickened with joy, and hope shone in her eyes.

"What guarantee can you offer me," she asked, "if I consent to give you that mission?"

"My love for you. Give me your orders: what must I do?"

"I don't know if I should tell you such a secret," she murmured hesitantly. "You're almost still a boy!"

"I see you need someone to vouch for me."

"I admit it would reassure me."

"Do you know Athos?"

"No."

"Porthos?"

"No."

"Aramis?"

"No. Who are those gentlemen?"

"They're musketeers. Do you know Monsieur de Tréville, their captain?"

"Yes, I do know him! Not personally, but I've often heard the queen speak of him as a brave and honorable gentleman."

"You're not afraid that he'd betray you to the cardinal, are you?"

"No, certainly not."

"Then tell him your secret, no matter how important, precious, or dangerous it may be, and ask him if you can safely tell it to me."

"But it's not my secret. I have no right to let anyone know it."

"You were going to tell it to your husband," d'Artagnan said resentfully.

"I wasn't going to tell him all of it, only enough of it for him to do what I wanted. It would have been like putting a letter in a hole in a tree, or tying it to a carrier pigeon or a dog's collar."

"But you can see I love you!"

"So you say."

"I'm a man of honor!"

"I believe it."

"I'm brave!"

"Oh, I'm sure of that!"

"Then put me to the test."

She looked at him, held back by a final hesitation. But there was such ardor in his eyes, and such persuasiveness in his voice, that she felt compelled to trust him. And she was in a situation where she had to take a great risk. The queen would be endangered by too much caution as surely as by too little. Finally, it must be admitted, her involuntary feelings for her young protector made her decide to speak.

"I'm going to trust you," she said. "But I swear to you

before God that if you betray me, and my enemies spare me, I'll kill myself and accuse you of my death.''

"And I swear to you before God that if I'm caught while carrying out your orders, I'll die rather than do or say anything that would compromise anyone.''

She told him the secret that chance had already partially revealed to him on the Pont-Neuf. This was their mutual declaration of love.

D'Artagnan was radiant with joy and pride. The secret he now possessed, the woman he loved, and the confidence she had shown in him made him feel like a giant.

"I'll leave immediately,'' he said.

"But what about your regiment, and your captain?''

"You'd made me forget all that, dear Constance! Yes, you're right, I must have a leave of absence.''

"Another obstacle,'' Madame Bonacieux murmured sorrowfully.

"Don't worry,'' d'Artagnan said after thinking for a moment, "I know how to solve that problem.''

"How?''

"I'll go to see Monsieur de Tréville this evening, and he'll ask Monsieur des Essarts, his brother-in-law, to give me a leave.''

"And now, there's something else . . .''

"What is it?'' he asked, seeing that she was reluctant to go on.

"Perhaps you have no money.''

"Your 'perhaps' is unnecessary,'' he said, smiling.

She opened a cupboard and took out the bag that her husband had caressed so lovingly half an hour earlier.

"Here, take this.''

"The money from the cardinal!'' he exclaimed, laughing, for, as we have said, he had overheard the whole conversation between Madame Bonacieux and her husband.

"Yes, it's from the cardinal,'' she replied. "So it's perfectly respectable.''

"It will be twice as amusing to save the queen with His Eminence's money!''

"You're a kind and charming young man,'' said Madame Bonacieux. "You can be sure that Her Majesty won't be ungrateful.''

"I've already been greatly rewarded! I love you and you've let me tell you so—that's more than I dared to hope for.''

"Quiet!'' she said with a sudden start.

"What is it?'' .

"I hear someone talking in the street."

"It's . . ."

"My husband! I recognize his voice!"

D'Artagnan ran to the door and bolted it.

"Don't let him in till I'm gone," he said.

"But I must go too. If I stayed, how could I explain why that money isn't here?"

"You're right, we'll both go."

"But how? He'll see us when we leave the house."

"We'll go up to my room."

"I'm frightened by the way you say that!"

D'Artagnan saw tears come into her eyes. A surge of tender emotion made him kneel at her feet.

"In my room," he said, "you'll be as safe as if you were in a church. I give you my word of honor."

"Then let's go. I trust you, my friend."

D'Artagnan cautiously unbolted the door. He and Madame Bonacieux slipped through the side door and climbed the stairs to his room.

Once they were inside, he barricaded the door. They went to the window and, through a slit in the shutter, saw Monsieur Bonacieux talking with a man in a cloak.

At the sight of this man, d'Artagnan half drew his sword and rushed toward the door.

It was the stranger he had encountered at Meung.

"Where are you going?" cried Madame Bonacieux. "We'll be lost if you're seen!"

"I've sworn to kill that man!" said d'Artagnan.

"Your life is no longer your own. In the name of the queen, I forbid you to take any risks not connected with your mission."

"And in your own name, do you have any orders for me?"

"In my name, I beg you to stay . . . Listen: I think they're talking about me."

D'Artagnan came back to the window and listened.

Monsieur Bonacieux had gone into the house, seen that his wife was no longer there, and returned to the man in the cloak.

"She's not here," he said. "She must have gone back to the Louvre."

"Are you sure she didn't guess why you left?" asked the stranger.

"She's not shrewd enough for that," Bonacieux answered smugly.

"Is your lodger at home?"

"I don't think so. As you can see, his shutter is closed and there's no light shining through it."

"Even so, we'd better make sure."

"How?"

"By knocking on his door."

"I'll ask his servant."

"Go."

Bonacieux went up the stairs that the two fugitives had just climbed and knocked on d'Artagnan's door.

There was no answer. Porthos had borrowed Planchet so that he could cut a better figure that evening. D'Artagnan, of course, gave no sign that he was at home. He and Madame Bonacieux stood still, with their hearts pounding.

"There's no one here," said Bonacieux.

"Let's go downstairs," said his companion. "It will be safer to talk there."

"We won't be able to hear anything more," Madame Bonacieux whispered to d'Artagnan.

"We'll hear even better," he assured her.

He knelt on the floor and uncovered the hollowed-out spot that made his room like the cave where Dionysius I, the tyrant of Syracuse, secretly listened to what was said by his prisoners. He then placed a carpet next to the opening and motioned Madame Bonacieux to kneel on it with him.

"Are you sure there's no one else in the house?" asked the stranger.

"Quite sure," replied Bonacieux.

"And you think your wife . . ."

"She's gone back to the Louvre."

"Without talking to anyone but you?"

"I'm certain of it."

"That's an important point, as you must understand."

"Then the news I brought you is valuable?"

"Very valuable, my dear Bonacieux."

"And the cardinal will be pleased with me?"

"I have no doubt of it."

"The great cardinal himself!"

"You're sure your wife didn't mention any names in her conversation with you?"

"I don't think so."

"She didn't mention Madame de Chevreuse, or the duke of Buckingham, or Madame de Vernet?"

"No, she only said she wanted to send me to London to serve the interests of an illustrious person."

"The traitor!" murmured Madame Bonacieux.

"Quiet!" whispered d'Artagnan. He took her hand, and, without thinking, she let him hold it.

"You were a fool not to pretend to accept the mission," the stranger said to Bonacieux. "You'd have the letter now, the threat to the state would be eliminated, and you—"

"And I?"

"The cardinal would have made you a nobleman."

"Did he tell you that?"

"Yes. He wanted to give you that pleasant surprise."

"Don't worry," said Bonacieux, "my wife adores me and there's still time."

"The idiot!" murmured Madame Bonacieux.

"Quiet!" d'Artagnan whispered again, squeezing her hand.

"How is there still time?" asked the stranger.

"I'll go to see my wife at the Louvre. I'll tell her I've thought it over and changed my mind. She'll give me the letter, and I'll take it to the cardinal."

"Hurry, then. I'll come back soon to learn if you've succeeded."

The stranger left.

"Oh, that vile traitor!" said Madame Bonacieux.

"Quiet!" d'Artagnan repeated, squeezing her hand even harder.

Their thoughts were interrupted by a terrible shriek. Bonacieux had just discovered that his bag of money was gone. He began shouting that he had been robbed.

"My God!" exclaimed Madame Bonacieux. "He'll stir up the whole neighborhood!"

Bonacieux went on shouting for a long time. But since such shouts from robbery victims were common, and since his house had recently acquired a rather bad reputation, no one came. Finally he left, still protesting at the top of his lungs. D'Artagnan and Madame Bonacieux heard his voice fade away in the direction of the Rue du Bac.

"Now that he's gone," said Madame Bonacieux, "you must go too. Be brave, but above all be careful, and remember that your life now belongs to the queen."

"To her and to you!" said d'Artagnan. "Don't worry, beautiful Constance, I'll come back worthy of her gratitude. But will I also come back worthy of your love?"

She answered only by blushing.

A few moments later d'Artagnan left the house, wrapped in a

big cloak that was jauntily raised on one side by the scabbard of his long sword.

From the window, Madame Bonacieux watched him with a look of love in her eyes. But when he had disappeared around the corner, she knelt, clasped her hands, and prayed, "Dear God, please protect the queen, and please protect me!"

19

Plans

D'Artagnan hurried to Monsieur de Tréville's house. Knowing that the cardinal would soon be alerted by that damned stranger, who seemed to be his agent, d'Artagnan rightly felt that there was not a moment to lose.

His heart was overflowing with joy. He had a chance to gain both glory and money, and he had been brought closer to the woman he adored. All this was more than he would have dared to ask of Providence.

Monsieur de Tréville was in his drawing room with his usual entourage of noblemen. Since d'Artagnan was known as a regular visitor to the house, he was allowed to go straight to the study. He sent word to Monsieur de Tréville that he was waiting for him there to discuss an important matter.

Five minutes later Tréville came into the study. Seeing d'Artagnan's elated expression, he realized that something new had happened.

On the way to the house, d'Artagnan had wondered if he would confide in Tréville, or if he would only ask to be given carte blanche for a secret mission. But Tréville had always been so kind to him, was so devoted to the king and the queen, and hated the cardinal so heartily that d'Artagnan had decided to tell him everything.

"You've asked to see me, my young friend?" said Tréville.

"Yes, sir, and I hope you'll forgive me for disturbing you when you learn the importance of what I have to say."

"I'm listening."

"What's at stake," said d'Artagnan, lowering his voice, "is nothing less than the queen's honor, and perhaps her life."

"What!" exclaimed Tréville. He glanced around to make sure they were alone, then gave d'Artagnan a questioning look.

"Chance has put me in possession of a secret . . ."

"Which I hope you'll guard with your life, young man."

"But I must tell it to you, sir, because I've just been given a mission for the queen and you're the only one who can help me to carry it out."

"Is it your secret?"

"No, sir, it's the queen's."

"Has she authorized you to tell it to me?"

"No, sir, my instructions are to let no one even suspect it."

"Then why do you want to tell it to me?"

"Because I can't do anything without your help and I'm afraid you won't give it to me unless you know why I'm asking it of you."

"Keep your secret, young man, and tell me what you want me to do."

"I want you to ask Monsieur des Essarts to give me a two-week leave of absence."

"Beginning when?"

"Tonight."

"You're leaving Paris?"

"Yes, for my mission."

"Can you tell me where you're going?"

"To London."

"Is it to anyone's interest that you shouldn't arrive there?"

"I believe the cardinal would give anything in the world to prevent me from succeeding."

"Will you be alone?"

"Yes."

"In that case I can promise you that you won't get any farther than Bondy."

"Why?"

"You'll be murdered."

"If so, I'll have died doing my duty."

"But your mission won't be accomplished."

"That's true," d'Artagnan acknowledged.

"Believe me," said Tréville, "for a mission of that kind, at least four men must start out if one is to get through."

"You're right, sir. You know Athos, Porthos, and Aramis, and you know whether I can take them with me."

"Without telling them the secret I refused to learn?"

"We've sworn always to trust each other blindly. And besides, if you tell them you have complete confidence in me, they won't question my mission any more than you've done."

"I can send a permit for a two-week leave to each of them: to Athos so that he can go and take the waters at Forges, because he's still suffering from his wound; and to Porthos and Aramis so that they can accompany their friend, because they wouldn't want to abandon him in his pain. Sending them their permits will show that I authorize their journey."

"Thank you, sir. It's very kind of you."

"Go to your friends now, and leave tonight. No, wait: before you go, write out your request to Monsieur des Essarts. You may have been followed by a spy, and in that case the cardinal already knows you've come here. With your written request, I can give a plausible explanation for your visit."

D'Artagnan wrote the request and gave it to Tréville, who assured him that all four leave permits would be delivered by two o'clock in the morning.

"Please send mine to Athos's apartment," said d'Artagnan. "I'm afraid I might have an unpleasant encounter if I went home."

"Very well," said Tréville. "Good-bye and good luck. Ah, one more thing . . ."

D'Artagnan, who had already started toward the door, turned back.

"Do you have money?" asked Tréville.

D'Artagnan jingled the bag of coins in his pocket.

"Is it enough?" Tréville insisted.

"Three hundred pistoles."

"Good; with that, you can go to the end of the world. Good-bye again."

D'Artagnan bowed, and Tréville held out his hand to him. D'Artagnan shook it with respect and gratitude. Ever since his arrival in Paris, he had found Monsieur de Tréville to be an honorable, forthright, and greathearted man.

D'Artagnan went to Aramis's apartment. It was the first time he had been there since the night he had followed Madame Bonacieux, and on the few occasions when he had seen him since then, Aramis had seemed deeply sad.

He was still up when d'Artagnan arrived. Again he seemed somber and thoughtful. D'Artagnan asked him why. Aramis replied that he was greatly preoccupied by a commentary that he had to write in Latin on the eighteenth chapter of Saint Augustine for the following week.

When the two friends had been talking for a few minutes, one of Monsieur de Tréville's servants came in with a sealed envelope.

"What's that?" asked Aramis.

"The leave permit that you requested, sir," answered the servant.

"I haven't asked for a leave permit."

"Be quiet and take it," said d'Artagnan. He turned to the servant. "Here's half a pistole for your trouble. Tell Monsieur de Tréville that Monsieur Aramis thanks him."

The servant bowed and left.

"What does this mean?" asked Aramis.

"Take what you'll need for a two-week journey and come with me."

"But I can't leave Paris without knowing . . ."

Aramis stopped short.

"Without knowing what's become of her, isn't that it?" asked d'Artagnan.

"Who?"

"The woman who was here, the woman with the embroidered handkerchief."

Aramis turned deathly pale.

"Who told you there was a woman here?"

"I saw her."

"And do you know who she is?"

"I think so."

"Since you know so many things, do you know what's become of her?"

"I presume she went back to Tours."

"To Tours? Yes, you know who she is . . . But why did she go back to Tours without telling me anything?"

"Because she was afraid of being arrested."

"Why didn't she write to me?"

"Because she was afraid it might be dangerous for you."

"D'Artagnan, you've brought me back to life! I thought she'd abandoned me for someone else. I was so happy to see her again! I couldn't believe she'd risked her freedom for me, and yet why else would she have come back to Paris?"

"She came back for the cause that's now about to make us go to England."

"And what is that cause?"

"You'll know some day, Aramis, but for now I'll imitate your discretion about the theologian's niece."

Aramis smiled, for he remembered the story he had told his friends one evening.

"Well, since you're sure she's left Paris," he said, "there's nothing to keep me here and I'm ready to go with you. Where did you say we were going?"

"To Athos's house, for the moment. If you want to come, you'd better hurry, because we've already lost too much time. By the way, notify Bazin."

"Bazin is coming with us?"

"Maybe. In any case I'd like him to follow us to Athos's house."

Aramis called Bazin, and after telling him to join him at Athos's house, he said to d'Artagnan, "Let's go."

He took his cloak, his sword, and his three pistols, then he opened several drawers to see if by chance they might contain a little money that he had overlooked before. When it became clear to him that his search was futile, he left with d'Artagnan, wondering how the young Gascon had discovered the identity of the woman who had stayed in his apartment, and how he knew more about what she had been doing than he himself did.

When they were outside the house, he put his hand on d'Artagnan's arm, looked at him insistently, and asked, "You haven't told anyone about that woman, have you?"

"I haven't mentioned her to anyone in the world."

"Not even Athos and Porthos?"

"No."

"Good."

With his mind at rest on this important point, Aramis continued on his way with d'Artagnan, and they were soon in Athos's apartment.

They found him holding his leave permit in one hand and a letter from Monsieur de Tréville in the other.

"Can you explain this permit and this letter I've just received?" he asked, puzzled. He read the letter aloud: " 'My dear Athos, since your health requires it, I am quite willing to let you rest for two weeks. Take the waters at Forges, or anywhere else you choose, and recover quickly. Affectionately, Tréville.' "

"The leave permit and the letter mean that you must come with me, Athos," said d'Artagnan.

"To Forges?"

"There or somewhere else."

"In the king's service?"

"Or the queen's; we serve both, you know."

Just then Porthos came in.

"This is odd!" he said. "Since when have musketeers been given leave without asking for it?"

"Since they've had friends who request it for them," replied d'Artagnan.

"Ah! So something new has happened!"

"Yes, we're leaving," said Aramis.

"Where are we going?"

"I have no idea," said Athos. "Ask d'Artagnan."

"We're going to London, gentlemen," d'Artagnan announced.

"London!" exclaimed Athos. "What are we going to do there?"

"I can't tell you. You'll have to trust me."

"But it takes money to go to London," said Porthos, "and I don't have any."

"Neither do I," said Aramis.

"Neither do I," said Athos.

"I have some," said d'Artagnan, taking his treasure from his pocket and putting it on the table. "There are three hundred pistoles in this bag. We'll each take seventy-five. That will be enough to go to London and back. But I don't think all of us will get there."

"Why not?"

"Because some of us will probably fall along the wayside."

"Then we're setting off on a campaign?"

"You can call it that. And it's going to be dangerous, I warn you."

"Since we're going to risk getting killed," said Porthos, "I'd at least like to know why."

"It wouldn't do you any good to know," said Athos.

"I agree with Porthos," said Aramis. "We ought to know."

"Does the king explain everything to you?" asked d'Artagnan. "No, he simply says to you, 'Gentlemen, there's fighting in Gascony or Flanders, go there and fight,' and you go. Why? You don't worry about that."

"D'Artagnan is right," said Athos. "We have our leave permits from Monsieur de Tréville and three hundred pistoles from I don't know where. Let's go and face death wherever we're told to. Is life worth all that concern? D'Artagnan, I'm ready to go with you."

"So am I," said Porthos.

"And so am I," said Aramis, "especially since I'll be glad to get away from Paris for a while. I'm beginning to be bored here."

"From now on you won't be bored, I can promise you that," said d'Artagnan.

"When are we leaving?" Athos asked him.

"Right now. There's no time to lose."

They all called their servants and told them to grease their boots and bring their horses from Monsieur de Tréville's house, for that was where each of them left his own horse and his servant's. Planchet, Grimaud, Mousequeton, and Bazin quickly left.

"Now let's make our plans," said Porthos. "Where are we going first?"

"To Calais," said d'Artagnan. "It's the most direct route to London."

"Well, then," said Porthos, "here's my opinion."

"Let's hear it."

"Four men traveling together would arouse suspicion. D'Artagnan will give each of us his instructions, then I'll leave first by the Boulogne road to act as a scout, Athos will leave two hours later by the Amiens road, and Aramis will follow by the Noyon road. As for d'Artagnan, he'll leave by whatever road he prefers, wearing Planchet's clothes, and Planchet will follow us, wearing d'Artagnan's uniform."

"I don't think we should involve our servants in this," said Athos. "Gentlemen may inadvertently give away a secret, but it's nearly always sold by servants."

"Porthos's plan doesn't seem feasible to me," said d'Artagnan, "because I myself don't know what instructions I could give you. I have a letter to deliver, that's all. I can't make three copies of it because it's sealed. So in my opinion we must travel together. I have the letter here, in this pocket. If I'm killed, one of you will take it and go on. If he's killed, another will take it, and so on. If one of us gets through, that's all that matters."

"Bravo, d'Artagnan!" said Athos. "I agree with you. And besides, by traveling together we can support the official reason for our journey: Monsieur de Tréville has told me to take the waters at Forges, or anywhere else I choose, and he's told you to go with me; I've chosen to go to the seaside, rather than to Forges. If anyone tries to arrest us, I'll show Monsieur de Tréville's letter and you'll show your leave permits; if we're attacked, we'll defend ourselves; if we're brought to trial, we'll insist that we had no other intention than going to bathe in the sea. Four isolated men could easily be overcome, but four men together make a troop. We'll arm our servants with pistols and muskets. If an army is sent against us, we'll fight, and anyone who survives will take the letter, as d'Artagnan says.''

"Well said, Athos!'' exclaimed Aramis. "You don't talk often, but when you do, you're worth listening to. I'm in favor of your plan. And you, Porthos?''

"I'm in favor of it too,'' said Porthos, "if it suits d'Artagnan. Since he has the letter, he's naturally the leader of the expedition. We'll do whatever he decides.''

"Well, then,'' said d'Artagnan, "my decision is that we'll adopt Athos's plan and leave in half an hour.''

"Agreed!'' said the three musketeers.

Each of them reached into the bag, took seventy-five pistoles, and began making preparations to leave.

20

The Journey

At two o'clock in the morning our four adventurers rode out of Paris by way of the Saint-Denis gate.

As long as it was night they remained silent; they were affected by the darkness in spite of themselves, and saw ambushes everywhere.

At dawn their tongues loosened. Their cheerfulness returned with the sun. It was as though they were on the eve of a battle: their hearts beat more rapidly, their eyes smiled, and they felt that the life they were perhaps about to leave was, on the whole, a good thing.

The little cavalcade had a formidable appearance. The musketeers' black horses, with the martial bearing and the regular gait that their training had given them, would have been enough to betray their riders if they had been traveling incognito.

The servants followed, armed to the teeth.

Everything went well till they stopped at Chantilly for breakfast at about eight o'clock. They dismounted in front of an inn with a sign showing Saint Martin giving a poor man half of his cloak. They told their servants not to unsaddle the horses and to be ready to set off again very soon.

They went into the dining room and sat down at a table where a gentleman who had just arrived by the Dammartin road was already eating. He made a few remarks about the weather; the four friends answered him. He drank to their health; they returned his politeness.

But when they were standing up to leave and Mousqueton had just come in to announce that the horses were ready, the stranger suggested to Porthos that they drink a toast to the cardinal. Porthos replied that he was quite willing, if the stranger would also drink a toast to the king. The stranger cried out that he knew no other king than His Eminence. Porthos called him a drunkard; the stranger drew his sword.

"You've made a foolish blunder," Athos told Porthos, "but it's too late to turn back now. Kill that man and rejoin us as soon as you can."

While Porthos was promising his adversary that he would perforate him with every kind of thrust known to the art of fencing, the three others remounted their horses and rode off.

"One down!" Athos said when they had ridden five hundred paces.

"Why do you think that man singled out Porthos, rather than one of us three?" asked Aramis.

"Because Porthos talks more loudly than any of us, so he assumed he was our leader," replied d'Artagnan.

"I've always said our young Gascon had a good head on his shoulders," remarked Athos.

They continued on their way.

At Beauvais they stopped to wait for Porthos and let their horses rest. After two hours, when Porthos still had not arrived and they had received no news of him, they set off again.

A few miles beyond Beauvais, at a place where the road was unpaved and squeezed in between two embankments, they came upon eight or nine men working on the road, though their work apparently consisted of digging holes and making muddy ruts.

Not wanting to dirty his boots in that artificial bog, Aramis sternly upbraided the workmen. Athos tried to restrain him, but it was too late. The workmen began jeering at the travelers. Their insolence made even Athos lose his head, and he spurred his horse toward one of them.

The workmen all ran to the ditch, took out muskets that had been hidden there and opened fire. One bullet went through

Aramis's shoulder, another hit Mousqueton in the left buttock. Mousqueton was the only one who fell off his horse, however— not that he was seriously wounded, but since he could not see his wound he evidently thought it more dangerous than it was.

"It's an ambush!"shouted d'Artagnan. "Don't shoot back! Let's go!"

Wounded though he was, Aramis rode off with the others, clinging to his horse's mane. Mousqueton's horse galloped along beside them, riderless.

"At least we have a spare horse now," said Athos.

"I'd rather have a hat," said d'Artagnan. "Mine was knocked off by a bullet. It's lucky the letter I'm carrying wasn't in it."

"They'll kill poor Porthos when he comes to that place!" said Aramis.

"If Porthos were still on his feet, he'd have caught up with us by now," said Athos. "I have a feeling that when he and the Cardinalist left the inn and began to fight, the drunkard suddenly became sober."

They galloped for two hours even though their horses became so tired that they seemed on the verge of refusing to go on.

They had taken a side road, hoping it would be safer, but at Crèvecoeur Aramis announced that he could go no further. If it had not been for the courage hidden behind his elegant appearance and polished manners, he would have had to stop much sooner. His face had turned increasingly white and his two companions now had to support him to keep him from falling off his horse. They took him to an inn and told Bazin, who, in a skirmish, would have been more of a hindrance than a help, to stay behind with him. They then rode on, intending to sleep at Amiens.

The troop was now reduced to d'Artagnan, Athos, Planchet, and Grimaud.

"I won't be taken in like that again!" said Athos. "They won't make me open my mouth or draw my sword between here and Calais. I swear I'll—"

"Let's not waste our breath swearing," said d'Artagnan. "Let's just keep riding, if our horses are willing."

They spurred their horses and this seemed to give them new strength. They reached Amiens at midnight and stopped at the Lis d'Or inn.

The innkeeper looked like the most honest, decent man in the world. He greeted his guests with a candlestick in one hand and his cotton nightcap in the other. He said he had an attractive room for each of the two gentlemen. Unfortunately these rooms were at opposite ends of the inn. D'Artagnan and Athos refused to take them. The innkeeper replied that he had no other rooms worthy of Their Excellencies. They said they would sleep in the common room, on mattresses on the floor. The innkeeper argued insistently, but they held firm, and finally he had to do as they wanted.

They had just put down their mattresses and barricaded the door from the inside when they heard a knock on the shutter that faced the courtyard. They asked who was there, recognized their servants' voices, opened the shutter, and saw Planchet and Grimaud.

"Grimaud can guard the horses," said Planchet, "and, if you like, I'll sleep in front of your door; that way, you can be sure you won't be attacked without warning."

"What will you sleep on?" asked d'Artagnan.

"Here's my bed," answered Planchet, holding up a bundle of straw.

"Come in, then," said d'Artagnan. "You're right to be suspicious. I don't like the innkeeper's face: it's too friendly."

"I think so too," said Athos.

Planchet climbed in through the window and lay down on his straw in front of the door. Grimaud went off to the stables after promising that he and the horses would be ready at five o'clock.

The night passed without serious incident. At two o'clock someone tried to open the door. Planchet awoke with a start and called out, "Who's there?" A man answered that he had come to the wrong room and walked away.

At four o'clock, however, there was an uproar in the stables. Grimaud had waked up the stablemen, and they were beating him. When Athos and d'Artagnan opened the window, they saw the poor man lying unconscious, with his head bleeding where it had been struck with a pitchfork handle.

Planchet went out to saddle the horses, but they were in no condition to be ridden. Only Mousqueton's horse, having carried no rider during the last four or five hours of the journey, would have been able to go on; but, by some inexplicable error, the veterinarian, who had apparently been summoned to bleed the innkeeper's horse, had bled Mousqueton's instead.

The situation was becoming alarming: all those setbacks might have happened by chance, but they might also have been the result of a plot. Athos and d'Artagnan came outside while Planchet went to ask if there were three horses for sale in the vicinity. In front of the inn he saw two fresh horses already saddled. That looked promising. He asked where the owners were and was told that they were paying the innkeeper after having spent the night at the inn.

Athos went to pay while d'Artagnan and Planchet remained at the front door. He went to the low-ceilinged room where he had been told he would find the innkeeper, walked into it, unsuspecting, and took out two pistoles to pay the bill. The innkeeper was seated at his desk, one of whose drawers was partly open. He took the two coins that Athos handed him and, after examining them, declared that they were counterfeit and that he was going to have Athos and his companion arrested as counterfeiters.

"You lying scoundrel!" roared Athos, moving toward him threateningly. "I'll cut off your ears!"

Just then four armed men came in through the side doors and rushed at him.

"I'm trapped!" he shouted at the top of his lungs. "Go, d'Artagnan, hurry!"

And he fired two pistol shots.

D'Artagnan and Planchet did not wait to be told twice. They untied the two horses waiting in front of the inn, leapt onto them, spurred them, and galloped away.

"Could you see what happened to Athos?" d'Artagnan asked Planchet.

"Yes, I saw through the glass of the door," Planchet answered. "He shot two men, and he was fencing with the others when we left."

"Brave as always," murmured d'Artagnan. "And to think we have to abandon him! Well, the same thing may be waiting for us at the next bend in the road. Planchet, you're a good man."

"As I told you, sir, we Picards only need a chance to show what we're worth. Besides, I'm in my home territory now, and that stirs up my courage."

They rode to Saint-Omer at full speed. There they let their horses rest awhile, but they held on to the reins, just to be safe. After quickly having a bite to eat, standing in the street, they rode on.

When they were within a hundred paces of the gates of Calais, d'Artagnan's horse collapsed, with blood flowing from his nose and eyes, and could not be made to stand up. There was still Planchet's horse, but he had stopped and refused to go on.

Luckily they were only a hundred paces from the town gates, as we have said. They left their horses on the road and ran to the harbor. Planchet called d'Artagnan's attention to a gentleman and his servant fifty paces in front of them.

They quickly caught up with them. The gentleman seemed to be in a great hurry. His boots were covered with dust and he was asking a ship's captain if he could take him to England immediately.

"I could easily take you," said the captain, whose ship was ready to set sail, "but this morning we were ordered not to let anyone leave without permission from the cardinal."

"I have that permission," said the gentleman, taking a sheet of paper from his pocket. "Here it is."

"Have it endorsed by the harbor master," said the captain, "and let me be the one to take you across."

"Where can I find the harbor master?"

"He's at home now."

"And where is his house?"

"About half a mile out of town. Look, you can see it from here, at the foot of that little hill: it's the house with the slate roof."

"Very well," said the gentleman.

He and his servant headed for the harbor master's house.

D'Artagnan and Planchet followed five hundred paces behind.

Once they were outside of town, d'Artagnan quickened his pace and caught up with the gentleman as he was entering a small wooded area.

"Sir," d'Artagnan said to him, "you seem to be in a hurry."

"Yes, sir, I'm in a great hurry."

"I'm sorry to hear that," said d'Artagnan, "because I'm also in a hurry and I wanted to ask a favor of you."

"What favor?"

"To let me leave for England ahead of you."

"That's impossible," said the gentleman. "I've traveled a hundred and fifty miles in forty-four hours and I must be in London tomorrow at noon."

"I've traveled the same distance in forty hours and I must be in London tomorrow morning at ten o'clock."

"I'm sorry, sir, but I came here first and I won't leave second."

"I'm sorry, sir, but I came here second and I'll leave first."

"I'm traveling in the king's service!" said the gentleman.

"I'm traveling in my own service!" said d'Artagnan.

"I believe you're trying to pick a quarrel with me."

"You're quite right."

"What do you want?"

"Would you really like to know?"

"Yes."

"I want your travel permit because I don't have one and I need one."

"I assume you're joking."

"I never joke."

"Let me pass!"

"No."

"A bullet will make you more accommodating, young man. Lubin! My pistols!"

"Planchet," said d'Artagnan, "take care of the servant and I'll take care of his master."

Emboldened by his first exploit, Planchet attacked Lubin, and since he was strong and agile, he quickly threw him to the ground and put his knee on his chest.

"I've done my work, sir," he said to d'Artagnan. "Now you can do yours."

Seeing what had happened, the gentleman drew his sword and rushed at d'Artagnan. But he had met his match. In three seconds d'Artagnan gave him three sword thrusts, saying, "One for Athos, one for Porthos, one for Aramis." With the third thrust, his adversary fell.

Thinking he was dead, or at least unconscious, d'Artagnan bent over him to take the travel permit. But the gentleman, who had not let go of his sword, gave him a thrust in the chest and said, "One for you!"

"And one more for me, the last one!" d'Artagnan said furiously, plunging his sword into his adversary's belly.

This time the gentleman closed his eyes and lost consciousness.

D'Artagnan reached into the pocket where he had seen him put the travel permit and took it. It was made out in the name of Count de Wardes.

Looking down at the handsome young man, no more than twenty-five, whom he was leaving dead or unconscious on the ground, d'Artagnan sighed at the thought of the strange destiny that made men destroy each other for the interests of people who did not know them, and often did not even know that they existed.

He was soon drawn from these reflections by Lubin, who was calling for help as loudly as he could.

Planchet gripped him by the throat and squeezed hard.

"Sir, he'll keep quiet as long as I'm holding him like this," said Planchet, "but he'll start yelling again as soon as I let go of him. I can see he's a Norman, and Normans are stubborn."

And it was true that even with Planchet choking him, Lubin was still trying to shout.

"Wait," said d'Artagnan.

He took out his handkerchief and gagged Lubin.

"Now let's tie him to a tree," said Planchet.

They did so, then pulled Count de Wardes close to his servant. Since night was falling and the two men were several paces inside the wood, it was obvious that they would not be found before morning.

"Now," said d'Artagnan, "let's go and see the harbor master."

"But you're wounded, sir," said Planchet.

"First things first. We'll worry about my wound later. Besides, I don't think it's very serious."

They rapidly walked to the harbor master's house, where d'Artagnan presented himself as Count de Wardes.

"Do you have a permit signed by the cardinal?" asked the harbor master.

"Yes, sir," replied d'Artagnan. "Here it is."

"I see it's perfectly in order."

"Of course. The cardinal has great confidence in me."

"It seems His Eminence wants to prevent someone from going to England."

"Yes, a Gascon named d'Artagnan who left Paris with three of his friends, intending to go to London."

"Do you know him personally?" asked the harbor master.

"Who?"

"That d'Artagnan."

"Yes, I know him very well."

"Then give me his description."

"I'll be glad to."

And d'Artagnan gave a detailed description of Count de Wardes.

"Is there anyone with him?" asked the harbor master.

"Yes, a servant named Lubin."

"We'll be on the lookout for them. If we get our hands on them, His Eminence can rest assured that they'll be taken back to Paris with a strong escort."

"If you do that, sir," said d'Artagnan, "you'll have earned the cardinal's gratitude."

"Will you see him when you return, Count?"

"Yes."

"Please tell him that I'm his faithful servant."

"I will, you can count on it."

Delighted by this promise, the harbor master endorsed the permit and handed it to d'Artagnan.

D'Artagnan wasted no time on useless conversation; he bowed to the harbor master, thanked him, and left.

He and Planchet hurried away. They made a detour around the little wood and entered the town through another gate.

The ship was still ready to put to sea, and the captain was waiting on the waterfront.

"Well?" he asked when he saw d'Artagnan.

"Here's my permit, endorsed by the harbor master."

"What about that other gentleman?"

"He won't leave today," said d'Artagnan, "but don't worry, I'll pay for both of us."

"In that case, let's go," said the captain.

"Let's go!" d'Artagnan repeated.

He and Planchet jumped into the rowboat. Five minutes later they boarded the ship.

It was none too soon: when they were a mile from shore, d'Artagnan saw a flash and heard an explosion. A cannon shot had announced that the harbor was closed.

Now it was time to have a look at his wound. Luckily, as he had thought, it was not very serious: the point of the sword had struck a rib and slid along it; his shirt had immediately stuck to the wound and only a few drops of blood had escaped.

D'Artagnan was exhausted. A mattress was put on the deck for him. He lay down on it and fell asleep.

At dawn the next morning they were still nearly ten miles from the coast of England. The wind had fallen off during the night and they had sailed very slowly.

At ten o'clock they dropped anchor in Dover harbor.

At half-past ten d'Artagnan set foot on English soil.

"I'm here at last!" he exclaimed.

But his journey was not yet over: he still had to go to London. In England, post horses were readily available. D'Artagnan and Planchet each rented one and set off, with a postilion riding in front of them. Four hours later they reached the gates of the capital.

D'Artagnan did not know London and he did not speak a word of English, but he wrote the duke of Buckingham's name on a piece of paper and passersby directed him to his house.

When he arrived there, d'Artagnan learned that the duke was at Windsor, hunting with the king. He asked for the duke's valet—who, having accompanied him on all his travels, spoke French fluently—and told him that he had just come from Paris for a matter of life and death and had to speak to his master without delay.

Patrick (that was the valet's name) was convinced by the confidence with which d'Artagnan spoke. He offered to take d'Artagnan to the duke and had two horses saddled. As for Planchet, he had been lifted off his horse, stiff as a board; he was at the end of his strength. But d'Artagnan seemed to be made of iron.

He and Patrick rode to the castle. They were told that the king and Buckingham were hawking in the marshes five or six miles away.

In twenty minutes they were there. Patrick soon heard his master's voice calling his falcon.

"How shall I announce you to His Grace?" he asked.

"Tell him I'm the young man who nearly fought him one night on the Pont-Neuf."

"That's a strange way to present yourself!"

"Perhaps, but you'll see that it's as good as any other."

Patrick rode to the duke and made the announcement as he had been told to do.

Buckingham immediately realized who the young man in question was, and suspected that he had come with important news from France. Following Patrick's directions, he rode toward d'Artagnan and soon recognized his uniform. Patrick followed at a discreet distance.

Buckingham's first words to d'Artagnan showed that his love was uppermost in his mind:

"Has anything happened to the queen?"

"I don't think so, Your Grace," replied d'Artagnan. "But I believe she's threatened by a great danger from which only you can save her."

"Just tell me what I must do!"

"First, read this letter."

"Who—"

"I think it's from Her Majesty."

Buckingham turned so pale that d'Artagnan thought he might be about to faint.

"From Her Majesty!" he exclaimed. Then he pointed to a hole in the letter and asked, "What's this?"

"I hadn't noticed it," said d'Artagnan. "Count de Wardes's sword must have made that hole on its way into my chest."

"You're wounded?" asked Buckingham, breaking the seal.

"It's nothing serious."

"My God!" the duke cried out when he had read the letter. "Patrick, stay here—no, go to the king and tell him that I humbly beg him to excuse me, but that I must go back to London for an extremely important matter." He turned to d'Artagnan. "Come, sir."

They both galloped off in the direction of London.

21

Lady de Winter

As they rode, d'Artagnan told the duke everything he knew about what had happened. There were few details in the queen's letter, but Buckingham was able to form a fairly clear idea of her desperate situation by comparing what he remembered with what d'Artagnan had told him.

He was surprised that the cardinal, having a great interest in preventing d'Artagnan from reaching England, had not succeeded in doing so. When he expressed his surprise, d'Artagnan told him about the precautions that had been taken and how, thanks to the devotion of the three friends who had fallen along the way, he had come through unscathed, not counting the sword thrust that had pierced the queen's letter, and for which he had made Count de Wardes pay so dearly. As he listened to this story the duke glanced at d'Artagnan in astonishment now and then, as if he could not understand how such a young man could be so brave, resolute, and resourceful.

Their horses galloped like the wind, and in a few minutes they were at the gates of London. D'Artagnan thought the duke would slow his pace when they entered the city, but he did not: he went on riding at full speed, not caring whether or not he knocked down people who were in his way. Two or three accidents of that kind happened as they rode through the streets, but Buckingham did not even look back to see what had become of his victims. Although d'Artagnan did not understand the words that were shouted after them, it was obvious to him that they were angry curses.

When they stopped in the courtyard of the duke's house, Buckingham leapt off his horse, tossed the reins onto the animal's neck, and rapidly strode toward the door. D'Artagnan did the same, in spite of his reluctance to abandon the horses without making sure they would be properly cared for. He was relieved when he saw them taken in hand by servants who came out of the kitchen and the stables.

The duke walked so swiftly that it was hard for d'Artagnan to keep up with him. They went through several drawing rooms furnished with an elegance that was unknown even to the greatest lords of France. Finally they came to a bedroom that was a marvel of luxury and good taste. In the alcove was a door hidden by a tapestry. The duke opened it with a little golden key that hung from his neck by a golden chain. D'Artagnan discreetly remained behind, but when the duke had gone through the door, he looked back, saw d'Artagnan's hesitation, and said, "Come in, and if you have the good fortune to be admitted into Her Majesty's presence, tell her what you've seen."

Encouraged by this invitation, d'Artagnan followed the duke, who closed the door behind them.

They were in a little chapel with hangings of Persian silk brocade, brightly lighted by a large number of candles. Above an altar, and under a blue velvet canopy surmounted by white and red feathers, was a life-sized portrait of the queen of France. It was such a perfect likeness that d'Artagnan gasped when he saw it, half expecting to hear the queen speak.

On the altar below the portrait was the rosewood box containing the diamond tags.

Buckingham approached the altar and knelt as though to pray, then he opened the box.

"These," he said, taking out a large bow of blue ribbon glittering with diamonds, "are the precious tags I've sworn to be buried with; but the queen gave them to me and now she's taking them back. May her will, like God's, be done in all things."

He gazed at the diamond tags from which he was about to be separated and began kissing them one by one. Suddenly he cried out so loudly that d'Artagnan was alarmed.

"What is it, Your Grace? What's happened?"

"A disaster!" said Buckingham, pale as a corpse. "Two of the tags are missing! There are only ten of them here!"

"Have you lost them, or do you think they were stolen?"

"They were stolen, and I'm sure the cardinal was behind it! Look: the ribbons that held them have been cut."

"Is there anyone you suspect? Maybe the thief still has them."

"Ah, I remember!" exclaimed the duke. "The only time I've ever worn them was a week ago, at the king's ball. I'd been on bad terms with Lady de Winter, but that night she came to me and acted as though she wanted a reconciliation. It was a jealous woman's revenge! I haven't seen her since then. She's an agent of the cardinal."

"He seems to have agents everywhere!"

"Yes, he's a terribly dangerous opponent," the duke said angrily. "But tell me about that ball in Paris. When is it going to take place?"

"Next Monday."

"Monday—we still have five days," said the Duke. "That's more than enough time." He opened the chapel door and called out: "Patrick!"

His confidential servant appeared.

"Send me my jeweler and my secretary."

Patrick left with a promptness and silence that showed he was accustomed to obeying his master blindly.

The secretary was the first to arrive, since he lived in the house. He found Buckingham sitting at a table in his bedroom, writing orders.

"Jackson," said the Duke, "go to the lord chancellor and tell him that I want these orders carried out immediately."

"But, Your Grace, if the lord chancellor asks me why you've taken such an extraordinary measure, what shall I tell him?"

"Tell him that I choose to do it and that I'm not obliged to explain my reasons to anyone."

"And is that also the answer that the lord chancellor is to give His Majesty," asked the secretary, smiling, "if His Majesty should happen to ask why no ships are allowed to leave England?"

"No, of course not," replied the duke, "and you're right to raise that question. If the king asks about the embargo, the lord chancellor is to tell him that I've decided on war, and that this is my first act of hostility against France."

The secretary bowed and left.

"There's one thing we needn't worry about," the duke said to d'Artagnan. "If the tags haven't yet been taken to France, they won't arrive there until after you do."

"Why not?"

"I've just put an embargo on all ships now in His Majesty's harbors. None of them can leave without special permission."

D'Artagnan stared in amazement at this man who, endowed with limitless power by his trusting sovereign, used it in the service of his love. Buckingham saw his expression, guessed what he was thinking, and smiled.

"Yes," he said, "Anne of Austria is my true queen. At a word from her, I'd betray my country, my king, even my God. She asked me not to send the Protestants of La Rochelle the help I'd promised them, and I didn't send it. I broke my word, but it didn't matter to me because I was obeying her wishes. And I was handsomely paid for my obedience: to show her appreciation, she gave me that portrait of herself."

D'Artagnan was filled with wonder at the thought that the fate of nations could sometimes hang by such fragile, unknown threads.

He was still turning this thought over in his mind when the jeweler arrived. He was an Irishman, highly skilled in his trade, who earned enough from the duke of Buckingham alone to make him enviably wealthy.

The duke led him into the chapel.

"O'Reilly," he said, "look at these diamond tags and tell me what each of them is worth."

The jeweler looked at them, noted their elegant settings, calculated the value of the diamonds, and named a figure.

"How long would it take to make two more like them?" asked the duke. "As you can see, two are missing."

"It would take a week, Your Grace."

"I'll pay twice as much as they're worth if I have them by day after tomorrow."

"You'll have them by then, Your Grace."

"You're a valuable man, O'Reilly. But there's one more thing: since I don't want it known that two of the tags have been replaced with duplicates, the new ones will have to be made here in this house."

"Then I'm afraid it can't be done, Your Grace, because there's no one but me who could do the work so well that no difference could be seen between the new ones and the old ones."

"In that case, my dear O'Reilly, you're my prisoner. You couldn't leave now if you wanted to, so make the best of it. Tell me which of your men you'll need, and which tools they must bring with them."

Knowing the duke, the jeweler realized it would be useless to protest.

"May I write to my wife?" he asked.

"Certainly," replied the duke. "You can even see her if you like. Don't worry, you'll be well treated during your captivity. And to compensate you for the inconvenience I'm causing you, take this—it's over and above the price I'll pay you for the tags."

He handed the jeweler a draft for an impressive sum.

D'Artagnan was more amazed than ever at this man who handled people and money with godlike ease.

The jeweler wrote a letter to his wife, enclosing the draft and asking her to send him his best apprentice, an assortment of diamonds of various weights and types, and the tools he would need.

Buckingham took him to the room he would occupy. In half an hour it was transformed into a workshop. Then he posted a sentry at each door, with orders not to let anyone come in except his valet Patrick. Needless to say, O'Reilly and his assistant would not be allowed to leave for any reason whatever.

Having settled this matter, the duke came back to d'Artagnan.

"Now, my young friend," he said, "England is at our disposal. What do you want?"

"A bed," replied d'Artagnan. "I must admit that's what I need most, for the moment."

Buckingham gave him a bedroom next to his own. He wanted to keep him close at hand, not because he mistrusted him, but because he wanted to have someone with whom he could talk about the queen.

An hour later his order was officially announced in London: no ship could leave for France, not even mail ships. Everyone regarded it as a declaration of war between the two countries.

Two days later, at eleven o'clock in the morning, the two diamond tags were finished. They were such exact copies that Buckingham could not distinguish between them and the old ones, and even the most highly trained expert would have seen no difference.

The duke sent for d'Artagnan.

"Here are the diamond tags you came to England for," he said, "and I want you to bear witness that I've done everything it was humanly possible to do."

"I'll report what I've seen, Your Grace. But aren't you going to put the tags back into their box?"

"No, the box would only be a hindrance to you. Besides, it's all the more precious to me now that it's all I have left. Please say that I'm keeping it."

"I will, Your Grace."

"And now," said Buckingham, looking at d'Artagnan intently, "how can I pay my debt to you?"

D'Artagnan blushed to the whites of his eyes. He realized that the duke wanted him to accept something and he was repelled by the idea of his friends' blood, and his own, being paid for with English gold.

"Let's consider the facts, Your Grace," he said, "so that there won't be any misunderstanding between us. I'm in the service of the king and queen of France and I belong to Monsieur des Essarts's company of guards. Like his brother-in-law Monsieur de Tréville, Monsieur des Essarts is strongly attached to Their Majesties. So everything I've done, Your Grace, was done for the queen, and not for you. Furthermore, I might not have done any of it if I hadn't wanted to please someone who's my lady, as the queen is yours."

"I think I know who that someone is," said the duke. "She's—"

"I didn't say her name, Your Grace," d'Artagnan quickly interrupted.

"That's true. So it's to her that I must be grateful for your devotion?"

"Yes, Your Grace, because now that there's talk of war, I must admit that I see you only as an Englishman and therefore as an enemy whom I'd rather meet on a battlefield than in Windsor Park or the halls of the Louvre. That won't prevent me from doing everything in my power to carry out my mission; I'm prepared to die for it if necessary. But you have no more reason to feel grateful to me for what I'm doing now than for what I did the first time we met."

"As we say in England, you're proud as a Scotsman."

"In France we say 'proud as a Gascon.' The Gascons are the Scotsmen of France."

D'Artagnan bowed to the duke and prepared to leave.

"Just a minute," said Buckingham. "How do you intend to get to France?"

"To tell you the truth, I hadn't thought of it."

"You Frenchmen don't worry about anything!"

"I was forgetting that England is an island and that you rule it."

"Go to the waterfront, find a brig named the *Sund,* and give this letter to the captain. He'll take you to a little French port where you can be sure that no one is watching for you, because ordinarily only fishing boats go there."

"What's the name of that port?"

"Saint-Valery. But wait, there's more. When you arrive there, go to the inn. It's a wretched, dirty place without a sign, without even a name, but you can't fail to find it because it's the only inn in town."

"And then?"

"Ask for the inkeeper and say 'forward' to him. That's the password. He'll give you a saddled horse and tell you where to go from there. You'll change horses three times along your way. Give your address in Paris each time; the first three horses will be sent to you there, and you can keep the fourth. You already know two of them: they're the ones we rode. The other two are just as good, take my word for it. All four will be fully equipped for a campaign. I'd like you to choose one of them for yourself and give the others to your three friends. Surely your pride will let you do that, since you can use the horses to go to war against us. After all, the end justifies the means."

"I'll accept your gifts, Your Grace, and, God willing, we'll make good use of them."

"And now, young man, give me your hand. We may soon meet again on a battlefield, but in the meantime I hope we'll part as friends."

"Yes, Your Grace, but with the hope of soon becoming enemies."

"That's something I can promise you."

"I'll count on your promise, Your Grace."

D'Artagnan bowed again and left.

Opposite the Tower of London he found the ship that the duke had indicated to him. He gave his letter to the captain, who had it endorsed by the harbor master, and the ship then got under way.

Fifty other ships were waiting, ready to leave. As he passed close to one of them, d'Artagnan thought he recognized the beautiful woman he had seen at Meung, the one the stranger had called "Milady." But because of the current and a stiff wind, his ship was moving so fast that he lost sight of her in a few moments.

The next day, at about nine o'clock in the morning, they reached Saint-Valery.

D'Artagnan immediately went off to find the inn. He was guided to it by the shouts he heard coming from it: war between England and France was regarded as certain and imminent, and the elated sailors were celebrating noisily.

Inside the inn, d'Artagnan made his way through the crowd, went up to the innkeeper, and said the word "forward." The innkeeper signaled him to follow, took him out into the courtyard, led him to the stables, where a saddled horse was waiting for him, and asked if he needed anything else.

"I need to know where to go from here," said d'Artagnan.

"First go to Blangy, and from there to Neufchâtel. At Neufchâtel, go to the Herse d'Or inn, say the password to the innkeeper, and he'll give you another saddled horse."

"How much do I owe you?"

"Everything has already been paid for, handsomely. Go, and may God be with you!"

"Amen," replied d'Artagnan.

He rode off at a gallop and reached Neufchâtel at four o'clock.

He followed the instructions he had been given and again found a saddled horse waiting for him. He intended to transfer the pistols from the saddle he had just used to the one he was about to use, but then he saw that the holsters of the new saddle already contained pistols exactly like the others.

"What's your address in Paris?" asked the innkeeper.

"The headquarters of Monsieur des Essarts's company of guards."

"Very well."

"Where do I go next?" asked d'Artagnan.

"Take the road to Rouen but pass to the left of the city. Stop at the little village of Ecouis and go to the inn. There's only one, the Ecu de France. Don't judge it by its appearance; in its stables you'll find a horse as good as this one."

"Same password?"

"Yes."

"Good-bye."

"Good-bye, sir. Do you need anything else?"

D'Artagnan shook his head and rode off.

At Ecouis the same scene was repeated: the obliging innkeeper gave him a fresh horse and asked him for his address. D'Artagnan rode to Pontoise, where he changed horses for the last time, and at nine o'clock he galloped into the courtyard of Monsieur de

Tréville's house. He had traveled nearly a hundred and fifty miles in twelve hours.

Monsieur de Tréville received him as if he had seen him that morning, except that he shook his hand a little more warmly than usual. He told him that Monsieur des Essarts's company was on duty in the Louvre and that he could go to his post.

22

The Merlaison Ballet

The next day, no one in Paris talked about anything but the ball that the municipal magistrates were giving for the king and queen, at which Their Majesties would dance the famous Merlaison ballet, the king's favorite.

For the past week, work had been going on to prepare the city hall for that great occasion. The city carpenter had erected platforms on which the invited ladies were to sit; the city grocer had provided two hundred white wax candles—an incredible luxury in those times—to light the rooms; twenty violinists had been hired, and they would be paid twice the usual amount because they were to play all night.

At ten o'clock in the morning Monsieur de La Coste, ensign of the king's guards, followed by two sergeants and several constables of the watch, came to ask the city clerk, named Clément, for the keys to all the inner and outer doors of the building. These keys were handed over to him, each bearing an identifying label. From then on, Monsieur de La Coste was charged with guarding all the doors and all the approaches to the building.

At twenty past eleven Duhallier, captain of the guards, arrived with fifty constables of the watch who dispersed throughout the city hall and took up their posts at the doors assigned to them.

At three o'clock came two companies of guards, one French and the other Swiss. Half the French company was made up of Monsieur Duhallier's men, the other half of Monsieur des Essarts's men.

At six o'clock the guests began arriving. When they entered, they were led into the great hall and shown to their places on the platforms that had been prepared for them.

At nine o'clock the wife of the president of Parliament arrived. Since, after the queen, she would be the most important woman at the ball, she was received by the municipal magistrates and placed in a box opposite the one that was to be occupied by the queen.

At ten o'clock a supper of preserves for the king was laid out in the little hall near the Saint-Jean church, facing the silver sideboard of the city, which was guarded by four constables.

At midnight loud shouts and cheering were heard: the king was coming to the city hall from the Louvre, along streets that were all lighted with colored lanterns.

The municipal magistrates, wearing their woolen robes and preceded by six sergeants carrying torches, went to meet the king on the front steps. The provost of the merchants of Paris welcomed him, and His Majesty apologized for being so late, though he put the blame on the cardinal, who had detained him till eleven o'clock to discuss affairs of state.

His Majesty, in ceremonial attire, was accompanied by his brother the duke d'Orléans, Count de Soissons, the grand prior, the duke de Longueville, the duke d'Elbeuf, Count d'Harcourt, Count de La Roche-Guyon, Monsieur de Liancourt, Monsieur de Baradas, Count de Cramail, and Chevalier de Souveray.

Everyone noticed that the king seemed sad and preoccupied.

A private dressing room had been prepared for His Majesty, and another for his brother. The clothes they were to wear at the ball had been laid out in their rooms. The same preparations had also been made for the queen and the wife of the president of Parliament. The lords and ladies of Their Majesties' retinues were to change clothes two by two in bedrooms fitted out for the purpose.

Before going into his dressing room, the king ordered that he be notified as soon as the cardinal arrived.

Half an hour later, new cheering announced the arrival of the queen. The municipal magistrates, again preceded by the sergeants, went out to meet her as they had met the king.

The queen came into the ballroom; it was noticed that, like the king, she seemed sad, and she also looked tired.

Just as she was entering, the curtain of a little gallery opened and the cardinal's pale face appeared. He was dressed as a Spanish cavalier. His eyes met the queen's and a smile of sinister joy passed over his lips: she was not wearing her diamond tags.

She stood for a time in the ballroom, receiving the compliments of the municipal magistrates and responding to the greetings of the ladies.

Suddenly the king appeared with the cardinal at one of the doors of the ballroom. The cardinal was speaking softly to him, and the king was very pale.

The king walked through the crowd, not wearing his mask and with the ribbons of his doublet half untied. He went up to the queen and said to her in a faltering voice, "Madame, will you tell me why you're not wearing your diamond tags, when you know it would have pleased me to see them?"

She looked around and saw the cardinal standing behind the king with a diabolical smile.

"Because I was afraid, Sire," she replied, also in a faltering voice, "that something might happen to them in the midst of this great crowd."

"You were wrong not to do as I asked! I gave them to you because I wanted you to wear them. I tell you that you were wrong!"

This time the king's voice quavered with anger. Everyone looked and listened in astonishment, not understanding what was taking place.

"I can have them brought from the Louvre," said the queen, "and then your wishes will be satisfied."

"Please have them brought as quickly as possible, because the ballet will begin in an hour."

The queen bowed as a sign of assent and went off with the ladies who were to show her to her dressing room.

The king went to his own dressing room.

There was a moment of embarrassment in the ballroom. Everyone had noticed that something was happening between the king and queen, but they had both spoken so softly that nothing had been overheard, since even those standing closest to them had respectfully remained at a distance of several paces. The violinists were now playing loudly, but no one listened to them.

The king was the first to come out of his dressing room. He wore an elegant hunting costume, as did his brother and the other lords. This was the costume that best suited the king; dressed in that way, he truly seemed to be the first gentleman of his kingdom.

The cardinal approached the king and handed him a box. The king opened it and saw two diamond tags.

"What's the meaning of this?" he asked.

"If the queen wears her diamond tags, which I doubt," replied the cardinal, "count them, Sire, and if there are only ten, ask her who could have stolen these two."

The king gave him a questioning look, but before he could say anything a cry of admiration burst from everyone's lips. While the king seemed to be the first gentleman of his kingdom, the queen was undoubtedly the most beautiful woman in France.

Her hunting costume was marvelously becoming to her. She wore a felt hat with blue feathers, a pearl-gray coat fastened with diamond clasps, and a blue satin skirt covered with silver embroidery. On her left shoulder glittered the diamond tags, attached to a bow of the same color as the feathers and her skirt.

The king felt a surge of joy, the cardinal a surge of anger. However, they were too far away from the queen to be able to count the tags. She was wearing them, that was certain, but did she have only ten of them or all twelve?

Just then the violins sounded the signal for the ballet to begin. The king went to the president's wife, with whom he was to dance while his brother danced with the queen. The partners took their places and the ballet began.

The king danced opposite the queen; each time he passed close to her, he eagerly looked at the diamond tags, but he was never able to count them. The cardinal's forehead was covered with cold sweat.

The ballet lasted an hour; it had sixteen scenes. It ended in the midst of applause from all over the ballroom. The gentlemen accompanied their ladies back to their seats; but the king, using his royal prerogative, abandoned his partner and hurried to the queen.

"Madame," he said, "I thank you for the deference you've shown to my wishes, but I believe two of your tags are missing and I've brought them to you."

He held out the two tags that the cardinal had given him.

"You're giving me two more, Sire?" said the young queen, pretending surprise. "Now I have fourteen!"

The king counted the tags on her shoulder: there were twelve.

He called the cardinal to him and said sternly, "What does this mean, Your Eminence?"

"It means, Sire, that I wanted to give Her Majesty those two tags, but, not daring to give them to her myself, I used this means of having her accept them."

"And I'm all the more grateful to you, Cardinal," Anne of

Austria said with a smile that proved that she was not taken in by his ingenious gallantry, "because I'm sure that these two tags cost you as much as the twelve others cost His Majesty."

She bowed to the king and the cardinal and went to her dressing room to change out of the clothes she had worn for the ballet.

Till now, because of the attention we were obliged to give the illustrious persons who appeared at the beginning of this chapter, we have said nothing about the man to whom Anne of Austria owed her spectacular triumph over the cardinal. Mingling unnoticed with the crowd at one of the doors, d'Artagnan had watched the scene that was comprehensible to only four people in the ballroom: himself, the king, the queen, and the cardinal.

The queen had just gone back to her dressing room and d'Artagnan was about to leave when he felt someone lightly touch his shoulder. He turned around and saw a young woman beckoning him to follow her. She wore a black velvet mask, but in spite of that precaution—which she had taken for others, not for him—he instantly recognized the alert and quick-witted Madame Bonacieux.

The day before, he had gone to the Louvre and asked Germain, the gatekeeper, to send for her. But he had been able to exchange only a few words with her before she hurried off to give the queen the good news of her messenger's safe and successful return. So he now followed her with feelings of both love and curiosity.

As the corridors became more deserted he tried to stop her, hold her, contemplate her, if only for a moment; but she always slipped away from him, and each time he tried to speak she silenced him by putting her finger on his lips in an imperious yet charming gesture that reminded him that he was sworn to blind obedience and had no right to complain. Finally, after several minutes of walking through the labyrinth of corridors, she opened a door and led him into a dark room. Again she put her finger on his lips, then she opened another door, hidden by a tapestry, and left him. The door remained open, but the doorway was blocked by the tapestry, through which light shone from the next room.

D'Artagnan stood still and wondered where he was; but soon the warm, fragrant air that came to him from the doorway, the elegant, respectful conversation of two or three women, and the words "Your Majesty," repeated several times, told him clearly that he was next to the queen's dressing room. He went on waiting in the shadows.

The queen seemed cheerful and happy, which evidently surprised the women with her, who were used to always seeing her sad and worried. She told them that she was in a good mood because she had enjoyed the ball and especially the ballet, and since they knew they must never contradict the queen, whether she was smiling or weeping, they enthusiastically praised the graciousness of the municipal magistrates.

Although d'Artagnan did not know the queen, he distinguished her voice from the others by her slight foreign accent, and also by the tone of authority in which all sovereigns naturally speak. He heard her come toward the doorway, then walk away from it, and two or three times he saw her shadow pass across the tapestry.

Suddenly a shapely hand and arm came through an opening in the tapestry. D'Artagnan realized that this was his reward. He fell to his knees, took the hand, and respectfully pressed his lips to it. Then the hand withdrew, leaving in his an object that he recognized as a ring. The door was closed and he found himself in total darkness.

He put the ring on his finger and waited again; it was obvious to him that everything was not yet over. Now that he had been rewarded for his devotion, he was going to be rewarded for his love. Although the ballet had been performed, the ball had scarcely begun; there would be a supper at three o'clock, and the clock of the Saint-Jean church had already struck a quarter to three.

D'Artagnan heard the sound of voices die away as the queen and her entourage left through another door. Then the tapestry was pushed aside and Madame Bonacieux returned to him.

"At last!" he cried.

"Quiet!" she said, putting her hand over his mouth. "Leave by the way you came."

"But where and when will I see you again?"

"You'll learn that from a note you'll find when you go home. But now you must leave!"

She opened the door to the corridor and pushed him out of the room. He obeyed like a child, without resistance or protest, which proved that he was really in love.

23

The Rendezvous

D'Artagnan ran all the way home, and although it was past three in the morning and he had to go through some of the most dangerous parts of Paris, he had no unpleasant encounters. As is well known, there is a god for drunkards and lovers.

He found the side door of the house unlocked, climbed his private staircase and gently knocked on his door in the way that he and his servant had agreed on. Planchet, whom he had sent back from the city hall two hours earlier with orders to wait for him, opened the door.

"Has someone brought a letter for me?" d'Artagnan asked eagerly.

"No, sir," replied Planchet, "but a letter came all by itself."

"What are you talking about, you imbecile?"

"I had the key to your apartment in my pocket and it never left me, but when I came back I found a letter on the table in your bedroom."

"Where is it?"

"I left it where it was, sir. It's not natural for letters to come in all by themselves like that. If the window had been open or only unlocked, there wouldn't be any mystery about it, but the window was closed and locked, the same as the door. Be careful, sir, because I'm sure that letter got here by some kind of magic."

While Planchet was talking, d'Artagnan had rushed into the bedroom and opened the letter. It was from Madame Bonacieux:

> *I want to thank you for myself and someone else. Be in Saint-Cloud at ten o'clock tomorrow night, across the street from the bungalow at the corner of Monsieur d'Estrées's house.*

When he read this, d'Artagnan felt his heart gripped by the sweet spasm that tortures and caresses the hearts of lovers. It was the first time a woman had ever given him a rendezvous. Drunk

with joy, he felt as if he were about to faint on the threshold of
the earthly paradise known as love.

"I was right, wasn't I, sir?" asked Planchet, who had seen his
master's face turn first red, then white. "There's something
diabolical about that letter, isn't there?"

"No, you're completely mistaken, Planchet," replied d'Artagnan, "and to prove it, here's an écu for you. Take it and drink
to my health."

"Thank you, sir. I promise I'll follow your instructions. But I
still say that letters that come into locked rooms . . ."

"They fall from heaven, my friend, they fall from heaven."

"Then there's nothing wrong, sir?"

"Nothing at all, my dear Planchet: I'm the happiest man on
earth!"

"Since you're so happy, sir, is it all right for me to go to bed
now?"

"Of course. Good night."

"I hope all the blessings of heaven fall on you, sir, but it's
still true that letters . . ."

Planchet left his sentence unfinished and withdrew, shaking
his head with a doubt that had not been entirely dispelled by
d'Artagnan's generosity.

When he was alone, d'Artagnan read his letter over and over
again, then he repeatedly kissed those lines written by the woman
he loved. Finally he went to bed, fell asleep, and dreamed
golden dreams.

At seven o'clock in the morning he got up and called Planchet,
who came in at the second call with his face still showing traces of
the uneasiness he had felt the night before.

"Planchet," d'Artagnan said to him, "I may be gone all day.
You're free till seven o'clock this evening. But at seven o'clock,
be ready with two horses."

"That sounds as if we're going to have another chance to get
holes made in our skin."

"Bring your musket and your pistols."

"I knew it!" exclaimed Planchet. "It's that damned letter!"

"Calm down, you idiot. Our trip will be only for pleasure."

"Yes, I know, like that trip the other day, when bullets were
flying all around us and we couldn't go half a mile without
falling into an ambush."

"If you're afraid, Monsieur Planchet," said d'Artagnan, "I'll
go without you. I'd rather travel alone than with someone who's
trembling in his boots."

"You're being unfair to me, sir. You've seen me in action."

"Yes, but I thought you'd used up all your courage at once."

"You'll see that I still have some left if I need it, sir. But don't make me waste it too much if you want it to last a long time."

"Do you think you'll have some that you can use tonight?"

"I hope so."

"Good, I'll count on you."

"I'll be ready at seven, sir. But I thought you had only one horse at the guards' stables."

"I may have only one there now, but by this evening there will be four."

"Is that why we made that trip? To get horses?"

"Exactly," said d'Artagnan.

And he left.

Monsieur Bonacieux was standing on his doorstep. D'Artagnan intended to pass by without speaking to him, but the draper gave him such a friendly greeting that he felt obliged not only to return the greeting but also to stop and talk with him. And besides, how could he not have had a certain amount of good will toward the man whose wife had given him a rendezvous for that evening in Saint-Cloud, across the street from Monsieur d'Estrées's bungalow?

The conversation naturally turned to the poor man's incarceration. Not knowing that d'Artagnan had heard his conversation with the stranger from Meung, Bonacieux told him about the persecutions of that monster Monsieur de Laffemas, whom he referred to as the cardinal's executioner, and he talked at length about the Bastille, with its locks, spy holes, air holes, iron bars, and instruments of torture.

D'Artagnan listened with exemplary patience till he had finished, then asked, "And what about Madame Bonacieux? Have you found out who abducted her? I haven't forgotten that it was because of her abduction, regrettable though it was, that I had the good fortune of making your acquaintance."

"They didn't give me the slightest hint about who did it," said Bonacieux, "and my wife swears she doesn't know. But what about you?" he went on good-naturedly. "What were you all doing the last few days? I didn't see you or your friends, and I don't think it was in the streets of Paris that you picked up all the dust I saw Planchet wiping off your boots yesterday."

"You're right, my dear Monsieur Bonacieux, my friends and I left the city for a little while."

"Did you go far away?"

"No, only about a hundred and twenty miles. Monsieur Athos went to take the waters at Forges. We went with him and my friends stayed there."

"But you came back," Bonacieux remarked with a sly look. "A handsome young man like you doesn't get very long leaves from his mistress. You were impatiently awaited in Paris, weren't you?"

"I must confess it's true," replied d'Artagnan, laughing, "since I see I can't hide anything from you. Yes, I was awaited, and very impatiently."

A light cloud passed over Bonacieux's face, so light that d'Artagnan did not notice it.

"And now you're going to be rewarded for your diligence, aren't you?" the draper asked with a slight quaver in his voice, which d'Artagnan did not notice any more than he had noticed the cloud that had briefly darkened his face.

"You don't disapprove of me, do you?" said d'Artagnan, laughing again. "Don't try to pretend that you've never been in the same situation yourself!"

"No, I don't disapprove; I only asked because I wanted to know if you'd come home late."

"But why do you want to know? Are you planning to wait up for me?"

"No, no, it's just that ever since my arrest and the robbery that was committed in my house, I'm frightened whenever I hear a door open, especially at night. You'll have to excuse me: I'm not a swordsman, like you."

"Well, don't be frightened if I come home at one o'clock in the morning, or two or three o'clock, or if I don't come home at all."

This time Bonacieux turned so pale that d'Artagnan could not fail to notice it. He asked what was wrong.

"Nothing," replied Bonacieux. "Since my misfortunes I've been subject to sudden fits of weakness, and I just had one. Don't worry about me; concentrate on trying to be happy."

"I don't have to try: I'm already happy."

"Your real happiness won't come till tonight."

"Yes, but meanwhile I can look forward to it. And maybe you're also looking forward to this evening. Maybe Madame Bonacieux will visit you then."

"Madame Bonacieux won't be free this evening," her husband said gravely. "Her duties will keep her at the Louvre."

"Well, I suppose it can't be helped," said d'Artagnan. "When I'm happy, I want everyone else to be happy too, but it seems that's impossible."

He walked away, laughing at the joke which he thought that only he understood.

"Enjoy yourself," Bonacieux said grimly.

But d'Artagnan was already too far away to hear him; and even if he had heard him, in his frame of mind, he would not have noticed anything unusual in his tone.

D'Artagnan went to Monsieur de Tréville's house. His last visit to him had been too short to allow much discussion.

He found Monsieur de Tréville in an excellent mood. The king and queen had treated him graciously at the ball; the cardinal had been plunged in gloom, and had left at one o'clock, saying he did not feel well. Their Majesties had stayed till six in the morning.

"Now, let's talk about you, my young friend," said Tréville, lowering his voice and looking around the room to make sure they were alone, "because it's obvious that your safe return had something to do with the king's joy, the queen's triumph, and the cardinal's humiliation. You must be on your guard."

"What do I have to fear," asked d'Artagnan, "as long as I have the good fortune to be in favor with the king and queen?"

"You have everything to fear, believe me. The cardinal isn't the kind of man who'll forget a prank like that till he's settled his scored with the prankster, and I strongly suspect that the prankster is a certain young Gascon I know."

"Do you think the cardinal shares your suspicion? Does he know I'm the one who went to London?"

"Ah, so you went to London! Is that where you got that beautiful diamond ring you're wearing? Be careful, my dear d'Artagnan: it's not good to take a gift from an enemy. I think there's something on that subject in a Latin poem . . . Let's see now . . ."

"Yes, I'm sure some Latin poet must have written about it," said d'Artagnan. He had never been able to master even the first page of his Latin grammar, and his ignorance had driven his tutor to despair.

"I'll remember it in a moment," said Tréville, who had a smattering of literary knowledge. "Monsieur de Benserade quoted it to me only the other day . . . Ah! Here it is: '. . . *timeo Danaos et dona ferentes*.' Which means: 'Beware of an enemy who gives you presents.' "

"This ring didn't come from an enemy, sir," said d'Artagnan. "It came from the queen."

"The queen? Yes, I can see it's a royal jewel: it's worth at least a thousand pistoles. Who brought it to you?"

"The queen gave it to me herself."

"Where?"

"In the room next to the one where she changed clothes."

"How?"

"She held out her hand for me to kiss, and she was holding the ring in it."

"You kissed the queen's hand!" exclaimed Tréville, looking at d'Artagnan.

"Yes, sir, she did me the honor of granting me that favor."

"In front of witnesses? That was rash of her!"

"No, sir, don't worry: no one saw her," said d'Artagnan. And he told Tréville how it had happened.

"Ah, women! Women!" said the old soldier. "They all have the same romantic imagination. They're delighted by anything that has a touch of mystery . . . So you saw only a hand and an arm; if you met the queen, neither of you would recognize the other."

"No, but because of this diamond ring . . ."

"Would you like me to give you some good advice, some friendly advice?"

"I'd be honored, sir."

"Go to the first jeweler you can find and sell that ring for whatever he's willing to give you. No matter how stingy he may be, he's sure to pay you at least eight hundred pistoles for it. Money has no name, young man, but that ring bears an awesome one and it can betray anyone who wears it."

"Sell a ring given to me by my queen? Never!"

"Then at least turn it around so that the diamond doesn't show. Everyone knows that young Gascons aren't given jewels like that by their mothers."

"Then you really think I have something to fear?"

"Compared to you, a man sleeping on a mine with a lighted fuse is safe."

"What must I do?" asked d'Artagnan, who was beginning to be worried by Tréville's tone of conviction.

"Stay on your guard at all times. The cardinal has a long memory and a powerful hand. He'll do something against you, you can be sure of that."

"But what will it be?"

"How should I know? He's as devious and crafty as the devil himself. The least that can happen to you is that you'll be arrested."

"Would they really dare to arrest a man in the king's service?"

"They didn't mind arresting Athos! Take the word of a man who's been at court for thirty years: if you let yourself be lulled into a feeling of security, you're lost. Expect to find enemies everywhere. If someone tries to pick a quarrel with you, don't let him do it, even if he's a ten-year-old child; if you're attacked at any time, day or night, retreat without shame; if you cross a bridge, test the planks to make sure they won't break under you; if you come home late, have your servant follow you, armed—if you're sure of his loyalty. Be suspicious of everyone: your brother, your mistress; especially your mistress."

D'Artagnan blushed.

"Why should I mistrust my mistress more than anyone else?"

"Because mistresses are one of the cardinal's favorite weapons, and one of his most effective. A woman will betray you for ten pistoles. Remember Samson and Delilah—you know the Bible, don't you?"

D'Artagnan thought of the rendezvous Madame Bonacieux had given him for that night, but it must be said to his credit that Tréville's bad opinion of women in general did not make him suspicious of her for one moment.

"But you haven't yet told me what became of your three friends," Tréville went on.

"I was going to ask you if you'd heard anything from them."

"No, nothing."

"I left them along the way: Porthos in Chantilly with a duel on his hands, Aramis in Crèvecoeur with a bullet in his shoulder, and Athos in Amiens with an accusation of counterfeiting against him."

"You see! And how did you escape?"

"Only by a miracle, sir, I must admit. Just outside of Calais, Count de Wardes wounded me in the shoulder. I ran him through and left him there."

"That's more proof of what I'm saying! Count de Wardes is one of the cardinal's men, and Rochefort's cousin. I have an idea, my friend."

"Please tell me what it is, sir."

"While the cardinal is having his men look for you in Paris, I think you should quietly slip out of the city, take the road to

Picardy and go to find out what's become of your three friends. That's the least you can do for them, after what they've done for you.''

"You're right, sir. I'll leave tomorrow."

"Tomorrow? Why not today?"

"I must be in Paris tonight, for a very important matter."

"Ah, young man, I can guess what that important matter is! It's a love affair, don't deny it. Let me tell you again that you must be on your guard. Women have been causing trouble ever since the Garden of Eden. If you take my advice, you'll leave today."

"I can't, sir."

"You've given your word?"

"Yes, sir."

"Then that's different. But promise me that if you're not killed tonight, you'll leave tomorrow."

"I promise."

"Do you need money?"

"I still have fifty pistoles. I think that's enough."

"But what about your friends?"

"They must not be short of money either. We left Paris with seventy-five pistoles each."

"Will I see you before you leave?"

"I don't think so, sir, unless there's something new."

"Then good-bye and good luck."

"Thank you, sir."

D'Artagnan took leave of Monsieur de Tréville, touched more than ever by his fatherly concern for his musketeers.

He went to his three friends' apartments; neither they nor their servants had returned, and no one had any news of them.

He would have gone to their mistresses to ask about them, but he did not know Porthos's or Aramis's mistress, and Athos did not have one.

As he was passing the guards' headquarters he looked into the stables: three of the four horses were already there. Planchet, amazed, had groomed two of them and was now working on the third.

"Ah, I'm glad to see you, sir!" he said when he caught sight of d'Artagnan.

"Why?" asked the young man.

"Do you trust our landlord, Monsieur Bonacieux?"

"No, not at all."

"You're right not to!"

"Why do you say that?"

"Because while you were talking with him, sir, I was watching the two of you, without listening, of course, and I saw his face change color two or three times."

"Well, what of it?"

"You must not have noticed, sir, because you were thinking about the letter you received. But I was still worried about the strange way that letter came into your bedroom, so I was on my guard and I watched his face very carefully."

"And how did his face seem to you?"

"Treacherous, sir."

"Really?"

"Yes, and as soon as you'd left him and turned the corner of the street, he took his hat, locked his door, and ran off in the opposite direction."

"You're right, Planchet: that seems highly suspicious. But don't worry, we won't pay our rent till he's given us a satisfactory explanation of his conduct."

"You're joking, sir, but you'll see."

"What do you expect me to do, Planchet? I can only follow where destiny leads me."

"Does that mean you're not going to change your plans for tonight?"

"You've made me less inclined to change them than ever. The more reason I have to dislike Monsieur Bonacieux, the more determined I am to obey the instructions given to me in that letter you're so upset about."

"If your mind is made up, sir . . ."

"It is, Planchet, and there's nothing more to be said. I'll come by for you here at nine o'clock tonight. Be ready."

Seeing that there was no hope of making his master give up his plans, Planchet sighed deeply and went back to grooming the third horse.

Since d'Artagnan was a cautious young man in most circumstances, instead of going home he went to have dinner with the Gascon priest who had once fed the four friends in their time of financial distress.

24

The Bungalow

At nine o'clock d'Artagnan returned to the guards' headquarters. Planchet was waiting for him, armed with his musket and a pistol. The fourth horse had arrived.

D'Artagnan already had his sword; he slipped two pistols into his belt, then he and Planchet mounted their horses and rode off as quietly as they could. It was dark and no one saw them leave. Planchet began riding ten paces behind his master.

They followed the river, left the city by way of the Conférence gate and took the Saint-Cloud road, which was much more beautiful then than it is today.

As long as they had been in the city, Planchet had respectfully kept his distance behind d'Artagnan, but when the road became darker and more deserted, he began gradually moving closer, and by the time they entered the Bois de Boulogne he was riding beside his master. We must not conceal the fact that he was made extremely uneasy by the swaying of the big trees and eerie glints of moonlight in the darkness beneath them. D'Artagnan became aware of his uneasiness.

"What's the matter, Planchet?" he asked.

"Haven't you ever noticed, sir, that forests are like churches?"

"In what way?"

"They both make you feel you have to talk softly."

"Why do you feel you must talk softly, Planchet? Is it because you're afraid?"

"Yes, sir, afraid of being heard."

"I don't see why you should be afraid of that, since our conversation is perfectly innocent. No one who heard it could object to it."

"There's something shifty about that Monsieur Bonacieux's eyebrows," said Planchet, coming back to the idea that refused to leave his mind.

"Bonacieux?" asked d'Artagnan, puzzled. "What made you think of him?"

"I can't help what I think of, sir. It's beyond my control."

"That's because you're fainthearted."

"Let's not confuse faintheartedness with prudence. Prudence is a virtue."

"And you're virtuous, aren't you, Planchet?"

"Look over there—isn't that a musket barrel shining in the moonlight? Maybe we'd better put our heads down."

In spite of himself, d'Artagnan remembered Monsieur de Tréville's warnings. "If I go on listening to Planchet," he thought, "he'll make me afraid too."

He spurred his horse into a trot. Planchet did the same, following him as if he were his shadow, and continued riding beside him.

"Are we going on like this all night, sir?" he asked.

"No, because you're stopping here."

"I am? And what about you, sir?"

"I'm going a little further."

"You're going to leave me here alone, sir?"

"Are you afraid?"

"No, sir, but I'd like to point out that it's a cold night, that chills cause rheumatism, and that a servant with rheumatism isn't of much use, especially to a master as active as you are, sir."

"If you're cold, you can go into one of those taverns over there and meet me in front of it at six o'clock tomorrow morning."

"I don't have the écu you gave me last night, sir. I spent it on food and drink. So I have no money to buy what I'll need to protect myself from chills."

"Here's half a pistole. I'll see you tomorrow."

D'Artagnan dismounted, tossed the reins of his horse to Planchet, wrapped himself in his cloak, and rapidly walked away.

"My God, but I'm cold!" Planchet muttered as soon as he had lost sight of his master. And, wanting to warm himself without delay, he hastened to knock on the door of a house that showed every sign of being a suburban tavern.

D'Artagnan walked along a side road till he reached Saint-Cloud. But instead of following the main street, he turned behind the castle, took an isolated little street, and soon found himself opposite the bungalow mentioned in Madame Bonacieux's letter. It was a deserted place. The bungalow stood at the corner of a high wall that ran along one side of the street; on the other side, a hedge screened a garden with a little hut at its far end.

He had arrived at his rendezvous, and since he had not been told to announce his presence by any kind of signal, he waited.

There was not a sound to be heard; it was as if he were hundreds of miles from Paris. He stood with his back to the hedge, after glancing behind him. Beyond the hedge, the garden, and the hut, dark fog enveloped the vast space in which the city slept, with a few pinpoints of light shining like forlorn stars.

But to d'Artagnan everything he saw was charming, all his thoughts were delightful, and the shadows were translucent, for the time of his meeting with the woman he loved was close at hand.

The bell of the Saint-Cloud steeple slowly boomed out ten o'clock. There was something mournful about that bronze voice lamenting in the night, but each of the strokes announcing the hour that d'Artagnan had been so eagerly awaiting resounded harmoniously in his heart.

He kept his eyes fixed on the bungalow. All its windows were closed by shutters, except for one on the second floor. From that window shone a soft light that cast a silvery glow on the quivering leaves of the linden trees that stood in a group outside the park. It was obvious to d'Artagnan that the lovely Madame Bonacieux was waiting for him behind that pleasingly lighted window.

Lulled by this sweet thought, he waited half an hour without the slightest impatience, looking at the attractive little house. Through the window he could see part of a ceiling with gilded moldings that testified to the elegance of the rest of the room.

The bell in the Saint-Cloud steeple struck half-past ten.

This time, without understanding why, d'Artagnan shuddered. Perhaps the chilly night air was beginning to affect him and he was mistaking a purely physical reaction for an emotional one.

Then it occurred to him that he might have misread the letter and that the rendezvous was for eleven o'clock, rather than ten. He stepped closer to the window, stood in a ray of light, took the letter from his pocket, and reread it. He had not been mistaken: the rendezvous was for ten o'clock.

He went back to the hedge. The silence and loneliness of the place now made him feel a little ill at ease.

When the clock struck eleven, he began to be afraid that something had happened to Madame Bonacieux. He clapped his hands three times, a common signal with lovers; but there was no answer, not even an echo. He felt a certain resentment at the thought that Madame Bonacieux might have fallen asleep while she was waiting for him. He went to the wall and tried to climb it, but it had been freshly plastered, and he only broke his fingernails on it in vain. Then he looked at the linden trees on which the light from the windows was still shining, and since one of them jutted out over the street it seemed to him that from its branches he would be able to see into the bungalow.

The tree was easy to climb, especially since d'Artagnan was barely twenty years old and still had his boyhood skills. In a few moments he was standing on a branch, looking into the bungalow through the windowpanes.

He shuddered from head to foot at what he saw: the gentle lamplight illuminated a scene of terrifying disorder. One of the windowpanes had been shattered; the door of the bedroom had been broken open and now hung askew from its hinges; a table that had evidently held an elegant supper had been overturned; broken bottles and crushed fruit were strewn over the floor. Everything in the room bore witness to a violent, desperate struggle. D'Artagnan even thought he saw shreds of clothing in the sinister debris, and bloodstains on the tablecloth and curtains.

He climbed down from the tree with his heart pounding horribly. He wanted to see if he could find other traces of violence.

The light still shone softly in the calm of the night. He saw something that he had not noticed before, since there had been no reason for him to look for it: the ground had been trampled by men and horses. He also saw deep wheel-marks in the soft earth, apparently made by a carriage that had come from the direction of Paris, then turned around and gone back in the same direction.

Finally, near the wall, he found a woman's torn glove. Except where it had touched the muddy ground, it was impeccably clean and fresh. It was a perfumed glove of the kind that lovers like to pull from a pretty hand.

As he continued his search, cold sweat broke out on his forehead, his heart was gripped by terrible anxiety, and his breathing became irregular; yet he tried to convince himself that the bungalow might have no connection with Madame Bonacieux, that she had intended to meet him in front of it rather than inside it, and that she might have been prevented from coming there by her service in the Louvre, or perhaps by her husband's jealousy.

But all this reasoning was overturned and destroyed by that feeling of intimate grief that sometimes takes possession of our whole being and cries out to us that a greater disaster is hanging over us.

D'Artagnan was thrown into a frenzy that bordered on madness. He ran along the street, then along the road he had taken when he came to the bungalow, and continued till he came to the ferry. He questioned the ferryman, who told him that at seven o'clock he had taken a woman across the river; she was wrapped in a black cloak and seemed greatly concerned not to be recognized, but precisely for that reason he had examined her closely and seen that she was young and pretty.

In those days, as now, there were many pretty young women who went to Saint-Cloud and were concerned not to be recognized, yet d'Artagnan did not doubt for one moment that it was Madame Bonacieux who had been noticed by the ferryman.

By the light of the lamp in the ferryman's shelter, he reread her letter to make sure he was not mistaken, that the rendezvous was in Saint-Cloud and not somewhere else, in front of Monsieur d'Estrées's bungalow and not on another street.

Everything combined to convince him that his foreboding of disaster had been right.

He ran back to the bungalow, thinking that during his absence there might have been some new occurrence that would help him to learn what had happened.

The street was still deserted, and the light from the window was as calm as before.

D'Artagnan thought of the hut behind the hedge: perhaps there was someone in it who had seen something. The gate was locked, but he leapt over the hedge and approached the hut despite the barking of a dog chained in front of it.

He knocked on the door. No answer. There was dead silence inside the hut, as in the bungalow. But since the hut was his only hope of getting information, he stubbornly went on knocking.

He heard a timid stirring inside. He stopped knocking and began to plead in a tone that was humble, earnest, and beseeching enough to reassure the most fearful listener. Finally a decrepit shutter was pushed ajar, then quickly closed again as soon as the light from a wretched lamp in a corner had shone on d'Artagnan's sword and pistols. But rapid though this movement was, d'Artagnan had time to glimpse an old man's face.

"In the name of heaven, listen to me!" he said. "I've been waiting for someone who hasn't come, and I'm dying of anxiety! Has anything happened near here? Please tell me!"

The window opened slowly, and the same face appeared again, even paler than before.

D'Artagnan candidly told his story, without mentioning any names; he told how a young woman had given him a rendezvous in front of the bungalow and how, after waiting for her in vain, he had climbed the linden tree and seen the disorder in the lamplit room.

The old man listened attentively, occasionally making a gesture to show that he understood; then, when he had heard the end of the story, he shook his head in a way that made d'Artagnan's blood run cold.

"You know something!" cried d'Artagnan. "Tell me what it is! Please! You must tell me!"

"Don't ask me anything, sir, because I'm sure nothing good would happen to me if I told you what I saw."

"Then you *did* see something!" said d'Artagnan, taking a pistole from his pocket and handing it to him. "Please, in the name of heaven, tell me what you saw! I give you my word of honor that I won't repeat anything you say."

The old man saw such sincerity and anguish in d'Artagnan's face that he motioned him to come closer and began speaking in an undertone:

"At about nine o'clock I heard a noise in the street and wanted to find out what it was. As I was walking toward my door I heard someone trying to get in. I'm not afraid of being robbed, because I'm a poor man, so I opened the door. I saw three men. Behind them was a carriage with horses harnessed to it, and some saddled horses. The three men were dressed for riding, so the saddled horses obviously belonged to them.

" 'What can I do for you, gentlemen?' I asked them.

" 'You must have a ladder,' said the one who seemed to be the leader.

" 'Yes, sir,' I answered, 'I have one that I use for picking fruit.'

" 'Give it to us and stay in your house,' he said. 'Here's an écu for your trouble. But remember this: if you say one word about what you're going to see and hear—because I know you'll look and listen, no matter how much we threaten you—you're lost.'

"He threw me an écu, I picked it up, and he took my ladder.

"After closing and locking the gate of the hedge behind them, I went back into my house, but then I slipped out the back door and hid in a clump of elder bushes, where I could see without being seen.

"The three men brought the carriage closer to the bungalow without making a sound. A short, fat man with gray hair and dark, shabby clothes got out of the carriage, climbed the ladder up to the second floor of the bungalow and looked through the window. When he came back down, he said, 'She's there!' The man who'd talked to me went to the door of the bungalow, unlocked it with a key that he took out of his pocket, and went inside. The two others climbed the ladder. The fat man stood by the carriage. The coachman held the carriage horses, and a servant held the saddled ones.

"Suddenly I heard a scream from the bungalow. A woman ran to the window and opened it as if she were going to jump out, but then she saw the two men on the ladder and stepped back. They went in through the window.

"I couldn't see anything now, but I heard furniture being knocked over. The woman called for help, but soon her voice was muffled. The three men carried her to the window. Two of them took her down the ladder and into the carriage, then the fat man got in. The man who'd stayed in the house closed the window, came out through the door a little later, and looked into the carriage to make sure the woman was there. The two others were waiting for him on their horses. He got on his horse, and the servant sat down on the seat beside the coachman. The carriage and the three riders galloped away. Since then I haven't seen or heard anything else."

Overwhelmed by this terrible news, d'Artagnan stood motionless and silent while all the demons of anger and jealousy shrieked in his heart.

"Don't lose hope, sir," the old man said to him, more deeply moved by his silent despair than he would have been by wails and tears. "They didn't kill her, and that's all that really matters."

"What can you tell me about the man who seemed to be the leader?" asked d'Artagnan.

"I don't know him."

"But since he talked to you, you must have seen him."

"Ah, you want me to describe him?"

"Yes."

"He was a tall, dark, slender man with a black mustache, and he seemed to be a gentleman."

"I knew it!" cried d'Artagnan. "The same man again! Always the same man! And the other one?"

"Which one?"

"The short, fat man."

"Oh, *he's* not a gentleman, I'm sure of that. He wasn't wearing a sword, and the others treated him without respect."

"He must have been a servant," murmured d'Artagnan. "Oh, poor woman, poor woman! What have they done with her?"

"Remember that you promised not to repeat anything I said."

"Don't worry: I'm a gentleman, and a gentleman always keeps his word."

D'Artagnan left, heartbroken, and began walking toward the ferry. His thoughts fluctuated: sometimes he could not believe it was Madame Bonacieux who had been taken from the bungalow, and he hoped to see her again the next day in the Louvre; sometimes he was afraid she had been having an affair with another man and that her jealous lover had learned of her rendezvous and had her abducted. He was pulled first in one direction, then in another, and his uncertainty increased his despair. "If only my friends were here!" he thought. "Then I'd at least have some hope of finding her. But I don't know what's become of them either!"

It was about midnight. He had to rejoin Planchet. He began going into all the taverns from which light was showing; he did not find Planchet.

At the sixth tavern, he decided that his search had little chance of being successful. Since Planchet was not supposed to meet him till six o'clock in the morning, he could be anywhere.

Besides, he reflected that if he stayed near the place where Madame Bonacieux had been abducted, he might learn something that would shed light on the mystery. So at the sixth tavern he ordered a bottle of good wine and sat down in a dark corner, intending to wait there till dawn. But again his hopes were disappointed: listening to the coarse jokes and good-natured insults exchanged by the workmen, servants, and carters in the tavern, he heard nothing that could be of the slightest use to him in learning where Madame Bonacieux had been taken. He finished off his bottle to avoid arousing suspicion, and because he had nothing else to do. Then he made himself as comfortable as possible in his corner and fell asleep. He was only twenty, as we have mentioned, and at that age it is difficult to resist the demands of sleep, even with a broken heart.

Toward six o'clock he woke up with the feeling of uneasiness that dawn usually brings after a bad night. It did not take him long to prepare himself for the new day; he checked to see if he had been robbed while he slept, and, having found his diamond ring on his finger, his purse in his pocket, and his pistols in his belt, he stood up, paid for his bottle of wine, and left, hoping that his luck in trying to find Planchet would be better this morning than it had been the night before. And it was: through the damp, grayish mist he saw Planchet holding the reins of the two horses, waiting in front of a disreputable little tavern that d'Artagnan had passed without even suspecting its existence.

25

Porthos

Instead of going directly home, d'Artagnan stopped at Monsieur de Tréville's house and rapidly climbed the stairs. This time he intended to tell him everything that had happened. Monsieur de Tréville would probably give him good advice, and since he saw the queen nearly every day, he might be able to learn something from her about Madame Bonacieux's abduction.

Monsieur de Tréville listened to d'Artagnan's story with a seriousness that showed that he saw more in it than an amorous intrigue.

"The whole affair reeks of the cardinal," he said.

"But what shall I do?" asked d'Artagnan.

"Nothing, for the moment, except to leave Paris as soon as you can, as I told you. The queen probably doesn't know the details of that poor woman's disappearance; I'll tell them to her and they'll guide her. When you come back, I may have some good news for you. You can count on me to do my best."

D'Artagnan knew that although Monsieur de Tréville was a Gascon, he did not often make promises, and that when he made one, he did even more than he had promised. D'Artagnan took leave of him, grateful for the past and the future. Tréville, who was strongly attached to this brave and resolute young man, affectionately shook his hand and wished him a good journey.

Determined to follow Monsieur de Tréville's advice without delay, d'Artagnan headed for home to have Planchet do his packing. As he was approaching his house he saw Monsieur Bonacieux standing on the doorstep dressed in morning clothes. Remembering what the prudent Planchet had told him about his landlord's sinister character, he looked at him more attentively than he had ever done before. He noticed the sickly, yellowish pallor caused by an infiltration of bile in the blood; that might not be significant, but he also noticed something cunning and treacherous in the wrinkles of his face. A criminal does not laugh in the same way as an honest man, a hypocrite does not shed the same tears as a man of good faith. Duplicity is a mask, and no matter how well made that mask may be, it can always be distinguished from the face with a little attention.

It thus seemed to d'Artagnan that Bonacieux was wearing a mask, and that it was very unpleasant to see.

His repugnance was so great that he decided to pass by without speaking to him, but Bonacieux called out to him as he had done the day before.

"Well, young man," he said, "I see you keep yourself busy at night. It's seven in the morning! You do things a little differently: you come home when most people are leaving."

"No one can accuse you of that," replied d'Artagnan. "Your life is a model of regularity. Of course, when a man has a pretty young wife he doesn't need to go out looking for happiness: it comes to him at home. Isn't that right, Monsieur Bonacieux?"

Bonacieux turned deathly pale and grimaced a smile.

"You always like to have your little joke, don't you? But tell me, where were you last night? It looks as though you'd traveled some bad roads."

D'Artagnan glanced down at his muddy boots. At the same time he also noticed Bonacieux's shoes and stockings: they were spotted with exactly the same kind of mud. An idea flashed into his mind: that short, fat, gray-haired man, treated without respect by the noblemen who abducted Madame Bonacieux, was Bonacieux himself! The husband had taken part in his wife's abduction!

D'Artagnan had a strong impulse to seize him by the throat and strangle him. He realized in time that he had to control himself, but his face had shown such fury that Bonacieux was frightened and tried to step back; he was stopped by the closed door behind him.

"It seems to me that you're in no position to make remarks about my boots," said d'Artagnan. "It's true that they need cleaning, but so do your shoes and stockings. Did you spend the night away from home, Monsieur Bonacieux? That would be inexcusable for a man of your age, especially one with a wife as young and pretty as yours."

"No, no, it's nothing like that," Bonacieux protested. "I need a servant, and yesterday I went to Saint-Mandé to ask about one. The roads were so bad that by the time I came home my shoes were covered with mud. I haven't yet had time to clean it off."

D'Artagnan's suspicion was strengthened by the fact that Bonacieux claimed to have gone to Saint-Mandé; he had said that, d'Artagnan believed, because Saint-Mandé was in the opposite direction from Saint-Cloud.

D'Artagnan drew hope from his suspicion: if Bonacieux knew where his wife was, drastic means could be used, if necessary, to make him tell his secret. But first that suspicion had to be turned into a certainty.

"Excuse me for imposing on you, Monsieur Bonacieux," said d'Artagnan, "but lack of sleep always makes me thirsty, and with your permission I'll go into your house and get myself a glass of water."

Without waiting for his landlord's permission, d'Artagnan went into the house, glanced at the bed, and saw that it had not been slept in. Bonacieux had not spent the night at home; he had come back only an hour or two earlier, after going with his wife to where she had been taken, or at least accompanying her on the first stage of the journey.

"Thank you, Monsieur Bonacieux," d'Artagnan said when he had drunk his glass of water, "that's all I wanted from you. I'm going upstairs to have Planchet clean my boots, and I'll send him down to you if you'd like him to clean your shoes."

He left Bonacieux taken aback and wondering if he had betrayed himself.

D'Artagnan found Planchet in a state of great agitation.

"Oh, I'm so glad you've come home, sir! I've got something to tell you!"

"What is it?" asked d'Artagnan.

"You'll never guess who came to see you!"

"When?"

"About half an hour ago, while you were at Monsieur de Tréville's house."

"And who was it?"

"Monsieur de Cavois."

"The captain of the cardinal's guards?"

"Yes, sir."

"Did he come to arrest me?"

"I think so, sir, in spite of the smooth-tongued way he talked. He said His Eminence had sent him to ask you to come to the Palais-Royal for a friendly visit."

"And what did you answer?"

"I told him it was impossible, since you weren't at home, as he could see for himself."

"What did he say then?"

"He told me to tell you to be sure to come and see him some time today, and then he said, 'Tell your master that His Eminence is very well disposed toward him, and that his fortune may depend on that visit.' "

"That was a rather crude trap, for the cardinal," remarked d'Artagnan, smiling.

"Yes, sir, and that's why I didn't have any trouble seeing it was a trap. I told Monsieur de Cavois that when you came home you'd be sorry to learn you'd missed him. He asked me where you'd gone and when you'd left. I said you'd left last night and gone to Troyes, in Champagne."

"Planchet, my friend, you're a very valuable man."

"I thought that if you should want to see Monsieur de Cavois, you could contradict me and say you hadn't gone away. I'm not a nobleman, so it's all right for me to lie."

"Don't worry, Planchet, you'll keep your reputation for truthfulness. We're leaving in a quarter of an hour."

"That's just what I was going to advise, sir. And where are we going, if you don't mind my curiosity?"

"In the opposite direction from where you said I went. Aren't you as eager to hear from Grimaud, Mousqueton, and Bazin as I am to know what's become of Athos, Porthos, and Aramis?"

"Yes, sir, and I'll leave whenever you say. I think the country air will be much healthier for us right now than the air of Paris."

"Then pack our things and we'll be off. I'll leave first, without carrying anything, so as not to arouse suspicion. You'll rejoin me at the guards' headquarters. Incidentally,

Planchet, I think you're right about our landlord: he's a miserable scoundrel.''

"When I tell you something, sir, you can believe it. I'm never mistaken about faces.''

D'Artagnan left first, as he had said he would do. To make sure he missed no chance to learn something about his three friends, he went to their houses, but he was told that there had been no news of them. The only information he acquired was that a perfumed letter, addressed in elegant handwriting, had arrived for Aramis. D'Artagnan took it, saying he would deliver it. Ten minutes later, Planchet rejoined him at the stables of the guards' headquarters, bringing their clothes and equipment. To avoid wasting time, d'Artagnan had already saddled his horse himself.

"Saddle the other three," he said to Planchet, "and we'll go.''

"Do you think we'll travel faster if we have two horses apiece?'' Planchet asked jokingly.

"Of course not, but with our four horses we can bring back our three friends—if we find them alive.''

"We'll be very lucky if we do, but we mustn't lose hope of God's mercy.''

"Amen,'' said d'Artagnan, mounting his horse.

They rode off in opposite directions. One of them was to leave Paris by the Villette gate, the other by the Montmartre gate, and they would meet past Saint-Denis.

This strategic maneuver was carried out precisely. D'Artagnan and Planchet entered Pierrefitte together.

It must be said that Planchet was braver by day than by night. But his natural prudence never abandoned him; remembering the incidents of the first journey, he considered that everyone they encountered on the road might be an enemy. As a result, he constantly had his hat in his hand and d'Artagnan kept reprimanding him for his servility because he was afraid it would make him seem to be the servant of an insignificant man.

Either because everyone was touched by Planchet's politeness or because this time no one had been posted along d'Artagnan's way, the two travelers reached Chantilly without incident and went to the Grand Saint Martin inn, the one where they had stayed during their first journey.

Seeing a young man followed by a servant and two extra horses, the innkeeper respectfully came out to greet him. Since d'Artagnan had already traveled nearly thirty miles, he decided to stop and eat at the inn, whether Porthos was there or not. He also decided it would be better not to ask about Porthos immediately. He told Planchet to take care of the horses, went into a little room intended for guests who wanted to be alone, and told the innkeeper to bring him a bottle of his best wine and as good a meal as possible.

This confirmed the innkeeper's favorable opinion of him. D'Artagnan was therefore served with miraculous speed. The guard companies were recruited from among the foremost noblemen of the kingdom, and d'Artagnan, followed by a servant and traveling with four magnificent horses, could not fail to make a great impression despite the simplicity of his uniform. The innkeeper served the wine himself. D'Artagnan asked for another glass and struck up a conversation with him.

"I told you to bring me your best wine," he said, filling the two glasses, "and if you've cheated me, you'll regret it because you're going to share the bottle with me; I don't like to drink alone. Here, take this glass and we'll drink a toast. Let's see, now, what shall we drink to? It must be something that won't offend anyone . . . I know: we'll drink to the prosperity of your inn."

"I'm greatly honored, sir," said the innkeeper, "and I thank you for your kindness."

"Don't thank me too much: there's a certain amount of selfishness in my toast, because I like to stay only at prosperous inns. An inn that's doing badly is an inn where everything is badly done, and the guests suffer from their host's difficulties. Since I travel a great deal, especially on this road, I'd like to see all innkeepers making a fortune."

"Now that you mention traveling on this road, sir, it seems to me that this isn't the first time I've had the honor of seeing you."

"I've passed through Chantilly a dozen times or so, and on three or four of those journeys I've stopped at your inn. The last time was less than two weeks ago. I was with friends, three musketeers, and one of them quarreled with a stranger for some reason that wasn't very clear to me."

"Ah, yes, I remember!" said the innkeeper. "You're referring to Monsieur Porthos, aren't you?"

"Yes, that's his name. Perhaps you can tell me what happened to him."

"Well, sir, you must have noticed that he wasn't able to continue on his way."

"Of course. He said he'd rejoin us, but we never saw him."

"He's done us the honor of staying with us."

"What! He's still here?"

"Yes, sir, and we're worried."

"About what?"

"About his bill . . ."

"He'll pay it."

"I can't tell you how glad I am to hear that, sir! His bill is quite large by now, and furthermore only this morning the doctor told me that if Monsieur Porthos didn't pay him, he'd hold me responsible for the debt, since I was the one who'd sent for him."

"A doctor? Is Porthos wounded?"

"I can't tell you, sir."

"What do you mean, you can't tell me? You ought to know better than anyone else."

"Yes, but an innkeeper doesn't always say what he knows, especially when he's been told that his ears will be cut off if he doesn't hold his tongue."

"May I see Porthos?"

"Certainly, sir. Go up to the second floor and knock on door number one. But be sure to say it's you."

"Why?"

"Because otherwise something unfortunate might happen."

"Something unfortunate?"

"Yes, sir. Monsieur Porthos might think you were someone from the staff of the inn, and be so angry that he'd run you through with his sword or blow your brains out with his pistol."

"What have you done to make him angry?"

"We've asked him for money."

"Ah, now I understand. Porthos doesn't like to be asked for money when he doesn't have any. But I know he had some when he came here."

"We thought so too, sir. We do things in an orderly way here, and we don't like to have any accounts remain unsettled for more than a week, so at the end of the first week I presented Monsieur Porthos with our bill. But it seems I came at a bad time, because as soon as I mentioned the bill he ordered me to go to hell. Perhaps it was a bad time because he'd gambled the day before."

"Gambled? With whom?"

"A gentleman who was passing through. That's all I can tell you; I don't know his name. Monsieur Porthos asked him if he'd like to play a game of lansquenet."

"And he lost everything he had, didn't he?"

"Yes, sir, even his horse. When the gentleman was about to leave, we saw that his servant was saddling Monsieur Porthos's horse. I pointed that out to him, but he said it was his horse and told me to mind my own business. I immediately informed Monsieur Porthos of what was happening. He called me some uncomplimentary names for doubting a gentleman's word, and told me that since this one had said the horse was his, it couldn't belong to anyone else."

"That sounds like Porthos," murmured d'Artagnan.

"When it became clear that we weren't going to come to terms about his bill," the innkeeper continued, "I asked him if he'd be kind enough to patronize the Aigle d'Or inn instead of mine. He answered that my inn was the best and he wanted to go on staying in it. I was so flattered that I couldn't insist on his leaving. I only asked him to give up the room he had, which is the best in the inn, and take an attractive though smaller one on the fourth floor. He said he was expecting his mistress at any moment, and that since she was one of the greatest ladies at court I could easily understand that even my best room was scarcely good enough for her.

"Although I didn't doubt what he said, I still felt I had to insist. But he refused to discuss the matter with me. He took out his pistol, put it on his bedside table and said he'd shoot anyone who said one more word to him about moving to another room or another inn. Since then, no one has gone into his room except his servant."

"Mousqueton is here?"

"Yes, sir. Five days after he left, he came back in a very bad humor; it seems that he also had some unpleasantness during his journey. Unfortunately he's not disabled, like his master; he turns the inn upside down to get what his master needs, because he thinks it might not be given to him if he asked for it, so he takes it without asking."

"Yes," said d'Artagnan, "I've always known that Mousqueton was very loyal and intelligent."

"Maybe so, sir, but if I meet a few more men as loyal and intelligent as he is, I'll be ruined."

"I've told you that Porthos will pay you."

"I hope you're right," the innkeeper replied in a tone that showed that he doubted it.

"He's the favorite of a very great lady who will think nothing of giving him the paltry sum he owes you."

"If I dared to say what I think about that . . ."

"Go on, tell me what you think."

"It's more than that: it's what I know, for certain."

"Well, what is it?"

"I know who that great lady is, sir."

"Have you seen her?"

"Oh, sir, if I thought I could rely on your discretion . . ."

"You can, I give you my word of honor."

"Well, sir, you understand that when people are worried they sometimes do things that . . ."

"What have you done?"

"Nothing that goes beyond what a creditor has a right to do, believe me."

"Yes, yes. Go on."

"Monsieur Porthos gave us a letter for that lady—a duchess, he said—and asked us to send it for him. This was before his servant came back. Since he couldn't leave his room, he had to ask us to do his errands for him. One of my servants happened to be going to Paris that day. Instead of putting Monsieur Porthos's letter in the post—which isn't always reliable, as you must know—I gave it to my servant and told him to deliver it to the duchess in person. Monsieur Porthos had told us to be very careful with the letter, so I was only doing what he wanted, wasn't I?"

"More or less, I suppose."

"Well, sir, do you know who that great lady is?"

"No; I've heard Porthos talk about her, but I've never met her."

"You don't know who that so-called duchess is?"

"No, I've already told you that."

"She's a lawyer's wife named Madame Coquenard. She's at least fifty but that doesn't stop her from being jealous. Ah, I thought it was odd for a duchess to be living on the Rue aux Ours!"

"Why do you say she's jealous?"

"Because she flew into a jealous rage when she read the letter. She accused Monsieur Porthos of being fickle and said he was wounded in a duel over another woman."

"He was wounded?"

"Good heavens, what have I said!"

"You said Porthos was wounded in a duel."

"Yes, but he ordered me not to breathe a word about it to anyone!"

"Why?"

"Because he bragged about how he was going to carve up that stranger he quarreled with, and instead the stranger left him lying on the ground. Since Monsieur Porthos is a very vain man, he doesn't want anyone to know he got the worst of a duel—anyone except his duchess, that is; he must have told her about it because he thought it would make him more interesting to her."

"So his wound is what's keeping him in bed?"

"Yes, sir, and it's no mere scratch, either. I don't know how he survived a wound like that. His soul must be bolted to his body!"

"You saw the duel?"

"I followed them out of curiosity and watched them from a place where they couldn't see me."

"What happened?"

"It didn't take long, believe me. They stood on guard, then the stranger feinted and lunged. He did it so quickly that before Monsieur Porthos could parry he had three inches of steel in his chest. He fell on his back. The stranger put the point of his sword to his throat, and Monsieur Porthos had to admit defeat. Then the stranger asked him his name. When he heard it was Porthos and not d'Artagnan, he offered him his arm, took him back to the inn, got on his horse, and rode away."

"So it was Monsieur d'Artagnan that the stranger wanted to fight?"

"Apparently so."

"Do you know what became of him?"

"No; I'd never seen him before and I haven't seen him since."

"Very well; I know what I wanted to know. You say Porthos's room is on the second floor, number one?"

"Yes, sir, the finest room in the house, a room I could have rented a dozen times since he took it."

"Don't worry," said d'Artagnan, "Porthos will pay you with Duchess Coquenard's money."

"Oh, sir, I wouldn't care if she was a duchess or a lawyer's wife if she opened her purse, but she answered Monsieur Porthos's letter by saying she was tired of his demands and his unfaithfulness, and she wasn't going to send him a single sou.''

"Did you give Porthos that message?''

"No, because then he'd have known I'd had his letter delivered in person.''

"So he's still waiting for his money?''

"Yes, sir. He wrote to her again yesterday, but this time his servant put the letter in the post.''

"You say she's old and ugly?''

"According to Pathaud, she's at least fifty and not at all pleasant to look at.''

"In that case you can put your mind at rest: she'll soon give in to Porthos. Besides, he must not owe you very much.''

"What! Not very much? He already owes me twenty pistoles, not counting the doctor! He has nothing but the best for himself; it's easy to see he's used to living well.''

"Even if his mistress abandons him, his friends won't, so go on giving him everything he needs and don't worry.''

"Remember, sir: you've promised not to say anything about his wound or the lawyer's wife.''

"You have my word.''

"He'd kill me if he knew I'd told you!''

"Don't be afraid, he's not as ferocious as he seems.''

Having said this, d'Artagnan climbed the stairs, leaving the innkeeper a little less worried about two things that seemed to mean a great deal to him: his money and his life.

On the second floor, a gigantic number one was written in black ink on the largest door. D'Artagnan knocked, was invited to come in, and did so.

Porthos was in bed, playing lansquenet with Mousqueton, just to keep his hand in. Two partridges were roasting on a spit in front of the fire, and on either side of the big fireplace two pots were boiling on charcoal stoves, giving off a delightful aroma of fish stew and fricassee of rabbit in white wine. The tops of a writing desk and a dresser were covered with empty bottles.

Porthos greeted his friend with a shout of joy. Mousqueton respectfully stood up to let d'Artagnan have his seat and went over to inspect the contents of the two pots.

"Ah, it's you!'' exclaimed Porthos. "Welcome! Excuse me for not getting up,'' he added, looking at d'Artagnan uneasily. "Do you know what happened to me?''

"No.''

"The innkeeper didn't tell you anything?''

"I only asked him where your room was, and came straight here," replied d'Artagnan. He saw a look of relief on Porthos's face. "What happened to you?"

"I'd wounded my opponent three times and I wanted to finish him off with a fourth thrust, but when I lunged at him, my foot slipped on a stone and I sprained my knee."

"Really?"

"Yes, and it was lucky for him, because otherwise I'd have killed him."

"What became of him?"

"I have no idea. He'd had enough, so he left as fast as he could. But what about you? What have you been doing?"

"So it's only your sprained knee that's keeping you in bed?" asked d'Artagnan, ignoring Porthos's question.

"Yes, that's all. But in a few days I'll be back on my feet."

"You must be terribly bored here. Why haven't you had someone take you back to Paris?"

"I intended to, but there's something I must confess to you."

"What is it?"

"Since I was terribly bored, as you say, and since I had the seventy-five pistoles you'd given me, I offered to play dice with a gentleman who'd just come to the inn. He accepted my offer, with the result that the seventy-five pistoles went from my pocket into his, and he took away my horse to boot. Now tell me about yourself."

"You can't be lucky in everything," said d'Artagnan. "You know the old saying: 'Unlucky in cards, lucky in love.' You're so lucky in love that you're bound to lose when you gamble. But what do you care about losing money? You still have your duchess and she's sure to help you."

"My streak of bad luck hasn't ended yet," Porthos said nonchalantly. "I wrote to her, told her about my situation, and asked her to send me fifty louis . . ."

"And?"

"She must have gone to her estate, because she hasn't answered me."

"She hasn't?"

"No. Yesterday I wrote her another letter, even more urgent than the first one . . . But here you are, my friend; let's talk about you. I must admit I was beginning to be a little worried about you."

"The innkeeper seems to be treating you well," said d'Artagnan, pointing to the full pots and the empty bottles.

"Fairly well. Several days ago he had the impertinence to bring me a bill. I ordered him to get out and take his bill with him. Since then, I've been like a conqueror in an occupied country. As you can see, I'm armed to the teeth in case there's a counterattack."

"But you evidently make sorties now and then," d'Artagnan said with a laugh, again pointing to the bottles and pots.

"I'm not the one who makes them, unfortunately," said Porthos. "My wretched knee keeps me in bed, but Mousqueton goes out foraging in the countryside and brings back supplies." He turned to his servant. "Mousqueton, my friend, now that reinforcements have arrived, we'll need more food."

"Mousqueton," said d'Artagnan, "I want you to do me a favor."

"What is it, sir?"

"Give Planchet your recipe; some day it may be my turn to withstand a siege, and if that happens I'd like him to do for me what you're doing for your master."

"There's really nothing to it, sir," Mousqueton said modestly. "You just have to know what you're doing, that's all. I grew up in the country, and my father did a little poaching in his spare time."

"What did he do the rest of the time?"

"He had an occupation that's always seemed rather clever to me."

"What was it?"

"It was in the time of the wars between the Catholics and the Huguenots. Since he saw Catholics slaughtering Huguenots and Huguenots slaughtering Catholics, in the name of religion, he adopted a mixed faith: he was sometimes a Catholic and sometimes a Huguenot. He used to go out walking with his blunderbuss on his shoulder, behind the hedges along the roads. Whenever he saw a Catholic coming toward him, alone, the Protestant religion took first place in his heart. He would aim his blunderbuss at the traveler and begin a conversation that almost always ended with the traveler giving up his purse to save his life. It goes without saying that when he saw a Huguenot coming, he felt such ardent Catholic zeal that he didn't understand how he could have doubted the superiority of our holy religion a quarter of an hour earlier. I'm a Catholic, sir, but my father was faithful to his principles: he made my older brother a Huguenot."

"And what became of that worthy man?" asked d'Artagnan.

"His career was ended by bad luck, sir. One day, on a road with embankments on both sides, he found himself caught between a Huguenot and a Catholic, two men he'd already practiced his occupation with. They both recognized him. They forgot their religious differences long enough to attack him together and hang him from a tree, then they went to brag about it in the tavern of the nearest village, where my brother and I were drinking."

"What did you do?"

"We let them talk. When they left the tavern, they went in opposite directions. My brother ran off to ambush the Catholic, and I did the same with the Protestant. Two hours later, it was all over. My brother and I had done what needed to be done, and we admired our father's foresight in raising each of us in a different religion."

"Your father seems to have been a very intelligent man, Mousqueton. And you say he was a poacher in his spare time?"

"Yes, sir, and he taught me to set a snare and bait a hook. So when the innkeeper here began feeding us coarse meat that was fit for hardy peasants but not for weakened stomachs like ours, I went back to my old trade. I took walks in Prince de Condé's woods and set snares on the trails; I lay down at the edge of His Highness's ponds and dropped fishlines into the water. And now, as you can see, we have partridges, rabbits, carp, and eels—light, nourishing foods that are suitable for invalids."

"But what about wine?" asked d'Artagnan. "Does the innkeeper supply it?"

"Yes and no."

"What do you mean?"

"He supplies it, but he doesn't know he has that honor."

"Explain yourself, Mousqueton; listening to you is instructive."

"It's like this, sir. In my wanderings I once happened to meet a Spaniard who'd been in many different countries, including several in the New World."

"What connection can there be between the New World and those bottles on the writing desk and the dresser?"

"Be patient, sir, and you'll see the connection."

"Very well, Mousqueton, I'm sure you'll make it clear to me. Go on."

"This Spaniard had a servant who'd been with him in Mexico. The servant was a Norman, like me, and we became friends all the more quickly because we had many things in common. We both liked hunting more than anything else. He told me that on the plains of South America the natives hunted tigers and bulls by throwing slipknots over their heads. At first I didn't believe it was possible to throw a lasso—that's what they call a rope with a slipknot at one end—so well that you could make the loop go where you wanted it to at a distance of twenty or thirty paces, but when my friend proved it to me, I had to admit he was telling the truth. He put a bottle on the ground, stood thirty paces away from it, and dropped the loop over it every time he threw his lasso. I began practicing it myself, and since I'm lucky enough to have certain natural abilities, I can now throw a lasso as well as any man in the world. Our innkeeper has a well-stocked wine cellar. The key to it is always in his pocket, but the cellar has a little window. I throw my lasso through the window. By now I know where the best bottles are and I take as many of them as I need. And that, sir, is the connection between the New World and the bottles on the dresser and the writing desk. If you like, you can try some of our wine and tell us what you think of it."

"No, thank you, Mousqueton. I just had lunch."

"Set the table, Mousqueton," said Porthos, "and while we eat, d'Artagnan will tell us what he's been doing in the ten days since he left us."

"I'll be glad to," said d'Artagnan.

While Porthos and Mousqueton ate with the hearty appetite of convalescents and the brotherly feeling that brings men closer together in times of adversity, d'Artagnan told how Aramis, wounded, had been forced to stop at Crèvecoeur, how he had left Athos at Amiens, fighting against four men who had accused him of being a counterfeiter, and how he, d'Artagnan, had been forced to run his sword through Count de Wardes in order to reach England.

But he did not explain why he had gone to England; he said only that he had brought back four magnificent horses, one for himself and one for each of his friends, and that the one he was giving Porthos was already in the stables of the inn.

Just then Planchet came in to tell his master that the horses were rested enough and that they still had time to reach Clermont and spend the night there.

Since d'Artagnan was now more or less reassured about Porthos and wanted to learn what had happened to his other two friends, he shook hands with him and told him that he was going to leave to continue his search. He added that since he intended to come back by the same road, if Porthos was still at the inn in seven or eight days, they would return to Paris together.

Porthos replied that his sprained knee probably would not allow him to leave before then. And besides, he had to stay at Chantilly to wait for an answer from his duchess.

D'Artagnan said he hoped the answer would be prompt and favorable. Then, after urging Mousqueton to take good care of Porthos, he paid his bill and set off with Planchet, leaving one of the spare horses behind.

26

Aramis's Thesis

D'Artagnan had said nothing to Porthos about his wound or the lawyer's wife. Despite his youth, he was a discreet and tactful man. He had pretended to believe everything the vain musketeer told him, for he was convinced that no friendship could withstand the strain of having a secret discovered, especially a secret that was kept in order to save face; and besides, knowing hidden details of someone's life always gives us a certain moral superiority over him.

Planning future intrigues and intending to use his three friends to further his advancement, d'Artagnan was pleased to know that he already had a grip on the invisible strings by which he expected to lead them.

Yet, as he rode along, there was also deep sadness in his heart. He thought of the young and pretty Madame Bonacieux who was to have given him the reward for his devotion; but let us hasten to add that his sadness came less from regret for his lost happiness than from fear of what might have happened to her. He had no doubt that she was a victim of the cardinal's revenge, and everyone knew that the cardinal was implacable in taking revenge. D'Artagnan did not know why His Eminence had spared him. Monsieur de Cavois would probably have explained it to him if he had found him at home when he came to see him.

Nothing shortens a journey and speeds the passage of time as much as being absorbed in thought. Distance and duration become meaningless; we simply leave one place and arrive at another, with no memories of the space between them except vague, confused images of trees, mountains, and landscapes. It was in a dreamlike state of this kind that d'Artagnan covered the fifteen or twenty miles from Chantilly to Crèvecoeur, riding at the speed his horse chose to take. When he arrived at Crèvecoeur, he remembered nothing he had seen along the way.

But then his mind cleared. He shook his head, saw the inn where he had left Aramis, made his horse trot to it, and stopped in front of the door.

This time he was received not by a host, but by a hostess. When he saw her cheerful face he knew he had nothing to fear from her and could speak openly.

"My good lady," he said, "can you tell me what's become of a friend of mine I had to leave here ten or twelve days ago?"

"A handsome, gentle, friendly young man about twenty-three or twenty-four years old?"

"Yes, and he's wounded in the shoulder."

"Then we're both talking about the same man. He's still here, sir."

"I'm very glad to hear that," said d'Artagnan, dismounting from his horse and tossing the reins to Planchet. "I'm eager to see my dear friend Aramis again. Where is he?"

"I'm sorry, sir, but I don't think he can see you now."

"Why not? Is he with a woman?"

"Good heavens, no! What a thing to ask about him! No, sir, he's not with a woman."

"Then who *is* he with?"

"The curate of Montdidier and the superior of the Jesuits of Amiens."

"My God!" exclaimed d'Artagnan. "Is he about to die?"

"No, sir, not at all. After his illness he was touched by divine grace, and he's now decided to take holy orders."

"Yes, I was forgetting that he was a musketeer only temporarily."

"Do you still want to see him, sir?"

"More than ever."

"Then take the staircase on the right in the courtyard and go to room number five, on the third floor."

D'Artagnan went in the direction the hostess pointed out to him and climbed an outside staircase of the kind that can still be seen in the courtyards of old inns. But it was not easy to enter the future priest's room, for the approaches to it were as well guarded as the garden of Armida: Bazin stood in the hall and barred the way all the more resolutely because, after many years of trials and tribulations, he felt that he was at last about to reach the goal for which he had been yearning so long.

Bazin's dream had always been to serve a churchman, and he had been impatiently waiting for the time when Aramis would exchange his musketeer's uniform for a cassock. Bazin had continued to serve a musketeer—at the risk of his salvation, he said—only because Aramis had promised him every day that he would soon become a priest.

And so Bazin was now overjoyed. This time it seemed that his master was really going to keep his promise. The combination of anguish and physical pain had produced the desired effect: Aramis, suffering in both his body and his soul, had finally turned all his thoughts to religion, and he had seen his two afflictions—the wound in his shoulder and the sudden disappearance of his mistress—as a warning from heaven.

Given these circumstances, it is easy to understand that nothing could have been more distressing to Bazin than d'Artagnan's arrival, since it might throw his master back into the whirlpool of worldly concerns that had held him so long. He was therefore determined to prevent d'Artagnan from going into Aramis's room. Having been betrayed by the hostess of the inn, he could not say that Aramis was absent, so instead he tried to prove to d'Artagnan that it would be intolerably discourteous to disturb his master in the pious conference that had begun that morning and that, according to Bazin, was sure to continue till evening.

But d'Artagnan was not at all convinced by Bazin's eloquent speech. Not wanting to argue with him, he simply pushed him aside with one hand and turned the doorknob of room number five with the other.

The door opened and he went into the room.

Aramis, wearing a black coat and a round, flat hat that closely resembled a priest's skullcap, was sitting at an oblong table covered with scrolls and enormous folio volumes. To his right sat the superior of the Jesuits and to his left the curate of Montdidier. The curtains were half closed and admitted only a dim, mysterious light, suitable for devout meditation. All the worldly objects that one would have expected to see in a young man's room, especially if the young man was a musketeer, had disappeared as though by magic; probably fearing that the sight of them might bring his master's thoughts back to the things of this world, Bazin had disposed of his sword, his pistols, his plumed hat, and everything adorned with embroidery and lace. And in a dark corner, hanging from a nail in the wall, was something that looked to d'Artagnan like a whip of the kind used for self-flagellation.

When d'Artagnan opened the door, Aramis looked up and recognized him. But, to d'Artagnan's surprise, his mind was evidently so detached from earthly matters that the sight of his friend seemed to make no great impression on him.

"Hello, my dear d'Artagnan," he said. "I'm glad to see you."

"I'm glad to see you too," said d'Artagnan, "though I'm not quite sure it's Aramis I'm talking to."

"It is, my friend. What makes you doubt it?"

"I was afraid I'd come into the wrong room. At first I thought it was a churchman's room, and then, when I saw you with these gentlemen, I thought you were gravely ill."

The two men in black understood what was behind d'Artagnan's words. They gave him an almost threatening look but he took no notice of it.

"Excuse me if I've disturbed you, Aramis," he went on. "It looks as if you're confessing to these gentlemen."

Aramis blushed slightly.

"You're not disturbing me at all, my friend. I'm happy to see you safe and sound."

D'Artagnan thought, "It's about time that occurred to him!"

"This gentleman is my friend," Aramis said to the two churchmen, "and he's just escaped from a mortal danger."

"Thank God, sir," they said, bowing to d'Artagnan.

"I've already done so, Your Reverences," he replied, returning their bow.

"You've come at a good time," said Aramis. "You can take part in our conversation and give us the benefit of your wisdom. The superior of Amiens, the curate of Montdidier, and I have been discussing certain theological questions that have greatly interested us for a long time. I'll be glad to hear your opinion."

"A soldier's opinion on such matters is worth very little," replied d'Artagnan, feeling uneasy at the turn the conversation had taken. "You'll do much better to listen to these gentlemen, believe me."

The two men in black bowed again.

"Your opinion will be valuable to us," said Aramis. "Here's the point at issue: the superior believes that my thesis should be primarily dogmatic and didactic."

"Your thesis? You're writing a thesis?"

"Of course," said the Jesuit. "A thesis is required for the examination preceding ordination."

"Ordination!" exclaimed d'Artagnan.

He still could not believe that Aramis really intended to become a priest, even though the hostess and Bazin had already told him so. He stared in amazement at the three men in front of him.

Aramis struck a graceful pose in his armchair, as if he were sitting in a bedroom, and looked with satisfaction at his hand, soft and white as a woman's, which he had held up to make the blood drain from it.

"As I told you, d'Artagnan," he said, "the superior would like my thesis to be dogmatic. But I'd like it to be idealistic. The superior has therefore proposed this theme for me: '*Utraque manus in benedicendo clericis inferioribus necessaria est.*' "

Although d'Artagnan's classical learning was nearly nonexistent, as we have seen, he did not let this Latin sentence disturb his poise any more than the one Monsieur de Tréville had quoted to him.

"Which means," Aramis obligingly added, " 'Both hands are necessary for priests of the lower orders when they give benediction.' "

"An admirable theme!" said the Jesuit.

"Admirable and dogmatic!" said the curate. With a knowledge of Latin not much greater than d'Artagnan's, he listened carefully to the Jesuit and echoed his words.

D'Artagnan did not share the two churchmen's enthusiasm.

"Yes, it's admirable!" said Aramis. "*Prorsus admirabile!* But it requires a thorough study of Scripture and the Church Fathers. As I've confessed to these learned gentlemen in all humility, my duties in the king's service have taken up so much of my time that I've somewhat neglected my studies. I'd therefore be more at ease, *facilius natans,* with a theme of my own choice, which would have the same relation to these arduous theological questions as ethics has to metaphysics in philosophy."

D'Artagnan was profoundly bored, and so was the curate.

"What an exordium!" exclaimed the Jesuit.

"Exordium," repeated the curate, unable to think of an appropriate comment.

"*Quemadmodum inter coelorum immensitatem.*"

Aramis glanced at d'Artagnan and saw him yawn in a way that threatened to dislocate his jaw.

"Let's speak French, Father," he said to the Jesuit, "so that

Monsieur d'Artagnan will enjoy our conversation even more.''

"I'm too tired from traveling," said d'Artagnan, "to be able to understand Latin.''

"Very well," the Jesuit said with a touch of annoyance while the curate gave d'Artagnan a grateful look. "Now, let's see what we can do with that theme . . . Moses, the servant of God—note that he's only a servant! Moses blesses with his hands; he has both his arms held up while the Hebrews defeat their enemies; he therefore blesses with both hands. Moreover, the Gospel says *imponite manus,*' and not *'manum,'* 'lay on hands,' and not 'a hand.' ''

" 'Lay on hands,' '' repeated the curate, making a gesture.

"And Saint Peter, of whom all the popes are successors, is told, *'Porrige digitos,'''* continued the Jesuit. '' 'Extend the fingers.' Now do you understand?''

"Yes," said Aramis, thoroughly enjoying himself. "But it's a subtle point.''

"The fingers!'' said the Jesuit. "Saint Peter blesses with his fingers. The pope also blesses with his fingers. And with how many fingers does he bless? With three: one for the Father, one for the Son, and one for the Holy Ghost.''

Aramis and the two churchmen crossed themselves; d'Artagnan felt obliged to follow their example.

"The pope is the successor of Saint Peter and represents the three divine powers; the rest, *ordines inferiores* in the ecclesiastical hierarchy, bless in the name of the angels and the holy archangels. The humblest clerics, such as our deacons and sacristans, bless with holy-water sprinklers, which simulate an indefinite number of blessing fingers. There, the theme is now simplified, *argumentum omni denudatum ornamento*. With that, I could write two volumes the size of this one.''

And, in his enthusiasm, the Jesuit pounded the Saint Chrysostom folio that nearly made the table collapse beneath its weight.

D'Artagnan shuddered.

"I recognize the beauties of that theme," said Aramis, "but I feel overwhelmed by it. Here's the theme I chose, d'Artagnan; tell me if it's to your liking: *'Non inutile est desiderium in oblatione,'* which can be rendered as: 'A little regret is not unfitting in an offering to the Lord.' ''

"Stop!'' cried the Jesuit. "That thesis borders on heresy! There's something quite similar to it in the heretic Jansenius's *Augustinus,* a book that will sooner or later be burned by the public executioner. Take care, my young friend: you're leaning toward false doctrines! Your soul is in danger.''

"Your soul is in danger," said the curate, woefully shaking his head.

"You're touching on the famous subject of free will, which is a deadly pitfall. You're approaching the insinuations of the Pelagians and the Semipelagians.''

"But, Father . . .'' said Aramis, a little dazed by the hail of objections falling on him.

"How can you prove," the Jesuit continued without giving him time to speak, "that we must regret giving up the world when we offer ourselves to God? Listen to this dilemma: God is God, and the world is the devil. To regret giving up the world is to regret giving up the devil; that's my conclusion.''

"It's mine too," said the curate.

"Please . . .'' said Aramis.

"Desideras diabolum, wretched sinner!'' cried the Jesuit.

"He regrets giving up the devil! Oh, my young friend,'' moaned the curate, "please don't do that, I beg you not to do that!''

D'Artagnan struggled to keep a grip on reality; he felt as if he were in a madhouse where the insanity of the inmates was contagious, but he could say nothing to them because he did not understand their language.

"Please listen to me," Aramis said politely, but with a hint of impatience in his voice. "I'm not saying that I regret giving up the world. I'll never say that, because it wouldn't be orthodox.''

The Jesuit threw up his arms and the curate did the same.

"But you must agree," Aramis went on, "that it would be ungracious to offer the Lord only things we dislike. Isn't that right, d'Artagnan?''

"It certainly is!" replied his friend.

The curate and the Jesuit started convulsively in their chairs.

"That's my point of departure," said Aramis. "It's a syllogism: the world has its attractions; I'm leaving the world; therefore I'm making a sacrifice. Scripture clearly tells us that we must make a sacrifice to the Lord.''

"That's true," acknowledged the Jesuit, seconded by the curate.

"I've written a little poem on the subject," said Aramis, pinching his ear to make it pink, after shaking his hands to make them white. "I showed it to the great Monsieur Voiture last year, and he complimented me highly.''

"A poem!" the Jesuit said disdainfully.

"A poem!" the curate said automatically.

"Let's hear it," suggested d'Artagnan. "At least it will be a change."

"No, it won't," replied Aramis, "because it's a religious poem. It's theology in verse."

D'Artagnan's face fell.

"Here it is," Aramis said with a modest expression that had a slight tinge of hypocrisy:

> *"Vous qui pleurez un passé plein de charmes,*
> *Et qui traînez des jours infortunés,*
> *Tous vos malheurs se verront terminés,*
> *Quand à Dieu seul vous offrirez vos larmes,*
> *Vous qui pleurez."**

D'Artagnan and the curate seemed pleased by what they had just heard. The Jesuit persisted in his disapproval.

"You must avoid secular tastes in theological writing. What is it that Saint Augustine says? *'Severus sit clericorum sermo.'*"

"Yes, let the sermon be clear!" said the curate.

Hearing his acolyte's blunder, the Jesuit hastened to go on: "Your thesis will please the ladies, that's all. You'll have the same kind of success as Patru, the lawyer, when he addresses the court."

"I hope so," said Aramis.

"You see!" cried the Jesuit. "The world still speaks loudly in you, *altissima voce.* You follow the lure of the world, and I'm afraid that grace may fail to save you."

"Have no fear, Father, I'm sure of myself."

"That's worldly presumption!"

"I know myself, Father. My decision is irrevocable."

"Then you still insist on writing that thesis?"

"I feel I've been called to write that one and no other, so I'll go on with it, and tomorrow I hope you'll be satisfied with the corrections I've made on the basis of what you've told me."

"Work slowly," said the curate. "We'll leave you in an excellent frame of mind."

---

*You who weep for a past full of charms,
  And drag out wretched days,
  All your woes will be ended
  When you offer your tears to God alone,
    You who weep.

"Yes, the soil is sown," said the Jesuit, "and we needn't fear that some of the seed has fallen on stones, and some has fallen along the way, and that the birds of the sky have eaten the rest, *aves coeli comederunt illam.*"

D'Artagnan was nearing the end of his self-control. "I hope his Latin sticks in his throat and chokes him!" he thought.

"Good-bye till tomorrow, my son," said the curate.

"Till tomorrow, my headstrong young friend," said the Jesuit. "You show promise of becoming one of the lights of the Church; may it please the Lord not to let that light become a devouring fire!"

D'Artagnan's exasperation during the last hour had made him chew his fingernails down to the quick.

The two men in black stood up, bowed to Aramis and d'Artagnan, and stepped toward the door. Bazin, who had been listening to the discussion with pious jubilation, rushed toward them, took the curate's breviary and the Jesuit's missal and respectfully walked in front of them to clear the way for them.

Aramis accompanied them downstairs, then returned to d'Artagnan. Now that they were alone together, there was an embarrassed silence between them. One of them had to break it, and since d'Artagnan seemed determined to leave that honor to his friend, Aramis said, "As you can see, I've come back to my fundamental ideas."

"Yes, you've been touched by grace, as that Jesuit would say."

"I've been planning to become a priest for a long time. You've heard me talk about it before, haven't you?"

"Of course, but I must admit I thought you were joking."

"Oh, d'Artagnan! I'd never joke about a thing like that!"

"Why not? People even joke about death."

"They shouldn't, because death is the door that leads to either salvation or damnation."

"I'm sure it is, but let's not talk theology, Aramis. You must have had enough of it to last you the rest of the day, and I've forgotten the little bit of Latin that I never really knew anyway. Besides, I haven't eaten anything since ten o'clock this morning and I'm hungry as a wolf."

"We'll have dinner soon. But let me remind you that today is Friday, so I can't eat meat, or even see any. I hope you can be satisfied with a very simple meal. It will consist of fruit and *Spinacia oleracea.*"

"What's that?" d'Artagnan asked uneasily.

"Spinach. But for your sake I'll add eggs, even though it's a serious violation of the rule: an egg is meat, since it engenders a chicken."

"It won't be a very appetizing meal, but I'll put up with it for the pleasure of staying with you."

"I'm grateful to you for your sacrifice," said Aramis. "Even if the meal doesn't please your body, however, you can be sure it will benefit your soul."

"So you're really going into the Church, Aramis. . . . What will our friends say? What will Monsieur de Tréville say? They'll call you a deserter, I warn you."

"I'm going *back* into the Church. I was a deserter when I left it. I acted against my nature when I became a musketeer, as you know."

"No, Aramis, I don't know anything about it."

"You don't know how I left the seminary?"

"No."

"Then I'll tell you my story. The Bible says we must confess to one another, and I'm going to confess to you, d'Artagnan."

"And I'm giving you absolution in advance. You see how good-natured I am?"

"You mustn't joke about holy things, my friend."

"Tell me your story. I'm listening."

"It was three days before my twentieth birthday. I'd been in the seminary since the age of nine, and it was taken for granted that I was going to be a priest. That evening I went to a house that I often visited with pleasure—I was young, and I had the weaknesses of youth. A certain officer came in unannounced. He'd watched me jealously in the past as I read the lives of the saints to the mistress of the house. On this particular evening I'd translated an episode from *Judith*. I'd just read it to the lady, who'd complimented me on it, and she was now rereading it with me, leaning on my shoulder. I admit it was a rather abandoned pose, and it offended the officer. He said nothing at the time, but when I left the house, he left a few moments later and caught up with me.

" 'Tell me, my pious friend,' he said to me, 'do you like being beaten with a cane?'

" 'I don't know,' I answered, 'because no one's ever dared to try it.'

" 'Listen carefully,' he said: 'I'll dare to do it if you ever go back to that house again.'

"I think I was frightened. I turned pale, my legs felt weak, and I tried to think of something to say, but I couldn't. The officer waited for my answer. When he saw I wasn't going to give him one, he laughed, turned away from me, and went back into the house. I returned to the seminary.

"I came from a long line of noble ancestors and I'm rather hot-blooded, as you may have noticed. Although no one else knew about the insult, I could feel it living and stirring in my heart. I told my superiors that I thought I wasn't yet adequately prepared for my ordination, and at my request it was postponed for a year.

"I went to the best fencing teacher in Paris and took a lesson from him every day for the next year. Then, on the anniversary of the day when I'd been insulted, I took off my cassock, dressed myself as a cavalier, and went to a ball, given by a lady who was one of my friends, where I knew my man was expected to be. It was on the Rue des Francs-Bourgeois, near La Force.

"My officer was there. I went up to him as he was singing a love song and looking tenderly at a woman, and I interrupted him in the middle of the second verse.

" 'Sir,' I said to him, 'are you still opposed to my returning to a certain house on the Rue Payenne, and will you still beat me with a cane if I choose to disobey you?'

"He looked at me in surprise and said, 'What do you want with me, sir? I don't know you.'

" 'I'm the seminary student,' I answered, 'who reads the lives of the saints and translates *Judith* into verse.'

" 'Ah, yes, I remember!' he said mockingly. 'Well, what do you want?'

" 'I'd like you to take a walk with me.'

" 'I'll be glad to accommodate you tomorrow morning.'

" 'No, not tomorrow morning: now.'

" 'If you really insist . . .'

" 'I do. In fact, I demand it.'

" 'Then let's go,' said the officer. He turned to the ladies and told them, 'I'll be gone just long enough to kill this gentleman, then I'll come back and finish my song.'

"We went out. I took him to the Rue Payenne, to the same spot where, a year before, he'd given me the compliment I've told you about. The moon was shining brightly. We drew our swords, and I killed him with my first thrust."

"That was quick work!" said d'Artagnan.

"Since the ladies didn't see their singer come back," Aramis continued, "and since he was found dead on the Rue Payenne with a wound in his heart, it was assumed that I was the one who'd killed him. There was a scandal that forced me to leave the seminary for the time being. I'd met Athos not long before, and Porthos had taught me a few useful tricks outside of my fencing lessons. They persuaded me to try to become a musketeer. The king had been very fond of my father, who was killed in the siege of Arras, and my request was granted. So you can understand why the time has now come for me to return to the Church.''

"No, I don't understand," said d'Artagnan. "Why now, rather than yesterday or tomorrow? What's happened to you now, to give you such disagreeable ideas?''

"That wound, my dear d'Artagnan, was a warning to me from heaven."

"But it's almost healed now, and I'm sure it's not the wound that's making you suffer most."

"What do you mean?" asked Aramis, his face coloring.

"You have a wound in your heart, much more painful than the other one, a wound given to you by a woman."

Aramis could not prevent his eyes from flashing.

"You ought to know me better than that," he said with a forced affability that failed to hide his emotion. "I never even think about such things. *Vanitas vanitatum!* Do you really believe I've lost my head over a woman, some seamstress or chambermaid I met in a garrison town?''

"No, Aramis, I think you have higher ambitions than that."

"Who am I to have high ambitions? I'm only a poor, obscure musketeer who hates worldly ties and feels out of place in society."

"Oh, Aramis . . ." said d'Artagnan, looking at him skeptically.

"Ashes to ashes, dust to dust," Aramis said gloomily. "Life is full of sorrow and humiliation. The threads that attach us to happiness are broken one by one, especially threads of gold. Take my advice, d'Artagnan," he went on, giving his voice a touch of bitterness. "When you're in pain, hide it. Silence is the only refuge of those who suffer. Never let anyone even catch a glimpse of your sorrow; inquisitive people drink tears as flies drink the blood of a wounded deer."

"When you talk about sorrow," d'Artagnan said with a deep sigh, "I know what you mean."

"Has something happened to make you . . ."

"Yes. The woman I love and adore has been taken away from

me by force. I don't know where she is, where she's been taken; she may be a prisoner, she may even be dead.''

"But at least you have the consolation of knowing that she didn't leave you voluntarily and that if you haven't heard from her it's because she has no way of communicating with you, whereas . . .''

"Whereas what?''

"Nothing,'' replied Aramis, "nothing. . . .''

"So you're really determined to renounce the world?''

"Yes, forever. You're my friend today, but tomorrow you'll be only a shadow to me, or rather you'll no longer exist at all. As for the world, it's a tomb, and nothing more.''

"What you're saying is very sad!''

"What else do you expect me to say? My vocation is drawing me away from the world.''

D'Artagnan smiled and made no reply. Aramis continued:

"And yet, while I'm still in the world, I'd have liked to talk with you about yourself and our friends.''

"And I'd have liked to talk about you, too,'' said d'Artagnan, "but you seem so detached from everything: love means nothing to you, your friends are shadows, the world is a tomb.''

"Alas, you'll discover that for yourself.''

"Then let's not talk about it any more, and let's burn your letter. It probably has nothing to tell you except that your seamstress or your chambermaid has been unfaithful to you again.''

"What letter?'' cried Aramis.

"A letter that came for you while you were gone. I took it to bring to you.''

"Who's it from?''

"Some tearful servant or heartbroken seamstress, I suppose. Or maybe it's Madame de Chevreuse's chambermaid; if so, she must have had to go back to Tours with her mistress, and she probably thought she'd make herself more attractive to you by writing on perfumed paper and sealing her letter with a duchess's coronet.''

"What . . .''

"I seem to have lost it,'' d'Artagnan said treacherously, pretending to search his pockets for the letter. "Well, it doesn't matter, since the world is a tomb, men and women are only shadows, and love means nothing to you.''

"D'Artagnan! You're killing me!''

"Ah, here it is.''

D'Artagnan took the letter from his pocket. Aramis snatched it out of his hand and read it, devoured it. His face became radiant.

"Thank you, d'Artagnan!" he cried out almost deliriously. "She was forced to go back to Tours, she's not unfaithful to me, she still loves me! Come, my friend, let me embrace you! I'm bursting with happiness!"

And the two friends began dancing around a volume of the works of the venerable Saint Chrysostom, trampling the pages of the thesis that had fallen on the floor.

Bazin came in with the spinach and the omelet.

"Get out, you dreary fool!" Aramis said, throwing his skull-cap at him. "Take that hideous vegetable and that repulsive omelet back where they came from and order a larded hare, a fat capon, a leg of mutton with garlic, and four bottles of old Burgundy!"

Bazin stared at his master, so shocked and bewildered that he dropped the spinach and the omelet.

"Now's the time to devote your life to the King of Kings," said d'Artagnan, "if you want to do it properly, because, as you said yourself, *'Non inutile est desiderium in oblatione.'* "

"Go to the devil with your Latin! Let's drink, d'Artagnan, because I've got a powerful thirst, and while we're drinking, you can tell me what's been going on in Paris."

27

Athos's Wife

"We still have to find out what's happened to Athos," d'Artagnan said to Aramis when he had told him everything that had taken place in Paris since their departure.

An excellent dinner had made d'Artagnan forget his fatigue, and Aramis his thesis.

"Don't you think he fought his way out of that trap he fell into?" asked Aramis. "He's so coolheaded, so brave, such a good swordsman . . ."

"No one has more respect for Athos's courage and skill than I do, but I'd rather feel steel against my sword than wood, and I'm afraid he may have been beaten by servants with sticks. Servants hit hard and keep at it a long time. So I'd like to leave as soon as possible.''

"I'll try to go with you," said Aramis, "although I'm not sure I feel well enough to ride a horse. Yesterday I tried some self-flagellation with that whip hanging on the wall, and it was so painful I couldn't go on with it very long.''

"You should have known you couldn't heal a gunshot wound with a whip. But you were sick, and sickness weakens the mind, so I'll excuse you.''

"When are you leaving?''

"Tomorrow morning at dawn. Get as much rest as you can tonight, and you'll leave with me if you're able to ride.''

"I'll give you the same advice," said Aramis, "because even though you're a man of iron, you must need some rest too.''

When d'Artagnan came into Aramis's room the next morning, he found him standing at the window.

"What are you looking at?'' he asked.

"I'm admiring the three magnificent horses that the stablemen are holding. It would be a royal pleasure to travel with horses like that!''

"You're going to have that royal pleasure, Aramis, because one of those horses is yours.''

"Really? Which one?''

"Whichever one you want. I have no preference.''

"And the rich trappings are mine too?''

"Of course.''

"You're joking, d'Artagnan, you're only making fun of me.''

"No, I haven't laughed at you since you stopped speaking Latin.''

"Those gilded holsters, that velvet saddlecloth, that silver-studded saddle—they're mine?''

"Yes. Everything that goes with your horse belongs to you. The other two are for Athos and me.''

"They're superb, all three of them!''

"I'm glad you like them.''

"Was it the king who gave them to you?''

"You can be sure it wasn't the cardinal. But don't worry about where they came from, just choose the one you want.''

"I'll take the one the red-haired stableman is holding.''

"Good.''

"Now I feel in the pink of health!'' said Aramis. "I'd ride

that horse even if I had a dozen bullets in my body! Ah, just look at those beautiful stirrups! Bazin! Come in here!"

Bazin, glum and languid, appeared in the doorway.

"Polish my sword, shape my hat, brush my cloak, and load my pistols," Aramis told him.

"That last order is useless," said d'Artagnan. "There are loaded pistols in your holsters."

Bazin sighed.

"Don't be upset, Bazin," d'Artagnan said to him. "A man doesn't have to be a priest to go to heaven."

"My master was already such a good theologian!" Bazin said almost tearfully. "He would have become a bishop and maybe even a cardinal."

"Just think a moment, Bazin. What's the use of becoming a churchman, since it doesn't mean you won't go to war? Cardinal Richelieu is going on the first campaign with a helmet on his head and a halberd in his hand. And what about Monsieur de Nogaret de La Valette? He's a cardinal too, but ask his servant how many times he's bandaged his wounds."

"Yes, I know, sir," Bazin said mournfully, "everything is in disorder nowadays."

Meanwhile the two young men and the servant had gone downstairs and out into the courtyard.

"Hold the stirrup for me, Bazin," said Aramis.

And he leapt into the saddle with his usual grace and lightness. But as soon as his horse had made a few high-spirited leaps and turns, he felt such unbearable pain that he turned pale and nearly fell from the saddle. D'Artagnan had been watching him, fearing this reaction. He ran to him, helped him to dismount, and led him back to his room.

"It's all right, Aramis," he said. "Stay here and take care of yourself. I can go and look for Athos without you."

"You're a man of iron, as I told you," said Aramis.

"No, I'm lucky, that's all. But how will you pass the time while I'm gone? You won't go back to writing your thesis or arguing about fingers and benedictions, will you?"

Aramis smiled.

"I'll write poetry," he said.

"Yes, poetry perfumed with the scent of that letter from Madame de Chevreuse's maid. You can teach Bazin the rules of versification; it will be a consolation to him. And ride for a few minutes every day, to get used to it again."

"Don't worry about that," said Aramis. "You'll find me ready to ride all day when you come back."

They said good-bye to each other and ten minutes later, after urging Bazin and the hostess to take good care of Aramis, d'Artagnan was on his way to Amiens.

How was he going to find Athos? Would he be able to find him at all? He had left him in a critical situation; perhaps he had not survived it. This thought darkened d'Artagnan's face, drew a sigh from him, and made him swear vengeance. Of all his friends, Athos was the oldest and would therefore have seemed to be the furthest from his tastes and inclinations, yet d'Artagnan had a marked preference for him. Athos's noble, distinguished air, the flashes of grandeur that occasionally burst from the shadows in which he enclosed himself, the even temper that made him the easiest companion in the world, his forced, caustic gaiety, his bravery, which could have been called blind if it had not been the result of an extraordinary self-control—all these qualities filled d'Artagnan with admiration, as well as earning his respect and friendship.

On the days when he was in a good humor, Athos could be compared favorably even with such an elegant and noble courtier as Monsieur de Tréville. He was of average height, but so well proportioned and solidly built that more than once he had emerged victorious from a bout of wrestling with Porthos, that giant whose physical strength was legendary among the musketeers. His face, with its piercing eyes, straight nose, and chin shaped like that of Brutus, gave a striking impression of majesty combined with graciousness. Although he did not take care of his hands in any way, they were the despair of Aramis, who cultivated his own hands with almond paste and perfumed oil. The sound of his voice was both penetrating and melodious.

He never thrust himself forward and seemed to prefer remaining in the background, but his command of the social graces was unmatched. He could organize a meal better than anyone else, seating each guest according to the rank that his ancestors had given him, or that he had earned for himself. In matters of heraldry he was the final authority, for he knew the names, genealogies, and branches of all the noble families in the kingdom, as well as the details and origins of their coats of arms. No point of etiquette was unfamiliar to him; he knew the rights of all the great landowners; he had a thorough knowledge of hunting and falconry, and one day, in a discussion of them, he had astonished King Louis XIII himself, who was a master of both arts.

Like all great noblemen of the time, he was a highly skilled rider and swordsman. He was so well educated, even in theology, which was rare among gentlemen, that he smiled when Aramis spoke a few words of Latin and Porthos pretended to understand them. Two or three times, to his friends' surprise, he had corrected Aramis on some point of Latin grammar. His integrity was unimpeachable, in a time when soldiers readily compromised with their religion and their conscience, lovers lacked the rigorous standards of honor that prevail today, and poor people often broke God's seventh commandment.

Athos was thus an extraordinary man. And yet, despite his distinction and refinement, he sometimes sank into sluggish apathy, as old men sink into physical and mental debility. In his periods of lethargy, and they were many, the radiant side of his nature disappeared, as though engulfed in darkness. Then, when the demigod had vanished, what remained was scarcely a man. With his head bowed, his eyes dull, and his speech heavy, he would sit for hours, staring at his bottle and glass, with an occasional glance at Grimaud, who, being used to obeying orders given by signs, always understood the wish expressed by his master's lackluster gaze and satisfied it immediately. If the four friends gathered during one of those periods, a few words, spoken with great effort, would be Athos's only contribution to the conversation. He would drink as much as the other three combined, though without showing any effects other than a more pronounced frown and a deeper sadness.

D'Artagnan's curious, inquisitive mind made him try to discover the cause of Athos's recurring despondency, but so far he had not succeeded. Athos never received any letters and never did anything that was not known to all his friends.

Although drinking deepened his sadness, it did not cause it, for he drank heavily only when his sadness had already begun. It could not be attributed to gambling because, unlike Porthos, whose moods ranged from triumph to despair, according to how his luck was running, Athos remained impassive whether he won or lost. One evening he had won three thousand pistoles, lost it all, along with his gold-embroidered swordbelt, then won it all back, plus a hundred louis, without showing the slightest sign of emotion or ceasing to carry on a calm, friendly conversation.

Nor was it the weather that affected his moods, as it does with our neighbors the English, for his sadness usually became more intense during the pleasant seasons of the year; June and July were his worst months.

He evidently had no reason for sorrow in the present, and he merely shrugged when anyone spoke to him of the future; it therefore seemed clear that his secret was in the past, as d'Artagnan had been vaguely given to understand.

The mystery that hung over Athos's life made him still more interesting; he had never revealed the slightest clue to it, even when he was drunk, no matter how adroitly he was questioned.

"Poor Athos may be dead now," d'Artagnan said to Planchet as they rode toward Amiens. "If so, it's my fault because I'm the one who dragged him into that affair. He didn't know the reason for it, he had nothing to gain from it, and he didn't even expect to know its outcome."

"And we probably owe our lives to him," said Planchet. "Remember how he shouted, 'I'm trapped! Go, d'Artagnan, hurry!' And after he'd fired his pistols, what a terrible noise he made with his sword! It sounded as if he were fighting twenty men, or twenty furious demons!"

These words redoubled d'Artagnan's eagerness to reach Amiens. He made his high-spirited horse break into a gallop.

At eleven o'clock in the morning he and Planchet came within sight of Amiens. At half-past eleven they reined up in front of the inn.

D'Artagnan had often contemplated vengeance against the treacherous innkeeper; the mere thought of it had been of some consolation to him. As he walked into the inn, he pulled his hat down low on his forehead, snapped his riding whip with his right hand, and put his left hand on the pommel of his sword.

"Do you recognize me?" he said to the innkeeper, who had come forward to greet him.

"I don't have the honor of knowing you, sir," replied the innkeeper, still dazzled by the luxurious trappings he had seen on d'Artagnan's horse.

"Ah, so you don't think you know me?"

"No, sir."

"A few words will restore your memory. What have you done with the gentleman you had the audacity to accuse of being a counterfeiter two weeks ago?"

The innkeeper turned pale, for d'Artagnan had taken his most threatening attitude and Planchet had followed suit.

"Oh, dear God, how I've paid for that mistake!" he wailed.

"Tell me what became of that gentleman."

"Please be kind enough to sit down and listen to me, sir. And I beg you to be merciful!"

D'Artagnan was speechless with anger and anxiety. He sat down and looked at the innkeeper with the menacing sternness of a judge. Planchet proudly leaned against his chair.

"I'll tell you the whole story, sir," said the innkeeper, trembling. "I recognize you now: you're the one who left just as I was having that unfortunate dispute with the gentleman you've referred to."

"Yes, and you can expect no mercy if you don't tell me the whole truth."

"I will, sir, please listen to me."

"I *am* listening."

"The authorities had warned me that a notorious counterfeiter was coming to my inn with several of his companions, all disguised as musketeers or guards. I'd been given a description of your horses, your servants, your faces . . ."

"Go on," said d'Artagnan, who had quickly realized where that description had come from.

"The authorities sent six men to help me and ordered me to take whatever measures I thought necessary to arrest the supposed counterfeiters."

"Don't use that word again!" said d'Artagnan; he found it irritating to his ears.

"Forgive me for saying such things, sir, but they're my excuse. The authorities had frightened me, and, as you know, an innkeeper must always try to stay on good terms with them."

"Never mind that! Just tell me about that gentleman! Where is he? Is he dead or alive?"

"Please be patient, sir," said the innkeeper. "I'm about to answer your questions. You know what was happening when you left. Your hurried departure made it seem that the authorities were right," he added, with a craftiness that did not escape d'Artagnan. "That gentleman, your friend, defended himself desperately. Unfortunately his servant had quarreled with the men sent by the authorities, disguised as stablemen . . ."

"You wretched scoundrel!" cried d'Artagnan. "You were all in the plot! I don't know what keeps me from slaughtering you all!"

"No, sir, we weren't all in the plot, as you'll see. Your friend—excuse me for not calling him by the honorable name I'm sure he bears, but I don't know what it is—put two men out of action with his pistols, then retreated, fighting with his sword. He disabled one of my men and knocked me unconscious with the flat of his blade."

"Come to the point! What happened to Athos?"

"As he retreated, he found himself at the top of the stairs that lead to the cellar. The key was in the cellar door, so he locked himself inside. Knowing he couldn't escape, the men left him there."

"They must not have been determined to kill him," said d'Artagnan. "They only wanted to imprison him."

"Imprison him, sir? Good heavens, no! He made himself a prisoner, I swear it's true! And he'd fought furiously before he locked himself in the cellar: one man killed and two seriously wounded. They were carried away by their companions, and I haven't heard of them since. When I came back to my senses, I went to the governor, told him what had happened, and asked him what I should do with the prisoner. But the governor seemed mystified. He told me he had no idea what I was talking about, that the orders I'd received hadn't come from him, and that if I ever told anyone he'd had anything to do with the incident, he'd have me hanged. Apparently I'd arrested the wrong man, and the man who was supposed to be arrested escaped."

"But what about Athos?" said d'Artagnan, whose impatience had been increased by learning that the authorities had dropped the whole matter. "What became of him?"

"Since I wanted to make amends to him as quickly as possible," the innkeeper continued, "I went down to the cellar to set him free. Oh, sir, he wasn't a man anymore, he was a devil! When I told him he could leave, he accused me of setting a trap for him and said he wouldn't come out of the cellar unless I agreed to certain conditions. I realized I'd put myself in a bad position by attacking one of His Majesty's musketeers, so I humbly told him I was willing to accept his conditions. 'First,' he said, 'I want you to send me my servant, fully armed.'

"We quickly obeyed that order because, as you can understand, sir, we were more than ready to do anything your friend wanted. Monsieur Grimaud—he told me his name, though he doesn't talk much—was wounded, but we took him down to the cellar. When his master had taken him inside, he barricaded the door again and ordered us to stay in our inn."

"But where is he?" said d'Artagnan. "Tell me where he is!"

"In the cellar, sir."

"What! You've kept him in the cellar all this time?"

"Heavens, no, sir! We haven't kept him in the cellar! You wouldn't say that if you knew what he's been doing there. Oh, sir, if you can make him leave, I'll be grateful to you the rest of my life, I'll worship you as my patron saint!''

"Then I'll find him in the cellar?"

"Yes, sir, since he's insisted on staying there. Every day we give him bread through the air hole, at the end of a pitchfork, and meat when he asks for it. I wish he were satisfied with bread and meat! Once I tried to go into the cellar with two of my men, but he flew into a terrible rage. I heard him cock his pistols, and his servant cock his blunderbuss. I asked him what he intended to do. He said that he and his servant had enough powder and lead for forty shots, and that they'd fire all of them before they'd let any of us set foot in the cellar. I went to complain to the governor. He told me I was only getting what I deserved, and that it would teach me not to insult honorable gentlemen who came to my inn.''

"And since then?" asked d'Artagnan, who could not help laughing at the pitiful look on the innkeeper's face.

"Since then, sir, we've led the saddest life you can imagine. I have to tell you that all our provisions are in the cellar: bottled wine, wine in casks, beer, olive oil, spices, bacon, sausages. Since he won't let us in, we have to refuse food and drink to all the travelers who come here, so every day we have fewer and fewer guests. Another week with your friend in the cellar and we'll be ruined!''

"And you deserve it," said d'Artagnan. "Couldn't you tell by looking at us that we weren't counterfeiters?"

"Yes, sir, you're right . . . Listen! He's losing his temper again.''

"Someone must have disturbed him."

"We have to disturb him! Two English gentlemen have just come in to the inn.''

"Well, what of it?"

"The English love good wine, as you know, sir. These two asked for the best. My wife must have gone down to ask Monsieur Athos for permission to get the wine, and he must have refused, as usual.''

D'Artagnan heard a loud noise from the direction of the cellar. He stood up. Preceded by the innkeeper, who was wringing his hands, and followed by Planchet holding his cocked blunderbuss, he walked toward the source of the tumult.

The two English gentlemen were exasperated; they had traveled a great distance and were dying of hunger and thirst.

"This is tyranny!" one of them said in correct French, though with a foreign accent. "That madman won't let these good people have their own wine! We'll break open the door, and if he's too rabid we'll kill him."

"One moment, gentlemen," said d'Artagnan, drawing his pistols from his belt. "You're not going to kill anyone."

"Let them come in," said Athos's calm voice from the other side of the door, "and we'll see how ferocious they are."

Brave though they seemed to be, the two Englishmen looked at each other hesitantly; it was as though they were outside the den of one of those gigantic, bloodthirsty ogres described in folk tales. There was a moment of silence. Finally they were ashamed to hold back any longer. The more irascible of the two went down the five or six steps that composed the staircase and gave the door a violent kick.

"Planchet," said d'Artagnan, cocking his pistols, "I'll take the one at the top of the stairs, you take the one at the bottom. So you want a battle, gentlemen! Very well, we'll give you one."

"My God!" exclaimed Athos's hollow voice. "I think I hear d'Artagnan!"

"Yes, I'm here, my friend!" d'Artagnan called out.

"Good! We'll deal with these door-breakers together!"

The Englishmen had drawn their swords, but they were caught between two fires. They hesitated again, and again pride won out. A second kick split the door.

"Stand back, d'Artagnan, I'm going to shoot!" shouted Athos.

"Be patient, Athos," said d'Artagnan, keeping his presence of mind. He turned to the Englishmen. "Gentlemen, consider what you're about to do. You're in a bad situation. All you can accomplish is to get yourselves riddled with bullets. My servant and I will fire three shots at you and three more will be fired from the cellar. Then my friend and I will still have our swords, and I assure you that we know how to use them. Let me handle this matter for you. I promise you that you'll soon have your wine."

"If there's any left," Athos said mockingly.

The innkeeper felt a chill run up his spine.

"If there's any left?" he murmured. "Does he mean . . ."

"Don't worry, there's still wine in your cellar," said d'Artagnan. "The two of them can't have drunk it all. Gentlemen, sheathe your swords."

"Put your pistols back in your belt!"

"I'll be glad to."

And d'Artagnan set the example. Then he turned to Planchet and motioned him to uncock his blunderbuss.

Reassured but still grumbling, the Englishmen sheathed their swords. D'Artagnan told them the story of Athos's imprisonment, and, since they were gentlemen, they put all the blame on the innkeeper.

"Now, gentlemen," said d'Artagnan, "go back to your rooms and I guarantee you that within ten minutes everything you want will be brought to you."

The Englishmen bowed and left.

"Now that they're gone, Athos," said d'Artagnan, "will you please open the door?"

"Certainly," replied Athos.

D'Artagnan heard a sound of clattering firewood and thudding beams: Athos was pulling down the barricade he had built.

The door swung open and Athos's pale face appeared. He quickly glanced around, as if to make sure no one was lurking in the vicinity.

D'Artagnan threw his arms around him. Then, when he tried to pull him out of the damp cellar, he noticed that he was unsteady on his feet.

"Are you wounded?" he asked.

"No, I'm dead drunk, that's all, and no one ever did more to achieve that result than I've done. I must have emptied at least a hundred and fifty bottles."

"Lord have mercy on us!" cried the innkeeper. "If your servant has drunk only half as much as you, I'm ruined!"

"Grimaud is a proper servant who wouldn't drink the same wine as his master: he only drank from the casks. I think he forgot to put the stopper back in the last one, though. Do you hear that? It's wine splashing on the floor."

D'Artagnan let out a burst of laughter that turned the innkeeper's chill into a fever.

Grimaud appeared behind his master with his blunderbuss on his shoulder, tilting his head to one side like the drunken satyrs in a Rubens painting. He was smeared front and back with a thick liquid that the innkeeper recognized as his best olive oil.

D'Artagnan led Athos and the two servants to the best room in the inn and took possession of it.

Meanwhile the innkeeper and his wife took lamps and hurried down to the cellar that had been denied to them so long. A hideous sight awaited them beyond the barricade that Athos had made of firewood, planks, beams, and empty casks: lying in puddles of olive oil and wine on the floor were the bones of all the hams that had been eaten; in one corner was a mound of broken bottles; a barrel was losing the last drops of its blood through the spigot that had been left open; of the fifty sausages that had hung from the ceiling, less than a dozen were left. The image of devastation and death, as an ancient poet said, reigned there as on a battlefield.

The shrieks of the innkeeper and his wife rose from the cellar. D'Artagnan himself was moved by them; Athos did not even turn his head.

But grief was followed by rage. The innkeeper armed himself with a skewer and, in his despair, came charging into the room where the two friends were sitting.

"Bring us some wine," Athos said when he saw him.

"You want more wine?" asked the innkeeper, taken aback. "You've already drunk more than a hundred pistoles' worth! I'm ruined, lost, destroyed!"

"Don't complain," said Athos, "we never drank enough to quench our thirst."

"It was bad enough that you drank all that wine, but you also broke the bottles!"

"You pushed me against a pile of bottles and they fell, so it's your fault."

"All my olive oil is gone!"

"Olive oil is a good balm, and poor Grimaud had to treat the wounds you gave him."

"All my sausages have been eaten!"

"It's amazing how many rats there are in that cellar."

"You're going to pay me for all that!" cried the innkeeper, exasperated.

"You'll see how I'm going to pay you!" said Athos, standing up threateningly. But he fell back into his chair; he had reached the end of his strength. D'Artagnan came to his aid by raising his riding whip. The innkeeper stepped back and burst into tears.

"This will teach you," said d'Artagnan, "to be more courteous to the guests God sends you."

"God? You mean the devil!"

"If you go on annoying us, my dear friend, all four of us will lock ourselves in your cellar and make sure the damage is really as great as you say it is."

"Gentlemen, I was wrong, I admit it, but no sin is unforgivable. You're noble lords and I'm only a poor innkeeper: have mercy on me."

"If you talk like that," said Athos, "you'll break my heart and tears will flow from my eyes as wine flowed from your casks. We're not as fierce as we look. Come here and let's talk it over."

The innkeeper approached, with anxiety.

"Don't be afraid," Athos went on. "When I was about to pay you, I put my purse on the table."

"Yes, sir."

"That purse contained sixty pistoles. Where is it?"

"It's been deposited in the records office, sir. The money in it was said to be counterfeit."

"Get it back for me and keep the sixty pistoles."

"Once the records office has something, it never lets go of it. You must know that, sir. If the coins really were counterfeit, there would be some hope, but unfortunately they're genuine."

"You'll have to solve that problem as best you can, my good man. It's your concern, not mine. If you don't get the purse, you won't get paid, because I have no other money than what was in it."

"Where's Monsieur Athos's horse?" asked d'Artagnan.

"In the stables," replied the innkeeper.

"How much is he worth?"

"Fifty pistoles, at most."

"He's worth eighty. Take him, and that will settle the account."

"What!" exclaimed Athos. "You're selling my horse, my Bajazet? How can I go to war? Will I have to ride Grimaud?"

"I've brought you another horse," said d'Artagnan.

"Another one?"

"A magnificent one!" said the innkeeper.

"Since I now have a better horse," said Athos, "take my old one. And bring us some wine."

"What kind, sir?" asked the innkeeper, whose outlook on life had now brightened.

"The kind that's at the back of the cellar, near the slats. There are still twenty-five bottles of it; the others were all broken when I fell. Bring up six of them."

The innkeeper turned toward the door and thought, "This man drinks like a fish! If he stays here two more weeks and pays for what he drinks, I'll be as well off as I was before."

"And take four bottles of the same wine to the English gentlemen," said d'Artagnan.

"And now, d'Artagnan," Athos said when the innkeeer had

left, "while we're waiting for our wine, tell me what's happened to the others."

D'Artagnan told him how he had found Porthos in bed with a sprained knee, and Aramis at a table with two theologians. As he was finishing his story the innkeeper came back with the wine and also a ham, which, luckily for him, he had not kept in the cellar.

"So much for Porthos and Aramis," said Athos, filling his glass and d'Artagnan's, "but you still haven't told me about yourself. You look gloomy to me."

"That's because I'm the unhappiest of all of us."

"You, unhappy? Why? Tell me about it."

"Later," said d'Artagnan.

"Why later? Because you think I'm drunk? The fact is that my mind is never clearer than when I've been drinking. Tell me what's wrong, I'm all ears."

D'Artagnan described his adventure with Madame Bonacieux.

Athos listened without showing any reaction; then, at the end of the story, he said, "That's only a trifle."

It was a word he used often.

"You think everything's a trifle!" said d'Artagnan. "You wouldn't think so if you'd ever been in love!"

A flame suddenly flared in Athos's eyes, but an instant later they became as dull and listless as before.

"You're right, I've never been in love," he said calmly.

"Since your heart is made of stone, you should be more indulgent to a tenderhearted man like me."

"Tender hearts were made to be broken," said Athos.

"What do you mean?"

"I mean that love is a lottery in which the prize is death. You've very lucky to have lost, d'Artagnan, believe me. And if you follow my advice, you'll always lose."

"She seemed to love me so much!"

"She seemed to."

"She *did* love me!"

"You're talking like a child! There's not one man who hasn't believed, like you, that his mistress loved him, and there's not one man whose mistress hasn't deceived him."

"Except you, Athos, since you've never had a mistress."

"That's true," Athos said after a moment of silence, "I've never had one. Let's drink."

"You're a philosopher," said d'Artagnan. "Give me the benefit of your knowledge. I need to be consoled."

"Consoled for what?"

"My misfortune."

"Your misfortune is laughable," said Athos, shrugging his shoulders. "I'd be curious to know what you'd say if I told you a love story."

"One that happened to you?"

"Or to one of my friends—what does it matter?"

"Tell it to me, Athos."

"I'd rather drink."

"You can do both."

"You're right, I can do both," said Athos. He emptied his glass and refilled it. "Drinking and telling stories go very well together."

"I'm listening," said d'Artagnan.

Athos collected his thoughts, and d'Artagnan saw him turn pale. He was at that stage of drunkenness where ordinary drinkers collapse and fall asleep. But he remained awake and dreamed aloud. There was something disquieting about that trancelike state.

"You really want me to tell you that story?" he asked.

"Yes, please do."

"Very well, since you insist. A friend of mine was . . ." Athos paused, then said with a somber smile, "I want it clearly understood that I'm talking about a friend, not about myself. This friend was one of the counts of Berry, my native province, and as noble as a Dandolo or a Montmorency. At twenty-five he fell in love with a breathtakingly beautiful girl of sixteen. Young though she was, she had a passionate nature and the mind of a poet. She was more than attractive, she was intoxicating. She lived in a little town with her brother, a priest. They'd been there only a short time. No one knew where they came from, but since she was so beautiful and her brother was so pious, no one thought to ask. They were said to be from a good family. My friend was the local lord; he could have seduced her or taken her by force if he'd wanted to. He had absolute power and no one would have come to the aid of two strangers. Unfortunately he was an honorable man: he married her, the fool, the idiot!"

"Why do you say that, since he loved her?" asked d'Artagnan.

"Wait and you'll understand. He took her into his castle and made her the first lady of the province. And in all fairness it must be said that she held her position admirably."

"Well, then?"

"One day when she was out hunting with her husband,"

Athos continued, speaking softly and rapidly, "she was thrown from her horse and knocked unconscious. The count hurried to help her. To loosen her clothes more quickly, he cut them with his dagger, and bared her shoulder. You'll never guess what was on her shoulder, d'Artagnan!" he said with a loud laugh.

"Then tell me."

"A fleur-de-lis. She'd been branded!"

Athos emptied his glass in one swallow.

"That's horrible!" exclaimed d'Artagnan.

"Horrible but true. The count's angel was a demon. A convicted thief."

"And what did the count do?"

"He was a great lord, with the right of justice in his domain. He finished cutting off her clothes, tied her hands behind her back, and hanged her from a tree."

"He murdered her!"

"Yes, he murdered her," said Athos, pale as death. "I seem to be running out of wine."

He picked up the last remaining bottle, raised it to his mouth and emptied it as though it were a glass. Then he slumped forward and buried his face in his hands. D'Artagnan stared at him, horror-stricken.

Athos raised his head and sat up straight.

"That cured me of beautiful, poetic, and amorous women," he said, abandoning the pretense of talking about a friend. "God grant that you'll be cured of them too! Let's drink!"

"So she's . . . she's dead . . ." d'Artagnan stammered.

"That's right. Hold out your glass. Ah, I see the wine's all gone. Well, if we can't drink, we'll eat some of that ham."

"What about her brother?" d'Artagnan asked timidly.

"Her brother?"

"Yes, the priest."

"I asked about him, intending to have him hanged too, but he'd already left."

"Did you ever find out who he was?"

"He was probably her first lover and her accomplice, pretending to be a priest so he could find a rich husband for her. I hope he's been drawn and quartered by now."

"My God, my God . . ." murmured d'Artagnan, feeling dazed from what he had heard.

Athos cut a slice of ham and put it on d'Artagnan's plate.

"Try some of this," he said, "it's delicious. I'm sorry there weren't three or four hams like this one in the cellar—I'd have drunk fifty more bottles of wine!"

D'Artagnan felt as if he would go mad if the conversation continued. He put his head down on the table and pretended to fall asleep.

"Today's young men can't hold their wine," said Athos, looking at him with pity, "and d'Artagnan's one of the best!"

28

The Return

D'Artagnan had been stunned by Athos's terrible story, but many things about it still seemed obscure to him. It had been told by a completely drunk man to one who was half drunk, and yet, despite the confusion engendered in the brain by two or three bottles of Burgundy, when d'Artagnan awoke next morning he remembered everything Athos had said as clearly as if each word had been engraved in his mind. Wanting to get rid of his uncertainty, he went to his friend's room with the intention of resuming their conversation. But Athos, sober now, was again the shrewdest and most inscrutable of men.

After shaking hands with d'Artagnan, he himself brought up the subject of what had taken place the night before.

"I was very drunk last night," he said. "I know it because my tongue was thick when I woke up this morning, and my pulse was still pounding. I must have said all sorts of ridiculous things."

He looked at his friend with a steadiness that embarrassed him.

"I don't think so," replied d'Artagnan. "If I remember right, you said only ordinary things."

"I'm surprised to hear that," said Athos. "I thought I'd told you some outrageous story."

And his look became still more intense.

"Then I must have been even drunker than you, because I don't remember anything like that."

Athos was not satisfied with his answer.

"As you must have noticed, drunkenness makes some people sad and others happy. It makes me sad. When I'm drunk, I begin telling all the gloomy stories my foolish nurse used to fill my head with. It's an annoying fault, I realize that, but otherwise I'm a good drinker."

D'Artagnan's conviction was shaken by the natural tone in which Athos had spoken, but he quickly tried to draw the truth from him.

"Yes, now I seem to remember vaguely that we talked about someone being hanged."

"You see?" said Athos, turning pale but trying to laugh. "I was sure of it! Hangings are my nightmare."

"My memory is coming back now . . . You told me . . . It was something about a woman . . ."

Athos's pallor increased.

"It must have been my story about the blond woman. When I tell that one, it means I'm dead drunk."

"Yes, it was a story about a blond, beautiful woman . . ."

"Who was hanged."

"By her husband, who was a friend of yours," d'Artagnan concluded, looking Athos in the eyes.

"You see how you can slander someone when you're too drunk to know what you're saying? I'm not going to get drunk any more. It's a bad habit."

D'Artagnan made no reply.

Athos abruptly changed the subject: "By the way, thank you very much for the horse you brought me."

"Do you like him?"

"Yes, but he didn't seem to be a horse that would have much endurance."

"You're mistaken: I did twenty-five miles with him in less than an hour and a half, and he was no more tired than if he'd only trotted around the Place Saint-Sulpice."

"Stop, you're making me regret what I did."

"What did you do?"

"I got rid of him."

"How?"

"I woke up at six o'clock this morning. You were sleeping like a log and I had nothing to do. My mind was still foggy from our drinking bout last night. I went down to the main hall and saw one of our Englishmen there. His horse had died of a stroke, and he was bargaining with a dealer to buy another one. I went up to him and heard that he was offering a hundred pistoles for a chestnut horse.

" 'Excuse me, sir,' I said to him, 'but I also have a horse for sale.'

" 'And a fine one, too,' he answered. 'I saw your friend's servant holding him yesterday.'

" 'Do you think he's worth a hundred pistoles?' I asked.

" 'Yes. Will you sell him to me at that price?''

" 'No, but I'll gamble with you for him.'

" 'What kind of gambling?'

" 'Dice.'

"So we played dice and I lost the horse. But I won back his trappings.''

D'Artagnan's face took on a rather disgruntled expression.

"Are you annoyed about it?'' asked Athos.

"Yes, I must admit I am. I intended for that horse to make us recognizable on a battlefield; he was a token, a souvenir. You shouldn't have gambled for him, Athos.''

"Put yourself in my place: I was bored; and besides, I don't like English horses. If you're only concerned about being recognized by someone, the saddle will take care of that—it's not a saddle that anyone could fail to notice. As for the horse, we'll think of some reason to explain his disappearance. After all, horses are mortal; let's say that mine died of glanders or farcy.''

D'Artagnan's face did not brighten.

"I'm sorry to know how much those horses mean to you,'' said Athos, "because I haven't finished my story yet.''

"What else have you done?''

"When I'd lost my horse, nine to ten—you see, I almost won—I had the idea of gambling for yours.''

"But you didn't act on that idea, did you?''

"Yes, I did.''

"And?'' asked d'Artagnan, worried.

"I lost.''

"You lost my horse?''

"That's right. Seven to eight. By only one point . . . But, as the saying goes, a miss is as good as a mile.''

"Athos, you're not in your right mind!''

"You should have said that last night, when I was telling you my silly stories, and not this morning. I forgot to mention that besides losing your horse, I also lost his harness, saddle, and trappings.''

"That's inexcusable! You . . .''

"Wait, there's more. I'd be an excellent gambler if I weren't so stubborn, but I never know when to stop. It's the same as when I'm drinking. So I went on gambling.''

"But how could you, when you had nothing left?"

"You're forgetting that we still had that diamond ring you're wearing. I noticed it yesterday."

"My ring!" cried d'Artagnan, putting his hand to it.

"I'm a good judge of diamonds, since I've had a few of my own. I estimated the value of your ring at a thousand pistoles."

"I hope you didn't mention my ring," d'Artagnan said apprehensively.

"I did, my friend. Don't you realize that it was our last resource? With that ring, I could win back our horses, and also win enough money for our journey."

"Tell me what happened!"

"Well, I told my partner about your ring. He'd noticed it too. After all, you can't wear a spectacular diamond like that and expect it to pass unnoticed."

"Never mind that, just tell me if you won or lost!"

"We divided the diamond into ten parts, each worth a hundred pistoles."

"You're joking, aren't you?" d'Artagnan said with anger rising inside him. "You just want to see how long I'll take you seriously."

"No, I'm not joking. Try to understand, d'Artagnan: I'd just spent two weeks alone with Grimaud in that cellar, with nothing to do but drink myself into a stupor."

"That's no reason to gamble with my ring!" said d'Artagnan, nervously clenching his fist.

"Let me finish. We agreed to throw the dice for a hundred pistoles each time. In thirteen throws I lost everything. Thirteen! That number has always been unlucky for me. It was on the thirteenth of July that . . ."

"My God!" exclaimed d'Artagnan, leaping to his feet; this morning's story had made him forget the one he had heard the night before.

"Be patient," said Athos. "I had a plan. The Englishman was a bit eccentric. I'd seen him talking with Grimaud, and Grimaud later told me that he'd tried to lure him away from my service and into his. So I staked Grimaud, the silent Grimaud, divided into ten parts."

"You're incredible!" said d'Artagnan, laughing in spite of himself.

"Yes, Grimaud himself! The whole of him isn't worth a silver ducat, but with ten parts of him I won back your diamond ring. Don't try to tell me that persistence isn't a virtue!"

"That's really funny!" said d'Artagnan, laughing again, this time more from relief than from amusement.

"Since my luck had changed, I staked the ring again."

D'Artagnan's laughter stopped abruptly.

"Oh, no . . ."

"I won back your harness, then your horse, then my harness, then my horse, then I lost again. Finally, when I had your harness and mine, I decided I'd done well enough, so I stopped."

D'Artagnan felt as if a weight as heavy as the inn had been lifted from his chest.

"Then I can keep my ring?" he asked timidly.

"Of course. We also have our harnesses."

"What good are harnesses without horses?"

"I have an idea about that."

"Your ideas make me shudder, Athos!"

"You haven't gambled for a long time, have you?"

"No, and I don't want to gamble now."

"You mustn't have a closed mind, d'Artagnan. Since you haven't gambled for a long time, you must have stored up a lot of good luck."

"That's one way of looking at it."

"The two Englishmen are still here. They seem to regret not having the harnesses and you seem to regret having lost your horse. I advise you to stake your harness against your horse."

"The Englishman wouldn't want only one harness."

"Stake mine too! I'm not selfish, like you."

"You'd let me stake yours?" said d'Artagnan. He was beginning to waver because he could not help being affected by Athos's confidence.

"Of course. Stake them both on one throw."

"But now that we've lost the horses, I'd very much like to keep the harnesses."

"Then stake your diamond ring."

"No! Never!"

"I'd suggest staking Planchet, but after what happened when I staked Grimaud, the Englishman probably wouldn't want to try it again."

"I'd really rather not risk anything."

"That's a pity," Athos said calmly. "The Englishman has more money than he knows what to do with. Come, d'Artagnan, just one throw of the dice! It will only take a minute!"

"What if I lose?"

"You'll win."

"You can't be sure of it."

"Well, if you lose, we won't have our harnesses anymore."

"All right, I'll do it. One throw."

Athos went off to find the Englishman and came upon him in the stables, looking covetously at the harnesses. Athos had found him at a good time. He made his proposition: both harnesses against one horse or a hundred pistoles. The Englishman quickly estimated that the harnesses were worth three hundred pistoles. He agreed to stake a horse against them.

D'Artagnan threw the dice with a trembling hand. He turned deathly pale when he saw the number three come up.

"That wasn't a good throw, my friend," said Athos. He turned to the Englishman. "Well, sir, it looks as if you'll have the horses with their harnesses."

The Englishman smiled triumphantly. He was so sure of winning that he threw the dice on the table without bothering to look at them. D'Artagnan had turned away to hide his chagrin.

"A very rare throw," Athos said quietly. "Offhand, I can recall having seen it only four times before: two aces."

The Englishman looked at the dice and scowled; d'Artagnan looked at them and was overjoyed.

"Yes, only four times," Athos went on. "Once in Monsieur de Chéquy's house; once in my castle in . . . when I had a castle; once in Monsieur de Tréville's house, where it surprised us all; and once in a tavern, where I was the one who threw it. It cost me a hundred louis and a supper."

"Well, sir, you've won a horse," said the Englishman. "Will you take back your own?"

"Of course," replied d'Artagnan.

"Shall we throw the dice again?"

"Only one throw: that was our agreement."

"That's true. The horse will be returned to your servant."

"Just a moment, sir," said Athos. "With your permission, I'd like to have a word with my friend."

"Certainly."

Athos took d'Artagnan aside.

"Are you trying to lead me into temptation again?" d'Artagnan asked him. "You want me to take another throw, don't you?"

"No, I want you to think."

"About what?"

"You said you were going to take back your horse."

"Is there anything wrong with that?"

"Yes. If I were you, I'd take the hundred pistoles. You staked the harnesses against a horse or a hundred pistoles, remember?''

"Yes."

"I'd take the hundred pistoles."

"I'm taking the horse."

"That would be a mistake. What could we do with one horse for the two of us? You can't expect us both to ride him: we'd look like two of Aymon's sons who'd lost their brothers. And I know you wouldn't want to humiliate me by riding that magnificent horse beside me while I walked. I'd take the hundred pistoles without a moment's hesitation. We need money to go back to Paris."

"I want that horse, Athos."

"You're not thinking clearly, d'Artagnan. Like any other horse, yours may get glanders or stumble and break a leg; he'll then be worthless and you'll have lost a hundred pistoles. And an owner has to feed his horse, whereas money feeds its owner."

"But how could we get back to Paris?"

"On our servants' horses, of course! Don't worry, no one will think we're servants ourselves: our faces will be enough to show that we're gentlemen."

"We'd cut a fine figure on those nags, with Aramis and Porthos riding their fiery steeds!"

"Aramis and Porthos!" exclaimed Athos, laughing.

D'Artagnan was puzzled.

"What's funny about them?" he asked.

"Nothing, nothing . . . Let's come back to the hundred pistoles."

"You really think I should take the money instead of my horse?"

"I certainly do. With a hundred pistoles we can feast till the end of the month. After what we've been through, we deserve a little rest."

"*I'm* not going to rest, Athos. As soon as I'm back in Paris I'll begin trying to find Madame Bonacieux."

"Which do you think will be more useful to you in trying to find her: a horse or a hundred pistoles? Take the money, my friend, take the money."

D'Artagnan was willing to change his mind for a good reason, and this one seemed excellent to him. Besides, he was afraid Athos would think he was selfish if he went on refusing. So he agreed to take the hundred pistoles.

The Englishman counted out the money and gave it to him.

Now it was time to leave. They settled with the innkeeper for six pistoles, besides Athos's old horse. D'Artagnan and Athos took their servants' horses. Planchet and Grimaud set off on foot, carrying the saddles on their heads.

Despite the poor quality of their mounts, the two friends soon pulled ahead of their servants and arrived at Crèvecoeur. They saw Aramis in the distance, leaning against his windowsill and mournfully gazing at the horizon, like Anne in *Bluebeard*.

"Aramis!" d'Artagnan called out to him. "What are you doing there?"

"Ah, it's you, d'Artagnan! And you, Athos! I was meditating on the fleeting nature of worldly goods. The thought was suggested to me by the sight of my English horse leaving in a cloud of dust. Life can be summed up in three words: *Erat, est, fuit*."

"What does that mean?" asked d'Artagnan, who was beginning to suspect what had happened.

"It means I've just made a fool's bargain: I took sixty louis for a horse than can trot twelve miles in an hour."

D'Artagnan and Athos burst out laughing.

"I hope you won't be too angry with me, d'Artagnan," said Aramis. "I had no choice. Besides, I've already been punished, because that vile dealer cheated me out of at least fifty louis. I see you two rode here on your servants' horses. It's wise of you to spare your fine horses by having your servants lead them slowly, in short stages."

Just then a wagon, coming from the direction of Amiens, stopped near the inn. Grimaud and Planchet got out of it with the saddles on their heads. The wagon was returning empty to Paris and the two servants had agreed to pay the driver for their transportation by buying him wine at frequent intervals along the way.

"What's this?" said Aramis. "Only saddles?"

"Now do you understand?" said Athos.

"My friends, I did the same as you: some instinct made me keep the harness. Bazin! Bring my harness and put it in the wagon."

"What have you done with your priests?" asked d'Artagnan.

"I invited them to dinner the next day and got them as drunk as I could; it was easy, because this inn has excellent wine. The curate ordered me never to trade my uniform for a cassock, and the Jesuit asked me to get him accepted into the musketeers."

"Without a thesis!" said d'Artagnan. "I'll ask for him to be accepted without a thesis!"

"Since then," Aramis went on, "I've been living pleasantly

here. I've begun a poem composed of one-syllable lines. It's difficult, but merit lies in overcoming difficulties. It's a love poem. I'll read you the first canto; it has four hundred lines and takes a minute to read.''

''If you make your poem as short as it is difficult,'' said d'Artagnan, who detested poetry almost as much as Latin, ''it will have two merits instead of one.''

''It's filled with honest passion,'' said Aramis. ''You'll see . . . So we're going back to Paris, my friends? Good, I'm ready. And I'll be glad to see Porthos again. I've missed that big oaf, can you believe it? There's one thing we can count on: *he* hasn't sold his horse, no matter how much he may have been offered for him. I'm impatient to see him on that horse, with his fine saddle. I'm sure he'll look like the Grand Mogul.''

They stayed for an hour to let the horses rest. Aramis paid his bill at the inn, put Bazin in the wagon with his comrades, and they all set off for Chantilly.

They found Porthos out of bed, and less pale than when d'Artagnan had seen him last. Although he was alone, he was sitting at a table set for four, with a dinner composed of enticingly prepared meats, choice wines, and superb fruit.

''You've come just in time, my friends!'' he said, standing up. ''I was just about to begin my dinner. You'll eat with me.''

''Mousqueton didn't lasso bottles of wine like that!'' said d'Artagnan. ''And look at that braised veal, and that fillet of beef!''

''I'm building up my strength,'' said Porthos. ''Nothing weakens you like one of those damned sprains. Have you ever had a sprain, Athos?''

''Never. But I remember that two weeks after I was wounded in our skirmish on the Rue Férou I felt the same as you do now.''

''That whole dinner wasn't for you alone, was it, Porthos?'' asked Aramis.

''No. I was expecting some gentlemen who live nearby, but they just sent word that they couldn't come. You'll replace them, and I'll be glad of the change. Mousqueton! Bring three more chairs, and more wine.''

Ten minutes after they had begun the meal, Athos asked, ''Do you know what we're eating?''

''I know what *I'm* eating,'' replied d'Artagnan. ''It's larded veal with cardoons and marrow.''

''And I'm eating fillet of lamb,'' said Porthos.

"And I'm eating a chicken breast," said Aramis.

"You're all mistaken, gentlemen," said Athos. "You're eating horse."

"Don't be ridiculous!" said d'Artagnan.

"Horse!" Aramis said with a grimace of disgust.

Porthos remained silent.

"Yes, horse," said Athos. "Isn't that right, Porthos? We may even be eating a harness, too!"

"No, I kept the harness," said Porthos.

"We're all birds of a feather," said Aramis. "It's as though we'd planned it in advance."

"What else could I have done?" said Porthos. "That horse made my visitors feel ashamed, and I didn't want to humiliate them!"

"And then your duchess is still away, isn't she?" asked d'Artagnan.

"Yes, she is. The governor of the province, one of the gentlemen I was expecting for dinner, seemed to want that horse so much that I gave him to him."

"*Gave* him?"

"That's the right word, yes. I'm sure the horse was worth a hundred and fifty louis, but that miser wouldn't pay me any more than eighty."

"Without the saddle?" asked Aramis.

"Without the saddle."

"Let me point out to you, gentlemen," said Athos, "that Porthos made a better bargain than any of the rest of us."

Porthos sat in perplexed silence while the others laughed, but they soon told him the reason for their mirth and he shared it—loudly, as usual.

"So we're all rich," said d'Artagnan.

"I'm not," said Athos. "I liked Aramis's Spanish wine so much that I had sixty bottles of it put into the wagon. That left me with a serious shortage of money."

"I gave everything I had," said Aramis, "down to the last sou, to the Montdidier church and the Jesuits of Amiens. I'd made commitments that I had to keep: I'd ordered masses for me and you, gentlemen. They'll be said, and I have no doubt that we'll benefit from them."

"And you don't think my sprained knee cost me nothing, do you?" said Porthos. "Not to mention Mousqueton's wound. I had to have it treated by a doctor twice a day, and he charged me double his usual fee because that idiot Mousqueton had managed to get himself shot in a place that's ordinarily shown only to an apothecary. I've told him to make sure he never gets wounded there again.''

''I see you've been generous with him,'' said Athos, exchanging a smile with d'Artagnan and Aramis. ''You're a good master.''

''When I'd paid all my expenses,'' Porthos went on, ''I had only thirty écus left.''

''And I had about ten pistoles,'' said Aramis.

''Well, d'Artagnan,'' said Athos, ''how much is left of your hundred pistoles?''

''First of all, I gave you fifty.''

''You think so?''

''I know it!''

''Yes, I remember now.''

''Then I gave the innkeeper six.''

''That innkeeper is contemptible! Why did you give him six pistoles?''

''You yourself told me to do it.''

''That's true. I'm too kind. You don't need to explain your other expenses, just tell me how much you have left.''

''Twenty-five pistoles.''

Athos took some small change from his pocket.

''And I have . . .''

''Nothing,'' said d'Artagnan.

''Yes, or so close to nothing that the difference isn't worth talking about. Now let's see how much we all have together. First you, Porthos.''

''Thirty écus.''

''Aramis?''

''Ten pistoles.''

''D'Artagnan?''

''Twenty-five.''

''What does that all add up to?'' asked Athos.

''Four hundred and seventy-five livres,'' replied d'Artagnan, who could calculate as well as Archimedes.

''When we get back to Paris,'' said Porthos, ''we'll still have more than four hundred, plus the harnesses.''

''But we'll need battle horses,'' said Aramis.

''We'll sell our servants' four horses, buy two battle horses with the money, and draw lots for them. The four hundred livres will buy half a horse for one of the two losers. Since d'Artagnan is lucky at dice, we'll give him all our loose change and he'll gamble with it in the first gambling house he can find. There, that's our plan.''

"Let's eat our dinner before it gets cold," said Porthos.

Reassured about their future, the four friends did full justice to the meal, and the leftovers were finished off by Mousqueton, Bazin, Planchet, and Grimaud.

When they arrived in Paris, d'Artagnan found a letter from Monsieur de Tréville informing him that the king had consented to let him leave Monsieur des Essarts's company of guards and enter the musketeers. No date had been set, so he did not know how long he would have to wait, but he was too happy to be upset by that. Becoming a musketeer was what he wanted most in the world—except, of course, for finding Madame Bonacieux safe and sound.

He hurried off to give his friends the news. They had been in high spirits when he left them half an hour earlier; he now found them sad and preoccupied. They had gathered in Athos's apartment to hold a council, which was something they did only in serious circumstances.

Monsieur de Tréville had just notified them that they must begin preparing their equipment immediately because His Majesty had decided to begin the campaign on the first of May.

The four friends looked at each other in dismay: they knew that Monsieur de Tréville was inflexible in matters of discipline.

"How much do you think we'll have to spend for our equipment?" asked d'Artagnan.

"I've added up the cost of what we'll need, keeping everything to the bare minimum," said Aramis, "and it comes to fifteen hundred livres for each of us."

"Four times fifteen is sixty: six thousand livres," said Athos.

"It seems to me," said d'Artagnan, "that fifteen hundred must not really be the bare minimum. I think we can get by with a thousand livres each."

"I've got an idea," Porthos said abruptly.

"That's better than nothing," said Athos. "I don't even have the shadow of an idea. As for d'Artagnan, his happiness at the prospect of becoming a musketeer has driven him mad. A thousand livres! That's ridiculous! I don't know about the rest of you, but I'll need at least two thousand."

"Let's accept that figure," said Aramis. "Eight thousand livres to buy equipment for the four of us. And we already have our saddles."

D'Artagnan left to go and thank Monsieur de Tréville.

Athos waited till he had closed the door behind him, then said, "We have more than our saddles: we also have that splendid diamond ring d'Artagnan is wearing. He's too good a friend to leave us short of money when he has a king's ransom on his finger."

29

The Search for Equipment

D'Artagnan was the most preoccupied of the four friends, even though he was still a guard and therefore needed less costly equipment than the lordly musketeers. Though he was thrifty almost to the point of stinginess, he was nearly as vain as Porthos. So he was preoccupied with the demands of his vanity, but he also had a less selfish concern: he still did not know what had happened to Madame Bonacieux. At Monsieur de Tréville's request, the queen had promised to make inquiries, but d'Artagnan had little hope that she could accomplish anything.

Athos stayed in his apartment; he had decided that he would not lift a finger to get equipment for himself.

"We still have two weeks," he said to his friends. "If I haven't found anything at the end of that time, or rather if nothing has come to find me, I won't shoot myself, because I'm too good a Catholic for that, but what I'll do instead is to pick a quarrel with four of the cardinal's guards, or eight Englishmen, and fight till one of them kills me, which is sure to happen, with that many opponents. I'll be said to have died for the king, so I'll have done my duty without having to get equipment."

"I'll try out my idea," said Porthos, pacing the floor with his hands behind his back.

Aramis looked worried and said nothing.

These details show that desolation reigned in the little community.

The servants shared their masters' sorrow. Mousqueton gathered crusts of bread; Bazin, who had always been strongly inclined toward piety, spent all his time in churches; Planchet stared into space; and although Grimaud still obeyed his master's order to speak only when absolutely necessary, he heaved sighs that would have brought tears from a stone.

While Athos maintained his refusal to make the slightest effort, the three others went out early every morning and came back late. They wandered through the streets, examining the pavement to see if someone might have happened to drop his purse. They were so attentive everywhere they went that they seemed like hounds on a trail. Whenever they met, they gave each other sad looks that asked the silent question, "Have you found anything?"

Since Porthos was the first to have an idea and work out a plan, he was the first to act; and besides, he had always been a man of action. One day d'Artagnan saw him walking toward the Saint-Leu church and followed him instinctively. Before going into the holy place, Porthos curled his mustache and smoothed his beard, which was always a sign that he intended to make a favorable impression on a lady. D'Artagnan was careful to stay out of sight, so Porthos did not know he was being followed. D'Artagnan went into the church behind him. Porthos stopped and leaned against a pillar; d'Artagnan, still unseen, leaned against the other side of the same pillar.

The church was crowded because a sermon was being preached. Porthos began eyeing the women. Thanks to Mousqueton's efforts, his appearance did not reflect his sad financial situation: his hat was a little shabby, its plume had lost some of its color and so had his embroidery, and his lace was frayed, but these flaws vanished in the dim light of the church, and Porthos was still the handsome Porthos.

D'Artagnan noticed a middle-aged woman in a black hat, sitting stiffly erect in the pew nearest to the pillar against which he and Porthos were leaning. Although she was a little too thin and her skin was rather sallow, she was still fairly attractive. From time to time Porthos glanced at her furtively, then went on looking over the other women in the congregation.

She also glanced at him now and then, and each time she did so he redoubled his attention to the other women. This obviously stung her to the quick because she bit her lips, scratched the end of her nose, and fidgeted nervously in her seat.

Seeing her reaction, Porthos again curled his mustache and smoothed his beard and began making signals to a beautiful lady near the chancel. Besides being beautiful, she was evidently a lady of high rank, for behind her was a little Negro boy who had brought the red cushion on which she was kneeling, and beside him was a maid holding the emblazoned bag containing her prayer book.

The lady in the black hat followed all the movements of Porthos's eyes and saw them come to rest on the lady with the red cushion, the Negro boy, and the maid.

Porthos exploited his advantage: he winked, touched his fingers to his lips, and smiled in a way that made the lady in the black hat frantic with jealousy. She moaned so loudly that everyone, even the lady with the red cushion, looked in her direction. Everyone except Porthos; he acted as if he had not heard her.

The lady with the red cushion made a strong impression on the other woman because she was seen as a dangerous rival; she also made a strong impression on Porthos because he found her much more beautiful than the lady in the black hat, and on d'Artagnan because he recognized her as the lady he had seen at Meung, where his persecutor, the man with the scar, had addressed her as Milady.

Without taking his eyes off her for very long at a time, he watched Porthos's maneuvers with amusement. He decided that the lady in the black hat must be Madame Coquenard, the lawyer's wife who lived on the Rue aux Ours, especially since the Saint-Leu church was not far from that street. He then concluded that Porthos was taking revenge on her for having refused to send him money when he was at Chantilly. But d'Artagnan noticed that no woman in the church showed any response to Porthos's flirtatious efforts. Madame Coquenard's suffering came from an illusion; but for real love and jealousy, is there any reality other than illusion?

When the sermon was over, she stood up and walked toward the holy-water basin. Porthos reached it first and, instead of one finger, put his whole hand into it. She smiled, thinking he had done it for her, but she was quickly and cruelly undeceived. When she was only three steps away from him, he turned his head and looked intently at the lady with the red cushion, who was coming toward him, followed by her Negro boy and her maid.

When she was close to him, he lifted his big hand, dripping with holy water. She touched it with her slender fingers, smiled, crossed herself, and left the church.

This was too much for Madame Coquenard; she no longer had any doubt that her rival had replaced her in Porthos's affections. If she had been a great lady, she would have fainted, but since she was only a lawyer's wife, she said with restrained fury, "Well, Monsieur Porthos, aren't you going to offer me holy water too?"

At the sound of her voice, Porthos acted as if he had just awakened with a start after a long sleep.

"Madame!" he exclaimed. "I didn't know you were here. How's your husband? Is he still as stingy as ever? I can't imagine why I never caught sight of you during the two hours that sermon lasted."

"I was sitting a few steps from you," she said, "but you didn't see me because you had eyes only for that beautiful lady you just gave holy water to."

Porthos pretended to be embarrassed.

"Ah, so you noticed . . ."

"I'd have had to be blind not to notice."

"That lady is a friend of mine, a duchess," Porthos said nonchalantly. "It's hard for us to meet, because of her husband's jealousy. She sent word to me that she was coming here today, to this little church in this out-of-the-way part of the city, just to see me."

"Monsieur Porthos," said Madame Coquenard, "will you be kind enough to offer me your arm and walk with me for a few minutes? I'd like to talk to you."

"Certainly," replied Porthos, feeling like a gambler about to fleece an unsuspecting victim.

Just then d'Artagnan went by, in pursuit of Milady. He glanced at Porthos and saw his triumphant expression. "It looks as if Porthos has a good chance of getting his equipment," he thought, reasoning in accordance with the strangely loose morality of the time.

Letting himself be guided by the pressure of Madame Coquenard's arm as a ship is guided by its rudder, Porthos reached the Saint-Magloire cloister, a secluded place with a turnstile at either end. During the day, it was nearly always deserted except for beggars who came there to eat, and children who came to play.

Madame Coquenard looked around to make sure no one else was there but the usual beggars and children.

"It seems you're a great lady-killer," she said.

"What makes you think so?" Porthos asked smugly.

"The looks you were giving that lady in church, and the way you offered her holy water. She must be at least a princess, with her Negro boy and her maid!"

"No, she's only a duchess."

"And what about that footman waiting for her at the door, and that carriage with a liveried coachman?"

Porthos had noticed neither the footman nor the carriage, but the jealous Madame Coquenard had missed nothing. He was now sorry he had not made the lady a princess.

"Women can't resist you," Madame Coquenard said with a sigh.

"With the physique that nature gave me, I'm bound to be successful with women."

"My God, how quickly men forget!" she exclaimed, raising her eyes to heaven.

"Not as quickly as women, it seems to me. Did you remember me when I lay wounded and dying and the doctors had given up hope for me? I, a man of noble birth, had trusted in your friendship till then. I nearly died in that wretched inn at Chantilly, first from my wounds and then from starvation, and you never deigned to answer the urgent letters I wrote you."

"But, Monsieur Porthos . . ." murmured Madame Coquenard. She was beginning to feel that, judging by what she had heard about the conduct of great ladies, she was in the wrong.

"And after I'd broken off with Countess de Penaflor for your sake!"

"Yes, I know."

"And Baroness . . ."

"Don't be unkind, Monsieur Porthos."

"And Duchess . . ."

"Please, Monsieur Porthos!"

"Very well, madame, I'll stop reminding you of the sacrifices I've made for you."

"It was because of my husband—he won't even consider lending money to anyone."

"Madame Coquenard," said Porthos, "don't you remember the first letter you wrote to me? Every word of it is engraved in my heart."

She moaned.

"It was also because the amount you asked to borrow was . . . rather large."

"I asked you for help when I could have written to a certain duchess whose name I won't mention because I never compromise a woman; I'll say only that if I'd written to her, she would have immediately sent me fifteen hundred."

Madame Coquenard shed a tear.

"You've punished me more than enough, Monsieur Porthos. I swear I'll help you if you're ever in such a situation again."

"Please, let's not talk about money," Porthos said as

though the subject were distasteful to him. "It's humiliating."

"So you don't love me any more?" she asked slowly and sadly.

Porthos maintained a majestic silence.

"You're not going to answer me? I know what that means . . ."

"You hurt me deeply, madame, I can still feel it here," he said, putting his hand over his heart.

"I'll make it up to you, my dear Porthos!"

He shrugged.

"I only asked you for a loan. Was that too much to expect? I'm not an unreasonable man. I know you're not rich; I know your husband has to squeeze his poor clients to get a few écus out of them. If you were a countess or a duchess, it would be different; in that case you'd be unforgivable."

"It's true that I'm only a lawyer's wife," she said, nettled, "but it's also true that I probably have more money than any of your ruined aristocratic ladies."

"Then your offense was worse than I thought," said Porthos, pulling her hand away from his arm. "If you're rich, there's no excuse for your refusal."

She saw that she had gone too far.

"I'm not really rich. That's not the right word. I'm well off, let's put it that way."

"I'd rather not discuss it. You've offended me and there can be nothing more between us."

"You're hardhearted and ungrateful!"

"You have no right to complain."

"Go back to your beautiful duchess! I'm not stopping you!"

"Maybe I will! She's not as bony as some women I know!"

"Monsieur Porthos, I'm going to ask you this for the last time. Do you still love me?"

Porthos took on his most melancholy expression.

"At a time when I'm about to go off to war, with a foreboding that I'll be killed . . ."

"Oh! Don't say such things!" exclaimed Madame Coquenard. She burst out sobbing.

"Something tells me that I won't come back," he continued, even more gloomily.

"That's not why you won't tell me if you still love me. It's because you love someone else."

"No, I'm being frank with you. I haven't fallen in love with anyone else. Deep in my heart, I still have tender feelings for you. But, as you may or may not know, the campaign will start in two weeks, and I'm terribly concerned about my equipment. I'm going to my family's estate in Brittany to get the money I'll need.'' Porthos paused to watch the final struggle between love and avarice in Madame Coquenard, then he went on: "The duchess you saw in church is also going to Brittany. She has land that borders on my family's. We'll travel together; a journey always seems much shorter when you share it with someone.''

"Don't you have any friends in Paris who would be willing to help you?'' asked Madame Coquenard.

"I thought so,'' he answered woefully, "but I found out I was mistaken.''

"You have one friend who will help you,'' she said with a surge of emotion that took her by surprise. "Come to the house tomorrow. You're my cousin, my aunt's son; you've come from Noyon, in Picardy, because you have several lawsuits in Paris, and you have no lawyer. Will you remember all that?''

"Yes, madame.''

"Come at lunch time.''

"Very well.''

"And be on your guard with my husband. He's very shrewd. He's seventy-six, but his mind is as sharp as ever.''

"Seventy-six! That's . . . the prime of life.''

"He passed his prime so long ago that he probably doesn't even remember it,'' said Madame Coquenard. "He may die at any moment and leave me a widow,'' she added, giving Porthos a meaningful look. "Luckily our marriage contract has a clause saying that everything will go to the surviving partner.''

"Everything?''

"Everything.''

"I see you're a woman who has the virtue of foresight,'' said Porthos, lovingly squeezing her hand.

"Are we reconciled now?'' she asked, simpering.

"Reconciled forever.''

"Good-bye, my fickle Monsieur Porthos.''

"Good-bye, my forgetful Madame Coquenard.''

"I'll see you tomorrow, my angel!''

"Till tomorrow, love of my life!''

30

Milady

D'Artagnan had followed Milady without letting her see him. He watched her get into her carriage and heard her order the coachman to go to Saint-Germain.

It would have been useless to try to follow the carriage on foot because its two powerful horses started off at a brisk trot, so d'Artagnan headed back toward the Rue Férou.

On the Rue de Seine he found Planchet standing in front of a pastry shop, gazing ecstatically at an appetizing bun. D'Artagnan told him to go to Monsieur de Tréville's stables, saddle two horses, and bring them to him at Athos's apartment. Monsieur de Tréville had put his stables at d'Artagnan's disposal. Planchet set off for the Rue du Colombier, and d'Artagnan for the Rue Férou.

Athos was at home, sadly emptying a bottle of the Spanish wine he had brought back from his journey to Picardy. He signaled Grimaud to bring a glass for d'Artagnan, and Grimaud obeyed as usual.

D'Artagnan told Athos everything that had happened in the church between Porthos and Madame Coquenard, and added that their friend was probably well on the way to getting his equipment.

"I'm sure of one thing," Athos remarked: "no woman is going to buy my equipment for me."

"But you're so handsome and aristocratic that you could have princesses and queens falling in love with you if you wanted to."

"You're very young, d'Artagnan," Athos said impassively.

He signaled Grimaud to bring another bottle.

Planchet modestly put his head through the half-open door and told d'Artagnan that the two horses were there.

"What horses?" asked Athos.

"Two horses that Monsieur de Tréville has lent me. I'm going to Saint-Germain."

"And what will you do there?"

D'Artagnan told Athos how he had seen the woman who obsessed him as much as the man with the scar on his temple.

"So now you're in love with her, as you used to be in love with Madame Bonacieux," said Athos, disdainfully shrugging his shoulders as though he felt sorry for human weakness.

"Not at all!" d'Artagnan protested. "I only want to clear up the mystery around her. I don't know her and she doesn't know me, yet for some reason I have a feeling that she's affecting my life."

"You're right to abandon Madame Bonacieux," said Athos. "No woman is worth the effort of trying to find her when she's lost. Madame Bonacieux is lost, but that's her concern, not yours."

"No, Athos, you're wrong. I love my poor Constance more than ever. I'd go to the ends of the earth to save her from her enemies if I knew where she was, but I don't. All my efforts to find her have failed. In the meantime, I still have to go on living."

"If having an adventure with Milady will brighten up your life, I wish you success."

"Athos, instead of staying in your apartment as if it were a prison, why not ride to Saint-Germain with me?"

"I ride when I own a horse, otherwise I walk."

D'Artagnan smiled at Athos's brusque refusal, which would have offended him if it had come from anyone else.

"I'm not as proud as you are," he said. "I ride any horse that comes my way. Good-bye, Athos."

"Good-bye," said the musketeer, motioning Grimaud to uncork the bottle he had just brought.

D'Artagnan and Planchet mounted their horses and set off for Saint-Germain.

As he rode along, d'Artagnan thought of what Athos had said about Madame Bonacieux. Although he was not very sentimental by nature, his tender feelings for her were quite genuine; as he had said, he was ready to go to the ends of the earth to find her. But, being round, the earth has many ends, so he did not know in which direction he should start.

Meanwhile he would try to find out who Milady was. She knew the man in the black cloak, since she had talked with him, and d'Artagnan was sure that man had abducted Madame Bonacieux the second time as well as the first. He was therefore not completely deluding himself in believing that by going in search of Milady he was also going in search of Constance Bonacieux.

Reflecting on all this and spurring his horse from time to time, he reached Saint-Germain. After passing the house where Louis XIV was to be born ten years later, he rode along a deserted street, looking for some trace of the beautiful Englishwoman. On the flowery terrace of a house that had no windows facing the street, as was common in that time, he saw a man who looked familiar to him. Planchet was the first to recognize him.

"You see that man standing there, staring at nothing in particular?" he said to d'Artagnan. "Don't you remember him?"

"No," replied d'Artagnan, "and yet I'm sure I've seen him before."

"You certainly have, sir. He's Lubin, the servant who was with Count de Wardes when you fought him a month ago, just outside of Calais."

"Ah, yes, now I remember him! Do you think he'll recognize you?"

"I doubt it, sir. He was so upset the last time he saw me that I don't think he has a very clear memory of what I looked like."

"Then go and talk with him and find out if his master is dead."

Planchet dismounted, walked over to Lubin, and struck up a conversation with him. As he expected, Lubin did not recognize him. D'Artagnan took the two horses into a side street, went around a house, and came back to eavesdrop on the conversation from behind a hazel hedge.

When he had been there a few moments, he heard the sound of wheels and saw Milady's carriage stop in front of the house. He would have recognized the carriage even if he had not seen Milady inside it. He hid behind his horse's neck so that he could see without being seen.

Milady put her charming blond head through the window and gave orders to her maid, who was sitting on the footboard, as was customary in those days.

The maid was an alert, lively, and pretty young woman in her early twenties who seemed worthy of serving a great lady. She leapt off the footboard, and d'Artagnan watched her walk to the terrace where he had seen Lubin.

Lubin had been called inside the house, and Planchet, standing alone on the terrace, was looking in all directions to see where d'Artagnan had gone. Mistaking him for Lubin, the maid handed him a note and said, "This is for your master."

"For my master?" Planchet asked in surprise.

"Yes, and it's urgent. Take it to him quickly."

She hurried back to the carriage, which had by now turned

around in the direction from which it had come. She jumped onto the footboard and the carriage set off.

Planchet turned the note over in his hands for a few moments. Then, being used to doing as he was told, he went off to deliver it. He walked down the side street and soon met d'Artagnan, who had seen everything and come toward him.

"For you, sir," said Planchet, handing him the note.

"For me? Are you sure?"

"Of course I'm sure. The maid said, 'This is for your master,' and you're the only master I have, so . . . She's a very pretty girl, that maid."

D'Artagnan opened the note.

> *Someone who is deeply interested in you would like to know when you will be well enough to take a walk in the forest. A servant in black and red will await your reply tomorrow in the Hôtel du Champ du Drap d'Or.*

When he had finished reading this, he said to himself, "Milady and I are apparently concerned about the health of the same person."

He turned to Planchet and asked, "How is Count de Wardes? He's not dead, is he?"

"No, sir. He's doing about as well as can be expected after the four wounds you gave him. He's still weak because he lost most of his blood. I told you I didn't think Lubin would recognize me, and he didn't. He told me the whole story of how his master was wounded."

"Planchet, you're the king of servants. Now get back on your horse and let's catch up with the carriage."

It did not take long: five minutes later they saw the carriage stopped on the side of the road. A richly dressed gentleman had reined up his horse beside it. His conversation with Milady was so animated that d'Artagnan stopped on the other side of the carriage without being noticed by anyone but the pretty maid.

The conversation was in English, a language d'Artagnan did not understand, but from Milady's tone he gathered that she was very angry. Finally she did something that left no doubt about her state of mind: she struck the gentleman with her fan, so hard that it broke. He laughed, and this seemed to exasperate her still more.

D'Artagnan decided it was time for him to intervene. He moved close to the window on his side of the carriage, respectfully took off his hat, and said, "Will you allow me to offer you my services, madame? This gentleman seems to have made you angry. You have only to say the word and I'll punish him for his discourtesy."

Milady had turned her head in his direction and looked at him in astonishment.

"Sir, I'd be glad to place myself under your protection," she said to him in excellent French, "if the man I'm quarreling with weren't my brother-in-law."

"Excuse me, madame," said d'Artagnan, "I naturally didn't know that."

"Why is this idiot meddling in our affairs," said the gentleman, leaning down from his horse to the carriage window, "and why doesn't he go on his way?"

"Idiot yourself!" said d'Artagnan, also bending down, and speaking through the other window. "I haven't gone on my way because I choose to stay here."

The gentleman said a few words to Milady in English.

"I've spoken to you in French," said d'Artagnan. "Please be so kind as to answer me in the same language. You're this lady's brother-in-law, but fortunately you're not mine."

One might have expected Milady to show the usual feminine reaction by trying to prevent the quarrel from going any further, but instead she leaned back in her seat and calmly told the coachman to take her home.

The pretty maid gave d'Artagnan a look of concern; his handsomeness had evidently produced its effect on her.

When the carriage started off, it left the two men facing each other with nothing between them. D'Artagnan now recognized Milady's brother-in-law as the Englishman who had won his horse, and nearly won his diamond ring, at Amiens. This increased his rage. When the Englishman made a movement to follow the carriage, d'Artagnan stopped him by seizing the bridle of his horse.

"You seem to be even more of an idiot than I am, sir," he said, "since you've apparently forgotten that there's a little quarrel between us."

"Ah, it's you: I remember you now," said the Englishman. "So you're ready to gamble again, are you?"

"Yes, I am. We haven't finished our game yet. But this time we'll use swords instead of dice."

"As you can see, I'm not carrying a sword. Are you trying to make a show of bravery against an unarmed man?"

"I hope you have swords at home. If not, I have two, and we can throw dice to see which one of them you'll use."

"There's no need for that: I have swords of my own."

"Then choose your longest one," said d'Artagnan, "and come and show it to me this evening."

"Where?"

"Behind the Luxembourg. It's an excellent place for the kind of gambling we're going to do."

"Very well, I'll be there."

"What time?"

"Six o'clock."

"By the way, you must have a friend or two . . ."

"I have three who will be honored to join in the game."

"Three?" said d'Artagnan. "What a lucky coincidence! That's exactly the number I have."

"And now, who are you?" asked the Englishman.

"I'm Monsieur d'Artagnan, a Gascon gentleman serving in the company of guards commanded by Monsieur des Essarts. And you?"

"I'm Lord de Winter."

"At your service, my lord," said d'Artagnan.

He spurred his horse into a gallop and rode back to Paris.

As he usually did on such occasions, he went straight to Athos's house.

He found Athos lying on a big sofa, still waiting for his equipment to come and find him, as he had said.

D'Artagnan told him everything that had just happened, omitting only the letter that had been meant for Count de Wardes.

Athos was delighted to learn that he was going to fight an Englishman; it was something he had wanted to do for a long time.

He and d'Artagnan sent their servants for Porthos and Aramis, and described the situation to them when they arrived.

Porthos drew his sword and began fencing against the wall, sometimes bending his legs like a dancer. Aramis, who was still working on his poem, shut himself up in Athos's study and asked not to be disturbed until it was time for the duel. Athos motioned for Grimaud to bring a bottle.

D'Artagnan was inwardly concocting a little plan, whose outcome will be shown later in the course of our story. It promised him a pleasing adventure, as could be seen from the smiles that brightened his face from time to time.

31

Englishmen and Frenchmen

When the time came, the four friends and their servants went to an enclosure behind the Luxembourg that was used for goats. Athos gave the goatherd a coin and asked him to leave, which he promptly did. The servants were posted as sentries.

A silent group came into the enclosure and joined the men waiting for them. Then, as was customary in England, the adversaries introduced themselves to each other. The Englishmen, all from noble and illustrious families, were surprised and disquieted when they heard the three musketeers' strange names.

"We still don't know who you are," said Lord de Winter. "We won't fight men who give us names like that. They're shepherds' names!"

"As I'm sure you realize," said Athos, "they're false names."

"Yes, and that makes us all the more determined to know your real ones."

"You didn't know my real name when you gambled with me at Amiens, and that didn't prevent you from winning two horses from me."

"But then I was risking only money; this time we're risking our blood. A gentleman will gamble with anyone, but he duels only with an equal."

"That's true," Athos acknowledged.

He took aside the Englishman he was to fight and whispered his name to him.

Porthos and Aramis did the same.

"Is that enough for you?" Athos asked his adversary. "Do you feel that I'm a great enough nobleman to do me the honor of crossing swords with me?"

"Yes, sir," replied the Englishman, bowing.

"And now will you allow me to tell you something?"

"Please do."

"It would have been better for you if you hadn't insisted on knowing who I am."

"Why?"

"Because I'm believed to be dead and I have reasons for not wanting it known that I'm alive, so I must kill you to make sure my secret will go no further."

The Englishman looked at Athos, thinking he was joking. But Athos was perfectly serious.

"Gentlemen," he said, addressing his companions and their adversaries, "are we ready?"

"Yes," answered the Englishmen and the Frenchmen.

"Then on guard!" said Athos.

Eight swords glittered in the rays of the setting sun and the fighting began, with a deadly intensity that was natural between men who were both personal and national enemies.

Athos fought as methodically as if he were in a fencing school.

Porthos, apparently cured of his overconfidence by his adventure at Chantilly, showed great finesse and caution.

Aramis, who had the third canto of his poem to finish, moved with the speed of a man in a hurry.

Athos was the first to down his adversary. He gave him only one thrust, but, as he had warned him, it was fatal, through the heart.

Then Porthos's adversary fell with a wound in the thigh. When he surrendered his sword without further resistance, Porthos picked him up and carried him to his carriage.

Aramis pushed his adversary so vigorously that after giving ground for nearly fifty paces he finally took to his heels and disappeared, pursued by the servants' jeering.

As for d'Artagnan, he limited himself to purely defensive tactics until he saw that his adversary was tired, then he disarmed him with a vigorous flanconade, making his sword fly through the air. Now that he was defenseless, Lord de Winter retreated several steps, but his foot slipped and he fell on his back.

D'Artagnan leapt toward him and put his sword to his throat.

"I could kill you, sir," he said, "but I'll spare your life for the sake of your sister-in-law."

D'Artagnan was overjoyed: he had just carried out the plan he had made in Athos's apartment, the plan that had brought smiles to his face.

Delighted by d'Artagnan's lack of vindictiveness, Lord de Winter embraced him and complimented the three musketeers.

Since Porthos's adversary was already in the carriage and Aramis's had decamped, the dead man was the only one who required any attention. While Porthos and Aramis were undressing him in the hope that his wound had not been fatal, a large purse fell from his belt. D'Artagnan picked it up and held it out to Lord de Winter.

"What the devil do you expect me to do with that?" asked the Englishman.

"You can give it to his family," said d'Artagnan.

"His family would care nothing for such a trifle: they're going to inherit an enormous income. Keep that purse for your servants."

D'Artagnan put it into his pocket.

"And now, my young friend, for I hope you'll allow me to call you that," said Lord de Winter, "I'll introduce you to my sister-in-law this evening, if you like. I want her to take you into her good graces, and since she's not without influence at court, a word or two from her may be useful to you in the future."

D'Artagnan flushed with pleasure and bowed his assent.

Athos came up to him and asked to speak with him in private.

"What are you going to do with that purse?" he said when they had stepped away from Lord de Winter.

"I'm going to give it to you, my dear Athos," replied d'Artagnan.

"To me? Why?"

"Because you killed the man it belonged to. You have a right to take it as booty."

"You expect me to take an enemy's money? What kind of a man do you think I am, d'Artagnan?"

"It's done in war, so why shouldn't it be done in dueling?"

"*I've* never done such a thing," said Athos, "even on a battlefield."

Porthos and Aramis had been listening to the conversation; the former shrugged indifferently, the latter nodded his approval of Athos.

"Well, then," said d'Artagnan, "let's give the money to the servants, as Lord de Winter told me to do."

"I'm willing," said Athos, "but we'll give it to the English servants, not to ours." He threw the purse to the coachman and called out, "That's for you and your comrades."

This magnanimous gesture by a man who had no money at all made a great impression even on Porthos. Lord de Winter and his friend later reported it everywhere they went, and it was admired by everyone except Grimaud, Mousqueton, Planchet, and Bazin.

Before leaving, Lord de Winter gave d'Artagnan his sister-in-law's address; she lived at 6 Place Royale, in what was then a very fashionable part of the city. He offered to take d'Artagnan there. They agreed to meet at eight o'clock, at Athos's apartment.

D'Artagnan's mind was filled with the prospect of being introduced to Milady. He recalled the strange way in which she had repeatedly turned up in his adventures. He was convinced that she was an agent of the cardinal, yet he was irresistibly drawn to her, by one of those feelings that one does not clearly understand. His only fear was that she might recognize him as the man she had seen in Meung and London; she would then know that he was a friend of Monsieur de Tréville and therefore devoted to the king, and this would make him lose the advantage of knowing more about her than she knew about him. As for what seemed to be the beginning of an affair between her and Count de Wardes, our presumptuous Gascon was unconcerned about it, even though the count was young, handsome, rich, and high in the cardinal's favor. D'Artagnan was only twenty and he was born in Tarbes, two facts that make his attitude less surprising.

He went home and changed into his best clothes, then he went to Athos's apartment and told him everything, as always. After listening to his plans, Athos shook his head and, with a kind of bitterness, urged him to be careful.

"You just lost a woman who, according to you, was good, charming, perfect in every way," he said, "and now you're already running after another one."

D'Artagnan recognized that the implied reproach was not entirely unfair.

"I loved Madame Bonacieux with my heart," he said, "and I love Milady with my head. My main reason for getting myself introduced to her is that I want to find out something about her position at court."

"Her position at court? That's not hard to guess, from what you've told me. She's an agent of the cardinal, a woman who will draw you into a lethal trap."

"It seems to me you're taking a very gloomy view of things, Athos."

"I mistrust women, that's all. And I have good reasons for it. I especially mistrust blond women. Didn't you say Milady is blond?"

"She has the most beautiful blond hair I've ever seen."

"Oh, my poor d'Artagnan . . ."

"I only want information from her. When I've learned what I want to know, I won't have anything more to do with her."

"Learn what you can," Athos said phlegmatically.

Lord de Winter arrived on time. Athos left the room before he came in, so he found d'Artagnan alone. They went out together, got into an elegant carriage drawn by two excellent horses, and reached the Place Royale a short time later.

Milady gave d'Artagnan a gracious reception. Her house was strikingly luxurious. Because of the impending war, most of the English people in France had either left the country or were about to do so, but Milady had just bought some new furniture for her house, which showed that the order expelling the English did not apply to her.

"This young gentleman," Lord de Winter said when he had introduced d'Artagnan to her, "had my life in his hands and refused to make use of his advantage, even though we were doubly enemies, since it was I who insulted him and I'm English. Thank him, then, if you have any friendship for me."

Milady frowned slightly and an almost imperceptible cloud passed over her face, then a strange smile appeared on her lips. D'Artagnan felt uneasy when he saw that abrupt change of expression.

Lord de Winter saw nothing, for he had turned to play with her pet monkey, which had tugged at his doublet.

"Welcome, sir," she said in a voice whose singular softness contrasted with the symptoms of ill-humor that d'Artagnan had just noticed. "What you did today has given you a right to my lifelong gratitude."

Lord de Winter turned back to her and described the duel in detail. She listened attentively, but despite her efforts to conceal her feelings it was easy to see that she was not pleased by the story. The blood rose to her face and she impatiently tapped her little foot on the floor beneath her dress.

Lord de Winter, however, failed to notice this. When he had finished, he went over to a table on which a bottle of Spanish wine and some glasses had been placed. He filled two glasses and made a gesture inviting d'Artagnan to drink.

Knowing that Englishmen were offended if anyone refused to drink with them, d'Artagnan went to the table and picked up one of the glasses, without losing sight of Milady. In a mirror he was able to see the change that took place in her expression. Now that she thought she was unobserved, her face was animated by something close to ferocity and she angrily bit her handkerchief.

The pretty maid who had already caught d'Artagnan's eye came in. She said a few words in English to Lord de Winter. He immediately asked d'Artagnan for permission to withdraw, saying that he had to deal with an urgent matter.

D'Artagnan shook hands with him and returned to Milady. Her amazingly mobile face now had a gracious expression, though a few little red spots on her handkerchief showed that she had bitten her lips—magnificent lips, the color of coral—hard enough to make them bleed. She seemed to have entirely regained her composure.

After a few minutes of light conversation, she told d'Artagnan that her husband, Lord de Winter's younger brother, had died, leaving her with one child. If Lord de Winter did not marry, this child would be his only heir. D'Artagnan had the feeling that she was hiding something from him, but he could not imagine what it might be.

When he had talked with her for half an hour, he became convinced that she was not English: she spoke French with an elegance and a total lack of foreign accent that clearly showed that it was her native language.

He began paying her flowery compliments and declaring his devotion to her in grandiloquent terms. She smiled indulgently at all this inane verbiage.

When it was time for him to go, he took leave of her and walked out of her drawing room, overflowing with elation and self-satisfaction.

On his way down the stairs, he saw the pretty maid coming up. She brushed against him as she passed, blushed to the whites of her eyes, and asked his pardon so charmingly that he granted it instantly.

He returned the next evening and was given an even friendlier welcome than before. This time Lord de Winter was not there and Milady talked with d'Artagnan alone. She seemed to take a great interest in him. She asked him where he was from, who his friends were, and whether he had not sometimes considered entering the service of the cardinal.

D'Artagnan, who was very shrewd for a young man of twenty, remembered his suspicions about her; he praised the cardinal and said he would have entered his guards instead of the king's if he had known Monsieur de Cavois, for example, instead of Monsieur de Tréville.

Milady deftly changed the subject and then casually asked d'Artagnan if he had ever been in England. He replied that he had been sent there by Monsieur de Tréville to discuss the purchase of some horses, and had brought back four of them as samples.

Milady pursed her lips two or three times in the course of the conversation; it had become plain to her that she was dealing with a wary opponent.

D'Artagnan left at the same time as he had done the night before, and in the hall he again met Kitty, the maid. She looked at him with a warm expression whose meaning was perfectly clear, but he was so preoccupied with Milady that he was unmindful of everything else.

He came back the following day, and the day after, and each time Milady received him graciously. And each time he met Kitty, the pretty maid, in the anteroom, on the stairs, or in the hall. But he still paid no attention to her persistence.

32

Lunch with the Coquenards

The duel in which Porthos had performed so well had not made him forget Madame Coquenard's invitation to lunch. A little before one o'clock the next day, he had Mousqueton give his clothes a final brush and then he eagerly set out for the Rue aux Ours.

His heart was beating fast, but not, like d'Artagnan's, from a young and impatient love. His excitement had a more material cause: he was about to cross the unknown threshold beyond which lay the fortune that Monsieur Coquenard had amassed through the years. He was going to see a certain chest that he had dreamed of many times, a long, deep chest locked shut and bolted to the floor, the chest that Madame Coquenard had mentioned to him so often. She was going to open it with her own hands—rather bony hands, it was true, but not without elegance—and let him admire its contents.

And he—a rootless wanderer, a man without family or fortune, a soldier used to inns and taverns, a gourmet who usually had to eat whatever food was offered to him—he was going to enjoy a home-cooked meal and the comforts of a well-run household, and savor the pampering that even the most hard-bitten trooper secretly longs for.

The future looked bright to Porthos: he saw himself, in his

assumed identity as Madame Coquenard's cousin, coming to the house every day for a good meal, ingratiating himself with the rich old lawyer, teaching the young law clerks the fine points of playing cards and dice, and being paid for his lessons by winning a month's savings from each of them.

He had heard some of the stories that were told about lawyers in those days, and have been told about them ever since: stories of stinginess, skimping, and meager meals. But except for a few times when Madame Coquenard had shown a deplorable tendency toward frugality, she had been generous to him—generous for a lawyer's wife, that is—and so he expected to be well fed in an opulent house.

When he reached the house, however, he had a few doubts. The approaches to it were not engaging: a dark, foul-smelling alley, a staircase with barred windows that admitted only dim, gray light from a courtyard, and on the first floor a low door studded with enormous nails like the main gate of the Grand-Châtelet.

Porthos knocked on it. It was opened by a tall clerk whose pale face was half hidden by a forest of disheveled hair. He bowed to Porthos grudgingly, as if he were forced to respect the strength shown by his powerful build, the military rank shown by his uniform, and the habit of good living shown by his ruddy complexion.

Behind the tall clerk stood a short one with another tall one behind him, and behind the third one was a twelve-year-old errand boy. In all, three and a half clerks, which in that time indicated a thriving law practice.

Although Porthos was not due to arrive till one o'clock, Madame Coquenard had been watching for him since noon, counting on his heart, and perhaps also his stomach, to make him come ahead of time.

She therefore came forward to meet him almost as soon as he stepped inside. He was relieved to see her because embarrassment had left him tongue-tied while the jagged line of clerks eyed him with unconcealed curiosity.

"This is my cousin," she announced loudly. "Come in, Monsieur Porthos, come in."

The clerks laughed when they heard Porthos's name, but he turned around and their faces became serious again.

Madame Coquenard led him out of the anteroom, where the clerks were, and through the office, a dark room filled with piles of paper, where they should have been. She then led him past the kitchen and into the reception room.

Porthos was not encouraged by these intercommunicating rooms: conversation could probably be overheard from a great distance through all those open doors. He had glanced into the kitchen as he passed and, to his regret and Madame Coquenard's shame, he had not seen the bustle and animation that should have reigned there if a good meal was being prepared.

Monsieur Coquenard had evidently been told that he was to have a visitor, for he showed no surprise when Porthos strode into the room and politely bowed to him.

"It seems we're cousins, Monsieur Porthos," said the lawyer, making an effort to sit erect in his wicker chair.

He wore a black doublet much too big for his thin, frail body. His grimacing mouth and little gray eyes seemed to be the only parts of his face that were still alive. Five or six months ago his legs had begun to fail him, and since then he had been more or less at his wife's mercy.

He accepted her cousin with resignation, but if he had been able-bodied, he would have rejected the idea of any kinship with Monsieur Porthos.

"Yes, sir, we're cousins," replied Porthos, undisturbed; he had not expected an enthusiastic reception from Madame Coquenard's husband.

"Cousins on the female side," the lawyer said slyly.

The joke passed over Porthos's head; he took it only as a naive remark and laughed to himself, behind his big mustache. Madame Coquenard, who knew that naive lawyers were a very rare species, smiled faintly and blushed heavily.

Ever since Porthos came in, Monsieur Coquenard had been glancing anxiously at a big chest in front of his oak desk. Porthos realized that this must be the chest he had dreamed of. It differed in shape and size from his image of it, but he was glad to discover that the reality was several feet higher than the dream.

Monsieur Coquenard did not carry his genealogical inquiries any further. He looked away from the chest and said to his wife, "I hope our cousin will be so kind as to have lunch with us some day before he leaves Paris."

Porthos felt this thrust in his stomach. Madame Coquenard was alarmed by it.

"He won't come back if he feels he's not welcome here," she said. "His stay in Paris will be so short that we must invite him to spend nearly all his free time with us."

"Oh, my poor legs, why have you deserted me?" murmured Coquenard. And he tried to smile.

Porthos was grateful to Madame Coquenard for having come to his defense when his gastronomic hopes were threatened.

Lunch was announced. He went into the big, dark dining room next to the kitchen.

The clerks, evidently having smelled unaccustomed aromas in the house, were already there. As they held their stools, ready to sit down, they moved their jaws in ravenous anticipation. Porthos looked at the three of them (the errand boy was naturally not allowed the honor of sharing the master's table) and thought, "If I were in my cousin's place, I wouldn't have gluttons like that in my house. They look like shipwrecked sailors who haven't eaten in six weeks."

Madame Coquenard pushed her husband into the dining room in his wheelchair. Porthos helped her bring him to the table.

The lawyer sniffed and moved his jaws like his clerks.

"Ah, that looks like a delicious soup!" he said.

Porthos did not understand how the soup could look delicious to anyone: it was a pale, watery liquid with nothing showing in it except pieces of bread crust, and there were so few of them that they floated like the widely scattered islands of an archipelago.

Madame Coquenard smiled and made a gesture, at which everyone quickly sat down.

She served her husband, Porthos, and herself, then she distributed the remaining pieces of crust, without soup, to the impatient clerks.

The door of the dining room swung open of its own accord, with its hinges creaking, and Porthos saw the errand boy; not being able to take part in the feast, he was eating his bread and seasoning it with the smells coming from the kitchen and the dining room.

After the soup, the maid brought in a boiled hen, an extravagant treat that made the clerks' eyes open so wide that they seemed in danger of falling from their sockets.

"I can see that you love your family," the lawyer said to his wife with an almost tragic smile. "I hope your cousin appreciates the lavish banquet you're giving in his honor."

The poor hen was scrawny and had one of those thick, rough skins that bones can never penetrate, despite all their efforts; it must have taken a long search to find her on the perch to which she had withdrawn to die of old age. "What a sad sight!"

thought Porthos. "I respect old age, but I don't really care for it when it's boiled or roasted."

He looked around the table to see if his opinion was shared, but he saw only eyes glowing at the thought of eating the elderly fowl he scorned.

Madame Coquenard pulled the dish toward her, cut off the hen's feet and put them on her husband's plate; then she cut off the head and neck for herself, gave Porthos a wing, and handed the dish to the maid. The hen was taken back into the kitchen, almost intact, before Porthos had time to study the different ways in which the clerks showed their disappointment, according to their individual temperaments.

Next came an enormous dish of beans, with a few mutton bones that looked as if they might have a little meat on them. But the clerks did not let themselves be deceived by appearances. Their faces took on an expression of profound resignation. Madame Coquenard doled out beans to them with the moderation of a good housekeeper.

Now it was time for the wine. Monsieur Coquenard picked up a narrow stone bottle and poured a third of a glassful for each of the clerks and himself. Then the bottle passed on to Porthos and Madame Coquenard.

The clerks poured water into their wine till their glasses were full, poured in more water when their glasses were half empty, and continued doing this till the end of the meal; by then, they were drinking something that was distinguishable from pure water only by a very faint pinkish tinge.

Porthos slowly ate his chicken wing and shuddered when he felt Madame Coquenard press her knee against his, under the table. He also drank half a glass of the sparingly dispensed wine, which he recognized as the abominable vintage of Montreuil, the terror of sensitive palates.

The lawyer sighed when he saw Porthos drink that unmixed wine.

"Would you like some of these beans, Cousin Porthos?" Madame Coquenard asked in a tone that meant, "Take my advice, don't even taste them."

Porthos inwardly swore that he would rather die than eat a single one of them.

"No, thank you," he said, "I really couldn't eat another bite."

There was a silence that made him feel uneasy. Monsieur Coquenard broke it by saying to his wife, "Congratulations on your lunch, my dear, it was a real feast! I can't remember the last time I ate so much!''

He had eaten his soup, the two chicken feet, and a bite of mutton from the only bone that had any meat on it.

Thinking he was the victim of a practical joke, Porthos frowned and curled his mustache; but Madame Coquenard's knee gently urged him to be patient.

He could not believe that the meal was already over, but the poor clerks knew it was all too true when they saw the lawyer give them a significant look, accompanied by a smile from his wife. They slowly stood up from the table, folded their napkins even more slowly, bowed, and left.

"Digest your meal while you're working," the lawyer called after them.

When the clerks were gone, Madame Coquenard went to the sideboard and took out a piece of cheese, some quince jam, and a cake she had made herself, with honey and almonds.

Monsieur Coquenard frowned because he saw too much food; Porthos pressed his lips together because he saw that there was not enough to make a meal. He looked to see if the dish of beans was still there. It had disappeared.

"Yes, a real feast!" said Monsieur Coquenard, fidgeting in his chair. *"Epulae epularum!* A meal worthy of the most discriminating gourmet!"

Porthos looked at the bottle in front of him, hoping he could take the edge off his hunger with wine, bread, and cheese. But when he picked up the bottle he saw that it was empty. His hosts did not seem to have noticed. "I know better than to expect another bottle," he thought.

He licked a spoonful of jam and sank his teeth into the sticky mass of Madame Coquenard's cake. "There, that's done," he told himself. "If it weren't for the hope of having Madame Coquenard open that chest for me . . ."

After what he regarded as his overindulgence, Monsieur Coquenard announced that he needed to take a nap. Porthos hoped he would do it right where he was, in his chair, but he demanded to be taken back to his room, and when he was there, he had himself wheeled so close to his chest that his feet touched it.

Madame Coquenard took Porthos into an adjoining room and began trying to solidify their reconciliation.

"You can come to lunch three times a week," she said.

"Thank you for the offer," said Porthos, "but I don't want to abuse your hospitality. And besides, my time will be taken up with trying to get my equipment."

"Ah, yes, your equipment . . ." she said sadly.

"I can't rest till I get it."

"What does it consist of, exactly?"

"Oh, all sorts of things. The musketeers are an elite corps, as you know, and we must have many things that the guards don't need."

"What are they? Give me a list of them."

Porthos did not want to let himself be drawn into a discussion of details; he preferred to go straight to the heart of the matter: money.

"I don't want to bore you with a long list," he said. "I'll just tell you what the total cost will be."

"How much?" she asked apprehensively. "I hope it's not more than . . ."

"No, it's not more than twenty-five hundred livres, and if I'm careful I think I can get by with two thousand."

"My God! Two thousand livres!" she cried. "That's a fortune!"

He made a meaningful grimace and she understood it.

"I asked you for a list of what you'll need," she said, "because I have many friends and relatives in business and I'm sure I can get things much cheaper than you could."

"Ah, so that's what you meant!"

"Yes, my dear Monsieur Porthos. Now, first of all you'll need a horse, won't you?"

"That's right."

"I know where I can get a very good one for you."

"Then I'll put my mind at ease about the horse," said Porthos, beaming. "I'll also need everything that goes with a horse, things that only a musketeer can buy. They won't come to more than three hundred livres."

"Very well, then, three hundred livres," Madame Coquenard said with a sigh.

Porthos smiled; since he still had the saddle that had come from the duke of Buckingham, he intended to slip the three hundred livres into his pocket.

"Then there's my servant's horse," he said, "and my valise. But don't worry about my weapons, I already have them."

"A horse for your servant?" Madame Coquenard asked hesitantly. "That's very aristocratic . . ."

"You don't think I'm a peasant, do you?" Porthos said haughtily.

"No, no, of course not. But a pretty mule sometimes looks as good as a horse, and it seems to me that if I got a pretty mule for Mousqueton . . ."

"Yes, get him one. After all, I've seen very great Spanish lords whose servants all rode mules. But for Mousqueton I want a mule with plumes and bells. You'll see to that, won't you?"

"Yes."

"There's still the valise."

"That's simple," said Madame Coquenard. "My husband has several valises and you can choose the best one. There's one that he always took when he traveled; it's big enough to hold a carriage."

"Is it empty?" Porthos asked with false innocence.

"Of course it's empty," Madame Coquenard replied with equally false innocence.

"But I need a well-filled valise, my dear."

Madame Coquenard sighed once again. Since Molière had not yet written *The Miser*, she was an earlier version of Harpagon.

Porthos bargained for the rest of his equipment in this same way, one item at a time. The upshot of the discussion was that Madame Coquenard would ask her husband for a loan of eight hundred livres and provide the horse and mule that would have the honor of carrying Porthos and Mousqueton on the path to glory.

When all this had been agreed upon, and the interest rate and date of repayment had been stipulated, Porthos took leave of Madame Coquenard. She tried to make him stay longer by giving him ardent looks, but he told her that his duties in the king's service required him to go, and she had to yield to His Majesty.

Porthos went home hungry and morose.

33

Maid and Mistress

Despite his own conscience and Athos's wise advice, d'Artagnan was falling more passionately in love with Milady from hour to hour. He went to pay court to her every day, convinced that sooner or later she would respond to his advances.

One evening when he arrived at her house with the buoyancy of a man expecting a shower of gold, he met Kitty, the pretty maid, in the carriage gateway. This time she did not merely smile at him in passing: she gently took his hand. "Milady has given her a message for me," he thought. "She wants to arrange a rendezvous with me and didn't have the courage to do it in person."

He looked at Kitty with boundless self-confidence.

"I need to talk to you, sir," she said hesitantly.

"I'm listening."

"Not here. What I have to say is too long, and too secret."

"Where shall we go?"

"Will you let me take you somewhere, sir?" she asked timidly.

"Yes, wherever you like."

"Then come, sir."

Still holding him by the hand, she led him up a dark spiral staircase. When they had climbed a dozen steps, she opened a door.

"Come in, sir," she said. "We'll be alone here and we can talk."

"What room is this?" asked d'Artagnan.

"It's my bedroom, sir. That door opens into my mistress's bedroom. But don't worry, she won't hear what we say, because she never goes to bed before midnight."

D'Artagnan looked around the little room and saw that it was clean and charmingly furnished. Then, in spite of himself, he stared at the door leading to Milady's bedroom.

Kitty guessed what he was feeling and sighed.

"You're in love with my mistress, aren't you, sir?"

"Yes! Madly in love with her!"

Kitty sighed again.

"That's a pity, sir."

"Why?"

"Because my mistress doesn't love you at all."

"What! Has she ordered you to tell me that?"

"Oh, no, sir! I decided to tell you on my own, in your interest."

"I appreciate your good intentions, Kitty, but don't expect me to thank you for what you've said. You must admit it's not very pleasant to hear."

"You don't believe it's true?"

"It's always hard to believe such things, if only because they hurt our pride."

"Do you believe me or not?"

"Unless you can give me some sort of proof . . ."

"Is this proof enough?" said Kitty, taking a letter from her bodice.

He snatched it from her hand and asked, "Is it for me?"

"No, it's for someone else."

"Another man?"

"Yes."

"Tell me his name!" demanded d'Artagnan.

"It's written on the envelope."

"Count de Wardes . . ."

The memory of the scene in Saint-Germain flashed into d'Artagnan's mind. He quickly tore open the envelope in spite of Kitty's cry when she saw what he was doing.

"No, sir, you mustn't!"

He ignored her and read:

You have not answered my first letter. Are you ill, or have you forgotten the looks you gave me at Madame de Guise's ball? Now is your chance, Count! Take it before it slips away.

D'Artagnan turned pale; he was wounded in his vanity, but thought he was wounded in his love.

"Poor Monsieur d'Artagnan!" Kitty said compassionately, squeezing his hand.

"You feel sorry for me?"

"Yes, with all my heart, because I know what it's like to be in love."

"You do?" he asked, looking at her attentively for the first time.

"Yes, unfortunately."

"Then instead of feeling sorry for me, you'd do better to help me get revenge on your mistress."

"What kind of revenge do you want?"

"I want to triumph over her, and take my rival's place."

"I'll never help you to do that, sir!" Kitty said forcefully.

"Why not?"

"For two reasons."

"What are they?"

"The first one is that my mistress will never love you."

"How do you know that?"

"You've hurt her too much."

"That's ridiculous! How could I have hurt her, when I've always been at her feet like a slave? Explain what you mean."

"I'll never explain it to anyone but the man who . . . can see into my heart!"

D'Artagnan examined Kitty closely for the second time. She had a freshness and beauty for which many a duchess would have given up her title.

"Then explain it to me, Kitty," he said, "because I'll see into your heart whenever you want me to."

And he gave her a kiss that made her turn as red as a cherry.

"No, you don't love me!" she said. "You love my mistress, you told me so yourself!"

"But that doesn't mean you can't tell me the second reason, does it?"

"The second reason," she answered, emboldened by his kiss and by the look she now saw in his eyes, "is that in love it's everyone for himself."

Only then did d'Artagnan remember her languid glances, his meetings with her in the anteroom, on the stairs, and in the hall, her stifled sighs, and the way she had brushed her hand against him each time she passed him. Absorbed in his desire to please the great lady, he had disdained her maid; a man hunting an eagle takes no notice of a sparrow. But now he suddenly realized the advantages he could gain from the love that Kitty had candidly confessed to him: he would be able to intercept letters addressed to Count de Wardes, get useful information from Kitty, and have access at any time to her bedroom, which adjoined Milady's. The treacherous young man was already planning to sacrifice Kitty in order to make Milady give in to him, willingly or unwillingly.

"Would you like me to give you proof of the love you doubt?" he said.

"What love?" asked Kitty.

"The love I'm ready to feel for you."

"How can you prove it?"

"Would you like me to spend the rest of this evening with you, rather than with your mistress?"

"Oh, yes!" said Kitty, clapping her hands.

"Then come here," he said, sitting down in an armchair, "and let me tell you that you're the prettiest girl I've ever seen."

And he told her this so eloquently and persistently that the poor girl, who asked nothing better than to believe him, did believe him. . . . But to his great surprise, she defended herself with a certain determination.

Time passes quickly when it is spent in such attacks and defenses.

The clock struck midnight, and at almost the same moment they heard the bell ring in Milady's room.

"Oh!" exclaimed Kitty. "My mistress is calling me! You must go! Hurry!"

He stood up and took his hat as though he intended to obey her, but then he quickly opened the door of a big wardrobe and hid himself among Milady's dresses and negligees.

"What are you doing?" cried Kitty.

D'Artagnan had taken the key. He locked himself in the wardrobe without answering.

"Are you asleep?" Milady's voice said sharply. "Why don't you come when I ring?"

D'Artagnan heard her throw open the door between the two rooms.

"Here I am, madame!" said Kitty, hurrying toward her.

They both went into the other room, and since the door was left open, d'Artagnan was able to hear Milady scolding Kitty. After a time her anger subsided and she began talking about him while Kitty prepared her for bed.

"I didn't see our Gascon this evening," Milady remarked.

"He didn't come, madame? Has he become fickle even before you've made him happy?"

"Oh, no, he must have been detained by Monsieur de Tréville or Monsieur des Essarts. I have a solid hold on him, believe me."

"What will you do with him, madame?"

"There's something between us that he doesn't know about:

he nearly made me lose favor with the cardinal. I'll make him pay for that!''

"I thought you loved him, madame."

"Love him? I hate him! He's a fool who had Lord de Winter's life in his hands and didn't kill him! That cost me an enormous income!''

"It's true," said Kitty, "your son is his uncle's only heir, and you'd have had control of his fortune till he came of age."

D'Artagnan had been struck by the hardness in Milady's voice, which she ordinarily tried to conceal, and he had shuddered when he heard her say she hated him for not having killed a man he had seen her treat as a close friend.

"For some reason the cardinal told me to be gentle with d'Artagnan," said Milady. "If it weren't for that, I'd have already taken my revenge on him."

"But you weren't gentle with the woman he loved, madame."

"The draper's wife? He's already forgotten her existence, so that's no revenge!"

D'Artagnan broke into a cold sweat. The woman was a monster! He went on listening, but unfortunately Kitty had finished her duties.

"Go back to your room now," said Milady, "and tomorrow, try to get an answer to the letter I gave you."

"The letter for Count de Wardes?"

"Of course."

"It seems to me that the count is just the opposite of Monsieur d'Artagnan."

"I didn't ask for your opinion," said Milady. "Go."

D'Artagnan heard the door close, then the sound of Milady bolting it shut. Kitty locked it from her side as quietly as she could. D'Artagnan came out of the wardrobe.

"What's the matter?" Kitty whispered anxiously. "You're so pale!"

"What a horrible creature she is!" he murmured.

"Quiet!" said Kitty. "You must leave! There's only a thin wall between my room and hers, and from either room you can hear what's being said in the other!"

"That's precisely why I won't leave."

"What do you mean?" asked Kitty, blushing.

"Or at least I won't leave till . . . later."

He drew her toward him. This time she could not resist—resistance would have made too much noise! And so she gave in to him.

It was a way of taking revenge on Milady. D'Artagnan found himself in complete agreement with the saying that revenge is the pleasure of the gods. With a little heart, he would have been satisfied with this new conquest; but he had only ambition and pride.

It must be said to his credit, however, that the first use he made of his influence over Kitty was to try to find out from her what had happened to Madame Bonacieux. But Kitty swore on his crucifix that she did not know; her mistress never revealed more than half her secrets to her, she said. The most she could say was that she did not think Madame Bonacieux was dead.

Nor could she explain Milady's remark that d'Artagnan had nearly made her lose favor with the cardinal. On this point d'Artagnan was better informed than Kitty: since he had seen Milady on a detained ship as he was leaving England, he suspected that the reason for her remark had something to do with the diamond tags.

But one thing was clear to him: the main cause of Milady's deep hatred of him was his failure to kill her brother-in-law.

He returned to her house the next evening. She was in a bad humor. He guessed that it was because she still had not received a reply from Count de Wardes. When Kitty came in, Milady spoke to her very harshly. Kitty gave d'Artagnan a look that seemed to say, "You see what I'm putting up with for your sake?"

Toward the end of the evening, however, Milady's mood softened. She smiled as she listened to d'Artagnan's compliments and even gave him her hand to kiss.

By the time he left, he no longer knew what to think; but since he was not a young man who could easily be made to lose his head, he had formed a little plan while he was paying court to Milady.

He found Kitty at the door and went up to her room with her to learn what news she had for him. She told him she had been violently scolded and accused of negligence. Milady was puzzled by Count de Wardes's silence and had ordered Kitty to come to her room at nine o'clock the next morning to take a third letter that she was going to write to him.

D'Artagnan made Kitty promise to bring him the letter that same morning. She was so madly in love with him that she was willing to do anything he wanted.

Things happened as they had the night before: d'Artagnan hid in the wardrobe, Milady rang for Kitty and sent her back to her room when she had finished preparing her for bed, and d'Artagnan did not go home till five in the morning.

At eleven o'clock Kitty came to him with Milady's new letter. This time she made no effort to prevent him from opening it; she belonged to him body and soul.

He read the letter:

> *This is the third time I have written to tell you I love you. I advise you not to make me write a fourth time to tell you I hate you.*
>
> *If you regret your conduct toward me, the girl who will bring you this letter will tell you how an honorable man can earn his pardon.*

D'Artagnan's face had changed color several times while he read these lines.

"Oh! You still love her!" said Kitty, who had not taken her eyes off him.

"No, Kitty, you're mistaken, I don't love her anymore. But I want revenge for her contempt."

"I know what kind of revenge you want. You told me about it."

"What difference does it make? You're the only one I love now."

"How can I know that?"

"From the contempt I'll show for her, when the time comes." Kitty sighed.

D'Artagnan picked up a pen and wrote:

> *Until now, madame, I doubted that your first two letters were really meant for me, because I did not consider myself worthy of such an honor. And furthermore I was so ill that I would have hesitated to answer in any case.*
>
> *But now I am forced to believe in your extreme kindness, since both your letter and your servant tell me that I have the good fortune to be loved by you.*
>
> *There is no need for your servant to tell me how an honorable man can earn his pardon. I will come to request mine at eleven o'clock this evening. If I were to delay my visit only one more day, I would feel that I had offended you again.*
>
> *You have made me the happiest of all men.*
>
> *Count de Wardes*

Writing this false letter was an unscrupulous act on d'Artagnan's part, and from the standpoint of our present morality it could even be regarded as infamous. But in those days there was less delicacy about such matters. Besides, d'Artagnan knew from Milady's own words that she was guilty of treachery greater than his, and he held her in low esteem. In spite of that, however, he still felt a burning passion for her, a passion that was mingled with contempt and perhaps better deserved the name of desire.

His plan was simple: from Kitty's bedroom he would go into Milady's and take advantage of her first moments of surprise, shame, and terror to triumph over her. Or perhaps he would fail, but he could not avoid leaving something to chance: since he would have to leave in a week, when the campaign began, he did not have time for a long, chivalrous courtship.

"Give this to Milady," he said to Kitty, handing her the sealed letter. "It's Count de Wardes's reply."

Kitty turned deathly pale; she suspected what was in the letter.

"Listen to me, my dear," said d'Artagnan. "It's too late for you to avoid taking any risks. You realize that, don't you? Milady may discover that you gave her first letter to my servant instead of the count's, and that I also opened the other two. If she finds that out, she'll dismiss you, but you know her well enough to be sure she won't stop there: she won't be satisfied till she's punished you with something much worse than dismissal."

"I'm running that risk for you!"

"Yes, I know, Kitty, and I'm very grateful to you, I swear."

"But what's in this letter?"

"Milady will tell you."

"Oh, you don't love me!" she cried. "I'm so unhappy . . ."

To this accusation there is a reply that always deceives women; d'Artagnan replied in a way that left Kitty completely in error.

Yet she wept a great deal before making up her mind to take the letter to Milady. Finally she agreed to do it, and that was all d'Artagnan wanted.

He promised her he would leave Milady earlier than usual that night, and come straight to her room. This promise swept away Kitty's last misgivings.

34

Equipment for Aramis and Porthos

Ever since the four friends had begun trying to get the equipment they needed, they saw each other much less often. They usually dined alone, wherever they happened to be, or rather wherever they could. Their military duties took up part of the precious time that was passing so quickly. They had agreed to meet once a week at about one o'clock, in Athos's apartment; Athos would not have met them anywhere else, because he was still keeping his vow not to cross his threshold.

One of these weekly meetings had been set for the day when Kitty visited d'Artagnan. As soon as she was gone, he left for the Rue Férou.

He found Athos and Aramis philosophizing. Aramis was again thinking of becoming a priest, though this time his thoughts were only tentative. Athos, as usual, argued neither for nor against the idea. He believed in letting everyone make his own decisions. He never gave advice unless he was asked for it, and even then he had to be asked twice.

"As a general rule," he had once said, "people ask for advice only in order not to follow it; or, if they do follow it, in order to have someone to blame for giving it."

Porthos arrived shortly after d'Artagnan. The group was now complete.

Each of the four friends had a different expression: Porthos looked serene, d'Artagnan hopeful, Aramis worried, Athos unconcerned.

After a few minutes of conversation in which Porthos gave the others to understand that a highly placed person had consented to solve the problem of his equipment for him, Mousqueton came in. He asked Porthos to go back to his apartment because, he said woefully, it was urgent for him to be there.

"Has my equipment come?" asked Porthos.

"Yes and no," replied Mousqueton.

"What does that mean?"

"Please come, sir."

Porthos stood up, bowed to his friends, and left with Mousqueton.

A few moments later, Bazin appeared in the doorway.

"What is it, my friend?" Aramis asked in the gentle tone he always used when his thoughts were turning back to the priesthood.

"A man is waiting for you at home, sir," answered Bazin.

"A man? Who is he?"

"A beggar."

"Give him some money, Bazin, and tell him to pray for a poor sinner."

"He insists on talking to you, sir, and he claims you'll be glad to see him."

"That's all he said?"

"No, sir. He also said, 'If Monsieur Aramis is reluctant to see me, tell him I just came from Tours.' "

"Tours!" exclaimed Aramis. "Please excuse me, gentlemen: I think that man has brought some news I've been waiting for."

He stood up and hurried away.

"It looks as if those two will soon have their equipment," Athos said when he and d'Artagnan had been left alone together. "What do you think?"

"I know that Porthos was already well on the way to getting his," said d'Artagnan, "and to tell you the truth, I've never been seriously worried about Aramis. But what about you, Athos? Now that you've so generously given away the Englishman's money that was rightfully yours, what are you going to do?"

"I'm glad I killed that Englishman: it serves him right for being English. But if I'd taken his money, it would have weighed on my conscience like remorse."

"Athos, I'll never understand you!"

"Don't bother to try. Monsieur de Tréville did me the honor of coming to see me yesterday, and he told me you'd been visiting some English friends of the cardinal. Is that true?"

"Not exactly. I've only been visiting an Englishwoman, the one I told you about."

"Ah, yes, the blond woman I advised you not to see any more. You've naturally ignored my advice."

"I gave you my reasons."

"I seem to recall that you thought you could get her to buy your equipment for you. Isn't that what you said?"

"Not at all! I'm convinced she had something to do with Madame Bonacieux's abduction."

"I see: you've decided to seduce one woman to find another. It takes longer that way, but it's more amusing."

For a moment d'Artagnan was on the verge of telling Athos everything, but then he decided against it: since Athos was a gentleman with a very strict code of honor, he was sure to be opposed to certain aspects of the little plan that d'Artagnan had worked out with regard to Milady. So d'Artagnan made no reply, and Athos, being the least inquisitive man on earth, let the subject drop.

Since the two friends now had nothing of any importance to say to each other, we will leave them and follow Aramis.

We have seen how quickly Aramis left when he learned that the man who wanted to talk to him had just come from Tours. He ran all the way from the Rue Feŕou to the Rue de Vaugirard.

He found his visitor waiting for him: a short man, with intelligent eyes, but dressed in rags.

"You asked to see me?"

"I asked to see Monsieur Aramis. Is that your name?"

"Yes. Do you have something for me?"

"Yes, if you show me a certain embroidered handkerchief."

Aramis took out a key and opened the little ebony box, inlaid with mother-of-pearl, in which he kept the handkerchief.

"Here it is," he said, showing it to the beggar.

"Very well. Send your servant away."

Curious to know what the beggar wanted, Bazin had run behind his master and arrived only a few moments later. It was a wasted effort because he had no choice but to obey when Aramis, at the beggar's request, motioned him to leave.

When Bazin was gone, the beggar looked around to make sure no one else was there, then he unbuckled the leather belt that held his threadbare coat, tore open a seam at the top of his doublet, and took out a letter.

Aramis nearly shouted for joy when he saw the seal. He kissed the letter with almost religious respect, opened it, and read the following:

> *My friend, fate has decreed that we must be separated a little longer, but the happy days of youth are not lost beyond recall. Do your duty in the field; I will do mine elsewhere. Take what my messenger brings you, prepare yourself to go off to war in a manner worthy of you, and think of me.*
> *Good-bye, until we meet again.*

The beggar was tearing open more seams. From the various places where they had been sewed into his dirty clothes, he took out a hundred and fifty Spanish double pistoles and put them on the table. Then he opened the door, bowed, and left while Aramis was still staring at him in astonished silence.

Aramis reread the letter and saw that it had a postscript:

> P.S.—*You can give my messenger an honorable reception: he is a count and a Spanish grandee.*

"You're right, my love: we're young and we still have happy days ahead of us!" Aramis cried out ecstatically. "Everything I have is yours—my blood, my love, my life! Everything, my beautiful mistress!"

He kissed the letter passionately, without even looking at the gold glittering on the table.

Bazin scratched on the door. Since Aramis no longer had any reason to keep him away, he told him to come in.

Bazin's amazement at the sight of the gold made him forget that he had come to announce a visit from d'Artagnan, whose curiosity had brought him there to find out why that beggar had wanted to see Aramis.

Seeing that Bazin had forgotten to announce him, d'Artagnan came in unannounced, for he never stood on ceremony with Aramis.

"If those are plums that were sent to you from Tours," he said when he saw the gold coins, "give my compliments to the gardener who grew them."

"You're mistaken," said Aramis, always discreet. "That's the payment my publisher sent me for my poem in one-syllable lines."

"Really? Then all I can say is that you have a generous publisher."

"I had no idea a poem was worth so much!" said Bazin. "It's unbelievable! You can do anything if you put your mind to it, sir—I'm sure you can become the equal of Monsieur de Voiture and Monsieur de Benserade. I'd like that very much because a poet is almost a priest. Oh, Monsieur Aramis, please become a poet!"

"Bazin, my friend," said Aramis, "I believe you're intruding in the conversation."

Realizing that he had overstepped the bounds of propriety, Bazin bowed his head and left.

"You're lucky to sell your poems at such a high price," d'Artagnan said with a smile. "Be careful not to lose the letter that's about to fall out of your pocket, because it must be from your publisher."

Aramis blushed to the whites of his eyes, pushed the letter more deeply into his pocket, and buttoned up his doublet.

"Let's go back to our friends," he said. "Since I'm rich now, we'll begin having dinner together again. I'll pay for it till the rest of you are rich too."

"I'm sure Athos and Porthos will appreciate your generosity as much as I do," said d'Artagnan. "It's been a long time since we had a decent meal. And I have a rather hazardous expedition ahead of me this evening, so I must admit I'd be glad to lift my spirits with a few bottles of old Burgundy."

"Then we'll add Burgundy to the menu," said Aramis. "I won't mind drinking some of it myself."

The gold had driven all thoughts of the priesthood from his mind. He put three or four of the double pistoles into his pocket to meet the needs of the moment and locked the others in the ebony box where he kept the handkerchief he had shown to the messenger.

The two friends first went to see Athos. Faithful to his vow not to leave his apartment, he said he would have a meal brought there. Knowing that he was a connoisseur of fine food, d'Artagnan and Aramis were happy to leave the matter in his hands.

They were on their way to Porthos's apartment when they met Mousqueton at the corner of the Rue du Bac. Looking crestfallen, he was driving a mule and a horse in front of him.

D'Artagnan cried out with surprise and joy.

"My yellow horse!" he said. "Aramis, look at that horse!"

"What a hideous old nag!" said Aramis.

"That's the horse I rode to Paris when I first came here."

"What!" exclaimed Mousqueton. "You know this horse, sir?"

"He has an unusual color," remarked Aramis. "I've never seen another horse with that color."

"Of course you haven't," said d'Artagnan, "and that's why I was able to sell him for three écus. The rest of him isn't worth that much, so it must have been because of his color. But how did you come to have him, Mousqueton?"

"I don't even like to think about it, sir!" said the servant. "Our duchess's husband played a horrible trick on us!"

"What are you talking about?"

"We're in high favor with a great lady, Duchess . . . Excuse me, I can't tell you her name because my master ordered me to be discreet. She insisted that we accept a gift from her, as a token of her esteem: a magnificent Spanish horse and an Andalusian mule. But her husband found out she was having them sent to us. He intercepted them on the way and sent us these two wretched animals instead!"

"And you're taking them back to him?" asked d'Artagnan.

"That's right, sir. We can't accept two mounts like these in place of the ones we were promised."

"Of course not, although I'd have liked to see Porthos on my old horse: it would have given me some idea of how I looked when I first arrived in Paris. But don't let us stop you, Mousqueton, go on with your mission. Is your master at home?"

"Yes, sir, but I warn you he's in a bad mood."

Mousqueton continued on his way toward the Quai des Grands-Augustins while the two friends went to the unfortunate Porthos's apartment and rang the doorbell. But Porthos had seen them crossing the courtyard and did not want to talk with them. After vainly waiting for him to open the door, they left.

Meanwhile Mousqueton crossed the Pont-Neuf, still driving the two animals in front of him, and reached the Rue aux Ours. There, following his master's orders, he tied the horse and the mule to the knocker of Monsieur Coquenard's door. Then, without worrying about their fate, he went back to Porthos and reported that he had accomplished his mission.

The two animals, who had not eaten since morning, made so much noise by raising the knocker and letting it fall back that the lawyer ordered his errand boy to make inquiries in the neighborhood and find out who owned them.

Madame Coquenard recognized her gift. At first she did not understand why the animals had been returned, but a visit from Porthos soon enlightened her. She was terrified when she saw the anger blazing in his eyes despite his efforts to control himself. Mousqueton had told him that he had met d'Artagnan and Aramis and that d'Artagnan had recognized the yellow horse as the one he had ridden to Paris and then sold for three écus.

Porthos told Madame Coquenard to meet him in the Saint-Magloire cloister, turned his back on her, and walked away. Seeing that he was leaving, her husband invited him to dinner. Porthos majestically declined the invitation.

Madame Coquenard trembled on her way to the cloister because she knew what lay in store for her there; but she was fascinated by Porthos's lordly manner.

Porthos assailed her with all the angry reproaches prompted by his wounded pride. She listened with her head bowed, then said meekly, "I thought it would turn out for the best. One of our clients is a horse dealer. He owed us money and we hadn't been able to make him pay. I told him I'd take a horse and a mule as payment of what he owed us. He agreed, and promised that they'd both be superb animals."

"Well, if he owed you more than five écus, he's a thief."

"It's not a crime to try to get things cheaply," she said in an effort to excuse herself.

"No, but people who try to get things cheaply have no right to complain if others abandon them because they prefer more generous friends."

Porthos turned and took a step away from her.

"Monsieur Porthos!" she cried out. "I was wrong, I admit it. I shouldn't even have considered the price when I was buying something for a great nobleman like you."

Without answering, he took another step.

Madame Coquenard suddenly had a vision of him surrounded by duchesses and countesses dropping bags of gold at his feet.

"Wait, Monsieur Porthos! Wait and let's talk."

"Talking with you brings me bad luck," said Porthos.

"Just tell me what you expect of me."

"I expect nothing of you, because I know that's what I'll get from you."

She clutched his arm and said with anguish in her voice, "Monsieur Porthos, I'm ignorant of all these things. I know nothing about horses and harnesses."

"Then you should have let me choose them for myself, because I know a great deal about them. But you wanted to save money, at my expense."

"I was wrong, I've already admitted that, and I swear I'll make it up to you."

"How?"

"Monsieur de Chaulnes has asked my husband to come and see him this evening, for a consultation that will last at least two hours. Come to the house while he's gone, and we'll settle everything to your satisfaction."

"Now you've finally said something worth listening to, my dear! I'll be there."

"Do you forgive me?"

"We'll see," Porthos said loftily.

And they parted with the understanding that they would meet again that evening.

As he walked away, Porthos thought, "I think I'm about to see the inside of that chest at last!"

35

All Cats Are Gray in the Dark

The evening awaited so impatiently by Porthos and d'Artagnan finally arrived.

D'Artagnan went to Milady's house at about nine o'clock, as usual. He found her in an excellent humor, and she welcomed him more warmly than she had ever done before. He concluded that this was an effect of his false letter, written in Count de Wardes's name.

Kitty came in to serve fruit juice. Milady greeted her with her most charming smile, but Kitty was so sad that she did not even notice it.

D'Artagnan looked at the two women and had to admit that Nature had made a mistake when she created them: she had given a vile, corrupt soul to the great lady, and a noble heart to the maid.

At ten o'clock Milady began to seem ill at ease. D'Artagnan knew why. She looked at the clock, stood up, sat down again, and gave him a smile that clearly meant, "You're pleasant company, but you'd be charming if you left now."

He stood up and took his hat. She gave him her hand to kiss. As he held it, he felt her squeeze his hand; he realized that she had done it not because she was trying to entice him, but because she was grateful to him for leaving. "She's head over heels in love with him," he thought, and walked out of the drawing room.

This time Kitty was not waiting for him in the anteroom, the hall, or the carriage gateway. He had to find the stairs and her little bedroom by himself.

Kitty was sitting with her face hidden in her hands, weeping. She heard d'Artagnan come in but did not look up. He went to her and took her hands. She burst out sobbing.

As he had presumed, Milady had been so delirious with joy when she received the letter that she had told Kitty everything; she had then given her a purse with money in it as a reward for bringing her the good news. Kitty had thrown the purse into a corner when she returned to her room. It was still there, open, disgorging several gold coins onto the floor.

She finally looked up when d'Artagnan spoke her name. He was alarmed by the emotion he saw in her face. She clasped her hands beseechingly, but without daring to say a word.

However insensitive his heart may have been, he was moved by that silent grief. But he was too intent on his plans, especially the one he intended to carry out tonight, to let anything interfere with them. He gave Kitty no hope of being able to make him change his mind; his only attempt to comfort her was to tell her that what he was about to do would be an act of revenge and nothing more.

His chances of success were increased by the fact that Milady, no doubt because she wanted to hide her blushes from her lover, had told Kitty that she was to put out all the lights, even in her own room, before Count de Wardes arrived. He would leave before daybreak, still in darkness.

D'Artagnan and Kitty heard Milady come into her room. He quickly stepped into the wardrobe. Milady rang.

Kitty went to her. This time she did not leave the door open, but the wall was so thin that d'Artagnan could hear nearly everything the two women said.

Milady seemed ecstatically happy. She made Kitty repeat every detail of her supposed meeting with Count de Wardes, asking her how he had acted when he received her letter, what he had said after reading it, how his face had looked, whether he had seemed to be truly in love. Poor Kitty tried to hide her feelings as she answered all these questions; she did not wholly succeed, but Milady was too absorbed in her own happiness to notice the sorrow in her maid's voice.

Finally, when it was nearly time for Count de Wardes to arrive, Milady told Kitty to put out all the lights, go back to her room, and show him in as soon as he came.

Kitty did not have to wait long. As she was closing the door behind her, d'Artagnan looked through the keyhole of the wardrobe, saw that the room was dark, and came out of his hiding place.

"What was that noise?" asked Milady.

"It's I, Count de Wardes," d'Artagnan said in an undertone.

A new wave of despair broke over Kitty. "He couldn't even wait for the time he set for himself!" she thought.

"Why don't you come in, Count?" Milady said in a trembling voice. "You know I'm expecting you."

D'Artagnan gently pushed Kitty aside and hurried into Milady's room.

It would be hard to imagine a more painful situation than that of a man who is with the woman he loves and hears her speaking words of passion to him in the belief that he is someone else. D'Artagnan was in that situation, and he had not foreseen the jealousy that now tore at his heart. He suffered nearly as much as Kitty, who was weeping in the next room.

"Yes, Count," Milady said softly, tenderly pressing his hand, "you've made me happy with the love I've seen in your eyes each time we've met. I love you too. Tomorrow I want you to give me something that will prove you think of me, and since you might forget me, take this."

She took a ring from her finger and slipped it onto d'Artagnan's. He remembered seeing her wear it; its setting was a magnificent sapphire surrounded by diamonds. His first impulse was to give it back to her, but she said, "No, keep it for my sake. By accepting it," she added in a voice vibrant with emotion, "you'll be doing me a greater service than you can imagine."

D'Artagnan thought, "This woman is full of mysteries."

At that moment he felt ready to reveal everything. He opened his mouth to tell her who he was and why he had come there to take revenge, but just then she said, "Poor angel, that Gascon monster nearly killed you!"

He was the Gascon monster.

"Are your wounds still painful?" she asked.

"Yes, very painful," he answered, not knowing what else to say.

"Don't worry," she murmured, "I'll avenge you—cruelly!"

It seemed obvious to d'Artagnan that this would not be a good time to reveal his true identity.

It took him quite some time to recover from this little dialogue. By then, all the ideas of revenge that he had brought with him had vanished. This woman had an incredible power over him. He hated and adored her at the same time. He would never have thought that two such contrary feelings could live in one heart and combine to form a strange and almost diabolical love.

The clock had struck one; they had to part. As he was leaving her, he felt only keen regret at having to be separated from her.

During their passionate farewell they agreed to meet again the following week.

Kitty had hoped to be able to say a few words to d'Artagnan when he came through her room, but Milady led him in the darkness herself and did not leave him till he reached the stairs.

The next morning, d'Artagnan went to see Athos. He had embarked on such a strange adventure that he wanted his advice. He told him everything. Athos frowned several times.

"Your Milady seems to me an infamous creature," he said, "but you were still wrong to deceive her like that. Sooner or later you're going to have a very dangerous enemy."

As he spoke, he looked attentively at the sapphire ring on d'Artagnan's finger. It had now taken the place of the queen's ring, which d'Artagnan had carefully put away in a jewel case.

"You're looking at my ring?" he asked, proud to show off such a valuable gift.

"Yes," said Athos, "it reminds me of one that used to be in my family."

"It's beautiful, isn't it?"

"It certainly is. I didn't think there could be two such magnificent sapphires . . . Did you trade your diamond ring for it?"

"No, it's a present from my beautiful Englishwoman, or rather my beautiful Frenchwoman, because although I haven't asked her, I'm sure she was born in France."

"Milady gave you that ring?" Athos asked with restrained emotion.

"Yes, she gave it to me last night."

"Let me see it."

"Here," said d'Artagnan, taking it off his finger.

Athos examined it and turned very pale. Then he tried it on the third finger of his left hand: it fitted as perfectly as if it had been made for him. A cloud of vindictive anger passed over his ordinarily serene face. "It can't be the same one," he thought. "How could Lady de Winter have gotten that ring? Yet it's hard to believe there could be two sapphire rings so exactly alike . . ."

"Have you seen that ring before?" asked d'Artagnan.

"I thought I recognized it," said Athos, "but I must have been mistaken."

He handed it back to d'Artagnan but went on looking at it.

"D'Artagnan," he said after a silence, "please either take off the ring or turn it around so that the setting doesn't show. It brings back such painful memories that the sight of it would keep me from thinking about the advice you said you wanted me to

give you . . . No, wait; let me see the ring again. The sapphire
in the one I was thinking of had a scratch on one of its facets, as
the result of an accident.''

D'Artagnan again took off the ring and handed it to him.

Athos started.

"Look at this," he said. "Strange, isn't it?"

And he showed d'Artagnan a scratch on one of the facets of
the sapphire.

"It must be the same ring you used to have," said d'Artagnan.
"How did you get it?"

"My mother gave it to me, and her mother gave it to her. It's
an old ring that was never supposed to leave the family.''

"And you . . . sold it?" d'Artagnan asked hesitantly.

"No," Athos said with an odd smile, "I gave it away during
a night of love, just as Milady gave it to you."

D'Artagnan was thoughtful for a moment; more than ever, it
seemed to him that there were dark, unknown depths in Milady's
soul.

Instead of putting the ring back on his finger, he put it in his
pocket.

"Listen to me," said Athos, taking his hand, "you know I
couldn't love you more if you were my son. Believe me when I
tell you that you must stop seeing that woman. I don't know her,
but a kind of intuition tells me there's something deadly about
her.''

"You're right," said d'Artagnan. "I admit I'm frightened of
her myself. I'll break off with her.''

"Will you have the courage to do it?''

"Yes. I'll do it very soon.''

"The sooner the better, my boy," said Athos, pressing
d'Artagnan's hand with almost fatherly affection. "She came
into your life only a short time ago; let's pray that it hasn't been
long enough for her to leave any tragic effects behind her.''

And he nodded to d'Artagnan in a way that showed he would
like to be left alone with his thoughts.

When d'Artagnan came home, he found Kitty waiting for him.
A month of fever could not have changed her more than she had
been changed by her night of insomnia and grief.

Her mistress, madly in love and overflowing with joy, had
sent her to ask Count de Wardes if he would come back to her
sooner than they had agreed.

Pale and trembling, Kitty waited for d'Artagnan's answer.

The advice he had been given by Athos, who had a strong

influence on him, as well as the promptings of his own heart, had made d'Artagnan decide not to see Milady again, now that he had saved his pride and satisfied his desire for revenge. He took a pen and wrote the following letter:

> *Do not count on me for a rendezvous in the near future. Since the end of my convalescence I have had so many engagements of that kind that I must arrange them in an orderly schedule. When your turn comes, I will have the honor of notifying you.*
> *I kiss your hands, madame.*
>
> Count de Wardes

Not a word about the sapphire ring. Did d'Artagnan want to keep it as a weapon against Milady? Or did he regard it as a last resource, to be sold, if necessary, in order to buy his equipment?

We should not judge one age from the viewpoint of another. Things that would now be considered unworthy of a gentleman were taken as a matter of course in d'Artagnan's time, when younger sons of excellent families were often kept by their mistresses.

D'Artagnan handed his letter to Kitty without closing it. At first she did not understand it, but when she had reread it she nearly went mad with joy.

She could scarcely believe her good fortune, until d'Artagnan had told her explicitly what was implied in the letter. Knowing Milady's violent temper, she realized it was going to be dangerous for her to deliver that letter, but this did not stop her from hurrying back to the Place Royale as fast as her legs could carry her. Even a kindhearted woman feels no compassion for a rival's suffering.

Milady opened the letter as eagerly as Kitty had brought it to her. She turned livid as soon as she began reading it. Then she angrily crumpled it and turned to Kitty with lightning in her eyes.

"What is this letter?" she said.

"Why, it's the answer to yours, madame," replied Kitty, trembling.

"Impossible!" cried Milady. "No gentleman could write such a letter to a woman!" She started. "My God! Could he know . . ." She stopped short and clenched her teeth.

Her face was ashen. She tried to walk over to the window to

breathe fresh air, but her legs gave way beneath her and she sank into a chair.

Thinking she had fainted, Kitty rushed forward to open her bodice. But Milady quickly stood up.

"What are you doing?" she said.

"I thought you'd fainted, madame, and I wanted to help you," Kitty answered, frightened by the terrible expression that had appeared on her mistress's face.

"You thought *I*'d fainted? I'm not that kind of weak, helpless woman. When I've been insulted I don't faint, I get revenge! Do you hear me? Revenge!"

And she made a gesture ordering Kitty to leave.

36

Dreams of Vengeance

That evening Milady gave orders that Monsieur d'Artagnan was to be shown in as soon as he came to pay his usual visit. But he did not come.

The next day Kitty went to see him again and told him what had happened the day before. He smiled; Milady's jealous anger was his revenge.

That evening Milady was even more impatient and gave the same order concerning d'Artagnan; but again she waited for him in vain.

Kitty came back the next day, not joyful and alert as she had been on the two previous days, but sad and downcast. D'Artagnan asked what was troubling her. Her only answer was to take a letter from her pocket and hand it to him.

It was from Milady, but this time it was addressed to d'Artagnan, not to Count de Wardes. He opened it and read:

> *My dear Monsieur d'Artagnan, it is unkind of you to neglect your friends as you have been doing, especially when you are about to leave them for so long. For the past two evenings my brother-in-law and I have waited for you in vain. Will it be the same this evening?*
> *Gratefully,*
>
>   *Lady de Winter*

"I was expecting a letter like this," said d'Artagnan. "I've risen in favor as a result of Count de Wardes's fall from grace."

"Will you go?" asked Kitty.

"It wouldn't be wise to refuse such a direct invitation," he said, trying to excuse himself in his own eyes for breaking the promise he had given Athos. "If I didn't go, Milady would wonder why I'd stopped my visits; she might suspect something, and who can say how far such a woman would go to get revenge?"

"You always put things in a way that makes you seem to be right!" said Kitty. "But I know what you'll try to do when you see her again, and if you succeed this time without trickery, without making her think you're someone else, it will be even worse than before!"

She was instinctively certain of what was going to happen, or at least part of it.

D'Artagnan reassured her as best he could and promised that he would be insensitive to Milady's seductive wiles.

He told Kitty to give Milady his answer to her letter: that he was honored by her wish to see him again and would come that evening. He did not answer with a letter of his own because he was afraid he would not be able to disguise his handwriting enough to deceive someone as shrewd and perceptive as Milady.

He arrived at her house on the stroke of nine. It was obvious that the servants waiting in the anteroom had been given instructions about him, because as soon as he appeared, even before he had asked if Milady was at home, one of them hurried off to announce him.

"Show him in," Milady said curtly, but loudly enough for d'Artagnan to hear her in the anteroom.

He was shown in.

"I'm not at home to anyone else," she told the servant, "no matter who may come."

The servant left.

D'Artagnan looked at her with curiosity: she was pale and her eyes were tired, either from weeping or from lack of sleep. Although there were fewer lights in the room than usual, she could not hide the traces of the torments she had suffered in the past two days.

D'Artagnan opened the conversation with his usual gallantry. She made a great effort to respond as she had always done before, but her ravaged face belied her calm, gracious smile.

When he asked about her health she answered, "It's bad, very bad."

"Then you need rest," he said, "and I mustn't stay any longer."

"No, don't go, Monsieur d'Artagnan. Your charming company will be a pleasant diversion for me."

She seemed friendlier than ever before, and to d'Artagnan this meant that he had to be on his guard.

Her manner became affectionate, her conversation sparkling. Her feverish emotion was still only just below the surface, however; it made her eyes shine and gave color to her cheeks and lips. D'Artagnan again saw her as the Circe who had cast her spell on him. He had thought his love was extinguished, but it had only been smoldering, and it was now rekindled in his heart. She smiled at him and he felt he would risk damnation for that smile.

There was a moment when he even felt something like remorse at what he had done to her.

She gradually began talking in a more intimate vein, and finally she asked him if he had a mistress.

He gave her his most soulful look and said, "How can you be so cruel as to ask me that question when I've lived and breathed only for you since the moment I met you?"

"So you love me?" she asked with a strange smile.

"Do I need to tell you? Haven't you seen it?"

"Yes, I have. But, as you know, the prouder a heart is, the harder it is to win."

"I'm not afraid of difficulties," said d'Artagnan. "Only impossibilities discourage me."

"Nothing is impossible for real love."

"Nothing, madame?"

"Nothing."

D'Artagnan thought, "Things are taking a new turn. Is she so fickle that she's already forgetting Count de Wardes and falling in love with me? Is she going to give me a sapphire ring like the one she gave me when she thought I was the count?"

He moved his chair closer to hers.

"What would you do to prove this love you claim to have for me?" she asked.

"Anything! Give me your orders, I'm ready to obey!"

"Anything?"

"Anything!" said d'Artagnan, knowing that he was not risking much by giving her this assurance.

Now she moved her chair closer to his.

"Well, then, let's have a talk," she said.

"I'm listening, madame."

She was undecided for a moment, then she seemed to make a sudden decision.

"I have an enemy," she said.

"*You* have an enemy, madame?" exclaimed d'Artagnan, pretending surprise. "How is that possible, good and beautiful as you are?"

"A mortal enemy."

"Really?"

"An enemy who's insulted me so cruelly that there's war to the death between us. May I count on your help?"

D'Artagnan realized what was in her vindictive mind.

"You may, because my life belongs to you, as well as my love," he said grandiloquently.

"In that case . . ."

"Yes?"

"In that case," Milady went on after a moment of silence, "you can forget about impossibilities."

"Oh! My heart is bursting with happiness!" cried d'Artagnan, kneeling before her.

While he was covering her hands with kisses, she thought, "What you don't know, you conceited fool, is that to me you're not a man, you're only a weapon I'm going to use for my revenge against that foul de Wardes. Once I've done that, I'll get rid of you."

And meanwhile d'Artagnan was thinking, "After you've coldly and deliberately thrown yourself into my arms, you vicious hypocrite, I'll laugh at you with the man you want me to kill."

He looked up at her.

"I'm ready," he said.

"Then you know what I want you to do?"

"I've guessed it."

"You'll use your sword for me?"

"Whenever you say."

"But how can I pay you for such a service? I know lovers: they don't do anything for nothing."

"You know the only answer I want," said d'Artagnan, "the only one that's worthy of you and me."

He gently drew her toward him. She scarcely resisted at all.

"You have an ulterior motive for helping me," she said, smiling.

He felt himself carried away by the passion she was still able to ignite in him.

"The happiness you've let me hope for seems so unlikely," he said, "that I'm afraid it will slip away from me like a dream, and so I'm eager to turn it into a reality as quickly as I can."

"First you must earn that happiness."

"I'm at your orders."

"Do you really mean that?" Milady asked with a lingering shadow of doubt.

"Just tell me the name of the heartless man who brought tears to your lovely eyes."

"What makes you think I've shed any tears?"

"Well, it seems to me that . . ."

"Women like me don't weep," said Milady.

"Good. Tell me the man's name."

"His name is my whole secret . . ."

"But you have to tell me who he is."

"Yes, and I *will* tell you. You see how much I trust you?"

"I'm honored by your trust. What's his name?"

"You know him."

"I do?"

"Yes."

"He's not one of my friends, is he?" asked d'Artagnan, pretending hesitation to support his pretense of ignorance.

A hard glint appeared in Milady's eyes.

"If he were one of your friends, would you hesitate?"

"No!" said d'Artagnan. "Not even if he were my brother!"

He spoke as if he were committing himself blindly, but in fact he knew where he was going.

"I love your devotion," said Milady.

"Is that all you love in me?"

"I love you for yourself, too," she said, taking his hand.

Her touch made him quiver, as if her fever had passed into him.

"You love me!" he cried. "If it's really true, it's enough to make me lose my reason!"

He took her in his arms. She did not try to move her lips away from his, but she did not return his kiss. Her lips were cold. It seemed to him that he had kissed a statue, but he still felt drunk with joy. He almost believed she loved him; and he almost believed that de Wardes was guilty of a vile crime. If he had seen de Wardes in front of him at that moment, he would have killed him.

Milady seized the opportunity.

"My enemy's name is . . ."

"De Wardes, I know," d'Artagnan blurted out.

"*How* do you know?" she asked, taking both his hands and looking intensely into his eyes.

He realized his impetuous blunder.

"Tell me," she insisted. "How do you know?"

"How do I know?"

"Yes."

"I know because yesterday I was at a social gathering where de Wardes showed everyone a ring and said it was a present from you."

"He's even more contemptible than I thought!" cried Milady.

D'Artagnan could not help being unpleasantly affected by the word "contemptible."

"I'll avenge you against that scoundrel," he said with the pomposity of Don Japhet in Scarron's play.

"Thank you, my brave friend. And when will I be avenged?"

"Tomorrow, or immediately—whenever you like."

Milady was about to say, "Immediately," but then it occurred to her that such haste might make d'Artagnan doubt the sincerity of her feelings by giving him the impression that she was anxious to be rid of him. Furthermore she needed time to take precautions and explain to him that he must avoid saying certain things to de Wardes in front of witnesses.

She was relieved when d'Artagnan himself chose not to act till the next day.

"Tomorrow," he said, "either you'll be avenged or I'll be dead."

"I'll be avenged. You won't be dead, because he's a coward."

"With women, maybe, but not with men. I know that from experience."

"You also know from experience that you're a better swordsman than he is."

"Luck was with me the last time we fought. It may not be with me the next time."

"Does that mean you're reluctant to fight him again?"

"No, of course not. But would it be fair for you to send me to possible death without giving me something more than hope?"

She looked at him in a way that told him he had only to ask for what he wanted. Then she added words to her look:

"No, it wouldn't be fair," she said tenderly.

"You're an angel!"

"Then it's all settled?"

"Everything except what I'm asking of you," said d'Artagnan.

"I've already told you that you can count on my love."

"I can't wait till tomorrow. For me, there may be no tomorrow."

"Quiet! I hear my brother-in-law. It will be better if he doesn't see you here."

She rang the bell. Kitty came in.

"Go out this way," Milady told d'Artagnan, opening a hidden door. "Come back at eleven o'clock and we'll finish our conversation. Kitty will bring you to my bedroom."

Poor Kitty nearly fainted when she heard this.

"Don't just stand there like a statue!" Milady rebuked her. "Show Monsieur d'Artagnan out, and show him in again at eleven o'clock, do you understand?"

D'Artagnan thought, "Eleven o'clock seems to be the time when she makes all her bedroom appointments. I suppose it's become a habit."

Milady held out her hand to him and he kissed it lovingly.

Kitty accompanied him down the stairs. He was so absorbed in thought that he scarcely heard her reproaches. "You mustn't let Milady make a fool of you," he warned himself. "She's a dangerous, treacherous woman. Be careful!"

37

Milady's Secret

In spite of Kitty's pleas, d'Artagnan left the house without going up to her room. He did this for two reasons: first, he wanted to avoid listening to her recriminations and entreaties; and second, he wanted time to collect his wits and try to guess exactly what was in Milady's mind.

One thing was clear to him: he was passionately in love with her and she did not love him at all. For a moment he realized that what he should do was to go home and write Milady a letter telling her that, as far as her reason for wanting revenge was concerned, he and de Wardes were the same man, and so he could not kill de Wardes without committing suicide. But he too

was goaded by a fierce desire for revenge; he wanted to possess
Milady under his own name, and since that kind of revenge
seemed especially attractive to him, he was not willing to give it
up.

He walked around the Place Royale five or six times, stopping
often to look at the light shining from the window of Milady's
drawing room; she was obviously less eager to go to her bedroom than she had been when she was expecting Count de
Wardes.

Finally the light vanished, and so did d'Artagnan's last qualms.
His heart pounded with excitement as he thought back over the
details of the first night. He went into the house and hurried up
to Kitty's room.

Deathly pale and trembling in every limb, Kitty tried to stop
him from going to Milady. But Milady, listening intently, had
heard him arrive. She opened the door between the two rooms.

"Come," she said.

It was all so incredibly brazen, so monstrously shameless, that
he could scarcely believe it was really happening. He felt as if he
were having one of those fantastic adventures that ordinarily
occur only in dreams. But his feeling of unreality did not prevent
him from rushing toward Milady; he was irresistibly drawn to
her, as iron is drawn to a magnet.

When the door had closed behind them, Kitty threw herself
against it. Suffering the torments of jealousy, rage, and hurt
pride, she was tempted to tell Milady the truth about her night
with the man she had thought to be Count de Wardes. But she
would be lost if she admitted taking part in that machination,
and, still worse, d'Artagnan would be lost to her forever. So she
forced herself to accept this last sacrifice.

D'Artagnan had reached the height of his desires: this time,
Milady did not love him in the belief that he was someone else,
but seemed to love him as himself. An inner voice told him that
he was only an instrument of revenge that she was caressing
before using it against her enemy. But his pride, his vanity, and
his mad passion silenced that voice. Self-confident as always, he
compared himself with de Wardes and decided there was no
reason not to believe that Milady could love him as himself.

He abandoned himself to the sensations of the moment. He no
longer saw Milady as a dangerous, treacherous woman: she was
now an ardent, passionate, unrestrained mistress who seemed to
feel genuine love for him. Two hours went by in this way.

Finally the two lovers became calmer. Milady, who did not

have d'Artagnan's reasons for wanting to forget, was the first to return to reality. She asked him if he had decided how he would provoke de Wardes into fighting a duel with him the next day. But d'Artagnan had not yet regained his coolheadedness: he foolishly said he could not think about that kind of dueling when he was engaged in a much more pleasant kind.

Milady was alarmed by his indifference to the only concern that was on her mind. She began pressing him with questions. Since he had never given any serious thought to the duel he had no intention of fighting, he tried to change the subject, but he was no match for her iron will. She refused to let him distract her from the matter she was determined to settle.

Secretly admiring his own cleverness, he advised her to forgive de Wardes and give up her plan for revenge. As soon as she heard this, she started furiously and drew away from him.

"Are you afraid, by any chance, my dear d'Artagnan?" she said in a shrill, mocking voice that resounded strangely in the darkness.

"You know I'm not," he replied. "But what if poor Count de Wardes were less guilty than you think?"

"The exact degree of his guilt doesn't matter," Milady said gravely. "He's insulted me, and for that he deserves to die."

"Then he'll die, since you've condemned him," d'Artagnan said in such a firm tone that she took it as proof of unshakable devotion.

And she again moved close to him.

We cannot say how long the night seemed to Milady, but to d'Artagnan it seemed that he had been with her no more than two hours when the pale glow of dawn began seeping into the room through the cracks in the blinds.

When he was about to leave her, she reminded him of his promise to avenge her against de Wardes.

"I'll keep my promise," he said, "but first I'd like to be sure of one thing."

"What is it?"

"That you love me."

"Haven't I proved it to you?"

"Yes, forgive me for doubting it," he said. "And now I belong to you body and soul."

"Thank you, my brave lover! But since I've proved my love, you'll prove yours too, won't you?"

"You can count on me for that. But if you love me as you say you do, aren't you a little afraid for me?"

"Why should I be afraid?"

"I may be seriously wounded, or even killed."

"That's impossible," said Milady. "You're too good a swordsman to lose a duel against de Wardes."

"But wouldn't you prefer a different kind of revenge, one that would make that duel unnecessary?"

She looked at him in silence. The wan light of daybreak gave her eyes a strangely funereal expression.

"Now I really believe you're wavering," she said.

"No, I'm not wavering. But I feel sorry for poor de Wardes now that you don't love him anymore, and it seems to me that the loss of your love must be such a cruel punishment that he doesn't need any other."

"What makes you think I ever loved him?" asked Milady.

"At least I can say now, without too much conceit, that you love someone else. And I feel you should be lenient with him."

"Why?"

"Because I know . . ."

"What do you know?"

"That he's far from having offended you as much as you think."

"Really?" Milady said uneasily. "What do you mean? Explain yourself."

D'Artagnan was still holding her in his arms. She drew back and looked at him with a disquieting light in her eyes.

He made his decision: he was going to tell her the truth and clear up everything between them.

"I'm a man of honor," he began, "and now that I have your love—I do have it, don't I?"

"Yes, go on."

"My happiness would be complete if something weren't weighing on my mind. I have a confession to make."

"A confession?"

"I wouldn't make it to you if I doubted your love. You do love me, don't you?"

"Of course."

"If I've done something wrong because I love you too much, you'll forgive me, won't you?"

"Perhaps."

He tried to kiss her, but she pushed him away.

"Tell me what you have to confess," she said, turning pale.

"You had a rendezvous with Count de Wardes last Thursday, in this same room, didn't you?"

"No, I didn't," she said so firmly, and with such an impassive face, that d'Artagnan would have doubted the truth if he had not had such perfect proof of it.

"There's no use lying, my beautiful angel," he said, smiling. "I hold nothing against you."

"But tell me . . ."

"De Wardes has nothing to boast about."

"Why do you say that? You told me yourself that he'd shown that ring . . ."

"I have that ring, my love. The Count de Wardes of last Thursday and the d'Artagnan of today are the same man."

He expected surprise mingled with shame, followed by a brief storm that would end in tears. He was terribly mistaken, and it did not take him long to find it out.

Milady's face was pale with rage. She violently shoved d'Artagnan away from her and leapt out of bed.

By now it was nearly broad daylight.

He clutched her thin batiste negligee to hold her back, intending to beg her to forgive him, but she tugged against him with all her strength. The negligee tore, leaving her shoulders bare. And d'Artagnan was horrified to see that one of those beautiful white shoulders had been branded with a fleur-de-lis, the infamous, indelible mark of a convicted criminal.

"My God!" he cried out, letting go of the negligee.

He then sat silent and motionless on the bed. But from his exclamation Milady realized what he had seen. Now he knew her secret, the terrible secret that no one else knew.

She turned on him like a wounded panther.

"First you played a despicable trick on me, and now you've discovered my secret!" she said. "You're going to die!"

She ran to an inlaid box on the dressing table, opened it with a trembling hand, took out a little gold-handled dagger with a sharp, slender blade, and rushed at the half-naked d'Artagnan.

Although he was brave, as we know, he was terror-stricken at the sight of her livid face, contorted by fury, with its bloodred lips and horribly dilated pupils. He retreated to the other side of the bed, as though a snake were crawling toward him. He groped in the space between the bed and the wall until his hand, damp with sweat, touched his sword. He drew it from its scabbard.

Ignoring his sword, Milady tried to climb up onto the bed to stab him. She did not stop till she felt the sharp point against her throat. She tried to seize the blade with her hand, but he kept it out of her grasp. Moving it rapidly back and forth between her eyes and her chest, he slid off the bed and began backing toward the door to Kitty's room, intending to escape through it.

Meanwhile Milady screamed and roared at him as she frenziedly tried to attack him.

He began to feel as if he were fighting a duel, and this restored his courage.

"Calm down, my fair lady," he said, "or, by God, I'll cut another fleur-de-lis into your other shoulder!"

"I'll kill you!" she shrieked.

But he continued to hold her at bay while he tried to find the door, without taking his eyes off her. Now and then he stepped behind a piece of furniture and she overturned it in an effort to get at him.

Hearing all this noise, Kitty opened the door. D'Artagnan was now within three steps of it. He suddenly darted into Kitty's room, slammed the door, and held it shut with his shoulder while Kitty bolted it.

Milady hurled herself against the door with strength far beyond any ordinary woman's; then, when she realized she could not break it open, she began stabbing it, sometimes driving the point of her dagger all the way through it. And with each blow she shouted a terrible curse.

"Get me out of the house," d'Artagnan whispered to Kitty. "If I'm not gone by the time she starts thinking clearly, she'll have me killed by her servants."

"But you can't go out like that," said Kitty. "You're almost naked."

Only then did he notice how he was dressed, insofar as he was dressed at all.

"You're right," he said. "Get me some clothes, anything will do. But hurry, it's a matter of life and death! You understand?"

Kitty understood all too well. A few moments later he was decked out in a flowered dress, a big bonnet, and a short cape, with slippers over his bare feet. She led him downstairs, in the nick of time: Milady had already rung her bell and awakened the whole household. The doorkeeper had just let d'Artagnan out, at Kitty's request, when Milady, still half naked, shouted from her window:

"Don't open the door!"

38

How Athos Got His Equipment without Effort

Milady could do nothing but make threatening gestures while d'Artagnan fled from the house. When she lost sight of him, she fell to the floor in a faint.

Goaded by terror, the shouts of policemen pursuing him, and the jeers of early-rising people on their way to work, d'Artagnan ran across half of Paris, so distraught that he gave no thought to what might happen to Kitty, and did not stop till he came to Athos's house.

He crossed the courtyard, climbed the stairs, and pounded on the door.

Grimaud opened it, his eyes puffy from sleep. D'Artagnan stepped inside so hurriedly that he nearly knocked him over.

This time Grimaud broke his usual silence.

"Where do you think you're going, miss?" he asked indignantly.

D'Artagnan opened his cape and pushed back his bonnet. Seeing his mustache and sword, Grimaud realized he was a man and thought he must be a robber.

"Help! Help!" he shouted.

"Quiet, you fool! I'm d'Artagnan, don't you recognize me? Where's your master?"

"You're Monsieur d'Artagnan?" exclaimed Grimaud, bewildered. "That's impossible!"

"Grimaud," said Athos, coming out of his bedroom in a dressing gown, "I believe you've taken the liberty of speaking."

"Yes, sir, but I . . ."

"Silence."

Grimaud closed his mouth and pointed to d'Artagnan.

Athos recognized his friend and, phlegmatic though he usually was, burst out laughing at the sight of d'Artagnan standing there with his bonnet awry, his skirt hanging down to his slippers, his sleeves rolled up, and his mustache quivering with emotion.

"Don't laugh!" protested d'Artagnan. "Believe me, there's nothing to laugh about!"

"Are you wounded? You're very pale!"

"No, but something horrible just happened. Are you alone, Athos?"

"Of course. Who do you think would be here at this hour?"

D'Artagnan quickly went into Athos's bedroom.

"Tell me what's happened," said Athos, coming in behind him and bolting the door so that they would not be disturbed. "Is the king dead? Have you killed the cardinal? You're in a terrible state! Tell me, I'm dying of anxiety!"

D'Artagnan took off the clothes Kitty had given him. He was now dressed only in his shirt.

"Prepare yourself to hear an incredible story," he said.

"First take this dressing gown."

D'Artagnan put it on, after distractedly thrusting his arm into the wrong sleeve.

"Well?" said Athos.

D'Artagnan leaned close to his ear and lowered his voice.

"Milady has a fleur-de-lis branded on her shoulder."

Athos cried out as if he had been shot.

"Are you sure that woman is really dead?" asked d'Artagnan.

"What woman?" Athos said almost inaudibly.

"The one you told me about in Amiens."

Athos moaned and put his head between his hands.

"This one," d'Artagnan went on, "is between twenty-six and twenty-eight years old."

"She's blond, isn't she?"

"Yes."

"Does she have light blue, strangely bright eyes, and dark eyebrows and lashes?"

"Yes."

"Is she tall and well made, and does she have a tooth missing on the left side of her upper jaw?"

"Yes."

"Is the fleur-de-lis small and reddish-brown, and has she tried to make it less visible with some sort of paste?"

"Yes."

"But you said she was English!"

"She's called Milady, but she may be French. And Lord de Winter is only her brother-in-law."

"I want to see her, d'Artagnan."

"Be careful, Athos. You tried to kill her once; she's perfectly capable of killing you for revenge."

"She won't dare to say anything, because she'd be denouncing herself."

"She wouldn't let anything stop her! Have you ever seen her in a rage?"

"No," said Athos.

"She's a tigress, a panther! Oh, Athos, I'm afraid I've exposed us both to the danger of a terrible vengeance!"

And d'Artagnan told everything that had happened, ending by describing Milady's violent fury and threats to kill him.

"You're right," said Athos. "My life isn't worth much now. It's lucky we're going to leave Paris day after tomorrow. We'll probably be sent to La Rochelle, and once we're gone . . ."

"She'll follow you to the end of the earth if she recognizes you. Let me be the only target of her hatred."

"What does it matter if she kills me? You don't think I care about life, do you?"

"There's some horrible mystery behind this, Athos. She's one of the cardinal's spies, I'm sure of it!"

"In that case, be on your guard. If the cardinal doesn't admire you for what you did in London, he hates you for it. If he hates you, he can't attack you openly, but you can be sure he won't rest till he's satisfied his hatred! You must constantly be on the alert. Don't go out alone; take precautions when you eat; be wary of everything, even your shadow."

"All we have to do is survive till day after tomorrow. When we're at war, I hope we'll have only men to fear."

"In the meantime," said Athos, "I'll give up my seclusion and stay with you everywhere. You need to go home now; I'll go with you."

"Even though it's not far, I can't go there like this."

"That's true," Athos acknowledged. He rang the bell.

Grimaud came in. Athos told him, by gestures, to go to d'Artagnan's apartment and bring back some clothes. Grimaud replied, also by gestures, that he understood, and left.

"As far as getting our equipment is concerned," said Athos, "we're worse off than ever. If I'm not mistaken, you've left your uniform at Milady's house, and I doubt that she'll be so kind as to return it to you. Luckily you still have the sapphire ring."

"That ring is yours, Athos. Didn't you tell me it was a family heirloom?"

"Yes, my father bought it for two thousand écus, he once told me. It was one of the wedding presents he gave to my mother. It's a magnificent ring. My mother gave it to me, and instead of treasuring it as a precious keepsake, I stupidly gave it to that vile woman.''

"Then take it back, my friend. I'm sure it means a great deal to you.''

"Take it back after *she's* worn it? Never! That ring is sullied, d'Artagnan.''

"Sell it, then.''

"I couldn't sell a ring that my mother gave me. That would be desecration.''

"Then pawn it. You can borrow at least a thousand écus on it. That will be more than enough for what you need. As soon as you get some more money, you'll redeem it and then it won't be sullied any more, because it will have passed through a moneylender's hands.''

Athos smiled.

"You're a delightful friend, d'Artagnan. Your good humor is an antidote to despair. Very well, we'll pawn the ring, but on one condition.''

"What is it?''

"Each of us will take five hundred écus.''

"Don't be ridiculous, Athos. I'm in the guards: I only need a quarter of that amount, and I can get it by selling my saddle. All I lack now is a horse for Planchet. And you're forgetting that *I* have a ring too.''

"Yes, and you value yours even more highly than I value mine; or at least I have that impression.''

"You're right, because it can save us not only from poverty but also from danger. It's not just a diamond ring, it's a magic talisman.''

"I don't know what you mean, but I'll take your word for it. Let's come back to my ring, or rather yours. Either you take half the money we can borrow on it or I'll throw it into the Seine, and I doubt that any fish will obligingly bring it back to us, like the one that returned Polycrates' ring.''

"All right, then, I'll take the money,'' said d'Artagnan.

Just then Grimaud came in. With him was Planchet. Worried about his master and curious to know what had happened to him, Planchet had brought the clothes himself.

D'Artagnan got dressed and so did Athos. When they were both ready to leave, Athos turned to Grimaud and made the gesture of a man raising a gun to his shoulder. Grimaud took his musket and prepared to accompany his master.

Athos and d'Artagnan, followed by their servants, reached the

Rue des Fossoyeurs without incident. Bonacieux was standing on the front steps. He gave d'Artagnan a sly look and said, "Hurry, my dear tenant, there's a pretty girl waiting for you, and you know women don't like to be kept waiting."

"It's Kitty!" cried d'Artagnan.

He rushed up to his apartment and found her huddled against the door, trembling.

"You promised to protect me, to save me from her anger," she said when she saw him. "You're the one who got me into this!"

"Yes, I know. But don't worry, Kitty. What happened after I left?"

"I didn't stay very long to find out. The servants came running when they heard her screams. She was in such a rage that she was like a raving lunatic. You can't imagine the curses she shrieked against you! I knew she'd realize I was your accomplice when she remembered that you'd come into her room through mine, so I took my best clothes, and what little money I had, and ran away."

"Poor Kitty! But what can I do with you? I'm leaving day after tomorrow."

"It doesn't matter, just get me out of the country, or at least out of Paris!"

"I can't take you with me to the siege of La Rochelle."

"No, but you can arrange for me to work somewhere in the provinces, for some lady you know—in your province, for example."

"In my province, ladies don't have chambermaids . . . But I know what to do! Planchet, go and ask Aramis to come here immediately. We have something very important to tell him."

"I understand," said Athos. "But why not Porthos? It seems to me that his marquise . . ."

"His marquise uses her husband's clerks as chambermaids," said d'Artagnan, laughing. "And besides, Kitty wouldn't want to live on the Rue aux Ours, would you, Kitty?"

"I'll live anywhere you like," she answered, "as long as I can stay hidden and *she* doesn't know where I am."

"Now that we're about to part, Kitty, and there's no longer any reason for you to be jealous of me . . ."

"Whether we're together or apart," she interrupted, "I'll always love you."

"Constancy turns up in unlikely places," murmured Athos.

"And I'll always love you too," said d'Artagnan. "But now I

want to ask you an important question. Have you ever overheard anything about a young woman who was abducted one night?''

"Let me think . . . Oh! Are you still in love with that woman?"

"No, it's one of my friends who loves her. It's Athos, here, as a matter of fact."

"What!" Athos exclaimed with a look of horror, as if he had just seen that he was about to step on a snake.

"No use denying it," said d'Artagnan, pressing Athos's hand. "And you know how much we're concerned about poor Madame Bonacieux. Kitty won't say anything, will you, Kitty? Madame Bonacieux is the wife of that ugly little man you saw in front of the house when you came here.''

"I was so frightened when I saw him!" said Kitty. "I hope he didn't recognize me!"

"Recognize you? Then you've seen him before?"

"He came to Milady's house twice."

"When?"

"The first time was two or three weeks ago."

"I see . . ."

"And the second time was last night."

"Last night?"

"Yes, a little while before you came."

"Athos, we're surrounded by spies!" said d'Artagnan. "And you think he may have recognized you, Kitty?"

"I pulled my bonnet down over my face when I saw him, but maybe it was too late."

"He's less suspicious of you than of me, Athos; go downstairs and see if he's still there."

Athos left and came back a few moments later.

"He's gone," he said, "and the front door is locked."

"He must have gone to report that all the chickens are in the coop.''

"Then let's fly the coop," said Athos. "We'll leave only Planchet here, to let us know what happens."

"But what about Aramis? Planchet has gone to bring him."

"Yes, that's true. We'll wait till he comes."

Aramis walked in at that very moment.

D'Artagnan explained the situation to him and told him how urgent it was for him to find a place for Kitty in the household of one of his lofty acquaintances.

Aramis thought for a moment, then asked, blushing, "Is it really important to you, d'Artagnan?"

"I'll be grateful to you the rest of my life!"

"Well, then, Madame de Bois-Tracy recently asked me if I knew of a reliable chambermaid for a friend of hers who lives somewhere in the provinces, I believe. If you can vouch for this girl . . ."

"Oh, sir," cried Kitty, "I'll be completely devoted to anyone who makes it possible for me to leave Paris!"

"Very well, then," said Aramis.

He sat down at a table, wrote a brief letter, sealed it with a ring and handed it to Kitty.

"And now, Kitty," said d'Artagnan, "you know it's no safer for us here than it is for you, so we must part. We'll meet again in better times."

"And whenever or wherever we meet again," she said, "you'll find me still loving you as I do now."

"Naturally," Athos said ironically as d'Artagnan accompanied Kitty downstairs.

A short time later, Athos, d'Artagnan, and Aramis left, after agreeing to meet at Athos's house at four o'clock. Planchet stayed behind to stand guard.

Aramis returned home. Athos and d'Artagnan went to pawn the sapphire ring.

As d'Artagnan expected, they were easily able to borrow three hundred pistoles on it. And the pawnbroker said that since it would go very well with a pair of earrings he had, he would pay five hundred pistoles for it if they were willing to sell it.

Diligent and knowledgeable as they were, Athos and d'Artagnan took only three hours to buy all of the musketeer's equipment. Whenever something suited him, Athos paid whatever price was asked for it, without deigning to bargain over it. D'Artagnan tried to persuade him to be more careful with his money, but Athos smiled and put his hand on his shoulder, and d'Artagnan understood that while haggling over prices might be permissible for a young man from the minor Gascon nobility, it was out of the question for a great aristocrat.

Athos found a superb jet-black five-year-old Andalusian horse with flaring nostrils and slender, elegant legs. He examined it, judged it to be flawless, and bought it for a thousand livres. Perhaps he could have had it for less; but while d'Artagnan was discussing the price with the dealer, Athos counted out the hundred pistoles on the table.

For three hundred livres, he bought a strong, stocky Picard horse for Grimaud.

But when he had bought Grimaud's saddle and weapons, not

one sou was left of his hundred and fifty pistoles. D'Artagnan offered to lend him part of his share of the money they had borrowed on the sapphire ring. Athos merely shrugged in reply.

"How much did the pawnbroker say he'd pay for the ring if we wanted to sell it to him?" he asked.

"Five hundred pistoles."

"That makes two hundred pistoles more: a hundred for you and a hundred for me. That's a small fortune, my friend! Go back to the pawnbroker."

"What? Do you mean you want to . . ."

"That ring would bring back too many unhappy memories. And besides, we'll never have three hundred pistoles to redeem it with, so we'd lose two hundred if we didn't sell it. Go to the pawnbroker, tell him the ring is his and come back with the two hundred pistoles."

"Think it over, Athos."

"Money is scarce these days, and we have to make sacrifices. Go, d'Artagnan; Grimaud will escort you with his musket."

Half an hour later, d'Artagnan safely returned with the money.

And now we know how Athos found unexpected resources.

39

A Vision

At four o'clock, the four friends were gathered in Athos's apartment. Their concern for their equipment had vanished and each of them now had only his own secret worries; future anxiety is always hidden behind present happiness.

Planchet suddenly came in with two letters addressed to d'Artagnan.

One of them was small, folded lengthwise, and closed with a pretty green wax seal showing a dove with a green twig in its beak. The other was large and square, and bore the imposing coat of arms of His Eminence the cardinal.

D'Artagnan's heart leapt when he saw the small one, for he was sure he recognized the handwriting on it; although he had seen that handwriting only once before, the memory of it was engraved in his mind.

He quickly opened the small letter and read it:

Take a ride on the Chaillot road Wednesday evening between six and seven o'clock, and look carefully into all the carriages that pass, but if you value your life and the lives of those who love you, do nothing to show that you have recognized the woman who will be exposing herself to great danger in order to see you for a moment.

There was no signature.

"It's a trap," said Athos. "Don't go."

"But I think I recognize the handwriting," said d'Artagnan.

"It may be a forgery. Between six and seven o'clock, the Chaillot road is completely deserted. You might as well be in the Bondy forest."

"But suppose we all go!" said d'Artagnan. "They can't devour all four of us, plus four servants, plus our horses, plus our weapons."

"It will give us a chance to show off our equipment," remarked Porthos.

"But if it's a woman who's written to you," said Aramis, "and if she doesn't want to be seen, you'd be compromising her by bringing the rest of us with you. That would be unworthy of a gentleman."

"We'll stay back," said Porthos, "and only d'Artagnan will go forward."

"Yes, but it doesn't take long to fire a pistol from a carriage."

"They'll miss me," d'Artagnan said confidently. "Then we'll overtake the carriage and exterminate the men in it. At least we'll have lowered the number of our enemies."

"He's right," said Porthos. "We'll fight! After all, we have to try out our weapons."

"Let's do it," Aramis said with his gentle, nonchalant expression. "Why miss a chance to enjoy ourselves?"

"I'm willing," said Athos.

"Gentlemen," said d'Artagnan, "it's half-past four. We barely have time to be on the Chaillot road by six o'clock."

"If we leave too late," said Porthos, "no one will see us, and that would be a shame. Let's get ready, gentlemen."

"But what about the other letter, d'Artagnan?" said Athos. "You're forgetting it, and its seal shows that it's well worth opening. I don't mind telling you that I'm much more interested in it than in the little note you just slipped into your pocket, next to your heart.''

D'Artagnan blushed.

"All right, gentlemen," he said, "let's see what His Eminence wants with me."

He unsealed the letter.

> *Monsieur d'Artagnan, of the des Essarts company of the king's guards, is expected at the Palais-Cardinal this evening at eight o'clock.*
>
> *La Houdinière*
> *Captain of the Guards*

"That's a much more alarming appointment than the other one!" said Athos.

"I'll go to it after the first one," said d'Artagnan. "One is for seven o'clock, the other for eight; I'll have time for both."

"I wouldn't go to the second one if I were you," said Aramis. "A gallant gentleman can't miss an appointment given to him by a lady, but a cautious man can apologize for not being able to pay a visit to His Eminence, especially when he has reason to believe that His Eminence doesn't want to see him just to have a friendly chat."

"I agree with Aramis," said Porthos.

"I've already had another invitation from His Eminence, delivered by Monsieur de Cavois," said d'Artagnan. "I ignored it, and something terrible happened: Constance disappeared! This time I'm going."

"If your mind's made up, then go," said Athos.

"But what if you end up in the Bastille?" asked Aramis.

"You'll get me out," replied d'Artagnan.

"Yes, of course," Porthos said casually, as though rescuing someone from the Bastille were the simplest thing in the world, "but since we're supposed to leave day after tomorrow, you'd better not take that chance."

"We'll stay with him all evening," said Athos. "Each of us will wait at a gate of the palace with three musketeers behind him, and if we see a suspicious-looking closed carriage come out, we'll stop it. We haven't had a fight with the cardinal's guards for a long time. Monsieur de Tréville must think we're dead."

"You should have been a general, Athos," said Aramis. "What do you think of his plan, gentlemen?"

Porthos and d'Artagnan declared that it was an admirable plan.

"I'll go to headquarters and tell our friends to be ready at eight o'clock," said Porthos. "We'll meet in front of the Palais-Cardinal. Meanwhile, have your servants saddle your horses."

"I don't have a horse," said d'Artagnan, "but I'll borrow one from Monsieur de Tréville."

"No, take one of mine instead," said Aramis.

"One of yours? How many do you have?" asked d'Artagnan.

"Three," Aramis answered with a smile.

"Three!" exclaimed Athos. "You must be the only poet in France with three horses!"

"You don't need that many," said d'Artagnan. "I don't understand why you bought three horses."

"I only bought two," said Aramis.

"And the third one just appeared out of thin air?"

"No, it was brought to me this morning by an unliveried servant who wouldn't tell me where it had come from. He said only that he'd been ordered by his master . . ."

"Or his mistress," d'Artagnan interrupted.

"It makes no difference," said Aramis, blushing. "He said his mistress had ordered him to put that horse into my stable without telling me who had sent it."

"Things like that happen only to poets," Athos said solemnly.

"Now you have a horse for yourself, one for Bazin, and one left over," said d'Artagnan. "Which will you ride: the one you bought for yourself or the one that was given to you?"

"The one that was given to me, of course," replied Aramis. "If I didn't ride that one, it would be insulting to . . ."

"Your unknown benefactor," said d'Artagnan.

"Or benefactress," said Athos.

"So the one you bought is now useless to you?" d'Artagnan continued.

"I suppose so."

"You chose it yourself."

"Yes, and very carefully. As you know, a horseman's safety nearly always depends on his horse."

"Sell it to me for whatever you paid."

"I was about to suggest that. You can take the horse now and pay me whenever you have the money. There's no hurry."

"How much did you pay for it?"

"Eight hundred livres."

"Here are forty double pistoles," said d'Artagnan, taking the sum from his pocket. "I know those are the coins with which you're paid for your poems."

"I see your financial situation has improved."

"I'm rich, my friend, very rich!" said d'Artagnan.

And he jingled the other pistoles in his pocket.

"Send your saddle to headquarters and have your horse brought here with ours."

"All right, but let's not waste any more time: it's nearly five o'clock."

A quarter of an hour later, Porthos appeared at the end of the Rue Férou on a magnificent Spanish horse, with Mousqueton riding behind him on a small but sturdy Auvergnat horse. Porthos was beaming with joy and pride.

At the same time, Aramis appeared at the other end of the street on a superb English charger. Behind him was Bazin on a roan horse, leading the vigorous Mecklenburger that was d'Artagnan's new mount.

The two musketeers met in front of the door while Athos and d'Artagnan watched them from the window.

"That's a fine horse you have there, Porthos!" said Aramis.

"Yes," replied Porthos, "it's the one that was supposed to have been sent to me in the first place. The husband sent the other one as a joke, but he's been punished for it and I've been given full satisfaction."

Planchet and Grimaud arrived, leading their masters' horses. D'Artagnan and Athos came out and the four friends rode off together, Athos on the horse he owed to his wife, Aramis on the horse he owed to his mistress, Porthos on the horse he owed to the attorney's wife, and d'Artagnan on the horse he owed to Lady Luck, the best mistress of all.

The servants followed.

As Porthos had expected, the cavalcade made a good impression. If Madame Coquenard had been there to see what a fine figure he cut on his handsome Spanish horse, she would not have regretted having bled her husband's strongbox.

Near the Louvre they met Monsieur de Tréville, who had just come back from Saint-Germain. He stopped them to compliment them on their horses, and within a few moments they were surrounded by a crowd of onlookers.

D'Artagnan took this opportunity to tell Monsieur de Tréville about the letter with the big red seal and the cardinal's coat of arms. He did not breathe a word, of course, about the other letter he had received.

Monsieur de Tréville approved of his decision and told him that if he had not returned by the next morning, he would find him, no matter where he was.

Just then the Samaritaine clock struck six. The four friends excused themselves, saying they had an appointment, and took leave of Monsieur de Tréville.

By the time they had galloped to the Chaillot road, daylight was beginning to fade. Carriages were passing in both directions. D'Artagnan looked into each of them, guarded by his friends from a distance, without seeing a familiar face.

Finally, after a quarter of an hour, when darkness was falling, a carriage came toward him at a gallop from the Sèvres road. He had a presentiment that this was the one he had been waiting for. He was surprised by the violence with which his heart began pounding. A woman's face appeared at the window of the carriage. She put two fingers to her lips, either to urge him to be silent or to throw him a kiss. He uttered a cry of joy: that woman, or rather that fleeting vision, for the carriage had passed with the speed of lightning, was Constance Bonacieux.

Involuntarily, despite the warning in the letter, he rode after the carriage and soon caught up with it. But a curtain had been drawn across the window; the vision had disappeared.

He then remembered the warning: "If you value your life and the lives of those who love you, do nothing to show that you have recognized the woman who will be exposing herself to great danger in order to see you for a moment."

He stopped, trembling, not for himself, but for the poor woman who had obviously risked her life to see him.

The carriage continued on its way, plunged into Paris, and vanished.

D'Artagnan sat motionless on his horse, not knowing what to think. If Madame Bonacieux was going back to Paris, why that rendezvous that lasted only for an instant, why that mere exchange of glances, why that kiss carried away by the wind? But what if it had not been Madame Bonacieux? It was possible, after all, since the dim light would have made it easy for him to be mistaken. In that case, perhaps he had fallen into a trap that his enemies had set for him, taking advantage of his love for Constance.

His three friends rode up to him. They had all seen a woman's face at the carriage window, but only Athos knew Constance Bonacieux. Less preoccupied than d'Artagnan with that pretty face, Athos thought he had also glimpsed a man in the carriage.

"If so," said d'Artagnan, "they must be taking her from one prison to another. But what do they want to do with that poor woman, and how can I ever find her again?"

"My friend," Athos said gravely, "remember that only the dead are impossible to meet again on this earth. You and I both know that, don't we? If your mistress isn't dead, if she really was the woman you just saw, you'll find her sooner or later. And," he added, with his usual misanthropy, "it may be sooner than you'd like."

It was half-past seven; the carriage had passed later than the time mentioned in the letter. D'Artagnan's friends reminded him that he had another appointment, and at the same time pointed out that it was still not too late to send word that he was unable to keep it.

But he was both stubborn and curious. He had taken it into his head that he would go to the Palais-Cardinal and find out what His Eminence wanted to tell him. Nothing could make him change his decision.

They rode to the Rue Saint-Honoré, and in front of the Palais-Cardinal they found the twelve musketeers Porthos had asked to come there. Only now was the situation explained to them.

The musketeers all knew that d'Artagnan would some day be one of them, so they regarded him as a comrade in advance and enthusiastically agreed to do what was expected of them, especially since it would probably give them a chance to inflict a defeat on the cardinal and his men.

Athos divided them into three groups, one led by himself, another by Aramis, and the third by Porthos, then each group went to keep watch on one of the palace gates.

D'Artagnan bravely walked in through the main entrance. Even though he knew he could count on vigorous support in case of danger, he was not without anxiety as he climbed the great staircase. His conduct toward Milady bore a certain resemblance to treachery, and he suspected that she was politically allied with the cardinal. Furthermore, de Wardes, whom he had treated so badly, was one of the cardinal's faithful partisans, and d'Artagnan knew that while His Eminence was ruthless against his enemies, he was also loyal to his friends.

"If de Wardes has told the cardinal about what happened between us, as he surely has, and if the cardinal has recognized me in the story, which is likely, I'm doomed," thought d'Artagnan, shaking his head. "But why didn't he send for me sooner? It must be because Milady has complained to him about me, with the hypocritical sorrow that can make her so appealing, and he felt that my latest crime was the last straw. Luckily my friends are waiting outside; they'll fight to save me if the cardinal tries to have me taken away. But Monsieur de Tréville's musketeers can't wage war against the cardinal by themselves. He has the whole army at his disposal, the queen is powerless against him, and the king is too weak-willed to resist him. D'Artagnan, my friend, you're brave, you have all sorts of good qualities, but women will be your downfall!"

He had just reached this sad conclusion when he came into the anteroom. He handed his letter to the usher on duty, who led him into the waiting room and then left.

There were five or six of the cardinal's guards in the waiting room. Recognizing d'Artagnan as the man who had wounded Jussac, they looked at him and smiled in a way that seemed ominous to him. But he was not easily intimidated; or at least, with his Gascon pride, he did not show his feelings if there was anything like fear in them. He stood boldly in front of the guards with one hand on his hip, in a pose that had a certain majesty about it.

The usher returned and told d'Artagnan to follow him. As he left the waiting room, it seemed to d'Artagnan that the guards were whispering to each other.

He walked along a hall, through a big drawing room, and into a library, where he found himself facing a man writing at a desk.

The usher left without a word. At first d'Artagnan thought the man at the desk might be a judge examining a dossier, but then he saw that he was writing, or rather revising, lines of uneven length and scanning them by tapping his fingers. The man was a poet. After a few moments he closed his manuscript, whose title was written on its cover: *Mirame, a Tragedy in Five Acts*.

He looked up, and d'Artagnan recognized the cardinal.

40

The Cardinal

The cardinal rested his elbow on his manuscript and his cheek on his hand, and looked at the young man a long time. No one had a more deeply penetrating gaze than Cardinal Richelieu. D'Artagnan felt ill at ease, but he put up a good front, holding his hat in his hand and waiting with neither too much pride nor too much humility.

"Are you one of the d'Artagnans of Béarn?" asked the cardinal.

"Yes, Monseigneur."

"There are several branches of the family in Tarbes and the surrounding area. Which one do you belong to?"

"I'm the son of the d'Artagnan who fought in the religious wars with the great King Henry, father of His Gracious Majesty."

"Ah, yes . . . So you're the one who left home seven or eight months ago to seek your fortune in Paris?"

"Yes, Monseigneur."

"You came by way of Meung and something happened to you there; I don't remember exactly what it was, but I know something happened."

"I'll tell you about it, Monseigneur. I . . ."

"Never mind," the cardinal said with a smile that showed that he knew the story as well as d'Artagnan himself did. "You had a letter of introduction to Monsieur de Tréville, didn't you?"

"Yes, Monseigneur, but in that unfortunate incident at Meung . . ."

"The letter was lost, I know. But Monsieur de Tréville is a good judge of character. He can size up a man at first sight. He placed you in the company of his brother-in-law, Monsieur des Essarts, and gave you hope of being able to become a musketeer some day."

"You're very well informed, Monseigneur."

"Since then, many things have happened to you. You took a stroll behind the Carmes-Deschaux monastery one day when it would have been better for you to be elsewhere. Then you went with your friends to take the waters at Forges; they stopped along the way, but you went on traveling until you reached England. You had business there.''

"Monseigneur," said d'Artagnan, taken aback, "I went . . .''

"You went hunting at Windsor, or somewhere else; it doesn't concern anyone but you. I know about it because it's my duty to know everything. When you came back, you paid a visit to a lady of very high rank, and I'm pleased to see that you've kept the present she gave you.''

D'Artagnan was wearing the queen's diamond ring; he quickly turned it around to hide its setting, but it was too late.

"The next day," the Cardinal continued, "Cavois came to see you, but you weren't at home. He left you an invitation to come to the palace. You didn't come; that was a mistake.''

"I was afraid I'd displeased you, Your Eminence.''

"Why? Because you'd carried out your superiors' orders with exceptional courage and intelligence? Why should I have been displeased with you for having done something praiseworthy? I punish people when they don't obey, not when they obey . . . too well. To convince you of that, I'll ask you to remember the day when I sent Cavois to tell you to come and see me, and then remember what happened that night.''

That was the night when Madame Bonacieux was abducted. D'Artagnan shivered; and he recalled seeing the poor woman pass by in a carriage only half an hour earlier, evidently still a captive of the same people who had abducted her.

"Since I hadn't heard anything about you for some time," the cardinal went on, "I wanted to know what you'd been doing. And you have reason to thank me: you must have noticed how gently you've been treated in all circumstances.''

D'Artagnan bowed respectfully.

"I've been lenient with you not only because I have a natural sense of fairness," said the cardinal, "but also because I have plans for you.''

D'Artagnan listened with increasing surprise.

"I wanted to tell you about those plans on the day when you received my first invitation, but you didn't come. Fortunately nothing has been lost by that delay, and I'm now going to tell you what I have in mind. Sit down, Monsieur d'Artagnan; a man from a family as noble as yours doesn't need to remain standing in my presence.''

The cardinal pointed out a chair to d'Artagnan, who was so astonished by the turn the conversation had taken that he did not sit down till His Eminence had repeated his gesture.

"You're brave, Monsieur d'Artagnan, and you're also prudent, which is even better. I like men who have both intelligence and courage. But you're young and inexperienced, and you have strong enemies; if you're not careful, they'll crush you."

"I'm afraid that won't be hard for them to do, Monseigneur," replied d'Artagnan, "because they have powerful connections and I have none."

"Yes, that's true; but even without connections you've already done a great deal, and I'm sure you'll do still more. However, I think you need to be guided in the adventurous course you've chosen, because unless I'm mistaken you came to Paris with the ambitious idea of making your fortune."

"I'm still at the age of foolish hopes, Monseigneur."

"Foolish hopes are only for fools, and you're a clever man, Monsieur d'Artagnan. What would you say if I offered to make you a lieutenant in my guards, and place you in command of a company after the campaign?"

"Oh, Monseigneur!"

"Then you accept my offer?"

"Well, Monseigneur . . ." d'Artagnan said with a look of embarrassment.

"What!" exclaimed the cardinal. "You refuse?"

"I'm in His Majesty's guards, Monseigneur, and I have no reason to regret it."

"But my guards are also His Majesty's, and a man who belongs to any French corps is serving the king."

"You misunderstood me, Your Eminence."

"You want an excuse for leaving His Majesty's guards, is that it? Very well: the campaign is about to begin and I'm offering you a promotion. That's your public reason, the one you can give to the world. There's also a private reason: you need protection. It's time you knew, Monsieur d'Artagnan, that I've received serious complaints against you. You don't spend all your days and nights in the king's service."

D'Artagnan's face flushed.

"I have a whole dossier on you," the cardinal continued, putting his hand on a stack of papers. "But I wanted to talk with you before I read it. You're a tenacious, strong-willed young man. If you're given proper guidance, you can rise to great heights, rather than stumbling into pitfalls. Think it over."

"I'm overwhelmed by your kindness, Monseigneur, but if you'll allow me to speak frankly . . ."

D'Artagnan stopped.

"Go on," said the cardinal.

"Your Eminence, all my friends are in either the musketeers or His Majesty's guards, and for some reason that I'm at a loss to explain, all my enemies are in your service, so if I accepted your offer I'd be unwelcome to the men around me and my friends would look down on me."

"Are you so arrogant as to think that I'm not offering you as much as you're worth?" the cardinal asked with a scornful smile.

"Not at all, Your Eminence; the fact is that I don't think I've yet done enough to be worthy of your kindness. You'll be able to watch me during the siege of La Rochelle. If I'm lucky enough to distinguish myself in some way, I'll feel I've earned the right to be honored by your protection. I don't want to act prematurely. Later, I may be entitled to give you my services, but now I'd seem to be selling them to you."

"In other words, you refuse to serve me," the cardinal said with a mixture of resentment and grudging respect. "Very well, then, you're free to keep your same friends and enemies."

"Monseigneur, I . . ."

"I don't hold it against you. I do my best to defend and reward my friends; I owe nothing to my enemies, but I'm going to give you some advice: be very careful, Monsieur d'Artagnan, because your life will be hanging by a thread as soon as I've withdrawn my support from you."

"I'll try to follow your advice, Monseigneur," d'Artagnan replied confidently.

"If something . . . unfortunate should happen to you later," Richelieu said pointedly, "remember that I sent for you and did what I could to prevent it."

D'Artagnan put his hand over his heart and bowed.

"No matter what happens, Your Eminence, I'll always be grateful to you for what you've offered me."

"We'll see each other after the campaign, Monsieur d'Artagnan," said the cardinal. He pointed to the magnificent armor he was going to wear. "I'll be at La Rochelle, and I'll have my eye on you. We'll settle things between us when we come back."

"Please spare me the burden of your disfavor, Monseigneur," said d'Artagnan. "Be neutral toward me, if you feel that I've behaved honorably."

"Young man," said Richelieu, "if I can again tell you what I've told you this evening, I promise you that I will."

These words expressed a terrible doubt; they alarmed d'Artagnan more than a threat would have done, because they were a warning. The cardinal was trying to save him from some danger that hung over him. D'Artagnan opened his mouth to reply, but the cardinal dismissed him with a haughty gesture.

D'Artagnan stood up and walked toward the door. When he reached it, he felt such sudden apprehension that he nearly turned back. But then the image of Athos's stern face came into his mind: if he accepted the pact that the cardinal had offered him, Athos would never again take his hand, Athos would disown him.

It was this fear that held him back; such is the powerful influence that a man of truly great character exercises on everyone around him.

D'Artagnan went downstairs. At the main gate of the palace he found Athos and his four musketeers. They had begun to worry as they waited for d'Artagnan to return. He reassured them with a few words, and Planchet hurried off to tell the others that they could now leave their posts because his master had come out of the Palais-Cardinal safe and sound.

When the four friends were back in Athos's apartment, Aramis and Porthos asked d'Artagnan to explain the reason for that strange summons. He replied only that the cardinal had sent for him to offer to take him into his guards with the rank of lieutenant, and that he had refused.

"And you were right!" Porthos and Aramis said in unison.

Athos seemed lost in thought and remained silent. Later, however, when he was alone with d'Artagnan, he said to him, "You did what you had to do. But maybe it was a mistake."

D'Artagnan sighed; he had a presentiment that disaster lay in store for him, and that feeling was strengthened by what Athos had just said.

The next day was spent in making preparations to leave. D'Artagnan went to say good-bye to Monsieur de Tréville. At that time it was thought that the separation of the guards and the musketeers would be only temporary; the king had summoned Parliament for that day and was to leave the next day. So Monsieur de Tréville merely asked d'Artagnan if he needed anything. D'Artagnan proudly replied that he lacked nothing.

That night there was a gathering of all the musketeers and all the guards of Monsieur des Essarts's company who had made friends with each other. They were about to be separated, and God alone knew when or if they would meet again. It was a tumultuous night, for in such cases great unconcern is the only remedy for great apprehension.

At the first sound of the trumpets the next morning, the friends parted. The musketeers went to Monsieur de Tréville's house, the guards to Monsieur des Essarts's. Each commander took his company to the Louvre to be inspected by the king.

The king looked gloomy and ill. He had been stricken with a fever the day before, during a formal session of Parliament. He was nevertheless determined to leave that evening. Though he had been advised against it, he insisted on inspecting his troops, hoping that he could overcome his illness by ignoring it.

When the inspection was over, the guards marched off. The musketeers were under orders to remain behind and leave later with the king.

This gave Porthos a chance to show off his superb equipment on the Rue aux Ours. Madame Coquenard saw him riding past on his beautiful horse, wearing his new uniform. She loved him too much to let him leave without saying good-bye, so she motioned him to stop and come into her house.

Porthos was magnificent; his spurs jingled, his armor gleamed and his sword swung boldly at his side. This time he looked so ferocious that the clerks had no inclination to laugh.

He was taken to Monsieur Coquenard, whose little gray eyes flashed with anger when he saw his new cousin. But one thing consoled him: everyone said it was going to be a hard-fought campaign, and he secretly hoped that Porthos would be killed in it.

Porthos paid his respects to Monsieur Coquenard and bade him good-bye. Monsieur Coquenard wished him all sorts of good luck. As for Madame Coquenard, she could not hold back her tears; but no shameful conclusions were drawn from her sorrow because it was known that she was strongly attached to her relatives and that they had always been a subject of painful discord between her and Monsieur Coquenard.

But the real farewells took place in her bedroom, and they were heartrending.

As she watched Porthos ride away she waved her handkerchief to him from a window and seemed on the verge of jumping out to run after him. He took this as a matter of course, giving the impression that he was used to such demonstrations of tender feeling. Only when he was about to turn the corner did he take off his hat and wave back to her.

Meanwhile Aramis was writing a long letter. To whom? No

one knew. Kitty was in the next room, waiting for that mysterious letter. She was to leave for Tours that evening.

Athos was slowly drinking up his last bottle of Spanish wine.

D'Artagnan was riding with his company. When they reached the Faubourg Saint-Antoine he turned around to look lightheartedly at the Bastille. But since his attention was focused on the Bastille, he did not see Milady. Sitting on a bay horse, she pointed him out to two sinister-looking men who immediately moved closer to him to make sure they would recognize him later. When they gave her a questioning glance, she nodded to let them know that they had singled out the right man. Then, satisfied that her orders would be executed without mistake, she spurred her horse and disappeared.

The two men followed the company on foot. As they were leaving the Faubourg Saint-Antoine, they mounted two horses that an unliveried servant had been holding while he waited for them.

41

The Siege of La Rochelle

The siege of La Rochelle was one of the great political events in the reign of Louis XIII and one of the cardinal's great military undertakings. We must say a few words about it because some of its details are so important to our story that we cannot pass over them in silence.

The cardinal had momentous political aims when he began the siege. We will examine them first, and then consider the personal aims that may have been equally important to him.

Of the large towns given to the Huguenots as places of safety by Henry IV, only La Rochelle remained. It was the last bulwark of Calvinism, a dangerous leaven that was constantly mingled with ferments of domestic rebellion and foreign wars, and so it had to be destroyed.

Discontented Spaniards, Englishmen, and Italians, adventurers from all nations and soldiers of fortune from every sect flocked to the banners of the Protestants and formed a vast association with branches all over Europe.

La Rochelle, which had taken on new importance with the ruin of the other Calvinist towns, was thus a hotbed of dissension and ambition. Furthermore, its harbor was the last door open to the English in all of France; in closing it to England, France's eternal enemy, the cardinal was completing the work of Joan of Arc and the duke de Guise.

And so Bassompierre, one of the military leaders in the siege of La Rochelle, who was a Protestant by conviction and a Catholic as commander of the Order of the Holy Spirit, German by birth and French in his heart, said to several other Protestant noblemen as he was about to lead them on a charge, "You'll see, gentlemen: we'll be foolish enough to take La Rochelle!"

And he was right: the artillery attack on the Ile de Ré presaged the persecution of Protestants in Cévennes; the taking of La Rochelle was a preface to the revocation of the Edict of Nantes.

But, as we have said, in addition to these objectives of the leveling, simplifying statesman, which belong to history, a chronicler must also acknowledge the lesser aims of the jealous rival.

The cardinal, as is well known, had been in love with the queen. We cannot say whether his love had a simple political goal or whether it was one of the deep passions that Anne of Austria aroused in those around her, but in any case we know that the duke of Buckingham had won out over him before the beginning of this story and that in later circumstances, particularly in the affair of the diamond tags, thanks to the three musketeers' devotion and d'Artagnan's courage, the duke had outwitted him.

The cardinal therefore intended to rid France of an enemy and take vengeance on a rival at the same time; and it had to be a resounding vengeance, worthy of a man who wielded the forces of a whole kingdom as if they were his sword.

Richelieu knew that in fighting England he would be fighting Buckingham, that in triumphing over England he would be triumphing over Buckingham, and that in humiliating England in the eyes of Europe he would be humiliating Buckingham in the eyes of the queen.

Buckingham professed concern for the honor of England, but he was also driven by motives similar to the cardinal's. He too was pursuing personal vengeance. Having failed in all his efforts to return to France as an ambassador, he now wanted to return to it as a conqueror.

The first advantage had gone to the duke of Buckingham. He had arrived unexpectedly at the Ile de Ré with ninety ships and twenty thousand men. Count de Toiras, the king's commander on the island, had been taken by surprise, and after a bloody battle Buckingham had made his landing.

Let us note in passing that Baron de Chantal died in that battle, leaving his eighteen-month-old daughter an orphan. That little girl later became Madame de Sévigné.

Count de Toiras withdrew with his garrison to the Saint-Martin citadel and left a hundred men in a little fort called the fort of La Prée.

This had hastened the cardinal's decisions. He and the king were not yet able to go and take command of the siege of La Rochelle, which had already been planned, but the cardinal had sent Monsieur* to direct the first operations and ordered all available troops to go there at once.

D'Artagnan was part of this detachment sent as an advance guard.

The king was to follow as soon as the formal session of Parliament was over, but at the end of that session, on June 28, he had become ill with a fever. He had nevertheless insisted on leaving, but his condition had worsened, and he had been forced to stop at Villeroi.

Wherever the king stopped, the musketeers stopped also, and so d'Artagnan, who was only in the guards, found himself temporarily separated from his friends Athos, Porthos, and Aramis. Though he regarded that separation only as an annoyance, he would have been seriously worried by it if he had known the dangers that surrounded him.

He arrived safely, however, on September 10, 1627, at the camp before La Rochelle.

The situation was unchanged: the duke of Buckingham and his English troops, masters of the Ile de Ré, were still unsuccessfully besieging the Saint-Martin citadel and the fort of La Prée. Hostilities with La Rochelle had begun two or three days earlier, prompted by a fort that the duke d'Angoulême had just built near the town.

Monsieur des Essarts's company of guards were billeted at Les Minimes.

Because he was so absorbed in his ambition to be a musketeer that he had made few friends among his companions in the guards, d'Artagnan was now left alone with his thoughts.

They were not cheerful thoughts. Since his arrival in Paris a

---

*Title given to the king's oldest brother. (Translator's note.)

year earlier, he had become involved in public affairs, but his private affairs, so far as love and fortune were concerned, had made little headway.

Madame Bonacieux, the only woman he loved, had disappeared, and he had been unable to discover what had become of her.

He had made an enemy of the cardinal, before whom the most powerful men in the kingdom trembled, including the king himself. The cardinal could crush him, but had not done so. To a mind as shrewd as d'Artagnan's, that indulgence was a hopeful sign for the future.

He had also made another enemy, less powerful than the cardinal, but one he instinctively felt was not to be taken lightly: Milady.

In exchange for all that, he had acquired the protection and goodwill of the queen; but as things stood at that time, her goodwill was only another cause of persecution, and her protection protected very little: witness Chalais and Madame Bonacieux.

His most certain gain was the diamond ring, worth five or six thousand livres, that he wore on his finger. If he kept it for the future, however, hoping to further his ambition someday by using it as a sign of recognition with the queen, he could not sell it, and so it was now worth no more to him than the pebbles he stepped on.

We say "than the pebbles he stepped on" because these thoughts had come to him as he was taking a solitary walk along the little road that led from the camp to the village of Angoutin. His thoughts had taken him farther than he had intended. Twilight was approaching when, in the rays of the setting sun, he thought he saw the glitter of a musket barrel behind a hedge.

Quick-witted as always, he realized that the musket had not come there by itself and that the man holding it had not hidden behind a hedge with friendly intentions. He had just decided to take to his heels when he saw the muzzle of a second musket on the other side of the road, behind a rock.

It was obviously an ambush.

He glanced at the first musket and was alarmed to see that it was being turned in his direction. As soon as it stopped, he threw himself to the ground. A shot was fired, and he heard a bullet whine past above him.

There was no time to lose. He leapt to his feet, and an instant later a bullet from the other musket sent up a spray of pebbles from the spot where he had been lying.

D'Artagnan was not one of those uselessly brave men who

seek a ridiculous death in order to have it said of them that they stood firm in the face of danger. And besides, courage was not called for here, since he had fallen into an ambush.

"If there's a third shot," he thought, "I'm lost!"

He began running back toward the camp, with a speed that justified the Gascons' reputation for agility. But the man who had fired first had now had time to reload. He shot again, this time so accurately that the bullet went through d'Artagnan's hat and sent it flying ten paces in front of him. Since it was the only hat he had, he picked it up as he ran.

He reached his quarters pale and out of breath, sat down without saying anything to anyone, and began thinking.

There were three possible explanations for the ambush.

The most natural one was that he had been attacked by enemy soldiers, who would have been glad to kill one of His Majesty's guards, not only because it would reduce the number of their enemies by one, but also because he might have a well-filled purse in his pocket.

D'Artagnan took off his hat, examined the bullet hole in it and shook his head: the bullet was not of the right caliber to have come from a military weapon; the accuracy of the shot had already given him the idea that it had been fired from a civilian's gun. So he had not been attacked by soldiers.

The ambush might have been a little surprise from the cardinal. It will be recalled that just before the providential ray of sunlight had enabled him to see the musket barrel, d'Artagnan had been thinking about the cardinal's seemingly inexplicable forbearance toward him. But again he shook his head: His Eminence seldom resorted to such methods with people he could put out of the way by simpler means.

It might have been an act of vengeance on Milady's part. That seemed more likely. He tried to remember something about the two men who had shot at him: their faces, their clothes; but he had run away so quickly that he had not had time to see them clearly. He thought of his three absent friends and murmured, "How I wish you were here! How I need you now!"

He spent a bad night. Three or four times he awoke with a start, imagining that someone was coming toward his bed to stab him. Daylight finally came; nothing had happened during the hours of darkness, but he strongly suspected that he had only been given a reprieve that could end at any moment.

He remained in his quarters all day. The excuse he gave himself was that the weather was bad.

*   *   *

Two days later, at nine o'clock in the morning, the drums beat a general salute. The duke d'Orléans was inspecting the posts. The guards assembled under arms and d'Artagnan took his place among his companions.

Monsieur passed down the ranks, then all the senior officers, including Monsieur des Essarts, approached him to pay him their respects.

A few moments later it seemed to d'Artagnan that Monsieur des Essarts was motioning him to come over to him. He waited, fearing he might have been mistaken. When Monsieur des Essarts repeated his gesture, d'Artagnan stepped toward him to receive his orders.

"Monsieur is going to ask for volunteers for a dangerous mission that will bring honor to those who carry it out. Be ready."

"Thank you, sir!" replied d'Artagnan, who asked nothing better then to distinguish himself in the eyes of the lieutenant general.

The enemy had made a sortie during the night and recaptured a bastion that the Royalist army had captured two days earlier. A patrol was needed to go and see how the bastion was being guarded.

A few moments later Monsieur raised his voice and said, "For this mission I'll need three or four volunteers led by a reliable man."

"I have the leader for you, sir," said Monsieur des Essarts, pointing to d'Artagnan. "As for the other volunteers, you have only to make your intentions known and you'll have more men than you need."

"Four volunteers to come and face death with me!" said d'Artagnan, raising his sword.

Two of his companions in the guards immediately came forward, and they were joined by two soldiers. Feeling that these were enough, d'Artagnan refused all others, not wanting to be unfair to the first four who had volunteered.

It was not known whether, after recapturing the bastion, the enemy had evacuated it or left a garrison in it. It would have to be examined from rather close range to find out.

D'Artagnan set off with his four men and followed the trench. The two guards walked abreast of him while the two soldiers brought up the rear.

Taking cover behind the revetments, they were able to come

within a hundred paces of the bastion. There, d'Artagnan looked back and saw that the two soldiers had disappeared. He assumed they had become frightened and stayed behind. He and the two others continued to move forward.

At a bend in the counterscarp, they found themselves about sixty paces from the stone bastion. It seemed abandoned. They were discussing whether to go any closer when suddenly a ring of smoke encircled the bastion and a dozen bullets whizzed past them.

Now that they knew the bastion was guarded, there was nothing to be gained by staying in that dangerous place any longer. They turned around and began a hurried withdrawal.

When they reached the corner of the trench that was going to serve as their rampart, one of the guards fell with a bullet in his chest. The other, unscathed, continued running toward the camp.

D'Artagnan did not want to abandon his companion. He bent down to help him return to safety, but just then two shots were fired. One bullet struck the wounded guard in the head and the other flattened itself against a rock after passing within two inches of d'Artagnan.

He spun around, because the attack could not have come from the bastion, which was hidden behind the angle of the trench. He thought of the two soldiers who had left him, and suddenly realized that they reminded him of the men who had tried to kill him two days before. He decided that this time he would find out who his attackers were. He fell across the body of his companion as though he were dead.

He saw two heads rise above an abandoned outwork thirty paces away and recognized the two soldiers. His suspicion was justified: they had come with him only to murder him, hoping his death would be attributed to the enemy. Since he might be only wounded, and therefore able to denounce their crime, they were now coming to finish him off if necessary. Luckily, however, taken in by his ruse, they had neglected to reload their muskets.

When they were ten paces away, d'Artagnan leapt to his feet and rushed toward them, holding the sword he had been careful not to let go of when he fell.

They realized that if they ran back to camp without having killed him, he would report what they had done, so their first thought was to pass over to the enemy. One of them took his musket by the barrel and swung it at d'Artagnan, using it as a club. D'Artagnan dodged the blow, but his movement allowed the soldier to slip past him and run toward the bastion. Since its

defenders did not know why he was coming to them, they fired
at him and he fell with his shoulder broken by a bullet.

Meanwhile d'Artagnan had attacked the second soldier with his
sword. The fight did not last long because his adversary had only
his unloaded musket with which to defend himself. D'Artagnan's
sword slipped along the barrel of the useless weapon and pierced
the murderer's thigh. He fell. D'Artagnan put the point of his
sword to his throat.

"Don't kill me!" cried the soldier. "Spare me, sir! I'll tell
you everything!"

"Is your secret valuable enough to make it worthwhile for me
to let you go on living?" asked d'Artagnan, withdrawing his
sword.

"Yes, if you think life is valuable to a man who's young,
brave, and handsome, as you are."

"Then talk quickly. Who sent you to kill me?"

"A woman. I don't know her, but she's called Milady."

"If you don't know her, how do you know her name?"

"My friend knew her and that's what he called her. She dealt
with him, not me. He has a letter from her in his pocket. From
what I've heard, that letter would be very interesting to you."

"How did you become involved in that ambush?"

"He offered to take me into it with him and I agreed."

"And how much did she give you for that noble mission?"

"A hundred louis."

"I'm glad to know she thinks I'm worth something!" said
d'Artagnan, laughing. "A hundred louis! That's a huge sum of
money to men like you two, so I can understand why you
accepted her offer and I'll spare you, but on one condition."

"What condition?" the soldier asked uneasily.

"I want you to bring me the letter your friend has in his
pocket."

"That's only another way of killing me! How do you expect
me to go and get that letter under fire from the bastion?"

"If you don't, you'll die here."

"Please don't kill me, sir!" cried the soldier. He rose to his
knees but had to support himself with one hand because he was
weakened by loss of blood from his wound. "Spare me for the
sake of the lady you love! You may think she's dead, but she's
not!"

"How did you know I loved a lady and thought she was
dead?"

"From the letter in my friend's pocket."

"Then I'm more determined than ever to have that letter. I won't wait any longer. I don't like the thought of dirtying my sword again with the blood of a vile scoundrel like you, but I swear I will if you don't do as I say."

With these words, d'Artagnan made such a threatening gesture that the soldier quickly stood up in spite of his wound.

"Stop!" he said, gaining courage from his fear. "I'll go! I'll go!"

D'Artagnan took the soldier's gun, which was not a military musket, and drove him toward his companion by pricking him in the back with his sword.

Already pale from the death that he felt awaited him, the soldier left a trail of blood behind him as he tried to crawl to his accomplice's body without being seen. He had broken into a cold sweat, and he seemed so terrified that d'Artagnan took pity on him, looked at him scornfully, and said, "I'm going to show you the difference between a brave man and a coward like you. Stay here, I'll go."

Moving stealthily, watching the enemy's movements, and taking advantage of every irregularity in the ground, d'Artagnan made his way to the other soldier.

There were two ways he could accomplish his purpose: he could either search the man where he lay or carry him back, using his body as a shield, and search him in the trench.

He chose the second way. The enemy opened fire just as he picked the man up on his shoulders. A slight jolt, the dull sound of three bullets burying themselves in flesh, a last cry and a death tremor proved to d'Artagnan that the man who had tried to kill him had just saved his life.

He returned to the trench and dropped the corpse beside the deathly pale wounded man.

His search yielded a leather wallet, a purse that obviously contained part of the money the assassin had been paid, a dice box, and a pair of dice. He left the box and the dice where they had fallen on the ground, tossed the purse to the wounded man, and eagerly opened the wallet.

Among some unimportant papers, he found the letter that he had risked his life to get:

Since you lost track of the woman and she is now safe in a convent that you should never have let her reach, try at least not to let the man escape you. If you do, I will make you pay dearly for the hundred louis you received from me. This is no idle threat, as you well know.

No signature. But it was obvious that the letter was from Milady, and d'Artagnan decided to keep it as evidence against her. Sheltered in the trench, he began questioning the wounded man, who confessed that he and his companion, the one who had just been killed, had agreed to abduct a young woman who was to leave Paris by way of the La Villette gate, but that they had stopped for a drink in a tavern and missed the carriage by ten minutes.

"But what were you going to do with that woman?" d'Artagnan asked anxiously.

"We were supposed to take her to a house on the Place Royale."

"Ah, yes," murmured d'Artagnan, "Milady's house!"

He shuddered when he realized the terrible thirst for revenge that drove Milady to destroy him and those who loved him, and how much she knew about court affairs, since she had discovered everything. She probably owed her information to the cardinal.

But he was elated to know that the queen had finally learned where Madame Bonacieux was being held prisoner because of her devotion and had succeeded in freeing her. He now understood the letter he had received from Madame Bonacieux, and her brief appearance on the Chaillot road.

Athos had proved to be right: d'Artagnan could find her again. And a convent was not impregnable.

This thought put him in a benevolent mood. He turned to the wounded man, who had been anxiously watching all the expressions on his face, and held out his arm to him.

"I won't abandon you here," he said. "Lean on me and we'll go back to camp."

It was hard for the soldier to believe in this magnanimity.

"But will you have me hanged when we get there?" he asked.

"No, I give you my word. I'm sparing your life for the second time."

The wounded man knelt to kiss his savior's feet, but d'Artagnan, no longer having any reason for staying so close to the enemy, cut short that demonstration of gratitude.

The guard who had run back to camp when the enemy first opened fire had reported that his four companions were dead, so there was surprise and joy in the regiment when d'Artagnan was seen returning safely.

He explained his companion's sword wound by inventing a sortie from the bastion, described the death of the other soldier, and told of the dangers they had faced. His story was a triumph

for him. The whole army talked about it for the rest of the day,
and Monsieur sent his congratulations.

And since every good deed has its reward, d'Artagnan's le-
niency had the effect of giving him back the peace of mind he
had lost. He felt there was no longer any need for him to worry,
because one of his two attackers was dead and the other was now
devoted to him.

His serenity proved one thing: he did not yet know Milady.

42

The Anjou Wine

The alarming reports on the king's condition finally gave way to
rumors of his convalescence; and it was said that since he was
eager to be at the scene of the siege in person, he would go there
as soon as he was again able to ride a horse.

Knowing that he would soon be replaced at the head of the
army by the duke d'Angoulême, Bassompierre, or Schomberg,
who were vying with each other for the position of commander,
Monsieur did little beyond sending out patrols to prove the
enemy's strength. He held back from taking any decisive action
to drive the English from the Ile de Ré, where they were still
besieging the Saint-Martin citadel and the fort of La Prée while
the French continued to besiege La Rochelle.

As we have said, d'Artagnan's mind was more at ease, now
that the danger from Milady seemed to have passed. His only
concern was that he had not heard from his friends.

But one morning, early in November, everything was explained by this letter, sent from Villeroi:

Monsieur d'Artagnan,
  *After amusing themselves greatly in my establishment
one night, Messieurs Athos, Porthos, and Aramis caused
such a commotion that the provost marshal, a very strict
man, had them confined to quarters for several days. I
am now obeying their order to send you a dozen bottles*

of my Anjou wine, which they appreciated highly. They want you to drink to their health with their favorite wine.

   Your respectful and obedient servant,
                    Godeau,
         Innkeeper to the Musketeers

"That makes me feel better!" exclaimed d'Artagnan. "They think of me when they're enjoying themselves, just as I think of them in my boredom! I'll gladly drink to their health, but I won't do it alone."

He went to two guards with whom he had become friendlier than with the others and invited them to share the delicious Anjou wine that had just arrived from Villeroi. One of them already had an invitation for that evening, the other had one for the following evening, and so they agreed to meet two days later.

As soon as d'Artagnan returned to his quarters, he had the twelve bottles of wine sent to an inn, with orders that it be carefully kept for him there.

At nine o'clock in the morning of the day when the meal was planned for noon, he sent Planchet to make all the preparations. Proud of having been raised to the rank of majordomo, Planchet was determined to perform his duties well. He enlisted the aid of Fourreau, the servant of one of d'Artagnan's guests, and Brisemont, the false soldier who had tried to kill d'Artagnan. Belonging to no unit, Brisemont had been in d'Artagnan's service, or rather Planchet's, ever since his life had been spared.

The two guests arrived and took their places at the heavily laden table. Planchet served the food with a napkin draped over his arm, Fourreau uncorked the bottles, and Brisemont poured the wine into glass decanters. It seemed to have deposited a sediment as the result of having been shaken during the journey. The first bottle was a little turbid. Brisemont poured the dregs into a glass, and d'Artagnan let him drink it, for he was still quite weak.

The guests had eaten their soup and were about to take their first sip of the wine when suddenly they heard cannons firing from Fort Louis and Fort Neuf. Thinking there had been a surprise attack by either the English or the troops in the besieged town, they seized their swords. D'Artagnan followed suit, and the three of them ran out to go to their posts.

But as soon as they were outside the inn, they learned the cause of the tumult: they heard drums beating and shouts of "Long live the king!" and "Long live the cardinal!" from all directions.

The king, impatient to be at the scene of the siege, had traveled without stopping in the last part of his journey and had just arrived with his whole household and ten thousand troops. He was preceded and followed by his musketeers. Standing along the line of march with his company, d'Artagnan greeted his friends with an expressive gesture, which they answered with their eyes. He also greeted Monsieur de Tréville, who recognized him as he passed.

When the reception ceremony was over, d'Artagnan and his friends embraced each other.

"You couldn't have come at a better time," said d'Artagnan. "The food hasn't even had time to get cold. Isn't that right, gentlemen?" he added, turning to the two guards, whom he introduced to his friends.

"Ah, so we're having a banquet!" said Porthos.

"I hope you haven't invited any women," said Aramis.

"Is there any drinkable wine here?" asked Athos.

"Of course!" replied d'Artagnan. "I still have your wine."

Athos seemed surprised.

"*Our* wine?"

"Yes, the wine you sent me."

"We sent you some wine?"

"Yes, that good Anjou."

"I know the kind you mean, but . . ."

"It's your favorite."

"I suppose it is, when I have neither champagne nor Chambertin."

"Well, since there's no champagne or Chambertin here, you'll have to be satisfied with Anjou."

"So you sent for some Anjou, did you?" said Porthos. "I always knew you were a gourmet!"

"No, *I* didn't send for it, *you* did. I mean, you had it sent to me."

"Was it you who had it sent, Aramis?" asked Athos.

"No. And you, Porthos?"

"No. And you, Athos?"

"No."

"It came from your innkeeper," said d'Artagnan.

"Our innkeeper?"

"Yes. He signed his letter 'Godeau, Innkeeper to the Musketeers.'"

"I don't care where it came from," said Porthos. "Let's taste it, and if it's good, we'll drink it."

"No," said Athos, "let's not drink wine from an unknown source."

"You're right, Athos," said d'Artagnan. "None of you told Godeau to send me wine?"

"No. But he claimed we told him to send it?"

"Here's his letter!" said d'Artagnan.

And he handed it to his friends.

"He didn't write this!" exclaimed Athos. "I know his handwriting because I'm the one who paid his bill before we left."

"It's a false letter," said Porthos. "We weren't confined to quarters."

"D'Artagnan," Aramis said reproachfully, "how could you have believed that we caused a commotion?"

D'Artagnan turned pale and trembled convulsively.

"What's the matter?" Athos asked with concern.

"Come, my friends, hurry!" said d'Artagnan. "I have a horrible suspicion! Could it be that woman's vengeance again?"

Athos also turned pale.

D'Artagnan ran back to the inn, followed by the three musketeers and the two guards.

The first thing he saw when he went into the dining room was Brisemont writhing on the floor. Planchet and Fourreau were trying to help him, but it was obvious that he was beyond help: his contracted features showed that he had begun his death agony.

"You pretended to spare my life," he cried out when he saw d'Artagnan, "and then you poisoned me!"

"I poisoned you? What are you saying?"

"I'm saying you gave me that wine and told me to drink it because you wanted to kill me for revenge!"

"You mustn't believe that, Brisemont, I swear . . ."

"God will punish you! Dear God, make him suffer some day the way I'm suffering now!"

"I swear I didn't know that wine was poisoned!" said d'Artagnan, rushing over to him. "I was going to drink it too!"

"I don't believe you," said Brisemont. And he died in a final spasm of pain.

"It's abominable!" murmured Athos, while Porthos broke the

bottles and Aramis gave somewhat belated orders to go and bring a confessor.

"My friends, you've saved my life again!" said d'Artagnan. "And you've saved these gentlemen's lives too." He turned to the two guards. "Gentlemen, I ask you to keep silent about all this. Powerful people may be involved in it and we'll all be safer if we say nothing about it."

"Oh, sir, I . . . I had a narrow escape!" stammered Planchet, looking as if he were more dead than alive.

"What! You were going to drink my wine?" d'Artagnan said sternly.

"I was going to drink just one little glass, sir, to the king's health. But before I could do it, Fourreau told me someone was asking for me."

"I wanted to get him out of the way so I could drink the wine myself," Fourreau admitted, his teeth chattering with terror.

"Gentlemen," said d'Artagnan, speaking to the guards again, "I'm sure you realize that a feast after what's just happened could only be gloomy, so please accept my apology and let me postpone our meal to another day."

The guards courteously accepted his apology. Then, seeing that the four friends wanted to be alone together, they left.

D'Artagnan and the three musketeers looked at each other with an expression that showed that they knew the seriousness of the situation.

"First of all," said Athos, "let's leave this room. A dead man is a bad companion, especially one who died a violent death."

"Planchet," said d'Artagnan, "see to it that this poor devil is buried in hallowed ground. He committed a crime, it's true, but he repented of it."

The four friends walked out, leaving Planchet and Fourreau to handle the details of Brisemont's burial.

The innkeeper gave them another room and served them hard-boiled eggs. Athos went to bring water from the fountain. In a few words, d'Artagnan described the situation to Porthos and Aramis.

"As you can see," he said to Athos, "it's war to the death."

Athos nodded. "Yes, I see. But are you sure she's . . . the woman you think she is?"

"I'm certain."

"I must admit I still have doubts."

"But what about the fleur-de-lis branded on her shoulder?"

"She may be an Englishwoman who committed a crime in France and was branded for it."

"She's your wife, Athos. Don't you remember how closely the two descriptions matched?"

"I never would have thought she was still alive, after I hanged her myself."

D'Artagnan shook his head.

"What are we going to do?" he asked.

"We can't go on like this, with a sword constantly hanging over our heads," said Athos. "We have to put an end to it."

"But how?"

"Try to see her again and settle things with her once and for all. Say to her, 'Either it's peace or it's war! I'll give you my word as a gentleman that I'll never say or do anything against you if you'll swear to remain neutral toward me. Otherwise I'll go to the chancellor, the king, and the executioner, I'll rouse the whole court against you, I'll denounce you as having been branded, I'll have you brought to trial, and if you're acquitted, I'll kill you in the street, as I'd kill a mad dog!' "

"I like that plan," said d'Artagnan. "But how can I see her again?"

"You'll have to wait for a chance. You'll be like a gambler raising his bets during a losing streak: if you can hold out long enough, you're sure to win."

"Yes, but in the meantime we'll be surrounded by murderers, poisoners . . ."

"God has protected us so far," said Athos, "and he'll go on protecting us."

"Maybe we'll come through," said d'Artagnan. "We're men, and we're used to risking our lives. But what about her?" he added in an undertone.

"Who?"

"Constance."

"Ah, yes, Madame Bonacieux!" said Athos. "I was forgetting that you're in love, my poor friend."

"But you told us she's in a convent, according to the letter you found in the dead man's wallet," said Aramis, "so why should you be worried about her? The religious life is deeply rewarding. As soon as the siege is over, I'll . . ."

"Yes, Aramis," Athos interrupted, "we know that the religious life is all you long for."

"I'm a musketeer only temporarily," Aramis said humbly.

"He evidently hasn't heard from his mistress in a long time,"

Athos whispered to d'Artagnan. "Don't pay any attention to him; you know how he is at times like this."

"It seems to me that there's a simple way to rescue Madame Bonacieux," said Porthos.

"What is it?" asked d'Artagnan.

"You say she's in a convent?"

"Yes."

"Well, then, as soon as the siege is over, we'll go there and take her away."

"But first we'll have to know which convent she's in."

"That's true," Porthos acknowledged.

"Now that I think of it," said Athos, "didn't you tell us the queen had chosen the convent for her?"

"That's what I believe, at least."

"Then Porthos can help us."

"How?" asked Porthos.

"Through your marquise, your duchess, your princess; she must have influence in high places."

"Of course she does," said Porthos, "but I think she's a Cardinalist, so we mustn't let her know anything about this."

"I'll find out which convent it is," said Aramis.

"How?" The other three all asked at once.

"Through the queen's chaplain," he answered, blushing. "I'm on close terms with him."

With this assurance the four friends, who had finished their modest meal, parted after agreeing to meet again that evening. D'Artagnan returned to Les Minimes and the three musketeers went to the king's headquarters, where they had to see about having lodgings prepared for them.

43

The Colombier-Rouge Inn

The king was eager to face the enemy, and he had even stronger reasons than the cardinal for hating Buckingham. As soon as he arrived in camp, he began making preparations to drive the English from the Ile de Ré and press the siege of La Rochelle. But he was delayed by the dissension that resulted from

Bassompierre's and Schomberg's opposition to the duke d'An-goulême.

Bassompierre and Schomberg were marshals of France and maintained that they were entitled to command the army under the king's orders. The cardinal knew Bassompierre's Protestant convictions and feared that he might make only halfhearted efforts to defeat the English and the defenders of La Rochelle, his coreligionists. His Eminence therefore supported the duke d'Angoulême, whom the king, at the cardinal's instigation, had promoted to lieutenant general. The upshot of all this was that, to prevent Bassompierre and Schomberg from leaving the army, each of the three men had to be given his own command: Bassompierre's sector was north of the town, from La Leu to Dompierre; the duke d'Angoulême's was east of it, from Dompierre to Périgny; and Schomberg's was to the south, from Périgny to Angoutin.

Monsieur's headquarters were at Dompierre, the king's were sometimes at Etré and sometimes at La Jarrie, and the cardinal's were on the coast, near Pont de La Pierre, in a simple house with no entrenchments. Bassompierre could therefore be watched by Monsieur, the duke d'Angoulême by the king, and Schomberg by the cardinal.

Once these arrangements had been made, the commanders turned their attention to dislodging the English from the island.

It was a favorable time. The English, who needed good food in order to be good soldiers, had been eating only salted meat and stale biscuits, and many of them had fallen ill. Furthermore, since the sea was always rough along the coast at that time of year, scarcely a day went by without the sinking of a small English ship, and at each tide the beach from Pointe de l'Aiguillon to the trench was littered with the wreckage of shallops, feluccas, and other small craft. It was obvious that even if the king's army stayed in camp, Buckingham, who was clinging to the island only out of stubbornness, would sooner or later have to abandon it.

But when Monsieur de Toiras reported that preparations for a new assault were being made in the enemy camp, the king decided it was time for decisive action and gave orders accordingly.

Since our intention is not to write a detailed account of the siege but to describe only those aspects of it that directly concern our story, we will simply say that the operation succeeded, to the great surprise of the king and the great glory of the cardinal. The English, driven back step by step, beaten in all encounters and crushed in the channel of the Ile de Loix, were forced to take to their ships, leaving behind them on the battlefield two thousand men, including five colonels, three lieutenant colonels, two hundred and fifty captains, and twenty noblemen of high rank, as well as four cannons and sixty flags. The flags were taken to Paris by Claude de Saint-Simon and hung from the ceiling of the cathedral of Notre-Dame with great pomp and ceremony.

Te Deums were sung in the French camp, and from there they were repeated all over France.

The cardinal was now free to continue the siege without having anything to fear from the English. But it was only a momentary respite. The capture of one of Buckingham's messengers, a man named Montague, had revealed that the Empire, Spain, England, and Lorraine had formed a league against France. Papers confirming the existence of this league were found in Buckingham's headquarters, which he had been forced to abandon more hurriedly than he expected. According to the cardinal in his memoirs, these papers seriously compromised Madame de Chevreuse, and therefore the queen.

Full responsibility lay on the cardinal's shoulders, for one cannot wield absolute power without being responsible. Night and day he used all the resources of his vast genius to gather every rumor, however slight, from the great kingdoms of Europe.

He was well aware of Buckingham's diligence and hatred. If the league that threatened France should triumph, the cardinal would lose all his influence. Spanish policy and Austrian policy had supporters, and so far no adversaries, in the cabinet at the Louvre; Richelieu—the French minister, the national minister par excellence—would be lost. Although the king obeyed him like a child, he also hated him as a child hates his master, and would abandon him to the vengeance of Monsieur and the queen. So he would be lost, and perhaps France would be lost with him. He had to take steps to prevent all that.

At all hours of the day and night, increasingly numerous messengers came in and out of the little house near Pont de La Pierre where the cardinal had established his residence. Some of them were monks who wore their robes so awkwardly that they were easily recognized as members of the church militant; others were women ill at ease in pages' clothes, with loose trunk hose that did not entirely conceal their curves; still others were men dressed as peasants, with dirty hands, who could be spotted as noblemen from a mile away.

The cardinal also had less pleasant visitors; it was rumored that there had been several attempts to kill him. His enemies claimed that the would-be assassins were acting on his orders and that he had instigated those unsuccessful attempts in order to have a pretext for reprisals, if the need arose; but one should not always believe a minister's enemies any more than the minister himself.

Whether they were genuine or false, the attempts on his life did not prevent the cardinal, whose personal bravery had never been questioned by even his most rabid detractors, from often going out at night, sometimes to give important orders to the duke d'Angoulême, sometimes to confer with the king, and sometimes to meet a messenger he did not want to enter his house.

As for the musketeers, their duties were light because they had little to do with the siege, and they were often free to enjoy themselves as they pleased. This was especially easy for Athos, Porthos, and Aramis: they were friends of Monsieur de Tréville and he usually gave them special permission to stay out later than the time when the camp was closed for the night.

One night when d'Artagnan had been unable to go with them because he was on trench duty, the three musketeers went to the Colombier-Rouge, an inn that Athos had discovered on the La Jarrie road two days earlier. As they rode back toward camp on their battle horses, wearing their uniform cloaks, each of them kept his hand on the butt of his pistol. They were on their guard: an ambush was always possible. When they were about half a mile from the village of Boisnar, they heard hoofbeats coming toward them. They immediately stopped and waited in the middle of the road, close together. Just as the moon came out from behind a cloud, they saw two riders appear at a bend in the road. They too stopped, and seemed to be discussing whether to turn back or continue on their way. Their hesitation made the three friends suspicious. Athos rode forward a few paces and called out, "Who goes there?"

"Who goes there yourself!" replied one of the two riders.

"That's no answer!" said Athos. "Who goes there? Answer, or we'll charge you!"

"Take care what you're about to do, gentlemen!" said a resonant voice that seemed to be accustomed to commanding.

"It must be some high-ranking officer making his night rounds," Athos said to his friends. "What shall we do?"

"Who are you?" said the same voice in the same tone of command. "Answer, or you'll regret your disobedience."

"We're musketeers," replied Athos, more and more convinced that the man who was questioning him had the right to do so.

"Which company?"

"Monsieur de Tréville's."

"Come closer and tell me what you're doing here at this hour."

The three friends rode forward, somewhat crestfallen, for they were now certain that they were dealing with someone of superior rank. Porthos and Aramis were glad to let Athos do the talking.

The rider who had questioned Athos was ten paces in front of his companion. Athos motioned Porthos and Aramis to stop and continued alone.

"Excuse me, sir," he said, "but we didn't know who you were and, as you saw, we were keeping close watch on the road."

"What's your name?" asked the stranger, whose face was partially covered by his cloak.

"But what about you, sir," said Athos, beginning to rebel against this inquisition. "Please give me some proof that you have the right to question me."

"What's your name?" the stranger repeated, letting his cloak fall away from his face.

"The cardinal!" Athos cried out in amazement.

"What's your name?" His Eminence asked for the third time.

"Athos."

The cardinal signaled to his companion, who rode up to him.

"These three musketeers will come with us," he said to him in an undertone. "I don't want it known that I've left the camp. This way, we can be sure they won't tell anyone."

"We're gentlemen, Monseigneur," said Athos. "Ask us for our word to say nothing, and then put your mind at rest. We can keep a secret."

The cardinal fixed his piercing eyes on this bold musketeer.

"You have sharp ears, Monsieur Athos. It's not because I mistrust you that I want you to come with me, it's for my own safety. Your companions are no doubt Monsieur Porthos and Monsieur Aramis, aren't they?"

"Yes, Your Eminence," said Athos, while the two musketeers who had remained behind rode forward with their hats in their hands.

"I know you, gentlemen," said the cardinal. "I know you're

not exactly friends of mine, and I regret it, but I also know that you're brave and loyal gentlemen who can be trusted. Do me the honor of accompanying me, all three of you, and I'll have an escort that even His Majesty will envy, if we should meet him.''

The three musketeers bowed over the necks of their horses.

"You're right to take us with you, Your Eminence," said Athos. "We've seen some unpleasant-looking men on the road and we even had a quarrel with four of them at the Colombier-Rouge.''

"A quarrel?" said the cardinal. "Why? You know I don't like quarrelers.''

"That's precisely why I'm reporting it to you, Your Eminence: otherwise you might hear a false report of it and think we were at fault.''

"And what were the results of that quarrel?" asked the cardinal, frowning.

"My friend Aramis got a slight sword wound in the arm, but that won't prevent him from storming the walls tomorrow, if you should order an escalade.''

"You're not the kind of men to let yourselves be wounded without giving a few wounds in return," said the cardinal. "Be frank, gentlemen, confess. As you know, I have the right to give absolution.''

"For my part, Monseigneur," said Athos, "I didn't even draw my sword, but I did pick up the man I was fighting and throw him out the window. It seems that when he fell," he went on hesitantly, "he broke his leg.''

"I see," said the cardinal. "And you, Monsieur Porthos?"

"Knowing that dueling is forbidden, Monseigneur, I picked up a bench and hit one of those bandits with it. I believe it broke his shoulder.''

"Very well. And you, Monsieur Aramis?"

"Since I have a very gentle nature, Monseigneur, and since, as you may not know, I'm about to take holy orders, I tried to separate my friends from their adversaries, but then one of the scoundrels treacherously plunged his sword into my left arm and I lost patience. I drew my sword just as he was attacking me again, and I believe he spitted himself on it. In any case, he fell, and it seems to me that he was carried away by his two companions.''

"Three men put out of action in a tavern brawl!" exclaimed the cardinal. "You gentlemen don't do things halfway! How did the quarrel start?"

"The wretches were drunk," said Athos. "They knew that a woman had arrived at the inn this evening and they tried to break open her door."

"Break open her door! Why?"

"To do her violence, no doubt. As I said, they were drunk."

"And was the woman young and pretty?" the cardinal asked with a certain anxiety.

"We didn't see her, Monseigneur," said Athos.

"Ah! Very good!" the cardinal said quickly. "You were right to defend a woman's honor, and since the Colombier-Rouge is where I'm going, I'll find out whether you've told me the truth."

"Monseigneur," Athos said proudly, "we're gentlemen and we wouldn't tell a lie to save our lives."

"I know, Monsieur Athos, and I don't doubt for a moment what you've said . . . Tell me, was that lady alone?"

"There was a man in the room with her," said Athos, "but since he didn't come out in spite of all the noise, he's presumably a coward."

"The Scriptures tell us not to judge hastily," said the cardinal.

"And now, gentlemen," His Eminence went on, "I know what I wanted to know. Come with me."

He again wrapped his face in his cloak and rode off, staying nine or ten paces ahead of the four other men.

They soon arrived at the inn. It was silent and deserted; evidently the innkeeper had been expecting his illustrious visitor and had sent away everyone whose presence might have been unwanted.

Just before they reached the door, where a saddled horse was tied, the cardinal motioned his escort to stop. He knocked three times on the door in a certain way.

A man wearing a cloak immediately came out, exchanged a few quick words with the cardinal, mounted the waiting horse and rode off in the direction of Surgères, which was also the direction of Paris.

"Come forward, gentlemen," the cardinal said to the three musketeers. "You told me the truth, and it won't be my fault if our meeting tonight isn't advantageous to you. Meanwhile, follow me."

He dismounted, and so did the three musketeers. He tossed the reins of his horse to his attendant, while the musketeers tied their horses to the window shutter.

The innkeeper was standing on the threshold; to him, the cardinal was only an officer coming to visit a lady.

"Do you have a room on the ground floor where these gentlemen can wait for me in front of a good fire?" asked the cardinal.

The innkeeper opened the door of a spacious room in which a bad stove had recently been replaced with a large and excellent fireplace.

"I have this one," he replied.

"Very well," said the cardinal. "Please wait for me here, gentlemen. I'll be back in no more than half an hour."

And while the three musketeers went into the room on the ground floor, the cardinal began climbing the stairs without asking the innkeeper for directions to where he wanted to go, which showed that he already knew the way.

44

The Usefulness of Stovepipes

It was obvious that although they had acted only because they were chivalrous and always ready for adventure, the three musketeers had helped someone the cardinal honored with his personal protection.

Who was that someone? They wondered about it for a time, then gave up, unable to think of a satisfactory answer. Porthos called the innkeeper and asked for a pair of dice.

Porthos and Aramis sat down at a table and began playing. Athos paced back and forth, thinking. As he did so, he repeatedly passed the stovepipe that had been broken in the middle. Its other end was in the room above. Each time he passed it, he heard a hum of voices. Finally the sound caught his attention. He stopped next to the stovepipe and was able to make out several words. They apparently interested him because he signaled his friends to be silent and stood with his ear close to the open end of the pipe.

"Milady," the cardinal was saying, "this is an important matter. Sit down and let's talk."

"Milady!" murmured Athos.

"I'm listening, Your Eminence," replied a woman's voice that made Athos start convulsively.

"A small ship with an English crew, and a captain who's one of my agents, is waiting for you at the mouth of the Charente, near the fort of La Pointe. It will set sail tomorrow morning."

"Then I must go to it tonight?"

"Yes, as soon as I've given you my instructions. Two men will be waiting at the door to escort you. I'll leave first, then you'll leave half an hour later."

"Yes, Monseigneur. And now let's come back to the mission you're giving me. Since I want to go on deserving your confidence, please explain it to me clearly and precisely, so I won't make any mistakes."

There was a moment of silence; the cardinal was thinking over what he had to say, and Milady was concentrating her attention to make sure she would understand and remember his instructions.

Athos told his friends to bolt the door, then come and listen with him.

Porthos and Aramis, who liked to be comfortable, brought three chairs. They all sat down, put their heads near the end of the stovepipe, and listened intently.

"You're going to London," said the cardinal, "and when you're there, you'll go to see Buckingham."

"Let me point out to you, Your Eminence," said Milady, "that the duke has suspected and mistrusted me ever since the affair of the diamond tags."

"This time you won't need to win his confidence: you'll present yourself to him openly and honestly as a negotiator."

"Openly and honestly," Milady repeated in an indescribable tone of duplicity.

"Yes, openly and honestly," the cardinal said in the same tone. "The negotiations must be carried on without concealing anything."

"I'll follow your instructions to the letter, Your Eminence."

"You'll go to Buckingham on my behalf and tell him that I know about all the preparations he's made, but that they don't disturb me because as soon as he makes his first move I'll bring on the queen's ruin."

"Will he believe you're in a position to carry out that threat?"

"Yes, because I have proof of her guilt."

"I must be able to tell him what the proof is and let him judge it for himself."

"Of course. Tell him that I'll make public Bois-Robert and

the Marquis de Beautru's report on his meeting with the queen at a masked ball given by the high constable's wife. And to make sure he has no doubts, tell him that he came in the Grand Mogul's costume that the chevalier de Guise was to wear, and which he bought from him for three thousand pistoles."

"Very well, Monseigneur."

"I know all the details of how he entered and left the Louvre one night in the disguise of an Italian fortune-teller. Tell him that under his cloak he was wearing a white robe with black tears, skulls, and crossbones on it, so that in case of emergency he could pretend to be the ghost of the White Lady, who, as everyone knows, returns to the Louvre whenever some great event is about to happen."

"Is that all, Monseigneur?"

"Tell him that I also know all the details of the Amiens adventure, and that I'll have a witty story written about it, with a plan of the garden and portraits of the main actors in that nocturnal scene."

"I'll tell him all that."

"Add that Montague has been captured and is in the Bastille, and that while it's true that no letter was found on him, torture can make him tell what he knows . . . and even what he doesn't know."

"That's excellent."

"And finally, tell him that in his hasty departure from the Ile de Ré he left behind a certain letter from Madame de Chevreuse that seriously compromises the queen because it proves not only that Her Majesty is capable of loving the king's enemies, but also that she conspires with the enemies of France . . . Do you remember everything I've told you?"

"Judge for yourself, Your Eminence: the masked ball, the night in the Louvre, the Amiens adventure, Montague's arrest, Madame de Chevreuse's letter."

"Perfect," said the cardinal. "You have an admirable memory, Milady."

"But what if the duke won't give in to your . . . persuasion, and goes on threatening France?"

"The duke is madly, or stupidly, rather, in love," Richelieu said with deep bitterness. "Like the knights of old, he undertook this war only for the sake of his fair lady. When he knows that the war can destroy her honor and perhaps even put an end to her freedom, I promise you that he'll have second thoughts about it."

"But suppose he still refuses to stop it," Milady said with a persistence that showed that she wanted to examine every possibility of her mission.

"If he refuses . . . That's very unlikely."

"But it's not impossible."

"If he refuses . . ." The cardinal paused. "In that case, I'll hope for one of those events that change the course of a nation's destiny."

"If you'll give me a few examples of such events, Your Eminence," said Milady, "perhaps I'll share your confidence in the future."

"Here's one example: In 1610, for a reason more or less the same as Buckingham's, King Henry the Fourth was about to invade Flanders and Italy so that he could attack Austria from two sides, but then something happened that saved Austria. Why shouldn't the present king of France be as lucky as the emperor?"

"I assume you're referring to Ravaillac's assassination of Henry the Fourth."

"Precisely."

"But don't you think that the horrible way in which Ravaillac was executed is enough to discourage anyone who might have the idea of imitating him?"

"In all countries, especially those divided by religion, there will always be fanatics eager to become martyrs. And now that I think of it, the English Puritans are furious with the duke of Buckingham; their preachers call him the Antichrist."

"Well?" asked Milady.

"One could begin," Richelieu said casually, "by finding a young, beautiful, and clever woman who had some reason for wanting to take revenge against the duke. It shouldn't be hard to find someone like that. The duke has had affairs with many women; at first they may have believed in his promises of eternal devotion, but some of them must have come to hate him for his constant unfaithfulness."

"You're right, such a woman could be found," Milady said calmly.

"And if she persuaded a fanatic to follow the example of Ravaillac or Jacques Clément, she would save France."

"Yes, but she'd be an assassin's accomplice."

"Were Ravaillac's or Jacques Clément's accomplices ever discovered?"

"No, but it may have been because they were in such high

places that no one dared to go after them there. Burning the Palais de Justice is something that wouldn't be done for everyone."

"Do you believe that the Palais de Justice wasn't burned by accident?" Richelieu asked as if it were a question of no importance.

"I don't believe anything, Monseigneur," replied Milady. "I'm only stating a fact. And I'll mention that if I were Mademoiselle de Montpensier or Queen Marie de Médicis, rather than being merely Lady de Winter, I wouldn't need all the precautions that I must take now."

"That's quite true," said Richelieu. "What would you like?"

"I'd like an order authorizing me to do whatever I feel is required for the good of France."

"But first the woman would have to be found, the one who wants to take revenge against the duke."

"She's already found," said Milady.

"And then the vile fanatic who will serve as the instrument of God's justice."

"He'll be found."

"When that's been done," said the cardinal, "it will be time to discuss giving you the order you mentioned just now."

"You're right, Monseigneur," said Milady, "and I was wrong to see my mission as different from what it is: I'm to tell the duke that you know the disguise he wore when he was with the queen at the masked ball; that you have proof of her meeting in the Louvre with a certain Italian astrologer who was none other than the duke of Buckingham; that you're prepared to have a witty story written about the Amiens adventure, with a plan of the garden where it took place and portraits of the people involved in it; that Montague is in the Bastille and that torture can make him tell what he remembers, and even things he doesn't remember; and finally, that you have a certain letter from Madame de Chevreuse, found in the duke's headquarters, which compromises not only its writer but also the woman in whose name it was written. That's as far as my mission goes. If the duke refuses to change his plans when he's heard what I have to say, all I can do is pray for a miracle that will save France. Isn't that right, Monseigneur?"

"Yes," the cardinal replied curtly.

Milady did not seem to notice the change in his attitude toward her.

"Now that you've given me your instructions regarding your

enemies," she said, "will you allow me to say a few words about mine?"

"You have enemies?" asked Richelieu.

"Yes, Monseigneur, and you owe me your protection against them, because I acquired them by serving you."

"Who are they?"

"First, a little schemer named Constance Bonacieux."

"She's in the Mantes prison."

"She *was* there," said Milady, "but the queen intercepted an order from the king and was able to have her taken to a convent."

"A convent?"

"Yes."

"Which one?"

"I don't know. The secret has been well kept."

"It won't be kept from *me*."

"When you find out which convent that woman is in, Your Eminence, will you tell me?"

"If you like."

"Good. And now, let me tell you about another enemy who's much more dangerous to me than that little Madame Bonacieux."

"Who is it?"

"You know him well, Your Eminence," said Milady, and anger rose in her voice as she continued: "He's your enemy as well as mine. He's the man who gave victory to the musketeers in a fight against your guards; he's the man who wounded Count de Wardes, your emissary, and made your plans fail in the affair of the diamond tags; and he's the one who's sworn to kill me because he knows it was I who had Madame Bonacieux taken away from him."

"Yes, I know the man you mean."

"I mean that wretched d'Artagnan."

"He's a brave young fighter," said the cardinal.

"That's precisely why he's dangerous."

"We ought to have some evidence of his collusion with Buckingham."

"I'll have enough to prove it a dozen times!" said Milady.

"Then it's a perfectly simple matter. Get the evidence for me and I'll send him to the Bastille."

"I'll get it, Monseigneur. But what then?"

"For someone in the Bastille," the cardinal said ominously, "there's no 'then.' If I could rid myself of my enemy as easily as I can rid you of yours, and if it were against such people that you wanted me to protect you . . ."

"Monseigneur," Milady interrupted, "I'll trade you a life for a life, a man for a man: rid me of this one and I'll rid you of the other."

"I don't know what you mean," said the cardinal, "and I don't want to know. But since I'd like to be of service to you, I'm willing to do as you wish with regard to that insignificant d'Artagnan, especially since I gather from what you've told me that he's a libertine, a dueler, and a traitor."

"Yes, he's an infamous traitor, Monseigneur!"

"Then give me pen and paper," said the cardinal.

"Here, Monseigneur."

There was a silence while the cardinal was either writing a letter or thinking of the terms in which he would write it. Athos, who had not missed a word of the conversation, took his two friends by the hand and led them to the other end of the room.

"What do you want?" asked Porthos. "Why didn't you let us hear the rest?"

"Quiet," Athos said softly. "We already know all we need to know. You can listen to the rest if you want to, but I must leave now."

"You're leaving? The cardinal is sure to ask where you are. What shall we tell him?"

"Don't wait for him to ask: tell him I went on ahead to act as a scout because certain things the innkeeper said made me think the road might not be safe. I'll say a few words about it to the man who came here with the cardinal. I know what I'm doing, believe me."

"Be careful, Athos!" said Aramis.

"Don't worry," replied Athos, "you know you can always count on me to be coolheaded."

Porthos and Aramis went back to the stovepipe.

Athos left the inn openly, untied his horse, and convinced the cardinal's companion that a scout would be necessary for his return. Then he ostentatiously checked the priming of his pistols, drew his sword, and rode off along on the road that led to the camp.

45

A Conjugal Scene

As Athos had expected, the cardinal soon came downstairs. Opening the door of the room into which the musketeers had gone, he found Porthos and Aramis absorbed in a game of dice. A quick look around the room showed him that Athos was missing.

"Where's Monsieur Athos?" he asked.

"He's gone off to act as a scout for you, Monseigneur," replied Porthos. "The innkeeper said some things that made him think the road might not be safe."

"And what have you been doing, Monsieur Porthos?"

"I've won five pistoles from Aramis."

"Are you ready to go back with me now?"

"We're at your orders, Monseigneur."

"Then let's go, gentlemen. It's getting late."

The cardinal's companion was at the door, holding the reins of his horse. A little farther on, two men were waiting in the shadows with three horses; they were the men who were to take Milady to the fort of La Pointe and see to it that she boarded the ship.

What Porthos had said about Athos was confirmed by the cardinal's companion. His Eminence made a gesture of approval and rode off, taking the same precautions as before.

We will now leave him on the road back to the camp, protected by his three escorts, and return to Athos.

He had ridden a hundred paces away from the inn, and then, when he was out of sight, he had turned to the right, circled back, and stopped in a thicket to watch for the little troop. He soon recognized his friends' hats and the cardinal's gold-fringed cloak. After waiting till the riders had disappeared around a bend in the road, he galloped back to the inn.

The innkeeper recognized him and let him come inside.

"I have a message for the lady on the second floor," said Athos. "My officer forgot to tell her something important, and he sent me back to do it for him."

"Go up to her room," said the innkeeper, "she's still there."

Athos silently climbed the stairs. The door was ajar; he looked in and saw Milady putting on her hat. He slipped into the room, closed the door behind him, and bolted it.

Milady turned her head when she heard the sound. Athos stood in front of the door, wrapped in his cloak, with his hat pulled down over his eyes. She was frightened at the sight of that silent, motionless figure.

"Who are you?" she cried out. "What do you want?"

"Yes, it's really her," Athos murmured to himself.

He took off his cloak and hat and walked toward her.

"Do you recognize me?" he asked.

Milady took a step forward, then leapt back as if she had seen a snake.

"Good," said Athos. "I see you do recognize me."

"Count de La Fère!" she gasped. Her face turned deathly pale, and she backed away from him till she was stopped by the wall.

"Yes, Milady, Count de La Fère in person. I've come back from the next world for the pleasure of seeing you. Sit down and let's talk, as the cardinal says."

Overwhelmed by inexpressible terror, Milady sat down without a word.

"Are you a demon sent to earth?" said Athos. "Your power is great, I know that; but with God's help men have often overcome the most terrible demons. I thought I killed you the first time you crossed my path, but either I was mistaken or the devil resurrected you."

His words brought back unbearable memories to Milady. She bowed her head and moaned softly.

"Yes, the devil resurrected you," Athos went on. "He's made you rich, given you another name, and almost even given you another face. But he hasn't cleansed your vile soul or wiped away the mark of infamy on your body."

Milady's eyes flashed fire, and she sprang to her feet. Athos remained seated.

"You thought I was dead," he went on, "just as I thought you were dead; and the name of Athos hid Count de La Fère, just as the name of Lady de Winter hid Anne de Breuil. That was your name when your honorable brother arranged our marriage, wasn't it?" He laughed. "How strange our situation is! We've gone on living only because each thought the other was dead.

Memories are less bothersome than people, though memories can sometimes be devastating!''

"But why have you come back to me?" Milady said dully. "What do you want?"

"I want to tell you that although you haven't seen me again till now, I've had my eye on you."

"You know what I've been doing?"

"I can describe your actions day by day, from the time you entered the cardinal's service."

An incredulous smile passed over Milady's pale lips.

"It was you," said Athos, "who cut the two diamond tags off the duke of Buckingham's shoulder. You were in love with de Wardes and, thinking you were going to spend the night with him, you opened your bedroom door to Monsieur d'Artagnan. Thinking de Wardes had offended you, you tried to have him killed by d'Artagnan. When d'Artagnan had discovered your shameful secret, you sent two men to murder him. Then, when you learned that their bullets had missed him, you sent poisoned wine to him, with a false letter to make him think the wine was from his friends. And finally you came here, to this room, and in exchange for the cardinal's promise to let you murder d'Artagnan with impunity, you promised to have the duke of Buckingham murdered."

Milady was livid.

"To know all that, you must be Satan himself!"

"Perhaps I am," said Athos. "Whether I am or not, listen to me carefully. I don't care if you have the duke of Buckingham killed, or kill him yourself. I don't know him; and besides, he's an Englishman. But d'Artagnan is my loyal friend and I'm as devoted to him as he is to me. If you touch one hair on his head, I swear to you that you won't live to commit another crime."

"Monsieur d'Artagnan has cruelly insulted me," Milady said grimly. "He will die."

"Is it really possible to insult you?" said Athos, laughing.

"He will die," Milady repeated. "After *she* has died."

Athos was seized with a kind of dizziness. The sight of this creature, who had only the outward appearance of a woman, forced him to remember that one day, in a situation less dangerous than this one, he had tried to sacrifice her to his honor. His bloodthirsty rage returned and took possession of him like a burning fever. He stood up, drew his pistol, and cocked it.

Pale as a corpse, Milady tried to cry out, but her tongue was frozen, and she was able to make only a hoarse sound that bore no resemblance to human speech. Pressing her back against the dark tapestry on the wall, with her hair disheveled, she was a living image of terror.

Athos slowly raised his pistol and moved it forward till its muzzle was almost touching her forehead. Then he said in a voice that was all the more terrible because it had the calm of inflexible determination, "Give me the letter the cardinal wrote for you, or I swear I'll put a bullet through your head."

With any other man, Milady might have had doubts, but she knew Athos. Even so, she did not move.

"You have one second to make up your mind," he said.

She saw from the contraction of his face that he was about to shoot. She quickly reached into her bodice, took out a sheet of paper, and handed it to him.

"Take it and be damned!" she said.

He put the pistol back in his belt, went over to the lamp, unfolded the paper, and read:

> *The bearer of this letter has acted under my orders and for the good of the State.*
>
> *Richelieu*

Athos put on his cloak and hat.

"Now that I've pulled out your fangs, you viper," he said, "bite if you can."

And he walked out of the room without looking back.

At the door of the inn he saw the two men waiting with a horse for Milady.

"As you know, gentlemen," he said to them, "your orders are to take that woman to the fort of La Pointe and stay with her till she boards the ship."

Since this tallied with the orders they had actually received, they nodded and asked no questions.

Athos leapt into the saddle and galloped off. But instead of following the road he cut across the fields, spurring his horse and stopping now and then to listen.

During one of these stops he heard the hoofbeats of several horses on the road. He had no doubt that it was the cardinal and his escorts. He rode on a little farther, halted to rub down his horse with heather and leaves, then took up a position in the middle of the road about two hundred paces from the edge of the camp.

"Who goes there?" he called out when he saw the riders.

"I believe that's our brave musketeer," said the cardinal.

"It is, Your Eminence," replied Athos.

"Thank you for keeping such a good watch, Monsieur Athos. Gentlemen, I'll leave you now. Go in through the left-hand gate. The password is 'king and Ré.' "

The cardinal nodded to the three friends and rode off to the right, followed by his companion; tonight, even His Eminence was going to sleep in camp.

"He wrote the letter she wanted," Porthos said when the cardinal was out of earshot.

"I know," Athos said calmly. "Here it is."

Except when they gave the password to the sentries, the three friends said nothing more till they reached their quarters. Then they sent Mousqueton to tell Planchet that they wanted his master to come to them as soon as he was off duty.

Milady found the two men waiting for her in front of the inn and rode off with them. For a moment she had been tempted to go to the cardinal and tell him everything, but a revelation from her would have brought a revelation from Athos; if she said that he had tried to kill her, he would say that she was branded. She had decided it would be better to remain silent, leave discreetly, carry out her difficult mission with her usual skill, and then, when everything had been accomplished to the cardinal's satisfaction, come back and claim her revenge.

After traveling all night, she reached the fort of La Pointe at seven o'clock in the morning. At eight she boarded the ship, which was supposedly about to leave for Bayonne with a letter of marque and reprisal from the cardinal. At nine it weighed anchor and set sail for England.

46

The Saint-Gervais Bastion

When d'Artagnan came to his friends' quarters, he found the three of them gathered in one room. Athos was thinking, Porthos was curling his mustache, and Aramis was reading prayers from an attractive little book of hours bound in blue velvet.

"I hope that what you have to tell me is worth hearing," d'Artagnan said to them, "because otherwise I warn you that I won't forgive you for making me come here instead of letting me sleep after I spent the night capturing and demolishing a bastion. I wish you'd been there, gentlemen. You wouldn't have been bored."

"We were somewhere else, and we weren't bored there either," said Porthos, turning up his mustache at the angle he preferred.

"Not so loud!" said Athos.

D'Artagnan understood his slight frown.

"I see that something new has happened," he said.

"Aramis, you ate at the Parpaillot inn day before yesterday, didn't you?" asked Athos.

"Yes."

"How was it there?"

"I had a very bad meal. It was supposed to be a meatless day, but they had no fish."

"Really? No fish, in a seaport?"

"They say," Aramis replied, turning his eyes back to his pious book, "that the dike built by the cardinal has driven all the fish away from the coast."

"In any case, I wasn't asking you about the quality of your meal. What I want to know is whether you were left alone at the Parpaillot, whether your privacy was respected."

"We weren't disturbed. I see what you mean, Athos. Yes, we can talk in private at the Parpaillot."

"Then let's go there," said Athos, "because the walls are like paper here."

Knowing his friend as he did, d'Artagnan could always tell from his manner when something serious was afoot. He took his arm and left with him in silence. Porthos and Aramis followed, talking casually with each other.

On the way they met Grimaud. Athos motioned him to come along. As usual, Grimaud obeyed without a word; the poor man had nearly forgotten how to speak.

They reached the Parpaillot inn at seven o'clock, just as the sun was beginning to rise. They ordered breakfast and went into a room where, according to the innkeeper, they would not be disturbed.

Unfortunately it was a bad time for a conference. Reveille had just sounded and the inn was crowded with soldiers who had come in for a drink to jolt themselves awake and ward off the damp chill of the morning air. Dragoons, Swiss mercenaries, guards, musketeers, and light-horsemen came and went at a rapid rate that pleased the innkeeper but thwarted the plans of our four friends, who were so annoyed that they gave surly replies to the greetings, toasts, and jokes of the men around them.

"If we're not careful, we'll have a quarrel on our hands," said Athos, "and that's the last thing we need now. D'Artagnan, tell us about your night and we'll tell you about ours later."

"Yes, you guards were on trench duty last night," said a light-horseman standing nearby, holding a glass of brandy that he had been slowly sipping, "and I've heard you had a brush with the enemy. Is that true?"

D'Artagnan looked at Athos to find out whether he should answer this intruder who had just broken into their conversation.

"Didn't you hear Monsieur de Busigny's question?" said Athos. "Tell us what happened last night, since these gentlemen want to know about it."

"You took a bastion, didn't you?" asked a Swiss who was drinking rum from a beer glass.

"Yes, sir, we had that honor," d'Artagnan replied. "As you may have heard, we put a barrel of gunpowder under one of its corners, and it made a very nice breach when it exploded. Since it was an old bastion, the rest of it was also badly shaken."

"Which bastion was it?" asked a dragoon who had brought a goose that he wanted to have cooked for him and was holding it impaled on his saber.

"The Saint-Gervais bastion," answered d'Artagnan. "The enemy had been harassing our labor batallions from it."

"Did they put up a stiff fight?"

"Yes, they did. We lost five men, they lost nine or ten."

The Swiss said something unintelligible that was evidently meant to be an exclamation of surprise; he had an admirable collection of German oaths but had not yet learned to swear in French.

"They'll probably send men to repair the bastion this morning," said the light-horseman.

"Probably so."

"Gentlemen, let's make a bet!" said Athos.

"I like to make bets," remarked the Swiss.

"Wait for me," said the dragoon, who had just laid his saber across the two big andirons in the fireplace, to hold his goose above the fire. "I want to be in on the bet. Innkeeper! Bring me a pan to put under this goose. I don't want to lose one drop of its grease.''

"You're right," said the Swiss. "Goose grease is very good with jam."

"Now I'm ready," said the dragoon, coming back from the fireplace. "Tell us about the bet, Monsieur Athos."

"Yes, tell us!" said the light-horseman.

"Monsieur de Busigny," said Athos, "I'll bet you that my three friends and I will eat our breakfast in the Saint-Gervais bastion and that we'll stay there an hour, no matter how hard the enemy may try to dislodge us."

Porthos and Aramis looked at each other; they were beginning to understand.

"Are you trying to get us killed?" d'Artagnan whispered in Athos's ear.

"We're more likely to be killed if we stay here," Athos whispered back.

"Well, gentlemen, what do you say to that bet?" asked Porthos, leaning back in his chair and twirling his mustache.

"I'll take it," replied Monsieur de Busigny. "Now let's decide on the stakes."

"There are four of you, gentlemen," said Athos, "and four of us. Shall we make the stakes a dinner for eight?"

"Excellent!" said Monsieur de Busigny.

"I'm willing," said the dragoon.

"It suits me," said the Swiss.

The fourth man, who had remained silent through the conversation, nodded his assent.

"Your breakfast is ready, gentlemen," said the innkeeper.

"Then bring it in," said Athos.

The innkeeper obeyed. Athos called Grimaud, pointed to a big basket that was lying in the corner and went through the motions of wrapping the food in the napkins. Grimaud understood that he was to make preparations for a picnic. He packed the food and wine in the basket and picked it up.

"Where are you going to eat?" asked the innkeeper.

"What does it matter to you," said Athos, "as long as we pay you?"

And he majestically tossed two pistoles onto the table.

"Shall I bring you change, sir?"

"No. Just add two bottles of champagne and the difference will be for the napkins."

The innkeeper realized that he was not going to make as much profit as he had thought at first, but he made things a little better for himself by slipping two bottles of Anjou wine into the basket, instead of champagne.

"Monsieur de Busigny," said Athos, "will you set your watch by mine, or allow me to set mine by yours?"

"Of course," said the light-horseman, taking out a handsome watch set with diamonds. "I have seven-thirty."

"And I have twenty-five to eight. We'll know that my watch is five minutes ahead of yours."

The four friends bowed to the astonished onlookers and set off for the Saint-Gervais bastion. Grimaud followed them, carrying the basket. He did not know where he was going, but Athos had made him so accustomed to passive obedience that he did not even think to ask.

As long as they were inside the camp they said nothing to each other; behind them walked a throng of curious men who knew about the bet and wanted to see how they would go about trying to win it. But when they had passed the last line of fieldworks and were in open terrain, d'Artagnan, who still did not know what Athos had in mind, decided it was time to ask for an explanation.

"And now, Athos," he said, "will you be so kind as to tell me where we're going?"

"We're going to the bastion, as you can see."

"Yes, but what are we going to do there?"

"We're going to eat breakfast, as you know."

"But why couldn't we have eaten at the inn?"

"Because we have important things to discuss and it was impossible to talk for five minutes at the inn, with all those intruders greeting us and trying to strike up a conversation. In the bastion, no one will disturb us."

"It seems to me that we could have found some isolated spot on the beach," said d'Artagnan, showing the caution that was one part of his nature, along with his reckless courage.

"Yes, a place where the four of us would have been seen together, so that within fifteen minutes the cardinal's spies would have told him we were having a conference."

"Athos is right," said Aramis. *"Animadvertuntur in desertis."*

"A desert would have been pretty good," said Porthos, "but we might have had trouble finding one."

"There's no wilderness where a bird can't fly overhead, or a fish can't jump out of the water, or a rabbit can't come out of its hole, and I wouldn't be surprised if the cardinal had birds, fish, and rabbits spying for him. It's better to go on with what we're doing. Besides, we couldn't turn back now without disgracing ourselves. We've made a bet, a bet that couldn't have been foreseen, and I defy anyone to guess its real purpose. To win it, we're going to spend an hour in the bastion. Either we'll be attacked or we won't. If we're not attacked, we'll have time to talk and no one will overhear us, because I assure you those walls don't have ears; if we *are* attacked, we'll have our talk anyway, and in fighting back against the attackers we'll cover ourselves with glory. Either way, things will turn out to our advantage.''

''Unless we're shot,'' said d'Artagnan, ''and there's a good chance of that.''

''You know very well that the enemy's bullets aren't the ones we have to worry about most.''

''But it seems to me that for such an expedition we should have brought our muskets,'' said Porthos.

''Porthos, my friend, you're talking like a fool. Why should we carry a useless burden?''

''When I'm facing the enemy, I don't think there's anything useless about a good musket, a dozen bullets, and a powder flask.''

''Didn't you hear what d'Artagnan said?''

''What did he say?'' asked Porthos.

''He said that in the attack last night we lost five men and the enemy lost nine or ten.''

''Well, what of it?''

''No one had time to take anything from the dead men, because everyone had more urgent things to do.''

''Yes, but . . .''

''We'll take their guns, powder, and bullets; instead of four muskets, we'll have fifteen, and we'll be able to fire at least a hundred shots.''

''Athos,'' said Aramis, ''you're a truly great man.''

Porthos nodded in agreement. D'Artagnan did not seem convinced.

Grimaud, who till now had not been sure of their destination, evidently shared d'Artagnan's misgivings. Seeing that they were walking straight toward the bastion, he tugged at his master's coattail and asked, by gestures, ''Where are we going?''

Athos pointed to the bastion.

''But we'll be killed!'' Grimaud protested, still in the same silent language.

Athos looked up and pointed to heaven.

Grimaud put his basket on the ground and sat down beside it, shaking his head. Athos took a pistol from his belt, cocked it, and pressed its muzzle against Grimaud's ear. Grimaud leapt to his feet as though moved by a spring. Athos motioned him to pick up his basket and lead the way. Grimaud obeyed. All the poor man had gained from his pantomime was the privilege of going from the rear to the vanguard.

When they reached the bastion, they looked back. Over three hundred men from all branches of the army had gathered at the gate of the camp. Monsieur de Busigny, the dragoon, the Swiss, and the fourth bettor were standing in a separate group.

Athos took off his hat, put it on the tip of his sword, and waved it. All the spectators returned his greeting, accompanied by a loud cheer.

The four friends disappeared into the bastion, where Grimaud had already preceded them.

47

The Musketeers' Conference

As Athos had foreseen, the bastion was occupied only by a dozen dead men.

"Gentlemen," said Athos, who had taken command of the expedition, "while Grimaud is setting the table, let's begin by gathering the guns and ammunition. We can talk at the same time. These gentlemen," he added, pointing to the dead men, "won't listen to us."

"We can throw them into the moat," said Porthos, "after searching their pockets."

"We'll have Grimaud do it," said Aramis.

"All right, then," said d'Artagnan, "Grimaud will search them and throw them over the wall."

"No," said Athos. "They can be useful to us."

"The dead men can be useful to us?" said Porthos. "You've lost your mind, my friend!"

"The Bible and the cardinal tell us not to judge hastily. How many muskets do we have, gentlemen?"

"Twelve," answered Aramis.

"How much ammunition?"

"Enough for a hundred shots."

"That's as much as we need. Let's load the muskets."

The four friends set to work. Just as the last musket was loaded, Grimaud gestured that the meal was ready.

Athos nodded and motioned him to go to a small turret and act as a sentry. To relieve the boredom of his duty, he let him take a loaf of bread, two cutlets, and a bottle of wine.

"And now, let's eat," Athos said to his friends.

The four of them sat down cross-legged on the floor.

"Now that you don't have to worry about being overheard, Athos," said d'Artagnan, "I hope you'll tell us your secret."

"And I hope I've brought you both enjoyment and glory, gentlemen," said Athos. "We've had a pleasant stroll, we're about to eat a delicious meal, and five hundred people, as you can see through the loopholes, are waiting to see what will become of us, thinking we must be either lunatics or heroes, though there's not much difference between the two."

"But what's your secret?" d'Artagnan insisted.

"My secret," replied Athos, "is that I saw Milady last night."

D'Artagnan had just raised his glass to his lips, but when he heard Milady's name, his hand trembled so much that he had to put down the glass to avoid spilling the wine.

"You saw your wi . . ."

"Sh!" Athos interrupted. "You're forgetting that Porthos and Aramis don't know about my family affairs, as you do. I saw Milady."

"Where?"

"About five miles from here, in the Colombier-Rouge inn."

"Then I'm lost," said d'Artagnan.

"No, not yet, because by now she should have left France."

D'Artagnan began breathing more easily.

"But who *is* this Milady?" asked Porthos.

"She's a charming woman," said Athos, and took a sip of sparkling wine. "That innkeeper's a thief!" he exclaimed. "He gave us Anjou instead of champagne, and he thinks we won't know the difference!" Then he continued calmly: "She's a charming woman who was very kind to our friend d'Artagnan. He offended her in some way or other and now she wants revenge. A month ago she tried to have him shot, a week ago she tried to poison him, and last night she asked the cardinal for his head."

"What!" cried d'Artagnan, pale with terror.

"It's the gospel truth," said Porthos. "I heard her with my own ears."

"So did I," said Aramis.

"In that case, there's no use going on," d'Artagnan said with a disheartened gesture. "I may as well blow my brains out and be done with it."

"That would be a stupid mistake," said Athos, "and the only one for which there's no remedy."

"But I won't survive anyway," said d'Artagnan, "not with the enemies I've made: first I quarreled with that stranger in Meung, then I wounded de Wardes, discovered Milady's secret, and foiled the cardinal's plan in London."

"Well, that's only four enemies," said Athos, "and there are four of us: we're evenly matched. But judging from the signs Grimaud is making to us, we'll soon be dealing with many more enemies than your four. What is it, Grimaud? Considering the seriousness of the situation, I'll allow you to speak, but please be brief. What do you see?"

"Men."

"How many."

"Twenty."

"Are they soldiers?"

"Sixteen workmen, four soldiers."

"How far away are they?"

"Five hundred paces."

"Good, we still have time to finish this chicken and drink to your health, d'Artagnan."

"To your health!" repeated Porthos and Aramis.

"To my health, then, though I don't think your toast will do it much good."

"Don't worry," said Athos. "God is great, as the Mohammedans say, and the future is in his hands."

After emptying his glass and setting it down on the floor, he casually stood up, took the nearest musket, and went over to a loophole.

Porthos, Aramis, and d'Artagnan followed suit. Grimaud was ordered to stand behind the four friends, ready to reload their guns.

They saw the enemy detachment coming toward them along a trench that connected the bastion with the town.

"I don't see why we had to interrupt our meal for twenty wretches armed with picks and shovels," said Athos. "If Grimaud had just waved his arms to tell them to go away, I'm sure they'd have left us alone.''

''I doubt it,'' remarked d'Artagnan, ''because they seem quite determined. Besides, along with the workmen there are four soldiers and a corporal, armed with muskets.''

''They seem determined because they haven't seen us yet,'' said Athos.

''I don't like the idea of shooting at those poor civilians,'' said Aramis.

''You'll be a bad priest if you feel sorry for heretics!'' said Porthos.

''Aramis is right,'' said Athos. ''I'm going to warn them.''

''What are you doing?'' cried d'Artagnan. ''You'll get yourself shot!''

But Athos ignored him. He stood up in the breach with his musket in one hand and his hat in the other.

Surprised by his sudden appearance, the soldiers and workmen stopped short, about fifty paces from the bastion.

''Gentlemen,'' he called out to them, bowing courteously, ''my friends and I are having breakfast in this bastion. As I'm sure you know, nothing is more unpleasant than being disturbed during breakfast, so if it's really necessary for you to come here, we'll be grateful to you if you'll wait till we've finished our meal, or go away and come back later—unless you should have a wholesome desire to abandon your rebellion and join us in drinking a toast to the king of France.''

''Look out, Athos!'' said d'Artagnan. ''Don't you see they're taking aim at you?''

''Yes, I see,'' replied Athos, ''but they're not professional soldiers. They can't shoot well enough to hit me.''

Four shots were fired. They all missed Athos. A moment later there were four answering shots, more accurate than the first ones: three soldiers fell dead and one workman was wounded.

''Grimaud, another musket!'' said Athos, still in the breach.

Grimaud quickly obeyed. The three others had reloaded their guns. A second volley killed the corporal and two workmen. The survivors ran away.

''Come, gentlemen, let's make a sortie,'' said Athos.

They rushed out of the bastion and picked up the four soldiers' muskets and the corporal's pike. Then, convinced that the others would not stop running till they reached the town, they went back into the bastion, carrying the trophies of their victory.

''Reload the muskets, Grimaud,'' said Athos. ''And now,

gentlemen, we'll continue our meal and our conversation. Where were we?''

"You'd just told us that Milady had left France," said d'Artagnan. "Where's she going?"

"To England."

"Why?"

"She intends to kill Buckingham, or have him killed."

"That's infamous!" d'Artagnan exclaimed with surprise and indignation.

"It doesn't bother me at all," said Athos. He turned to Grimaud. "Now that you've finished reloading, take the corporal's pike, tie a napkin to it, and plant it at the top of our bastion, so the rebels will see that they're dealing with brave and loyal soldiers of the king."

Grimaud obeyed without answering. A short time later the white flag was floating above the four friends' heads. Its appearance was greeted with thunderous applause from the camp; half the army had gathered at the gates.

"It doesn't bother you that she's going to have the duke of Buckingham killed?" d'Artagnan protested. "The duke is our friend!"

"He's English," said Athos, "and he's fighting against us. I don't care what she does to him. He means no more to me than this empty bottle."

And he threw away the bottle whose last drop of wine he had just poured into his glass.

"I'm not abandoning Buckingham like that," said d'Artagnan. "He gave us four magnificent horses."

"And four beautiful saddles," said Porthos, who was wearing the braid from his saddle on his cloak.

"Furthermore," said Aramis, "God wants sinners to be converted, not killed."

"Amen," said Athos. "We can discuss it later if you like, but first let me tell you that my main concern—and I'm sure you'll understand me, d'Artagnan—was to get a letter she'd made the cardinal give her, a letter that would enable her to get rid of you, and perhaps us also, with impunity."

"That woman must be some sort of demon!" said Porthos, holding out his plate to Aramis, who was carving a chicken.

"And did you get the letter?" asked d'Artagnan.

"Yes. I won't say it was easy, because I'd be lying."

"Athos," said d'Artagnan, "I can't count the number of times you've saved my life."

"So that's why you left us!" said Aramis. "You wanted to see her after the cardinal had gone."

"Exactly."

"Do you still have the letter?" asked d'Artagnan.

"Here it is."

Athos took the precious sheet of paper from the pocket of his cloak.

D'Artagnan unfolded it without trying to hide the trembling of his hands and read it aloud:

> *"The bearer of this letter has acted under my orders and for the good of the State.*
>
>   *Richelieu"*

"That's complete absolution for anything she may do," said Aramis.

"We have to tear it up!" said d'Artagnan, who saw the letter as his death warrant.

"No, you're mistaken," said Athos. "We must keep it and make sure we don't lose it. I wouldn't sell it for enough gold to cover it."

"What will she do now?" asked d'Artagnan.

"She'll probably write to the cardinal," Athos replied nonchalantly, "to say that the letter was taken from her by that damned musketeer named Athos. She'll advise him to get rid of Athos, along with his two friends Porthos and Aramis. The cardinal will remember that those are the men who keep getting in his way. One fine day he'll have d'Artagnan arrested, and then, so he won't be bored by having to stay in the Bastille all by himself, he'll send us there to keep him company."

"I must say I don't appreciate your joke," said Porthos.

"I wasn't joking," said Athos.

"In my opinion," Porthos went on, "it would be much less of a sin to wring that damned Milady's neck than to kill those poor Huguenots whose only crime is to sing hymns in French that we sing in Latin."

"What does our priest say to that?" Athos asked calmly.

"I agree with Porthos," replied Aramis.

"And I agree with him completely!" said d'Artagnan.

"I'm glad she's far away," remarked Porthos. "I must admit I'd feel a little uneasy if she were here."

"She makes me feel uneasy whether she's in England or in France," said Athos.

"I'd still feel uneasy about her if she went to the other side of the world," said d'Artagnan.

"Why did you let her get away last night?" Porthos asked Athos. "Why didn't you drown her, or strangle her, or hang her? Dead people are the only ones who never come back."

"You think so, Porthos?" Athos said with a somber smile that only d'Artagnan understood.

"I have an idea," said d'Artagnan.

"What is it?" the three musketeers all asked at once.

"We're being attacked!" shouted Grimaud.

The young men leapt up and ran to their muskets.

A detachment of twenty to twenty-five men was coming toward them, but this time there were no workmen: they were all soldiers from the garrison.

"Shall we go back to camp?" Porthos suggested. "It seems to me that the two sides aren't very evenly matched."

"We can't go back now, for three reasons," said Athos. "First, we haven't finished our breakfast; second, we still have some important matters to discuss; and third, we have ten more minutes to spend here before the hour is up."

"Let's at least decide on a plan of battle," said Aramis.

"It's quite simple," said Athos. "As soon as they're within musket range, we'll open fire. If they keep coming, we'll fire again and go on firing as long as we have loaded muskets. If the men who are left still want to attack the bastion, we'll wait till they're in the moat and then we'll push down this section of wall on them. It's still standing only by a miracle of balance."

"Bravo!" cried Porthos. "Athos, you were born to be a general! The cardinal thinks he's a great military leader, but he's nothing compared to you!"

"We mustn't waste any of our shots by firing two of them at one target," said Athos. "I want each of you to pick out his man."

"I have mine," said d'Artagnan.

"So have I," said Porthos.

"And so have I," said Aramis.

"Then fire!" said Athos.

The four shots made a single explosion and four men fell.

The drum beat, and the little troop charged. The shooting continued from the bastion with the same accuracy, but the attackers went on running forward, as though they knew the numerical weakness of the defenders.

Three more shots brought down two more men, yet those still on their feet did not slow their pace.

When they reached the foot of the bastion, there were still twelve to fifteen of them left. A final volley failed to stop them. They leapt down into the moat and prepared to climb into the breach.

The four friends, aided by Grimaud, began pushing on an enormous section of the wall with the barrels of their muskets. It tilted as though blown by the wind, broke off at its base and went crashing down into the moat. There was a loud shriek, a cloud of dust rose into the sky, and that was all.

"Could we have crushed every one of them?" asked Athos.

"It looks that way," said d'Artagnan.

"No," said Porthos, "I see a few of them limping away."

Three or four soldiers, covered with mud and blood, were fleeing along the road that led back to the town. They were all that remained of the detachment.

Athos looked at his watch.

"Gentlemen," he said, "we've been here an hour. We've won our bet, but we may as well stay a little longer and win it with a flourish. Besides, d'Artagnan hasn't yet told us his idea."

And, with his usual calm, he sat down in front of what was left of their meal.

"My idea?"

"Yes," said Athos. "You told us you had one, remember?"

"Ah, yes; I'll go back to England and warn the duke of Buckingham about the plot against his life."

"You won't do that, d'Artagnan," Athos said firmly.

"Why not? I've already gone to the duke once before."

"Yes, but we weren't at war then, and the duke was an ally, not an enemy. If you went to him now, you'd be accused of treason."

D'Artagnan recognized the strength of this argument and made no reply.

"I've got an idea too," said Porthos.

"Silence for Porthos's idea!" said Aramis.

"I'll ask Monsieur de Tréville for a leave. You can invent a reason for me; I'm not very good at that kind of thing. Milady doesn't know me, so I'll be able to come near her without alarming her, and when I find her, I'll strangle her."

"I'm not far from accepting that idea," said Athos.

"How can you even think of such a shameful thing as killing a woman, Porthos?" said Aramis. "No, I have the right idea."

"What is it, Aramis?" asked Athos, who had great respect for him.

"We must warn the queen."

"Yes!" exclaimed d'Artagnan. "I think that *is* the right idea!"

"Warn the queen?" said Athos. "How? We have no connections at court. We couldn't send anyone there without having it known in camp. It's three hundred and fifty miles from here to Paris; we'd all be in a dungeon before our letter got to Angers."

"I can see to it that a letter reaches the queen safely," said Aramis. "I know a resourceful person in Tours . . ."

He stopped short when he saw Athos smile.

"Shall we adopt that plan, Athos?" asked d'Artagnan.

"I'm not completely opposed to it," said Athos. "But I'd like to point out a few things to you, Aramis. You can't leave camp. Any messenger except one of us would be unreliable. Within two hours after he left, all the cardinal's agents would know your letter by heart. You and your resourceful person would both be arrested."

"Not to mention," said Porthos, "that although the queen would save the duke of Buckingham, she wouldn't save us."

"Gentlemen," said d'Artagnan, "Porthos has just raised a very sensible objection!"

"Listen!" said Athos. "What's happening in the town?"

"They're sounding a call to arms!"

They all heard the drum.

"They're going to send a whole regiment against us, you'll see," said Athos.

"You don't intend to hold off a regiment, do you?" asked Porthos.

"Why not? I feel in good form. I'd hold off an army if we'd only taken the precaution of bringing along another dozen bottles."

"The drum is coming closer," said d'Artagnan.

"Let it come," said Athos. "It takes a good quarter of an hour to get here from the town, and that's more time than we'll need to work out our plan. If we leave here now, we'll never find such a good place again. And it so happens that I've just had an excellent idea."

"Tell us about it."

"First let me give Grimaud some necessary orders."

Athos beckoned to Grimaud.

"Grimaud," he said, pointing to the dead men lying in the bastion. "I want you to take these gentlemen and stand them up against the wall with hats on their heads and muskets in their hands.''

"Yes, you're a great man!" said d'Artagnan. "I understand!"

"You do?" said Porthos.

"And you, Grimaud," said Aramis, "do *you* understand?"

Grimaud nodded.

"That's all it takes," said Athos. "Let's come back to my idea."

"I still wish I understood about those dead men," said Porthos.

"There's no need for you to understand."

"Let's hear Athos's idea," said Aramis.

"D'Artagnan, I believe you told me that woman, that demon, has a brother-in-law."

"Yes. I know him quite well, and I don't think he's very fond of her."

"There's nothing wrong with that," said Athos. "It would be even better if he hated her."

"He does."

"I wish you'd explain what Grimaud is doing," said Porthos.

"Quiet, Porthos!" said Aramis.

"What's her brother-in-law's name?"

"Lord de Winter."

"Where is he now?"

"He went back to London as soon as there was talk of war."

"He's just the man we need," said Athos. "He's the one we'll warn. We'll let him know that his sister-in-law is about to murder someone, and ask him to keep an eye on her. In London there must be something like the Madelonnettes in Paris, a place where he can have her held to keep her out of trouble. Once he's put her into it, we can stop worrying."

"Yes, till she comes out," said d'Artagnan.

"You're asking too much, d'Artagnan. I've done the best I could, but now I'm out of ideas."

"I think we've found the best solution," said Aramis. "We'll warn both the queen and Lord de Winter."

"But who will deliver the two letters, to Tours and London?"

"Bazin can take one of them," said Aramis.

"And Planchet the other," said d'Artagnan.

"You're right," said Porthos. "We can't leave camp, but our servants can."

"Of course," said Aramis. "We'll write the letters today, give the servants some money, and send them on their way."

"Money?" said Athos. "Where will we get it?"

The four friends looked at each other and their faces darkened.

"Here they come!" d'Artagnan suddenly exclaimed. "Look at those black and red dots over there! You said they'd send a regiment against us, Athos, but that's an army!"

"Yes, there they are," said Athos. "They're marching without drums or trumpets, hoping to take us by surprise. Have you finished, Grimaud?"

Grimaud nodded and pointed to the dozen dead men he had placed in lifelike attitudes: some had their muskets resting on their shoulders, others seemed to be aiming them, still others held drawn swords.

"Very good!" said Athos. "It does credit to your imagination."

"I still don't understand," said Porthos.

"First, we'll get out of here," said d'Artagnan, "and you can understand later."

"Just a moment, gentlemen," said Athos. "Let's give Grimaud time to pack up the dishes and what's left of our breakfast."

"Those black and red dots are getting much bigger," Aramis pointed out. "I agree with d'Artagnan: let's go back to camp without wasting any more time."

"I have nothing against a retreat now," said Athos. "We bet that we'd stay here an hour, and we've stayed an hour and a half. We've won our bet with a generous margin to spare. Let's go."

Grimaud had already left, carrying the basket that contained the remains of the meal.

The four friends followed him, but they had taken no more than a dozen steps outside the bastion when Athos suddenly said, "Stop, gentlemen. We've forgotten something."

"What?" asked Aramis.

"Our flag. We mustn't let a flag fall into the enemy's hands, even if it's only a napkin."

Athos ran back into the bastion, climbed to the top, and took the flag. The enemy soldiers were now within musket range. They began shooting at the man who seemed totally unconcerned as he exposed himself to their fire. But it was as though Athos had a charmed life: bullets whizzed all around him and not one of them hit him.

He turned his back on the enemy, faced the camp, and waved his flag. He heard cheering in front of him and cries of rage behind him. A second volley was fired. The napkin acquired three bullet holes that turned it into a real battle flag.

Everyone in the camp began shouting to him: "Come down! Come down!"

He came down. His friends, who had been waiting for him with great anxiety, were overjoyed when they saw him leave the bastion.

"Let's go," said d'Artagnan. "Hurry! It would be stupid for us to be killed now that we've worked out everything except how we'll get the money."

But Athos continued to walk majestically, no matter what his friends said. Seeing that it was useless to argue with him, they adjusted their pace to his. Grimaud had gone on ahead with his basket and was now out of range.

They soon heard the sound of furious firing.

"What's that?" asked Porthos. "What are they shooting at? I don't hear any bullets passing, and I don't see anyone."

"They're shooting at our dead men," replied Athos.

"But our dead men won't shoot back."

"Precisely. The enemy will be afraid of falling into some sort of trap. They'll talk it over and finally send a spokesman with a flag of truce. By the time they find out about the little joke we've played on them, we'll be beyond reach of their bullets. That's why there's no use tiring ourselves by hurrying."

"Ah, *now* I understand!" Porthos said admiringly.

"It's about time," said Athos, shrugging his shoulders.

When the men in camp saw them coming back with no sign of haste, they cheered still more loudly.

Finally there was another burst of gunfire. This time bullets glanced off rocks near the four friends and whined mournfully. The enemy had just taken possession of the bastion.

"What incompetent soldiers they are!" said Athos. "How many of them did we shoot? Twelve?"

"Maybe fifteen."

"How many did we crush in the moat?"

"Nine or ten."

"And in exchange for all that, not one of us was even scratched . . . No, I see that's not quite true. Isn't that blood on your hand, d'Artagnan?"

"It's nothing," said d'Artagnan.

"Were you grazed by a bullet?"

"No."

"Then what happened?"

As we have said, Athos loved d'Artagnan as if he were his

son; and, somber and inflexible though he was, he sometimes felt fatherly concern for him.

"I cut my hand on the diamond in my ring," said d'Artagnan.

"That's what comes of wearing a diamond ring," Athos said disdainfully.

"A diamond!" exclaimed Porthos. "Since there's a diamond in your ring, why are we complaining about not having any money?"

"Yes, why?" said Aramis.

"You're right, Porthos!" said Athos. "This time you've had a good idea."

Porthos threw out his chest with pride at Athos's compliment.

"It's simple," he said, "we'll sell the ring."

"But it was given to me by the queen," d'Artagnan objected.

"All the more reason to sell it," said Athos. "Through that ring the queen will save Buckingham, her lover, and us, her friends. Nothing could be more right and proper than that. What does our priest think about it? I won't ask for Porthos's opinion because we already know it."

"I think," said Aramis, blushing, "that since the ring wasn't given to d'Artagnan by his mistress, and therefore isn't a token of love, he can sell it."

"You reason like the learned theologian you are, my friend. So your opinion is . . ."

"That we should sell the ring."

"Then it's settled," d'Artagnan said lightheartedly. "We'll sell it."

The firing still continued, but they were now out of range; the enemy were shooting at them only for the sake of form.

"We can thank Porthos for having that excellent idea," said Athos. "We're almost back at the camp; not a word about all this to anyone, gentlemen. Look: they're watching us, they're coming out to meet us, they're going to carry us back in triumph."

The whole camp was in a state of great excitement. More than two thousand people had watched the spectacle of the four friends' bravado, without suspecting the real reason for it. There were shouts of "Hurrah for the guards! Hurrah for the musketeers!" Monsieur de Busigny came forward to shake Athos's hand and acknowledge that he had lost the bet. He was followed by the dragoon and the Swiss, who were in turn followed by everyone else. There were endless congratulations, handshakes, and embraces, and uproarious laughter at the expense of the enemy. The tumult became so great that the cardinal thought a riot must be taking place and sent La Houdinière, his captain of the guards, to find out about it. The exploit was described to La Houdinière with enthusiastic embellishments.

"Well?" the cardinal asked when his captain returned.

"Three musketeers and a guard," replied La Houdinière, "made a bet with Monsieur de Busigny that they would go and eat their breakfast in the Saint-Gervais bastion. They did it, held off the enemy for two hours, and killed I don't know how many of them."

"Did you ask the names of the three musketeers?"

"Yes, Monseigneur."

"Who are they?"

"Their names are Athos, Porthos, and Aramis."

"Those three again!" murmured the cardinal. "And the guard?"

"He's Monsieur d'Artagnan."

"That young rascal again! I must have those four men in my service . . ."

That evening the cardinal spoke with Monsieur de Tréville about the exploit, which was still the talk of the camp. Monsieur de Tréville had been informed of it by the four heroes themselves; he related it to the cardinal in detail, including the episode of the napkin.

"Please have that napkin brought to me," said the cardinal. "I'll have three gold fleurs-de-lis embroidered on it, then I'll give it to your company as a banner."

"That would be unfair to the guards, Monseigneur," said Monsieur de Tréville. "Monsieur d'Artagnan isn't in my company: he's in Monsieur des Essarts's."

"Then take him," said the cardinal. "Since those four brave soldiers like each other so much, they ought to be in the same company."

That same evening Tréville announced the news to d'Artagnan and the three musketeers, and invited them to have lunch with him the next day.

D'Artagnan was beside himself with joy. As we know, becoming a musketeer was the dream of his life. His three friends shared his elation.

"That was a brilliant idea you had," he told Athos. "It turned out just as you said it would: we covered ourselves with glory and we were able to have a very important conversation in private."

"And we can continue that conversation without being sus-

pected because, with God's help, from now on we'll be regarded
as Cardinalists.''

Later that evening d'Artagnan went to pay his respects to
Monsieur des Essarts and tell him about his transfer. Monsieur
des Essarts, who was very fond of him, offered to help him with
the expenses of the new uniform and equipment he would have
to buy.

D'Artagnan declined the offer but took advantage of the opportunity to give his diamond ring to Monsieur des Essarts and have
it sold for him.

At eight o'clock the next morning, Monsieur des Essarts's
servant came to d'Artagnan with a bag containing seven thousand livres in gold—the price of the diamond ring that had been
given to him by the queen.

48

A Family Matter

Athos had found the right expression to use: a family matter. A
family matter was not subject to investigation by the cardinal,
concerned no one outside the family, and could be dealt with
openly.

And so Athos had found the expression: a family matter.

Aramis had found the idea: the servants.

Porthos had found the means: the diamond ring.

Only d'Artagnan, usually the most inventive member of the
foursome, had found nothing; but it must be said that the mere
mention of Milady's name was enough to paralyze him.

No, we are mistaken: d'Artagnan had found a way to sell the
ring.

Conversation during the lunch with Monsieur de Tréville was
animated and cheerful. D'Artagnan was already wearing his
musketeer's uniform. Aramis, handsomely paid by the publisher
of his poem, had bought two of everything, and since he and
d'Artagnan were about the same size, he had given him a
uniform and all the equipment that went with it.

D'Artagnan would have been completely happy if the thought
of Milady had not loomed on his mental horizon like a black cloud.

After lunch, the four friends agreed to meet that evening in Athos's quarters to make their final arrangements.

D'Artagnan spent the day showing off his musketeer's uniform all over the camp.

That evening, he met with his friends as they had agreed. Only three things remained to be decided: what they would write to Milady's brother-in-law, what they would write to Aramis's resourceful person in Tours, and which of the servants would deliver the letters.

Each of the four friends proposed his own servant. Athos extolled Grimaud's discretion; Grimaud, he said, never opened his mouth without his master's permission. Porthos praised Mousqueton's strength, saying that four men of average size were no match for him. Aramis, confident of Bazin's resourcefulness, spoke grandiloquently in favor of his candidate. D'Artagnan had complete faith in Planchet's courage and described his behavior in the thorny episode at Boulogne.

These four virtues were discussed at great length and gave rise to magnificent speeches that we will not repeat here, for fear of boring the reader.

"The ideal solution," Athos finally said, "would be to send someone with all four of those qualities."

"But where could we find such a servant?"

"Nowhere, I know that," said Athos. "So take Grimaud."

"Take Mousqueton."

"Take Bazin."

"Take Planchet. He's brave and resourceful: that gives him two out of the four qualities."

"Gentlemen," said Aramis, "the most important thing we have to decide is not which of our servants is the most discreet, the strongest, the most resourceful, or the bravest, but which of them loves money most."

"That's very sensible," said Athos. "It's better to count on people's faults than on their virtues. Father Aramis, you're a great philosopher!"

"It's true that what I said is sensible," replied Aramis. "We must choose the right man, not only to succeed but also to avoid failure, because if we fail it's not the servants' lives that will be in danger, it's . . ."

"Lower your voice!" said Athos.

"Yes, you're right . . . It's *our* lives that will be in danger. Are our servants devoted enough to risk their lives for us? No."

"I'd almost answer for Planchet," said d'Artagnan.

"In that case, reward his natural devotion with a respectable sum of money and you can answer for him twice instead of once."

"No, even then you couldn't count on him," said Athos, who was optimistic about things but pessimistic about people. "It's the same with all our servants. For money, they'll promise to do anything, but fear will stop them from carrying it through. When they're caught, they'll give in to pressure and tell what they know. We shouldn't expect anything else; after all, we're not children. To get to England," he went on, almost in a whisper, "our messenger will have to cross France, and France is swarm- .ing with the cardinal's spies and agents. He'll need a permit to board a ship. In England, he'll have to know English well enough to ask the way to London. The difficulties are enormous."

"Not at all," said d'Artagnan, who urgently wanted the plan to be carried out. "It all seems easy to me. Needless to say, if we send Lord de Winter a letter that's full of state secrets and lurid stories about the cardinal's horrible crimes . . ."

"Not so loud!" said Athos.

" . . . we'll all be hanged," d'Artagnan continued in an undertone. "But don't forget what you said yourself, Athos: we're writing to him about a family matter; we only want to tell him that as soon as Milady arrives in London he must put her in a place where she won't be able to harm us. I'll write the letter, and here's what I'll say . . ."

"Yes, let's hear what you'll write," said Aramis, taking on a critical expression in advance.

" 'My dear friend . . .' "

"Ah, yes, 'dear friend' to an Englishman!" Athos interrupted. "That's a good beginning! Congratulations, d'Artagnan! Those two words alone will be enough to save you from being hanged: you'll be drawn and quartered instead!"

"All right, then, I'll just begin with 'Dear Sir.' "

" 'My Lord' would be better," said Athos, a stickler for etiquette.

" 'My Lord, do you remember the little enclosure behind the Luxembourg?' "

"The Luxembourg? They'll think it's a reference to the queen mother! That's very clever."

"Then I'll just write, 'My Lord, do you remember a certain little enclosure where your life was spared?' "

"D'Artagnan, you'll never know how to write a letter," said Athos. " 'Where your life was spared!' You mustn't remind an honorable man of something like that! It's a sure way to offend him!''

''Athos, you're unbearable! If you go on objecting to every word, I won't write the letter.''

''I'm glad to hear that. Stick to your sword and musket, you handle them very well, but let Aramis wield the pen for us. That's his specialty.''

''Yes, let Aramis do it,'' said Porthos. ''He even knows how to write in Latin.''

''I'm willing,'' said d'Artagnan. ''Write the letter for us, Aramis. But be careful, because I warn you that now *I'm* going to be critical of every word!''

''I'm not worried,'' Aramis replied with the naive self-confidence that is part of every poet's nature. ''But I need to know more details. I gather that Lord de Winter's sister-in-law is an evil woman, and I heard evidence of it myself, during her conversation with the cardinal, but . . .''

''Lower your voice!'' Athos said again.

''But I don't know exactly what she's done,'' Aramis concluded.

''Neither do I,'' said Porthos.

D'Artagnan and Athos looked at each other in silence. Athos thought for a few moments and turned even paler than usual. Finally he nodded, and d'Artagnan understood that he had been given permission to speak.

''Here's the gist of what we want to say: 'My Lord, your sister-in-law is an evil woman. She tried to have you killed so she could inherit from you, but her marriage to your brother was invalid because she already had a husband in France, and . . .' ''

D'Artagnan stopped and looked questioningly at Athos.

''And her husband in France had sent her away,'' said Athos.

''Because she'd been branded,'' continued d'Artagnan.

''Branded!'' exclaimed Porthos. ''And she tried to have her brother-in-law killed?''

''Yes.''

''She already had another husband when she married Lord de Winter's brother?'' asked Aramis.

''Yes.''

''And her first husband saw that she had a fleur-de-lis branded on her shoulder?'' asked Porthos.

''Yes.''

It was Athos who had answered ''Yes'' three times, in an increasingly grim tone.

''Who else has seen that fleur-de-lis?'' asked Aramis.

"D'Artagnan and I," replied Athos, "or rather I and d'Artagnan, to put it in chronological order."

"And that horrible woman's first husband is still alive?"

"He is."

"Are you sure?"

"I'm certain."

There was a silence during which each of the four friends was absorbed in his own feelings. Athos was the first to speak again.

"This time d'Artagnan has done better. The letter should begin with what he said, more or less."

"Yes, but it's important to have the right wording," said Aramis, "and that's a delicate matter. Even the chancellor would find it hard to write such a letter, with all his skill in drawing up reports. Be quiet, all of you, and let me think."

He picked up a pen, stared into space for a few moments, and then began writing in a graceful, feminine hand. When he had finished, he read the letter aloud, so slowly that he seemed to be carefully weighing each word:

> *My Lord,*
> *The man who is writing this to you once had the honor of crossing swords with you in a small enclosure on the Rue d'Enfer. Since you were later kind enough to call yourself his friend, he feels that he must show his gratitude for your friendship by giving you a warning. On two occasions you have nearly been killed by a close relative of yours. You believe that she is entitled to inherit from you, but you do not know that before marrying in England she had already married in France. She is about to make a third attempt on your life. She has left La Rochelle for England. Watch for her arrival, because she has great and terrible plans. If you want to know what she is capable of, read her past on her left shoulder.*

"Excellent!" said Athos. "Aramis, you write like a secretary of state! Lord de Winter will be on his guard—if the letter reaches him. But even if the cardinal intercepts it, it won't put us in danger. Since the servant who takes it may be tempted to stop at Châllerault and tell us he's been to London, we'll pay him only half the money in advance and promise to give him the other half when he brings back a reply. Do you have the diamond ring, d'Artagnan?"

"I have something better than the ring: I have the money I got for it."

And d'Artagnan dropped the bag on the table. At the sound of the gold coins, Aramis looked up and Porthos started. Athos remained impassive.

"How much is in that bag?" he asked.

"Seven thousand livres in twelve-franc louis."

"Seven thousand!" exclaimed Porthos. "That little diamond was worth seven thousand livres?"

"Apparently so," said Athos, "since the money is here in front of us. I assume our friend d'Artagnan hasn't added any money of his own to it."

"We're forgetting about the queen, gentlemen," said d'Artagnan. "Let's give a little thought to the health of her dear Buckingham; that's the least we owe her."

"Yes," said Athos, "but that's Aramis's affair."

"What shall I do?" asked Aramis, blushing.

"It's quite simple," replied Athos. "Write a letter to that resourceful person who lives in Tours."

Aramis picked up his pen again, thought for a moment, wrote another letter, and began reading it to his friends: " 'My dear cousin . . .' "

"So that resourceful person is related to you!" said Athos.

"She's my first cousin."

"I see."

Aramis continued reading:

"My dear cousin,
  His Eminence the cardinal—may God preserve him for the happiness of France and the dismay of her enemies!—is about to finish off the heretical rebels of La Rochelle. It is likely that the English fleet will not even come within sight of the town; I am certain, in fact, that the duke of Buckingham will be prevented from leaving by a great event. His Eminence is the most illustrious statesman who has ever lived, and there will probably never be anyone like him in the future. He would extinguish the sun if it were a hindrance to him. Give this good news to your sister, my dear cousin. I dreamed that cursed Englishman was dead. I cannot remember whether he was stabbed or poisoned, but I am sure I dreamed he was dead, and, as you know, my dreams are never wrong, so you may expect to see me come back soon."

"Excellent again!" said Athos. "Aramis, you're the king of poets. That letter has the ring of gospel truth. Now all you have to do is address it."

He neatly folded the letter and wrote: "To Mademoiselle Marie Michon, Linen-draper, Tours."

His three friends looked at each other and laughed; he had outwitted them.

"And now, gentlemen," said Aramis, "you can understand that only Bazin can take this letter to Tours; he's the only one my cousin knows and trusts. Anyone else would fail. Besides, Bazin is ambitious and learned. He's read history and knows that Sixtus the Fifth became pope after starting in life as a swineherd. He intends to enter the Church when I do, and he has hopes of some day becoming pope, or at least a cardinal. A man with aims like that won't let himself be caught—or, if he *is* caught, he'll undergo martyrdom rather than betray us."

"I'm perfectly willing to have Bazin take the letter for Tours," said d'Artagnan, "but let Planchet take the one for London. Milady once had him beaten and thrown out of her house; he has a good memory, and I promise you that if he sees a chance of getting revenge, he won't let anything stop him. What happens in Tours is your affair, Aramis, and what happens in London is mine. So I ask that Planchet be sent to London. He's been there once before, with me, and he knows English well enough to say, 'London, sir, if you please,' and 'my master, Lord d'Artagnan.' That's all he needs to get there and back, take my word for it."

"Your word is good enough for me," said Athos. "We'll give Planchet seven hundred livres when he leaves and seven hundred when he comes back. For Bazin, it will be three hundred when he leaves and three hundred when he comes back. That brings us down to five thousand. Each of us will take a thousand to use as he sees fit, and Aramis will keep the extra thousand for emergencies or added expenses. Does that suit you?"

"Athos," said Aramis, "you speak like Nestor, who, as everyone knows, was the wisest of the Greeks."

"Then it's settled," said Athos. "Planchet and Bazin will take the letters. To tell you the truth, I'm not sorry that Grimaud is going to stay with me; he's used to my ways and I'd miss him. He must still be badly shaken from our picnic in the bastion yesterday, and I'm afraid a dangerous journey would be the end of him."

Planchet was summoned and given his instructions. D'Artagnan had already told him that he might be sent on a mission; he had first mentioned the glory it involved, then the money, and finally the danger.

"I'll carry the letter in the cuff of one of my coat sleeves," said Planchet, "and if I'm stopped, I'll swallow it."

"But then you won't be able to deliver it," said d'Artagnan.

"Give me a copy of it tonight, and tomorrow I'll know it by heart."

D'Artagnan looked at his friends as though to say, "You see? What did I tell you?"

"You have eight days to reach Lord de Winter and eight days to return," he said to Planchet. "That makes sixteen in all. If you're not back by eight o'clock on the evening of the sixteenth day, no money, not even if you come at five minutes past eight."

"Then buy me a watch, sir," said Planchet.

"Take this one," said Athos, giving him his own with casual generosity, "and be brave. Remember that if you talk loosely or dawdle on the way, you'll be killing your master, who trusts you so much that he's given us his word that you won't fail. And remember this too: if anything happens to d'Artagnan because of you, I'll find you, no matter where you are, and slice open your belly."

"Oh, sir!" cried Planchet, humiliated by Athos's suspicion and frightened by his air of calm determination.

"And I'll skin you alive," said Porthos, glaring at him with his big eyes.

"Oh, sir!"

"And I'll roast you over a slow fire," Aramis said in his gentle, melodious voice.

"Oh, sir!"

Planchet burst into tears; we cannot say whether it was from terror at the threats he had just received or because he was deeply moved to see the four friends so closely united.

D'Artagnan took his hand and embraced him.

"You mustn't misunderstand, Planchet. These gentlemen said all that because they're my loyal friends, but they like you."

"Either I'll succeed, sir, or I'll be cut to pieces, and if that happens, you can be sure that not one piece of me will talk."

It was decided that Planchet would leave at eight o'clock the next morning, so that he could learn the letter by heart during the night, as he had said he would. It was still understood that he was to be back no later than eight o'clock in the evening of the sixteenth day.

The next morning, when Planchet was about to leave, d'Artagnan took him aside.

"When you've given the letter to Lord de Winter," said d'Artagnan, who still had a weak spot in his heart for Buckingham, "and when he's read it, say to him, 'Watch over the duke of Buckingham, because he's in danger of being murdered.' That's such a serious and important secret, Planchet, that I didn't even want to let my friends know I was going to tell it to you, and I wouldn't put it in writing for a captain's commission."

"Don't worry, sir," said Planchet, "you'll see that you can count on me."

He mounted an excellent horse and galloped off. The plan was for him to ride fifty miles and then take a stagecoach. He was still a little dismayed by the threats of d'Artagnan's three friends, but otherwise he was in a buoyant mood.

Bazin left the next morning for Tours, having been given eight days in which to carry out his mission.

While Planchet and Bazin were gone, the four friends were more intensely on the alert than ever. They spent their time eavesdropping on conversations, keeping an eye on the cardinal, and watching for messengers. More than once they trembled when they were summoned for some unexpected duty. They were also concerned about their own safety; Milady was like a ghost that kept people from sleeping peacefully once they had seen it.

On the morning of the eighth day, Bazin walked into the Parpaillot inn, smiling as usual, just as the four friends had begun eating breakfast.

"Monsieur Aramis, here's the answer from your cousin," he announced, using the words he had been told to say if his mission was successful.

The four friends exchanged happy looks; half of the task had been done, though they realized that it was the shortest and easiest half.

Blushing in spite of himself, Aramis took the letter. It was awkwardly written.

"I have no hope of ever teaching that poor Marie to write like Monsieur de Voiture," he said, laughing.

"Who's that poor Marie?" asked the Swiss mercenary, who

had been talking with the four friends when Bazin brought the letter.

"No one important," said Aramis, "only a little linen-draper I was once very fond of. I asked her to write me a letter as a souvenir."

"She has the handwriting of an aristocrat," remarked the Swiss.

Aramis read the letter and gave it to Athos.

"Look what she's written to me," he said.

Athos glanced over the letter and then, to dispel any suspicion that it might have aroused, he read it aloud:

> *"My dear cousin,*
>   *My sister and I are very good at interpreting dreams and we are terribly afraid of them, but I hope that yours will prove to be false.*
>   *Take care of yourself and let us hear from you now and then.*
>
>   *Marie Michon"*

"What dream is she talking about?" asked the dragoon, who had come over to the table when Athos began reading the letter.

"Yes, what dream?" said the Swiss.

"One of my dreams," answered Aramis. "I told her about it."

"I never have any dreams," said the Swiss.

"You're lucky," said Athos, standing up. "I wish I could say the same."

"I never dream," said the Swiss, delighted to know that a man like Athos envied him for something. "Never!"

Seeing Athos stand up, d'Artagnan did the same, took his arm, and left the inn with him.

Porthos and Aramis stayed behind to answer the joking remarks of the dragoon and the Swiss.

As for Bazin, he lay down to sleep on a bundle of straw, and since he had more imagination than the Swiss, he dreamed that Aramis had become pope and made him a cardinal.

But, as we have said, Bazin's successful return had relieved only part of the anxiety that tormented the four friends. Days of waiting are long, and d'Artagnan, especially, felt that each day now contained forty-eight hours. He forgot the slowness of travel by sea and exaggerated Milady's power. He thought of her as a demon and attributed supernatural helpers to her. At the slightest sound, he imagined that Planchet was being brought to him and that he and his friends were about to be arrested. His confidence in Planchet, which had been unshakable, was now weakening day by day. His apprehension was so great that Porthos and Aramis could not help sharing it. Only Athos remained impassive, as if there were no danger around him and he had only ordinary concerns on his mind.

When the sixteenth day arrived, d'Artagnan, Porthos, and Aramis were so agitated that they could not stay still. They wandered like shadows on the road by which Planchet was to return.

"If you're so frightened by a woman," Athos said to them, "you must be children, not men! What is there to be afraid of, after all? Being imprisoned? We'll be taken out of prison, just as Madame Bonacieux was. Being beheaded? Every day in the trench we expose ourselves to worse than that, because a cannon ball can smash your leg, and I'm sure a surgeon makes you suffer more by cutting off your leg than an executioner does by cutting off your head. Don't worry: in two hours, or four, or six at the latest, Planchet will be here. He promised he would, and I have faith in his promise. He doesn't seem to me the kind of man who would let you down."

"But what if he doesn't come?" said d'Artagnan.

"If he doesn't come today, it will mean that he's been delayed, that's all. He may have been thrown off his horse; he may have slipped and fallen on the deck of the ship; he may have traveled so strenuously that he caught a chill and had to stop somewhere to recover. We must make allowance for unexpected events, gentlemen. Life is a series of little mishaps and a philosopher takes them with a smile. Be philosophical, like me. Sit down and have a drink; the future always looks brighter when you see it through a glass of Chambertin."

"Maybe so," said d'Artagnan, "but I'm tired of having to be afraid that the wine I drink may have come from Milady's cellar."

"You're hard to please," said Athos. "She's such a beautiful woman!"

"Yes, a woman of the very finest brand!" Porthos said with a loud laugh.

Athos started, wiped the sweat off his forehead, and stood up with a nervousness that he could not control.

The day finally went by; evening came slowly, but it came. The taverns filled with customers. Athos, having pocketed his share of the money from the diamond ring, had been spending most of his evenings at the Parpaillot. Monsieur de Busigny gave the four friends a magnificent dinner there. Athos had found him to be a worthy gambling opponent. They were gambling together, as usual, when the clock struck seven. Soldiers walked past, on their way to reinforce the guard posts. At half-past seven, tattoo was sounded.

D'Artagnan leaned close to Athos's ear and said, "We're lost."

"You mean we've lost," Athos said calmly, taking four pistoles from his pocket and tossing them onto the table. "Gentlemen, it's time for us to go."

He walked out of the Parpaillot with d'Artagnan. Aramis and Porthos followed. Aramis recited poetry under his breath; now and then Porthos expressed his despair by pulling a few whiskers from his mustache.

Suddenly they saw a shadowy form in the darkness and a familiar voice said to d'Artagnan, "I've brought you your cloak, sir, because it's chilly this evening."

"Planchet!" d'Artagnan exclaimed joyfully.

"Planchet!" repeated Porthos and Aramis.

"Yes, it's Planchet," said Athos. "What's so surprising about it? He promised to be back by eight o'clock and that's exactly what time it is now. Bravo, Planchet! You're a man of your word. If you ever leave your master's service, I'll be glad to take you into mine."

"Oh, no," said Planchet, "I'll never leave Monsieur d'Artagnan."

Just then d'Artagnan felt Planchet slip a letter into his hand.

He had a strong impulse to embrace him again, as he had done before he left, but he restrained himself because he was afraid that passersby might be taken aback by such a display of affection for his servant in the street.

"I have the reply," d'Artagnan told his friends.

"Good," said Athos. "Let's go back to our quarters and read it."

The letter was burning d'Artagnan's hand. He tried to hurry forward, but Athos took him by the arm and made him go on walking at the same pace.

Finally they came to the tent and went inside it. They lit a lamp, and while Planchet stood guard at the entrance to make sure they would not be taken by surprise, d'Artagnan broke the

seal with a trembling hand and opened the long-awaited letter.
The laconic message was in English:

Thank you. Don't worry.

Athos took the letter from d'Artagnan, set fire to it over the
lamp, and did not drop it until it had burned to ashes. He then
called Planchet inside and said to him, "Now you can claim
your seven hundred livres. But you weren't risking much with a
letter like that."

"You can't blame me for wanting to have it as short as
possible," said Planchet.

"Tell us about your journey," said d'Artagnan.

"It's a long story, sir."

"I'm sure it is," said Athos, "so we'd better leave it for later.
Tattoo has sounded and we'd be noticed if we kept our lamp
burning longer than the others."

"Yes, let's go to bed," said d'Artagnan. "Sleep well,
Planchet."

"I will, sir, and it will be the first time I've slept well since I
left."

"It will be the first time for me too!" said d'Artagnan.

"And for me!" said Porthos.

"And for me!" repeated Aramis.

"To tell you the truth," said Athos, "for me too!"

49

A Disastrous Setback

After the ship had set sail, Milady had stood on deck, seething
with the helpless fury of a caged lioness. She was tempted to
jump overboard and swim back to shore, because she could not
tolerate the thought that she had been insulted by d'Artagnan and
threatened by Athos, and was leaving France without having
taken vengeance on them. This thought soon became so unbearable that, ignoring the terrible consequences it might have for
her, she begged the captain of the ship to put her ashore
immediately. But the captain, knowing he was in danger from

both French and English warships, wanted to return to England as quickly as possible. He stubbornly refused to give in to what he regarded as a woman's whim. Since his passenger had been sent to him by the cardinal, however, he promised her that if the sea or the French did not prevent it, he would put her ashore at a port in Brittany, either Lorient or Brest. Meanwhile the wind was contrary, the sea was rough, and the ship had to make laborious progress by tacking.

Nine days after putting to sea, Milady, pale with chagrin and rage, saw the bluish coast of Finistère. She estimated that it would take at least three days to cross that part of France and return to the cardinal; with one day for reaching the coast and landing, that made four; and the nine days that had already passed made a total of thirteen days wasted—thirteen days during which so many important things might have happened in London. She realized that the cardinal would undoubtedly be furious with her for coming back and would therefore be more inclined to listen to complaints against her than to her accusations against others. So she watched Lorient and Brest pass by in the distance and did not hold the captain to his promise; and he said nothing to remind her of it. She continued her voyage and reached Portsmouth the same day Planchet boarded a ship there, on his way back to France.

The whole city was astir: four large ships, recently built, had just been launched. On the pier stood the duke of Buckingham, dazzlingly adorned as usual with gold and precious stones, wearing a hat whose white plume drooped down to his shoulder, and surrounded by staff officers dressed nearly as impressively as himself.

It was one of those beautiful and rare winter days when England remembers that there is a sun. Still radiant as it set on the horizon, the sun streaked the sea and the sky with crimson and cast a last golden ray on the towers and buildings of the city, making the windowpanes glitter as though from the reflection of a fire. Smelling the increasing fragrance of the air as the ship approached land, Milady contemplated the powerful force of vessels and men that she was expected to defeat by her own efforts, with only a few bags of gold to help her. She compared herself with Judith, the Jewish heroine, when she entered the Assyrian camp and saw the enormous mass of chariots, horses, men, and weapons that she was to dissipate like a puff of smoke with a single movement of her hand.

The ship came into the roadstead. As it was about to drop

anchor, a heavily armed little cutter approached and signaled that it was a coastal defense vessel. A boat was lowered from it, containing an officer, a boatswain, and eight oarsmen. Only the officer came aboard the ship, where he was received with the deference owed to his uniform.

He had a brief conversation with the captain and showed him a sheet of paper. The captain ordered the crew and passengers to assemble on deck.

When this order had been carried out, the officer loudly asked where the ship had come from, what course it had followed and where it had stopped along the way. The captain answered these questions without hesitation. The officer began examining the sailors and passengers one by one. He stepped in front of Milady and looked her over carefully, but without saying a word to her.

He went back to the captain and again spoke to him briefly. Then, as if he had taken command of the ship, he gave the crew an order that they promptly obeyed. The ship got under way again. The cutter stayed alongside it, threatening its side with six cannons. The boat followed in the wake of the ship, dwarfed by its huge mass.

While the officer had been scrutinizing Milady, she had, of course, scrutinized him with equal attention. But despite her skill in reading the thoughts of those whose secrets she needed to discover, this time she found a face so impassive that it told her nothing. The officer who had studied her so intently in silence was a young man of about twenty-five with deepset blue eyes and thin, firm lips; his prominent chin denoted that strength of will that, in the common British type, is usually only stubbornness; he had the high forehead of a poet, a visionary, or a military leader; his short, thin hair had the same dark reddish-brown color as the beard that covered the lower part of his face.

When the ship entered the harbor, darkness had already fallen. Fog made the night still darker and drew luminous circles around the lanterns on the pier, like the ring that surrounds the moon when rain is threatening. The damp, chilly air had a depressing effect on Milady; strong as she was, she shivered in spite of herself.

The officer had Milady's baggage lowered into the boat. He then held out his hand to her and asked her to climb down the ladder.

She looked at him and hesitated.

"Who are you?" she asked. "And why are you giving me this special attention?"

"My uniform should tell you who I am," he replied. "I'm an English naval officer."

"Is it customary for English naval officers to meet passengers coming into an English port and carry courtesy to the point of personally taking them ashore?"

"In time of war it's customary—as a precaution, not as a courtesy—to take foreigners to special inns and keep them there until the government has complete information on them."

Though these words were spoken calmly and politely, they did not put Milady at ease.

"But I'm not a foreigner," she said in flawless English, "and I find this treatment . . ."

"There are no exceptions to the rule."

"Very well, then, I'll go with you."

She took his hand, then climbed down the ladder to the waiting boat. He followed her. A large cloak had been spread out in the stern; he invited her to sit down on it and sat beside her.

At his order, the eight oarsmen began rowing. Their oars moved with perfect regularity, all dipping into the water at once, and the boat seemed to skim over the surface.

Five minutes later it reached shore.

The officer leapt onto the pier and held out his hand to Milady.

A carriage was waiting.

"Is that carriage for us?" she asked.

"Yes," replied the officer.

"How far is the inn?"

"It's on the other side of the city."

"Let's go," said Milady, and she resolutely got into the carriage.

The officer saw to it that her baggage was carefully tied to the outside, then he took his place beside her and closed the door.

Without being given an order or told where to go, the coachman started off the horses at a gallop.

Milady's strange reception had given her food for thought. Seeing that the young officer did not seem at all inclined to talk, she sat back in her corner of the carriage and began examining all the possibilities that came into her mind.

After a quarter of an hour, surprised by the length of the journey, she leaned toward the window to see where she was being taken. There were no houses in sight; trees filed past in the darkness like big black ghosts running after each other. She shuddered.

"We've left the city!" she said.

The officer remained silent.

"I warn you that I won't go any farther unless you tell me where you're taking me!"

Her threat brought no response from him.

"This is too much! Help! Help!"

Her cries went unanswered. The carriage continued rolling swiftly along. The officer seemed to have been turned into a statue.

Her eyes blazed in the darkness as she glared at him with a fierce expression that seldom failed to produce an effect. He showed no reaction.

She tried to open the door.

"Be careful," he said calmly, "you'll be killed if you jump out."

She sat back again. He leaned toward her and was surprised to see that her beautiful face was so contorted by anger that it had become almost hideous. Realizing that she must not reveal her true self to him, she composed her features and said plaintively, "In the name of heaven, tell me whether it's you, your government, or an enemy who's responsible for the violence that's being done to me!"

"No violence is being done to you. This is simply a precaution that we're obliged to take with everyone who comes into England."

"Then you don't know me?"

"This is the first time I've ever had the honor of seeing you."

"Will you swear on your honor that you have no reason to hate me?"

"None, I give you my word."

His tone was so serene and even gentle that she was reassured.

Finally, when they had been traveling nearly an hour, the carriage stopped in front of an iron gate that was quickly opened, revealing a graveled drive leading to a massive, grim-looking, isolated castle. As the wheels rolled over the gravel, Milady heard a vast roar that she recognized as the sound of the sea breaking against a steep coast.

The carriage passed under two arches and came to a halt in a dark, square courtyard. The officer opened the door, leapt out, and offered his hand to Milady. She leaned on it and stepped down rather calmly.

She glanced around her, then looked at the officer with a gracious smile.

"I'm still a prisoner," she said, "but my clear conscience and your courtesy assure me that it won't be for long."

He made no reply to her compliment. From his belt he took a little silver whistle like those used by boatswains on warships and blew it three times in three different tones. Three men appeared, unharnessed the steaming horses, and pulled the carriage into a shed.

Still with the same impassive politeness, the officer invited his prisoner to come inside. She smiled at him again, took his arm, and went with him through a low, arched doorway into a vaulted corridor, lighted only at the far end, that led to a stone spiral staircase. They stopped in front of a heavy door. When he had unlocked it and pushed it open, they went into the room that had been prepared for her.

She rapidly examined it. It seemed to be furnished too attractively for a prison cell and too austerely for a guest room. But the bars on the window and the bolts on the outside of the door made it clear to her that she was in a cell.

For a moment her vigorous inner strength abandoned her; she sank into an armchair, folded her arms, and bowed her head, expecting a judge to come in and question her.

But no one came in except three soldiers carrying her baggage. By gestures, the officer ordered them to put it down in a corner. It was as though speech had become unnecessary between him and his subordinates. When they had obeyed his orders, the three men left without a word.

Finally, unable to bear it any longer, Milady broke the silence.

"Tell me what all this means! Let me know where I stand! I have the courage to face danger or misfortune if I understand it. Where am I, and why am I here? If I'm free, why is the window barred? If I'm a prisoner, then what crime have I committed?"

"All I can tell you is that you're in the place where it was intended for you to be. My orders were to take you from the ship and bring you to this castle. I believe I've carried out those orders with military strictness, but also with the courtesy of a gentleman. I've now done my duty with regard to you, at least for the present; what happens next will be decided by someone else."

"Who is that someone else?" asked Milady. "Can't you tell me his name?"

Just then she heard spurs jingling on the staircase; voices arose and faded away, and footsteps approached the door.

"Here he is now," said the officer, stepping aside from the doorway. He stood at attention.

The door opened and a man appeared on the threshold. He was bareheaded, a sword hung at his side, and he had a handkerchief in one hand.

Though he stood in shadow, Milady thought she recognized him. She pressed one hand against the arm of her chair and leaned forward as though to confirm a certainty.

He slowly walked toward her. As he approached the circle of light cast by the lamp, she involuntarily drew back.

"You!" she cried out in amazement when she could no longer doubt his identity.

"Yes, it's I," said Lord de Winter, with a bow that was half courteous and half ironic.

"Then this castle . . ."

"It's mine."

"And this room . . ."

"It's yours."

"I'm your prisoner?"

"More or less."

"This is a shameful abuse of power!"

"Please don't make a speech," said Lord de Winter. "Let's have a calm, sensible family discussion." He turned toward the door and, seeing that the young officer was awaiting his orders, said to him, "Thank you, Felton. You may go now."

50

A Conversation between Relatives

Lord de Winter closed the door, then drew a chair close to his sister-in-law's.

Now that she knew into whose hands she had fallen, Milady had been examining her situation in that light. She knew that her brother-in-law was an ardent hunter, a reckless gambler, and a bold seducer, but she was sure that as far as intrigue was concerned he was no match for her. How had he been able to discover that she was coming to England, and have her seized? Why was he keeping her a prisoner?

From what Athos had told her, it was clear that her conversation with the cardinal had been overheard, but she could not believe that he had been able to organize such an effective counterattack so quickly.

She was afraid that her earlier operations in England had been discovered. Perhaps Buckingham had learned that it was she who had cut off the two diamond tags; it was not in his nature to do anything extreme against a woman, especially if he thought she had acted out of jealousy, but he might still want some sort of revenge.

This seemed to her the most likely explanation; she had probably been imprisoned to punish her for the past, not to prevent her from doing something in the future. And since she expected to outwit her brother-in-law without difficulty, she was glad to be dealing with him, rather than being directly confronted by a more intelligent enemy.

"Yes, let's talk," she said almost cheerfully; she needed information in order to make her plans and she was determined to get it from him no matter how he might try to mislead her.

"Why have you come back to England," asked Lord de Winter, "after telling me so often in Paris that you never wanted to set foot on English soil again?"

Milady evaded this question by asking another one.

"How did you keep such close watch on me that you knew not only that I was coming back, but also the exact date, time, and place of my arrival?"

He decided to use the same tactic, feeling that since she had used it, it must be good.

"What did you intend to do in England?"

"I came to see you," she said, hoping to make him more favorably disposed toward her by this lie and not realizing that it reinforced the suspicion aroused in his mind by d'Artagnan's letter.

He tried to show no reaction.

"You came to see me?"

"Yes. What's so surprising about that?"

"You had no other reason for coming to England?"

"No."

"So you crossed the Channel only to see me?"

"That's right."

"I'm touched by your affection, my dear sister-in-law."

"After all, I'm your closest relative," she said winsomely.

"Which means that you expect to inherit from me," he retorted, looking her straight in the eyes.

In spite of all her self-control she could not help quivering, and since he had laid his hand on her arm when he spoke, that quiver did not escape him.

His words had been a direct attack on her. The first thought that came into her mind was that Kitty had betrayed her, for she remembered that she had been foolish enough to display her dislike of her brother-in-law in front of her maid. She also remembered that she had shown her anger against d'Artagnan for having spared Lord de Winter's life.

"I don't understand," she said, hoping to gain time and make her adversary talk. "Is there some hidden meaning in what you just said?"

"No, no, of course not," he replied with apparent good humor. "I learned that you were coming to England because you wanted to see me, or at least I assumed you were coming for that reason, and to spare you all the tiresome annoyances of leaving a ship in a port at night, I sent one of my officers to meet you. I put a carriage at his disposal and he brought you here. Since I'm in command of this castle, I come here every day. I had a room prepared for you so that we could have the pleasure of seeing each other. Is there anything more surprising in that than in what you told me?"

"No. What surprises me is that you knew I was coming."

"It's quite simple. Didn't you notice that before entering the roadstead the captain of your ship sent a boat on ahead with his logbook and a list of his passengers and crew, to ask permission to come into the harbor? I'm the governor of the port, so the list was brought to me and I saw your name. My heart told me what you've just confirmed: that you'd braved the danger and fatigue of a sea voyage in order to see me. I sent my cutter out to meet your ship. You know the rest."

Milady knew he was lying and this alarmed her still more.

"Wasn't that the duke of Buckingham I saw on the pier when I arrived?" she asked.

"Yes, it was. I can understand why you were struck by the sight of him: you've come from a country where there must be a great deal of talk about him, and I know that his preparations for war against France are a matter of serious concern to your friend the cardinal."

"My friend the cardinal!" exclaimed Milady, taken aback to realize that Lord de Winter was also well informed on this point.

"He's not your friend?" de Winter asked nonchalantly. "Excuse me, I thought he was. We'll come back to the duke of Buckingham later, but first I'd like to go on discussing the pleasant topic of your visit. You've come to England only to see me, is that right?"

"Yes."

"Then you must be delighted to know that I've arranged things so that we can see each other every day."

"Are you going to keep me here forever?" she asked apprehensively.

"Aren't you comfortable here? Just ask for anything you need and I'll have it brought to you immediately."

"I have no maids, no servants . . ."

"That will be taken care of. Tell me how your household was organized when you lived with your first husband, and although I'm only your brother-in-law, I'll see to it that you're equally well served here."

"My first husband!" cried Milady, wide-eyed with fear.

"Yes, your French husband; I'm not referring to my brother. If you've forgotten the details of your household when you lived with him, I can write and ask him for the information I need, since he's still alive."

Cold sweat broke out on Milady's forehead.

"You're joking," she said in a choked voice.

"Do I seem to be joking?" asked de Winter, standing up and stepping back from her.

She clutched the arms of her chair and raised herself to her feet.

"Then you're insulting me!"

"Insulting you?" he said contemptuously. "Do you really think that's possible?"

"You're either drunk or insane. Get out, and send me a maid."

"Maids are so indiscreet! Why not let me serve as your attendant? That way, all our secrets will remain in the family."

"You insolent . . ."

She rushed toward him. He waited for her impassively, though with his hand on his sword.

"I know you're used to murdering people," he said, "but I warn you that I'll defend myself, even against you."

"I believe you. You're the kind of coward who would use force against a woman."

"Yes, I might," he replied, "but I'd have an excuse: I wouldn't be the first man to use force against you."

And he slowly pointed to her left shoulder, almost touching it with his finger.

She uttered a cry of rage and backed away from him, like a panther preparing to spring.

"Roar all you like," he said, "but don't try to bite, because you'll regret it if you do. There are no lawyers here to settle inheritances in advance, no knight-errant who will come and fight me over the fair lady I'm holding prisoner. But there are judges ready to deal with a woman shameless enough to slip into my brother's bed when she was already married to another man. They'll send you to a public executioner who will make your right shoulder the same as your left."

Her eyes blazed so fiercely that even though he was an armed man facing an unarmed woman, he felt a chill of fear. He continued, however, with growing anger:

"Yes, I can understand that after inheriting from my brother you'd have liked to inherit from me, but I've taken precautions against that. It will do you no good to kill me or have me killed, because you won't get your hands on one penny of my money. You already have a fortune, isn't that enough for you? Your only reason for doing evil is that it gives you pleasure. If the memory of my brother weren't sacred to me, you'd rot in a dungeon or be hanged at Tyburn. I'll say nothing about you to the authorities, but in return I expect you to bear your captivity without complaining. In two or three weeks I'll go to La Rochelle with the army. The day before I leave, you'll be put on a ship and deported to one of our southern colonies. And I'll send a man to keep an eye on you, with orders to shoot you on the spot if you make any attempt to come back to England or the Continent."

Milady listened to him with a concentration that dilated her inflamed eyes.

"But for the present," he went on, "you'll stay in this castle. The walls are thick, the doors are strong, the bars are solid, and from your window there's a sheer drop down to the sea, far below. Men who are unshakably loyal to me will be guarding this room and all passages leading to the courtyard. Even if you reached the courtyard, you'd still have to go through three iron gates. My men are under strict orders to shoot you at the slightest sign of any effort to escape. If they kill you, I think the authorities will be grateful to me for sparing them the trouble of doing it themselves. I see your face is becoming calm and confident again. You're saying to yourself, 'I have two or three weeks! With my inventive mind, I'm sure to think of something by then, and I can entice some fool into helping me. I'll be out of here in less than two weeks.' Well, all I can say to you is: try!''

Seeing that he had guessed her thoughts, Milady dug her fingernails into the palms of her hands to keep herself from showing any other feeling than anguish.

"The officer who brought you here is in command during my absence," Lord de Winter continued. "He knows how to obey an order, as you've already discovered, because I'm sure you didn't come here from Portsmouth without trying to make him talk. You couldn't have learned less from him if he'd been a statue, could you? You've tried your powers of seduction on many men and till now, unfortunately, you've always succeeded, but just try them on *this* man! If you succeed with him, I'll know you're a demon in the form of a woman!''

He went to the door, opened it, and called out, "Ask Lieutenant Felton to come here." He turned back to Milady. "I'm going to tell him what he can expect from you."

In the silence that fell between them, they heard slow, steady footsteps approaching. Then a figure appeared in the shadowy hall and a moment later the young lieutenant stopped in the doorway to await Lord de Winter's orders.

"Come in, John, and shut the door."

John Felton stepped into the room.

"Look at this woman," said de Winter. "She's young and beautiful, and she has every kind of charm imaginable; yet she's a monster who, at the age of twenty-five, has already committed as many crimes as you'll find in the records of our law courts for a year. Her voice speaks in her favor, her beauty lures her victims, and I must say in all fairness that her body pays what she's promised. She'll try to seduce you, she may even try to kill you. I rescued you from poverty, John, I had you commissioned as a lieutenant, I saved your life once, as you remember. I've been not only a protector to you, but also a friend; not only a benefactor, but also a father. This woman came back to England to plot against my life. She's as dangerous as a viper, but now I've captured her. John, my friend, my son, protect me, and especially yourself, against her. Swear to me that you'll keep her

here for the punishment she deserves. I trust your word, I believe
in your loyalty.''

"I swear I'll do as you wish, sir," said Felton, looking at
Milady with all the hatred he could find in his heart.

She received his look with such a gentle, submissive expression on her beautiful face that Lord de Winter scarcely recognized her as the tigress he had been prepared to fight only a short
time earlier.

"She must never leave this room, John. She will correspond
with no one and speak to no one but you—if you do her the
honor of speaking to her.''

"Yes, sir. I'll obey your orders to the letter.''

"And now," de Winter said to Milady, "try to make your
peace with God for the next world, because you've already been
judged in this one.''

Milady bowed her head as if she felt crushed by that judgment.
Lord de Winter walked out of the room, followed by Felton,
who locked the door behind him.

A few moments later Milady heard the heavy footsteps of the
guard in the hall, pacing back and forth with an axe in his belt
and a musket in his hand.

She remained in the same position for several minutes because
she thought that perhaps she was being watched through the
keyhole. Then she slowly raised her head. Her face now had an
expression of fierce defiance. After listening at the door and
looking through the window, she came back to her big armchair,
sat down in it, and became absorbed in thought.

51

Officer!

Meanwhile the cardinal was waiting for news from England, but
the only news that came was disturbing.

The siege of La Rochelle was well organized. The precautions
that had been taken, especially the dike that prevented all ships
from reaching the town, made success seem certain. But the
blockade might last a long time; that was an affront to the king's
army and a great annoyance to the cardinal. His Eminence no

longer had to be concerned with sowing discord between the king and the queen, since that goal had been achieved, but he now had to quell the antagonism between Monsieur de Bassompierre and the duke d'Angoulême.

As for Monsieur, who had begun the siege, he was content to let the cardinal finish it.

Despite the incredible tenacity of the town's mayor, some of its people had tried to rebel and surrender. The mayor had had the rebels hanged. This had calmed the others who favored surrender, and they had decided to await death by starvation, since it was slower and less certain than death by hanging.

Now and then the besiegers captured messengers sent from La Rochelle to Buckingham, or spies sent by Buckingham to La Rochelle. In either case, the trial was brief. The cardinal always gave the same sentence: "Hang him!" The king was invited to watch these executions. He went to them indolently and always sat in a place from which he could see all the details; to him, they were a diversion that helped to relieve the monotony of the siege. But he was still bored most of the time and kept talking about going back to Paris. If the cardinal had run out of messengers and spies, he would have been hard pressed to find another diversion for the king, despite all his imagination.

Time passed nevertheless. La Rochelle still refused to surrender. A spy was captured with a letter for Buckingham, telling him that the town could not hold out much longer; but instead of adding, "If your help does not arrive within two weeks, we will surrender," it added, "If your help does not arrive within two weeks, we will all die from starvation."

The people of La Rochelle had only one hope: Buckingham. They regarded him as their savior. It was obvious that if they ever learned with certainty that they could not count on him, their courage as well as their hope would be destroyed. The cardinal therefore waited impatiently for news from England announcing that Buckingham would not come.

The idea of trying to take the town by storm had often been debated in the king's council, and it had always been rejected. First of all, La Rochelle seemed to be impregnable. Furthermore, despite what he said, the cardinal knew that the horror of bloodshed in a battle of Frenchmen against Frenchmen would set the country back sixty years, from a political standpoint, and he was what is now called a man of progress. If, in 1628, the king's army were to sack La Rochelle and kill three or four thousand Huguenots, it would be too reminiscent of the Saint Bartholomew's

Day massacre in 1572. The king, a good Catholic, had no moral qualms about taking that extreme course, but his generals always opposed it with the argument that La Rochelle could not be captured by any means except starvation.

The cardinal could not help being apprehensive about his emissary, for he too was aware of Milady's disquieting ability to be a raging lioness one moment and a wily serpent the next. Had she betrayed him? Was she dead? He knew her well enough to be sure that whether she was working for or against him, whether she was his friend or his enemy, she would not remain inactive unless something serious had happened to her, but so far he had been unable to learn what had gone wrong.

Even so, he still counted on her. He had guessed that in her past there were terrible things that only his red cloak could cover, but he felt that she would be loyal to him because only he was powerful enough to protect her from the danger that threatened her.

He finally decided to carry on the war alone, without expecting any outside help, though he did not rule out the possibility that such help might come as a stroke of good luck. He went on building the famous dike that was to starve the people of La Rochelle. Meanwhile he considered the plight of that unfortunate town, which contained so much misery and heroism, and recalled the maxim of Louis XI, his political predecessor, just as he was Robespierre's: "Divide and rule."

When Henry IV was besieging Paris, he had food thrown over the walls to the people; the cardinal had leaflets thrown over the walls of La Rochelle, telling the people how unjust, selfish, and barbaric their leaders' conduct was. Those leaders had a large supply of grain but did not share it; they had adopted the principle that it did not matter how many women, children, and old men died, as long as the men who were to defend their walls remained strong and healthy. Although that principle was not accepted by everyone, it had been put into practice. Now it was shaken by the cardinal's leaflets. They reminded the able-bodied men that the children, women, and old men being starved were their sons, wives, and fathers, and that it would be more just if suffering were divided equally among the population, so that a shared situation would result in unanimous decisions.

These leaflets had the effect that the cardinal expected: they prompted a large number of the townspeople to open negotiations with the royal army.

But just as the cardinal's stratagem was beginning to succeed

and he was congratulating himself on having used it, a man
returned to La Rochelle from Portsmouth. God only knows how
he was able to slip through the royal lines in spite of the strict
surveillance maintained by Bassompierre, Schomberg, and the
duke d'Angoulême, who were in turn closely watched by the
cardinal. Be that as it may, the man reported that in Portsmouth
he had seen a magnificent fleet ready to set sail in less than a
week. He also had a letter from Buckingham to the mayor,
announcing that the great league against France was about to
take action and that the kingdom would be invaded by the
English, Imperial, and Spanish armies. This letter was read
aloud in all public squares, and copies of it were displayed at
street corners. Those who had opened negotiations now broke
them off and resolved to wait for the help that had been promised.

This setback revived the cardinal's previous apprehensions and
forced him to be concerned with what was happening on the other
side of the Channel.

The royal army, however, was unaffected by the cares of its
only real leader. The men were leading a joyous life. There was
no shortage of food or money in the camp. All units of the army
vied with each other in daring and gaiety. Capturing and hanging
spies, making hazardous excursions on the dike or at sea,
planning reckless exploits and coolheadedly performing them—
these were the pastimes that made the days seem short to the
army. Yet these were the same days that seemed so long not only
to the people of La Rochelle, who were gnawed by hunger and
anxiety, but also to the cardinal, who was stringently blockading
them.

The cardinal often rode out to inspect the siegeworks being
built under the supervision of engineers he had brought from all
parts of France. No matter how fast the work was progressing, it
was never as fast as he would have liked. During these outings
he sometimes encountered a musketeer from Tréville's company;
he would ride closer to him and scrutinize him, and then, not
recognizing him as one of our four friends, he would look away
from him and turn his thoughts to other matters.

One day, bored, still without news from England, and having
lost hope of negotiating with the town, the cardinal took a ride
outside the camp for lack of anything better to do, accompanied
by Cahusac and La Houdinière. As he rode slowly along the
coast, mingling the vastness of his daydreams with the vastness
of the ocean, he reached the top of a hill from which he saw
seven men lying on the sand, surrounded by empty bottles. It

was one of the sunny days so rare at that time of year. Four of those men were our musketeers. One of them had just received a letter and was about to read it aloud to the others. Three of their servants were opening an enormous demijohn of Collioure wine.

The cardinal was in a gloomy mood, and when he was in such a mood, nothing made him more peevish than seeing others enjoy themselves. Furthermore, one of his peculiarities was that he always believed others were happy precisely because of the things that made him sad. He motioned La Houdinière and Cahusac to stop, then he dismounted and walked toward those suspiciously cheerful men, hoping that the sand would muffle his footsteps and the hedge would conceal his approach enough to enable him to overhear their conversation. When he was ten paces away from the hedge, he recognized d'Artagnan's Gascon accent, and since he already knew that the three others were musketeers he had no doubt that they were those known as the inseparables: Athos, Porthos, and Aramis.

This discovery made him all the more eager to eavesdrop on their conversation. A strange look appeared in his eyes and he moved stealthily toward the hedge. So far he had been able to make out only a few isolated words that were not enough to give him the meaning of what was being said. Suddenly an exclamation startled him and drew the attention of the musketeers.

"Officer!" cried Grimaud.

"You've spoken!" Athos said sternly, raising himself on one elbow and glaring at him.

Grimaud said nothing more; he merely pointed in the direction of the cardinal and his escort. The four musketeers leapt to their feet and bowed respectfully.

The cardinal seemed furious.

"Apparently the musketeers post their own guards now!" he said. "Are the English coming by land, or do you regard yourselves as senior officers?"

In the midst of the panic around him, Athos had kept the lordly calm that never deserted him.

"Monseigneur," he said, "when musketeers aren't on duty, they drink and play dice, and to their servants they're officers of very high rank."

"Servants!" the cardinal said irascibly. "When servants are under orders to warn their master if anyone passes by, they're no longer servants: they're sentries!"

"If we hadn't taken that precaution, Monseigneur," Athos replied, "you might have passed by without our knowing it, and we'd have missed this chance to pay our respects to you and thank you for having brought the four of us together." He turned to d'Artagnan. "You were saying just now that you wished you could express your gratitude to His Eminence for having made you a musketeer. Here he is; take advantage of your opportunity."

Athos said all this with the imperturbable self-assurance that distinguished him in times of danger, and with the extreme courtesy that sometimes made him more majestic than a king.

D'Artagnan stepped forward and stammered a few words of thanks but soon fell silent before the cardinal's grim expression.

His Eminence showed no sign of having been mollified by the diversion that Athos had tried to create.

"I don't like ordinary soldiers who act like great lords simply because they belong to a privileged unit," he said. "Discipline is the same for them as for anyone else."

Athos bowed again and said, "I don't believe we've neglected discipline in any way, Monseigneur. We're not on duty now and we felt we were entitled to spend our time as we saw fit. If you have special orders for us, we're ready to obey." He frowned slightly, for he was beginning to lose patience at having to defend himself. "As you can see, we brought our weapons with us, to be prepared for any emergency."

He pointed to the four muskets stacked beside the drum on which the dice and cards were lying.

"Your Eminence," said d'Artagnan, "we'd have gone forward to meet you if we'd known it was you coming toward us with such a small escort."

The cardinal bit his mustache and a little of his upper lip.

"Do you know what you look like, armed and guarded by your servants?" he said. "You look like four conspirators."

"We *are* conspirators, Monseigneur," said Athos, "but as you saw the other morning, we conspire against the enemy."

"I might learn many things," said the cardinal, scowling, "if I could read your minds the way you were reading the letter you hid when you saw me coming."

Blood rose to Athos's face and he took a step toward the cardinal.

"You seem to be really suspicious of us, Monseigneur, and this seems to be a real interrogation. If so, please tell us the reason for it. Then we'll at least know where we stand."

"What if it *is* an interrogation, Monsieur Athos? I've interrogated others before you, and they've answered."

"We're ready to answer any questions you may want to ask us, Monseigneur."

"What's that letter you were about to read before you hid it, Monsieur Aramis?"

"It's a letter from a woman, Monseigneur."

"Ah, I understand!" said the cardinal. "One must be discreet with such letters. But they can be shown to a confessor, and, as you know, I've taken holy orders."

"Monseigneur," Athos said with a calm that was all the more impressive because he knew that what he was about to say might cost him his life, "the letter is from a woman, but it's not signed Marion de Lorme or Madame d'Aiguillon."*

The cardinal's eyes flashed and his face went livid. He turned around as though to give an order to Cahusac and La Houdinière. When Athos saw this movement, he stepped toward the muskets. His friends were already looking at them in a way that made it clear that they had no intention of letting themselves be arrested. The cardinal had only two men with him; the musketeers and their servants numbered seven. He judged that the odds against him were too great, especially since he now believed that the musketeers really had been conspiring and would therefore resist any attempt to arrest them. In one of those rapid turnabouts that he always had at his disposal, his anger melted into a smile.

"I didn't mean to give the impression that I doubted your loyalty, gentlemen," he said. "There's no harm in looking out for yourselves when you look out for others so well: I haven't forgotten the night when you escorted me to the Colombier-Rouge. If there were any danger on the road I'm about to travel now, I'd ask you to accompany me again, but there's none, so stay here and finish your bottles, your game, and your letter. Good-bye, gentlemen."

He mounted his horse, which Cahusac had brought to him, and rode off.

The four young men stood watching him in silence till he disappeared. Then they looked at each other. D'Artagnan, Porthos, and Aramis had an expression of dismay because they realized that despite the cardinal's friendly farewell he had gone off with rage in his heart. As for Athos, he smiled disdainfully.

"Grimaud took his time about warning us!" said Porthos, who felt like venting his ill-humor on someone.

---

*Two women who were reputed to have been the cardinal's mistresses. (Translator's note.)

Grimaud was about to apologize when Athos silenced him by raising a finger.

"Would you have given that letter to the cardinal, Aramis?" asked d'Artagnan.

"I'd made up my mind," Aramis replied in his gentle voice, "that if he demanded the letter I'd hold it out to him with one hand and run my sword through his body with the other."

"I thought you might have decided something like that," said Athos. "That's why I stood between you and the cardinal. It was rash of him to talk that way to men: he acts as if he'd never dealt with anyone but women and children."

"I admire you, Athos," said d'Artagnan, "but the fact is that we were in the wrong."

"In the wrong? What do you mean? Who owns the air we're breathing, and the ocean, and the sand we were lying on, and that letter? Does the cardinal own all that? No, he doesn't, but he thinks the whole world belongs to him! You stood there stammering, paralyzed, as if you saw the Bastille in front of you and the sight of it had turned you to stone. Does being in love mean that you're a conspirator? You're in love with a woman the cardinal has imprisoned, and you want to rescue her from him. It's a game between you and him, a deadly serious game. That letter is the highest card in your hand. Why should you show your opponent your highest card? If he can guess it, that's perfectly fair—after all, we've guessed some of the cards in *his* hand!"

"What you're saying is very sensible," d'Artagnan acknowledged.

"Then let's stop talking about what just happened. Aramis, go on reading the letter where you left off when the cardinal interrupted you."

Aramis took the letter from his pocket. His three friends moved closer to him and the three servants again gathered around the demijohn.

"You'd read only a line or two," said d'Artagnan, "so start over from the beginning."

"Very well," said Aramis, and he read aloud:

"My dear cousin,
    I think I will soon go to Béthune, where my sister has placed our little servant girl in the Carmelite convent. The poor girl has resigned herself because she knows she cannot live anywhere else without endangering the salvation of her

*soul. But if our family affairs are settled in the way we wish,
I believe she will run the risk of damnation and come back
to the people she misses, especially since she knows they
still think of her. In the meantime she is not too unhappy.
All she wants is a letter from her fiancé. I know it is not
easy to get such letters into a convent, but, as I have proven
to you, my dear cousin, I am rather resourceful, and I will
see to it that the letter is delivered. My sister was greatly
worried for a time, but her mind is a little more at ease now
that she has sent someone to make sure that nothing unexpected will happen.*

*Good-bye, my dear cousin. Let us hear from you as often
as you can, that is, whenever you believe you can do it
safely.*

Love,
Marie Michon''

"I'm so grateful to you, Aramis!" said d'Artagnan. "At last I
have news of my dear Constance! She's alive, she's safe in a
convent at Béthune! Where's Béthune, Athos?"

"It's not far from Lille. We can go there when the siege is
over."

"It shouldn't take much longer," said Porthos. "This morning they hanged a spy who said that people in La Rochelle are
eating their shoe leather now. I suppose that after they've eaten
the leather they'll eat the soles, and I don't see what they'll have
left then, unless they start eating each other."

Athos emptied a glass of excellent Bordeaux wine, which at
that time did not have the reputation it has today, but deserved it
nevertheless.

"Poor fools!" he said. "They don't seem to realize that
Catholicism is the most pleasant and advantageous of all religions!"
He paused to savor the aftertaste of the wine. "Even so, you
have to admire them . . . Aramis, why are you putting that letter
back in your pocket?"

"Athos is right," said d'Artagnan, "we mustn't keep it. Let's
burn it—though for all I know, the cardinal may have a way of
reading ashes."

"I wouldn't be at all surprised," said Athos.

"Then what shall we do with the letter?" asked Porthos.

Athos called Grimaud, who stood up and came over to him.

"Grimaud, my friend, as punishment for having spoken without permission, you're going to eat this letter, and then, as a

reward for the service you'll have rendered us by eating it, you'll drink this glass of wine. Here's the letter; chew it thoroughly."

Grimaud smiled. Looking at the glass that Athos had just filled to the brim with wine, he chewed the letter and swallowed it.

"Well done, Grimaud!" said Athos. "Here's your wine. I'll excuse you from thanking me."

Grimaud drank the Bordeaux in silence, but his eyes eloquently expressed his appreciation for it.

"And now," said Athos, "unless the cardinal has the ingenious idea of opening Grimaud's belly, I don't think there's any need for us to worry about that letter."

Meanwhile His Eminence continued his melancholy ride. Now and then he muttered in his mustache, "I must have those four men in my service!"

52

First Day of Captivity

Our brief look at events in France has made us lose sight of Milady. Let us now return to her.

We find her in the same desperate situation as when we left her, plunged in gloomy thought and almost without hope, for this was the first time she had ever felt uncertainty and fear.

Twice she had failed because her real intentions were discovered, and both those failures were the work of d'Artagnan, the man who seemed to have been sent by divine justice to combat her evil power.

After taking advantage of her love, humiliating her pride, and thwarting her ambition, he had now deprived her of her freedom and placed her in danger of losing her fortune and even her life. Furthermore, he had lifted one corner of her mask, destroying part of the secrecy that had been such an important advantage to her.

D'Artagnan had saved Buckingham—whom she hated as she hated everyone she had once loved—from the defeat that Richelieu had tried to inflict on him through the queen. D'Artagnan had treacherously made her believe he was de Wardes, for whom she had felt one of those fiery passions that sometimes seize women of her fierce temperament. D'Artagnan knew the terrible secret that she had sworn no one would ever know without dying. And finally, just when she had obtained a letter from the cardinal that would enable her to get revenge on her enemy with impunity, the letter had been taken away from her, and because of d'Artagnan she was being held prisoner, because of him she was going to be sent to Botany Bay or some other horrible penal colony.

Yes, d'Artagnan was behind all that, she had no doubt of it; who else could have brought such disaster down upon her head? Only he could have told Lord de Winter the incriminating secrets that fate had led him to discover one by one. He knew her brother-in-law; he must have written to him.

She sat motionless, her eyes glowing with murderous hatred. Now and then an angry sound like the low growl of a tigress rose from deep inside her and mingled with the roar of the waves breaking against the cliff on which the forbidding castle stood. As the lightning of her fury flashed in her soul she made magnificent plans, set in the vague future, for revenge against Madame Bonacieux, Buckingham, and especially d'Artagnan.

But to take revenge she would have to be free, and to be free she would have to make a hole in a wall or the floor, or remove the bars from the window; such things were possible for a strong, patient man, but she had neither the strength nor the patience required. It would also take time—months, maybe years—and according to Lord de Winter, her implacable jailer, she had only two weeks. Even so, if she were a man, she would make the attempt, and perhaps she would succeed. Why had fate made the mistake of putting her powerful spirit in this frail, delicate body?

The first moments of her captivity had been terrible for her, but a few convulsions of rage had been her only sign of feminine weakness. She had gradually brought her feelings under control and quelled the nervous tremors of her body. Now she was turned inward on herself, like a coiled snake.

"It was foolish of me to let myself be carried away like that," she thought as she stood facing her reflection in a mirror as though to question herself. "I mustn't give in to violent emotion; it comes from weakness. And I've never succeeded by violence. If I were fighting against women I might be able to attack them directly and overpower them, but I'm fighting against men. To them I'm only a woman, so I'll fight as a woman and turn my weakness into strength.''

As though to convince herself that she had not lost her ability to control her face, she made it take on a series of expressions, from a ferocious scowl to a sweet, seductive smile. Then she deftly arranged her hair in the way that she felt was most becoming to her. Finally she murmured, satisfied with herself, ''Nothing's lost yet. I'm still beautiful.''

It was about eight o'clock in the evening. She looked at the bed in her room. It occurred to her that a few hours' rest would not only help her to put her thoughts in order, but would also freshen her complexion. As she was about to lie down, however, she had a better idea. It would surely not be long before supper was brought to her. Not wanting to waste any time, she decided to take that opportunity to probe the characters of the men assigned to guard her.

When a streak of light appeared under the door, announcing the return of her jailers, she quickly sat down in the armchair with her head thrown back, her beautiful hair disheveled, and her bosom half bare beneath her rumpled lace; then she put one hand over her heart and let the other hang limply.

The door was unbolted and opened. Footsteps approached her.

''Put the table down there,'' said a voice that she recognized as John Felton's. The order was carried out. ''Now bring torches and have the guard relieved.''

Milady concluded from these orders that the men who served her, as well as those who guarded her, would be soldiers. And from the promptness with which the orders were obeyed, she concluded that Felton was a strict disciplinarian.

He turned and looked at her for the first time since he had come in.

''I see she's asleep,'' he said. ''Well, she can eat when she wakes up.''

He walked toward the door.

A soldier less stoical than the young lieutenant had stepped closer to Milady.

''She's not asleep, sir,'' he said.

''What do you mean? Can't you see that her eyes are closed?''

''She's fainted, sir. She's very pale and I can't hear her breathing.''

''You're right,'' said Felton, looking at Milady without making the slightest move toward her. ''Go and tell Lord de Winter

that his prisoner has fainted. He hasn't given me any instructions
for such a case."

The soldier left. Felton sat down on a chair near the door and
waited motionlessly. Like many women, Milady had become
skilled in the art of looking through her eyelashes without seeming to open her eyes. She saw Felton sitting with his back to her
and watched him for ten minutes during which he never turned
around.

Then she realized that Lord de Winter would soon be there,
and that his presence would give Felton new strength. Her first
attempt had failed, but she was by no means at the end of her
resources. She raised her head, opened her eyes, and sighed
weakly.

At this sigh, Felton finally turned around.

"I see you're awake," he said, "so there's no reason for me
to stay here. Call out if you need anything."

"Oh, how I've suffered!" she murmured in the harmonious
voice she used so well to bring men under her spell.

She sat up, in an even more graceful and abandoned pose than
when she had been lying back in her chair.

"You'll be served three meals a day," said Felton, standing
up, "at nine o'clock in the morning, one in the afternoon, and
eight in the evening. If you prefer different hours, the schedule
will be changed to suit you."

"Am I always going to be alone in this big, gloomy room?"
she asked.

"A woman who lives nearby will serve as your maid. She'll
be here tomorrow and she'll come whenever you want her."

"I'm very grateful to you, sir," Milady said humbly.

Felton bowed stiffly and turned to leave. As he was about to
go through the doorway, Lord de Winter appeared in the hall,
followed by the soldier who had gone to tell him that the
prisoner had fainted. He held a bottle of smelling salts.

"What's this?" he said mockingly, seeing that Milady was
awake and Felton was about to leave. "Our patient has revived
already? Didn't you realize she was playing you for a fool,
Felton? That was only her first performance: I'm sure she'll give
us many more chances to admire her talent as an actress."

"I suspected she was only pretending, sir," said Felton, "but
since she's a woman, I wanted to treat her with the consideration
that a gentleman owes to any woman, if not for her sake, then
for his own."

Milady shivered; Felton's words had sent a chill through her body.

"So you weren't seduced by that skillfully disarranged hair, that white skin, and those languid eyes?" said Lord de Winter, laughing. "You must be made of stone!"

"Believe me, sir," the young man replied, "it would take more than coquettish tricks to corrupt me."

"Then let's go to supper and leave her to think of something else. Don't worry, she has an excellent imagination: her next performance will be at least as good as the one you just saw."

Lord de Winter laughed again, took Felton's arm, and led him away.

Milady clenched her teeth and thought, "I'll find what it takes to get you in my power, you wretched monk in a soldier's uniform!"

Lord de Winter stopped in the doorway and turned back to her.

"Don't let this setback take away your appetite," he said. "Try the chicken and the fish. They're not poisoned, I give you my word. I'm on good terms with my cook, and since he doesn't expect to inherit from me, I trust him. You can trust him too. Good-bye, till the next time you faint."

This was more than Milady could bear: she gripped the arms of her chair with all her strength as she watched the door close behind the two men. As soon as she was alone, she was again overwhelmed with despair. She glanced up at the table, saw a knife, rushed over to it, and picked it up. But she was cruelly disappointed: the knife had a blunt tip and was made of flexible silver.

She heard loud laughter and saw that the door had opened again.

"What did I tell you, Felton?" said Lord de Winter. "She meant to use that knife on you. She'd have killed you, my boy. One of her little faults is that she always tries to find some way to get rid of people who bother her. If I'd listened to you, the knife would have been sharp and made of steel, and it would have put an end to your life. After stabbing you, she'd have stabbed everyone else who got in her way. As you can see, she knows how to hold a knife."

Milady was still clutching it firmly, but de Winter's scornful words suddenly made her feel so discouraged that she loosened her grip and the knife fell to the floor.

"You were right, sir," Felton said in a tone of disgust that deepened Milady's discouragement. "You were right and I was wrong."

And they both left again.

This time Milady listened more attentively than before. She heard their footsteps slowly fade away in the hall.

"I'm lost," she murmured, "I'll never be able to soften those men. They might as well be granite statues, for all the good it will do me to try. They know me too well; they're armored against all my weapons . . . But this *can't* end the way they want it to! No! It's impossible!"

She was already beginning to hope again, instinctively. With her, fear and weakness never lasted long. She sat down at the table, ate from several dishes, drank a little Spanish wine, and felt all her determination return to her.

Before going to bed she carefully recalled and analyzed all the words, gestures, movements, expressions, and even silences of her jailers, and from her shrewd, thorough study she decided that, on the whole, Felton was the more vulnerable of the two.

One remark seemed particularly significant to her: "If I'd listened to you . . ." Lord de Winter had said to Felton. This could only mean that Felton had spoken in her favor and that de Winter had refused to listen to him.

"Whether he's weak or strong," she thought, "Felton has a spark of pity in his soul. I'll fan that spark into a flame that will destroy him. De Winter is afraid of me because he knows what to expect if I ever escape from him, so it would be useless for me to try anything with him. But with Felton it's different. He's a naive young man and he seems to be virtuous; I'll find a way to make him do what I want."

She went to bed and fell asleep with a smile on her lips. Anyone seeing her would have taken her for a young girl dreaming of the wreath of flowers she would wear at the next village festival.

53

Second Day of Captivity

Milady was actually dreaming that she had d'Artagnan in her power at last and was watching his execution, and it was the sight of his odious blood flowing beneath the headsman's axe that had brought that charming smile to her lips.

She slept soundly, lulled by her first hope of escape.

When breakfast was brought to her the next morning, she was still in bed. Felton remained in the hall outside her room. He had brought the woman who was to serve as her maid. She went over to the bed and asked Milady what she could do for her.

Milady knew that her naturally pale complexion could make her seem ill to someone seeing her for the first time.

"I have a fever," she said. "I didn't sleep at all last night. I feel terribly ill. I hope you'll be kinder to me than my jailers were yesterday. All I ask is to be allowed to stay in bed."

"I'll send for a doctor if you want me to," the woman offered.

Felton was listening to the conversation through the open doorway.

Milady reflected that the more people there were around her, the more Lord de Winter would consider it necessary to keep close watch on her. Besides, a doctor might declare that her illness was a sham, and having failed in her first attempt to arouse Felton's pity, she did not want to fail in this one.

"Send for a doctor?" she said. "What good would that do? Yesterday my jailers thought I was only pretending, and it's obvious that they still think so, because otherwise they'd have sent for a doctor long before now."

"Just tell us what you'd like us to do," Felton said impatiently.

"I don't know what to tell you. I only know that I'm ill. Do whatever you think best."

"Go and bring Lord de Winter," Felton told the maid. His expression showed that he was tired of listening to Milady's complaints.

"Oh, no!" she cried out. "Please don't send for him! I'll

soon be well again, I don't need anything. Please don't send for him!"

She spoke with such a convincing show of distress that Felton was affected by it in spite of himself and came into the room. "I've made a crack in his armor," she thought.

"If you're *really* ill," said Felton, "we'll send for a doctor. If you're deceiving us, you'll regret it. But at least we'll be free of blame."

Milady's only reply was to lay her head back on the pillow and burst into tears.

Felton looked at her a few moments with his usual impassivity; then, judging that her sobbing might continue for some time, he turned away from her and left. The maid followed him. Lord de Winter did not appear.

"I think I'm on the right track," Milady thought with savage joy. She pulled the sheet over her face to hide her elation from anyone who might be spying on her.

Two hours went by.

"It's time for me to end my illness and get up," she told herself. "I must make some progress today. I have only two weeks, and by this evening two days will have passed."

She assumed that the soldiers would soon come to take away the table on which her breakfast had been served, and that she would then see Felton again.

She was not mistaken: Felton came back. Without looking to see whether she had eaten anything, he ordered his men to remove the table.

He stayed behind when they had left. She saw that he was holding a book.

Sitting languidly in an armchair near the fireplace, pale and resigned, she looked like a saintly virgin awaiting martyrdom.

Felton approached her and said, "Lord de Winter is a Catholic, like you. Not wanting to deprive you of the rites of your religion, he's decided to let you read your mass every day. Here's a book that contains it."

Noticing the way he put the book down on the little table beside her, and hearing the disdain in his voice when he said "your mass," Milady looked at him more attentively. From his severely cut hair and stony face, she realized that he was one of those somber Puritans she had met so often at the court of King James as well as at the court of the king of France, where they sometimes took refuge despite the memory of the Saint Bartholomew's Day massacre.

She had one of those sudden inspirations that come to people of genius at times when their fate hangs in the balance. The words "your mass" and her quick examination of Felton had shown her the importance of the reply she was about to make, and her swift intelligence brought it to her lips without hesitation.

"*My* mass?" she said with the same disdain she had heard in Felton's voice. "Lord de Winter is a corrupt Catholic. He knows I don't belong to his religion. This is some sort of trap he's trying to set for me."

Despite his great self-control, Felton could not entirely conceal his surprise.

"What is your religion?" he asked.

"I'll tell you that," she said with feigned emotion, "when I've suffered enough for my faith."

Felton's look told her how far those words had taken her, but he remained silent and motionless; only his eyes had spoken.

"I'm in the hands of my enemies," she went on in the fervent tone she knew to be common with Puritans. "May God save me, or may I perish for my God. Please take that answer to Lord de Winter. As for that book," she added, pointing to it without touching it, as if she were afraid it would sully her, "you can take it and use it yourself, because you must be Lord de Winter's accomplice in heresy as well as in persecution."

Felton did not answer. He picked up the book with the same repugnance he had shown before and walked out, deep in thought.

At about five o'clock Lord de Winter came in. Milady had spent the afternoon working out her plans; she received him confidently, with the feeling that she had regained all her advantages.

He sat down in a chair facing hers and nonchalantly stretched out his legs in front of the fire.

"It seems you've become an apostate," he said.

"What do you mean?"

"I mean that you've changed your religion since the last time I saw you. Have you married a third husband, a Protestant this time?"

"Explain yourself," she said majestically. "I don't understand."

He laughed sarcastically.

"Then you must have no religion at all. I'm glad to know that."

"If I really were an atheist, my beliefs would be closer to yours."

"You can believe whatever you like. It doesn't matter to me."

"Even if you didn't admit your indifference to religion, your debauchery and crimes would still proclaim it."

"Did I hear you mention debauchery, Messalina? And crimes, Lady Macbeth? I admire your effrontery!"

"You're talking like that because you know our conversation is being overheard," Milady said coldly. "You want to influence your jailers and executioners against me."

"My jailers and executioners? What a dramatic expression! Since your comic performance failed last night, you've decided to try tragedy. But in a little more than a week you'll be where you belong and my task will be finished."

"Yes, your sinful, infamous task will be finished!" Milady said in the exalted tone of an innocent victim defying her judge.

"I do believe you're going mad," said de Winter, standing up. "I advise you to calm yourself, because otherwise you'll spend the rest of your time here in a dungeon cell. Was it my Spanish wine that put you into this state? Well, it will soon wear off, and I hope you'll behave less foolishly when you're sober."

He walked out, swearing, which in those days was not regarded as ungentlemanly.

Milady had guessed correctly: Felton was in the hall and had not missed a word of the conversation.

"So you think I'm behaving foolishly, do you?" she muttered under her breath, looking at the door that had just closed behind Lord de Winter. "You'll find out how wrong you are, you imbecile, but then it will be too late for you to do anything about it!"

When Felton and the soldiers came to bring her supper two hours later, they found her reciting prayers that she had learned from a Puritan servant of her second husband. She seemed to be so absorbed in her pious occupation that she was unaware of anything happening around her. Felton motioned the soldiers not to disturb her. When they had put down the table, he left with them in silence.

Knowing she might be watched, Milady finished the last prayer she had begun. It seemed to her that the soldier on guard outside the door was no longer pacing back and forth but had stopped to listen.

For the moment, she was satisfied. She stood up from her kneeling position, sat down at the table, ate sparingly, and drank only water.

An hour later the soldiers came back to take away the table, but Milady noticed that this time Felton was not with them. "So he's afraid to see me too often!" she thought, and turned her face to the wall to smile, for the look of triumph on her face would have betrayed her.

She waited half an hour. There was no sound but the vast murmur of the ocean below the old castle. Then, in her pure, vibrant, harmonious voice she began singing a hymn that was in favor with the Puritans:

> *"If e'er we are forsaken by the Lord,*
> *'Tis but to try us if to sin we yield,*
> *And then our fortitude hath its reward*
> *From His own hand, by which all wounds are healed."*

This was not excellent poetry, far from it; but, as is well known, the Puritans did not pride themselves on being poetic.

As Milady sang, she listened: the soldier on guard at her door had stopped as if he had been turned to stone. From this she judged that she had produced the effect she wanted.

She went on singing with deep fervor. She felt that her voice was floating through the castle and casting a magic spell on her jailers. But the soldier on guard, no doubt a zealous Catholic, evidently broke the spell, because he called out to her through the door:

"Please stop, ma'am! Your song is as sad as a funeral march, and it's bad enough being on duty here without having to listen to things like that!"

"You're overstepping your orders!" said a deep voice that Milady recognized as Felton's. "No one told you to stop that woman from singing. You were told only to guard her and shoot her if she tried to escape. Obey your orders, but don't go beyond them."

An expression of joy brightened Milady's face, but it was as fleeting as a flash of lightning. Without seeming to have heard either Felton or the guard, though not a word of what they said had escaped her, she continued singing with all the seductive charm that the devil had put into her voice:

> *"I languish in this world of woe and tears.*
> *Bleak is my exile, heavy are my chains.*
> *But, steadfast in my faith through passing years,*
> *I know that God hath balm for all my pains."*

That voice, filled with sublime passion, gave the crude verses a magic and depth of meaning that even the most ardent Puritans seldom found in their hymns, which they usually had to adorn with all the resources of their imagination. To Felton, it was as if he were listening to the angel who comforted the three Hebrews in the fiery furnace.

> *"God is eternal, merciful, and just;*
> *He will deliver us from Satan's thrall.*
> *Our hearts grow weary, still we keep our trust.*
> *Midst harsh travail, we wait for our Lord's call."*

This verse, sung by the terrible enchantress with all the bewitching power at her command, brought the tumult in Felton's soul to such a pitch that he flung open the door. Milady saw him appear on the threshold with a strange glow in his eyes; he seemed almost demented.

"Why are you singing like that, in such a voice?" he said.

"Excuse me, sir," she replied softly. "I was forgetting that my hymns are out of place here. I must have offended your beliefs, but I didn't mean to, I assure you. Please forgive me; my offense was unintentional."

The religious rapture that seemed to have taken possession of her made her face so poignantly beautiful that Felton, dazzled, now felt as if he were seeing the angel he had only heard before.

"You . . . you're . . ." he stammered. "I . . . Your singing was . . . Yes, disturbing, you were disturbing the people in the castle."

The poor man was not even aware of his incoherence. Milady eyed him shrewdly for an instant, then bowed her head with gentle resignation and murmured, "I won't sing anymore."

"No, no, that's not what I meant," he said. "Just sing a little less loudly, especially at night."

Then, realizing that he could no longer maintain a stern attitude toward her, he turned and hurried out of the room.

"You're right, sir," the guard said to him. "Her singing upset me at first, but then I got used to it: her voice is so beautiful!"

54

Third Day of Captivity

Felton had come, and Milady knew he would come again; the next step was to make him stay longer. She had no clear idea of how she would do that.

She also had to make him talk, so that she could talk to him. She was well aware that her voice, which could range over all the tones of human and angelic speech, was one of her most powerful weapons of seduction.

Yet despite those weapons she might fail, because Felton had been warned against her. She would have to keep careful watch on everything she said and did; the movements of her eyes, her gestures, even her breathing, which could be interpreted as a sigh. Although she was a superbly talented actress, she was now playing a kind of part that she had never played before and a convincing performance would require attention to detail.

The part she would play with Lord de Winter was easier. She had already worked it out in her mind: she would remain quiet and dignified in his presence, irritate him now and then with a show of disdain or a scornful word, and provoke him to threats and violent outbursts that would contrast sharply with her noble resignation. Felton would see; he might say nothing, but he would see.

He came that morning as usual. She let him supervise the preparations for her breakfast without saying a word to him. She had a glimmer of hope as he was about to leave: she thought he was going to speak to her of his own accord. But though his lips moved, he held back the words that had nearly escaped from them. Then he left.

Toward noon, Lord de Winter came in.

It was a cloudless winter day. The rays of the pale English sun, which gives light but no warmth, were streaming in through the barred window. Milady stood looking out at the sea, pretending not to have heard the door open.

"At least you have some variety in your performances," said de Winter: "first comedy, then tragedy, and now melancholy."

She made no reply.

"I know what you're thinking," he went on. "You wish that you were free on that shore, or on a ship sailing across that emerald-green sea, and in either case you wish you were about to draw me into one of those deadly traps that you know how to set so well. But you won't have to be patient much longer: you're going to leave here sooner than I expected. In four days that sea will be open to you, more open than you'd like, because in four days England will be rid of you."

Milady clasped her hands, raised her eyes to heaven, and said with angelic sweetness, "O Lord, please forgive this man as I forgive him myself."

"Yes, pray, you demon," said Lord de Winter. "Your prayer is all the more generous because you're in the hands of a man who won't forgive you!"

And he walked away from her.

As he opened the door to leave she caught a glimpse of Felton quickly stepping aside, trying to avoid letting her see him.

She knelt and began praying aloud: "Dear God, thou knowest the holy cause for which I suffer; give me the strength to suffer."

The door opened again, gently. She showed no sign of having heard and went on praying: "God of vengeance, God of righteousness, wilt thou allow that man to succeed in his abominable plans?"

Then, pretending to have just become aware of Felton's presence, she quickly stood up, blushing as if she were ashamed of having been seen on her knees.

"I don't like to interrupt anyone's prayers," Felton said gravely. "Please don't let me disturb you."

"Prayers?" Milady said in a voice choked by a sob. "You're mistaken, sir, I wasn't praying."

"Do you think I'd prevent you from kneeling before your Creator? God forbid that I should ever feel I had a right to do such a thing! Repentant sinners are sacred to me, however great their guilt."

"Then you believe I'm guilty of a crime?" she said with a smile that would have disarmed the angel of the Last Judgment. "It's true that I'm being punished as if I were guilty, but, as you know, God loves martyrs and sometimes allows the innocent to be punished."

"If you're a martyr, you have all the more reason to pray, and I'll add my prayers to yours."

"Oh, you're a good man! I can't go on much longer because I'm afraid my strength will fail me when I must withstand the struggle and confess my faith. Listen to the plea of a woman in distress! You're being deceived . . . But that's not what matters. I ask only one favor of you, and if you grant it to me, I'll bless you in this world and in the next."

"You'll have to speak to my master," said Felton. "Neither pardon nor punishment is in my hands. God has given that responsibility to someone higher than myself."

"No, I must speak to you, to you alone. Listen to me, rather than being an accomplice in my shame."

"If you deserve that shame, you must endure it and accept God's will."

"What are you saying? Oh, you don't understand! You thought I was referring to something like imprisonment or execution. But I care nothing about such punishments, thank heaven!"

"You're right, I don't understand you."

"Or you're pretending not to," she said, smiling skeptically.

"I'm not pretending. I swear it on my honor as a soldier and a Christian."

"What? You don't know what Lord de Winter is planning to do to me?"

"I know nothing about it."

"That's impossible! He confides in you!"

"I never lie."

"But he doesn't bother to hide his intentions! You must have guessed them by now!"

"I don't try to guess anything. I wait to be told, and aside from what he's said in front of you, Lord de Winter has told me nothing."

"Then you're not his accomplice?" Milady asked with seemingly genuine surprise. "You don't know that he intends to plunge me into a shame more horrible than any punishment on earth?"

The blood rushed to Felton's face.

"You're mistaken. Lord de Winter is incapable of such a crime."

Milady thought, "Good: he calls it a crime even without knowing what I mean!"

Then she said, "A friend of the devil's disciple is capable of anything."

"The devil's disciple? Explain yourself."

"Does that name fit more than one man in England?"

Felton's eyes flashed.

"Do you mean George Villiers?"

"Yes, I mean the man whom heathens and unbelievers call the duke of Buckingham. I wouldn't have thought there was anyone in England who needed that explanation!"

"The hand of the Lord is upon him. He won't escape the punishment he deserves."

Felton was expressing the attitude of nearly everyone in England toward the duke of Buckingham. The Catholics called him an extortioner and a libertine; the Puritans simply called him Satan.

"O God," cried Milady, "when I ask thee to punish that man as he deserves, thou knowest that I ask it not for my own personal revenge, but for the deliverance of the whole English people!"

"Then you know him?" asked Felton.

Milady was delighted by the progress she had made. "At last he's questioning me!" she thought.

"Yes, I know him—to my despair!"

She wrung her hands as though she were overwhelmed with sorrow. Felton evidently felt his strength abandoning him, because he stepped toward the door. She rushed after him and stopped him.

"Be kind, be merciful," she implored him, "please listen to me. You remember the knife that Lord de Winter wouldn't let me have because he knew what I wanted to do with it . . . Stay! Hear me out! I beg you to bring me that knife. Hand it to me through the grille and leave the door locked—I have no wish to harm you. Oh, no! I'd never harm you: you're kind, just, and compassionate, and perhaps you'll be my savior! Let me have the knife for only a minute, then I'll give it back to you through the grille. Only a minute, Mr. Felton, and you'll have saved my honor!"

"You want to kill yourself!" he cried, too horrified to realize that she was clutching his hands.

"I've told you my secret," she said in a faltering voice. "You know everything. I'm lost!"

She collapsed to the floor. He stood looking down at her, motionless and undecided. "He still has doubts," she thought. "I wasn't convincing enough."

They heard footsteps in the hall. Milady recognized them as Lord de Winter's. So did Felton. Seeing him move toward the door, she leapt to her feet.

"Not one word to him about what I've told you," she said urgently, "or I'll be lost, and it will be you who . . ."

She stopped short, for fear Lord de Winter might hear her. She put her beautiful hand over Felton's mouth with a look of infinite terror. He gently pushed her away. She sat down on a chaise longue as if she no longer had the strength to stand.

Lord de Winter passed by the door without stopping. Deathly pale, Felton listened intently for a few moments, and then, when the sound of de Winter's footsteps had faded away, he took a deep breath, like a man who has just awakened from a dream, and hurried out of the room.

Milady heard him walk away in the direction from which de Winter had come. "I've finally got him under my thumb!" she thought. Then her face darkened. "If he tells de Winter what I said, everything I've accomplished will be undone. De Winter knows very well I won't kill myself. He'll give me a knife in front of Felton, and then Felton will know that my despair was only a pretense."

She stood up and went over to the mirror. She had never seen herself more beautiful. "Yes," she thought, smiling, "but he won't tell de Winter anything."

That evening, Lord de Winter came with the soldiers who brought her supper.

"Are your visits a necessary part of my imprisonment?" she said. "Can't you at least spare me that ordeal?"

"I'm surprised to hear you talk like that, my dear sister-in-law, after telling me you came to England only to see me. According to you, you risked storms, seasickness, and imprisonment for the pleasure of my company. Well, here I am, so enjoy my company to your heart's content. Besides, this time there's a reason for my visit."

Milady shuddered, thinking that Felton had talked to him. She had experienced many strong and conflicting emotions in her life, but never before had she felt her heart pound so violently.

He drew up a chair, sat down beside her, took a sheet of paper from his pocket, and slowly unfolded it.

"I've made out a kind of passport for you," he said. "You can use it as an identity paper in the life I'll allow you to lead." He began reading it aloud: " 'Order to conduct Charlotte Backson, convicted by French law but released after punishment, to . . .' The name of the place has been left blank. If you have a preference, I'll see to it that you're sent there, provided it's at least three thousand miles from London. 'She will remain there and never go more than ten miles away. If she tries to escape, she will be put to death. She will be given an allotment of five shillings a day for food and lodging.' ''

"That order doesn't concern me," Milady said coldly, "because it bears a name that isn't mine."

"A name? Do you really have one?"

"I have your brother's."

"You're mistaken: my brother was your second husband and your first one is still alive. Tell me his name and I'll put it in place of Charlotte Backson . . . You'd rather not tell me? Very well, then, you'll be deported under the name of Charlotte Backson."

This time Milady's silence was not an affectation. She was genuinely terrified because she thought that the order was to be carried out without delay, that very evening. For a moment she believed she had no chance to save herself. Then she noticed that there was no signature on the order.

Her joy was so great that she could not hide it from Lord de Winter.

"Yes, I know," he said, "you've seen that the order is unsigned and you've become hopeful again because you're thinking that I've shown it to you only to frighten you. Well, you're wrong: tomorrow this order will be sent to the duke of Buckingham, day after tomorrow it will come back with his signature and seal, and twenty-four hours later you'll be on your way. That's all I have to say to you."

"And all I have to say to you is that sending me into exile under a false name is an infamous abuse of power!"

"Would you rather be hanged under your real name? As you know, bigamy is a serious offense under English law. Tell me frankly what you prefer. Even though my name, or rather my brother's name, is involved in all this, I'm willing to risk the scandal of a public trial to make sure I'm rid of you."

Milady made no reply but turned as pale as a corpse.

"I see you prefer to travel," said de Winter. "Perhaps it will be good for you; there's an old saying that travel broadens the mind. You're right to prefer exile to death: after all, life is good. That's why I don't intend to let you take mine. I'll explain one more thing to you: your allotment of five shillings a day. I know you must feel I'm being a bit stingy, but it's because I wouldn't care to have you bribe your guards. You'll still have your seductive charms, however. You can always try them on your guards, if your failure with Felton hasn't discouraged you from making another attempt of that kind.''

Hearing this, Milady became still more hopeful. ''Felton hasn't talked to him,'' she thought.

''And now,'' said de Winter, ''good-bye till tomorrow, when I'll come to tell you that my messenger has left to have the deportation order signed by the duke of Buckingham.''

He stood up, bowed to her ironically, and walked out.

Milady sighed with relief: she had three days ahead of her. That would be long enough for her to finish bringing Felton under her spell.

Then a terrible thought struck her: maybe Felton himself would be sent to have the order signed by Buckingham. If so, his separation from her would break her power over him and she would not have enough time to build it up again.

But another thought brought back some of her confidence: Felton had said nothing to de Winter.

Not wanting to seem upset by de Winter's threats, she sat down at the table and ate. Then, as she had done the night before, she knelt and said her prayers aloud. Again, the guard stopped his pacing and stood still to listen.

She soon heard lighter footsteps than the guard's coming along the hall. They stopped in front of the door. ''He's come back,'' she thought.

And she began singing the hymn that had affected Felton so strongly before. But though her voice was as poignantly sweet as ever, the door remained closed. She furtively glanced at it and thought she saw Felton's eyes ardently watching her through the grille; but whether she had seen them or only imagined them, this time he had the strength of will to restrain himself from coming in.

A few moments after she had finished her hymn, she heard a deep sigh; then the same light footsteps moved off along the corridor, slowly and as though regretfully.

55

Fourth Day of Captivity

When Felton came into Milady's room the next day, he found her standing on a chair, holding a rope that she had made by tearing batiste handkerchiefs into strips, braiding them, and tying them end to end. At the sound of the opening door, she jumped down from the chair and tried to hide her improvised rope behind her.

Felton was even paler than usual, and his eyes, reddened by sleeplessness, showed that he had spent a feverish night. But his face had regained its austere composure.

Milady sat down. He slowly walked over to her and took one end of the rope that, whether inadvertently or deliberately, she had left protruding.

"What's this?" he asked coldly.

"Oh, it's nothing," she replied with a sorrowful smile. "As you must know, boredom is a prisoner's worst enemy. I was bored, so I passed the time by braiding this rope."

He looked up and saw a gilded hook, meant for holding clothes or weapons, set into the wall above the chair on which he had found her standing. He started, and she saw his reaction, for although she sat with her head bowed, nothing escaped her.

"Why were you standing on that chair?"

"What does it matter to you?"

"I . . . I want to know."

"Don't question me," said Milady. "You must know that we true Christians are forbidden to lie."

"Then I'll tell you what you were doing, or rather what you were about to do: you were going to commit the terrible sin you've been planning. It's true that our God forbids lying—and he forbids suicide even more sternly."

"When God sees one of his creatures unjustly persecuted and forced to choose between suicide and dishonor," Milady said in a tone of deep conviction, "he forgives suicide, because suicide is then martyrdom."

"You've said either too much or not enough. In heaven's name, explain yourself!"

"If I told you about my misfortune, you'd say I was lying; if I told you about my plans, you'd report them to my persecutor. No, I'll tell you nothing. And why should you care whether your prisoner lives or dies? You're responsible only for my body. If that body is dead, provided it's proved to be mine, you won't be blamed—and you may even be rewarded."

"Surely you don't believe I'd accept a reward for your death!" cried Felton. "You don't mean what you're saying!"

"You must be ambitious, Lieutenant Felton, like any other officer. If you let me die, you'll attend my funeral with the rank of captain."

"I can't take such a responsibility!" he protested. "In a few days you'll be far away from here. Your life will no longer be in my care, and then," he added with a sigh, "you can do with it as you please."

"So your only concern is not to be held accountable for my death!" Milady said indignantly. "And I thought you were a righteous, pious man!"

"It's my duty to guard your life, and I always do my duty."

"But don't you understand what you're doing? It would still be cruel if I were guilty—since I'm innocent, it's even worse."

"I'm a soldier. I obey my orders."

"At the Last Judgment, do you think that those who blindly carry out evil orders will be treated more leniently than those who give such orders? You won't let me kill my body, yet you're the willing servant of the man who wants to kill my soul!"

"You're in no more danger from Lord de Winter than you are from me," said Felton, shaken. "I can answer for him as confidently as for myself."

"How can you be so foolish as to answer for someone else when the wisest of men hesitate to answer for themselves? You've sided with a persecutor against his victim, with a strong man against a weak woman!"

Felton was stung by this reproach, but held firm.

"I can't do as you wish. As long as you're a prisoner, I won't let you escape; as long as you're alive, I won't let you take your own life."

"But I'll lose something I value much more highly than my life: my honor! And I'll hold you accountable, before God and men, for my shame!"

Despite his efforts to remain impassive, Felton was unable to resist the secret influence that was already taking possession of him. Seeing this beautiful woman grief-stricken was too much for a visionary whose mind had been undermined by the ardent dreams of an ecstatic faith, and whose heart had been corroded by a burning love of heaven and a consuming hatred of humanity.

Milady looked at that young fanatic's agitation and sensed the contrary passions that were warring within him. Like an able general who sees his enemy ready to retreat and marches against him with a cry of victory, she stood up and stepped toward him with the sensuous grace of a pagan priestess and the radiance of a saintly Christian virgin, modestly holding her dress across her bosom with one hand and pointing at him accusingly with the other, her eyes illuminated by the fire that had already thrown his senses into disorder. Then she sang in the stern, implacable tone that she could give to her voice when the occasion demanded it:

> *"All those who persecute the innocent*
> *And mercilessly mock their victims' fear,*
> *The Lord of Justice shall make them repent*
> *When they before His judgment must appear."*

Felton stood as though petrified by this strange assault.

"Who are you?" he cried, clasping his hands. "Have you been sent from heaven or from hell? Are you an angel or a demon?"

"Don't you see what I am? I'm neither an angel nor a demon, I'm only an earthly woman who shares your faith."

"Yes, oh yes! I still doubted you, but now I believe you!"

"You believe me, yet you're the accomplice of that son of Belial, Lord de Winter! You believe me, yet you leave me in the hands of my enemies, of England's enemy, and God's enemy! You believe me, yet you deliver me to the man who defiles the world with his heresy and debauchery, that wicked libertine whom the spiritually blind call the duke of Buckingham, and believers call the Antichrist!"

"You accuse *me* of delivering you to Buckingham? How can you say that?"

" 'They have eyes to see, and see not; they have ears to hear, and hear not.' "

"Yes," said Felton, passing his hand over his forehead as though to wipe away his last doubt, "I recognize the voice that speaks to me in my dreams; I recognize the face of the angel who appears to me each night and cries out to my sleepless soul, 'Strike! Save England, save yourself, lest you die without appeasing God's wrath!' Speak, speak to me, I can understand you now!''

A glow of triumph appeared in Milady's eyes but vanished in an instant. Fleeting though it was, Felton saw it, and he started as if it had given him a glimpse into the depths of her heart. He suddenly recalled Lord de Winter's warnings and Milady's efforts to lead him astray as soon as she had arrived. He stepped back from her and bowed his head, but without ceasing to look at her; he was so fascinated by her that he could not turn his eyes away from hers.

She saw his hesitation and knew what was behind it, for she was still a shrewd observer in the midst of her theatrical display of emotion. Not wanting to continue the conversation at that same difficult level of intensity, she let her arms fall at her sides, as though her womanly weakness had prevailed over her zeal.

"No," she said, "I'm not called upon to be the Judith who will strike down that Holofernes. The sword of the Almighty is too heavy for my arm. Let me escape dishonor by death, let me take refuge in martyrdom. I don't ask you for freedom, as I would if I were guilty, or for revenge, as I would if I were a pagan. Let me die—that's all I ask of you. I beg it of you! Let me die, and with my last breath I'll bless you as my savior.''

Hearing her soft, pleading voice and seeing her timid, downcast eyes, Felton moved closer to her. The enchantress had again taken on the magic power of her beauty and distress, heightened by the irresistible attraction of sensuality mingled with religious fervor.

"All I can do for you," said Felton, "is to pity you if you prove to me that you're an innocent victim. I feel drawn to you: you're a Christian, you share my faith. I've found the world to be full of treacherous, impious people, and I've been devoted only to my benefactor. You're beautiful and you seem to be pure in heart, yet Lord de Winter must have serious grievances against you, because otherwise he wouldn't treat you so harshly. Have you done wicked things?''

'' 'They have eyes to see,' '' Milady repeated in a tone of deep sorrow, '' 'and see not; they have ears to hear, and hear not.' ''

"Tell me what you mean! Tell me everything!''

"You're a man and I'm a woman—how can you expect me to

tell you about my shame?'' she said, putting her hand over her eyes as though to shield herself from his gaze. "No, no, I couldn't do that!''

"But I'm your brother in faith!''

She looked at him a long time with an expression that he interpreted as doubt, though she was actually observing him and, at the same time, trying to strengthen the fascination she already exercised on him. By his own expression, he silently begged her to speak.

"Yes,'' she finally said, "I'll dare to trust my brother.''

Just then they heard Lord de Winter's footsteps. This time he did not merely walk past: he stopped, exchanged a few words with the guard, opened the door, and came in.

Meanwhile Felton had quickly stepped away from Milady.

De Winter scrutinized them both as he slowly walked toward them.

"You've been here a long time, John,'' he said. "Has she been telling you all her crimes? If so, I can understand the length of your visit.''

Felton started, and Milady realized that she would be lost if she did not intervene.

"Are you afraid your prisoner will escape?'' she said. "Ask your jailer what I was begging him to do for me.''

"She wants you to do her a favor?'' de Winter asked suspiciously.

"Yes, sir,'' Felon replied with embarrassment.

"What does she want?''

"She wants me to give her a knife, and she says she'll give it back to me a minute later, through the grille.''

"Is there someone hiding in this room, someone she wants to kill?'' de Winter said mockingly.

"I want to kill myself,'' said Milady.

"I've given you a choice between deportation and hanging. Since you want to die, choose hanging: it's more reliable than stabbing yourself.''

Felton turned pale, remembering that she had been holding a rope when he came in.

"I know,'' she said, "I've already thought of that . . . And I won't forget it,'' she added in an undertone.

Felton shuddered. De Winter saw his reaction and said to him, "Be careful, John. Remember that I'm trusting you as my friend. I've warned you against her! Be firm for three more days and then we'll be rid of her. Where I'm sending her, she won't be able to harm anyone."

"Do you hear him?" Milady said loudly, in such a way that Felton knew she was speaking to him, but de Winter thought she was addressing God.

Felton bowed his head and became lost in thought.

De Winter took him by the arm and led him away, looking back to keep Milady in sight till they had left the room.

"I haven't made as much progress as I thought," she said to herself, when the door had closed behind them. "De Winter's usual stupidity has turned into wariness. His desire for revenge has sharpened his wits! As for Felton, he's still wavering. He's not a man like that damned d'Artagnan! A Puritan worships virgins and wouldn't dare to touch them; a musketeer likes women and takes them in his arms."

She waited impatiently, convinced that she would see Felton again before the day was over.

An hour later she heard a murmur of voices in the hall, then the door opened and Felton appeared. He walked rapidly into the room, leaving the door open and telling her by a gesture not to speak. He seemed distraught.

"What do you want?" she asked.

"I sent the guard away," he said in a low voice, "so that I could come here without having it known, and talk to you without being overheard. Lord de Winter has told me a horrible story."

She gave him the smile of a resigned victim and shook her head.

"Either you're a demon," Felton continued, "or Lord de Winter, my benefactor, the man who's been a father to me, is a monster. I've known you for only four days and I've loved him for ten years, so it's understandable that I should hesitate between the two of you. Don't be alarmed by what I'm saying. I need to be convinced. I'll come to see you tonight, after midnight, and you'll convince me."

"No, Felton, my brother, I can't ask such a great sacrifice of you. I know what it would cost you. I'm doomed and I don't want you to share my fate. I'll be more eloquent in death than in life; the silence of my corpse will convince you better than anything I could say now."

"You mustn't talk like that! I've come here to make you swear, by everything you hold sacred, that you won't take your own life."

"I won't swear to that. No one respects a promise more than I
do, and if I gave you my word, I'd have to keep it."

"Then promise only to wait till you've seen me again.
Afterward, if you haven't changed your mind, you'll be free to
do what you want, and I'll give you the knife you asked me for."

"Very well, then," said Milady, "I'll wait for you."

"Will you give me your word on it?"

"I swear it by our God. Are you satisfied?"

"Yes," said Felton. "Good-bye till tonight."

He swiftly walked out of the room, closed the door, and
waited in front of it, holding the soldier's pike, as though
standing guard in his place.

When the soldier returned, Felton handed him his pike and
left.

Looking through the grille, Milady saw him cross himself
fervently and walk off along the hall in a transport of joy.

She went back to her chair with a smile of savage contempt on
her lips, blasphemously speaking the name of God, by whom she
had sworn without ever having learned to know him.

"That brainless fanatic!" she muttered. "He can have his God
and I'll have mine. *My* God is myself, and anyone who helps me
to get my revenge!"

56

Fifth Day of Captivity

Milady's strength was redoubled by her certainty that she was
well on the way to achieving her goal.

Till now, she had won easy victories over men accustomed to
the amorous intrigues of life at court and therefore quick to let
themselves be seduced. She was beautiful enough not to encounter any resistance of the flesh, and intelligent enough to allay any
misgivings of the mind. But this time she had overcome a sullen,
fiercely restrained, inhumanly austere nature. Piety and peni-
tence had made Felton inaccessible to ordinary means of seduction.
Such vast, tumultuous plans swirled in his overheated brain that
there was no room in it for earthly, physical love, which blos-
soms in leisure and grows in depravity.

With her false virtue, Milady had begun to change his initially hostile attitude toward her; and, chaste and pure though he was, he could not prevent his heart and senses from responding to her beauty. Nature and religion had combined to make him the most difficult challenge she had ever faced. In her efforts to conquer him, she had used resources that she herself had not known she possessed.

That evening, however, she often despaired of fate and herself. She did not invoke God, as we know, but she had faith in the spirit of evil, that vast power that governs all the details of human life and, as in the Arab fable, can reconstruct a lost world out of a pomegranate seed.

Being already well prepared to receive Felton, Milady was able to lay her plans for the next day. She had only two more days in which to act. She knew that once Buckingham had signed the deportation order—and he would sign it all the more readily because it bore a false name that would mean nothing to him—Lord de Winter would put her on a ship. She also knew that women condemned to deportation had much less effective weapons of seduction than women free to live in the fashionable world, where they could present an appearance of virtue, set off their beauty and wit to best advantage, and bask in a flattering reflection of aristocracy. Undergoing a shameful punishment in wretched circumstances does not prevent a woman from being beautiful, but it is an obstacle to her ever becoming powerful again. Like all capable people, Milady knew the surroundings that best suited her nature. Poverty was repugnant to her, degradation took away most of her ascendancy over others. She was a queen only among queens. She did not enjoy being dominant unless her pride was satisfied; to her, dominating inferiors was a humiliation rather than a pleasure.

If she was deported, she would come back some day; she had no doubt of that. But how long would her exile last? With her active, ambitious temperament, she felt that any day not spent in moving forward was a waste of time, and the thought of help-lessly drifting backward, day after day, was completely intolerable to her. She might be away for a year, two years, three years—an eternity, as far as she was concerned. Then, when she came back, she might find d'Artagnan and his friends happy and triumphant after being rewarded by the queen for the services they had rendered her. This prospect tormented Milady beyond endurance. If her body had been as strong as the stormy passions that raged inside her, she would have broken through the walls of her prison with her bare hands.

Being unable to communicate with the cardinal was another source of torment for her. Since he was mistrustful and suspicious even in the best of circumstances, she did not like to think of how he might be interpreting her silence. She had counted on him as her only protector, the man who would enable her to gain wealth and take revenge on her enemies. Knowing him as she did, she had no illusions about the reception he would give her when she came back to him after failing in her mission. It would do her no good to tell him about her imprisonment and dramatically describe her sufferings; he would listen to her with his usual skepticism and then say mockingly, "You shouldn't have let yourself be caught."

Her thoughts returned to Felton and she concentrated all her determination on him. He was the only ray of hope that penetrated to the dark depths into which she had fallen. Like a snake coiling and uncoiling to test its strength, she enveloped Felton in all the treacherous convolutions of her imagination.

Meanwhile time was passing. Each stroke of the bell that marked the hours resounded in her heart.

At nine o'clock Lord de Winter came in. He examined the fireplace, the doors, and the bars on the window, then sounded the floor and the walls. During that long, careful inspection, neither he nor Milady spoke. They both realized that the situation had become too serious for useless words and futile anger.

"At least I know you won't escape tonight," de Winter said as he left.

At ten o'clock Felton came to post a guard. Milady now recognized his footsteps as if he were her lover, yet she hated and despised that weak fanatic.

He did not come in; it was not yet time.

Two hours later, on the stroke of midnight, the guard was relieved.

Now the time had come. Milady waited with growing impatience.

The new guard began pacing back and forth in the hall.

Ten minutes later Felton came back. Milady listened intently.

"Don't leave this door for any reason," she heard him say to the guard. "Last night Lord de Winter punished a soldier for being away from his post only a few minutes, even though I stood guard in his place while he was gone."

"Yes, sir, I know," said the guard.

"Be alert at all times," Felton continued. "I'm going into the prisoner's room. There's a danger that she may try to take her own life and I've been ordered to keep close watch on her."

"Good," thought Milady, "my austere Puritan has begun to lie!"

The soldier smiled.

"You're lucky to have an order like that, sir," he said, "especially if you're supposed to watch her even when she's in bed."

Felton's face turned red; at any other time he would have reprimanded the soldier for making such a joke, but now his conscience was so troubled that the reprimand died on his lips.

"Come in if I call you," he said, "and notify me if you hear anyone coming."

"Yes, sir."

Felton opened the door and went into the room. Milady stood up.

"It's you!" she said.

"I promised I'd come, and I did."

"You also promised me something else."

"What . . . what do you mean?" asked Felton; beads of sweat broke out on his forehead and his knees trembled.

"You promised to bring me a knife and leave it with me after our conversation."

"Don't talk about that! No situation, however desperate, can ever give us the right to take away the life that God has given us. I've thought it over and I now know that I mustn't be an accomplice in such a crime."

"Ah, so you've thought it over," she said, sitting down in her amrchair with a disdainful smile. "Well, I've been thinking too."

"About what?"

"I've decided that I have nothing to say to a man who doesn't keep his word."

"In the name of heaven . . ." Felton murmured weakly.

"You may as well go now. I won't tell you anything."

"Here's the knife!" he said, taking it from his pocket. He had brought it, as he promised, but he still hoped he could avoid giving it to her.

"Let me see it."

"Why?"

"I swear I'll give it back to you in a few moments. You can put it on that table and stay between me and it."

He handed the knife to her. She examined it carefully and tested its point on her finger.

"This one is made of steel," she said, returning it to him. "You're a true friend."

He put the knife on the table while she watched him with an expression of satisfaction.

"And now," she said, "listen to me."

He stood in front of her, eagerly awaiting her words.

"Felton," she began in a solemn, melancholy tone, "suppose your sister, your own father's daughter, came to you and said, 'When I was young and unfortunately rather pretty, a man lured me into a trap, but I resisted. He tried to overcome my resistance by every means, from violence to deceit; I held firm. He blasphemed against my God and my religion because I called on them for help; still I resisted. He continued his outrages, to no avail. Unable to corrupt my soul, he still wanted to sully my body . . .' "

She stopped and a bitter smile passed over her lips.

"Go on," said Felton, "what did he do next?"

"He decided to paralyze my resistance, since he couldn't destroy it. One evening a powerful drug was mixed with my drinking water. As soon as I'd finished my meal I felt a strange torpor coming over me. I didn't yet suspect anything, but a vague fear made me struggle against sleep. I stood up, intending to run to the window and call for help, but my legs trembled so much that I couldn't even walk. I felt as if the ceiling had fallen on my head. I stretched out my arms and tried to speak; I could only mumble inarticulate sounds. I began to feel numb. I clutched a chair to keep from falling, but my arms were too weak to support me. I sank down on one knee, then on the other. I tried to pray, but my tongue was frozen. God must not have seen or heard me. I fell to the floor and a minute later I was in the grip of a sleep that was like death.

"When I woke up, I had no memory of what had happened during that sleep and I didn't know how long it had lasted. I was in a round, magnificently furnished bedroom. Light came into it only through an opening in the ceiling, and it seemed to have no doors. It was like a luxurious dungeon.

"It took me a long time to become aware of the details I just described to you. My mind seemed powerless to shake off the heavy torpor that still weighed down on me. Vague recollections began coming to me: a journey, the rumble of a carriage, some sort of nightmare in which my strength was exhausted. But it was all so indistinct that it seemed to be part of another life that had somehow become mingled with mine.

"For a time, it was hard for me to believe that I wasn't dreaming. I got up. My legs were still weak. I saw my clothes on a chair beside the bed, but I didn't remember undressing or going to bed. My surroundings gradually became real to me and my lethargy gave way to fear. As far as I could judge from the sunlight, it was late afternoon, which meant that my sleep had lasted nearly twenty-four hours! What had happened to me during that time?

"I got dressed as quickly as I could but my movements were still slow and clumsy. The effects of the drug hadn't yet worn off. I saw that the room had been furnished for a woman, and so attractively that no woman could have found fault with it. I was sure it had held other captives before me. But, as you can understand, Felton, the beauty of that prison increased my terror.

"Yes, it was a prison, as I learned when I tried to leave it. I tapped on the walls, hoping to discover a hidden door; the walls were solid everywhere. I went around the room a dozen times, looking for some sort of opening; there was none. Finally I sank into an armchair, exhausted, and apprehensive.

"Meanwhile night was falling, and with darkness my fears increased. I stayed in my chair, feeling that unknown dangers were waiting to pounce on me if I moved. I hadn't eaten since the day before, but I was too frightened to be hungry.

"There were no sounds that would have helped me to guess what time it was, but I thought it must be somewhere between seven and eight o'clock in the evening, since it was October and the darkness was now complete.

"I suddenly started when I heard a door turning on its hinges. A lamp appeared above the opening in the ceiling and lit up the room. I was terrified to see a man standing a few feet away from me. Then I saw that a table set for two had come to the middle of the room as though by magic.

"The man standing before me was the man who'd been pursuing me for a year. He'd sworn to dishonor me, and the first words from his mouth now told me that he'd done it the night before."

"The vile scoundrel!" murmured Felton.

"Oh, yes, he was vile!" said Milady, pleased to see that Felton was hanging on every word of her strange story. "He thought it was enough to have triumphed over me during my sleep: he expected me to accept my shame because it was already consummated. He'd come to offer me his fortune in exchange for my love.

"I poured out all the contempt and scorn that a woman's heart can contain. He was evidently used to such reproaches because he listened to me calmly with his arms folded, smiling. Then, when he thought I'd said everything I had to say, he stepped toward me. I ran to the table, snatched up a knife, and held its point against my chest.

" 'If you take one more step,' I said, 'you'll have my death on your conscience, as well as my dishonor!'

"He must have sensed my determination from my voice and my gestures, because he stopped.

" 'Your death?' he said. 'Oh, no, you're such a charming mistress that I wouldn't want to lose you like that, after possessing you only once. Good-bye, my beautiful spitfire. I'll wait till you're in a better mood before I pay you another visit.'

"He blew a whistle. The light disappeared and I was again in darkness. I heard the sound of a door being opened and closed; then the light appeared again and I found myself alone. It was a terrible moment. If I'd had any doubts before, they had now vanished: I was in the power of a man I hated and despised, a man who had already given me cruel proof that he would stop at nothing."

"But who was that man?" asked Felton.

"I spent the night on a chair," Milady went on without answering his question, "starting at the slightest sound, because the lamp had gone out at about midnight and I was in darkness again. But my persecutor didn't come back that night. At dawn, I saw that the table was gone. But I still had the knife in my hand. That knife was my hope.

"I was crushed by fatigue and my eyes were smarting because I hadn't dared to sleep for one moment all night. Daylight reassured me. I lay down on the bed after hiding the knife under the pillow.

"When I woke up, the table was there again, with another meal on it. This time, in spite of my fear and anguish, I was ravenously hungry. I hadn't eaten anything for forty-eight hours. I ate some bread and fruit. But, remembering how I'd been drugged, I didn't touch the water that was on the table. Instead, I filled my glass from a marble fountain set into the wall above the washstand. Even so, I waited anxiously after I'd drunk the water. My fears proved to be groundless: I felt none of the symptoms I dreaded. I poured out half of the water in the pitcher so that the precaution I'd taken wouldn't be noticed.

"Evening came. My eyes were now becoming accustomed to the darkness in the room and I was able to see the table sink down through the floor. About fifteen minutes later it came up again with my supper on it, and then the room was lighted by the lamp.

"I was determined to eat only food that couldn't have been drugged. After eating two eggs and some fruit, I filled my glass from the fountain. The taste of the water seemed to have changed since that morning. I became suspicious and stopped, but I'd already drunk half the glass. I poured out the rest of it and waited in horror, with cold sweat on my forehead.

"Someone must have been watching me when I drank water from the fountain that morning. My persecutor had decided to take advantage of my confidence and make me helpless to prevent him from dishonoring me again.

"Within less than half an hour the same symptoms returned. This time, since I'd drunk only half a glass of water, I struggled longer, and instead of becoming completely unconscious I remained in a state of heavy lethargy that left me aware of my surroundings but made me too weak to defend myself.

"I staggered toward the bed to get the only thing that could save me: my knife. But before I could reach it I fell to my knees, clutching one of the bedposts. I knew I was lost."

Felton turned ghastly pale and shuddered convulsively.

"The worst of it was that this time I was conscious of the danger that threatened me," Milady continued in an unsteady voice, as though she were reliving the anguish of her terrible experience. "My mind was awake while my body slept. I could still see and hear. It was as if everything were a dream, but that made it all the more frightening.

"I saw the lamp being taken away, leaving me in darkness. Then I heard the door creak as it opened; it was a sound I knew well, even though I'd heard it only twice before. I instinctively felt someone coming toward me, as people in the American wilderness are said to feel the approach of a deadly snake. I tried to scream. With an enormous effort of my will, I stood up, but I immediately fell—into the arms of my persecutor."

"Who was that man?" Felton asked again. "Tell me!"

Milady saw that she was torturing him by dwelling on each detail of her story, but she did not want to spare him. The more she made him suffer, the more surely he would avenge her. She went on as if she had not heard him:

"But this time he wasn't dealing with a completely unconscious woman. As I told you, I was aware of my danger even though I wasn't in full control of my body. I struggled with all the strength I had left. In spite of my weakness I evidently put up a long resistance, because I heard him say, 'These damned Puritan women! It's as hard to seduce them as it is to convert them!'

"But I felt my strength abandoning me, and I knew my desperate resistance couldn't last much longer. I fainted, and that vicious beast took advantage of my unconsciousness."

Felton had been listening in silence, except for a kind of low growl that escaped from him now and then. Sweat trickled down his forehead. He had thrust one hand under his coat and was now clawing at his chest in an effort to hold himself in check.

"The first thing I did after coming back to my senses was to reach for the knife under my pillow. I hadn't been able to defend myself with it, but at least I could use it to expiate my dishonor. Then, when I picked it up, a terrible thought came to me . . . I promised to tell you everything, Felton, and I will, even if the truth turns you against me."

"You thought of revenge, didn't you?" said Felton.

"Yes, I did. I know it wasn't a Christian thought. It must have been put into my mind by Satan. But I must tell you," she added in a tone of self-accusation, "that once it had come to me, it stayed with me. I'm now being punished for that murderous thought."

"Go on," said Felton, "I'm impatient to hear about your revenge."

"I was sure he'd come back the following night and I intended to take my revenge then. During the day I had nothing to fear, so when my breakfast came I didn't hesitate to eat and drink. Since I wasn't going to eat anything that evening—my plan was to make a pretense of eating then, without swallowing anything—I needed to build up strength for my fast. I hid a glass of the water that had been brought with my breakfast because thirst had made me suffer more than hunger during the forty-eight hours I'd spent without eating or drinking.

"My determination became even stronger as the day went by, but I was careful not to let my face show what was in my mind, because I had no doubt that I was being watched. Sometimes I found myself smiling. I'm afraid to tell you what made me smile, Felton; you'd be horrified . . ."

"Never mind," said Felton. "Just tell me what happened."

"When evening came, my supper was served in darkness, as usual, then the lamp appeared and I sat down at the table. I ate only a little fruit. I pretended to pour some water, but I drank only the water I'd kept in my glass. I did this deftly enough to deceive anyone who might be watching me.

"A little later, I showed the same signs of drowsiness as the night before, but this time I acted as if I weren't surprised by what was happening to me. I dragged myself over to the bed and pretended to fall asleep. As I lay there, I gripped the handle of my knife under the pillow.

"Two hours went by. I began to be afraid he wouldn't come—how strange that idea would have seemed to me the night before! Finally the lamp was withdrawn. I strained my eyes to see in the darkness. For ten minutes I heard nothing but the beating of my heart while I prayed he would come. Then I heard the familiar sound of the door opening and closing, and despite the thickness of the carpet I heard a floorboard creak. In the darkness I saw a shadow coming toward my bed."

"Tell me what happened!" Felton cried out. "Can't you see I'm dying to know?"

"I summoned up all my strength. The time for revenge, or rather justice, had come. I saw myself as another Judith. I tensed my muscles, still holding the knife. When I saw him beside me, groping to find me on the bed, I tried to stab him in the chest. But he'd known what to expect: his chest was covered with chain mail! My knife struck it without so much as scratching him.

"He seized my arm, took the knife away from me and said, 'Ah, so you want to kill me, my beautiful Puritan! That's more than hatred: it's ingratitude! Come, come, calm yourself. I thought you'd become more docile. But I'm not one of those tyrants who keep women by force. You don't love me. I doubted it, with my usual conceit, but now I'm convinced. Tomorrow you'll be free.'

"All I wanted now was for him to kill me.

" 'Be careful,' I said, 'because my freedom will mean your dishonor. As soon as I leave here I'll tell everything: the violence you've used against me, the way you've held me prisoner. You're a powerful man, but not powerful enough to escape justice. Above you is the king, and above the king is God!'

"Anger broke through his self-control. I couldn't see the

expression of his face, but my hand was on his arm and I felt it quiver.

" 'In that case, you won't leave here,' he said.

" 'Then the scene of my ordeal will be the scene of my death,' I answered. 'I'll die here. You're alarmed by my threat to expose you, but you'll be terrified by my accusing ghost.'

" 'You won't have a weapon.'

" 'There's one weapon that despair provides for anyone who has the courage to use it. I'll die of starvation.'

" 'Why don't we settle this peacefully?' he said. 'I'll set you free and proclaim your virtue from the housetops; I'll call you the Lucretia of England.'

" 'And I'll call you the Sextus of England. I'll accuse you before human justice as I've already accused you before God, and if, like Lucretia, I must sign my accusation with my blood, I won't hesitate to do it.'

" 'Then I withdraw my offer,' he said mockingly. 'After all, you're comfortable here and you lack nothing. If you die of starvation, it will be your own fault.'

"With those words, he left. I heard the door open and close. I was overwhelmed, but less by sorrow, I must confess, than by anger at having failed to get revenge.

"He didn't come back the following night. For two days I neither ate nor drank. I was determined to die of starvation, as I had told him. I prayed day and night, hoping that God would forgive me for my suicide.

"On the second night the door opened. I was lying on the floor; my strength had begun to abandon me. At the sound of the door I sat up, supporting myself with one hand.

" 'Have you softened your attitude?' said a voice that I recognized all too well. 'Are you willing to pay for your freedom with a promise of silence? I'm a fair and reasonable man. Although I don't like Puritans—unless they're pretty women—I know they can be trusted to keep an oath. If you swear on the Cross that you won't say anything against me, I'll set you free.'

"I stood up, because the sound of that hated voice had given me back my strength.

" 'Yes, I'll swear on the Cross!' I said. 'I swear on the Cross that no promise, threat, or torture will silence me! I swear on the Cross that I'll denounce you as a savage brute and a vile seducer! I swear on the Cross that if I ever leave here, I'll demand vengeance against you!'

" 'Be careful!' he said in a threatening tone that I'd never heard him use before. 'I have a way of closing your mouth, or at least making sure that no one will believe a word you say, and I'll use it if you leave me no other choice.'

"I answered him only with a scornful laugh. He saw that it was war between us, war to the death.

" 'I'll give you the rest of this night and all day tomorrow to think it over,' he said. 'If you promise to be silent, you'll have wealth, respect, and a high position in society. If you threaten to speak, I'll condemn you to inescapable infamy for the rest of your life.'

"I thought he'd gone mad.

" 'Get out!' I said. 'Leave me, or I'll break my head against the wall before your eyes!'

" 'Very well,' he said. 'Good-bye till tomorrow night.'

" 'Till tomorrow night,' I answered.

"I sank to the floor and lay there, grinding my teeth with rage."

Felton was leaning against a table. To her demonic joy, Milady saw that he was near the breaking point. She wondered if he could hold out till she had finished telling her story.

57

A Superb Dramatic Performance

After a moment of silence during which Milady observed Felton, she continued her story:

"I hadn't eaten or drunk anything for nearly three days. Sometimes a cloud seemed to pass before my eyes. I was close to becoming delirious.

"By that evening I was so weak that I'd begun fainting now and then, and each time it happened I thanked God because I thought I was going to die. As I was sinking into one of those faints I heard the door open. Terror brought me back to my senses. My persecutor came in, followed by a masked man. He himself was also masked, but I recognized his step and the imposing air that the devil gave him, to the world's misfortune.

" 'Well,' he said, 'have you decided to give me the promise I want?'

" 'We Puritans keep our word, as you know,' I answered, 'and I've already given you mine: I'll accuse you before human justice and before God.'

" 'You won't change your mind?'

" 'With God as my witness, I swear that I'll denounce your crime until I find an avenger.'

" 'You're a prostitute,' he said loudly, 'and you'll be given the punishment of a prostitute! When you've been branded, try to make anyone believe you! There's no one in the world who won't think you're either lying or insane.' He turned to the man who had come in with him. 'Executioner, do your duty.' "

"His name!" Felton cried out. "Tell me his name!"

"I began to realize that something worse than death was about to happen to me. The executioner seized me. I screamed and struggled, but he threw me on the floor and held me down. I was choked by my sobbing, and half unconscious. I called out to God for help; he didn't hear me. Suddenly I shrieked with pain and shame when the executioner's red-hot iron branded my shoulder."

Felton roared with anger.

"Look!" said Milady, standing up with the majesty of a queen. "Look at the martyrdom that was invented for a pure young girl who'd been the victim of a scoundrel's brutality. Learn to know men's hearts, and don't let them make you the instrument of their unjust revenge."

She quickly opened her dress, tore the batiste that covered her bosom and, with feigned shame and rage, showed him the indelible mark that dishonored her beautiful shoulder.

"But that's a fleur-de-lis!" he exclaimed.

"Yes, and that's precisely why it's so infamous," said Milady. "If he'd put the English brand on me, he'd have had to prove which court had sentenced me. But with this French fleur-de-lis I can't prove that I was branded unjustly."

This was too much for Felton. Crushed by that terrible revelation and dazzled by the beauty of the woman who had uncovered herself to him with an immodesty that he found sublime, he knelt before her as the early Christians knelt before those saintly young women who were publicly martyred in Rome for the entertainment of the bloodthirsty, lascivious populace. He no longer saw the brand on her shoulder; only her beauty remained.

"Forgive me!" he cried.

Milady saw love in his eyes.

"Forgive you for what?" she asked.

"For having joined your persecutors."

She held out her hand to him. He covered it with kisses.

"So young, so beautiful . . ." he said.

She gave him one of those looks that can turn a slave into a king. But Felton was a Puritan: he let go of her hand and began kissing her feet. He no longer loved her, he worshiped her.

When he began to regain his composure, she seemed to regain hers also, though actually she had never lost it. She drew her dress back over the amorous treasures she had exposed to him. Now that they were hidden from him, he desired them all the more ardently.

"And now," he said, "I have only one thing to ask of you: the name of your persecutor."

"Must I tell you his name? Haven't you guessed it already?"

"What! Do you mean to say that he's . . ."

"He's the man who's ravaged England, persecuted true believers, and destroyed the honor of countless women, the man who's plunged two kingdoms into bloody war to satisfy a whim of his depraved heart, the man who protects the Protestants today and will betray them tomorrow."

"Buckingham!" Felton said furiously. "Yes, it's Buckingham!"

Milady hid her face in her hands, as though she could not bear the shame that this name brought back to her.

"O Lord," said Felton, "Buckingham has tormented this angelic woman, and thou hast not destroyed him! He is still honored, still in full possession of the power he uses for the degradation of mankind!"

"God abandons those who abandon themselves," said Milady.

"He'll suffer the punishment of the damned," Felton continued with growing fervor, "but first he'll be struck down by human vengeance!"

"Human vengeance spares him because he's feared."

"I don't fear him and I won't spare him!"

Hearing this, Milady felt a surge of triumphant joy.

After a moment of silence, Felton asked, "But how is Lord de Winter, my fatherly protector, involved in all this?"

"To explain that," said Milady, "I must tell you about a man as noble and magnanimous as Buckingham is brutal and contemptible. I loved him, he loved me, and we were engaged to be married. He was a man like you, Felton, with a heart like yours. He was also a great lord who stood on an equal footing with Buckingham. After my ordeal, I went to him and told him everything. Knowing me as he did, he didn't doubt me for one moment. He said nothing; he simply put on his sword and cloak and went to Buckingham's house.''

"He was right," said Felton, "though a dagger, not a sword, is the weapon to use with men like that.''

"Buckingham wasn't there: he'd just been sent to Spain to ask for the Infanta's hand for Charles the First, who was then Prince of Wales. My fiancé came back and said to me, 'He's not in England, so for the moment he's safe from my vengeance. In the meantime we'll be married, and as surely as I bear the noble name of de Winter, you can count on me to uphold my wife's honor and my own.' ''

"De Winter!'' exclaimed Felton.

"Yes. Now you understand everything, don't you? Buckingham was gone for more than a year. A week before he came back, my husband died suddenly, leaving me to inherit everything from him. How did he die? God knows the answer to that question, but I accuse no one . . .''

"Oh, what an abyss of evil!'' said Felton.

"My husband died without having told the terrible secret to his brother: he'd intended to keep it hidden from everyone till the day of vengeance. Your protector had been distressed to see his elder brother marry a penniless young girl. Now that his hope of an inheritance had been disappointed, I felt I could expect no support from him. I went to France, intending to stay there the rest of my life. But my entire fortune is in England. When communications were cut off by the war, I ran short of money. I had to come back to England, and six days later I landed at Portsmouth.''

"And then?'' asked Felton.

"Buckingham must have learned of my return and told Lord de Winter, who was already prejudiced against me, that his sister-in-law was a prostitute, a branded woman. My husband was no longer there to defend me. Lord de Winter believed everything he was told, especially since it was to his interest to believe it. He had you arrest me and bring me here to be imprisoned. You know the rest: day after tomorrow he'll have me deported, sent off to live in shame. Ah, it's a clever plot! Since my honor will be destroyed forever, I have no choice but to die. Felton, give me that knife!''

As though her strength had been exhausted, she languidly fell into Felton's arms. Intoxicated with love and anger, aflame with sensual feelings that he had never known before, he clasped her to his chest. A tremor ran through him when he felt the warmth of her breath and the touch of her palpitating bosom.

"No," he said, "you'll live in honor, you'll live to triumph over your enemies!"

She slowly pushed him away with her hand and drew him toward her with her eyes. He clung to her and gazed at her imploringly, as if she were a divinity.

"Better death than shame," she said, lowering her eyes and voice. "Felton, my friend, my brother, please let me die!"

"No! You'll live, you'll be avenged!"

"I bring misfortune to everyone around me. Abandon me, Felton, let me die!"

"Then we'll die together!" he said, and pressed his lips to hers.

There was a knock at the door. This time she pushed him away in earnest.

"Listen!" she said. "Our conversation has been overheard! We're lost!"

"No," said Felton, "it's only the guard notifying me that someone is coming."

"Then hurry to the door and open it."

He obeyed; she was already in complete possession of his heart and mind.

He found himself facing a sergeant in command of a patrol.

"What is it?" asked Felton.

"You told me to open the door if you called, sir," said the guard, "but you forgot to give me the key. I heard you shouting, but I couldn't understand what you were saying. I tried to open the door. It was locked from inside, so I called the sergeant."

"And here I am," said the sergeant.

Felton was so distraught that he remained speechless. Milady realized she would have to take control of the situation. She ran to the table and picked up the knife that Felton had left on it.

"What right do you have to prevent me from dying?" she said.

"Oh, no!" Felton cried out in horror, seeing the knife in her hand.

Just then there was a burst of ironical laughter from the hall. Having heard the noise, Lord de Winter had come to investigate. He appeared on the threshold in his dressing gown, with his sword under his arm.

"I see we've reached the last act of the tragedy," he said.

"Didn't I tell you that you could expect a great dramatic performance from her, Felton? But don't worry, no blood will flow."

Milady knew she would be lost if she did not give Felton immediate and impressive proof of her determination.

"You're mistaken," she said, "blood *will* flow, and I hope it will fall on the heads of those who made me shed it!"

Felton uttered a heartrending cry and rushed toward her. It was too late; she had already stabbed herself.

But luckily, or rather skillfully, she had thrust the point of her knife against the metal busk that in those days defended a woman's bosom like a breastplate. The blade slipped off the busk, ripped her dress, and penetrated at an angle between two of her ribs.

A second later, her dress was bloodstained. She fell backward and seemed unconscious.

Felton pulled out the knife.

"She's dead, sir," he said solemnly. "She was in my care, and I let her kill herself!"

"No, she's not dead," said Lord de Winter. "Demons don't die so easily. You can put your mind at ease. Go and wait for me in my study."

"But, sir . . ."

"I order you to go."

Felton obeyed. But as he left he slipped the knife under his coat, next to his chest.

Lord de Winter sent for the woman who served as Milady's maid and, when she came, told her to take care of the prisoner, who still appeared to be unconscious. He then walked out of the room, leaving the two women alone together.

Despite his suspicion, he decided there was a chance that Milady's wound might be serious. He sent a man on horseback to bring a doctor.

58

Escape

As Lord de Winter had thought, Milady's wound was not dangerous. She opened her eyes as soon as her maid began undressing her. She had to make a show of weakness and pain, but that was easy for an actress of her ability. The maid was completely taken in and insisted on staying with her all night, in spite of Milady's efforts to convince her that it was not necessary.

But the maid's presence did not prevent Milady from thinking.

She had no doubt that Felton believed her story and was now so devoted to her that if an angel had appeared before him to accuse her, he would have taken him for a demon sent by Satan. She smiled at this thought because Felton was her only hope, her only means of escape. But then she wondered if Lord de Winter might have begun to suspect him and decided to have him watched.

The doctor arrived at about four o'clock in the morning. Since Milady's wound had now had time to close, he could not determine its depth or direction, but from her pulse it was clear to him that her condition was not serious.

At daylight she sent the maid away, saying that she had not slept all night and needed to be left alone so that she could rest. She hoped to see Felton when her breakfast was brought to her. But he did not come.

Were her fears justified? Did Lord de Winter suspect Felton? Would Felton be unable to help her at the decisive time? She had only one more day: de Winter had said she would leave on the twenty-third, and it was now the morning of the twenty-second.

She waited for her midday meal, trying to hold her impatience in check. The meal was brought at the usual time, even though she had eaten no breakfast. She was alarmed to see that the soldiers wore different uniforms. When she ventured to ask one of them what had become of Felton, she was told only that he had ridden away from the castle an hour earlier. She asked if Lord de Winter had also left. The soldier said that he was still in the castle and had given orders that he was to be notified if the prisoner wanted to speak to him. Milady replied that she was too weak for a visit and wanted only to be left alone.

The soldiers went out, leaving the meal on the table.

Felton had been sent away and different soldiers had been assigned to guard her. This could only mean that Felton was under suspicion. She began to lose hope.

Till now she had stayed in bed, keeping up her pretense of being gravely wounded, but she suddenly felt that she could not bear to go on lying there any longer. She got up and looked at the door; Lord de Winter had had a board nailed over the grille; he must have been afraid that, by some diabolical means, she might still succeed in seducing her guards through that opening. She smiled at the thought that she could now give vent to her feelings without being observed. She began pacing the floor like a madwoman or a caged tigress. If she had still had the knife, she would have planned to use it, not to kill herself, but to kill Lord de Winter.

At six o'clock he came in, armed to the teeth. Before her imprisonment, she had regarded him as a rather foolish and gullible gentleman, but he had now become an excellent jailer who seemed to guess all his prisoner's intentions and take precautions against them.

One look at her was enough to tell him what was in her mind.

"You won't kill me today," he said. "You have no weapon, and besides I'm on my guard. You'd begun to pervert my poor Felton. He was already under your diabolical influence, but I'm trying to save him. He'll never see you again. Pack your things: you're leaving tomorrow. I was going to send you away on the twenty-fourth, but I decided it would be safer to do it earlier. By noon tomorrow I'll have your deportation order, signed by Buckingham. If you say one word to anyone before you're on the ship, my sergeant will shoot you. Those are his orders. And the captain of the ship has agreed to have you thrown overboard if you speak to anyone without his permission. That's all I have to tell you today. I'll come back tomorrow to say good-bye."

He left.

Milady had listened to him with a disdainful smile on her lips, but rage in her heart.

When her supper was brought in, she ate because she felt she needed to keep up her strength. She did not know what might happen during the night that lay ahead. It promised to be a stormy night: dark clouds scudded across the sky and lightning flashed in the distance.

Toward ten o'clock the storm broke. Milady was comforted to see nature share her agitation. Thunder roared like the anger in her soul, and she seemed to feel the rain buffeting her face while the wild lament of the wind echoed her despair.

Suddenly she heard someone tap on her windowpane, and in the glare of a lightning flash she saw a man's face on the other side of the bars.

She ran to the window and opened it.

"Felton! I'm saved!"

"Yes," said Felton, "but we must keep our voices down. I'll need time to cut through the bars with my file. Be careful they don't see you through the grille."

"They've nailed a board across the grille—that proves the Lord is with us!"

"God has taken away their reason."

"But what must I do?" asked Milady.

"Just close the window and go to bed with your clothes on. I'll tap on the glass when I've finished. But will you be able to go with me?"

"Oh, yes!"

"What about your wound?"

"It's still painful, but it won't prevent me from walking."

"Be ready to go as soon as you hear my signal."

Milady closed the window, put out the lamp, and got into bed. Amid the moans of the gale she heard Felton's file grating on the bars, and each time the lightning flashed she saw his shadow in the window.

She lay still for an hour, scarcely daring to breathe. Anxiety gripped her heart at each sound she heard from the hall. It was one of those hours that seem to last a year.

Finally she heard Felton's signal, leapt out of bed, and opened the window. Where two bars were missing there was now an opening large enough for a man to pass through.

"Are you ready?" asked Felton.

"Yes. Shall I take anything with me?"

"Gold, if you have any."

"I have some. Luckily they let me keep what I had."

"Good, because I've spent all my money chartering a ship."

"Here," she said, handing him a bag of gold. He dropped it to the ground below.

"And now, let's go."

She stood on a chair, put the upper part of her body through the window and saw Felton suspended high above the ground on a rope ladder.

For the first time, sudden fear reminded her that she was a woman. She stared in horror at the sheer drop below her.

"I thought you might have that reaction," said Felton.

"Never mind, it's nothing. I'll climb down with my eyes closed."

"Do you trust me?"

"Of course."

"Put your arms in front of you and cross your wrists."

He tied her wrists together with his handkerchief, then with a rope over the handkerchief.

"What are you doing?" she asked with surprise.

"Put your arms around my neck and don't be afraid."

"But I'll make you lose your balance, and we'll both fall!"

"Don't worry. I'm a sailor."

There was no time to lose. She put her arms around his neck and let herself slide out of the window. He began slowly climbing down the ladder. Despite the weight of their two bodies, they swayed in the wind.

Suddenly he stopped.

"What's the matter?" she asked.

"Quiet. I hear footsteps."

"They've seen us!"

They were both silent for a few moments.

"No," he said, "it's nothing to worry about."

"But what's that noise?"

"A patrol. They're only making their rounds."

"Are they coming this way?"

"Yes. They'll pass under us."

"They'll see us!"

"Not if there's no lightning."

"They'll run into the bottom of the ladder!"

"It's higher than their heads."

"Here they come!"

"Quiet!"

They hung motionless and held their breath while the soldiers walked past, laughing and talking, twenty feet below them. It was a terrible moment for the two fugitives.

"We're safe now," Felton said when the sound of the soldiers' voices and footsteps had faded away.

Milady heaved a sigh and fainted.

Felton continued climbing down the ladder. When he came to

the bottom, he hung by his hands from the last rung and dropped to the ground. He picked up the bag of gold, gripped it between his teeth, and, carrying Milady in his arms, swiftly walked off in the direction from which the patrol had come. He soon left the path and went down among the rocks to the shore, where he blew his whistle.

He was answered by an identical signal. Five minutes later he saw a boat with four men in it. It came close to the shore but could not reach it because the water was too shallow. Felton waded out to it, not wanting to entrust his precious burden to anyone.

The storm was beginning to die down, but the sea was still rough. The boat bobbed on the waves like a nutshell.

"To the sloop," said Felton, "and row as fast as you can."

The four men began rowing. Their progress through the big waves was slow and laborious. But they were moving away from the castle, and that was what counted. Soon the shore was nearly invisible in the darkness; it then seemed safe to assume that the boat could not be seen from the shore.

A moving black dot appeared on the surface of the sea. It was the sloop.

The oarsmen continued rowing with all their strength. Felton untied Milady's wrists, then cupped his hand, dipped it into the sea and sprinkled water on her face. She sighed and opened her eyes.

"Where am I?"

"You're saved."

"Saved!" she exclaimed. "Yes, I see the sky, and the sea! The air I'm breathing is the air of freedom! Oh, thank you, Felton, thank you!"

He pressed her to his heart.

"But why are my wrists so sore?" she said. "They feel as if they'd been crushed in a vise."

She raised her arms; her wrists had been bruised by the rope with which Felton had tied them together.

"I'm sorry," he said, looking at her beautiful hands and shaking his head.

"It's nothing," she said. "Now I remember."

She looked around her as if she had lost something.

"It's here," said Felton, pushing the bag of gold with his foot.

They were nearing the sloop. The sailor on watch hailed the boat, and Felton answered.

"What ship is that?" asked Milady.

"The one I've chartered for you."

"Where will it take me?"

"Wherever you like, after it first takes me to Portsmouth."

"What are you going to do in Portsmouth?"

"I'm going to carry out Lord de Winter's instructions," Felton said with a grim smile.

"What instructions?"

"Haven't you guessed?"

"No. Please tell me."

"Since Lord de Winter mistrusted me, he decided to guard you himself, so he sent me to have your deportation order signed by Buckingham."

"But if he mistrusted you, why did he let you have the deportation order?"

"He thought I didn't know what it was."

"I see. And you're going to Portsmouth?"

"Yes, and I have no time to lose: tomorrow is the twenty-third, the day when Buckingham intends to leave with the fleet."

"Where is he going?"

"To La Rochelle."

"He mustn't leave!" cried Milady, forgetting her usual presence of mind.

"Don't worry, he won't."

Milady started with joy. She had just seen into the depths of Felton's heart, and Buckingham's death was written plainly there.

"Felton, you're as great as Judas Maccabaeus. All I can say is that if you die, I'll die with you."

"Quiet!" he said, for the boat had now touched the side of the sloop.

He climbed up the ladder and gave Milady his hand while the sailors steadied her from below, because the sea was still rough.

A few moments later they were on the deck of the sloop.

"Captain," said Felton, "this is the lady you agreed to take to France."

"For a thousand pistoles," said the captain.

"I've already given you five hundred."

"That's true."

"And here's the other five hundred," said Milady, taking the bag of gold.

"No," said the captain. "Once I've made a bargain I stick to it, and my bargain with this young man was that I wouldn't get the rest of the money till we reached Boulogne."

"And are you sure we'll get there?"

"We'll get there safe and sound, sure as my name's Jack Butler!"

"If we do, I'll give you not five hundred pistoles, but a thousand!"

"You're the kind of passenger I like!" said the captain. "May God send me many more like you!"

"But first," said Felton, "you must put me ashore in the little bay of Chichester, near Portsmouth, as we agreed."

The captain replied by giving orders to set sail for the bay.

The little ship dropped anchor in it at about seven o'clock in the morning.

During the voyage, Felton had told Milady everything: how, instead of going to Portsmouth, he had chartered the sloop; how he had come back; how he had scaled the wall of the castle by driving spikes into the cracks between stones and using them as footholds; and how he had tied the rope ladder to two of the window bars. Milady knew the rest.

She tried to encourage him in his plan, but from the first words he said in reply she realized that the young fanatic needed to be cautioned rather than encouraged.

It was agreed that she would wait for him aboard the sloop till ten o'clock; if he had not come back by then, she would leave without him, and later, if he was able to escape from England, he would rejoin her in France, at the Carmelite convent in Béthune.

59

What Happened in Portsmouth on August 23, 1628

Felton took leave of Milady calmly, as if he were a brother saying good-bye to his sister before going out for a walk.

Though he outwardly maintained his composure, his eyes shone as if he had a fever, he was paler than usual, he clenched his teeth now and then, and he spoke with an abruptness that showed that he was preoccupied with something.

During the whole time he was in the boat taking him to shore, he looked back at Milady, who stood watching him from the deck of the sloop. They were not worried about being pursued: no one ever came into Milady's room before nine o'clock, and it would take three hours to go from the castle to Portsmouth.

Felton stepped ashore, climbed to the top of the cliff, waved to Milady one last time, and began walking toward the town. When he had gone a hundred paces downhill, he could see only the mast of the sloop.

He quickened his pace. In front of him, about half a mile away, he saw the towers and houses of Portsmouth in the morning mist. Beyond, the sea was covered with vessels whose masts swayed in the wind like a forest of poplars stripped by winter.

As he strode swiftly along, he thought of all the true or false accusations against the duke of Buckingham that he had gathered from ten years of ascetic meditation and many conversations with his fellow Puritans. It seemed to him that Buckingham's secret crimes, which Milady had revealed to him, were even more abominable than his public crimes, which were known all over Europe. Felton's strange, ardent love for Milady made him attribute lurid reality to her imaginary accusations, as if he were looking at specks of dust through a magnifying glass and seeing them as hideous monsters.

The exertion of his rapid pace, the thought that the woman he loved, or rather worshiped as a saint, was exposed to the danger of a terrible vengeance, the tumultuous emotions of the past few days, his present fatigue—all these things combined to put him in a state of exaltation beyond ordinary human feelings.

He came into Portsmouth at about eight o'clock in the morning. The whole population was up and about. Drums were beating in the streets and on the waterfront: troops were marching toward the ships that would take them to France.

He arrived at the Admiralty covered with dust and streaming with sweat; his face, usually so pale, had now turned red from heat and anger. The sentry tried to turn him back, but Felton called the sergeant of the guard, took the deportation order from his pocket, and said, "An urgent message from Lord de Winter."

Knowing that Lord de Winter was one of Buckingham's closest friends, and seeing that Felton wore the uniform of a naval officer, the sergeant let him pass.

Felton hurried into the building. At the same time, another man came in. He too was dusty and out of breath. The horse he had left at the gate had fallen to its knees from exhaustion.

He and Felton both spoke to Patrick, the duke of Buckingham's confidential servant. Felton announced that he had been sent by Lord de Winter; the stranger refused to give any name and said that he could identify himself only to the duke in person.

Patrick, who knew that the duke had both friendly and official relations with Lord de Winter, gave precedence to the man who had come in his name. The stranger had to wait, and it was easy to see his exasperation at this delay.

Felton followed the servant through a large room in which deputies from La Rochelle, led by the prince de Soubise, were waiting. Patrick then went into a little room where the duke was dressing himself, with his usual painstaking care, after a bath.

"Lieutenant Felton, with a message from Lord de Winter."

"From Lord de Winter?" said Buckingham. "Show him in."

When Felton entered, the duke had just taken off a gold brocade dressing gown and was putting on a blue velvet doublet embroidered with pearls.

"Why didn't Lord de Winter come himself?" asked Buckingham. "I was expecting him this morning."

"He told me to tell you, Your Grace," replied Felton, "that he regrets not having the honor of seeing you this morning, but that he must stay at the castle to supervise the guarding of a prisoner."

"Yes, I know he has a prisoner."

"I've come to speak to you about that prisoner, Your Grace."

"I'm listening."

"What I have to say must be heard only by you."

"Leave us, Patrick," said Buckingham, "but stay where you can hear the bell. I'll ring for you shortly."

Patrick left.

"We're alone now," said the duke. "You can speak freely."

"Your Grace," said Felton, "Lord de Winter wrote to you the other day asking you to sign an order to deport a young woman named Charlotte Backson."

"Yes, and I answered that I'd sign the order when it was brought to me."

"Here it is, Your Grace."

"Let me see it."

The duke took the sheet of paper from Felton's hand and glanced over it to make sure it was the order that had been described to him. He then put it on the table, picked up a pen, and prepared to sign it.

"Excuse me, Your Grace," said Felton, "but do you know that Charlotte Backson is not that woman's real name?"

"Yes, I do," replied the duke, dipping his pen in ink.

"Then you know her real name?"

"Yes."

The duke lowered his pen toward the paper.

"And, knowing her real name, are you still going to sign that order?"

"Knowing who she is makes me all the more willing to sign it."

"I can't believe, Your Grace," Felton said with an effort, as if he were struggling to keep from choking, "that you know she's Lady de Winter."

"I know it very well, but I'm surprised that *you* know it!"

"You'll sign that order without remorse?"

The duke gave Felton a haughty look.

"You're asking me some strange questions! I've already answered more of them than you had any right to expect."

"Answer this one, Your Grace: the situation is more serious than you may realize."

Thinking that Felton must be speaking in Lord de Winter's name, Buckingham softened his attitude.

"I'll sign the order without the slightest remorse," he said. "Lord de Winter knows as well as I do that his sister-in-law is a dangerous criminal and that limiting her punishment to deportation is almost the same as pardoning her."

He put his pen to the paper.

"You won't sign that order, Your Grace," said Felton, stepping toward him.

"I won't sign it? Why not?"

"Because you'll examine your conscience and do justice to Lady de Winter."

"If I did her justice, I'd have her hanged at Tyburn. She's a demon."

"No, Your Grace, she's an angel, and you know it. I ask you to set her free."

"You must be mad to speak to me like this!"

"Excuse me, Your Grace; I'm restraining myself as much as I can. But if you don't reconsider what you're about to do, I can't answer for the consequences."

"What!" exclaimed Buckingham. "I believe you're threatening me!"

"No, Your Grace, I'm still pleading with you. I'll only point out that one drop is enough to make a full glass overflow, and that a small offense can bring punishment to someone who has so far been spared in spite of many crimes."

"Lieutenant Felton," said Buckingham, "leave this room and place yourself under arrest, immediately."

"Hear me out, Your Grace. You seduced Lady de Winter before her marriage, you violated her, sullied her. If you make amends for your crime by letting her leave freely, I won't demand anything more of you."

The duke stared at Felton in amazement.

"You won't *demand*?"

"Take care, Your Grace," said Felton, becoming more impassioned as he spoke, "all England is weary of your iniquity. You've abused the royal power that you've almost usurped. You're abhorrent to men and God. God will punish you later, but I'll punish you today."

"This is too much!" said Buckingham, walking toward the door.

Felton stepped in front of him.

"I humbly ask you to sign an order for Lady de Winter's release," he said. "Remember that she's the woman you dishonored."

"Leave, or I'll ring for my servant and tell him to have the guards put you in irons!"

"You won't ring for anyone," said Felton, placing himself between the duke and the bell that stood on a silver-inlaid pedestal table. "Take care, Your Grace, you're in God's hands now."

"In the devil's hands, you mean," said Buckingham, raising his voice to make himself heard by the servants, without calling them directly.

Felton held out a sheet of paper to him.

"Sign Lady de Winter's release, Your Grace."

"Do you think you can make me sign it by force? You must be joking! Patrick! Come here, Patrick!"

"Sign it, Your Grace!"

"Never!"

"Never?"

The duke called out to Patrick again and reached for his sword. But Felton did not give him time to draw it. From under his doublet he took the knife with which Milady had stabbed herself.

Just as Felton lunged at the duke, Patrick came into the room and said, "Your Grace! A letter from France!"

"From France!" exclaimed Buckingham, forgetting everything else.

Felton took advantage of this moment to plunge his knife into Buckingham's side.

"Traitor!" cried the duke. "You've killed me . . ."

"Murder! Murder!" shouted Patrick.

Felton looked around for a way to escape and saw that there was no one in front of the door. He darted into the next room, where the deputies from La Rochelle were waiting. He ran through it and headed for the stairs, but as he started down them he nearly collided with Lord de Winter.

Seeing Felton wild-eyed and livid, with blood on his hand and face, de Winter seized him and said, "I knew it! I knew it, and yet I've come a minute too late!"

Felton put up no resistance. Lord de Winter turned him over to the guards. Pending further orders, they took him to a small terrace overlooking the sea. De Winter ran toward Buckingham's dressing room.

When the man Felton had met in the anteroom heard Patrick's shout, he rushed into the dressing room. He found the duke lying on a sofa, pressing his hand over his wound.

"La Porte," Buckingham said in a feeble voice, "have you come from *her*?"

"Yes, Your Grace," replied Anne of Austria's faithful servant, "but I may have come too late."

"Quiet, La Porte! You might be heard. Patrick, don't let anyone come in . . . Oh, I'm dying, I'll never know what her message was . . ."

And the duke fainted.

Lord de Winter, the deputies, the leaders of the expedition, and the officers of Buckingham's staff burst into the room. Cries of grief arose.

The news quickly filled the whole building with lamentations, then spread through the town. A cannon shot announced that something unexpected had happened.

Lord de Winter was in despair.

"Too late!" he wailed. "Only a minute too late! Oh, my God, what a disaster!"

Having been notified at seven o'clock that a rope ladder was hanging from one of the windows of the castle, he had gone straight to Milady's room and found it empty, with the window open and the bars cut. He had then remembered the warning given to him by d'Artagnan's messenger. Fearing for the duke's life, he had run to the stable, leapt onto the first horse he saw, galloped to the Admiralty, dismounted in the courtyard, hurried up the stairs, and met Felton at the top.

Meanwhile the duke was still alive. He regained consciousness and opened his eyes. Those around him began to hope.

"Gentlemen," he said, "leave me alone with Patrick and La Porte . . . Ah, you're here, de Winter! That was a strange messenger you sent me this morning! He had a bad effect on me, as you can see."

"Oh, Your Grace," cried Lord de Winter, "I'll never . . ."

"Your grief will pass, my friend. No man deserves to be mourned all through another man's lifetime. But please leave me now."

Lord de Winter walked out of the room, sobbing.

Only La Porte and Patrick were now with the duke.

Servants had run off in search of a doctor, but so far none had been found.

La Porte knelt beside the sofa on which Buckingham lay, with blood still flowing from his wound.

"You'll live, Your Grace, you'll live!"

"What has she written to me?" Buckingham asked weakly, struggling against his pain to speak of the woman he loved. "Read me her letter."

"But Your Grace . . ."

"Do as I say, La Porte. Don't you see that time is running short?"

La Porte broke the seal and held the letter in front of Buckingham's eyes. The duke vainly tried to read it.

"Read it to me," he said. "My sight is failing. Hurry, because soon my hearing will fail too, and I don't want to die without knowing what she's written to me."

La Porte read aloud:

> *"Your Grace,*
>   *By everything that I have suffered since I met you, suffered because of you and for you, I beg you, if my peace of mind means anything to you, to stop arming England against France and put an end to this war. Its cause is publicly said to be religion, but privately everyone says that its real cause is your love for me. Not only may it bring great disaster to both France and England, but it may also bring you personal misfortunes that I would regret forever.*

Be on your guard; your life is in danger, and it will be dear to me when I am no longer obliged to regard you as an enemy.

Affectionately,
Anne"

Buckingham had summoned up all his remaining strength to listen to La Porte's reading of the letter.

"Don't you have anything to tell me in person, La Porte?" he asked, as though the letter had been a bitter disappointment to him.

"Yes, Your Grace: the queen told me to warn you to be careful, because she'd learned that plans were being made to assassinate you."

"Is that all?" Buckingham asked impatiently.

"She also told me to tell you that she still loves you."

"Thank God! My death won't be a stranger's death to her."

La Porte burst into tears.

"Patrick," said the duke, "bring me the box that held the diamond tags."

Patrick brought the box, and La Porte recognized it as having belonged to the queen.

"Now the white satin bag with her pearl-embroidered monogram on it."

Patrick obeyed again.

"La Porte," said Buckingham, "these are my only mementos of her: this box and these two letters. Give them back to her. And as a last keepsake from me, give her . . ."

He looked around for some precious object, but his eyes, dimmed by the approach of death, encountered only the bloody knife that Felton had dropped.

"Give her that knife," he said, clasping La Porte's hand.

He found the strength to put the knife and the satin bag into the box, then he shook his head to tell La Porte that he could no longer speak.

A final convulsion, which this time he was unable to control, made him fall from the sofa onto the floor.

Patrick cried out in alarm.

Buckingham tried to smile, but death stopped his thought and it remained engraved on his face like a last kiss of love.

Just then the duke's doctor arrived in a state of great agitation; he had already been aboard the flagship and it had taken all this time to bring him from there.

He took the duke's hand, held it a moment, and then dropped it.

"There's nothing to be done," he said. "He's dead."

"Dead! Dead!" cried Patrick.

At this cry, the crowd came back into the room. Everyone was thrown into consternation.

As soon as Lord de Winter saw that Buckingham had died, he ran to the terrace where the guards were still keeping Felton. Now that he had stabbed the duke, Felton had regained the calm that was never to leave him again.

"What have you done, you wretched fool!" de Winter said to him.

"I've taken vengeance," he replied.

"That woman used you for her diabolical plans! But I swear that this crime will be her last!"

"I don't know what you mean, sir," Felton said serenely. "No woman had anything to do with it. I killed the duke of Buckingham because he twice refused your request to have me promoted to captain. I punished him for his unfairness, that's all."

De Winter stared at him in bewilderment, not knowing what to think of such cold-bloodedness.

Only one thing disturbed Felton's tranquility: at each sound he heard, the naive Puritan was afraid that Milady had come to throw herself into his arms, confess her complicity in his act, and die with him.

He looked out over the sea, which was visible to a great distance from the terrace on which he stood. Suddenly he started: he had just seen something that anyone without his experience as a sailor would have taken for a seagull floating on the waves, but he recognized it as the sloop heading for the coast of France.

Realizing that he had been betrayed, he turned pale and put his hand over his aching heart.

"Will you do me one last favor, sir?" he asked Lord de Winter.

"What is it?"

"Please tell me what time it is."

De Winter took out his watch.

"It's ten minutes to nine," he said.

Milady had left an hour and a half earlier than she had agreed. When she heard the cannon shot announcing the fateful event, she had ordered the captain to weigh anchor.

The sloop was now sailing along beneath a blue sky, far off the coast.

"It was God's will," Felton said with a fanatic's resignation. But he could not take his eyes off the sloop, and he imagined that he could see a woman on its deck, the woman to whom he had sacrificed his life.

De Winter followed his gaze, sensed his suffering, and guessed everything.

Two guards took hold of Felton and began leading him away. He kept his eyes fixed on the sea.

"Your accomplice has escaped for now, and you'll be punished alone," de Winter said to him, "but I swear by the memory of my beloved brother that she too will be punished as she deserves!"

Felton bowed his head and said nothing.

De Winter hurried down the stairs and went to the waterfront.

60

In France

When the king of England, Charles I, learned of Buckingham's death, his first fear was that the terrible news might dishearten the people of La Rochelle. He tried to keep it from them as long as possible, Richelieu says in his memoirs, by closing all the ports of his kingdom; until the departure of the army that Buckingham had prepared, no other vessels were to be allowed to leave. Now that Buckingham was dead, the king himself undertook to supervise that departure.

He went so far as to detain the Danish ambassador when he had already taken official leave, and the Dutch resident ambassador, who was to have taken back to Vlissingen the ships of the East Indies fleet, which Charles I had decided to return to the United Provinces.

But since he did not think of issuing these orders till two o'clock in the afternoon, more than five hours after Buckingham's death, two ships had already set sail. One of them was the sloop that Felton had chartered for Milady. When she left, she already believed she knew what had happened, and her belief soon became a certainty when she saw a black flag flying from the mast of a warship.

As for the other ship, we will later see who was aboard it and how it left.

Meanwhile there was nothing new in the camp before La Rochelle, except that the king, bored as always, decided to go incognito to Saint-Germain for the Saint Louis festival. He asked the cardinal to prepare an escort of twenty musketeers. Since the cardinal was sometimes infected by the king's boredom, he was glad to have him leave. His Majesty promised to be back by about September 15.

As soon as the cardinal had informed him of the journey, Monsieur de Tréville packed the things he would need for it. Without knowing their reason, he was aware that the four friends were eager to return to Paris, so he naturally made them part of the escort.

They were the first men to whom he gave the news, only a quarter of an hour after learning it himself. D'Artagnan now had even more reason to be glad that he had become a musketeer: if he had remained in the guards, he would have had to stay in camp while his friends went off without him.

They had been impatiently waiting for a chance to leave camp because they knew that Madame Bonacieux would be in great danger if she encountered Milady, her mortal enemy, in the convent at Béthune. Aramis had written to Marie Michon, the linen-draper in Tours who had such good connections, to ask her to obtain the queen's permission for Madame Bonacieux to leave the convent and go either to Lorraine or to Belgium. Nine or ten days later he received this reply:

My dear cousin,
    Here is my sister's authorization to take our servant from the Béthune convent, since you think the air is bad for her there. My sister is glad to send you this authorization because she is very fond of the girl and intends to help her later.

Tenderly yours,
Marie Michon

Enclosed with this letter was the following authorization:

    The abbess of the Béthune convent will release into the custody of the bearer of this note the novice who entered the convent on my recommendation and under my patronage.
The Louvre, August 10, 1628.

Anne

Aramis's three friends were greatly amused by his kinship with a linen-draper who called the queen his sister. But after Porthos's heavy-handed jokes had several times made him blush to the whites of his eyes, Aramis asked that the subject be dropped and declared that if one more word was said about it, he would never again use his cousin as an intermediary in such matters.

And so the four musketeers made no further mention of Marie Michon. In any case, they had what they wanted: the order to withdraw Madame Bonacieux from the Carmelite convent at Béthune. This order was of little use to them, however, as long as they were encamped before La Rochelle, at the other end of France. D'Artagnan was on the verge of asking Monsieur de Tréville for leave, and telling him his reason for wanting it, when he and his friends received the news that they were going to be among the twenty musketeers who would escort the king to Paris. They were overjoyed.

They sent their servants on ahead with their baggage and left on the morning of the sixteenth.

The cardinal accompanied His Majesty from Surgères to Mauzé, where they took leave of each other with a great display of friendship.

The king wanted to travel as fast as possible and reach Paris by the twenty-third, but he also wanted to enjoy himself along the way, so he stopped now and then to hunt with his hawk. It was a pastime that he had learned from the duke de Luynes and he was still very fond of it. Sixteen of the twenty musketeers were delighted by these breaks in the journey; the other four cursed and grumbled.

D'Artagnan often had a buzzing in his ears; Porthos explained it in this way: "A great lady once told me it means that someone is talking about you somewhere."

Finally they reached Paris on the night of the twenty-third. The king thanked Monsieur de Tréville and authorized him to grant four-day leaves, on condition that none of the men who received them would appear in any public place, under penalty of being sent to the Bastille.

Our four friends were, of course, the first men to be granted leave. Athos even persuaded Monsieur de Tréville to give them six days instead of four, plus two extra nights. Tréville postdated their leaves to the morning of the twenty-fifth, but they left on the twenty-fourth at five o'clock in the afternoon.

"It seems to me that we're making too much of a simple

matter," said d'Artagnan, who, as we know, never had doubts about anything. "By riding two horses to death—and I can afford it, now that I have money—I can get to Béthune in two days. I'll give the queen's letter to the abbess of the convent and leave with Madame Bonacieux. I won't take her to Lorraine or Belgium: I'll bring her back to Paris. It will be better to hide her there, especially as long as the cardinal is at La Rochelle. When the siege is over, the queen will do as we want, partly because of what we've done for her and partly because of Aramis's cousin. The rest of you may as well go back and wait for me in Paris. Planchet and I by ourselves can easily do what needs to be done."

"We have money, too," said Athos. "I haven't yet drunk up my share of the diamond ring, and Porthos and Aramis haven't yet eaten up theirs. But don't forget that the cardinal has told Milady to go to Béthune and that she brings disaster wherever she goes. If you were dealing with four men, d'Artagnan, I'd tell you to go alone, but since you'll be dealing with that woman, the rest of us will go too, and may God grant that even with our servants there won't be too few of us!"

"You sound as if you were really worried," said d'Artagnan. "What is there to be afraid of?"

"Everything," replied Athos.

D'Artagnan looked at Porthos and Aramis. Like Athos, they seemed apprehensive. They all continued riding swiftly along the road without saying anything more.

They reached Arras on the evening of the twenty-fifth. D'Artagnan went into the Herse d'Or inn for a glass of wine. A minute later a man rode out of the courtyard of the post house, where he had just taken a fresh horse, and galloped off in the direction of Paris. As he was passing the door of the inn, the wind lifted his hat and blew open the cloak he was wearing even though it was August. He caught his hat in time to keep it from being blown away and quickly pulled it down over his eyes.

Seeing him pass, d'Artagnan turned pale and dropped his glass.

"What's the matter, sir?" said Planchet. "Oh! Come here, gentlemen! My master's about to faint!"

D'Artagnan's three friends hurried into the inn and saw that instead of fainting he was running toward his horse. They stopped him in the doorway.

"Where the devil are you going?" said Athos.

"There he goes!" cried d'Artagnan, livid with anger. "Let me ride after him!"

"But who is he?"

"That man!"

"Which man?"

"The one who's always appeared like an evil spirit when something terrible is about to happen, the one who was with Milady the first time I saw her, the one I was looking for when I got into a quarrel with Athos, the one I saw on the morning of the day when Madame Bonacieux disappeared—the man from Meung! I saw him! I recognized him when the wind blew open his cloak!"

"So you really saw him . . ." Athos said thoughtfully.

"Let's go! We'll ride after him and catch him!"

"He's going in the opposite direction from ours," said Aramis. "Our horses are tired and his is fresh. We'd only kill our horses without having a chance to catch him. Let him go, d'Artagnan. Saving Madame Bonacieux is the most important thing we have to do now."

"Stop, sir!" shouted a stableman, running after the stranger. "Here's a piece of paper that fell out of your hat!"

"I'll give you half a pistole for that piece of paper!" d'Artagnan called out to him.

"It's yours!" said the stableman. "Here it is."

He went back into the courtyard, delighted with his profitable bargain.

D'Artagnan unfolded the paper.

"Well?" asked his friends, gathering around him.

"There's only one word on it," said d'Artagnan.

"Yes," said Aramis, "but it's the name of a town or a village."

" 'Armentières,' " read Porthos. "Armentières . . . I've never heard of it."

"It's in her handwriting!" exclaimed Athos.

"We'll take good care of this piece of paper," said d'Artagnan. "Maybe I didn't waste that half-pistole. Gentlemen, let's be on our way!"

The four friends galloped off along the road to Béthune.

61

The Carmelite Convent at Béthune

Great criminals have a kind of predestination that enables them to surmount all obstacles and escape all dangers—till the time set by Providence for their downfall.

So it was with Milady: she slipped past the warships of two nations and reached Boulogne without incident.

On her arrival at Portsmouth, she had posed as an English-woman driven from La Rochelle by French persecution; when she landed at Boulogne after a two-day crossing, she posed as a Frenchwoman who in Portsmouth had been a victim of English hatred of France. She had a combination of advantages more effective than any passport: her beauty, her air of distinction, and the generosity with which she handed out money.

Having been spared the usual formalities by the elderly governor of the port, who kissed her hand and did his best to please her with his most gallant manners, she stayed in Boulogne only long enough to send off a letter to the cardinal:

> *Your Eminence,*
> *You may be certain that the duke of Buckingham will not leave for France.*
> *Boulogne, August 25.*
>
> *Lady de———*
>
> *P.S.—In accordance with your wishes I am going to the Carmelite convent at Béthune and will await your orders there.*

She left Boulogne that evening, spent the night at an inn, and set off again at five o'clock the next morning. Three hours later she arrived at Béthune. She asked for directions to the Carmelite convent and went there immediately.

The abbess came to meet her. Milady showed her the cardinal's order. The Abbess gave her a room and had breakfast served to her.

The past had now faded from Milady's mind; she looked toward the future and saw only the great reward that the cardinal would give her for having served him so well in that murderous affair, without involving his name in any way. With its unending succession of consuming passions, her life was like a storm cloud passing over the earth, leaving devastation and death behind it.

When Milady had finished her breakfast, the abbess came to see her. There are few diversions in a convent, and the good abbess was eager to make her acquaintance. Milady charmed her with her gracious manner and varied conversation.

The abbess, a lady of noble birth, was especially interested in stories of life at court, which seldom reached the outer limits of the kingdom and almost never penetrated the walls of a convent isolated from worldly affairs. Milady was quite familiar with aristocratic intrigues, having lived in the midst of them for the past five or six years. She told the abbess about social activities at the French court, described the king's exaggerated show of piety, related various scandals involving great lords and ladies whom the abbess knew by name, and touched lightly on the love affair between the queen and Buckingham, hoping that by talking freely she would induce the abbess to do the same.

Although the abbess listened and smiled without saying anything, it was obvious that she enjoyed the stories she was hearing, so Milady went on telling them. She brought up the subject of the cardinal. Not knowing whether the abbess was a Cardinalist or a Royalist, she steered a cautious middle course. But the abbess was even more cautious: she made no comments and merely bowed her head each time Milady spoke the cardinal's name. Milady began to think she was going to be bored to tears during her stay at the convent.

She decided to take a risk in order to find out where the abbess stood with regard to the cardinal. She began speaking against him, vaguely at first, then more specifically. She told about his love affairs with Madame d'Aiguillon, Marion de Lorme, and other licentious women. The abbess listened attentively, gradually became more animated, and continued to smile. "Good, she's still enjoying my stories," thought Milady. "If she's a Cardinalist, she's at least not fanatical about it."

They talked about the cardinal's persecution of his enemies. The abbess crossed herself, expressing neither approval nor disapproval. This strengthened Milady's suspicion that she was more of a Royalist than a Cardinalist. She pursued the subject, giving even more appalling examples.

"I know nothing of all those things," the abbess finally said, "but even though we're far from the court and outside of all worldly interests, we still see some very sad examples of the things you're describing. One of our novices has suffered greatly from the cardinal's persecution."

"Then I pity her!" said Milady.

"And she deserves your pity. She's been imprisoned, threatened, mistreated . . . But perhaps the cardinal had good reasons for doing what he's done to her. She looks like an angel, but we mustn't always judge people by appearances."

Milady thought, "Maybe I'm going to discover something here. It looks as if I'm in luck."

She tried to give herself an expression of perfect candor.

"Yes, I know that people say we shouldn't judge by appearances, but what can we believe in, if not in the Lord's noblest handiwork: the human face? Maybe I'll often be disappointed or deceived, but I'll always trust someone whose face appeals to me."

"Then you're inclined to believe that woman is innocent?" asked the abbess.

"Evil isn't the only thing the cardinal punishes: there are virtues that he punishes more severely than certain crimes."

"Allow me to express my surprise."

"At what?" Milady asked naively.

"At the way you're talking."

Milady smiled.

"What's so surprising about the way I'm talking?"

"You're a friend of the cardinal, since he's sent you here, and yet . . ."

"And yet I speak badly of him?"

"Well, at least you haven't spoken well of him."

"That's because I'm not his friend," Milady said with a sigh. "I'm his victim."

"But the letter recommending you to me . . ."

"It's actually an order telling me to remain in captivity here until one of his underlings comes to take me away."

"Why haven't you escaped from him?"

"Where could I go? Do you think there's any place on earth that's beyond the cardinal's reach if he takes the trouble to put out his hand? If I were a man, I might try it, but what can a woman do? Has your novice tried to escape?"

"No, but with her it's different: I think a love affair is keeping her in France."

"If she's in love," Milady said with a sigh, "she can't be completely unhappy."

The abbess looked at her with growing interest.

"Then you're another poor victim of persecution?"

"Unfortunately, yes."

The abbess frowned, as if a disquieting thought had just occurred to her.

"You're not . . . an enemy of our holy faith, are you?" she asked uneasily.

"I, a Protestant?" exclaimed Milady. "Oh, no! With God as my witness, I'm a devout Catholic."

"Then our convent won't be a harsh prison for you," said the abbess, smiling. "We'll do everything we can to make you enjoy your captivity. And you'll have the company of that young woman who's probably being persecuted because of some court intrigue. She's gracious and charming."

"What's her name?"

"She was recommended to me, by someone of high rank, under the name of Kitty. I haven't tried to learn her other name."

"Kitty! Are you sure?"

"I'm sure she came here under that name. Do you know her?"

Without answering, Milady smiled inwardly at the thought that the novice might be her former maid. Then she remembered her anger against Kitty. For an instant her desire for revenge showed in her face, but her talent for dissimulation quickly brought back her calm, friendly expression.

"I know I'm going to like that young woman," she said. "When can I meet her?"

"This evening, or even sooner," replied the abbess. "But you told me you'd been traveling for four days and got up at five o'clock this morning, so you must need rest. Why don't you take a nap now? We'll wake you when it's time for lunch."

Even though Milady could have done without sleep, since she was sustained by the excitement that the prospect of a new adventure always aroused in her, she accepted the abbess's suggestion; her body was still able to resist her fatigue but she had been through so much emotional turmoil in the past two weeks that her mind needed rest.

The abbess left, and Milady lay down on her bed, lulled by

the thoughts of revenge that the mention of Kitty's name had revived in her. She recalled that the cardinal had promised her almost unlimited freedom of action if she succeeded in her mission. She had succeeded, and now she could take revenge against d'Artagnan.

Only one thing made her apprehensive: her husband, Count de La Fère, whom she had thought to be dead or at least in exile, had reappeared under the identity of Athos, d'Artagnan's best friend. But since he was d'Artagnan's friend, he must have been involved in all the machinations that had enabled the queen to thwart the cardinal's plans, and he was therefore the cardinal's enemy, which meant that she could probably make him share d'Artagnan's fate when the time came for her revenge.

These thoughts were so sweet to Milady that they had a soothing effect on her, and she soon drifted into peaceful sleep.

She was awakened by a soft voice from the foot of her bed. She opened her eyes and saw the abbess, accompanied by a young woman with blond hair and a fresh complexion who was looking at her with friendly curiosity.

This woman's face was completely unknown to Milady. They examined each other attentively as they exchanged polite remarks. They were both beautiful, but in sharply different ways. Milady was pleased to note her own superiority so far as distinction and aristocratic manners were concerned, though it was true that the young stranger, being dressed as a novice, was not able to show herself to best advantage.

The abbess introduced them to each other. Then she left to attend to her duties. The novice turned to follow her but Milady stopped her by saying, "Please don't deprive me of your company already. I've been counting on it to help me pass the time I must spend here."

"I was afraid I'd come at a bad time," said the novice. "You were asleep and you must still be tired."

"What's better than to be awakened by a pleasant surprise?" said Milady. "Stay and let me enjoy it a little longer."

She took her by the hand and drew her toward a chair beside the bed. The novice sat down.

"I'm so unlucky!" she said. "I've been here for six months, bored the whole time, and now, just when you've come and I finally have someone to keep me company, I'm probably going to leave at any moment."

"You're leaving soon?" asked Milady.

"I hope so, at least," the novice replied with a happiness that she made no attempt to conceal.

"I gather that you've suffered because of the cardinal. That would have been a bond between us."

"Yes, the abbess has told me that you've also been a victim of that evil man."

"Sh! We mustn't talk about him that way, even here. All my trouble came from saying something like what you just said, in front of a woman I regarded as my friend. She betrayed me. Were you betrayed too?"

"No," said the novice. "My trouble came from my devotion to a woman I'd gladly give my life for."

"And she abandoned you?"

"I was unjust enough to think so, but a few days ago I was given proof that it's not true, thank God! I'd have been terribly hurt if she'd forgotten me. But you seem to be free—why should you stay if you don't want to?"

"Where would I go, with no friends or money, in a part of France where I've never been before?"

"You're so beautiful, and you seem so kind, that I'm sure you'll always have friends wherever you go!"

"Thank you for the compliment," Milady said with an expression of angelic sadness, "but the fact remains that I'm alone and persecuted."

"You mustn't lose hope. There always comes a time when God rewards us for the good we've done. And it may be lucky for you that you've met me: I have no power of my own, but I have powerful friends. They've been working to save me, and once I'm out of here, they can work to save you too."

Milady decided to go on talking about herself in the hope of drawing information from the novice.

"When I said I was alone, I didn't mean it literally. I have several acquaintances in high places. But they all tremble before the cardinal. Even the queen doesn't dare to stand up to him. More than once she's had to watch helplessly while he persecuted people who'd served her well."

"The queen may seem to have abandoned those people," said the novice, "but the more they're persecuted the more she thinks about them, and often, when they expect it least, they have proof that she hasn't forgotten them."

"I believe it: she has such a good heart."

"You must know our beautiful and noble queen, to talk about her like that!" the novice exclaimed enthusiastically.

"Well, no, I don't have the honor of knowing her personally," Milady said cautiously, "but I know quite a few of her closest friends. I know Monsieur de Putange; I met Monsieur Dujart in England; I know Monsieur de Tréville . . ."

"Monsieur de Tréville! You know *him*?"

"Yes. I know him well, in fact."

"The captain of the King's Musketeers?"

"That's right."

"You and I are going to be friends, I'm sure of it! Since you know Monsieur de Tréville, you must have been in his house."

"Often," said Milady, deciding to carry her lie through to the end, since it seemed to be succeeding.

"Then you must have seen some of his musketeers there."

"All those who are usually there," replied Milady. She was beginning to take a real interest in this conversation.

"Tell me some of the ones you know, and we'll see if I know them too."

"Well," said Milady, a bit disconcerted, "I know Monsieur de Louvigny, Monsieur de Courtivron, Monsieur de Férussac . . ." She stopped and seemed to hesitate.

"Do you know a gentleman named Athos?" asked the novice.

Milady turned as white as the sheet on which she was lying. Despite her self-control she could not help uttering an exclamation, seizing the novice's hand, and staring at her intently.

"What's the matter?" the poor young woman asked in dismay. "Have I said something that offended you?"

"No, it's just that I once knew that gentleman, and it seemed strange to find someone else who knew him."

"Yes, I know him well, and also his friends: Monsieur Porthos and Monsieur Aramis."

"Really?" said Milady, feeling a chill in her heart. "I know them too."

"Then you must know that they're brave and honorable men— why don't you ask them to help you?"

"You see, I . . . I don't know them very well personally," stammered Milady. "I know them mainly from having heard a great deal about them from one of their friends, Monsieur d'Artagnan."

"You know Monsieur d'Artagnan!" cried the novice. Then, seeing Milady's strange expression, she added, "Excuse me, but would you mind telling me on what terms you know him?"

"Why, we're . . . we're friends, that's all . . ."

"You're not telling me the truth! You've been his mistress!"

"No, *you've* been his mistress!" Milady said forcefully. "I know who you are now: you're Madame Bonacieux!"

The novice shrank back in surprise and alarm.

"Don't try to deny it!" said Milady.

"It's true. I love him. Are we rivals?"

Milady's eyes flashed so savagely that in other circumstances Madame Bonacieux would have fled in terror, but now she was completely absorbed in her jealousy.

"Tell me whether or not you've been his mistress," she said with a firmness that was not ordinarily in her character.

"Oh, no!" Milady replied in a tone that made it impossible to doubt her sincerity. "Never!"

"I believe you. But why were you so angry just now?"

Milady had already recovered her presence of mind.

"I wasn't angry, I was surprised," she said. "Don't you understand?"

"How can I understand when I don't know anything about your . . . friendship with Monsieur d'Artagnan?"

"Don't you understand that since he's my friend, he's confided in me?"

"What has he told you?"

"Everything. I know that you were abducted from a little house in Saint-Cloud, that he and his friends were in despair, that all their efforts to find you have been in vain, that he loves you with all his heart. He's told me so much about you that I thought of you as my friend before I'd ever seen you. *Now* you understand my surprise, don't you? Nothing could have been more unexpected than finding you here, in this convent! My dear Constance, I've met you at last!"

Milady held out her arms to Madame Bonacieux, who was so convinced by what she had just heard that her jealousy had vanished and she now saw her only as a sincere and devoted friend.

"Oh, forgive me!" she said, resting her head on Milady's shoulder. "I love him so much!"

For a few moments the two women embraced each other. If Milady's strength had been as great as her hatred, Madame Bonacieux would not have come out of that embrace alive. But, not being able to crush her, she smiled at her.

"Oh, I'm so glad to have found you!" she said. "Let me look at you." She scrutinized her face. "Yes, it's really you. I clearly recognize you now, from what he said about you."

Madame Bonacieux had no way of knowing the cruel thoughts

that lay behind the apparent compassion she saw in Milady's eyes.

"Then you know how I've suffered," she said, "since he's told you how he's suffered. But suffering for him is happiness."

"Yes, of course," Milady said distractedly; her mind was on other matters.

"But my ordeal is about to end," Madame Bonacieux continued. "Tomorrow, or maybe even tonight, I'll see him again, and then the past will be wiped away."

"Tonight? Tomorrow?" said Milady, jolted out of her reverie. "What do you mean? Are you expecting news from him?"

"I'm expecting him in person."

"D'Artagnan is coming *here*?"

"Yes."

"But that's impossible! He's at the siege of La Rochelle with the cardinal, he won't come back till the siege is over!"

"Nothing is impossible for my d'Artagnan."

"Oh, no! I can't believe it!"

Carried away by her happiness and pride, Madame Bonacieux handed Milady a letter.

"Then read this," she said.

Milady looked at the letter and thought, "Madame de Chevreuse's handwriting! I was sure they had contacts in that direction!" And she avidly read these lines:

> *Be ready, my dear child: our friend will soon come to take you away from the prison where your safety required you to hide. Prepare to leave, and never lose hope in us.*
> *Our charming Gascon has just proved himself to be brave and loyal, as always. Tell him that his warning was received with deep gratitude.*

"Yes," said Milady, "the letter is quite specific . . . Do you know the warning it refers to?"

"No, but I suppose he must have warned the queen about one of the cardinal's plots."

"Yes, that must be it," said Milady, returning the letter to Madame Bonacieux.

She let her head fall back onto the pillow and for a moment she was lost in thought. Then she heard the hoofbeats of a galloping horse.

"Oh!" cried Madame Bonacieux, running over to the window. "Has he come already?"

Milady remained in her bed, petrified by surprise; so many unexpected things were happening that for once she had lost her self-possession. She lay still, staring into space.

"Can it really be that he's here?" she murmured.

"No," Madame Bonacieux said with bitter disappointment, "it's a man I don't know. But he seems to be coming here. Yes, he's slowing down . . . He's stopping at the gate . . . He's about to ring the bell."

Milady leapt out of bed.

"Are you sure it's not d'Artagnan?" she said.

"Yes, very sure."

"Maybe you couldn't see him well enough to recognize him."

"I'd recognize him if I saw only the feather in his hat or the edge of his cloak!"

Milady was now getting dressed.

"But you say it's a man who's coming here?"

"Yes. He's already gone inside."

"He's come either for you or for me."

"You seem so upset!"

"I *am* upset, I admit it. I'm not as confident as you are. With the cardinal against me, I'm afraid of everything."

"Sh! Someone's coming!" said Madame Bonacieux.

The door opened and the abbess came in.

"You came here from Boulogne, didn't you?" she asked Milady.

"Yes," replied Milady, trying to regain her composure. "Who wants to see me?"

"A man who won't give his name. He says he was sent by the cardinal."

"Are you sure I'm the one he wants to see?"

"He says he has a message for a lady who just came from Boulogne."

"Then please show him in."

"Do you think he has bad news for you?" Madame Bonacieux asked with concern.

"I'm afraid so."

"I'll leave you to talk with him but, if you don't mind, I'll come back as soon as he's gone."

"Please do."

The abbess and Madame Bonacieux left the room.

Milady stood with her eyes fixed on the door. A moment later she heard the jingling of spurs on the stairs, then the sound of approaching footsteps. The door opened and a man appeared.

Milady cried out with joy when she recognized him as Count de Rochefort, the cardinal's right-hand man.

62

Two Types of Demon

"Ah, it's you!" Rochefort and Milady both exclaimed at once.

"Where have you come from?" asked Milady.

"La Rochelle. And you?"

"England."

"The duke of Buckingham . . ."

"He's either dead or seriously wounded. I wasn't able to see him, but just as I was leaving England he was stabbed by a fanatic."

"What a stroke of good luck!" Rochefort said, smiling. "His Eminence will be delighted. Have you told him?"

"I wrote to him from Boulogne. But why are you here?"

"His Eminence sent me because he was worried about you."

"I arrived only yesterday."

"And what have you been doing since then?"

"I haven't wasted my time."

"I'm sure you haven't."

"I've met someone here. Try to guess who it is."

"I can't even try."

"It's that young woman the queen took out of prison."

"D'Artagnan's mistress?"

"Yes. Madame Bonacieux. The cardinal didn't know where she was hiding."

"More good luck! The cardinal can't complain that he's not getting his share!"

"You can imagine my surprise when I found her here."

"Does she know who you are?"

"No."

"Then she regards you as a stranger?"

Milady smiled.

"I'm already her best friend!"

"No one but you can work miracles like that," said Rochefort.

"It's turned out to be a useful miracle: from my friendly conversation with her, I learned that tomorrow or the day after they're coming to take her away, with an order from the queen."

"Who's coming?"

"D'Artagnan and his friends."

"I think we'll have to send them to the Bastille for their trouble."

"Why hasn't that been done already?"

"I wish I could tell you. The cardinal has a weakness for those men that I don't understand."

"Really?"

"Yes."

"Then tell him this, Rochefort: tell him that our conversation at the Colombier-Rouge was overheard by those men; that after he left, one of them came back and took away the letter he'd given me; that they told Lord de Winter I was coming to England, and almost made my mission fail again, as they did in the case of the diamond tags. And tell him that of those four men only two are dangerous: d'Artagnan and Athos. Aramis is Madame de Chevreuse's lover; he must be allowed to live, because we know his secret and it may be useful to us. Porthos is nothing but a conceited fool, so there's no need for the cardinal to bother with him."

"But those four men are supposed to be at the siege of La Rochelle."

"I thought so too, but now I've seen a letter from Madame de Chevreuse that proves they're coming to take Madame Bonacieux from this convent. She was foolish enough to show me the letter herself."

"We'll have to do something . . ."

"What are your orders from the cardinal?"

"He told me to take any messages you might have for him, written or oral, and come back. When he knows what you've done, he'll decide what you're to do next."

"Must I stay here?" asked Milady.

"Here or somewhere nearby."

"You can't take me with you?"

"No. The cardinal specifically told me not to do that. If you were in the vicinity of the camp, you might be recognized and your presence would arouse suspicion, especially after what just happened in England. Tell me in advance where you'll be waiting for word from the cardinal, so I'll always know where to find you."

"I probably won't be able to go on staying in this convent."

"Why not?"

"Because my enemies may arrive at any moment."

"That's true . . . But then, will that woman escape from the cardinal?"

"I'm her best friend, remember?" Milady said with her own special smile.

"Yes, of course. So I can tell the cardinal . . ."

"Tell him not to worry about her."

"Is that all?"

"He'll know what I mean."

"Or at least he'll guess it. And now, what shall I do?"

"Leave immediately. It seems to me that the news I have for the cardinal is worth a little haste."

"My post chaise broke down as I was coming into Lillers."

"Good!"

"Why is that good?"

"Because I need your post chaise."

"Then how will I travel?"

"On horseback."

"That's easy for you to say, but for me it means riding more than four hundred miles!"

"It can be done."

"All right, I'll do it."

"When you pass through Lillers on your way back, send the post chaise to me and tell your servant to place himself at my disposal."

"Very well."

"You have a written order from the cardinal, haven't you?"

"I have one giving me full powers."

"Show it to the abbess; tell her that someone will come for me in your name either today or tomorrow, and that I must go with him."

"Very well," Rochefort repeated.

"And when you tell her all that, be sure to speak harshly of me."

"Why?"

"Because I'm supposed to be one of the cardinal's victims. I want Madame Bonacieux to go on trusting me."

"Of course. And now will you write a report on everything that's happened?"

"I've already told you everything and you have a good memory: just repeat what I said. A written report can get lost."

"You're right. Now tell me where I can find you, so I won't have to do any unnecessary searching."

"Let me think . . ."

"Do you want a map?"

"I don't need one. I know this region like the back of my hand."

"You do? When were you ever here before?"

"I was brought up here."

"Really?"

"Yes. Sometimes it's useful to have been brought up somewhere."

"Where will you be waiting for me?"

"Just a minute . . . Yes: Armentières."

"What's that?"

"A little town on the Lys. All I'll have to do is cross the river and I'll be out of France."

"Excellent! But you won't cross the river unless you're in danger, will you?"

"No."

"But if you do, how will I know where you are?"

"You can do without your servant, can't you?"

"Yes."

"Is he reliable?"

"Completely."

"Then let me take him with me. No one knows him. If I cross the river, I'll leave him behind and he'll tell you where I've gone."

"Good. Otherwise I'll meet you in Argentières."

"Armentières," she corrected him.

"Write it down for me, in case I forget. There's nothing compromising about the name of a town, is there?"

"We can't be sure," said Milady, "but I'll take the risk anyway."

She wrote the name on half a sheet of paper. Rochefort took it, folded it, and put it in the lining of his hat.

"Don't worry," he said, "I'll keep repeating the name to myself, like a schoolboy learning a lesson, so I'll still know it even if I lose the paper. Is there anything else you need to tell me?"

"I don't think so."

"Let's make sure I've remembered everything: Buckingham is

dead or seriously wounded; your conversation with the cardinal was overheard by the four musketeers; Lord de Winter was warned that you were coming to Portsmouth; d'Artagnan and Athos must be put in the Bastille; Aramis is Madame de Chevreuse's lover; Porthos is a conceited fool; you've found Madame Bonacieux; I'm to send you my post chaise, place my servant at your disposal, and make you out to be one of the cardinal's victims when I talk to the abbess; Armentières, on the Lys. Is that right?''

"You have a prodigious memory, my dear Rochefort. Now that I think of it, though, there's one more thing . . .''

"Yes?''

"I saw some woods that must touch the garden of the convent. Tell the abbess that I'm allowed to take walks in those woods. Who knows, I may have to leave by the back door.''

"You think of everything.''

"And you've forgotten something.''

"What is it?''

"You've forgotten to ask me if I need money.''

"Ah, yes. How much do you want?''

"All the gold you have.''

"I have about five hundred pistoles.''

"And I have about the same. With a thousand pistoles, I can cope with anything. Empty your pockets.''

"Here.''

"Thank you. When are you leaving?''

"In an hour or so, when I've had time to eat something and send for a post horse.''

"That will be soon enough. Good-bye, Rochefort.''

"Good-bye, Lady de Winter.''

"Give my regards to the cardinal,'' said Milady.

"And give mine to Satan,'' replied Rochefort.

They exchanged a smile and parted.

An hour later Rochefort galloped off. After riding for five hours he stopped at Arras. We have already seen how d'Artagnan recognized him there, and how this recognition alarmed the four musketeers and made them hasten their journey.

63

The Drop of Water

Almost as soon as Rochefort had left, Madame Bonacieux came back into the room. Milady smiled at her.

"What you were afraid of has happened," said Madame Bonacieux. "The cardinal is going to send someone for you tonight or tomorrow."

"What makes you think so?"

"I heard the messenger say it to the abbess."

"Come here and sit down beside me," said Milady. Madame Bonacieux did as she was told. "And now . . . But first let me make sure no one is listening."

"Why . . ."

"You'll soon understand."

Milady stood up, went to the door, opened it, and looked into the hall. Then she came back and sat down beside Madame Bonacieux.

"He played his part well," she said.

"Who?"

"The man who told the abbess he'd been sent by the cardinal."

"He was only playing a part?"

"That's right."

"Do you mean he really wasn't . . ."

"That man," said Milady, lowering her voice, "is my brother."

"Your brother!" exclaimed Madame Bonacieux.

"Yes. You're the only one who knows that secret. If you tell it to anyone, I'll be lost, and perhaps you will be too."

"Oh!"

"Listen carefully; here's what happened. My brother was on his way here to take me away by force if necessary. He met one of the cardinal's men who was also coming here to take me away. He followed him. When they were on a lonely road, he drew his sword and ordered the messenger to give him the papers he was carrying. The messenger tried to resist and my brother killed him."

"Oh, no!" cried Madame Bonacieux, shuddering.

"There was no other way. Then my brother decided to use deception instead of force. He took the papers, came here, and introduced himself as the cardinal's messenger. In an hour or two, a carriage will come to take me away, under orders from the cardinal."

"I understand: the carriage will actually be sent by your brother."

"Precisely. But that's not all. The letter you received, the one you thought was from Madame de Chevreuse . . ."

"What about it?"

"It's a forgery."

"A forgery?"

"Yes. Its purpose is to prevent you from making any resistance when they come for you."

"But d'Artagnan is coming!"

"No, he's not. He and his friends are still at the siege of La Rochelle."

"How do you know that?"

"My brother met some of the cardinal's agents dressed as musketeers. They plan to have you called to the door, make you think they were sent by your friends, then take you to Paris."

"Oh, dear God! My head is spinning with all these evil schemes!" said Madame Bonacieux. She put her hands to her forehead. "If I hear any more, I'll go mad!"

"Listen . . ."

"What is it?"

"I hear a horse. My brother must be leaving. I want to tell him good-bye. Come."

Milady opened the window and Madame Bonacieux stood beside her.

Rochefort galloped past.

"Good-bye, Georges!" Milady called out to him.

He looked back, saw the two young women, and waved his hand.

Milady closed the window.

"He's always been such a good brother to me!" she said with affection in her voice and a melancholy expression on her face.

She sat down again and seemed to become lost in personal thoughts.

"Excuse me for disturbing you," said Madame Bonacieux, "but I must ask you for advice. You have more experience than I do. Please tell me what I should do."

"First of all," said Milady, "I have to tell you that I may be mistaken: it's possible that d'Artagnan and his friends really will come for you.''

''That would be too good to be true!''

''But if they *are* coming, it will simply be a question of time: if your friends are the first to arrive, you'll be saved; if it's the cardinal's men, you'll be lost.''

''Yes, lost! They'd show me no mercy! Oh, what shall I do?''

''There's one way you can protect yourself.''

''How?''

''Hide somewhere nearby and wait to see who comes to ask for you.''

''Where can I hide?''

''I'm going to hide too, a few miles from here, till my brother rejoins me. You can come with me and we'll wait together.''

''But they won't let me leave the convent. I'm almost a prisoner here.''

''Since they'll believe I'm leaving by order of the cardinal, they won't think you have any desire to go with me.''

''No, but . . .''

''When the carriage is in front of the gate, you'll stand on the footboard to tell me good-bye and embrace me one last time. I'll have told my brother's servant what to do. When he sees you on the footboard, he'll signal to the postilion and we'll gallop off.''

''But what if d'Artagnan comes later?''

''We'll know it.''

''How?''

''It's quite simple. We'll send my brother's servant back to Béthune; we can count on him. He'll disguise himself and rent a room across the street from the convent. If he sees the cardinal's men come, he won't move; if he sees d'Artagnan and his friends, he'll bring them to where we are.''

''Does he know them?''

''Of course. He's seen d'Artagnan in my house.''

''Ah, yes . . . You're right, that seems to be the best plan. But let's not go very far away from here.''

''We can go less than twenty miles and be just this side of the border; then, if there's any sign of danger, we can quickly cross the border and be outside of France.''

''And what shall we do till we leave?''

''Wait.''

''What if the cardinal's men come?''

''My brother's carriage will get here first.''

"Suppose I'm not with you when it comes—it may come during lunch or dinner, for example."

"Tell the abbess you want to spend as much time as possible with me before I leave, and ask her for permission to have your meals with me."

"Will she let me do that?"

"I see no reason why she shouldn't."

"What a good idea! That way, we can be together all the time."

"Go and talk to the abbess. In the meantime I'll take a walk in the garden; I have a headache."

"Where shall I meet you?"

"Here, in an hour."

"I'll be here then. Oh, you're so kind, and I'm so grateful to you!"

"It's only natural that I should want to help you: besides being pretty and charming, you're the friend of one of my best friends."

"Dear d'Artagnan! How he'll thank you when he knows what you've done!"

"I hope so. Well, now that everything's settled, let's go."

"You're going to the garden?"

"Yes."

"Follow the hall till you come to a little staircase; it will take you to a door that opens into the garden."

"Thank you."

The two women parted after exchanging friendly smiles.

Milady had told the truth when she said she had a headache, because hastily contrived plans were swirling in her brain. The immediate future still seemed vague to her; she needed to be alone, in quiet surroundings, to put her confused thoughts in order and shape them into a definite course of action.

The first thing to do was to take Madame Bonacieux away and put her in a safe place where she could be used as a hostage if necessary. Milady was beginning to be apprehensive about the outcome of that terrible duel in which her enemies were as tenacious as she was ruthless. She sensed that the final combat was approaching, like a violent storm about to break.

Having Madame Bonacieux in her power was her strongest advantage. Since Madame Bonacieux was the woman d'Artagnan loved, she could be used as a means of negotiating if anything went wrong.

Milady was sure that Madame Bonacieux would trustingly leave the convent with her. Once she was hidden in Armentières, it would be easy to make her believe that d'Artagnan had not come to Béthune. Rochefort would be back in two weeks at the most. During that time Milady would decide how to go about settling her score with the four friends. She would not be bored, because she would have the most enjoyable of all occupations for a woman of her nature: making plans for revenge.

As she turned these things over in her mind, she memorized the exact layout of the garden. She was like a good general who envisages both victory and defeat and is ready either to advance or to retreat, depending on how the battle develops.

When she had been in the garden for an hour, she heard Madame Bonacieux's gentle voice calling her. The good abbess had naturally given her consent, and they were going to have dinner together.

As they were crossing the courtyard they heard the sound of carriage wheels.

"Do you hear that?" asked Milady.

"Yes, a carriage is stopping at the gate."

"It's the one sent by my brother."

"Oh! Then it's already time . . ."

"Don't let your courage fail you now."

The bell at the gate rang loudly.

"Go up to your room," said Milady. "You must have some jewelry that you want to take with you."

"I have some letters."

"Go and get them, then come to my room. We'll eat a quick dinner, because we may travel a good part of the night without stopping."

Madame Bonacieux put her hand to her chest.

"My heart is pounding," she murmured. "I can't get my breath . . ."

"This is no time to weaken! In a few minutes you'll be saved! Do what you have to do, and remember that you'll be doing it for him."

"Oh, yes, for him! You've given me back all my strength by reminding me of that!"

They separated. Milady hurried up to her room, where she found Rochefort's servant already waiting for her. She gave him her instructions. He was to wait at the gate; if the musketeers arrived, the carriage would set off at a gallop, go to a village on the other side of the woods and wait for her there. She would go through the garden and walk to the village; as we have seen, she was thoroughly familiar with the region. If the musketeers did not arrive, things would go as she had planned: Madame Bonacieux would get into the carriage on the pretext of telling her good-bye and the carriage would take them away together.

Madame Bonacieux came in. To allay her suspicions, if she had any, Milady repeated the last part of her instructions to the servant. She then asked about the carriage and learned that it was a three-horse chaise driven by a postilion, and that Rochefort's servant would go ahead of it as an outrider.

Milady was wrong to think that Madame Bonacieux might be suspicious: the poor young woman was too guileless to suspect another woman of such treachery. The name of Lady de Winter, which she had heard from the abbess, was completely unknown to her. She did not even know that a woman had played such a great part in her misfortunes.

"Everything's ready," Milady said when the servant had left. "The abbess thinks I'm going to be taken away by order of the cardinal. My brother's servant will give the postilion his instructions. We'll eat something and drink a little wine, then we'll go."

"We'll go," Madame Bonacieux echoed, as if she were in a daze.

Milady motioned her to sit down and served her a glass of Spanish wine and a chicken breast.

"Look," she said, "things are turning out just right for us: it's already getting dark. By dawn tomorrow we'll be in our hiding place and no one will know where we are."

Madame Bonacieux distractedly ate a few mouthfuls and took a sip of wine.

"You need to eat more than that," said Milady. "Follow my example."

She picked up her glass, but stopped when it was halfway to her lips: she had just heard distant hoofbeats and a moment later it seemed to her that she also heard horses whinnying. She felt as if she had just been awakened from a beautiful dream by a thunderclap. She turned pale and ran to the window. Madame Bonacieux stood up, trembling, and steadied herself by clutching the back of her chair.

Milady could not yet see anything, but the hoofbeats were coming closer.

"Who is it?" asked Madame Bonacieux.

"It's either our friends or our enemies," Milady replied impassively. "Stay where you are; I'll tell you who they are as soon as I can see them."

Madame Bonacieux stood motionless and silent, white as a statue.

The hoofbeats continued to grow louder. When the horses seemed to be within a hundred paces of the convent, Milady still could not see them, because of a bend in the road, but the sound was so distinct that she could almost count their number. She stared intently at the road, hoping there would still be enough light for her to identify the riders when they appeared.

Suddenly she saw plumed hats at the bend in the road. She counted two, then five, then eight riders. One of them was ahead of the others by two horses' lengths. She tried to stifle the cry of rage that burst from her throat when she recognized him as d'Artagnan.

"What's the matter?" Madame Bonacieux asked anxiously.

"They're in the uniform of the cardinal's guards!" said Milady. "Let's go, while there's still time!"

"Yes, let's go!" said Madame Bonacieux, but she could not move; she was frozen by terror.

They heard the horsemen ride past the window.

"Come!" said Milady, trying to lead her by the arm. "We can escape through the garden: I have the key. But we must hurry, before it's too late!"

Madame Bonacieux took two steps and fell to her knees. Milady tried to pick her up and carry her but did not have the strength for it. Then they heard the rumble of carriage wheels: the postilion had driven off at the sight of the musketeers. Several shots were fired.

"For the last time, are you coming?" Milady said furiously.

"I can't. I'm too weak . . . You must go without me."

"And leave you here?" said Milady. "Never!"

Suddenly her eyes flashed. She ran over to the table, deftly took a little reddish pellet from the setting of a ring she was wearing and dropped it into Madame Bonacieux's glass of wine. The pellet promptly dissolved.

"Here, drink some wine," she said, holding the glass to Madame Bonacieux's lips. "It will give you strength."

Madame Bonacieux drank obediently.

Milady put the glass back onto the table with a diabolical smile. "This isn't the kind of revenge I wanted," she thought, "but I'll have to settle for what I can get."

And she ran out of the room.

Madame Bonacieux watched her leave but was unable to follow her; it was as if she were having one of those nightmares in which one remains rooted to the spot while some terrible danger approaches.

A few minutes passed. She heard loud shouts from the convent gate. She kept expecting to see Milady come back, but she waited for her in vain. Cold sweat broke out on her forehead and she attributed it to her fear.

Finally she heard the creaking of the gate as it was opened, then the sound of boots and spurs on the stairs and a murmur of approaching voices, in the midst of which she thought she could make out someone saying her name.

Suddenly she cried out with joy and ran to the door: she had recognized d'Artagnan's voice.

"D'Artagnan! D'Artagnan!" she called to him. "Is it really you? I'm here!"

"Constance! Constance! Where are you? Oh, my God!"

The door was flung open and several men burst into the room. Madame Bonacieux had sunk into a chair; she was now unable to move. D'Artagnan dropped the pistol he was holding and fell to his knees before her. Athos put his pistol back in his belt. Porthos and Aramis sheathed their swords.

"Oh, d'Artagnan, my love! You've come at last, you didn't desert me! It's really you!"

"Yes, Constance, we're together again!"

"She said you wouldn't come, but I went on hoping. I didn't want to run away with her. How right I was to stay! Oh, I'm so happy!"

Athos had calmly sat down; hearing the word "she," he sprang to his feet.

"Who do you mean by 'she'?" asked d'Artagnan.

"The woman who was here with me. We became friends. She wanted to save me from the cardinal, but she mistook you for some of the cardinal's guards and ran away."

D'Artagnan turned as white as the veil his mistress wore.

"Who is she?"

"She said she was your friend and that you'd told her everything. Her carriage was at the gate when you came."

"But what's her name? My God! Don't you know her name?"

"Yes, I heard the abbess say it. It's . . . Just a moment, my head feels so strange . . . I can hardly see . . ."

"Help me!" d'Artagnan said to his friends. "Her hands are like ice! She's fainting!"

While Porthos called for help at the top of his lungs, Aramis ran to the table to get a glass of water, but he stopped short when he saw the change that had come over Athos's face. Standing in front of the table, Athos was staring at one of the glasses with an expression of horror.

"No, it's impossible!" he said. "God wouldn't permit such a crime!"

"Water! Water!" shouted d'Artagnan.

"Poor woman," Athos murmured in a broken voice.

Madame Bonacieux opened her eyes beneath d'Artagnan's kisses.

"She's recovering!" he said. "Oh, thank God!"

"Madame," said Athos, "who drank from this glass?"

"I did," she replied weakly.

"And who poured the wine into it?"

"She did."

"Who is she? What's her name?"

"Ah, I remember now," said Madame Bonacieux. "Lady de Winter."

The four friends all cried out at once, but Athos's voice rose above the others.

Just then Madame Bonacieux's face turned ashen and she was shaken by a spasm of pain. She slumped forward in her chair. Porthos and Aramis were unable to catch her before she fell to the floor. She lay still, gasping for breath.

D'Artagnan gripped Athos's hands with indescribable anguish.

"Do you think . . ." he began, then his voice was choked by a sob.

Athos bit his lip.

"I can't bear to say what I think."

"D'Artagnan! D'Artagnan!" said Madame Bonacieux. "Where are you? Don't leave me! Can't you see I'm dying?"

D'Artagnan let go of Athos's hands and rushed over to her.

Her beautiful face was contorted by pain, her eyes were already glazed, she was trembling convulsively, and sweat trickled down her forehead.

"In the name of heaven, go and bring help!" said d'Artagnan. "Porthos, Aramis, bring help!"

"That would be futile," said Athos. "There's no antidote for the poison she uses."

"Yes, help . . ." murmured Madame Bonacieux.

Summoning up all her remaining strength, she took d'Artagnan's head between her hands, looked at him for a moment with eyes in which all her waning vitality seemed to be concentrated, then sobbed and pressed her lips to his.

"Constance! Constance!" he moaned.

She sighed and he felt the warmth of her breath for the last time: that sigh was her pure, loving soul leaving her body and rising to heaven.

He now held only a corpse in his arms.

He uttered a loud cry and fell unconscious beside her.

Porthos wept, Aramis shook his fist toward heaven, Athos crossed himself.

Just then a man appeared in the doorway, almost as pale as those in the room. He saw Madame Bonacieux dead and d'Artagnan unconscious.

He had come at that moment of stupefaction that follows a great catastrophe.

"I wasn't mistaken," he said. "There's Monsieur d'Artagnan, and you're his friends, Messieurs Athos, Porthos, and Aramis."

The three men looked at him in astonishment, feeling that they had seen him before.

"Gentlemen," he went on, "you and I are looking for the same woman. She must have been here," he added with a grim smile, "because I see a corpse."

The three friends remained silent. His face and voice seemed familiar to them, but they could not recall when or where they had met him.

"Since you can't or won't recognize a man who has probably owed his life to you twice," he continued, "I must introduce myself: I'm Lord de Winter, that woman's brother-in-law."

The three friends started with surprise.

Athos stood up and held out his hand to Lord de Winter.

"Welcome," he said, "you're one of us."

"I left Portsmouth five hours after she did," said de Winter, "and arrived three hours after her in Boulogne. I missed her by twenty minutes at Saint-Omer. Finally I lost her trail at Lillers. I was wandering at random, asking everyone I met for information, when I saw you ride past and recognized Monsieur d'Artagnan. I called out to you, but you didn't answer; I tried to follow you, but my horse was too tired to keep up with yours. You were riding as fast as you could, and yet it seems you've arrived too late!"

"Yes, as you can see," said Athos, pointing to Madame Bonacieux while Porthos and Aramis tried to revive d'Artagnan.

"Are they both dead?" asked de Winter.

"No, fortunately," replied Athos. "D'Artagnan has only fainted."

"Ah, thank God!"

At that moment d'Artagnan opened his eyes. He pushed Porthos and Aramis aside and desperately clung to the body of his mistress.

Athos slowly walked over to him and tenderly embraced him. When d'Artagnan burst out sobbing, Athos said to him in his noble, persuasive voice, "Be a man, my friend. Women weep for the dead, men avenge them."

"Yes!" said d'Artagnan. "If it's to avenge her, I'm ready to go with you anywhere!"

Taking advantage of this moment of strength that the hope of revenge had given his grief-stricken friend, Athos told Porthos and Aramis to go and bring the abbess.

They found her in the hall, still bewildered by the tumult that had erupted in her convent. She had brought several nuns with her. After their years of seclusion, they were disconcerted to find themselves in the presence of five men.

"Reverend Mother," Athos said to the abbess, taking d'Artagnan's arm, "we'll leave this poor woman's body to your pious care. She was an angel on earth before becoming an angel in heaven. Treat her as if she were one of your sisters. We'll come back some day to pray at her grave."

D'Artagnan hid his face against Athos's chest and began sobbing again.

"Weep," said Athos, "weep, young heart filled with love, youth, and life! How I wish I could weep as you do!"

And he led his friend away, affectionate as a father, comforting as a priest, greathearted as a man who has suffered much.

The four friends, their servants, and Lord de Winter left the convent and began walking toward Béthune. They stopped at the first inn they saw on the outskirts of the town.

"But aren't we going after that woman?" said d'Artagnan.

"Later," replied Athos. "There are some things I must do first."

"She'll get away! She'll escape from us, and it will be your fault!"

"I take responsibility for her," said Athos.

D'Artagnan had such confidence in his word that he bowed his head and followed him into the inn without saying anything more.

Porthos and Aramis looked at each other, puzzled by Athos's self-assurance. Lord de Winter thought he had spoken that way only to ease d'Artagnan's grief.

"And now, gentlemen," Athos said when he had made sure there were accommodations for them at the inn, "let's all go to our rooms. D'Artagnan needs to be alone with his sorrow, and you need to sleep. I'll take care of everything; put your minds at rest."

"But it seems to me," said Lord de Winter, "that if there's something to be done against Lady de Winter, it concerns me: she's my sister-in-law."

"And she's my wife," said Athos.

D'Artagnan started: he realized that Athos must be sure of his revenge, to reveal such a secret. Porthos and Aramis exchanged a look. Lord de Winter thought Athos was mad.

"Go to your rooms," Athos went on, "and leave everything in my hands. As her husband, I'm the one who must deal with her. D'Artagnan, if you haven't lost it, give me the piece of paper that fell out of that man's hat, with the name of a town on it."

"Ah, yes, I understand!" said d'Artagnan. "The name of a town, written in her hand . . ."

"You see?" said Athos. "There really is a God in heaven!"

64

The Man in the Red Cloak

Athos's despair had given way to an intense concentration that made his brilliant mind even more lucid. He was totally absorbed in thoughts of how he could meet the responsibility he had assumed.

He went to his room, asked the innkeeper to bring him a map of the province, studied it carefully, saw that four different roads went from Béthune to Armentières, and summoned the servants.

Planchet, Grimaud, Mousqueton, and Bazin came into his room. He gave them clear, precise orders. They were to leave at dawn the next morning and go to Armentières, each by a different road. Planchet, the most intelligent of the four, would follow the road on which the carriage accompanied by Rochefort's servant had been quickly driven away from the convent while the four friends shot at it.

Athos had decided that the servants would be the first to go into action not only because he had come to appreciate their varied merits but also because he knew that servants questioning passersby would arouse less mistrust than their masters, and would therefore be more likely to get the needed information. Furthermore, Milady knew the masters but not the servants, while the servants knew her by sight.

At eleven o'clock the next day, they were to meet at a certain place. If they had discovered where Milady was hiding, three of them would stay to keep watch on her while the fourth went back to Béthune to notify Athos and serve as the four friends' guide.

When they had received these orders, the servants went to bed.

Athos stood up, put on his sword and cloak, and went out. It was nearly ten o'clock. At that time of night, the streets of a provincial town are nearly deserted. Athos was obviously looking for someone to question. Finally he saw a man, went up to him, and said a few words to him. The man stepped back in alarm but gave Athos the directions he wanted. He then refused Athos's offer of half a pistole to accompany him.

Athos walked along the street that had been pointed out to him. When he came to a crossroads he hesitated, not knowing which way to go, and since he had a better chance of encountering someone at a crossroads than anywhere else, he stopped there. Soon a night watchman came along. Athos asked him the same question he had already asked the first man he had met. The watchman showed the same alarm, also refused to accompany him, and pointed out the way to him.

Athos walked in that direction till he came to the edge of the town. Here he again hesitated and stopped. Luckily a beggar approached him to ask for alms. Athos offered him an écu to go with him to his destination. The beggar refused at first, but the sight of the silver coin gleaming in the darkness made him change his mind. He walked in front of Athos to show him the way.

When they came to a corner, the beggar pointed to an isolated, sinister-looking little house in the distance. Athos went toward it while the beggar, who had received his pay, hurried off in the opposite direction.

Athos had to walk around the house before he could find the door. No light came through the cracks of the shutters, and there was no sound from inside the house to indicate that it was inhabited; it was as dark and silent as a tomb.

Athos knocked three times without getting an answer. Then he heard footsteps approaching. The door opened and he saw a tall, pale man with a black beard. After they had exchanged a few words, the tall man motioned Athos to come in. Athos stepped across the threshold, and the door closed behind him.

The man whom Athos had found with such difficulty led him into his laboratory, where he had been wiring together the clattering bones of a skeleton. The body was assembled and the head lay on the table.

Everything else in the room showed that he was devoted to the study of the natural sciences: there were labeled jars with snakes in them; dried lizards in black wooden frames gleamed like cut emeralds; bundles of fragrant herbs, no doubt endowed with powers unknown to ordinary men, hung from the ceiling.

There were no relatives or servants in the house; the tall man lived there alone.

Athos looked indifferently at the things we have just described. Then, at the tall man's invitation, he sat down and told him the reason for his visit and what he wanted him to do. The stranger, who had remained standing in front of Athos, shrank back in terror and refused. Athos showed him a small piece of paper on which two lines were written, with a signature and a seal below them. When the tall man had read the lines, seen the signature, and recognized the seal, he bowed to show that he was ready to obey.

Athos asked nothing more of him. He stood up, bowed to him, left the house, walked back to the inn, and went straight to his room.

At dawn, d'Artagnan came in and asked what he should do.

"Wait," replied Athos.

A short time later a message came from the abbess of the convent, announcing that Madame Bonacieux's funeral would take place at noon. As for the murderess, there was no news of her. She had evidently escaped through the garden, because her footprints had been recognized on the ground there, the gate had been found locked, and the key had disappeared.

At noon, Lord de Winter and the four friends arrived at the convent. All the bells were ringing, the chapel door was open, and the gate of the chancel was closed. In the middle of the chancel lay Madame Bonacieux's body, dressed as a novice. The Carmelite nuns were gathered on either side of the chancel, behind gates that opened onto the convent. They listened to the service and sang with the priests, without seeing the laymen in the chapel or being seen by them.

At the chapel door, d'Artagnan felt his courage failing him again. He looked around for Athos, but Athos had disappeared.

Faithful to his mission of revenge, Athos had asked to be taken to the garden. There he saw the light footprints of the woman who had left death behind her wherever she went. He followed them to the gate on the other side of the garden, had it unlocked for him, and headed into the forest.

His suspicion was confirmed: the road that the carriage had taken skirted the forest. He walked along it and saw dark stains where blood had fallen, either from one of the horses or from the man who had gone ahead of the carriage as an outrider. When he had walked nearly two miles and was about fifty paces from the village of Festubert, he saw a bloodstain larger than the others, at a place where the road had been trampled by the hooves of horses that had come to a halt. Between the road and the edge of the forest, a little behind the place where the road had been trampled, he saw the same small footprints he had seen in the garden; the carriage had stopped there.

This was where Milady had come out of the forest and gotten into the carriage.

Satisfied with this discovery that showed that he had guessed correctly, he went back to the inn and found Planchet impatiently waiting for him.

Planchet's report gave Athos further proof that he was right. Planchet had followed the road and, like Athos, had noticed the bloodstains and the place where the horses had stopped. But he had gone farther than Athos. While he was having a drink at an inn in the village of Festubert, he had gathered some precious information without having to question anyone: at half-past eight the night before, a man accompanying a lady traveling in a post chaise had been forced to stop because he was wounded and unable to go on. The man claimed to have been wounded by robbers who had stopped the post chaise in the forest. He had stayed in the village, but the lady had taken fresh horses and continued on her way.

Planchet went in search of the postilion who had driven the post chaise. He found him and learned that he had taken the lady to Fromelles, and that from there she had gone on to Armentières.

Planchet took a short cut and reached Armentières at seven in the morning. There was only one inn, the Hôtel de la Poste. He went to it and introduced himself as an unemployed servant looking for work. In less than ten minutes of conversation he learned that a woman had come to the inn at eleven o'clock the night before, taken a room, and told the innkeeper that she intended to stay in the vicinity for some time.

That was all Planchet needed to know. He met the three other servants at the place Athos had designated, posted them as sentries to watch all the exits of the inn, and hurried back to Béthune.

He had just finished giving Athos his report when the three other musketeers came in. They were all scowling darkly, even Aramis, whose face ordinarily looked so gentle.

"What are we going to do?" asked d'Artagnan.

"Wait," Athos answered once again.

They went back to their rooms.

At eight o'clock that evening, Athos gave orders to saddle the horses and sent word to his friends and Lord de Winter that it was time to leave.

They were all ready in a few minutes. Each of them made sure his weapons were in good condition. When Athos came out of the inn, he found d'Artagnan already in the saddle.

"You'll have to be patient a little longer," said Athos. "One member of our expedition isn't here yet."

The four others stared at him in perplexity; as far as they knew, no one else was coming with them.

Just then Planchet brought Athos's horse and the musketeer leapt lightly into the saddle.

"Wait for me," he said, "I'll be back soon."

He rode away.

A quarter of an hour later he returned, accompanied by a masked man wearing a big red cloak.

Lord de Winter and the three other musketeers looked at each other questioningly. None of them knew who the man was, but they did not doubt that Athos had a good reason for bringing him.

At nine o'clock, guided by Planchet, the little troop set off along the road that had been taken by the carriage.

They rode in silence, each absorbed in his own thoughts, looking as bleak as despair and as stern as punishment.

65

The Trial

It was a dark, stormy night; the stars were hidden by big clouds racing across the sky, and the moon would not rise till midnight. From time to time a flash of lightning on the horizon revealed the white, deserted road, then everything was plunged back into darkness.

D'Artagnan kept pulling ahead of the other riders, and Athos kept calling him back. D'Artagnan now had only one thing in mind: to reach his destination.

They rode through the village of Festubert, where the wounded servant had stayed, and then they skirted the Richebourg forest. When they reached Herlies, Planchet, who was still guiding the troop, turned left.

Several times Lord de Winter, Porthos, and Aramis had tried to talk with the man in the red cloak, but at each question he had only bowed without answering. Finally they had ceased their efforts, realizing that he had some reason for remaining silent.

The storm was approaching; lightning flashes followed each other in quick succession, thunder could now be heard, and the wind was blowing briskly across the plain, ruffling the plumes of the musketeers' hats.

The riders made their horses break into a rapid trot.

Soon after they had passed Fromelles, the storm broke. They wrapped their cloaks around themselves. They still had seven miles to go, and they rode that distance in torrential rain.

D'Artagnan had taken off his hat, and he was the only one who had not put on his cloak. He liked feeling the cool water on his feverish forehead and body.

When they had passed Goskal and were nearing the relay station, a man who had taken shelter under a tree stepped into the middle of the road, stood in front of them, and put his finger to his lips. Athos was the first to recognize him as Grimaud.

"What's wrong?" asked d'Artagnan. "Has she left Armentières?"

Grimaud nodded. D'Artagnan clenched his teeth.

"Let me question him, d'Artagnan," said Athos, "since I've taken responsibility for everything. Where is she, Grimaud?"

Grimaud pointed in the direction of the Lys.

"How far?" asked Athos.

Grimaud held up his forefinger.

"Alone?"

Grimaud nodded.

"Gentlemen," said Athos, "she's one mile from here, alone, in the direction of the river."

"Lead us there, Grimaud," said d'Artagnan.

Grimaud set off across the fields, guiding the others. After about five hundred paces they came to a stream and forded it.

A lightning flash gave them a glimpse of the village of Erquinghem.

"Is that where she is?" asked d'Artagnan.

Grimaud shook his head.

"Quiet!" said Athos.

They continued on their way.

Lightning flashed again; Grimaud stretched out his arm, and in the bluish white glare they saw an isolated little house near the riverbank, a hundred paces from a ferry. One of its windows was lighted.

"We've arrived," said Athos.

At that moment a man who had been lying in the ditch stood up. It was Mousqueton.

"She's there," he said, pointing to the lighted window.

"And Bazin?" asked Athos.

"He's been watching the door while I watched the window."

"Good," said Athos, "you're all faithful servants."

He dismounted from his horse, handed the reins to Grimaud, and walked toward the window after motioning the others to approach from the direction of the door.

The little house was surrounded by a quickset hedge two or three feet high. Athos went through the hedge and stopped in front of the window. It had no shutters but its half-curtains were drawn. He climbed up on the stone sill to look over them.

In the light of a lamp he saw a woman wrapped in a dark cloak, sitting on a stool beside a dying fire, with her elbows on a rickety table and her chin resting on her ivory white hands.

Athos could not see her face, but a sinister smile passed over his lips: there could be no doubt that this was the woman he had been looking for.

Just then a horse neighed. Milady turned her head, saw Athos's pale face in the window and screamed. Realizing that he had been recognized, Athos broke open the window with his knee and his hand and leapt into the room. Milady felt as if the spirit of vengeance had suddenly appeared before her. She ran to the door, opened it, and found herself facing d'Artagnan, who seemed to her even more threatening than Athos.

She stepped back from him and screamed again. Afraid that she might have some way of escaping, he drew his pistol, but Athos raised his hand and said, "Put your pistol back in your belt, d'Artagnan. This woman must be tried, not murdered. Wait a little longer and you'll be satisfied. Come in, gentlemen."

D'Artagnan obeyed, for Athos had the solemn voice and powerful gestures of a judge sent by God himself.

Porthos, Aramis, Lord de Winter, and the man in the red cloak came into the room. The four servants took up their positions to guard the door and the window.

Milady had fallen into a chair, holding her hands in front of her as though to ward off a terrible apparition. She uttered a cry when she recognized Lord de Winter.

"Why are you here?" she asked.

"We've come for the woman who has been known as Charlotte Backson, Countess de La Fère, and Lady de Winter," replied Athos.

"What do you want with me?" she murmured, terrified.

"We want to try you for your crimes. You'll be free to answer our charges and justify yourself if you can. Monsieur d'Artagnan, you will be the first accuser."

D'Artagnan stepped forward.

"Before God and men," he said, "I accuse this woman of having poisoned Constance Bonacieux, who died last night."

He turned to Porthos and Aramis.

"We bear witness to that," they said together.

"Before God and men," d'Artagnan continued, "I accuse this woman of having tried to poison me with wine that she sent me from Villeroi with a false letter saying that the wine had been sent by my friends; God saved me, but a man named Brisemont died in my place."

"We bear witness to that," Porthos and Aramis repeated.

"Before God and men, I accuse this woman of having tried to make me murder Count de Wardes, and since no one else is here to bear witness to the truth of that accusation, I bear witness to it myself.

"Those are my charges against her."

D'Artagnan went to the other side of the room and stood with Porthos and Aramis.

"Now you, Lord de Winter," said Athos.

"Before God and men," he said, "I accuse this woman of having had the duke of Buckingham murdered."

"The duke of Buckingham!" exclaimed the others.

"Yes!" said de Winter. "After the letter of warning you wrote to me, I had her arrested and placed her under the guard of a man who was loyal to me. She corrupted that man and made him kill the duke, and at this very moment he may be paying for her crime with his life."

The others shuddered at this revelation of crimes that had been unknown to them.

"That's not all. After marrying her, my brother made her his sole heir. He died in three hours of a strange illness that left livid patches all over his body. Lady de Winter, how did your husband die?"

Porthos and Aramis cried out in horror.

"I demand justice against you," Lord de Winter said to Milady, "for the deaths of the duke of Buckingham, Felton, and my brother, and I declare that, if necessary, I will punish you myself."

He went to stand beside d'Artagnan, yielding his place to the next accuser.

Milady let her forehead fall onto her hands and tried to put her chaotic thoughts in order.

"Now it's my turn," said Athos, trembling before her like a lion before a snake. "I married this woman when she was a young girl. I married her against the objections of my whole family. I gave her my wealth and my name. One day I discovered that a fleur-de-lis had been branded on her left shoulder."

Milady leapt to her feet.

"I defy you to find the court that passed that infamous sentence on me!" she said. "I defy you to find the man who carried it out!"

"Silence!" said a voice. "That's for me to answer!"

And the man in the red cloak walked toward her.

"Who is this man?" cried Milady, choking with fear.

All eyes turned to him. He was unknown to everyone except Athos, but Athos looked at him with as much surprise as the others because he did not understand why he had come forward to speak at this point.

After slowly approaching Milady until only the table separated them, the stranger took off his mask.

Milady stared with growing terror at that pale, expressionless face framed by black hair and side-whiskers.

"Oh, no!" she suddenly cried out. She backed away from him till she was stopped by the wall. "It's a ghost! It can't be . . . Help! Help!" She turned to the wall as if she thought she could break through it.

"Tell us who you are!" d'Artagnan said to the man in the red cloak.

"Ask that woman," he replied. "You can see that she's recognized me."

"The executioner of Lille!" Milady shrieked wildly, pushing against the wall with her hands to keep from falling.

The other men stepped back from the stranger, leaving him standing alone in the middle of the room.

Milady sank to her knees.

"Have mercy on me! Forgive me!"

The man in the red cloak waited till she had fallen silent.

"I told you she'd recognized me," he said. "Yes, I'm the executioner of the city of Lille, and I'll tell you my story . . ."

The others all looked at him intently, waiting for him to go on speaking.

"This young woman was once a young girl as beautiful as she is now. She was a nun in the Benedictine convent at Templemar. The convent priest was a young man with a simple, believing heart. She set out to seduce him and she succeeded—she could have seduced a saint!

"They had both taken irrevocable religious vows, so their affair couldn't last long without bringing disaster to them. She persuaded him to run away with her. But to go to some other part of the country where they could live in peace because they were unknown, they needed money, and neither of them had any. The priest stole the sacred vessels and sold them. But as they were about to leave together, they were both arrested.

"A week later she seduced the jailer's son and escaped. The young priest was sentenced to be branded and then imprisoned for ten years in irons. I was the executioner of the city of Lille, as this woman has said. I had to brand the prisoner—and the prisoner, gentlemen, was my brother!

"I swore that the woman who had ruined his life, who was more than his accomplice, since she'd driven him to crime, would at least share his punishment. I thought I knew where she was hiding, and I was right, because I found her there. I tied her hands and feet, and branded her in the same way I'd branded my brother.

"The day after I returned to Lille, my brother also succeeded in escaping. I was accused of complicity and sentenced to remain in prison in his place till he gave himself up. He knew nothing of my sentence. He rejoined this woman and they went to Berry together. He became a parish priest there, and she passed herself off as his sister.

"The lord of the estate on which my brother's church was located met her and fell so deeply in love with her that he proposed to her. She abandoned her first victim, married her second, and became Countess de La Fère."

Everyone looked at Athos, whose real name had just been revealed. He nodded to show that everything the executioner had said was true.

"My brother went back to Lille in despair," the executioner continued. "She'd destroyed his honor and his happiness, and he had no desire to go on living. When he learned that I'd been imprisoned in his place, he gave himself up. That same evening he hanged himself in his cell.

"The authorities kept their word: I was released as soon as the body had been positively identified.

"Now you know the crime I accuse her of, and why I branded her."

"Monsieur d'Artagnan," said Athos, "what sentence do you demand against this woman?"

"Death," replied d'Artagnan.

"Lord de Winter," continued Athos, "what sentence do you demand against this woman?"

"Death."

"Monsieur Porthos and Monsieur Aramis, you're her judges. To what do you sentence her?"

"Death," the two musketeers said quietly but resolutely.

Milady screamed and dragged herself toward her judges on her knees.

Athos stopped her with a gesture.

"Anne de Breuil, Countess de La Fère, Lady de Winter," he said, "your crimes have gone beyond the endurance of men on earth and God in heaven. If you know a prayer, say it now, because you've been condemned to death and you're going to die."

At these words, which left her no hope, Milady stood up and

tried to speak, but her strength failed her. She felt a powerful hand seize her by the hair and pull her implacably toward the door. She left the house without putting up any resistance.

Lord de Winter, d'Artagnan, Athos, Porthos, and Aramis walked out behind her. The servants followed their masters, and the room was left empty, with its broken window, its open door, and its smoking lamp flickering mournfully on the table.

66

The Execution

It was nearly midnight. The waning moon, reddened by the last traces of the storm, was rising behind the little town of Armentières, whose dark houses and tall, thin steeple stood out in its dim glow. The Lys was like a river of molten tin. On the far bank, a black mass of trees was outlined against a stormy sky filled with copper-colored clouds that made a kind of twilight in the middle of the night. To the left rose an old, abandoned windmill; its sails were motionless and from somewhere inside it an owl screeched at regular intervals. The road followed by the sinister procession cut across a plain dotted with low, stocky trees that were like misshapen dwarfs crouching to spy on the travelers who had ventured into their territory at that late hour.

Now and then the whole horizon was illuminated as a broad streak of lightning slashed the sky like a monstrous saber. The air was heavy and still. All nature was crushed beneath a deathly silence. The ground was damp and slippery from the rain that had just fallen, and the refreshed plants gave off their fragrance with increased vigor.

Grimaud and Mousqueton were leading Milady, each holding her by an arm. The executioner walked behind her, followed by Lord de Winter, d'Artagnan, Athos, Porthos, and Aramis, with Planchet and Bazin bringing up the rear.

They were approaching the river. Milady said nothing but her eyes pleaded eloquently with Grimaud and Mousqueton as she looked at each of them in turn.

When she saw that the others had fallen a little behind, she said to the two servants, "I'll give each of you a thousand pistoles if you help me to escape. But if you let your masters kill me, I have friends near here who will make you pay dearly for my death.''

Grimaud looked at her uneasily. Mousqueton trembled.

Athos had heard her speak. He hurried forward, and so did Lord de Winter.

"These two aren't reliable, now that she's talked to them," said Athos.

Grimaud and Mousqueton were replaced by Planchet and Bazin.

When they reached the riverbank, the executioner tied Milady's hands and feet. She then broke her silence.

"You're cowards and murderers! There are ten of you to kill one woman! But you'd better reconsider—if I'm not rescued, I'll be avenged!''

"You're not a woman," Athos said coldly. "You don't belong to the human race: you're a demon from hell, and we're going to send you back there.''

"You're all pretending to be so righteous," she said vehemently, "but the one who kills me will be a murderer!''

"An executioner can kill without being a murderer," said the man in the red cloak, touching his broad sword. "He's the final judge, that's all: the *Nachrichter,* as our German neighbors say.''

Milady uttered a savage cry of rage that resounded strangely in the night and died away in the depths of the forest.

"If you really believe I committed the crimes you've accused me of, take me before a court! You're not judges! You have no right to sentence me!''

"I offered to send you to Tyburn," said Lord de Winter. "Why did you refuse to go there?''

"Because I don't want to die," she answered, struggling against her bonds, "because I'm too young to die!''

"The woman you poisoned at Béthune was even younger than you, but she died," said d'Artagnan.

"You were in a convent," said the executioner, "and you ran away from it to ruin my brother's life.''

Milady screamed in fear and fell to her knees. The executioner picked her up under the arms and took a step toward a boat tied to the bank.

"Oh, my God!" she shrieked. "Are you going to drown me?''

Her cries were so heartrending that d'Artagnan, who had at

first been the most relentless in pursuing her, sat down on a tree stump and put his hands over his ears, but he could still hear her.

He was the youngest of all those men; his heart failed him.

"I can't watch such a horrible thing!" he said. "I can't consent to having her killed this way!"

These words gave Milady a glimmer of hope.

"D'Artagnan!" she called out to him. "Remember that I loved you!"

He stood up and began walking toward her. But Athos suddenly drew his sword and stood in front of him.

"If you take one more step, d'Artagnan," he said, "you and I will cross swords."

D'Artagnan fell to his knees and prayed.

"Executioner," said Athos, "do your duty."

"I will, sir," said the man in the red cloak, "because as sure as I'm a good Catholic, I firmly believe I'll be serving justice by executing this woman."

"And you're right," said Athos.

He stepped toward Milady.

"I forgive you," he said, "for the harm you've done me; I forgive you for blighting my future, destroying my honor, defiling my love, and throwing me into such despair that I've endangered my salvation. Die in peace."

Lord de Winter came forward.

"I forgive you for poisoning my brother, having the duke of Buckingham murdered, causing poor Felton's death, and trying to kill me. Die in peace."

"Forgive me," said d'Artagnan, "for provoking your anger by a deceitful trick unworthy of a gentleman. In exchange, I forgive you for murdering the woman I love and trying to murder me. I forgive you and I pity you. Die in peace."

"I'm lost," murmured Milady. "I'm going to die."

Then her eyes flashed and she looked around her as if she expected to see someone coming to save her. She saw only her enemies. She listened and heard nothing.

"Where am I going to die?" she asked.

"On the other bank," replied the executioner.

He picked her up and placed her in the boat. As he was about to step into it himself, Athos gave him a sum of money.

"Here's your fee for the execution," he said. "I want to make it clear that we're acting as judges."

"Very well," said the executioner. "And now I want this woman to see that I'm acting only from a sense of duty."

He threw the money into the river.

The boat moved toward the left bank of the Lys, carrying Milady and the executioner. The others remained on the right bank and knelt to pray.

The boat glided slowly along the ferry rope, in the reflection of a pale cloud that hung low over the water. The two people in it were silhouetted against the reddish glow on the horizon. The men watching it saw it reach the other bank.

During the crossing, Milady had succeeded in slipping off the rope that bound her ankles together. When the boat touched land, she leapt out of it and ran. But when she reached the top of the slope, she slipped on the wet ground and fell to her knees.

Perhaps she was struck by a superstitious idea and took her fall as a sign that fate was against her; in any case, she remained as she had fallen, on her knees, with her head bowed and her hands still tied.

The silent witnesses on the other side of the river saw the executioner raise his arms. Moonlight glittered on the broad blade of his sword. There was a scream as he swiftly brought down his arms, then a truncated mass collapsed beneath the blow.

He took off his red cloak, spread it on the ground, placed the body and the head on it, tied its four corners together, lifted it onto his shoulder, and got back into the boat.

At midstream he stopped the boat, held up his burden, and said loudly, "God's justice be done!"

He dropped the body into the river. The water closed over it.

Three days later the four musketeers returned to Paris, just before their leave expired. That evening they went to pay the customary visit to Monsieur de Tréville.

"Well, gentlemen," he asked them, "did you enjoy yourselves during your trip?"

"Enormously," replied Athos, clenching his teeth.

67

Conclusion

On the sixth of the following month the king left Paris; he had told the cardinal that he would return to La Rochelle and he was faithful to his word. The news of Buckingham's assassination had just reached Paris. His Majesty was still taken aback by it.

Although she had been warned that the man she loved was in danger, the queen at first refused to believe the report of his death. She was even rash enough to exclaim, "It's not true! He just wrote to me!"

But the next day she was forced to believe it: La Porte, who had been detained in England like everyone else, by order of King Charles I, arrived with Buckingham's distressing last gift to her.

The king was overjoyed at the news. Far from making any effort to hide his feelings, he deliberately made a great show of them in front of the queen. Like all weak men, Louis XIII was vindictive.

But he soon sank back into his gloomy apathy; his cheerful moods never lasted very long. He knew that once he had returned to the camp he would resume his servitude, and yet he felt he had to go back. He was under the cardinal's spell, like a bird unable to escape from the hypnotic gaze of a snake.

The return to La Rochelle was therefore as dismal as a funeral procession. The other musketeers in the royal escort were surprised by the behavior of our four friends. They rode together, side by side, with melancholy faces and bowed heads. Only Athos looked up now and then: he would smile bitterly and a strange light would briefly appear in his eyes, then he would again become lost in somber thought.

As soon as the escort had stopped in a town and conducted the king to his lodgings, the four friends withdrew to their rooms or went to some isolated tavern where they neither drank nor gambled, but only talked among themselves in low voices, looking carefully to make sure no one could overhear them.

One day when the king had stopped along the way to hunt

with his falcon and the four friends had gone to a tavern on the highway rather than accompanying the others on the hunt, a man who had just ridden from La Rochelle came to the door for a glass of wine, looked inside, and saw them sitting at a table.

"Monsieur d'Artagnan!" he called out. "That *is* you, isn't it?"

D'Artagnan looked up and felt a surge of fierce joy: he had just recognized the man he called his phantom, the stranger he had seen at Meung, on the Rue des Fossoyeurs, and at Arras.

He drew his sword and ran toward the door. But this time, instead of hurrying away, the stranger leapt off his horse and came forward to meet him.

"At last I've caught up with you!" said d'Artagnan. "This time you won't escape from me!"

"I have no intention of escaping from you, because this time I've been looking for you. In the name of the king, I arrest you and order you to hand over your sword. I warn you that if you put up the slightest resistance, you'll be placing your life in danger."

"Who are you?" asked d'Artagnan, lowering his sword but not surrendering it.

"I'm Count de Rochefort, Cardinal Richelieu's equerry. I'm under orders to bring you to His Eminence."

Athos came up beside d'Artagnan.

"We're on our way back to His Eminence," he said, "and I'm sure you'll accept Monsieur d'Artagnan's word that he'll go straight to La Rochelle."

"My orders are to turn him over to a detachment of guards who will take him back to camp."

"We give you our word as gentlemen that we'll serve as his guards," said Athos. "We also give you our word as gentlemen," he added, frowning, "that we won't let you take him from us."

Rochefort glanced behind him and saw that Porthos and Aramis were standing between him and the door. He realized that he was completely at the mercy of these four men.

"Gentlemen," he said, "if Monsieur d'Artagnan will surrender his sword and join his word to yours, I'll accept your promise to take him to the cardinal."

"You have my word, sir," said d'Artagnan, "and here's my sword."

"This arrangement actually suits me quite well," said Rochefort, "because it will allow me to go on traveling without delay."

"If you're on your way to meet Milady," Athos said coldly, "you're wasting your time. You won't find her."

"Why not?" Rochefort asked anxiously. "What's happened to her?"

"Go back to camp and you'll find out."

Rochefort was thoughtful for a moment; then, since they were only a day's journey from Surgères, where the cardinal was to meet the king, he decided to follow Athos's advice and come back with the king and his escort. This would also have the advantage of enabling him to keep an eye on d'Artagnan.

They reached Surgères at three o'clock the following afternoon. The cardinal was already there. He and the king greeted each other with a lavish display of affection and commented enthusiastically on the stroke of good luck that had rid France of the ruthless enemy who had been stirring up Europe against her. The cardinal invited the king to come the next day and inspect the dike, which was now completed. He then took leave of His Majesty because Rochefort had told him that d'Artagnan had been arrested, and he was eager to see him.

When he returned that evening to his headquarters at Pont de La Pierre, he found d'Artagnan and his three friends standing in front of the house. D'Artagnan did not have his sword, but the others were armed.

This time, since he was in a position of strength, the cardinal looked at them sternly and motioned d'Artagnan to come with him.

D'Artagnan obeyed.

"We'll be waiting for you, d'Artagnan," said Athos, loudly enough for the cardinal to hear.

His Eminence frowned, stopped for a moment, then continued on his way without saying anything.

D'Artagnan followed him into the house, and Rochefort came in behind him; the door was guarded.

The cardinal went into the room that served as his study and signaled Rochefort to show d'Artagnan in. Rochefort did so and left.

D'Artagnan was now alone with the cardinal; it was his second interview with him, and he later admitted that he was convinced it would be his last.

His Eminence remained standing, leaning against the fireplace, with a table between him and d'Artagnan.

"Monsieur d'Artagnan, you've been arrested by my order."

"So I was told, Monseigneur."

"Do you know why?"

"No, Monseigneur, because there's only one thing I could have been arrested for, and you don't yet know about it."

Richelieu looked at d'Artagnan intently.

"What does that mean?"

"If you'll be so kind as to tell me what crimes I'm accused of, Your Eminence, I'll then tell you what I've done."

"You're accused of crimes that have brought more important men than you to the scaffold!"

"What are they, Monseigneur?" d'Artagnan asked with a calm that surprised the cardinal.

"You're accused of corresponding with enemies of the kingdom, intercepting state secrets, and attempting to thwart your general's plans."

D'Artagnan was sure these accusations had come from Milady.

"And who's accused me of all that, Monseigneur? A woman who was branded by French justice, a woman who married one man in France and another in England, a woman who poisoned her second husband, and tried to poison me!"

"What are you saying!" exclaimed the cardinal. "What woman are you referring to?"

"Lady de Winter, Your Eminence. I'm sure you didn't know about all her crimes when you honored her with your confidence."

"If she's committed the crimes you've mentioned, she'll be punished."

"She's already been punished, Monseigneur."

"And who punished her?"

"We did."

"Is she in prison?"

"She's dead."

"Dead!" repeated the cardinal. He could not believe his ears. "Did you say she was dead?"

"Yes, Monseigneur. Three times she tried to kill me, and I forgave her. But then she killed the woman I loved. My friends and I captured her, tried her, and sentenced her to death."

D'Artagnan described Madame Bonacieux's murder in the Carmelite convent at Béthune, the trial in the isolated house, and the execution on the bank of the Lys.

A shudder ran through the cardinal, who did not shudder easily. But then his somber face brightened, as though from the influence of some unexpressed thought.

"So you appointed yourselves judges," he said in a gentle tone that contrasted with the sternness of his words, "without stopping to think that by imposing the death penalty when you had no lawful right to do it, you became guilty of murder!"

"Monseigneur, I swear I've never had any intention of defending myself against you. I'll submit to whatever punishment you choose to give me. Life doesn't mean enough to me to make me fear death."

"Yes, I know you're a brave man," the cardinal said almost affectionately, "so I can tell you in advance that you'll be tried and convicted."

"Anyone else in my place might answer that he had his pardon in his pocket; I'll merely say, 'Give your orders, Monseigneur, I'm ready.' "

"Your pardon?" said the cardinal, surprised.

"Yes, Monseigneur."

"Signed by whom? The king?"

His Eminence spoke these words with a singular expression of contempt.

"No, Monseigneur, it's signed by you."

"By me? Are you mad?"

"I believe you'll recognize your handwriting, Monseigneur."

D'Artagnan handed him the precious letter that Athos had taken from Milady and later given to d'Artagnan as a safeguard.

The cardinal took it and slowly read it aloud, stressing each word:

"The bearer of this letter has acted under my orders and for the good of the State.

Richelieu"

He then became lost in thought, without giving the letter back to d'Artagnan. "He's trying to decide how he'll have me put to death," d'Artagnan told himself. "Well, he'll see how a nobleman dies!"

The young musketeer was in an excellent frame of mind for dying heroically.

The cardinal continued his reflections, rolling and unrolling the paper between his hands. Finally he looked up, fixed his hawklike gaze on d'Artagnan's forthright, intelligent face, and read in it the suffering he had endured for the past month; for the third or fourth time, he thought what a promising future lay before this boy of twenty-one, and what resources his energy, courage, and quick wit could offer to a good master.

Moreover, Milady's crimes, power, and diabolical genius had frightened the cardinal more than once. He felt something close to secret joy at being rid of that dangerous accomplice.

He slowly tore up the letter that d'Artagnan had so magnanimously given back to him.

D'Artagnan thought, "I'm lost," and bowed deeply to the cardinal, as though to say, "God's will be done."

The cardinal went over to the table and, without sitting down, wrote a few lines on a sheet of parchment already two-thirds covered with writing. He then placed his seal on it. "It's my death sentence," thought d'Artagnan. "He's going to spare me the boredom of the Bastille and the tedious delay of a trial. I can be grateful to him for that."

"Here," the cardinal said to him, "take this in exchange for the letter you just gave me. I've left a blank space for the name: you can write it in yourself."

D'Artagnan hesitantly took the parchment and looked at it. It was a lieutenant's commission in the musketeers. He fell to his knees before the cardinal.

"Monseigneur," he said, "from now on my life belongs to you; dispose of it as you wish. But I don't deserve the favor you've granted me. I have three friends who are much worthier of it."

The cardinal clapped him familiarly on the shoulder.

"You're a fine boy, d'Artagnan," he said, delighted to have vanquished that rebellious nature. "You can do whatever you like with that commission. But remember that although you can choose the name you want to write on it, it's to you that I'm giving it."

"I'll never forget, Monseigneur. You can be certain of that."

The cardinal turned and called out, "Rochefort!"

Rochefort, who had no doubt been standing on the other side of the door, immediately came into the room.

"Rochefort," said the cardinal, "I now count Monsieur d'Artagnan among my friends. I want you to embrace each other—and behave yourselves, if you want to keep your heads."

Rochefort and d'Artagnan embraced halfheartedly while the cardinal watched them vigilantly.

They walked out of the room together.

"We'll meet again, won't we?" Rochefort said to d'Artagnan.

"Whenever you like," replied d'Artagnan.

"We'll soon have a chance," Rochefort assured him.

Just then the cardinal opened the door behind them.

"What are you saying?" he asked suspiciously.

The two men smiled at each other, shook hands, and bowed to His Eminence.

"We were beginning to lose patience," Athos said when d'Artagnan came out of the house.

"Well, here I am, my friends!" said d'Artagnan. "I'm not only free, I'm also in good favor!"

"Tell us about it."

"I will, this evening."

That evening d'Artagnan went to Athos's quarters and found him emptying a bottle of Spanish wine, a ritual that he performed faithfully every night.

After telling him what had happened between himself and the cardinal, d'Artagnan took the commission from his pocket and said, "Take it, Athos. You have every right to it."

Athos gave him his gentle, charming smile.

"My friend," he said, "it's too much for Athos and not enough for Count de La Fère. Keep it, it's yours. God knows you've paid a high enough price for it."

D'Artagnan left Athos and went to Porthos.

Porthos was standing in front of a mirror, wearing a luxurious coat covered with rich embroidery.

"Ah, it's you, my friend!" he said. "How does this coat look on me?"

"It's magnificent," said d'Artagnan, "but I've come to offer you something that will look even better on you."

"What is it?"

"The uniform of a lieutenant in the musketeers."

D'Artagnan told him about his interview with the cardinal and took the commission from his pocket.

"Write your name on it," he said, "and treat me well when I'm under your orders."

Porthos took the commission and looked it over. Then, to d'Artagnan's great surprise, he handed it back to him.

"I'd be delighted to accept it," he said, "but I wouldn't have much time to enjoy it. My duchess's husband died while we were on our expedition to Béthune, and since his strongbox now belongs to his widow, I'm going to marry her. I was just trying on my wedding clothes when you came in. Keep the lieutenancy for yourself, my friend.''

D'Artagnan went to Aramis's quarters.

He found him kneeling at a prie-dieu, with his forehead resting on an open book of hours.

D'Artagnan again described his interview with the cardinal and took the commission from his pocket.

"Aramis, you're our guiding light, our quiet protector. Take this commission. You've earned it more than anyone else, with your wisdom and your sound advice that's always given such good results.''

"No, my friend," said Aramis, "our recent adventures have completely turned me against life as a man of the sword. This time my mind is made up irrevocably: as soon as the siege is over, I'm going to become a Lazarist. Keep the commission, d'Artagnan. The military life suits you. You'll be a brave and adventurous officer.''

D'Artagnan, his eyes moist with gratitude and shining with joy, went back to Athos, who was still sitting at his table, holding up his last glass of Malaga to the flame of the lamp.

"They both refused it too.''

"That's because no one is worthier of it than you," said Athos.

He took a pen and wrote d'Artagnan's name on the commission.

"I'll have no more friends," said d'Artagnan. "I'll have nothing but bitter memories . . .''

Tears rolled down his cheeks. He let his head fall between his hands.

"You're young," said Athos. "Your bitter memories still have time to turn into sweet ones.''

Epilogue

La Rochelle, deprived of the aid of the English fleet and the division promised by Buckingham, capitulated after a year's siege. The surrender was signed on October 28, 1628.

The king made his entry into Paris on December 23 of the same year. He was given a triumphal welcome, as though he had vanquished an enemy instead of other Frenchmen. He entered by way of the Faubourg Saint-Jacques, under arches of greenery.

D'Artagnan assumed his new rank.

Porthos left the musketeers and married Madame Coquenard the following year. The strongbox he had so ardently coveted contained eight hundred thousand livres.

Mousqueton was given a magnificent livery and had the satisfaction of achieving his lifelong ambition: to ride atop a gilded carriage.

After a journey to Lorraine, Aramis disappeared completely and stopped writing to his friends. It was later learned through Madame de Chevreuse, who told it to two or three of her lovers, that he had become a monk in a monastery in Nancy.

Bazin became a lay brother.

Athos remained a musketeer under d'Artagnan's command until 1633, when, after a journey to Touraine, he also left the service, saying that he had just received a small inheritance in Roussillon.

Grimaud went with him.

D'Artagnan fought three duels with Rochefort and wounded him three times.

"I'll probably kill you the next time," he told him after the third duel, as he held out his hand to help him to his feet.

"Then it will be better for both of us if we don't fight again," said his wounded adversary. "I'm more your friend than you think, because I could have had you beheaded after our first duel, simply by saying a few words to the cardinal."

They embraced, but this time it was wholeheartedly.

Rochefort made Planchet a sergeant in the guards.

Monsieur Bonacieux went on living peacefully, not knowing

what had happened to his wife, and caring very little. One day he made the foolish mistake of writing a letter to the cardinal to remind him of his existence. The cardinal replied with a promise to see to it that from now on he would never lack anything.

Monsieur Bonacieux left home at seven o'clock the next morning to go to the Louvre and never returned to his house on the Rue des Fossoyeurs. The opinion of those who seemed best informed was that he was being fed and lodged in some royal castle at the generous cardinal's expense.

Bantam Classics bring you the world's greatest litera-ture—books that have stood the test of time—at specially low prices. These beautifully designed books will be proud additions to your bookshelf. You'll want all these time-tested classics for your own reading pleasure.

☐	21264	SISTER CARRIE, Theodore Dreiser	$3.50
☐	21218	UNCLE TOM'S CABIN, Harriet Beecher Stowe	$2.95
☐	21116	LEAVES OF GRASS, Walt Whitman	$2.95
☐	21248	THE HOUSE OF MIRTH, Edith Wharton	$2.95
☐	21575	THE TELL-TALE HEART & OTHER WRITINGS, Edgar Allen Poe	$2.75

Titles by James Fenimore Cooper:

☐	21085	THE DEERSLAYER	$2.95
☐	21103	THE LAST OF THE MOHICANS	$2.50

Titles by Nathaniel Hawthorne:

☐	21270	THE HOUSE OF THE SEVEN GABLES	$2.50
☐	21009	THE SCARLET LETTER	$1.50

Bantam Classics bring you the world's greatest literature—books that have stood the test of time—at specially low prices. These beautifully designed books will be proud additions to your bookshelf. You'll want all these time-tested classics for your own reading pleasure.

Titles by Mark Twain:

☐ 21079	ADVENTURES OF HUCKLEBERRY FINN	$1.75
☐ 21128	ADVENTURES OF TOM SAWYER	$1.75
☐ 21195	COMPLETE SHORT STORIES	$4.50
☐ 21143	A CONNECTICUT YANKEE IN KING ARTHUR'S COURT	$1.95
☐ 21142	LIFE ON THE MISSISSIPPI	$1.95
☐ 21150	THE PRINCE AND THE PAUPER	$1.95
☐ 21158	PUDDIN'HEAD WILSON	$1.95

Titles by Herman Melville:

☐ 21094	BILLY BUDD	$1.95
☐ 21007	MOBY DICK	$1.95

Titles by Jack London:

☐ 21233	THE CALL OF THE WILD & WHITE FANG	$2.25
☐ 21225	THE SEA WOLF	$1.95
☐ 21212	MARTIN EDEN	$3.95
☐ 21213	TO BUILD A FIRE & OTHER STORIES	$2.95

Titles by Stephen Crane:

☐ 21011	THE RED BADGE OF COURAGE	$1.50
☐ 21198	MAGGIE: A GIRL OF THE STREETS & OTHER SHORT FICTION	$2.50

Bantam Classics bring you the world's greatest literature—books that have stood the test of time—at specially low prices. These beautifully designed books will be proud additions to your bookshelf. You'll want all these time-tested classics for your own reading pleasure.

Titles by Charles Dickens:

☐	21123	THE PICKWICK PAPERS	$4.95
☐	21223	BLEAK HOUSE	$3.95
☐	21086	NICHOLAS NICKLEBY	$4.50
☐	21189	GREAT EXPECTATIONS	$2.50
☐	21176	A TALE OF TWO CITIES	$2.25
☐	21016	HARD TIMES	$1.95
☐	21102	OLIVER TWIST	$2.50
☐	21126	A CHRISTMAS CAROL & OTHER VICTORIAN TALES	$2.95

Titles by Thomas Hardy:

☐	21191	JUDE THE OBSCURE	$2.95
☐	21024	THE MAYOR OF CASTERBRIDGE	$1.95
☐	21269	THE RETURN OF THE NATIVE	$2.25
☐	21168	TESS OF THE D'URBERVILLES	$2.95
☐	21131	FAR FROM THE MADDING CROWD	$2.75

Titles by Henry James:

☐	21153	THE BOSTONIANS	$2.95
☐	21127	PORTRAIT OF A LADY	$3.50
☐	21059	THE TURN OF THE SCREW	$1.95

Look for them at your bookstore or use this handy coupon:

Bantam Classics bring you the world's greatest literature—books that have stood the test of time—at specially low prices. These beautifully designed books will be proud additions to your bookshelf. You'll want all these time-tested classics for your own reading pleasure.

☐	21105	ROBINSON CRUSOE, Daniel Defoe	$1.95
☐	21232	GULLIVER'S TRAVELS & OTHER WRITINGS, Jonathan Swift	$2.95
☐	21032	THE HUNCHBACK OF NOTRE DAME, Victor Hugo	$1.95
☐	21247	FRANKENSTEIN, Mary Shelley	$1.95
☐	21148	DRACULA, Bram Stoker	$1.95

Titles by Robert Louis Stevenson:

☐	21200	DR. JEKYLL AND MR. HYDE	$2.50
☐	21260	KIDNAPPED	$1.95
☐	21249	TREASURE ISLAND	$1.95

Titles by Alexander Dumas:

☐	21230	THE COUNT OF MONTE CRISTO	$3.95
☐	21217	THE THREE MUSKETEERS	$4.50

Titles by H. G. Wells:

☐	21253	THE INVISIBLE MAN	$2.50
☐	21239	THE TIME MACHINE	$2.50

Titles by Rudyard Kipling:

☐	21190	CAPTAINS COURAGEOUS	$1.95
☐	21117	KIM	$2.25
☐	21199	THE JUNGLE BOOK & JUST SO STORIES	$3.95

Titles by Jules Verne:

☐	21145	AROUND THE WORLD IN EIGHTY DAYS	$2.25
☐	21252	20,000 LEAGUES UNDER THE SEA	$2.50